WHO COULD IMAGINE

—that a supermarket could be the place where humanity makes its last stand against unholy destruction?

—that a trip to the attic could turn into a journey to hell?

—that a woman driver could find a very scary shortcut to paradise?

—that an idyllic lake could be the home of bottomless evil?

—that a desert island could be the scene of the most gruesome struggle for survival ever waged?

Stephen King imagines all this, and more, in

SKELETON CREW

"King has the talent to lift adults' blinders to horror, and that's why his fans can't get enough of him. It's also what makes his stories as deliciously frightening as they are."

—*Cincinnati Enquirer*

"Stephen King lands you in a hurry and then leans back, chortling, while you shiver on his hook!" —*Playboy*

For more spirited acclaim, please turn page. . . .

SKELETON CREW

STEPHEN KING

A SIGNET BOOK

NEW AMERICAN LIBRARY

NAL BOOKS ARE AVAILABLE AT QUANTITY DISCOUNTS WHEN
USED TO PROMOTE PRODUCTS OR SERVICES. FOR INFORMATION
PLEASE WRITE TO PREMIUM MARKETING DIVISION, NEW AMERI-
CAN LIBRARY, 1633 BROADWAY, NEW YORK, NEW YORK 10019.

This book is for
Arthur and Joyce Greene

Contents

I'm your boogie man
that's what I am
and I'm here to do
whatever I can . . .

—K.C. and the Sunshine Band

Do you love?

Introduction

Wait—just a few minutes. I want to talk to you . . . and then I am going to kiss you. Wait . . .

I

Here's some more short stories, if you want them. They span a long period of my life. The oldest, "The Reaper's Image," was written when I was eighteen, in the summer before I started college. I thought of the idea, as a matter of fact, when I was out in the back yard of our house in West Durham, Maine, shooting baskets with my brother, and reading it over again made me feel a little sad for those old times. The most recent, "The Ballad of the Flexible Bullet," was finished in November of 1983. That is a span of seventeen years, and does not count as much, I suppose, if put in comparison with such long and rich careers as those enjoyed by writers as diverse as Graham Greene, Somerset Maugham, Mark Twain, and Eudora Welty, but it is a longer time than Stephen Crane had, and about the same length as the span of H. P. Lovecraft's career.

A friend of mine asked me a year or two ago why I still bother. My novels, he pointed out, were making very good money, while the short stories were actually losers.

"How do you figure that?" I asked.

He tapped the then-current issue of *Playboy*, which had occasioned this discussion. I had a story in it ("Word Processor of the Gods," which you'll find in here someplace), and had pointed it out to him with what I thought was justifiable pride.

"Well, I'll show you," he said, "if you don't mind telling me how much you got for the piece."

"I don't mind," I said. "I got two thousand dollars. Not exactly chicken-dirt, Wyatt."

(His name isn't really Wyatt, but I don't want to embarrass him, if you can dig that.) "No, you didn't get two thousand," Wyatt said.

"I didn't? Have you been looking at my bankbook?"

"Nope. But I know you got eighteen hundred dollars for it, because your agent gets ten percent."

"Damn right," I said. "He deserves it. He got me in *Playboy*. I've always wanted to have a story in *Playboy*. So it was eighteen hundred bucks instead of two thousand, big deal."

"No, you got $1,710."

"*What?*"

"Well, didn't you tell me your business manager gets five percent of the net?"

"Well, okay—eighteen hundred less ninety bucks. I still think $1,710 is not bad for—"

"Except it wasn't," this sadist pushed on. "It was *really* a measly $855."

"*What?*"

"You want to tell me you're not in a fifty-percent tax bracket, Steve-O?"

I was silent. He knew I was.

"And," he said gently, "it was *really* just about $769.50, wasn't it?"

I nodded reluctantly. Maine has an income tax which requires residents in my bracket to pay ten percent of their federal taxes to the state. Ten percent of $855 is $85.50.

"How long did it take you to write this story?" Wyatt persisted.

"About a week," I said ungraciously. It was really more like two, with a couple of rewrites added in, but I wasn't going to tell *Wyatt* that.

"So you made $769.50 that week," he said. "You know how much a plumber makes per week in New York, Steve-O?"

"No," I said. I hate people who call me Steve-O. "And neither do you."

"Sure I do," he said. "About $769.50, after taxes. And so, far as I can see, what you got there is a dead loss." He laughed like hell and then asked if I had any more beer in the fridge. I said no.

I'm going to send goodbuddy Wyatt a copy of this book with a little note. The note will say: *I am not going to tell you how much I was paid for this book, but I'll tell you this, Wyatt: my total take on "Word Processor of the Gods"*—net—*is now just over twenty-three hundred dollars, not even counting the $769.50 you hee-hawed so over at my house at the lake.* I will sign the note *Steve-O* and add a PS: *There really was more beer in the fridge, and I drank it myself after you were gone that day.*

That ought to fix him.

I

Except it's not the money. I'll admit I was bowled over to be paid $2,000 for "Word Processor of the Gods," but I was equally as bowled over to be paid $40 for "The Reaper's Image" when it was published in *Startling Mystery Stories* or to be sent twelve contributor's copies when "Here There Be Tygers" was published in *Ubris*, the University of Maine college literary magazine (I am of a kindly nature and have always assumed that *Ubris* was a cockney way of spelling *Hubris*).

I mean, you're glad of the money; let us not descend into total fantasy here (or at least not yet). When I began to publish short fiction in men's magazines such as *Cavalier*, *Dude*, and *Adam* with some regularity, I was twenty-five and my wife was twenty-three. We had one child and another was on the way. I was working fifty or sixty hours a week in a laundry and making $1.75 an hour. *Budget* is not exactly the word for whatever it was we were on; it was more like a modified version of the Bataan Death March. The checks for those stories (on publication, never on acceptance) always seemed to come just in time to buy antibiotics for the baby's ear infection or to keep the telephone in the apartment for another record-breaking month. Money is, let us face it, very handy and very heady. As Lily Cavenaugh says in *The Talisman* (and it was Peter Straub's line, not mine), "You can never be too thin or too rich." And if you don't believe it, you were never really fat or really poor.

All the same, you don't do it for money, or you're a monkey. You don't think of the bottom line, or you're a monkey. You don't think of it in terms of hourly wage, yearly wage, even lifetime wage, or you're a monkey. In the end you don't even do it for love, although it would be nice to think so. You do it because to not do it is suicide. And while that is tough, there are compensations I could never tell Wyatt about, because he is not that kind of guy.

Take "Word Processor of the Gods" as a for-instance. Not the best story I ever wrote; not one that's ever going to win any prizes. But it's not too bad, either. Sort of fun. I had just gotten my own word processor a month before (it's a big Wang, and keep your smart comments to yourself, what do you say?) and I was still exploring what it could and couldn't do. In particular I was fascinated with the INSERT and DELETE buttons, which make cross-outs and carets almost obsolete.

I caught myself a nasty little bug one day. What the hell, happens to the best of us. Everything inside me that wasn't nailed down came out from one end or the other, most of it at roughly the speed of sound. By nightfall I felt very bad indeed—chills, fever, joints full of spun glass. Most of the muscles in my stomach were sprung, and my back ached.

I spent that night in the guest bedroom (which is only four running steps from the bathroom) and slept from nine until about two in the morning. I woke up knowing that was it for the night. I only stayed in bed because I was too sick to get up. So there I lay, and I got thinking about my word processor, and INSERT and DELETE. And I thought, "Wouldn't it be funny if this guy wrote a sentence, and then, when he pushed DELETE, the subject of the sentence was deleted from the world?" That's the way just about all of my stories start; "Wouldn't it be funny if—?" And while many of them are scary, I never *told* one to people (as opposed to writing it down) that didn't cause at least some laughter, no matter what I saw as the final *intent* of that story.

Anyway, I started imaging on DELETE to begin with, not exactly making up a story so much as seeing pictures in my head. I was watching this guy (who is always to me just the

I-Guy until the story actually starts coming out in words, when you have to give him a name) delete pictures hanging on the wall, and chairs in the living room, and New York City, and the concept of war. Then I thought of having him *insert* things and having those things just pop into the world.

Then I thought, "So give him a wife that's bad to the bone—he can delete her, maybe—and someone else who's good to maybe insert." And then I fell asleep, and the next morning I was pretty much okay again. The bug went away but the story didn't. I wrote it, and you'll see it didn't turn out exactly as the foregoing might suggest, but then—they never do.

I don't need to draw you a picture, do I? You don't do it for money; you do it because it saves you from feeling bad. A man or woman able to turn his or her back on something like that is just a monkey, that's all. The story paid me by letting me get back to sleep when I felt as if I couldn't. I paid the story back by getting it concrete, which it wanted to be. The rest is just side effects.

3

I hope you'll like this book, Constant Reader. I suspect you won't like it as well as you would a novel, because most of you have forgotten the real pleasures of the short story. Reading a good long novel is in many ways like having a long and satisfying affair. I can remember commuting between Maine and Pittsburgh during the making of *Creepshow,* and going mostly by car because of my fear of flying coupled with the air traffic controllers' strike and Mr. Reagan's subsequent firing of the strikers (Reagan, it appears, is really only an ardent unionist if the unions in question are in Poland). I had a reading of *The Thorn Birds,* by Colleen McCullough, on eight cassette tapes, and for a space of about five weeks I wasn't even having an affair with that novel; I felt *married* to it (my favorite part was when the wicked old lady rotted and sprouted maggots in about sixteen hours).

A short story is a different thing altogether—a short story is like a quick kiss in the dark from a stranger. That is not, of course, the same thing as an affair or a marriage, but kisses can be sweet, and their very brevity forms their own attraction.

Writing short stories hasn't gotten easier for me over the years; it's gotten harder. The time to do them has shrunk, for one thing. They keep wanting to bloat, for another (I have a real problem with bloat—I write like fat ladies diet). And it seems harder to find the voice for these tales—all too often the I-Guy just floats away.

The thing to do is to keep trying, I think. It's better to keep kissing and get your face slapped a few times than it is to give up altogether.

4

All right; that's just about it from this end. Can I thank a few people (you can skip this part if you want to)?

Thanks to Bill Thompson for getting this going. He and I put *Night Shift*, the first book of short stories, together, and it was his idea to do this one. He's moved on to Arbor House since, but I love him just as well there as anywhere else. If there really is a gentleman left in the gentleman's profession of book publishing, it's this guy. God bless yer Irish heart, Bill.

Thanks to Phyllis Grann at Putnam for taking up the slack.

Thanks to Kirby McCauley, my agent, another Irishman, who sold most of these, and who pulled the longest of them, "The Mist," out of me with a chain fall.

This is starting to sound like an Academy Awards acceptance speech, but fuck it.

Thanks are due to magazine editors, as well—Kathy Sagan at *Redbook*, Alice Turner at *Playboy*, Nye Willden at *Cavalier*, the folks at *Yankee*, to Ed Ferman—my man!—at *Fantasy & Science Fiction*.

I owe just about everybody, and I could name them, but I won't bore you with any more. Most thanks are to you, Constant Reader, just like always—because it all goes out to you in the end. Without you, it's a dead circuit. If any of these do it for you, take you away, get you over the boring lunch hour, the plane ride, or the hour in detention hall for throwing spitballs, that's the payback.

5

Okay—commercial's over. Grab onto my arm now. Hold tight. We are going into a number of dark places, but I think I know the way. Just don't let go of my arm. And if I should kiss you in the dark, it's no big deal; it's only because you are my love.

Now listen:

April 15th, 1984
Bangor, Maine

The Mist

I. The Coming of the Storm

This is what happened. On the night that the worst heat wave
in northern New England history finally broke—the night of
July 19—the entire western Maine region was lashed with the
most vicious thunderstorms I have ever seen.

We lived on Long Lake, and we saw the first of the storms
beating its way across the water toward us just before dark.
For an hour before, the air had been utterly still. The American flag that my father put up on our boathouse in 1936 lay
limp against its pole. Not even its hem fluttered. The heat
was like a solid thing, and it seemed as deep as sullen
quarry-water. That afternoon the three of us had gone swimming, but the water was no relief unless you went out deep.
Neither Steffy nor I wanted to go deep because Billy couldn't.
Billy is five.

We ate a cold supper at five-thirty, picking listlessly at ham
sandwiches and potato salad out on the deck that faces the
lake. Nobody seemed to want anything but Pepsi, which was
in a steel bucket of ice cubes.

After supper Billy went out back to play on his monkey
bars for a while. Steff and I sat without talking much, smoking and looking across the sullen flat mirror of the lake to
Harrison on the far side. A few powerboats droned back and

forth. The evergreens over there looked dusty and beaten. In the west, great purple thunderheads were slowly building up, massing like an army. Lightning flashed inside them. Next door, Brent Norton's radio, tuned to that classical-music station that broadcasts from the top of Mount Washington, sent out a loud bray of static each time the lightning flashed. Norton was a lawyer from New Jersey and his place on Long Lake was only a summer cottage with no furnace or insulation. Two years before, we had a boundary dispute that finally wound up in county court. I won. Norton claimed I won because he was an out-of-towner. There was no love lost between us.

Steff sighed and fanned the top of her breasts with the edge of her halter. I doubted if it cooled her off much but it improved the view a lot.

"I don't want to scare you," I said, "but there's a bad storm on the way, I think."

She looked at me doubtfully. "There were thunderheads last night and the night before, David. They just broke up."

"They won't do that tonight."

"No?"

"If it gets bad enough, we're going to go downstairs."

"How bad do you think it can get?"

My dad was the first to build a year-round home on this side of the lake. When he was hardly more than a kid he and his brothers put up a summer place where the house now stood, and in 1938 a summer storm knocked it flat, stone walls and all. Only the boathouse escaped. A year later he started the big house. It's the trees that do the damage in a bad blow. They get old, and the wind knocks them over. It's mother nature's way of cleaning house periodically.

"I don't really know," I said, truthfully enough. I had only heard stories about the great storm of thirty-eight. "But the wind can come off the lake like an express train."

Billy came back a while later, complaining that the monkey bars were no fun because he was "all sweated up." I ruffled his hair and gave him another Pepsi. More work for the dentist.

The thunderheads were getting closer, pushing away the blue. There was no doubt now that a storm was coming. Norton had turned off his radio. Billy sat between his mother and me, watching the sky, fascinated. Thunder boomed, rolling slowly across the lake and then echoing back again. The clouds twisted and rolled, now black, now purple, now veined, now black again. They gradually overspread the lake, and I could see a delicate caul of rain extending down from them. It was still a distance away. As we watched, it was probably raining on Bolster's Mills, or maybe even Norway.

The air began to move, jerkily at first, lifting the flag and then dropping it again. It began to freshen and grew steady, first cooling the perspiration on our bodies and then seeming to freeze it.

That was when I saw the silver veil rolling across the lake. It blotted out Harrison in seconds and then came straight at us. The powerboats had vacated the scene.

Billy stood up from his chair, which was a miniature replica of our director's chairs, complete with his name printed on the back. "Daddy! Look!"

"Let's go in," I said. I stood up and put my arm around his shoulders.

"But do you see it? Dad, what is it?"

"A water-cyclone. Let's go in."

Steff threw a quick, startled glance at my face and then said, "Come on, Billy. Do what your father says."

We went in through the sliding glass doors that give on the living room. I slid the door shut on its track and paused for another look out. The silver veil was three-quarters of the way across the lake. It had resolved itself into a crazily spinning teacup between the lowering black sky and the surface of the water, which had gone the color of lead streaked with white chrome. The lake had begun to look eerily like the ocean, with high waves rolling in and sending spume up from the docks and breakwaters. Out in the middle, big whitecaps were tossing their heads back and forth.

Watching the water-cyclone was hypnotic. It was nearly on top of us when lightning flashed so brightly that it printed everything on my eyes in negative for thirty seconds afterward. The telephone gave out a startled *ting!* and I turned to see my wife and son standing directly in front of the big picture window that gives us a panoramic view of the lake to the northwest.

One of those terrible visions came to me—I think they are

reserved exclusively for husbands and fathers—of the picture window blowing in with a low hard coughing sound and sending jagged arrows of glass into my wife's bare stomach, into my boy's face and neck. The horrors of the Inquisition are nothing compared to the fates your mind can imagine for your loved ones.

I grabbed them both hard and jerked them away. "What the hell are you doing? Get away from there!"

Steff gave me a startled glance. Billy only looked at me as if he had been partially awakened from a deep dream. I led them into the kitchen and hit the light switch. The phone ting-a-linged again.

Then the wind came. It was as if the house had taken off like a 747. It was a high, breathless whistling, sometimes deepening to a bass roar before glissading up to a whooping scream.

"Go downstairs," I told Steff, and now I had to shout to make myself heard. Directly over the house thunder whacked mammoth planks together and Billy shrank against my leg.

"You come too!" Steff yelled back.

I nodded and made shooing gestures. I had to pry Billy off my leg. "Go with your mother. I want to get some candles in case the lights go off."

He went with her, and I started opening cabinets. Candles are funny things, you know. You lay them by every spring, knowing that a summer storm may knock out the power. And when the time comes, they hide.

I was pawing through the fourth cabinet, past the half-ounce of grass that Steff and I bought four years ago and had still not smoked much of, past Billy's wind-up set of chattering teeth from the Auburn Novelty Shop, past the drifts of photos Steffy kept forgetting to glue in our album. I looked under a Sears catalogue and behind a Kewpie doll from Taiwan that I had won at the Fryeburg Fair knocking over wooden milk bottles with tennis balls.

I found the candles behind the Kewpie doll with its glazed dead man's eyes. They were still wrapped in their cellophane. As my hand closed around them the lights went out and the only electricity was the stuff in the sky. The dining room was lit in a series of shutterflashes that were white and purple.

Downstairs I heard Billy start to cry and the low murmur of Steff soothing him.

I had to have one more look at the storm.

The water-cyclone had either passed us or broken up when it reached the shoreline, but I still couldn't see twenty yards out onto the lake. The water was in complete turmoil. I saw someone's dock—the Jassers', maybe—hurry by with its main supports alternately turned up to the sky and buried in the churning water.

I went downstairs. Billy ran to me and clung to my legs. I lifted him up and gave him a hug. Then I lit the candles. We sat in the guest room down the hall from my little studio and looked at each other's faces in the flickering yellow glow and listened to the storm roar and bash at our house. About twenty minutes later we heard a ripping, rending crash as one of the big pines went down nearby. Then there was a lull.

"Is it over?" Steff asked.

"Maybe," I said. "Maybe only for a while."

We went upstairs, each of us carrying a candle, like monks going to vespers. Billy carried his proudly and carefully. Carrying a candle, carrying the *fire*, was a very big deal for him. It helped him forget about being afraid.

It was too dark to see what damage had been done around the house. It was past Billy's bedtime, but neither of us suggested putting him in. We sat in the living room, listened to the wind, and looked at the lightning.

About an hour later it began to crank up again. For three weeks the temperature had been over ninety, and on six of those twenty-one days the National Weather Service station at the Portland Jetport had reported temperatures of over one hundred degrees. Queer weather. Coupled with the grueling winter we had come through and the late spring, some people had dragged out that old chestnut about the long-range results of the fifties A-bomb tests again. That, and of course, the end of the world. The oldest chestnut of them all.

The second squall wasn't so hard, but we heard the crash of several trees weakened by the first onslaught. As the wind began to die down again, one thudded heavily on the roof, like a fist dropped on a coffin lid. Billy jumped and looked apprehensively upward.

"It'll hold, champ," I said.

Billy smiled nervously.

Around ten o'clock the last squall came. It was bad. The wind howled almost as loudly as it had the first time, and lightning seemed to be flashing all around us. More trees fell, and there was a splintering crash down by the water that made Steff utter a low cry. Billy had gone to sleep on her lap.

"David, what was that?"

"I think it was the boathouse."

"Oh. Oh, Jesus."

"Steffy, I want us to go downstairs again." I took Billy in my arms and stood up with him. Steff's eyes were big and frightened.

"David, are we going to be all right?"

"Yes."

"Really?"

"Yes."

We went downstairs. Ten minutes later, as the final squall peaked, there was a splintering crash from upstairs— the picture window. So maybe my vision earlier hadn't been so crazy after all. Steff, who had been dozing, woke up with a little shriek, and Billy stirred uneasily in the guest bed.

"The rain will come in," she said. "It'll ruin the furniture."

"If it does, it does. It's insured."

"That doesn't make it any better," she said in an upset, scolding voice. "Your mother's dresser . . . our new sofa . . . the color TV . . ."

"Shhh," I said. "Go to sleep."

"I can't," she said, and five minutes later she had.

I stayed awake for another half hour with one lit candle for company, listening to the thunder walk and talk outside. I had a feeling that there were going to be a lot of people from the lakefront communities calling their insurance agents in the morning, a lot of chainsaws burring as cottage owners cut up the trees that had fallen on their roofs and battered through their windows, and a lot of orange CMP trucks on the road.

The storm was fading now, with no sign of a new squall coming in. I went back upstairs, leaving Steff and Billy on the bed, and looked into the living room. The sliding glass door had held. But where the picture window had been there was now a jagged hole stuffed with birch leaves. It was the top of the old tree that had stood by our outside basement access for as long as I could remember. Looking at its top, now visiting in our living room, I could understand what Steff had meant by saying insurance didn't make it any better. I had loved that tree. It had been a hard campaigner of many winters, the one tree on the lakeside of the house that was exempt from my own chainsaw. Big chunks of glass on the rug reflected my candle-flame over and over. I reminded myself to warn Steff and Billy. They would want to wear their slippers in here. Both of them liked to slop around barefoot in the morning.

I went downstairs again. All three of us slept together in the guest bed, Billy between Steff and me. I had a dream that I saw God walking across Harrison on the far side of the lake, a God so gigantic that above the waist He was lost in a clear blue sky. In the dream I could hear the rending crack and splinter of breaking trees as God stamped the woods into the shape of His footsteps. He was circling the lake, coming toward the Bridgton side, toward us, and all the houses and cottages and summer places were bursting into purple-white flame like lightning, and soon the smoke covered everything. The smoke covered everything like a mist.

II. After the Storm. Norton. A Trip to Town.

"Jeee-pers," Billy said.

He was standing by the fence that separates our property from Norton's and looking down our driveway. The driveway runs a quarter of a mile to a camp road which, in its turn, runs about three-quarters of a mile to a stretch of two-lane blacktop, called Kansas Road. From Kansas Road you can go anywhere you want, as long as it's Bridgton.

I saw what Billy was looking at and my heart went cold.

"Don't go any closer, champ. Right there is close enough."

Billy didn't argue.

The morning was bright and as clear as a bell. The sky, which had been a mushy, hazy color during the heat wave, had regained a deep, crisp blue that was nearly autumnal. There was a light breeze, making cheerful sun-dapples move back and forth in the driveway. Not far from where Billy was standing there was a steady hissing noise, and in the grass there was what you might at first have taken for a writhing bundle of snakes. The power lines leading to our house had fallen in an untidy tangle about twenty feet away and lay in a burned patch of grass. They were twisting lazily and spitting. If the trees and grass hadn't been so completely damped down by the torrential rains, the house might have gone up. As it was, there was only that black patch where the wires had touched directly.

"Could that lectercute a person, Daddy?"

"Yeah. It could."

"What are we going to do about it?"

"Nothing. Wait for the CMP."

"When will they come?"

"I don't know." Five-year-olds have as many questions as Hallmark has cards. "I imagine they're pretty busy this morning. Want to take a walk up to the end of the driveway with me?"

He started to come and then stopped, eyeing the wires nervously. One of them humped up and turned over lazily, as if beckoning.

"Daddy, can lectricity shoot through the ground?"

A fair question. "Yes, but don't worry. Electricity wants the ground, not you, Billy. You'll be all right if you stay away from the wires."

"Wants the ground," he muttered, and then came to me. We walked up the driveway holding hands.

It was worse than I had imagined. Trees had fallen across the drive in four different places, one of them small, two of them middling, and one old baby that must have been five feet through the middle. Moss was crusted onto it like a moldy corset.

Branches, some half-stripped of their leaves, lay everywhere in jackstraw profusion. Billy and I walked up to the camp road, tossing the smaller branches off into the woods on either side. It reminded me of a summer's day that had been maybe twenty-five years before; I couldn't have been much older than Billy was now. All my uncles had been here, and they had spent the day in the woods with axes and hatchets and Darcy poles, cutting brush. Later that afternoon they had all sat down to the trestle picnic table my dad and mom used to have and there had been a monster meal of hot dogs and hamburgers and potato salad. The 'Gansett beer had flowed like water and my uncle Reuben took a dive into the lake with all his clothes on, even his deck-shoes. In those days there were still deer in these woods.

"Daddy, can I go down to the lake?"

He was tired of throwing branches, and the thing to do with a little boy when he's tired is to let him go do something else. "Sure."

We walked back to the house together and then Billy cut right, going around the house and giving the downed wires a large berth. I went left, into the garage, to get my McCullough. As I had suspected, I could already hear the unpleasant song of the chainsaw up and down the lake.

I topped up the tank, took off my shirt, and was starting back up the driveway when Steff came out. She eyed the downed trees lying across the driveway nervously.

"How bad is it?"

"I can cut it up. How bad is it in there?"

"Well, I got the glass cleaned up, but you're going to have to do something about that tree, David. We can't have a tree in the living room."

"No," I said. "I guess we can't."

We looked at each other in the morning sunlight and got giggling. I set the McCullough down on the cement areaway, and kissed her, holding her buttocks firmly.

"Don't," she murmured. "Billy's—"

He came tearing around the corner of the house just then. "Dad! Daddy! Y'oughta see the—"

Steffy saw the live wires and screamed for him to watch out. Billy, who was a good distance away from them, pulled up short and stared at his mother as if she had gone mad.

"I'm okay, Mom," he said in the careful tone of voice you use to placate the very old and senile. He walked toward us, showing us how all right he was, and Steff began to tremble in my arms.

"It's all right," I said in her ear. "He knows about them."

"Yes, but people get killed," she said. "They have ads all the time on television about live wires, people get—Billy, I want you to come in the house right now!"

"Aw, come on, Mom! I wanna show Dad the boathouse!" He was almost bug-eyed with excitement and disappointment. He had gotten a taste of poststorm apocalypse and wanted to share it.

"You go in right now! Those wires are dangerous and—"

"Dad said they want the ground, not me—"

"Billy, don't you argue with me!"

"I'll come down and look, champ. Go on down yourself." I could feel Steff tensing against me. "Go around the other side, kiddo."

"Yeah! Okay!"

He tore past us, taking the stone steps that led around the west end of the house two by two. He disappeared with his shirttail flying, trailing back one word—"Wow!"—as he spotted some other piece of destruction.

"He knows about the wires, Steffy." I took her gently by the shoulders. "He's scared of them. That's good. It makes him safe."

One tear tracked down her cheek. "David, I'm scared."

"Come on! It's over."

"Is it? Last winter . . . and the late spring . . . they called it a black spring in town . . . they said there hadn't been one in these parts since 1888—"

"They" undoubtedly meant Mrs. Carmody, who kept the Bridgton Antiquary, a junk shop that Steff liked to rummage around in sometimes. Billy loved to go with her. In one of the shadowy, dusty back rooms, stuffed owls with gold-ringed eyes spread their wings forever as their feet endlessly grasped varnished logs; stuffed raccoons stood in a trio around a "stream" that was a long fragment of dusty mirror; and one moth-eaten wolf, which was foaming sawdust instead of saliva around his muzzle, snarled a creepy eternal snarl. Mrs. Carmody claimed the wolf was shot by her father as it came to drink from Stevens Brook one September afternoon in 1901.

The expeditions to Mrs. Carmody's Antiquary shop worked well for my wife and son. She was into carnival glass and he was into death in the name of taxidermy. But I thought that the old woman exercised a rather unpleasant hold over Steff's mind, which was in all other ways practical and hardheaded. She had found Steff's vulnerable spot, a mental Achilles' heel. Nor was Steff the only one in town who was fascinated by Mrs. Carmody's gothic pronouncements and folk remedies (which were always prescribed in God's name).

Stump-water would take off bruises if your husband was the sort who got a bit too free with his fists after three drinks. You could tell what kind of a winter was coming by counting the rings on the caterpillars in June or by measuring the thickness of August honeycomb. And now, good God protect and preserve us, THE BLACK SPRING OF 1888 (add your own exclamation points, as many as you think it deserves). I had also heard the story. It's one they like to pass around up here—if the spring is cold enough, the ice on the lakes will eventually turn as black as a rotted tooth. It's rare, but hardly a once-in-a-century occurrence. They like to pass it around, but I doubt that many could pass it around with as much conviction as Mrs. Carmody.

"We had a hard winter and a late spring," I said. "Now we're having a hot summer. And we had a storm but it's over. You're not acting like yourself, Stephanie."

"That wasn't an ordinary storm," she said in that same husky voice.

"No," I said. "I'll go along with you there."

I had heard the Black Spring story from Bill Giosti, who owned and operated—after a fashion—Giosti's Mobil in Casco Village. Bill ran the place with his three tosspot sons (with occasional help from his four tosspot grandsons . . . when they could take time off from tinkering with their snowmobiles and dirtbikes). Bill was seventy, looked eighty, and could still drink like twenty-three when the mood was on him. Billy and I had taken the Scout in for a fill-up the day after a surprise mid-May storm dropped nearly a foot of wet, heavy snow on the region, covering the new grass and flowers. Giosti had been in his cups for fair, and happy to pass along the Black Spring story, along with his own original twist. But we get snow in May sometimes; it comes and it's gone two days later. It's no big deal.

Steff was glancing doubtfully at the downed wires again. "When will the power company come?"

"Just as soon as they can. It won't be long. I just don't want you to worry about Billy. His head's on pretty straight. He forgets to pick up his clothes, but he isn't going to go and step on a bunch of live lines. He's got a good, healthy dose of self-interest.'' I touched a corner of her mouth and it obliged by turning up in the beginning of a smile. "Better?''

"You always make it seem better,'' she said, and that made me feel good.

From the lakeside of the house Billy was yelling for us to come and see.

"Come on,'' I said. "Let's go look at the damage.''

She snorted ruefully. "If I want to look at damage, I can go sit in my living room.''

"Make a little kid happy, then.''

We walked down the stone steps hand in hand. We had just reached the first turn in them when Billy came from the other direction at speed, almost knocking us over.

"Take it easy,'' Steff said, frowning a little. Maybe, in her mind, she was seeing him skidding into that deadly nest of live wires instead of the two of us.

"You gotta come see!'' Billy panted. "The boathouse is all bashed! There's a dock on the rocks . . . and trees in the boat cove . . . Jesus *Christ!*''

"Billy Drayton!'' Steff thundered.

"Sorry, Ma—but you gotta—wow!'' He was gone again.

"Having spoken, the doomsayer departs,'' I said, and that made Steff giggle again. "Listen, after I cut up those trees across the driveway, I'll go by the Central Maine Power office on Portland Road. Tell them what we got. Okay?''

"Okay,'' she said gratefully. "When do you think you can go?''

Except for the big tree—the one with the moldy corset of moss—it would have been an hour's work. With the big one added in, I didn't think the job would be done until eleven or so.

"I'll give you lunch here, then. But you'll have to get some things at the market for me . . . we're almost out of milk and butter. Also . . . well, I'll have to make you a list.''

Give a woman a disaster and she turns squirrel. I gave her a hug and nodded. We went on around the house. It didn't take more than a glance to understand why Billy had been a little overwhelmed.

"Lordy,'' Steff said in a faint voice.

From where we stood we had enough elevation to be able

to see almost a quarter of a mile of shoreline—the Bibber property to our left, our own, and Brent Norton's to our right.

The huge old pine that had guarded our boat cove had been sheared off halfway up. What was left looked like a brutally sharpened pencil, and the inside of the tree seemed a glistening and defenseless white against the age-and-weather-darkened outer bark. A hundred feet of tree, the old pine's top half, lay partly submerged in our shallow cove. It occurred to me that we were very lucky our little Star-Cruiser wasn't sunk underneath it. The week before, it had developed engine trouble and it was still at the Naples marina, patiently waiting its turn.

On the other side of our little piece of shorefront, the boathouse my father had built—the boathouse that had once housed a sixty-foot Chris-Craft when the Drayton family fortunes had been at a higher mark than they were today—lay under another big tree. It was the one that had stood on Norton's side of the property line, I saw. That raised the first flush of anger. The tree had been dead for five years and he should have long since had it taken down. Now it was three-quarters of the way down; our boathouse was propping it up. The roof had taken on a drunken, swaybacked look. The wind had swirled shingles from the hole the tree had made all over the point of land the boathouse stood on. Billy's description, "bashed," was as good as any.

"That's Norton's tree!" Steff said. And she said it with such hurt indignation that I had to smile in spite of the pain I felt. The flagpole was lying in the water and Old Glory floated soggily beside it in a tangle of lanyard. And I could imagine Norton's response: Sue me.

Billy was on the rock breakwater, examining the dock that had washed up on the stones. It was painted in jaunty blue and yellow stripes. He looked back over his shoulder at us and yelled gleefully, "It's the Martinses', isn't it?"

"Yeah, it is," I said. "Wade in and fish the flag out, would you, Big Bill?"

"Sure!"

To the right of the breakwater was a small sandy beach. In 1941, before Pearl Harbor paid off the Great Depression in blood, my dad hired a man to truck in that fine beach sand—six dumptrucks full—and to spread it out to a depth that is about nipple-high on me, say five feet. The workman charged eighty bucks for the job, and the sand has never moved. Just as well, you know, you can't put a sandy beach in on your land now. Now that the sewerage runoff from the booming cottage-building industry has killed most of the fish and made the rest of them unsafe to eat, the EPA has forbidden installing sand beaches. They might upset the ecology of the lake, you see, and it is presently against the law for anyone except land developers to do that.

Billy went for the flag—then stopped. At the same moment I felt Steff go rigid against me, and I saw it myself. The Harrison side of the lake was gone. It had been buried under a line of bright-white mist, like a fair-weather cloud fallen to earth.

My dream of the night before recurred, and when Steff asked me what it was, the word that nearly jumped first from my mouth was *God.*

"David?"

You couldn't see even a hint of the shoreline over there, but years of looking at Long Lake made me believe that the shoreline wasn't hidden by much; only yards, maybe. The edge of the mist was nearly ruler-straight.

"What is it, Dad?" Billy yelled. He was in the water up to his knees, groping for the soggy flag.

"Fogbank," I said.

"On the *lake?*" Steff asked doubtfully, and I could see Mrs. Carmody's influence in her eyes. Damn the woman. My own moment of unease was passing. Dreams, after all, are insubstantial things, like mist itself.

"Sure. You've seen fog on the lake before."

"Never like that. That looks more like a cloud."

"It's the brightness of the sun," I said. "It's the same way clouds look from an airplane when you fly over them."

"What would do it? We only get fog in damp weather."

"No, we've got it right now," I said. "Harrison does, anyway. It's a little leftover from the storm, that's all. Two fronts meeting. Something along that line."

"David, are you sure?"

I laughed and hauled my arm around her neck. "No, actually, I'm bullshitting like crazy. If I was sure, I'd be doing the weather on the six-o'clock news. Go on and make your shopping list."

She gave me one more doubtful glance, looked at the fogbank for a moment or two with the flat of her hand held up to shade her eyes, and then shook her head. "Weird," she said, and walked away.

For Billy, the mist had lost its novelty. He had fished the flag and a tangle of lanyard out of the water. We spread it on the lawn to dry.

"I heard it was wrong to ever let the flag touch the ground, Daddy," he said in a businesslike, let's-get-this-out-of-the-way tone.

"Yeah?"

"Yeah. Victor McAllister says they lectercute people for it."

"Well, you tell Vic he's full of what makes the grass grow green."

"Horseshit, right?" Billy is a bright boy, but oddly humorless. To the champ, everything is serious business. I'm hoping that he'll live long enough to learn that in this world that is a very dangerous attitude.

"Yeah, right, but don't tell your mother I said so. When the flag's dry, we'll put it away. We'll even fold it into a cocked hat, so we'll be on safe ground there."

"Daddy, will we fix the boathouse roof and get a new flagpole?" For the first time he looked anxious. He'd maybe had enough destruction for a while.

I clapped him on the shoulder. "You're damn tooting."

"Can I go over to the Bibbers' and see what happened there?"

"Just for a couple of minutes. They'll be cleaning up, too, and sometimes that makes people feel a little ugly." The way I presently felt about Norton.

"Okay. Bye!" He was off.

"Stay out of their way, champ. And Billy?"

He glanced back.

"Remember about the live wires. If you see more, steer clear of them."

"Sure, Dad."

I stood there for a moment, first surveying the damage, then glancing out at the mist again. It seemed closer, but it was very hard to tell for sure. If it was closer, it was defying all the laws of nature, because the wind—a very gentle breeze—was against it. That, of course, was patently impossible. It was very, very white. The only thing I can compare it to would be fresh-fallen snow lying in dazzling contrast to the deep-blue brilliance of the winter sky. But snow reflects hundreds and hundreds of diamond points in the sun, and this peculiar fogbank, although bright and clean-looking, did not sparkle. In spite of what Steff had said, mist isn't uncommon on clear days, but when there's a lot of it, the suspended moisture almost always causes a rainbow. But there was no rainbow here.

The unease was back, tugging at me, but before it could deepen I heard a low mechanical sound—*whut-whut-whut!* —followed by a barely audible "Shit!" The mechanical sound was repeated, but this time there was no oath. The third time the chuffing sound was followed by "Mother-fuck!" in that same low I'm-all-by-myself-but-boy-am-I-pissed tone.

Whut-whut-whut-whut—

—Silence—

—then: "You cunt."

I began to grin. Sound carries well out here, and all the buzzing chainsaws were fairly distant. Distant enough for me to recognize the not-so-dulcet tones of my next-door neighbor, the renowned lawyer and lakefront-property-owner, Brenton Norton.

I moved down a little closer to the water, pretending to stroll toward the dock beached on our breakwater. Now I could see Norton. He was in the clearing beside his screened-in porch, standing on a carpet of old pine needles and dressed in paint-spotted jeans and a white strappy T-shirt. His forty-dollar haircut was in disarray and sweat poured down his face. He was down on one knee, laboring over his own chainsaw. It was much bigger and fancier than my little $79.95 Value House job. It seemed to have everything, in fact, but a starter button. He was yanking a cord, producing the listless *whut-whut-whut* sounds and nothing more. I was gladdened in my heart to see that a yellow birch had fallen across his picnic table and smashed it in two.

Norton gave a tremendous yank on the starter cord.

Whut-whut-whutwhutwhut-WHAT! WHAT! WHAT! . . . *WHAT!* . . . *Whut.*

Almost had it there for a minute, fella.

Another Herculean tug.

Whut-whut-whut.

"Cocksucker," Norton whispered fiercely, and bared his teeth at his fancy chainsaw.

I went back around the house, feeling really good for the first time since I got up. My own saw started on the first tug, and I went to work.

Around ten o'clock there was a tap on my shoulder. It was Billy with a can of beer in one hand and Steff's list in the other. I stuffed the list in the back pocket of my jeans and took the beer, which was not exactly frosty-cold but at least cool. I chugged almost half of it at once—rarely does a beer taste that good—and tipped the can in salute at Billy. "Thanks, champ."

"Can I have some?"

I let him have a swallow. He grimaced and handed the can back. I offed the rest and just caught myself as I started to crunch it up in the middle. The deposit law on bottles and cans has been in effect for over three years, but old ways die hard.

"She wrote something across the bottom of the list, but I can't read her writing," Billy said.

I took out the list again. "I can't get WOXO on the radio," Steff's note read. "Do you think the storm knocked them off the air?"

WOXO is the local automated FM rock outlet. It broadcast from Norway, about twenty miles north, and was all that our old and feeble FM receiver would haul in.

"Tell her probably," I said, after reading the question over to him. "Ask her if she can get Portland on the AM band."

"Okay, Daddy, can I come when you go to town?"

"Sure. You and Mommy both, if you want."

"Okay." He ran back to the house with the empty can.

I had worked my way up to the big tree. I made my first cut, sawed through, then turned the saw off for a few moments to let it cool down—the tree was really too big for it, but I thought it would be all right if I didn't rush it. I wondered if the dirt road leading up to Kansas Road was clear of falls, and just as I was wondering, an orange CMP truck lumbered past, probably on its way to the far end of our little road. So that was all right. The road was clear and the power guys would be here by noon to take care of the live lines.

I cut a big chunk off the tree, dragged it to the side of the driveway, and tumbled it over the edge. It rolled down the slope and into the underbrush that had crept back since the long-ago day when my dad and his brothers—all of them artists, we have always been an artistic family, the Draytons—had cleared it away.

I wiped sweat off my face with my arm and wished for another beer; one really only sets your mouth. I picked up the chainsaw and thought about WOXO being off the air. That was the direction that funny fogbank had come from. And it was the direction Shaymore (pronounced *Shammore* by the locals) lay in. Shaymore was where the Arrowhead Project was.

That was old Bill Giosti's theory about the so-called Black Spring: the Arrowhead Project. In the western part of Shaymore, not far from where the town borders on Stoneham, there was a small government preserve surrounded with wire. There were sentries and closed-circuit television cameras and God knew what else. Or so I had heard; I'd never actually seen it, although the Old Shaymore Road runs along the eastern side of the government land for a mile or so.

No one knew for sure where the name Arrowhead Project came from and no one could tell you for one hundred percent sure that that really was the name of the project—if there was a project. Bill Giosti said there was, but when you asked him how and where he came by his information, he got vague. His niece, he said, worked for the Continental Phone Company, and she had heard things. It got like that.

"Atomic things," Bill said that day, leaning in the Scout's window and blowing a healthy draught of Pabst into my face. "That's what they're fooling around with up there. Shooting atoms into the air and all that."

"Mr. Giosti, the air's full of atoms," Billy had said. "That's what Mrs. Neary says. Mrs. Neary says everything's full of atoms."

Bill Giosti gave my son Bill a long, bloodshot glance that finally deflated him. "These are *different* atoms, son."

"Oh, yeah," Billy muttered, giving in.

Dick Muehler, our insurance agent, said the Arrowhead Project was an agricultural station the government was running, no more or less. "Bigger tomatoes with a longer growing season," Dick said sagely, and then went back to showing me how I could help my family most efficiently by dying young. Janine Lawless, our postlady, said it was a geological survey having something to do with shale oil. She knew for a fact, because her husband's brother worked for a man who had—

Mrs. Carmody, now . . . she probably leaned more to Bill Giosti's view of the matter. Not just atoms, but *different* atoms.

I cut two more chunks off the big tree and dropped them over the side before Billy came back with a fresh beer in one hand and a note from Steff in the other. If there's anything Big Bill likes to do more than run messages, I don't know what it could be.

"Thanks," I said, taking them both.

"Can I have a swallow?"

"Just one. You took two last time. Can't have you running around drunk at ten in the morning."

"Quarter past," he said, and smiled shyly over the top of the can. I smiled back—not that it was such a great joke, you know, but Billy makes them so rarely—and then read the note.

"Got JBQ on the radio," Steffy had written. "Don't get drunk before you go to town. You can have one more, but that's it before lunch. Do you think you can get up our road okay?"

I handed him the note back and took my beer. "Tell her the road's okay because a power truck just went by. They'll be working their way up here."

"Okay."

"Champ?"

"What, Dad?"

"Tell her everything's okay."

He smiled again, maybe telling himself first. "Okay."

He ran back and I watched him go, legs pumping, soles of his zori showing. I love him. It's his face and sometimes the way his eyes turn up to mine that make me feel as if things are really okay. It's a lie, of course—things are not okay and never have been—but my kid makes me believe the lie.

I drank some beer, set the can down carefully on a rock, and got the chainsaw going again. About twenty minutes later I felt a light tap on my shoulder and turned, expecting to see

Billy again. Instead it was Brent Norton. I turned off the chainsaw.

He didn't look the way Norton usually looks. He looked hot and tired and unhappy and a little bewildered.

"Hi, Brent," I said. Our last words had been hard ones, and I was a little unsure how to proceed. I had a funny feeling that he had been standing behind me for the last five minutes or so, clearing his throat decorously under the chainsaw's aggressive roar. I hadn't gotten a really good look at him this summer. He had lost weight, but it didn't look good. It should have, because he had been carrying around an extra twenty pounds, but it didn't. His wife had died the previous November. Cancer. Aggie Bibber told Steffy that. Aggie was our resident necrologist. Every neighborhood has one. From the casual way Norton had of ragging his wife and belittling her (doing it with the contemptuous ease of a veteran matador inserting *banderillas* in an old bull's lumbering body), I would have guessed he'd be glad to have her gone. If asked, I might even have speculated that he'd show up this summer with a girl twenty years younger than he was on his arm and a silly my-cock-has-died-and-gone-to-heaven grin on his face. But instead of the silly grin there was only a new batch of age lines, and the weight had come off in all the wrong places, leaving sags and folds and dewlaps that told their own story. For one passing moment I wanted only to lead Norton to a patch of sun and sit him beside one of the fallen trees with my can of beer in his hand, and do a charcoal sketch of him.

"Hi, Dave," he said, after a long moment of awkward silence—a silence that was made even louder by the absence of the chainsaw's racket and roar. He stopped, then blurted: "That tree. That damn tree. I'm sorry. You were right."

I shrugged.

He said, "Another tree fell on my car."

"I'm sorry to h—" I began, and then a horrid suspicion dawned. "It wasn't the T-Bird, was it?"

"Yeah. It was."

Norton had a 1960 Thunderbird in mint condition, only thirty thousand miles. It was a deep midnight blue inside and out. He drove it only summers, and then only rarely. He loved that Bird the way some men love electric trains or model ships or target-shooting pistols.

"That's a bitch," I said, and meant it.

He shook his head slowly. "I almost didn't bring it up. Almost brought the station wagon, you know. Then I said what the hell. I drove it up and a big old rotten pine fell on it. The roof of it's all bashed in. And I thought I'd cut it up . . . the tree, I mean . . . but I can't get my chainsaw to fire up . . . I paid two hundred dollars for that sucker . . . and . . . and . . ."

His throat began to emit little clicking sounds. His mouth worked as if he were toothless and chewing dates. For one helpless second I thought he was going to just stand there and bawl like a kid on a sandlot. Then he got himself under some halfway kind of control, shrugged, and turned away as if to look at the chunks of wood I had cut up.

"Well, we can look at your saw," I said. "Your T-Bird insured?"

"Yeah," he said, "like your boathouse."

I saw what he meant, and remembered again what Steff had said about insurance.

"Listen, Dave, I wondered if I could borrow your Saab and take a run up to town. I thought I'd get some bread and cold cuts and beer. A lot of beer."

"Billy and I are going up in the Scout," I said. "Come with us if you want. That is, if you'll give me a hand dragging the rest of this tree off to one side."

"Happy to."

He grabbed one end but couldn't quite lift it up. I had to do most of the work. Between the two of us we were able to tumble it into the underbrush. Norton was puffing and panting, his cheeks nearly purple. After all the yanking he had done on that chainsaw starter pull, I was a little worried about his ticker.

"Okay?" I asked, and he nodded, still breathing fast. "Come on back to the house, then. I can fix you up with a beer."

"Thank you," he said. "How is Stephanie?" He was regaining some of the old smooth pomposity that I disliked.

"Very well, thanks."

"And your son?"

"He's fine, too."

"Glad to hear it."

Steff came out, and a moment's surprise passed over her

face when she saw who was with me. Norton smiled and his eyes crawled over her tight T-shirt. He hadn't changed that much after all.

"Hello, Brent," she said cautiously. Billy poked his head out from under her arm.

"Hello, Stephanie. Hi, Billy."

"Brent's T-Bird took a pretty good rap in the storm," I told her. "Stove in the roof, he says."

"Oh, no!"

Norton told it again while he drank one of our beers. I was sipping a third, but I had no kind of buzz on; apparently I had sweat the beer out as rapidly as I drank it.

"He's going to come to town with Billy and me."

"Well, I won't expect you for a while. You may have to go to the Shop-and-Save in Norway."

"Oh? Why?"

"Well, if the power's off in Bridgton—"

"Mom says all the cash registers and things run on electricity," Billy supplied.

It was a good point.

"Have you still got the list?"

I patted my hip pocket.

Her eyes shifted to Norton. "I'm very sorry about Carla, Brent. We all were."

"Thank you," he said. "Thank you very much.'

There was another moment of awkward silence which Billy broke. "Can we go now, Daddy?" He had changed to jeans and sneakers.

"Yeah, I guess so. You ready, Brent?"

"Give me another beer for the road and I will be."

Steffy's brow creased. She had never approved of the one-for-the-road philosophy, or of men who drive with a can of Bud leaning against their crotches. I gave her a bare nod and she shrugged. I didn't want to reopen things with Norton now. She got him a beer.

"Thanks," he said to Steffy, not really thanking her but only mouthing a word. It was the way you thank a waitress in a restaurant. He turned back to me. "Lead on, Macduff."

"Be right with you," I said, and went into the living room. Norton followed, and exclaimed over the birch, but I wasn't interested in that or in the cost of replacing the window just then. I was looking at the lake through the sliding glass panel that gave on our deck. The breeze had freshened a little and the day had warmed up five degrees or so while I was cutting wood. I thought the odd mist we'd noticed earlier would surely have broken up, but it hadn't. It was closer, too. Halfway across the lake now.

"I noticed that earlier," Norton said, pontificating. "Some kind of temperature inversion, that's my guess."

I didn't like it. I felt very strongly that I had never seen a mist exactly like this one. Part of it was the unnerving straight edge of its leading front. Nothing in nature is that even; man is the inventor of straight edges. Part of it was that pure, dazzling whiteness, with no variation but also without the sparkle of moisture. It was only half a mile or so off now, and the contrast between it and the blues of the lake and sky was more striking than ever.

"Come on, Dad!" Billy was tugging at my pants.

We all went back to the kitchen. Brent Norton spared one final glance at the tree that had crashed into our living room.

"Too bad it wasn't an apple tree, huh?" Billy remarked brightly. "That's what my mom said. Pretty funny, don't you think?"

"Your mother's a real card, Billy," Norton said. He ruffled Billy's hair in a perfunctory way and his eyes went to the front of Steff's T-shirt again. No, he was not a man I was ever going to be able to really like.

"Listen, why don't you come with us, Steff?" I asked. For no concrete reason I suddenly wanted her to come along.

"No, I think I'll stay here and pull some weeds in the garden," she said. Her eyes shifted toward Norton and then back to me. "This morning it seems like I'm the only thing around here that doesn't run on electricity."

Norton laughed too heartily.

I was getting her message, but tried one more time. "You sure?"

"Sure," she said firmly. "The old bend-and-stretch will do me good."

"Well, don't get too much sun."

"I'll put on my straw hat. We'll have sandwiches when you get back."

"Good."

She turned her face up to be kissed. "Be careful. There might be blowdowns on Kansas Road too, you know."

"I'll be careful."

"You be careful, too," she told Billy, and kissed his cheek.

"Right, Mom." He banged out of the door and the screen cracked shut behind him.

Norton and I walked out after him. "Why don't we go over to your place and cut the tree off your Bird?" I asked him. All of a sudden I could think of lots of reasons to delay leaving for town.

"I don't even want to look at it until after lunch and a few more of these," Norton said, holding up his beer can. "The damage has been done, Dave old buddy."

I didn't like him calling me buddy, either.

We all got into the front seat of the Scout (in the far corner of the garage my scarred Fisher plow blade sat glimmering yellow, like the ghost of Christmas yet-to-come) and I backed out, crunching over a litter of storm-blown twigs. Steff was standing on the cement path which leads to the vegetable patch at the extreme west end of our property. She had a pair of clippers in one gloved hand and the weeding claw in the other. She had put on her old floppy sunhat, and it cast a band of shadow over her face. I tapped the horn twice, lightly, and she raised the hand holding the clippers in answer. We pulled out. I haven't seen my wife since then.

We had to stop once on our way up to Kansas Road. Since the power truck had driven through, a pretty fair-sized pine had dropped across the road. Norton and I got out and moved it enough so I could inch the Scout by, getting our hands all pitchy in the process. Billy wanted to help but I waved him back. I was afraid he might get poked in the eye. Old trees have always reminded me of the Ents in Tolkien's wonderful Rings saga, only Ents that have gone bad. Old trees want to hurt you. It doesn't matter if you're snow-shoeing, cross-country skiing, or just taking a walk in the woods. Old trees want to hurt you, and I think they'd kill you if they could.

Kansas Road itself was clear, but in several places we saw

more lines down. About a quarter-mile past the Vicki-Linn Campground there was a power pole lying full-length in the ditch, heavy wires snarled around its top like wild hair.

"That was some storm," Norton said in his mellifluous, courtroom-trained voice; but he didn't seem to be pontificating now, only solemn.

"Yeah, it was."

"Look, Dad!"

He was pointing at the remains of the Ellitches' barn. For twelve years it had been sagging tiredly in Tommy Ellitch's back field, up to its hips in sunflowers, goldenrod, and Lolly-come-see-me. Every fall I would think it could not last through another winter. And every spring it would still be there. But it wasn't anymore. All that remained was a splintered wreckage and a roof that had been mostly stripped of shingles. Its number had come up. And for some reason that echoed solemnly, even ominously, inside me. The storm had come and smashed it flat.

Norton drained his beer, crushed the can in one hand, and dropped it indifferently to the floor of the Scout. Billy opened his mouth to say something and then closed it again— good boy. Norton came from New Jersey, where there was no bottle-and-can law; I guess he could be forgiven for squashing my nickel when I could barely remember not to do it myself.

Billy started fooling with the radio, and I asked him to see if WOXO was back on the air. He dialed up to FM 92 and got nothing but a blank hum. He looked at me and shrugged. I thought for a moment. What other stations were on the far side of that peculiar fog front?

"Try WBLM," I said.

He dialed down to the other end, passing WJBQ-FM and WIGY-FM on the way. They were there, doing business as usual . . . but WBLM, Maine's premier progressive-rock station, was off the air.

"Funny," I said.

"What's that?" Norton asked.

"Nothing. Just thinking out loud."

Billy had tuned back to the musical cereal on WJBQ. Pretty soon we got to town.

The Norge Washateria in the shopping center was closed, it being impossible to run a coin-op laundry without electricity,

but both the Bridgton Pharmacy and the Federal Foods Supermarket were open. The parking lot was pretty full, and as
always in the middle of the summer, a lot of the cars had
out-of-state plates. Little knots of people stood here and there
in the sun, noodling about the storm, women with women,
men with men.

I saw Mrs. Carmody, she of the stuffed animals and the
stump-water lore. She sailed into the supermarket decked out
in an amazing canary-yellow pantsuit. A purse that looked the
size of a small Samsonite suitcase was slung over one forearm. Then an idiot on a Yamaha roared past me, missing my
front bumper by a few scant inches. He wore a denim jacket,
mirror sunglasses, and no helmet.

"Look at that stupid shit," Norton growled.

I circled the parking lot once, looking for a good space.
There were none. I was just resigning myself to a long walk
from the far end of the lot when I got lucky. A lime-green
Cadillac the size of a small cabin cruiser was easing out of a
slot in the rank closest to the market's doors. The moment it
was gone, I slid into the space.

I gave Billy Steff's shopping list. He was five, but he could
read printing. "Get a cart and get started. I want to give your
mother a jingle. Mr. Norton will help you. And I'll be right
along."

We got out and Billy immediately grabbed Mr. Norton's
hand. He'd been taught not to cross the parking lot without holding an adult's hand when he was younger and
hadn't yet lost the habit. Norton looked surprised for a
moment, and then smiled a little. I could almost forgive
him for feeling Steff up with his eyes. The two of them
went into the market.

I strolled over to the pay phone, which was on the wall
between the drugstore and the Norge. A sweltering woman in
a purple sunsuit was jogging the cutoff switch up and down. I
stood behind her with my hands in my pockets, wondering
why I felt so uneasy about Steff, and why the unease should
be all wrapped up with that line of white but unsparkling fog,
the radio stations that were off the air . . . and the Arrowhead
Project.

The woman in the purple sunsuit had a sunburn and freckles on her fat shoulders. She looked like a sweaty orange

baby. She slammed the phone back down in its cradle, turned toward the drugstore and saw me there.

"Save your dime," she said. "Just dah-dah-dah." She walked grumpily away.

I almost slapped my forehead. The phone lines were down someplace, of course. Some of them were underground, but nowhere near all of them. I tried the phone anyway. The pay phones in the area are what Steff calls Paranoid Pay Phones. Instead of putting your dime right in, you get a dial tone and make your call. When someone answers, there's an automatic cutoff and you have to shove your dime in before your party hangs up. They're irritating, but that day it did save me my dime. There was no dial tone. As the lady had said, it was just dah-dah-dah.

I hung up and walked slowly toward the market, just in time to see an amusing little incident. An elderly couple walked toward the IN door, chatting together. And still chatting, they walked right into it. They stopped talking in a jangle and the woman squawked her surprise. They stared at each other comically. Then they laughed, and the old guy pushed the door open for his wife with some effort—those electric-eye doors are heavy—and they went in. When the electricity goes off, it catches you in a hundred different ways.

I pushed the door open myself and noticed the lack of air conditioning first thing. Usually in the summer they have it cranked up high enough to give you frostbite if you stay in the market more than an hour at a stretch.

Like most modern markets, the Federal was constructed like a Skinner box—modern marketing techniques turn all customers into white rats. The stuff you really needed, staples, like bread, milk, meat, beer, and frozen dinners, was all on the far side of the store. To get there you had to walk past all the impulse items known to modern man—everything from Cricket lighters to rubber dog bones.

Beyond the IN door is the fruit-and-vegetable aisle. I looked up it, but there was no sign of Norton or my son. The old lady who had run into the door was examining the grapefruits. Her husband had produced a net sack to store purchases in.

I walked up the aisle and went left. I found them in the third aisle, Billy mulling over the ranks of Jello-O packages and instant puddings. Norton was standing directly behind him, peering at Steff's list. I had to grin a little at his nonplussed expression.

I threaded my way down to them, past half-loaded carriages (Steff hadn't been the only one struck by the squirreling impulse, apparently) and browsing shoppers. Norton took two cans of pie filling down from the top shelf and put them in the cart.

"How are you doing?" I asked, and Norton looked around with unmistakable relief.

"All right, aren't we, Billy?"

"Sure," Billy said, and couldn't resist adding in a rather smug tone: "But there's lots of stuff Mr. Norton can't read either, Dad."

"Let me see." I took the list.

Norton had made a neat, lawyerly check beside each of the items he and Billy had picked up—half a dozen or so, including the milk and a six-pack of Coke. There were maybe ten other things that she wanted.

"We ought to go back to the fruits and vegetables," I said. "She wants some tomatoes and cucumbers."

Billy started to turn the cart around and Norton said, "You ought to go have a look at the checkout, Dave."

I went and had a look. It was the sort of thing you sometimes see photos of in the paper on a slow newsday, with a humorous caption beneath. Only two lanes were open, and the double line of people waiting to check their purchases out stretched past the mostly denuded bread racks, then made a jig to the right and went out of sight along the frozen-food coolers. All of the new computerized NCRs were hooded. At each of the two open positions, a harried-looking girl was totting up purchases on a battery-powered pocket calculator. Standing with each girl was one of the Federal's two managers, Bud Brown and Ollie Weeks. I liked Ollie but didn't care much for Bud Brown, who seemed to fancy himself the Charles de Gaulle of the supermarket world.

As each girl finished checking her order, Bud or Ollie would paperclip a chit to the customer's cash or check and toss it into the box he was using as a cash repository. They all looked hot and tired.

"Hope you brought a good book," Norton said, joining me. "We're going to be in line for a while."

I thought of Steff again, at home alone, and had another flash of unease. "You go on and get your stuff," I said. "Billy and I can handle the rest of this."

"Want me to grab a few more beers for you too?"

I thought about it, but in spite of the rapprochement, I didn't want to spend the afternoon with Brent Norton getting drunk. Not with the mess things were in around the house.

"Sorry," I said. "I've got to take a raincheck, Brent."

I thought his face stiffened a little. "Okay," he said shortly, and walked off. I watched him go, and then Billy was tugging at my shirt.

"Did you talk to Mommy?"

"Nope. The phone wasn't working. Those lines are down too, I guess."

"Are you worried about her?"

"No," I said, lying. I was worried, all right, but had no idea why I should be. "No, of course I'm not. Are you?"

"No-ooo . . ." But he was. His face had a pinched look. We should have gone back then. But even then it might have been too late.

III. The Coming of the Mist.

We worked our way back to the fruits and vegetables like salmon fighting their way upstream. I saw some familiar faces—Mike Hatlen, one of our selectmen, Mrs. Reppler from the grammar school (she who had terrified generations of third-graders was currently sneering at the cantaloupes), Mrs. Turman, who sometimes sat Billy when Steff and I went out—but mostly they were summer people stocking up on no-cook items and joshing each other about "roughing it." The cold cuts had been picked over as thoroughly as the dimebook tray at a rummage sale; there was nothing left but a few packages of bologna, some macaroni loaf, and one lonely, phallic kielbasa sausage.

I got tomatoes, cukes, and a jar of mayonnaise. She wanted bacon, but all the bacon was gone. I picked up some of the bologna as a substitute, although I've never been able to eat the stuff with any real enthusiasm since the FDA reported that each package contained a small amount of insect filth—a little something extra for your money

"Look," Billy said as we rounded the corner into the fourth aisle. "There's some army guys."

There were two of them, their dun uniforms standing out against the much brighter background of summer clothes and sportswear. We had gotten used to seeing a scattering of army personnel with the Arrowhead Project only thirty miles or so away. These two looked hardly old enough to shave yet.

I glanced back down at Steff's list and saw that we had everything . . . no, almost but not quite. At the bottom, as an afterthought, she had scribbled: *Bottle of Lancers?* That sounded good to me. A couple of glasses of wine tonight after Billy had sacked out, then maybe a long slow bout of love-making before sleep.

I left the cart and worked my way down to the wine and got a bottle. As I walked back I passed the big double doors leading to the storage area and heard the steady roar of a good-sized generator.

I decided it was probably just big enough to keep the cold cases cold, but not large enough to power the doors and cash registers and all the other electrical equipment. It sounded like a motorcycle back there.

Norton appeared just as we got into line, balancing two six-packs of Schlitz Light, a loaf of bread, and the kielbasa I had spotted a few minutes earlier. He got in line with Billy and me. It seemed very warm in the market with the air conditioning off, and I wondered why none of the stockboys had at least chocked the doors open. I had seen Buddy Eagleton in his red apron two aisles back, doing nothing and piling it up. The generator roared monotonously. I had the beginnings of a headache.

"Put your stuff in here before you drop something," I said.

"Thanks."

The lines were up past the frozen food now; people had to cut through to get what they wanted and there was much excuse-me-ing and pardon-me-ing. "This is going to be a cunt," Norton said morosely, and I frowned a little. That sort of language is rougher than I'd like Billy to hear.

The generator's roar muted a little as the line shuffled forward. Norton and I made desultory conversation, skirting around the ugly property dispute that had landed us in district court and sticking with things like the Red Sox's chances and the weather. At last we exhausted our little store of small talk and fell silent. Billy fidgeted beside me. The line crawled along. Now we had frozen dinners on our right and the more expensive wines and champagnes on our left. As the line progressed down to the cheaper wines, I toyed briefly with the idea of picking up a bottle of Ripple, the wine of my flaming youth. I didn't do it. My youth never flamed that much anyway.

"Jeez, why can't they hurry up, Dad?" Billy asked. That pinched look was still on his face, and suddenly, briefly, the mist of disquiet that had settled over me rifted, and something terrible peered through from the other side—the bright and metallic face of terror. Then it passed.

"Keep cool, champ," I said.

We had made it up to the bread racks—to the point where the double line bent to the left. We could see the checkout lanes now, the two that were open and the other four, deserted, each with a little sign on the stationary conveyor belt, signs that read PLEASE CHOOSE ANOTHER LANE and WINSTON. Beyond the lanes was the big sectioned plate-glass window which gave a view of the parking lot and the intersection of Routes 117 and 302 beyond. The view was partially obscured by the white-paper backs of signs advertising current specials and the latest giveaway, which happened to be a set of books called *The Mother Nature Encyclopedia*. We were in the line that would eventually lead us to the checkout where Bud Brown was standing. There were still maybe thirty people in front of us. The easiest one to pick out was Mrs. Carmody in her blazing-yellow pantsuit. She looked like an advertisement for yellow fever.

Suddenly a shrieking noise began in the distance. It quickly built up in volume and resolved itself into the crazy warble of a police siren. A horn blared at the intersection and there was a shriek of brakes and burning rubber. I couldn't see—the angle was all wrong—but the siren reached its loudest as it approached the market and then began to fade as the police car went past. A few people broke out of line to look, but not many. They had waited too long to chance losing their places.

Norton went; his stuff was tucked into my cart. After a few moments he came back and got into line again. "Local fuzz," he said.

Then the town fire whistle began to wail, slowly cranking

up to a shriek of its own, falling off, then rising again. Billy grabbed my hand—clutched it. "What is it, Daddy?" he asked, and then, immediately: "Is Mommy all right?"

"Must be a fire on the Kansas Road," Norton said. "Those damned live lines from the storm. The fire trucks will go through in a minute."

That gave my disquiet something to crystallize on. There were live lines down in *our* yard.

Bud Brown said something to the checker he was supervising; she had been craning around to see what was happening. She flushed and began to run her calculator again.

I didn't want to be in this line. All of a sudden I very badly didn't want to be in it. But it was moving again, and it seemed foolish to leave now. We had gotten down by the cartons of cigarettes.

Someone pushed through the IN door, some teenager. I think it was the kid we almost hit coming in, the one on the Yamaha with no helmet. "The fog!" he yelled. "Y'oughta see the fog! It's rolling right up Kansas Road!" People looked around at him. He was panting, as if he had run a long distance. Nobody said anything. "Well, y'oughta see it," he repeated, sounding defensive this time. People eyed him and some of them shuffled, but no one wanted to lose his or her place in line. A few people who hadn't reached the lines yet left their carts and strolled through the empty checkout lanes to see if they could see what he was talking about. A big guy in a summer hat with a paisley band (the kind of hat you almost never see except in beer commercials with backyard barbecues as their settings) yanked open the OUT door and several people—ten, maybe a dozen—went out with him. The kid went along.

"Don't let out all the air conditioning," one of the army kids cracked, and there were a few chuckles. I wasn't chuckling. I had seen the mist coming across the lake.

"Billy, why don't you go have a look?" Norton said.

"No," I said at once, for no concrete reason.

The line moved forward again. People craned their necks, looking for the fog the kid had mentioned, but there was nothing on view except bright-blue sky. I heard someone say that the kid must have been joking. Someone else responded that he had seen a funny line of mist on Long Lake not an hour ago. The first whistle whooped and screamed. I didn't like it. It sounded like big-league doom blowing that way.

More people went out. A few even left their places in line, which speeded up the proceedings a bit. Then grizzled old John Lee Frovin, who works as a mechanic at the Texaco station, came ducking in and yelled: "Hey! Anybody got a camera?" He looked around, then ducked back out again.

That caused something of a rush. If it was worth taking a picture of, it was worth seeing.

Suddenly Mrs. Carmody cried in her rusty but powerful old voice, "Don't go out there!"

People turned around to look at her. The orderly shape of the lines had grown fuzzy as people left to get a look at the mist, or as they drew away from Mrs. Carmody, or as they milled around, seeking out their friends. A pretty young woman in a cranberry-colored sweatshirt and dark-green slacks was looking at Mrs. Carmody in a thoughtful, evaluating way. A few opportunists were taking advantage of whatever the situation was to move up a couple of places. The checker beside Bud Brown looked over her shoulder again, and Brown tapped her shoulder with a long finger. "Keep your mind on what you're doing, Sally."

"Don't go out there!" Mrs. Carmody yelled. "It's death! I feel that it's death out there!"

Bud and Ollie Weeks, who both knew her, just looked impatient and irritated, but any summer people around her stepped smartly away, never minding their places in line. The bag-ladies in big cities seem to have the same effect on people, as if they were carriers of some contagious disease. Who knows? Maybe they are.

Things began to happen at an accelerating, confusing pace then. A man staggered into the market, shoving the IN door open. His nose was bleeding. "Something in the fog!" he screamed, and Billy shrank against me—whether because of the man's bloody nose or what he was saying, I don't know. "Something in the fog! Something in the fog took John Lee! Something—" He staggered back against a display of lawn food stacked by the window and sat down there. *"Something in the fog took John Lee and I heard him screaming!"*

The situation changed. Made nervous by the storm, by the police siren and the fire whistle, by the subtle dislocation any power outage causes in the American psyche, and by the

steadily mounting atmosphere of unease as things somehow
. . . somehow *changed* (I don't know how to put it any better
than that), people began to move in a body.

They didn't bolt. If I told you that, I would be giving you
entirely the wrong impression. It wasn't exactly a panic. They
didn't run—or at least, most of them didn't. But they went.
Some of them just went to the big show window on the far
side of the checkout lanes to look out. Others went out the IN
door, some still carrying their intended purchases. Bud Brown,
harried and officious, began yelling: "Hey! You haven't paid
for that! Hey, you! Come back here with those hot-dog
rolls!"

Someone laughed at him, a crazy, yodeling sound that
made other people smile. Even as they smiled they looked
bewildered, confused, and nervous. Then someone else laughed
and Brown flushed. He grabbed a box of mushrooms away
from a lady who was crowding past him to look out the
window—the segments of glass were lined with people now,
they were like the folks you see looking through loopholes
into a building site—and the lady screamed, "Give me back
my mushies!" This bizarre term of affection caused two men
standing nearby to break into crazy laughter—and there was
something of the old English Bedlam about all of it, now.
Mrs. Carmody trumpeted again not to go out there. The fire
whistle whooped breathlessly, a strong old woman who had
scared up a prowler in the house. And Billy burst into tears.

"Daddy, what's that bloody man? Why is that bloody
man?"

"It's okay, Big Bill, it's his nose, he's okay."

"What did he mean, something in the fog?" Norton asked.
He was frowning ponderously, which was probably Norton's
way of looking confused.

"Daddy, I'm scared," Billy said through his tears. "Can
we please go home?"

Someone bumped past me roughly, jolting me off my feet,
and I picked Billy up. I was getting scared, too. The confusion was mounting. Sally, the checker by Bud Brown, started
away and he grabbed her back by the collar of her red smock.
It ripped. She slap-clawed out at him, her face twisting. *"Get
your fucking hands off me!"* she screamed.

"Oh, shut up, you little bitch," Brown said, but he sounded
totally astounded.

He reached for her again and Ollie Weeks said sharply: "Bud! Cool it!"

Someone else screamed. It hadn't been a panic before—not quite—but it was getting to be one. People streamed out of both doors. There was a crash of breaking glass and Coke fizzed suddenly across the floor.

"What the Christ *is* this?" Norton exclaimed.

That was when it started getting dark . . . but no, that's not exactly right. My thought at the time was not that it was getting dark but that the lights in the market had gone out. I looked up at the fluorescents in a quick reflex action, and I wasn't alone. And at first, until I remembered the power failure, it seemed that was it, that was what had changed the quality of the light. Then I remembered they had been out all the time we had been in the market and things hadn't seemed dark before. Then I knew, even before the people at the window started to yell and point.

The mist was coming.

It came from the Kansas Road entrance to the parking lot, and even this close it looked no different than it had when we first noticed it on the far side of the lake. It was white and bright but nonreflecting. It was moving fast, and it had blotted out most of the sun. Where the sun had been there was now a silver coin in the sky, like a full moon in winter seen through a thin scud of cloud.

It came with lazy speed. Watching it reminded me somehow of last evening's waterspout. There are big forces in nature that you hardly ever see—earthquakes, hurricanes, tornadoes—I haven't seen them all but I've seen enough to guess that they all move with that lazy, hypnotizing speed. They hold you spellbound, the way Billy and Steffy had been in front of the picture window last night.

It rolled impartially across the two-lane blacktop and erased it from view. The McKeons' nice restored Dutch Colonial was swallowed whole. For a moment the second floor of the ramshackle apartment building next door jutted out of the whiteness, and then it went too. The KEEP RIGHT sign at the entrance and exit points to the Federal's parking lot disappeared, the black letters on the sign seeming to float for a moment in limbo after the sign's dirty-white background was gone. The cars in the parking lot began to disappear next.

"What the Christ *is* this?" Norton asked again, and there was a catch in his voice.

It came on, eating up the blue sky and the fresh black hottop with equal ease. Even twenty feet away the line of demarcation was perfectly clear. I had the nutty feeling that I was watching some extra-good piece of visual effects, something dreamed up by Willys O'Brian or Douglas Trumbull. It happened so quickly. The blue sky disappeared to a wide swipe, then to a stripe, then to a pencil line. Then it was gone. Blank white pressed against the glass of the wide show window. I could see as far as the litter barrel that stood maybe four feet away, but not much farther. I could see the front bumper of my Scout, but that was all.

A woman screamed, very loud and long. Billy pressed himself more tightly against me. His body was trembling like a loose bundle of wires with high voltage running through them.

A man yelled and bolted through one of the deserted lanes toward the door. I think that was what finally started the stampede. People rushed pell-mell into the fog.

"Hey!" Brown roared. I don't know if he was angry, scared, or both. His face was nearly purple. Veins stood out on his neck, looking almost as thick as battery cables. *"Hey you people, you can't take that stuff. Get back here with that stuff, you're shoplifting!"*

They kept going, but some of them tossed their stuff aside. Some were laughing and excited, but they were a minority. They poured out into the fog, and none of us who stayed ever saw them again. There was a faint, acrid smell drifting in through the open door. People began to jam up there. Some pushing and shoving started. I was getting an ache in my shoulders from holding Billy. He was good-sized; Steff sometimes called him her young heifer.

Norton started to wander off, his face preoccupied and rather bemused. He was heading for the door.

I switched Billy to the other arm so I could grab Norton's arm before he drifted out of reach. "No, man, I wouldn't," I said.

He turned back. "What?"

"Better wait and see."

"See what?"

"I don't know," I said.

"You don't think—" he began, and a shriek came out of the fog.

Norton shut up. The tight jam at the OUT door loosened and then reversed itself. The babble of excited conversation, shouts and calls, subsided. The faces of the people by the door suddenly looked flat and pale and two dimensional.

The shriek went on and on, competing with the fire whistle. It seemed impossible that any human pair of lungs could have enough air in them to sustain such a shriek. Norton muttered, "Oh my God," and ran his hands through his hair.

The shriek ended abruptly. It did not dwindle; it was cut off. One more man went outside, a beefy guy in chino workpants. I think he was set on rescuing the shrieker. For a moment he was out there, visible through the glass and the mist, like a figure seen through a milkscum on a tumbler. Then (and as far as I know, I was the only one to see this) something beyond him appeared to move, a gray shadow in all that white. And it seemed to me that instead of running into the fog, the man in the chino pants was *jerked* into it, his hands flailing upward as if in surprise.

For a moment there was total silence in the market.

A constellation of moons suddenly glowed into being outside. The parking-lot sodium lights, undoubtedly supplied by underground electrical cables, had just gone on.

"Don't go out there," Mrs. Carmody said in her best gore-crow voice. "It's death to go out there."

All at once, no one seemed disposed to argue or laugh.

Another scream came from outside, this one muffled and rather distant-sounding. Billy tensed against me again.

"David, what's going on?" Ollie Weeks asked. He had left his position. There were big beads of sweat on his round, smooth face. "What is this?"

"I'll be goddammed if I have any idea," I said. Ollie looked badly scared. He was a bachelor who lived in a nice little house up by Highland Lake and who liked to drink in the bar at Pleasant Mountain. On the pudgy little finger of his left hand was a star-sapphire ring. The February before, he won some money in the state lottery. He bought the ring out of his winnings. I always had the idea that Ollie was a little afraid of girls.

"I don't dig this," he said.

"No. Billy, I have to put you down. I'll hold your hand, but you're breaking my arms, okay?"

"Mommy," he whispered.

"She's okay," I told him. It was something to say.

The old geezer who runs the secondhand shop near Jon's Restaurant walked past us, bundled into the old collegiate letter-sweater he wears year-round. He said loudly: "It's one of those pollution clouds. The mills at Rumford and South Paris. Chemicals." With that, he made off up the Aisle 4, past the patent medicines and toilet paper.

"Let's get out of here, David," Norton said with no conviction at all. "What do you say we—"

There was a thud. An odd, twisting thud that I felt mostly in my feet, as if the entire building had suddenly dropped three feet. Several people cried out in fear and surprise. There was a musical jingle of bottles leaning off their shelves and destroying themselves upon the tile floor. A chunk of glass shaped like a pie wedge fell out of one of the segments of the wide front window, and I saw that the wooden frames banding the heavy sections of glass had buckled and splintered in some places.

The fire whistle stopped in mid-whoop.

The quiet that followed was the bated silence of people waiting for something else, something more. I was shocked and numb, and my mind made a strange cross-patch connection with the past. Back when Bridgton was little more than a crossroads, my dad would take me in with him and stand talking at the counter while I looked through the glass at the penny candy and two-cent chews. It was January thaw. No sound but the drip of meltwater falling from the galvanized tin gutters to the rain barrels on either side of the store. Me looking at the jawbreakers and buttons and pinwheels. The mystic yellow globes of light overhead showing up the monstrous, projected shadows of last summer's battalion of dead flies. A little boy named David Drayton with his father, the famous artist Andrew Drayton, whose painting *Christine Standing Alone* hung in the White House. A little boy named David Drayton looking at the candy and the Davy Crockett bubble-gum cards and vaguely needing to go pee. And outside, the pressing, billowing yellow fog of January thaw.

The memory passed, but very slowly.

"You people!" Norton bellowed. "All you people, listen to me!"

They looked around. Norton was holding up both hands, the fingers splayed like a political candidate accepting accolades.

"It may be dangerous to go outside!" Norton yelled.

"Why?" a woman screamed back. "My kids're at home! I got to get back to my kids!"

"It's death to go out there!" Mrs. Carmody came back smartly. She was standing by the twenty-five-pound sacks of fertilizer stacked below the window, and her face seemed to bulge somehow, as if she were swelling.

A teenager gave her a sudden hard push and she sat down on the bags with a surprised grunt. "Stop saying that, you old bag! Stop rappin' that crazy bullshit!"

"Please!" Norton yelled. "If we just wait a few moments until it blows over and we can see—"

A babble of conflicting shouts greeted this.

"He's right," I said, shouting to be heard over the noise. "Let's just try to keep cool."

"I think that was an earthquake," a bespectacled man said. His voice was soft. In one hand he held a package of hamburger and a bag of buns. The other hand was holding the hand of a little girl, maybe a year younger than Billy. "I really think that was an earthquake."

"They had one over in Naples four years ago," a fat local man said.

"That was in Casco," his wife contradicted immediately. She spoke in the unmistakable tones of a veteran contradictor.

"Naples," the fat local man said, but with less assurance.

"Casco," his wife said firmly, and he gave up.

Somewhere a can that had been jostled to the very edge of its shelf by the thump, earthquake, whatever it had been, fell off with a delayed clatter. Billy burst into tears. "I want to go *home!* I want my MOTHER!"

"Can't you shut that kid up?" Bud Brown asked. His eyes were darting rapidly but aimlessly from place to place.

"Would you like a shot in the teeth, motormouth?" I asked him.

"Come on, Dave, that's not helping," Norton said distractedly.

"I'm sorry," the woman who had screamed earlier said.

"I'm sorry, but I can't stay here. I've got to get home and see to my kids."

She looked around at us, a blond woman with a tired, pretty face.

"Wanda's looking after little Victor, you see. Wanda's only eight and sometimes she forgets . . . forgets she's supposed to be . . . well, watching him, you know. And little Victor . . . he likes to turn on the stove burners to see the little red light come on . . . he likes that light . . . and sometimes he pulls out the plugs . . . little Victor does . . . and Wanda gets . . . bored watching him after a while . . . she's just eight . . ." She stopped talking and just looked at us. I imagine that we must have looked like nothing but a bank of merciless eyes to her right then, not human beings at all, just eyes. *"Isn't anyone going to help me?"* she screamed. Her lips began to tremble. "Won't . . . won't anybody here see a lady home?"

No one replied. People shuffled their feet. She looked from face to face with her own broken face. The fat local man took a hesitant half-step forward and his wife jerked him back with one quick tug, her hand clapped over his wrist like a manacle.

"You?" the blond woman asked Ollie. He shook his head. "You?" she said to Bud. He put his hand over the Texas Instruments calculator on the counter and made no reply. "You?" she said to Norton, and Norton began to say something in his big lawyer's voice, something about how no one should go off half-cocked, and . . . and she dismissed him and Norton just trailed off.

"You?" she said to me, and I picked Billy up again and held him in my arms like a shield to ward off her terrible broken face.

"I hope you all rot in hell," she said. She didn't scream it. Her voice was dead tired. She went to the OUT door and pulled it open, using both hands. I wanted to say something to her, call her back, but my mouth was too dry.

"Aw, lady, listen—" the teenage kid who had shouted at Mrs. Carmody began. He held her arm. She looked down at his hand and he let her go, shamefaced. She slipped out into the fog. We watched her go and no one said anything. We watched the fog overlay her and make her insubstantial, not a human being anymore but a pencil-ink sketch of a human being done on the world's whitest paper, and no one said anything. For a moment it was like the letters of the KEEP RIGHT sign that had seemed to float on nothingness; her arms and legs and pallid blond hair were all gone and only the misty remnants of her red summer dress remained, seeming to dance in white limbo. Then her dress was gone, too, and no one said anything.

IV. The Storage Area. Problems with the Generators. What Happened to the Bag-Boy.

Billy began to act hysterical and tantrummy, screaming for his mother in a hoarse, demanding way through his tears, instantly regressing to the age of two. Snot was lathered on his upper lip. I led him away, walking down one of the middle aisles with my arm around his shoulders, trying to soothe him. I took him back by the long white meat cabinet that ran the length of the store at the back. Mr. McVey, the butcher, was still there. We nodded at each other, the best we could do under the circumstances.

I sat down on the floor and took Billy on my lap and held his face against my chest and rocked him and talked to him. I told him all the lies parents keep in reserve for bad situations, the ones that sound so damn plausible to a child, and I told them in a tone of perfect conviction.

"That's not regular fog," Billy said. He looked up at me, his eyes dark-circled and tear-streaked. "It isn't, is it, Daddy?"

"No, I don't think so." I didn't want to lie about that.

Kids don't fight shock the way adults do; they go with it, maybe because kids are in a semipermanent state of shock until they're thirteen or so. Billy started to doze off. I held him, thinking he might snap awake again, but his doze deepened into a real sleep. Maybe he had been awake part of the night before, when we had slept three-in-a-bed for the first time since Billy was an infant. And maybe—I felt a cold eddy slip through me at the thought—maybe he had sensed something coming.

When I was sure he was solidly out, I laid him on the floor and went looking for something to cover him up with. Most of the people were still up front, looking out into the thick blanket of mist. Norton had gathered a little crowd of listeners, and was busy spellbinding—or trying to. Bud Brown stood rigidly at his post, but Ollie Weeks had left his.

There were a few people in the aisles, wandering like ghosts, their faces greasy with shock. I went into the storage area through the big double doors between the meat cabinet and the beer cooler.

The generator roared steadily behind its plywood partition, but something had gone wrong. I could smell diesel fumes, and they were much too strong. I walked toward the partition, taking shallow breaths. At last I unbuttoned my shirt and put part of it over my mouth and nose.

The storage area was long and narrow, feebly lit by two sets of emergency lights. Cartons were stacked everywhere—bleach on one side, cases of soft drinks on the far side of the partition, stacked cases of Beefaroni and catsup. One of those had fallen over and the cardboard carton appeared to be bleeding.

I unlatched the door in the generator partition and stepped through. The machine was obscured in drifting, oily clouds of blue smoke. The exhaust pipe ran out through a hole in the wall. Something must have blocked off the outside end of the pipe. There was a simple on/off switch and I flipped it. The generator hitched, belched, coughed, and died. Then it ran down in a diminishing series of popping sounds that reminded me of Norton's stubborn chainsaw.

The emergency lights faded out and I was left in darkness. I got scared very quickly, and I got disoriented. My breathing sounded like a low wind rattling in straw. I bumped my nose on the flimsy plywood door going out and my heart lurched. There were windows in the double doors, but for some reason they had been painted black, and the darkness was nearly total. I got off course and ran into a stack of the bleach cartons. They tumbled and fell. One came close enough to my head to make me step backward, and I tripped over another carton that had landed behind me. I fell down, thumping my head hard enough to see bright stars in the darkness. Good show.

I lay there cursing myself and rubbing my head, telling myself to just take it easy, just get up and get out of here, get back to Billy, telling myself nothing soft and slimy was going to close over my ankle or slip into one groping hand. I told myself not to lose control, or I would end up blundering around back here in a panic, knocking things over and creating a mad obstacle course for myself.

I stood up carefully, looking for a pencil line of light between the double doors. I found it, a faint but unmistakable scratch on the darkness. I started toward it, and then stopped.

There was a sound. A soft sliding sound. It stopped, then started again with a stealthy little bump. Everything inside me went loose. I regressed magically to four years of age. That sound wasn't coming from the market. It was coming from behind me. From outside. Where the mist was. Something that was slipping and sliding and scraping over the cinderblocks. And, maybe, looking for a way in.

Or maybe it was already in, and it was looking for me. Maybe in a moment I would feel whatever was making that sound on my shoe. Or on my neck.

It came again. I was positive it was outside. But that didn't make it any better. I told my legs to go and they refused the order. Then the quality of the noise changed. Something *rasped* across the darkness and my heart leaped in my chest and I lunged at that thin vertical line of light. I hit the doors straight-arm and burst through into the market.

Three or four people were right outside the double doors—Ollie Weeks was one of them—and they all jumped back in surprise. Ollie grabbed at his chest. "David!" he said in a pinched voice. "Jesus Christ, you want to take ten years off my—" He saw my face. "What's the matter with you?"

"Did you hear it?" I asked. My voice sounded strange in my own ears, high and squeaking. "Did any of you hear it?"

They hadn't heard anything, of course. They had come up to see why the generator had gone off. As Ollie told me that, one of the bag-boys bustled up with an armload of flashlights. He looked from Ollie to me curiously.

"I turned the generator off," I said, and explained why.

"What did you hear?" one of the other men asked. He worked for the town road department; his name was Jim something.

"I don't know. A scraping noise. Slithery. I don't want to hear it again."

"Nerves," the other fellow with Ollie said.

No. It was not nerves.

"Did you hear it before the lights went out?"

"No, only after. But . . ." But nothing. I could see the way they were looking at me. They didn't want any more bad news, anything else frightening or off-kilter. There was enough of that already. Only Ollie looked as if he believed me.

"Let's go in and start her up again," the bag-boy said, handing out the flashlights. Ollie took his doubtfully. The bag-boy offered me one, a slightly contemptuous shine in his eyes. He was maybe eighteen. After a moment's thought, I took the light. I still needed something to cover Billy with.

Ollie opened the doors and chocked them, letting in some light. The bleach cartons lay scattered around the half-open door in the plywood partition.

The fellow named Jim sniffed and said, "Smells pretty rank, all right. Guess you was right to shut her down."

The flashlight beams bobbed and danced across cartons of canned goods, toilet paper, dog food. The beams were smoky in the drifting fumes the blocked exhaust had turned back into the storage area. The bag-boy trained his light briefly on the wide loading door at the extreme right.

The two men and Ollie went inside the generator compartment. Their lights flashed uneasily back and forth, reminding me of something out of a boys' adventure story—and I illustrated a series of them while I was still in college. Pirates burying their bloody gold at midnight, or maybe the mad doctor and his assistant snatching a body. Shadows, made twisted and monstrous by the shifting, conflicting flashlight beams, bobbed on the walls. The generator ticked irregularly as it cooled.

The bag-boy was walking toward the loading door, flashing his light ahead of him. "I wouldn't go over there," I said.

"No, I know *you* wouldn't."

"Try it now, Ollie," one of the men said. The generator wheezed, then roared.

"Jesus! Shut her down! Holy crow, don't that *stink!*"

The generator died again.

The bag-boy walked back from the loading door just as they came out. "Something's plugged that exhaust, all right," one of the men said.

"I'll tell you what," the bag-boy said. His eyes were shining in the glow of the flashlights, and there was a devil-may-care expression on his face that I had sketched too many times as part of the frontispieces for my boys' adventure series. "Get it running long enough for me to raise the loading door back there. I'll go around and clear away whatever it is."

"Norm, I don't think that's a very good idea," Ollie said doubtfully.

"Is it an electric door?" the one called Jim asked.

"Sure," Ollie said. "But I just don't think it would be wise for—"

"That's okay," the other guy said. He tipped his baseball cap back on his head. "I'll do it."

"No, you don't understand," Ollie began again. "I really don't think anyone should—"

"Don't worry," he said indulgently to Ollie, dismissing him.

Norm, the bag-boy, was indignant. "Listen, it was my idea," he said.

All at once, by some magic, they had gotten around to arguing about who was going to do it instead of whether or not it should be done at all. But of course, none of them had heard that nasty slithering sound. "Stop it!" I said loudly.

They looked around at me.

"You don't seem to understand, or you're trying as hard as you can *not* to understand. This is no ordinary fog. Nobody has come into the market since it hit. If you open that loading door and something comes in—"

"Something like what?" Norm said with perfect eighteen-year-old macho contempt.

"Whatever made the noise I heard."

"Mr. Drayton," Jim said. "Pardon me, but I'm not convinced you heard anything. I know you're a big-shot artist with connections in New York and Hollywood and all, but that doesn't make you any different from anyone else, in my book. Way I figure, you got in here in the dark and maybe you just . . . got a little confused.''

"Maybe I did," I said. "And maybe if you want to start screwing around outside, you ought to start by making sure that lady got home safe to her kids.'' His attitude—and that of his buddy and of Norm the bag-boy—was making me mad and scaring me more at the same time. They had the sort of light in their eyes that some men get when they go shooting rats at the town dump.

"Hey," Jim's buddy said. "When any of us here want your advice, we'll ask for it.''

Hesitantly, Ollie said: "The generator really isn't that important, you know. The food in the cold cases will keep for twelve hours or more with absolutely no—''

"Okay, kid, you're it," Jim said brusquely. "I'll start the motor, you raise the door so that the place doesn't stink up too bad. Me and Myron will be standing by the exhaust outflow. Give us a yell when it's clear.''

"Sure," Norm said, and bustled excitedly away.

"This is crazy," I said. "You let that lady go by herself—''

"I didn't notice you breaking your ass to escort her,'' Jim's buddy Myron said. A dull, brick-colored flush was creeping out of his collar.

"—but you're going to let this kid risk his life over a generator that doesn't even matter?''

"Why don't you just shut the fuck up!'' Norm yelled.

"Listen, Mr. Drayton," Jim said, and smiled at me coldly. "I'll tell you what. If you've got anything else to say, I think you better count your teeth first, because I'm tired of listening to your bullshit.''

Ollie looked at me, plainly frightened. I shrugged. They were crazy, that was all. Their sense of proportion was temporarily gone. Out there they had been confused and scared. In here was a straightforward mechanical problem: a balky generator. It was possible to solve this problem. Solving the problem would help make them feel less confused and helpless. Therefore they would solve it.

Jim and his friend Myron decided I knew when I was licked and went back into the generator compartment. "Ready, Norm?'' Jim asked.

Norm nodded, then realized they couldn't hear a nod. "Yeah," he said.

"Norm," I said. "Don't be a fool."

"It's a mistake," Ollie added.

He looked at us, and suddenly his face was much younger than eighteen. It was the face of a boy. His Adam's apple bobbed convulsively, and I saw that he was scared green. He opened his mouth to say something—I think he was going to call it off—and then the generator roared into life again, and when it was running smoothly, Norm lunged at the button to the right of the door and it began to rattle upward on its dual steel tracks. The emergency lights had come back on when the generator started. Now they dimmed down as the motor which lifted the door sucked away the juice.

The shadows ran backward and melted. The storage area began to fill with the mellow white light of an overcast late-winter day. I noticed that odd, acrid smell again.

The loading door went up two feet, then four. Beyond I could see a square cement platform outlined around the edges with a yellow stripe. The yellow faded and washed out in just three feet. The fog was incredibly thick.

"Ho up!" Norm yelled.

Tendrils of mist, as white and fine as floating lace, eddied inside. The air was cold. It had been noticeably cool all morning long, especially after the sticky heat of the last three weeks, but it had been a summery coolness. This was *cold*. It was like March. I shivered. And I thought of Steff.

The generator died. Jim came out just as Norm ducked under the door. He saw it. So did I. So did Ollie.

A tentacle came over the far lip of the concrete loading platform and grabbed Norm around the calf. My mouth dropped wide open. Ollie made a very short glottal sound of surprise —*uk!* The tentacle tapered from a thickness of a foot—the size of a grass snake—at the point where it had wrapped itself around Norm's lower leg to a thickness of maybe four or five feet where it disappeared into the mist. It was slate gray on top, shading to a fleshy pink underneath. And there were rows of suckers on the underside. They were moving and writhing like hundreds of small, puckering mouths.

Norm looked down. He saw what had him. His eyes bulged. *"Get it off me! Hey, get it off me! Christ Jesus, get this frigging thing off me!"*

"Oh my God," Jim whimpered.

Norm grabbed the bottom edge of the loading door and yanked himself back in. The tentacle seemed to bulge, the way your arm will when you flex it. Norm was yanked back against the corrugated steel door—his head clanged against it. The tentacle bulged more, and Norm's legs and torso began to slip back out. The bottom edge of the loading door scraped the shirttail out of his pants. He yanked savagely and pulled himself back in like a man doing a chin-up.

"Help me," he was sobbing. "Help me, you guys, please, please."

"Jesus, Mary, and Joseph," Myron said. He had come out of the generator compartment to see what was going on.

I was the closest, and I grabbed Norm around the waist and yanked as hard as I could, rocking back on my heels. For a moment we moved backward, but only for a moment. It was like stretching a rubber band or pulling taffy. The tentacle yielded but gave up its basic grip not at all. Then three more tentacles floated out of the mist toward us. One curled around Norm's flapping red Federal apron and tore it away. It disappeared back into the mist with the red cloth curled in its grip and I thought of something my mother used to say when my brother and I would beg for something she didn't want us to have—candy, a comic book, some toy. "You need that like a hen needs a flag," she'd say. I thought of that, and I thought of that tentacle waving Norm's red apron around, and I got laughing. I got laughing, except my laughter and Norm's screams sounded about the same. Maybe no one even knew I was laughing except me.

The other two tentacles slithered aimlessly back and forth on the loading platform for a moment, making those low scraping sounds I had heard earlier. Then one of them slapped against Norm's left hip and slipped around it. I felt it touch my arm. It was warm and pulsing and smooth. I think now that if it had gripped me with those suckers, I would have gone out into the mist too. But it didn't. It grabbed Norm. And the third tentacle ringleted his other ankle.

Now he was being pulled away from me. "Help me!" I shouted. "Ollie! Someone! Give me a hand here!"

But they didn't come. I don't know what they were doing, but they didn't come.

I looked down and saw the tentacle around Norm's waist

working into his skin. The suckers were *eating* him where his shirt had pulled out of his pants. Blood, as red as his missing apron, began to seep out of the trench the pulsing tentacle had made for itself.

I banged my head on the lower edge of the partly raised door.

Norm's legs were outside again. One of his loafers had fallen off. A new tentacle came out of the mist, wrapped its tip firmly around the shoe, and made off with it. Norm's fingers clutched at the door's lower edge. He had it in a death grip. His fingers were livid. He was not screaming anymore; he was beyond that. His head whipped back and forth in an endless gesture of negation, and his long black hair flew wildly.

I looked over his shoulder and saw more tentacles coming, dozens of them, a forest of them. Most were small but a few were gigantic, as thick as the moss-corseted tree that had been lying across our driveway that morning. The big ones had candy-pink suckers that seemed the size of manhole covers. One of these big ones struck the concrete loading platform with a loud and rolling *thrrrrap!* sound and moved sluggishly toward us like a great blind earthworm. I gave one gigantic tug, and the tentacle holding Norm's right calf slipped a little. That was all. But before it reestablished its grip, I saw that the thing was eating him away.

One of the tentacles brushed delicately past my cheek and then wavered in the air, as if debating. I thought of Billy then. Billy was lying asleep in the market by Mr. McVey's long white meat cooler. I had come in here to find something to cover him up with. If one of those things got hold of me, there would be no one to watch out for him—except maybe Norton.

So I let go of Norm and dropped to my hands and knees.

I was half in and half out, directly under the raised door. A tentacle passed by on my left, seeming to walk on its suckers. It attached itself to one of Norm's bulging upper arms, paused for a second, and then slid around it in coils.

Now Norm looked like something out of a madman's dream of snake charming. Tentacles twisted over him uneasily almost everywhere . . . and they were all around me, as well. I made a clumsy leapfrog jump back inside, landed on my shoulder, and rolled. Jim, Ollie and Myron were still there. They stood like a tableau of waxworks in Madame Tussaud's, their faces pale, their eyes too bright. Jim and Myron flanked the door to the generator compartment.

"Start the generator!" I yelled at them.

Neither moved. They were staring with a drugged, thanatotic avidity at the loading bay.

I groped on the floor, picked up the first thing that came to hand—a box of Snowy bleach—and chucked it at Jim. It hit him in the gut, just above the belt buckle. He grunted and grabbed at himself. His eyes flickered back into some semblance of normality.

"Go start that fucking generator!" I screamed so loudly it hurt my throat.

He didn't move; instead he began to defend himself, apparently having decided that, with Norm being eaten alive by some insane horror from the mist, the time had come for rebuttals.

"I'm sorry," he whined. "I didn't know, how the hell was I supposed to know? You said you heard something but I didn't know what you meant, you should have said what you meant better. I thought, I dunno, maybe a bird, or something—"

So then Ollie moved, bunting him aside with one thick shoulder and blundering into the generator room. Jim stumbled over one of the bleach cartons and fell down, just as I had done in the dark. "I'm sorry," he said again. His red hair had tumbled over his brow. His cheeks were cheese-white. His eyes were those of a horrified little boy. Seconds later the generator coughed and rumbled into life.

I turned back to the loading door. Norm was almost gone, yet he clung grimly with one hand. His body boiled with tentacles, and blood pattered serenely down on the concrete in dime-size droplets. His head whipped back and forth and his eyes bulged with terror as they stared off into the mist.

Other tentacles now crept and crawled over the floor inside. There were too many near the button that controlled the loading door to even think of approaching it. One of them closed around a half-liter bottle of Pepsi and carried it off. Another slipped around a cardboard carton and squeezed. The carton ruptured and rolls of toilet paper, two-packs of Delsey wrapped in cellophane, geysered upward, came down, and rolled everywhere. Tentacles seized them eagerly.

One of the big ones slipped in. Its tip rose from the floor and it seemed to sniff the air. It began to advance toward Myron and he stepped mincingly away from it, his eyes rolling madly in their sockets. A high-pitched little moan escaped his slack lips.

I looked around for something, anything at all long enough to reach over the questing tentacles and punch the SHUT button on the wall. I saw a janitor's push broom leaning against a stack-up of beer cases and grabbed it.

Norm's good hand was ripped loose. He thudded down onto the concrete loading platform and scrabbled madly for a grip with his one free hand. His eyes met mine for a moment. They were hellishly bright and aware. He knew what was happening to him. Then he was pulled, bumping and rolling, into the mist. There was another scream, choked off. Norm was gone.

I pushed the tip of the broom handle onto the button and the motor whined. The door began to slide back down. It touched the thickest of the tentacles first, the one that had been investigating in Myron's direction. It indented its hide—skin, whatever— and then pierced it. A black goo began to spurt from it. It writhed madly, whipping across the concrete storage-area floor like an obscene bullwhip, and then it seemed to flatten out. A moment later it was gone. The others began to withdraw.

One of them had a five-pound bag of Gaines dog food, and it wouldn't let go. The descending door cut it in two before thumping home in its grooved slot. The severed chunk of tentacle squeezed convulsively tighter, splitting the bag open and sending brown nuggets of dog food everywhere. Then it began to flop on the floor like a fish out of water, curling and uncurling, but ever more slowly, until it lay still. I prodded it with the tip of the broom. The piece of tentacle, maybe three feet long, closed on it savagely for a moment, then loosened and lay limp again in the confused litter of toilet paper, dog food, and bleach cartons.

There was no sound except the roar of the generator and Ollie, crying inside the plywood compartment. I could see him sitting on a stool in there with his face clutched in his hands.

Then I became aware of another sound. The soft, slithery sound I had heard in the dark. Only now the sound was multiplied tenfold. It was the sound of tentacles squirming over the outside of the loading door, trying to find a way in.

Myron took a couple of steps toward me. "Look," he said. "You got to understand—"

I looped a fist at his face. He was too surprised to even try to block it. It landed just below his nose and mashed his upper lip into his teeth. Blood flowed into his mouth.

"You got him killed!" I shouted. "Did you get a good look at it? Did you get a good look at what you did?"

I started to pummel him, throwing wild rights and lefts, not punching the way I had been taught in my college boxing classes but only hitting out. He stepped back, shaking some of them off, taking others with a numbness that seemed like a kind of resignation or penance. That made me angrier. I bloodied his nose. I raised a mouse under one of his eyes that was going to black just beautifully. I clipped him a hard one on the chin. After that one, his eyes went cloudy and semi-vacant.

"Look," he kept saying, "look, look," and then I punched him low in the stomach and the air went out of him and he didn't say "look, look" anymore. I don't know how long I would have gone on punching him, but someone grabbed my arms. I jerked free and turned around. I was hoping it was Jim. I wanted to punch Jim out, too.

But it wasn't Jim. It was Ollie, his round face dead pale, except for the dark circles around his eyes—eyes that were still shiny from his tears. "Don't, David," he said. "Don't hit him anymore. It doesn't solve anything."

Jim was standing off to one side, his face a bewildered blank. I kicked a carton of something at him. It struck one of his Dingo boots and bounced away.

"You and your buddy are a couple of stupid assholes," I said.

"Come on, David," Ollie said unhappily. "Quit it."

"You two assholes got that kid killed."

Jim looked down at his Dingo boots. Myron sat on the floor and held his beer belly. I was breathing hard. The blood was roaring in my ears and I was trembling all over. I sat down on a couple of cartons and put my head down between my knees and gripped my legs hard just above the ankles. I sat that way for a while with my hair in my face, waiting to see if I was going to black out or puke or what.

After a bit the feeling began to pass and I looked up at Ollie. His pinky ring flashed subdued fire in the glow of the emergency lights.

"Okay," I said dully. "I'm done."

"Good," Ollie said. "We've got to think what to do next."

The storage area was beginning to stink of exhaust again. "Shut the generator down. That's the first thing."

"Yeah, let's get out of here," Myron said. His eyes appealed to me. "I'm sorry about the kid. But you got to understand—"

"I don't got to understand anything. You and your buddy go back into the market, but you wait right there by the beer cooler. And don't say a word to anybody. Not yet."

They went willingly enough, huddling together as they passed through the swinging doors. Ollie killed the generator, and just as the lights started to fail, I saw a quilted rug—the sort of thing movers use to pad breakable things—flopped over a stack of returnable soda bottles. I reached up and grabbed it for Billy.

There was the shuffling, blundering sound of Ollie coming out of the generator compartment. Like a great many overweight men, his breathing had a slightly heavy wheezing sound.

"David?" His voice wavered a little. "You still here?"

"Right here, Ollie. You want to watch out for all those bleach cartons."

"Yeah."

I guided him with my voice and in thirty seconds or so he reached out of the dark and gripped my shoulder. He gave a long, trembling sigh.

"Christ, let's get out of here." I could smell the Rolaids he always chewed on his breath. "This dark is . . . is bad."

"It is," I said. "But hang tight a minute, Ollie. I wanted to talk to you and I didn't want those other two fuckheads listening."

"Dave . . . they didn't twist Norm's arm. You ought to remember that."

"Norm was a kid, and they weren't. But never mind, that's over. We've got to tell them, Ollie. The people in the market."

"If they panic—" Ollie's voice was doubtful.

"Maybe they will and maybe they won't. But it will make

them think twice about going out, which is what most of them want to do. Why shouldn't they? Most of them will have people they left at home. I do myself. We have to make them understand what they're risking if they go out there.''

His hand was gripping my arm hard. ''All right,'' he said. ''Yes, I just keep asking myself . . . all those tentacles . . . like a squid or something . . . David, what were they hooked to? *What were those tentacles hooked to?''*

''I don't know. But I don't want those two telling people on their own. That *would* start a panic. Let's go.''

I looked around, and after a moment or two located the thin line of vertical light between the swing doors. We started to shuffle toward it, wary of scattered cartons, one of Ollie's pudgy hands clamped over my forearm. It occurred to me that all of us had lost our flashlights.

As we reached the doors, Ollie said flatly: ''What we saw . . . it's impossible, David. You know that, don't you? Even if a van from the Boston Seaquarium drove out back and dumped out one of those gigantic squids like in *Twenty Thousand Leagues Under the Sea,* it would die. *It would just die.''*

''Yes,'' I said. ''That's right.''

''So what happened? Huh? What happened? What is that damned mist?''

''Ollie, I don't know.''

We went out.

V. An Argument with Norton.
A Discussion Near the Beer Cooler.
Verification.

Jim and his good buddy Myron were just outside the doors, each with a Budweiser in his fist. I looked at Billy, saw he was still asleep, and covered him with the ruglike mover's pad. He moved a little, muttered something, and then lay still again. I looked at my watch. It was 12:15 P.M. That seemed utterly impossible; it felt as if at least five hours had passed since I had first gone in there to look for something to cover him with. But the whole thing, from first to last, had taken only about thirty-five minutes.

I went back to where Ollie stood with Jim and Myron.

Ollie had taken a beer and he offered me one. I took it and gulped down half the can at once, as I had that morning cutting wood. It bucked me up a little.

Jim was Jim Grondin. Myron's last name was LaFleur—that had its comic side, all right. Myron the flower had drying blood on his lips, chin, and cheek. The eye with the mouse under it was already swelling up. The girl in the cranberry-colored sweatshirt walked by aimlessly and gave Myron a cautious look. I could have told her that Myron was only dangerous to teenage boys intent on proving their manhood, but saved my breath. After all, Ollie was right—they *had* only been doing what they thought was best, although in a blind, fearful way rather than in any real common interest. And now I needed them to do what *I* thought was best. I didn't think that would be a problem. They had both had the stuffing knocked out of them. Neither—especially Myron the flower—was going to be good for anything for some time to come. Something that had been in their eyes when they were fixing to send Norm out to unplug the exhaust vent had gone now. Their peckers were no longer up.

"We're going to have to tell these people something," I said.

Jim opened his mouth to protest.

"Ollie and I will leave out any part you and Myron had in sending Norm out there if you'll back up what he and I say about . . . well, about what got him."

"Sure," Jim said, pitifully eager. "Sure, if we don't tell, people might go out there . . . like that woman . . . that woman who . . ." He wiped his hand across his mouth and then drank more beer quickly. "Christ, what a mess."

"David," Ollie said. "What—" He stopped, then made himself go on. "What if they get in? The tentacles?"

"How could they?" Jim asked. "You guys shut the door."

"Sure," Ollie said. "But the whole front wall of this place is plate glass."

An elevator shot my stomach down about twenty floors. I had known that, but had somehow been successfully ignoring it. I looked over at where Billy lay asleep. I thought of those tentacles swarming over Norm. I thought about that happening to Billy.

"Plate glass," Myron LaFleur whispered. "Jesus Christ in a chariot-driven sidecar."

I left the three of them standing by the cooler, each working a second can of beer, and went looking for Brent Norton. I found him in sober-sided conversation with Bud Brown at Register 2. The pair of them—Norton with his styled gray hair and his elderly-stud good looks, Brown with his dour New England phiz—looked like something out of a *New Yorker* cartoon.

As many as two dozen people milled restlessly in the space between the end of the checkout lanes and the long show window. A lot of them were lined up at the glass, looking out into the mist. I was again reminded of the people that congregate at a building site.

Mrs. Carmody was seated on the stationary conveyor belt of one of the checkout lanes, smoking a Parliament in a One Step at a Time filter. Her eyes measured me, found me wanting, and passed on. She looked as if she might be dreaming awake.

"Brent," I said.

"David! Where did you get off to?"

"That's what I'd like to talk to you about."

"There are people back at the cooler drinking beer," Brown said grimly. He sounded like a man announcing that X-rated movies had been shown at the deacons' party. "I can see them in the security mirror. This has simply got to stop."

"Brent?"

"Excuse me for a minute, would you, Mr. Brown?"

"Certainly." He folded his arms across his chest and stared grimly up into the convex mirror. "It *is* going to stop, I can promise you that."

Norton and I headed toward the beer cooler in the far corner of the store, walking past the housewares and notions. I glanced back over my shoulder, noticing uneasily how the wooden beams framing the tall, rectangular sections of glass had buckled and twisted and splintered. And one of the windows wasn't even whole, I remembered. A pie-shaped chunk of glass had fallen out of the upper corner at the instant of that queer thump. Perhaps we could stuff it with cloth or something—maybe a bunch of those $3.59 ladies' tops I had noticed near the wine—

My thoughts broke off abruptly, and I had to put the back of my hand over my mouth, as if stifling a burp. What I was really stifling was the rancid flood of horrified giggles that wanted to escape me at the thought of stuffing a bunch of shirts into a hole to keep out those tentacles that had carried Norm away. I had seen one of those tentacles—a small one—squeeze a bag of dog food until it simply ruptured.

"David? Are you okay?"

"Huh?"

"Your face—you looked like you just had a good idea or a bloody awful one."

Something hit me then. "Brent, what happened to that man who came in raving about something in the mist getting John Lee Frovin?"

"The guy with the nosebleed?"

"Yes, him."

"He passed out and Mr. Brown brought him around with some smelling salts from the first-aid kit. Why?"

"Did he say anything else when he woke up?"

"He started in on that hallucination. Mr. Brown conducted him up to the office. He was frightening some of the women. He seemed happy enough to go. Something about the glass. When Mr. Brown said there was only one small window in the manager's office, and that that one was reinforced with wire, he seemed happy enough to go. I presume he's still there."

"What he was talking about is no hallucination."

"No, of course it isn't."

"And that thud we felt?"

"No, but, David—"

He's scared, I kept reminding myself. Don't blow up at him, you've treated yourself to one blowup this morning and that's enough. Don't blow up at him just because this is the way he was during that stupid property-line dispute . . . first patronizing, then sarcastic, and finally, when it became clear he was going to lose, ugly. Don't blow up at him because you're going to need him. He may not be able to start his own chainsaw, but he looks like the father figure of the Western world, and if he tells people not to panic, they won't. So don't blow up at him.

"You see those double doors up there beyond the beer cooler?"

He looked, frowning. "Isn't one of those men drinking beer the other assistant manager? Weeks? If Brown sees that,

I can promise you that man will be looking for a job very soon.''

"Brent, will you listen to me?"

He glanced back at me absently. "What were you saying, Dave? I'm sorry."

Not as sorry as he was going to be. "Do you see those doors?"

"Yes, of course I do. What about them?"

"They give on the storage area that runs all the way along the west face of the building. Billy fell asleep and I went back there to see if I could find something to cover him up with . . ."

I told him everything, only leaving out the argument about whether or not Norm should have gone out at all. I told him what had come in . . . and finally, what had gone out, screaming. Brent Norton refused to believe it. No—he refused to even entertain it. I took him over to Jim, Ollie, and Myron. All three of them verified the story, although Jim and Myron the flower were well on their way to getting drunk.

Again, Norton refused to believe or even to entertain it. He simply balked. "No," he said. "No, no, no. Forgive me, gentlemen, but it's completely ridiculous. Either you're having me on"—he patronized us with his gleaming smile to show that he could take a joke as well as the next fellow—"or you're suffering from some form of group hypnosis."

My temper rose again, and I controlled it—with difficulty. I don't think that I'm ordinarily a quick-tempered man, but these weren't ordinary circumstances. I had Billy to think about, and what was happening—or what had already happened—to Stephanie. Those things were constantly gnawing at the back of my mind.

"All right," I said. "Let's go back there. There's a chunk of tentacle on the floor. The door cut it off when it came down. And you can *hear* them. They're rustling all over that door. It sounds like the wind in ivy."

"No," he said calmly.

"What?" I really did believe I had misheard him. "What did you say?"

"I said no, I'm not going back there. The joke has gone far enough."

"Brent, I swear to you it's no joke."

"Of course it is," he snapped. His eyes ran over Jim,

Myron, rested briefly on Ollie Weeks—who held his glance with calm impassivity—and at last came back to me. "It's what you locals probably call 'a real belly-buster.' Right, David?"

"Brent . . . look—"

"No, you look!" His voice began to rise toward a court-room shout. It carried very, very well, and several of the people who were wandering around, edgy and aimless, looked over to see what was going on. Norton jabbed his finger at me as he spoke. "It's a joke. It's a banana skin and I'm the guy that's supposed to slip on it. None of you people are exactly crazy about out-of-towners, am I right? You all pretty much stick together. The way it happened when I hauled you into court to get what was rightfully mine. You won that one, all right. Why not? Your father was the famous artist, and it's your town. I only pay my taxes and spend my money here!"

He was no longer performing, hectoring us with the trained courtroom shout; he was nearly screaming and on the verge of losing all control. Ollie Weeks turned and walked away, clutching his beer. Myron and his friend Jim were staring at Norton with frank amazement.

"Am I supposed to go back there and look at some ninety-eight-cent rubber-joke novelty while these two hicks stand around and laugh their asses off?"

"Hey, you want to watch who you're calling a hick," Myron said.

"I'm *glad* that tree fell on your boathouse, if you want to know the truth. *Glad.*" Norton was grinning savagely at me. "Stove it in pretty well, didn't it? Fantastic. Now get out of my way."

He tried to push past me. I grabbed him by the arm and threw him against the beer cooler. A woman cawed in surprise. Two six-packs of Bud fell over.

"You dig out your ears and listen, Brent. There are lives at stake here. My kid's is not the least of them. So you listen, or I swear I'll knock the shit out of you."

"Go ahead," Norton said, still grinning with a kind of insane palsied bravado. His eyes, bloodshot and wide, bulged from their sockets. "Show everyone how big and brave you are, beating up a man with a heart condition who is old enough to be your father."

"Sock him anyway!" Jim exclaimed. "Fuck his heart

condition. I don't even think a cheap New York shyster like him has got a heart."

"You keep out of it," I said to Jim, and then put my face down to Norton's. I was kissing distance, if that had been what I had in mind. The cooler was off, but it was still radiating a chill. "Stop throwing up sand. You know damn well I'm telling the truth."

"I know . . . no . . . such thing," he panted.

"If it was another time and place, I'd let you get away with it. I don't care how scared you are, and I'm not keeping score. I'm scared, too. But I need you, goddammit! Does that get through? I need you!"

"Let me *go!*"

I grabbed him by the shirt and shook him. "Don't you understand anything? People are going to start leaving and walk right into that thing out there! For Christ's sake, don't you understand?"

"Let me go!"

"Not until you come back there with me and see for yourself."

"I told you, *no!* It's all a trick, a joke, I'm not as stupid as you take me for—"

"Then I'll haul you back there myself."

I grabbed him by the shoulder and the scruff of his neck. The seam of his shirt under one arm tore with a soft purring sound. I dragged him toward the double doors. Norton let out a wretched scream. A knot of people, fifteen or eighteen, had gathered, but they kept their distance. None showed any signs of wanting to interfere.

"Help me!" Norton cried. His eyes bulged behind his glasses. His styled hair had gone awry again, sticking up in the same two little tufts behind his ears. People shuffled their feet and watched.

"What are you screaming for?" I said in his ear. "It's just a joke, right? That's why I took you to town when you asked to come and why I trusted you to cross Billy in the parking lot—because I had this handy fog all manufactured, I rented a fog machine from Hollywood, it cost me fifteen thousand dollars and another eight thousand dollars to ship it, all so I could play a joke on you. Stop bullshitting yourself and open your eyes!"

"Let . . . me . . . go!" Norton bawled. We were almost at the doors.

"Here, here! What is this? What are you doing?"

It was Brown. He bustled and elbowed his way through the crowd of watchers.

"Make him let me go," Norton said hoarsely. "He's crazy."

"No. He's not crazy. I wish he were, but he isn't." That was Ollie, and I could have blessed him. He came around the aisle behind us and stood there facing Brown.

Brown's eyes dropped to the beer Ollie was holding. "You're *drinking!*" he said, and his voice was surprised but not totally devoid of pleasure. "You'll lose your job for this."

"Come on, Bud," I said, letting Norton go. "This is no ordinary situation."

"Regulations don't change," Brown said smugly. "I'll see that the company hears of it. That's my responsibility."

Norton, meanwhile, had skittered away and stood at some distance, trying to straighten his shirt and smooth back his hair. His eyes darted between Brown and me nervously.

"Hey!" Ollie cried suddenly, raising his voice and producing a bass thunder I never would have suspected from this large but soft and unassuming man. *"Hey! Everybody in the store! You want to come up back and hear this! It concerns all of you!"* He looked at me levelly, ignoring Brown altogether. "Am I doing all right?"

"Fine."

People began to gather. The original knot of spectators to my argument with Norton doubled, then trebled.

"There's something you all had better know—" Ollie began.

"You put that beer down right now," Brown said.

"You shut up right now," I said, and took a step toward him.

Brown took a compensatory step back. "I don't know what some of you think you are doing," he said, "but I can tell you it's going to be reported to the Federal Foods Company! All of it! And I want you to understand—*there may be charges!*" His lips drew nervously back from his yellowed teeth, and I could feel sympathy for him. Just trying to cope; that was all he was doing. As Norton was by imposing a mental gag order on himself. Myron and Jim had tried by turning the whole thing into a macho charade—if the generator could be fixed, the mist would blow over. This was Brown's way. He was . . . Protecting the Store.

"Then you go ahead and take down the names," I said. "But please don't talk."

"I'll take down plenty of names," he responded. "Yours will be head on the list, you . . . you *bohemian.*"

"Mr. David Drayton has got something to tell you," Ollie said, "and I think you had better all listen up, in case you were planning on going home."

So I told them what had happened, pretty much as I told Norton. There was some laughter at first, then a deepening uneasiness as I finished.

"It's a lie, you know," Norton said. His voice tried for hard emphasis and overshot into stridency. This was the man I'd told first, hoping to enlist his credibility. What a balls-up.

"Of course it's a lie," Brown agreed. "It's lunacy. Where do you suppose those tentacles came from, Mr. Drayton?"

"I don't know, and at this point, that's not even a very important question. They're here. There's—"

"I suspect they came out of a few of those beer cans. That's what I suspect." This got some appreciative laughter. It was silenced by the strong, rusty-hinge voice of Mrs. Carmody.

"Death!" she cried, and those who had been laughing quickly sobered.

She marched into the center of the rough circle that had formed, her canary pants seeming to give off a light of their own, her huge purse swinging against one elephantine thigh. Her black eyes glanced arrogantly around, as sharp and balefully sparkling as a magpie's. Two good-looking girls of about sixteen with CAMP WOODLANDS written on the back of their white rayon shirts shrank away from her.

"You listen but you don't hear! You hear but you don't believe! Which one of you wants to go outside and see for himself?" Her eyes swept them, and then fell on me. "And just what do you propose to do about it, Mr. David Drayton? What do you think you can do about it?"

She grinned, skull-like above her canary outfit.

"It's the end, I tell you. The end of everything. It's the Last Times. The moving finger has writ, not in fire, but in lines of mist. The earth has opened and spewed forth its abominations—"

"Can't you make her shut up?" one of the teenage girls burst out. She was beginning to cry. "She's scaring me!"

"Are you scared, dearie?" Mrs. Carmody asked, and turned on her. "You aren't scared now, no. But when the foul creatures the Imp has loosed upon the face of the earth come for you—"

"That's enough now, Mrs. Carmody," Ollie said, taking her arm. "That's just fine."

"You let go of me! It's the end, I tell you! It's death! Death!"

"It's a pile of shit," a man in a fishing hat and glasses said disgustedly.

"No, sir," Myron spoke up. "I know it sounds like something out of a dope-dream, but it's the flat-out truth. I saw it myself."

"I did, too," Jim said.

"And me," Ollie chipped in. He had succeeded in quieting Mrs Carmody, at least for the time being. But she stood close by, clutching her big purse and grinning her crazy grin. No one wanted to stand too close to her—they muttered among themselves, not liking the corroboration. Several of them looked back at the big plate-glass windows in an uneasy, speculative way. I was glad to see it.

"Lies," Norton said. "You people all lie each other up. That's all."

"What you're suggesting is totally beyond belief," Brown said.

"We don't have to stand here chewing it over," I told him. "Come back into the storage area with me. Take a look. And a listen."

"Customers are not allowed in the—"

"Bud," Ollie said, "go with him. Let's settle this."

"All right," Brown said. "Mr. Drayton? Let's get this foolishness over with."

We pushed through the double doors into the darkness.

The sound was unpleasant—perhaps evil.

Brown felt it, too, for all his hardheaded Yankee manner; his hand clutched my arm immediately, his breath caught for a moment and then resumed more harshly.

It was a low whispering sound from the direction of the loading door—an almost caressing sound. I swept around gently with one foot and finally struck one of the flashlights. I bent down, got it, and turned it on. Brown's face was tightly drawn, and he hadn't even seen them—he was only hearing them. But I had seen, and I could imagine them twisting and climbing over the corrugated steel surface of the door like living vines.

"What do you think now? Totally beyond belief?"

Brown licked his lips and looked at the littered confusion of boxes and bags. "They did this?"

"Some of it. Most of it. Come over here."

He came—reluctantly. I spotted the flashlight on the shriveled and curled section of tentacle, still lying by the push broom. Brown bent toward it.

"Don't touch that," I said. "It may still be alive."

He straightened up quickly. I picked up the broom by the bristles and prodded the tentacle. The third or fourth poke caused it to unclench sluggishly and reveal two whole suckers and a ragged segment of a third. Then the fragment coiled again with muscular speed and lay still. Brown made a gagging, disgusted sound.

"Seen enough?"

"Yes," he said. "Let's get out of here."

We followed the bobbing light back to the double doors and pushed through them. All the faces turned toward us, and the hum of conversation died. Norton's face was like old cheese. Mrs. Carmody's black eyes glinted. Ollie was drinking beer; his face was still running with trickles of perspiration, although it had gotten rather chilly in the market. The two girls with CAMP WOODLANDS on their shirts were huddled together like young horses before a thunderstorm. Eyes. So many eyes. I could paint them, I thought with a chill. No faces, only eyes in the gloom. I could paint them but no one would believe they were real.

Bud Brown folded his long-fingered hands primly in front of him. "People," he said. "It appears we have a problem of some magnitude here."

VI. Further Discussion. Mrs. Carmody.
Fortifications.
What Happened to the Flat-Earth Society.

The next four hours passed in a kind of dream. There was a long and semihysterical discussion following Brown's confirmation, or maybe the discussion wasn't as long as it seemed;

maybe it was just the grim necessity of people chewing over the same information, trying to see it from every possible point of view, working it the way a dog works a bone, trying to get at the marrow. It was a slow coming to belief. You can see the same thing at any New England town meeting in March.

There was the Flat-Earth Society, headed by Norton. They were a vocal minority of about ten who believed none of it. Norton pointed out over and over again that there were only four witnesses to the bag-boy being carried off by what he called the Tentacles from Planet X (it was good for a laugh the first time, but it wore thin quickly; Norton, in his increasing agitation, seemed not to notice). He added that he personally did not trust one of the four. He further pointed out that fifty percent of the witnesses were now hopelessly inebriated. That was unquestionably true. Jim and Myron LaFleur, with the entire beer cooler and wine rack at their disposal, were abysmally shitfaced. Considering what had happened to Norm, and their part in it, I didn't blame them. They would sober off all too soon.

Ollie continued to drink steadily, ignoring Brown's protests. After a while Brown gave up, contenting himself with an occasional baleful threat about the Company. He didn't seem to realize that Federal Foods, Inc., with its stores in Bridgton, North Windham, and Portland, might not even exist anymore. For all we knew, the Eastern Seaboard might no longer exist. Ollie drank steadily, but didn't get drunk. He was sweating it out as rapidly as he could put it in.

At last, as the discussion with the Flat-Earthers was becoming acrimonious, Ollie spoke up. "If you don't believe it, Mr. Norton, that's fine. I'll tell you what to do. You go on out that front door and walk around to the back. There's a great big pile of returnable beer and soda bottles there. Norm and Buddy and I put them out this morning. You bring back a couple of those bottles so we know you really went back there. You do that and I'll personally take my shirt off and eat it."

Norton began to bluster.

Ollie cut him off in that same soft, even voice. "I tell you, you're not doing anything but damage talking the way you are. There's people here that want to go home and make sure their families are okay. My sister and her year-old daughter are at home in Naples right now. I'd like to check on them, sure. But if people start believing you and try to go home, what happened to Norm is going to happen to them.''

He didn't convince Norton, but he convinced some of the leaners and fence sitters—it wasn't what he said so much as it was his eyes, his haunted eyes. I think Norton's sanity hinged on not being convinced, or that he thought it did. But he didn't take Ollie up on his offer to bring back a sampling of returnables from out back. None of them did. They weren't ready to go out, at least not yet. He and his little group of Flat-Earthers (reduced by one or two now) went as far away from the rest of us as they could get, over by the prepared-meats case. One of them kicked my sleeping son in the leg as he went past, waking him up.

I went over, and Billy clung to my neck. When I tried to put him down, he clung tighter and said, ''Don't do that, Daddy. Please.''

I found a shopping cart and put him in the baby seat. He looked very big in there. It would have been comical except for his pale face, the dark hair brushed across his forehead just above his eyebrows, his woeful eyes. He probably hadn't been up in the baby seat of the shopping cart for as long as two years. These little things slide by you, you don't realize at first, and when what has changed finally comes to you, it's always a nasty shock.

Meanwhile, with the Flat-Earthers having withdrawn, the argument had found another lightning rod—this time it was Mrs. Carmody, and understandably enough, she stood alone.

In the faded, dismal light she was witchlike in her blazing canary pants, her bright rayon blouse, her armloads of clacking junk jewelry—copper, tortoiseshell, adamantine—and her thyroidal purse. Her parchment face was grooved with strong vertical lines. Her frizzy gray hair was yanked flat with three horn combs and twisted in the back. Her mouth was a line of knotted rope.

''There is no defense against the will of God. This has been coming. I have seen the signs. There are those here that I have told, but there are none so blind as those who will not see.''

''Well, what are you saying? What are you proposing?'' Mike Hatlen broke in impatiently. He was a town selectman, although he didn't look the part now, in his yachtsman's cap and saggy-seated Bermudas. He was sipping at a beer; a great many men were doing it now. Bud Brown had given up protesting, but he was indeed taking names—keeping a rough tab on everyone he could.

"Proposing?" Mrs. Carmody echoed, wheeling toward Hatlen. "Proposing? Why, I am proposing that you prepare to meet your God, Michael Hatlen." She gazed around at all of us. "Prepare to meet your God!"

"Prepare to meet shit," Myron LaFleur said in a drunken snarl from the beer cooler. "Old woman, I believe your tongue must be hung in the middle so it can run on both ends."

There was a rumble of agreement. Billy looked around nervously, and I slipped an arm around his shoulders.

"I'll have my say!" she cried. Her upper lip curled back, revealing snaggle teeth that were yellow with nicotine. I thought of the dusty stuffed animals in her shop, drinking eternally at the mirror that served as their creek. "Doubters will doubt to the end! Yet a monstrosity did drag that poor boy away! Things in the mist! Every abomination out of a bad dream! Eyeless freaks! Pallid horrors! Do you doubt? Then go on out! Go on out and say howdy-do!"

"Mrs. Carmody, you'll have to stop," I said. "You're scaring my boy."

The man with the little girl echoed the sentiment. She, all plump legs and scabby knees, had hidden her face against her father's stomach and put her hands over her ears. Big Bill wasn't crying, but he was close.

"There's only one chance," Mrs. Carmody said.

"What's that, ma'am?" Mike Hatlen asked politely.

"A sacrifice," Mrs. Carmody said—she seemed to grin in the gloom. "A blood sacrifice."

Blood sacrifice—the words hung there, slowly turning. Even now, when I know better, I tell myself that then what she meant was someone's pet dog—there were a couple of them trotting around the market in spite of the regulations against them. Even now I tell myself that. She looked like some crazed remnant of New England Puritanism in the gloom . . . but I suspect that something deeper and darker than mere Puritanism motivated her. Puritanism had its own dark grandfather, old Adam with bloody hands.

She opened her mouth to say something more, and a small,

neat man in red pants and a natty sport shirt struck her
openhanded across the face. His hair was parted with ruler
evenness on the left. He wore glasses. He also wore the
unmistakable look of the summer tourist.

"You shut up that bad talk," he said softly and tonelessly.

Mrs. Carmody put her hand to her mouth and then held it
out to us, a wordless accusation. There was blood on the
palm. But her black eyes seemed to dance with mad glee.

"You had it coming!" a woman cried out. "I would have
done it myself!"

"They'll get hold of you," Mrs. Carmody said, showing
us her bloody palm. The trickle of blood was now running
down one of the wrinkles from her mouth to her chin like a
droplet of rain down a gutter. "Not today, maybe. Tonight.
Tonight when the dark comes. They'll come with the night
and take someone else. With the night they'll come. You'll
hear them coming, creeping and crawling. And when they
come, you'll beg for Mother Carmody to show you what to
do."

The man in the red pants raised his hand slowly.

"You come on and hit me," she whispered, and grinned
her bloody grin at him. His hand wavered. "Hit me if you
dare." His hand dropped. Mrs. Carmody walked away by
herself. Then Billy did begin to cry, hiding his face against
me as the little girl had done with her father.

"I want to go home," he said. "I want to see my mommy."

I comforted him as best I could. Which probably wasn't
very well.

The talk finally turned into less frightening and destructive
channels. The plate-glass windows, the market's obvious weak
point, were mentioned. Mike Hatlen asked what other en-
trances there were, and Ollie and Brown quickly ticked them
off—two loading doors in addition to the one Norm had
opened. The main IN/OUT doors. The window in the manager's office (thick, reinforced glass, securely locked).

Talking about these things had a paradoxical effect. It
made the danger seem more real but at the same time made us
feel better. Even Billy felt it. He asked if he could go get a
candy bar. I told him it would be all right so long as he didn't
go near the big windows.

When he was out of earshot, a man near Mike Hatlen said,

"Okay, what are we going to do about those windows? The old lady may be as crazy as a bedbug, but she could be right about something moving in after dark."

"Maybe the fog will blow over by then," a woman said.

"Maybe," the man said. "And maybe not."

"Any ideas?" I asked Bud and Ollie.

"Hold on a sec," the man near Hatlen said. "I'm Dan Miller. From Lynn, Mass. You don't know me, no reason why you should, but I got a place on Highland Lake. Bought it just this year. Got held up for it, is more like it, but I had to have it." There were a few chuckles. "Anyway, I saw a whole pile of fertilizer and lawn-food bags down there. Twenty-five-pound sacks, most of them. We could put them up like sandbags. Leave loopholes to look out through . . . ."

Now more people were nodding and talking excitedly. I almost said something, then held it back. Miller was right. Putting those bags up could do no harm, and might do some good. But my mind went back to that tentacle squeezing the dog-food bag. I thought that one of the bigger tentacles could probably do the same for a twenty-five-pound bag of Green Acres lawn food or Vigoro. But a sermon on that wouldn't get us out or improve anyone's mood.

People began to break up, talking about getting it done, and Miller yelled: "Hold it! Hold it! Let's thrash this out while we're all together!"

They came back, a loose congregation of fifty or sixty people in the corner formed by the beer cooler, the storage doors, and the left end of the meat case, where Mr. McVey always seems to put the things no one wants, like sweetbreads and Scotch eggs and sheep's brains and head cheese. Billy wove his way through them with a five-year-old's unconscious agility in a world of giants and held up a Hershey bar. "Want this, Daddy?"

"Thanks." I took it. It tasted sweet and good.

"This is probably a stupid question," Miller resumed, "but we ought to fill in the blanks. Anyone got any firearms?"

There was a pause. People looked around at each other and shrugged. An old man with grizzled white hair who introduced himself as Ambrose Cornell said he had a shotgun in the trunk of his car. "I'll try for it, if you want."

Ollie said, "Right now I don't think that would be a good idea, Mr. Cornell."

Cornell grunted. "Right now, neither do I, son. But I thought I ought to make the offer."

"Well, I didn't really think so," Dan Miller said. "But I thought—"

"Wait, hold it a minute," a woman said. It was the lady in the cranberry-colored sweatshirt and the dark-green slacks. She had sandy-blond hair and a good figure. A very pretty young woman. She opened her purse and from it she produced a medium-sized pistol. The crowd made an *ahhhh*-ing sound, as if they had just seen a magician do a particularly fine trick. The woman, who had been blushing, blushed that much the harder. She rooted in her purse again and brought out a box of Smith & Wesson ammunition.

"I'm Amanda Dumfries," she said to Miller. "This gun . . . my husband's idea. He thought I should have it for protection. I've carried it unloaded for two years."

"Is your huband here, ma'am?"

"No, he's in New York. On business. He's gone on business a lot. That's why he wanted me to carry the gun."

"Well," Miller said, "if you can use it, you ought to keep it. What is it, a thirty-eight?"

"Yes. And I've never fired it in my life except on a target range once."

Miller took the gun, fumbled around, and got the cylinder to open after a few moments. He checked to make sure it was not loaded. "Okay," he said. "We got a gun. Who shoots good? I sure don't."

People glanced at each other. No one said anything at first. Then, reluctantly, Ollie said: "I target-shoot quite a lot. I have a Colt .45 and a Llama .25."

"You?" Brown said. "Huh. You'll be too drunk to see by dark."

Ollie said very clearly, "Why don't you just shut up and write down your names?"

Brown goggled at him. Opened his mouth. Then decided, wisely, I think, to shut it again.

"It's yours," Miller said, blinking a little at the exchange. He handed it over and Ollie checked it again, more professionally. He put the gun into his right-front pants pocket and slipped the cartridge box into his breast pocket, where it made a bulge like a pack of cigarettes. Then he leaned back against the cooler, round face still trickling sweat, and cracked a fresh beer. The sensation that I was seeing a totally unsuspected Ollie Weeks persisted.

"Thank you, Mrs. Dumfries," Miller said.

"Don't mention it," she said, and I thought fleetingly that if I were her husband and proprietor of those green eyes and that full figure, I might not travel so much. Giving your wife a gun could be seen as a ludicrously symbolic act.

"This may be silly, too," Miller said, turning back to Brown with his clipboard and Ollie with his beer, "but there aren't anything like flamethrowers in the place, are there?"

"Ohhh, *shit*," Buddy Eagleton said, and then went as red as Amanda Dumfries had done.

"What is it?" Mike Hatlen asked.

"Well . . . until last week we had a whole case of those little blowtorches. The kind you use around your house to solder leaky pipes or mend your exhaust systems or whatever. You remember those, Mr. Brown?"

Brown nodded, looking sour.

"Sold out?" Miller asked.

"No, they didn't go at all. We only sold three or four and sent the rest of the case back. What a pisser. I mean . . . what a shame." Blushing so deeply he was almost purple, Buddy Eagleton retired into the background again.

We had matches, of course, and salt (someone said vaguely that he had heard salt was the thing to put on bloodsuckers and things like that); and all kinds of O'Cedar mops and long-handled brooms. Most of the people continued to look heartened, and Jim and Myron were too plotzo to sound a dissenting note, but I met Ollie's eyes and saw a calm hopelessness in them that was worse than fear. He and I had seen the tentacles. The idea of throwing salt on them or trying to fend them off with the handles of O'Cedar mops was funny, in a ghastly way.

"Mike," Miller said, "why don't you crew this little adventure? I want to talk to Ollie and Dave here for a minute."

"Glad to." Hatlen clapped Dan Miller on the shoulder. "Somebody had to take charge, and you did it good. Welcome to town."

"Does this mean I get a kickback on my taxes?" Miller asked. He was a banty little guy with red hair that was receding. He looked like the sort of guy you can't help liking on short notice and—just maybe—the kind of guy you can't help not liking after he's been around for a while. The kind of guy who knows how to do everything better than you do.

"No way," Hatlen said, laughing.

Hatlen walked off. Miller glanced down at my son.

"Don't worry about Billy," I said.

"Man, I've never been so worried in my whole life," Miller said.

"No," Ollie agreed, and dropped an empty into the beer cooler. He got a fresh one and opened it. There was a soft hiss of escaping gas.

"I got a look at the way you two glanced at each other," Miller said.

I finished my Hershey bar and got a beer to wash it down with.

"Tell you what I think," Miller said. "We ought to get half a dozen people to wrap some of those mop handles with cloth and then tie them down with twine. Then I think we ought to get a couple of those cans of charcoal lighter fluid all ready. If we cut the tops right off the cans, we could have some torches pretty quick."

I nodded. That was good. Almost surely not good enough—not if you had seen Norm dragged out—but it was better than salt.

"That would give them something to think about, at least," Ollie said.

Miller's lips pressed together. "That bad, huh?" he said.

"That bad," Ollie agreed, and worked his beer.

By four-thirty that afternoon the sacks of fertilizer and lawn food were in place and the big windows were blocked off except for narrow loopholes. A watchman had been placed at each of these, and beside each watchman was a tin of charcoal lighter fluid with the top cut off and a supply of mop-handle torches. There were five loopholes, and Dan Miller had arranged a rotation of sentries for each one. When four-thirty came around, I was sitting on a pile of bags at one of the loopholes, Billy at my side. We were looking out into the mist.

Just beyond the window was a red bench where people sometimes waited for their rides with their groceries beside them. Beyond that was the parking lot. The mist swirled slowly, thick and heavy. There *was* moisture in it, but how dull it seemed, and gloomy. Just looking at it made me feel gutless and lost.

"Daddy, do you know what's happening?" Billy asked.

"No, hon," I said.

He fell silent for a bit, looking at his hands, which lay limply in the lap of his Tuffskin jeans. "Why doesn't somebody come and rescue us?" he asked finally. "The State Police or the FBI or someone?"

"I don't know."

"Do you think Mom's okay?"

"Billy, I just don't know," I said, and put an arm around him.

"I want her awful bad," Billy said, struggling with tears. "I'm sorry about the times I was bad to her."

"Billy," I said, and had to stop. I could taste salt in my throat, and my voice wanted to tremble.

"Will it be over?" Billy asked. "Daddy? Will it?"

"I don't know," I said, and he put his face in the hollow of my shoulder and I held the back of his head, felt the delicate curve of his skull just under the thick growth of his hair. I found myself remembering the evening of my wedding day. Watching Steff take off the simple brown dress she had changed into after the ceremony. She had had a big purple bruise on one hip from running into the side of a door the day before. I remembered looking at the bruise and thinking, *When she got that, she was still Stephanie Stepanek,* and feeling something like wonder. Then we had made love, and outside it was spitting snow from a dull gray December sky.

Billy was crying.

"Shh, Billy, shh," I said, rocking his head against me, but he went on crying. It was the sort of crying that only mothers know how to fix right.

Premature night came inside the Federal Foods. Miller and Hatlen and Bud Brown handed out flashlights, the whole stock, about twenty. Norton clamored loudly for them on behalf of his group, and received two. The lights bobbed here and there in the aisles like uneasy phantoms.

I held Billy against me and looked out through the loophole. The milky, translucent quality of the light out there hadn't changed much; it was putting up the bags that had made the market so dark. Several times I thought I saw something, but it was only jumpiness. One of the others raised a hesitant false alarm.

Billy saw Mrs. Turman again, and went to her eagerly, even though she hadn't been over to sit for him all summer. She had one of the flashlights and handed it over to him amiably enough. Soon he was trying to write his name in light on the blank glass faces of the frozen-food cases. She seemed as happy to see him as he was to see her, and in a little while they came over. Hattie Turman was a tall, thin woman with lovely red hair just beginning to streak gray. A pair of glasses hung from an ornamental chain—the sort, I believe, it is illegal for anyone except middle-aged women to wear—on her breast.

"Is Stephanie here, David?" she asked.

"No. At home."

She nodded. "Alan, too. How long are you on watch here?"

"Until six."

"Have you seen anything?"

"No. Just the mist."

"I'll keep Billy until six, if you like."

"Would you like that, Billy?"

"Yes, please," he said, swinging the flashlight above his head in slow arcs and watching it play across the ceiling.

"God will keep your Steffy, and Alan, too," Mrs. Turman said, and led Billy away by the hand. She spoke with serene sureness, but there was no conviction in her eyes.

Around five-thirty the sounds of excited argument rose near the back of the store. Someone jeered at something someone else had said, and someone—it was Buddy Eagleton, I think—shouted, "You're crazy if you go out there!"

Several of the flashlight beams pooled together at the center of the controversy, and they moved toward the front of the store. Mrs. Carmody's shrieking, derisive laugh split the gloom, as abrasive as fingers drawn down a slate blackboard.

Above the babble of voices came the boom of Norton's courtroom tenor: "Let us pass, please! Let us pass!"

The man at the loophole next to mine left his place to see what the shouting was about. I decided to stay where I was. Whatever the concatenation was, it was coming my way.

"Please," Mike Hatlen was saying. "Please, let's talk this thing through."

"There is nothing to talk about," Norton proclaimed. Now his face swam out of the gloom. It was determined and haggard and wholly wretched. He was holding one of the two flashlights allocated to the Flat-Earthers. The corkscrewed tufts of hair still stuck up behind his ears like a cuckold's horns. He was at the head of an extremely small procession— five of the original nine or ten. "We are going out," he said.

"Don't stick to this craziness," Miller said. "Mike's right. We can talk it over, can't we? Mr. McVey is going to barbecue some chicken over the gas grill, we can all sit down and eat and just—"

He got in Norton's way and Norton gave him a push. Miller didn't like it. His face flushed and then set in a hard expression. "Do what you want, then," he said. "But you're as good as murdering these other people."

With all the evenness of great resolve or unbreakable obsession, Norton said: "We'll send help back for you."

One of his followers murmured agreement, but another quietly slipped away. Now there was Norton and four others. Maybe that wasn't so bad. Christ Himself could only find twelve.

"Listen," Mike Hatlen said. "Mr. Norton—Brent—at least stay for the chicken. Get some hot food inside you."

"And give you a chance to go on talking? I've been in too many courtrooms to fall for that. You've psyched out half a dozen of my people already."

"Your people?" Hatlen almost groaned it. *"Your* people? Good Christ, what kind of talk is that? They're *people,* that's all. This is no game, and it's surely not a courtroom. There are, for want of a better word, there are *things* out there, and what's the sense of getting yourself killed?"

"Things, you say," Norton said, sounding superficially amused. "Where? Your people have been on watch for a couple of hours now. Who's seen one?"

"Well, out back. In the—"

"No, no, no," Norton said, shaking his head. "That ground has been covered and covered. We're going out—"

"No," someone whispered, and it echoed and spread, sounding like the rustle of dead leaves at dusk of an October evening. *No, no, no . . .*

"Will you restrain us?" a shrill voice asked. This was one of Norton's "people," to use his word—an elderly lady wearing bifocals. "Will you restrain us?"

The soft babble of negatives died away.

"No," Mike said. "No, I don't think anyone will restrain you."

I whispered in Billy's ear. He looked at me, startled and questioning. "Go on, now." I said. "Be quick."

He went.

Norton ran his hands through his hair, a gesture as calculated as any ever made by a Broadway actor. I had liked him better pulling the cord of his chainsaw fruitlessly, cussing and thinking himself unobserved. I could not tell then and do not know any better now if he believed in what he was doing or not. I think, down deep, that he knew what was going to happen. I think that the logic he had paid lip service to all his life turned on him at the end like a tiger that has gone bad and mean.

He looked around restlessly, seeming to wish that there was more to say. Then he led his four followers through one of the checkout lanes. In addition to the elderly woman, there was a chubby boy of about twenty, a young girl, and a man in blue jeans wearing a golf cap tipped back on his head.

Norton's eyes caught mine, widened a little, and then started to swing away.

"Brent, wait a minute," I said.

"I don't want to discuss it any further. Certainly not with you."

"I know you don't. I just want to ask a favor." I looked around and saw Billy coming back toward the checkouts at a run.

"What's that?" Norton asked suspiciously as Billy came up and handed me a package done up in cellophane.

"Clothesline," I said. I was vaguely aware that everyone in the market was watching us now, loosely strung out on the other side of the cash registers and checkout lanes. "It's the big package. Three hundred feet."

"So?"

"I wondered if you'd tie one end around your waist before you go out. I'll let it out. When you feel it come up tight, just tie it around something. It doesn't matter what. A car door handle would do."

"What in God's name for?"

"It will tell me you got at least three hundred feet," I said.

Something in his eyes flickered . . . but only momentarily. "No," he said.

I shrugged. "Okay. Good luck, anyhow."

Abruptly the man in the golf cap said, "I'll do it, mister. No reason not to."

Norton swung on him, as if to say something sharp, and the man in the golf cap studied him calmly. There was nothing flickering in *his* eyes. He had made his decision and there was simply no doubt in him. Norton saw it too and said nothing.

"Thanks," I said.

I slit the wrapping with my pocketknife and the clothesline accordioned out in stiff loops. I found one loose end and tied it around Golf Cap's waist in a loose granny. He immediately untied it and cinched it tighter with a good quick sheet-bend knot. There was not a sound in the market. Norton shifted uneasily from foot to foot.

"You want to take my knife?" I asked the man in the golf cap.

"I got one." He looked at me with that same calm contempt. "You just see to paying out your line. If it binds up, I'll chuck her."

"Are we all ready?" Norton asked, too loud. The chubby boy jumped as if he had been goosed. Getting no response, Norton turned to go.

"Brent," I said, and held out my hand. "Good luck, man."

He studied my hand as if it were some dubious foreign object. "We'll send back help," he said finally, and pushed through the OUT door. That thin, acrid smell came in again. The others followed him out.

Mike Hatlen came down and stood beside me. Norton's party of five stood in the milky, slow-moving fog. Norton said something and I should have heard it, but the mist seemed to have an odd damping effect. I heard nothing but the sound of his voice and two or three isolated syllables, like the voice on the radio heard from some distance. They moved off.

Hatlen held the door a little way open. I paid out the clothesline, keeping as much slack in it as I could, mindful of the man's promise to chuck the rope if it bound him up. There was still not a sound. Billy stood beside me, motionless but seeming to thrum with his own inner current.

Again there was that weird feeling that the five of them did not so much disappear into the fog as become invisible. For a moment their clothes seemed to stand alone, and then they were gone. You were not really impressed with the unnatural density of the mist until you saw people swallowed up in a space of seconds.

I paid the line out. A quarter of it went, then a half. It stopped going out for a moment. It went from a live thing to a dead one in my hands. I held my breath. Then it started to go out again. I paid it through my fingers, and suddenly remembered my father taking me to see the Gregory Peck film of *Moby Dick* at the Brookside. I think I smiled a little.

Three-quarters of the line was gone now. I could see the end of it lying beside one of Billy's feet. Then the rope stopped moving through my hands again. It lay motionless for perhaps five seconds, and then another five feet jerked out. Then it suddenly whipsawed violently to the left, twanging off the edge of the OUT door.

Twenty feet of rope suddenly paid out, making a thin heat across my left palm. And from out of the mist there came a high, wavering scream. It was impossible to tell the sex of the screamer.

The rope whipsawed in my hands again. And again. It skated across the space in the doorway to the right, then back to the left. A few more feet paid out, and then there was a ululating howl from out there that brought an answering moan from my son. Hatlen stood aghast. His eyes were huge. One corner of his mouth turned down, trembling.

The howl was abruptly cut off. There was no sound at all for what seemed to be forever. Then the old lady cried out—this time there could be no doubt about who it was. *"Git it offa me!"* she screamed. *"Oh my Lord my Lord get it—"*

Then her voice was cut off, too.

Almost all of the rope abruptly ran out through my loosely closed fist, giving me a hotter burn this time. Then it went completely slack, and a sound came out of the mist—a thick, loud grunt—that made all the spit in my mouth dry up.

It was like no sound I've ever heard, but the closest

approximation might be a movie set in the African veld or a South American swamp. It was the sound of a big animal. It came again, low and tearing and savage. Once more . . . and then it subsided to a series of low mutterings. Then it was completely gone.

"Close the door," Amanda Dumfries said in a trembling voice. "Please."

"In a minute," I said, and began to yank the line back in.

It came out of the mist and piled up around my feet in untidy loops and snarls. About three feet from the end, the new white clothesline went barn-red.

"Death!" Mrs. Carmody screamed. "Death to go out there! Now do you see?"

The end of the clothesline was a chewed and frayed tangle of fiber and little puffs of cotton. The little puffs were dewed with minute drops of blood.

No one contradicted Mrs. Carmody.

Mike Hatlen let the door swing shut.

VII. The First Night.

Mr. McVey had worked in Bridgton cutting meat ever since I was twelve or thirteen, and I had no idea what his first name was or his age might be. He had set up a gas grill under one of the small exhaust fans—the fans were still now, but presumably they still gave some ventilation—and by 6:30 P.M. the smell of cooking chicken filled the market. Bud Brown didn't object. It might have been shock, but more likely he had recognized the fact that his fresh meat and poultry wasn't getting any fresher. The chicken smelled good, but not many people wanted to eat. Mr. McVey, small and spare and neat in his whites, cooked the chicken nevertheless and laid the pieces two by two on paper plates and lined them up cafeteria-style on top of the meat counter.

Mrs. Turman brought Billy and me each a plate, garnished with helpings of deli potato salad. I ate as best I could, but Billy would not even pick at his.

"You got to eat, big guy," I said.

"I'm not hungry," he said, putting the plate aside.

"You can't get big and strong if you don't—"

Mrs. Turman, sitting slightly behind Billy, shook her head at me.

"Okay," I said. "Go get a peach and eat it, at least.'Kay?"

"What if Mr. Brown says something?"

"If he says something, you come back and tell me."

"Okay, Dad."

He walked away slowly. He seemed to have shrunk somehow. It hurt my heart to see him walk that way. Mr. McVey went on cooking chicken, apparently not minding that only a few people were eating it, happy in the act of cooking. As I think I have said, there are all ways of handling a thing like this. You wouldn't think it would be so, but it is. The mind is a monkey.

Mrs. Turman and I sat halfway up the patent-medicines aisle. People were sitting in little groups all over the store. No one except Mrs. Carmody was sitting alone; even Myron and his buddy Jim were together—they were both passed out by the beer cooler.

Six new men were watching the loopholes. One of them was Ollie, gnawing a leg of chicken and drinking a beer. The mop-handle torches leaned beside each of the watchposts, a can of charcoal lighter fluid next to each . . . but I don't think anyone really believed in the torches the way they had before. Not after that low and terribly vital grunting sound, not after the chewed and blood-soaked clothesline. If whatever was out there decided it wanted us, it was going to have us. It, or they.

"How bad will it be tonight?" Mrs. Turman asked. Her voice was calm, but her eyes were sick and scared.

"Hattie, I just don't know."

"You let me keep Billy as much as you can. I'm . . . Davey, I think I'm in mortal terror." She uttered a dry laugh. "Yes, I believe that's what it is. But if I have Billy, I'll be all right. I'll be all right for him."

Her eyes were glistening. I leaned over and patted her shoulder.

"I'm so worried about Alan," she said. "He's dead, Davey. In my heart, I'm sure he's dead."

"No, Hattie. You don't know any such thing."

"But I feel it's true. Don't you feel anything about Stephanie? Don't you at least have a . . . a feeling?"

"No," I said, lying through my teeth.

A strangled sound came from her throat and she clapped a hand to her mouth. Her glasses reflected back the dim, murky light.

"Billy's coming back," I murmured.

He was eating a peach. Hattie Turman patted the floor beside her and said that when he was done she would show him how to make a little man out of the peach pit and some thread. Billy smiled at her wanly, and Mrs. Turman smiled back.

At 8:00 P.M. six new men went on at the loopholes and Ollie came over to where I was sitting. "Where's Billy?"

"With Mrs. Turman, up back," I said. "They're doing crafts. They've run through peach-pit men and shopping-bag masks and apple dolls and now Mr. McVey is showing him how to make pipe-cleaner men."

Ollie took a long drink of beer and said, "Things are moving around out there."

I looked at him sharply. He looked back levelly.

"I'm not drunk," he said. "I've been trying but haven't been able to make it. I wish I could, David."

"What do you mean, things are moving around out there?"

"I can't say for sure. I asked Walter, and he said he had the same feeling, that parts of the mist would go darker for a minute—sometimes just a little smudge, sometimes a big dark place, like a bruise. Then it would fade back to gray. And the stuff is swirling around. Even Arnie Simms said he felt like something was going on out there, and Arnie's almost as blind as a bat."

"What about the others?"

"They're all out-of-staters, strangers to me," Ollie said. "I didn't ask any of them."

"How sure are you that you weren't just seeing things?"

"Sure," he said. He nodded toward Mrs. Carmody, who was sitting by herself at the end of the aisle. None of it had hurt her appetite any; there was a graveyard of chicken bones on her plate. She was drinking either blood or V-8 juice. "I think she was right about one thing," Ollie said. "We'll find out. When it gets dark, we'll find out."

But we didn't have to wait until dark. When it came, Billy saw very little of it, because Mrs. Turman kept him up back.

Ollie was still sitting with me when one of the men up front gave out a shriek and staggered back from his post, pinwheeling his arms. It was approaching eight-thirty; outside the pearl-white mist had darkened to the dull slaty color of a November twilight.

Something had landed on the glass outside one of the loopholes.

"Oh my Jesus!" the man who had been watching there screamed. *"Let me out! Let me out of this!"*

He tore around in a rambling circle, his eyes starting from his face, a thin lick of saliva at one corner of his mouth glimmering in the deepening shadows. Then he took off straight up the far aisle past the frozen-food cases.

There were answering cries. Some people ran toward the front to see what had happened. Many others retreated toward the back, not caring and not wanting to see whatever was crawling on the glass out there.

I started down toward the loophole, Ollie by my side. His hand was in the pocket that held Mrs. Dumfries' gun. Now one of the other watchers let out a cry—not so much of fear as disgust.

Ollie and I slipped through one of the checkout lanes. Now I could see what had frightened the guy from his post. I couldn't tell what it was, but I could see it. It looked like one of the minor creatures in a Bosch painting—one of his hellacious murals. There was something almost horribly comic about it, too, because it also looked a little like one of those strange creations of vinyl and plastic you can buy for $1.89 to spring on your friends . . . in fact, exactly the sort of thing Norton had accused me of planting in the storage area.

It was maybe two feet long, segmented, the pinkish color of burned flesh that has healed over. Bulbous eyes peered in two different directions at once from the ends of short, limber stalks. It clung to the window on fat sucker-pads. From the opposite end there protruded something that was either a sexual organ or a stinger. And from its back there sprouted oversized, membranous wings, like the wings of a housefly. They were moving very slowly as Ollie and I approached the glass.

At the loophole to the left of us, where the man had made the disgusted cawing sound, three of the things were crawling on the glass. They moved sluggishly across it, leaving sticky snail trails behind them. Their eyes—if that is what they were—joggled on the end of the finger-thick stalks. The biggest was maybe four feet long. At times they crawled right over each other.

"Look at those goddam things," Tom Smalley said in a sickened voice. He was standing at the loophole on our right. I didn't reply. The bugs were all over the loopholes now, which meant they were probably crawling all over the building . . . like maggots on a piece of meat. It wasn't a pleasant image, and I could feel what chicken I had managed to eat now wanting to come up.

Someone was sobbing. Mrs. Carmody was screaming about abominations from within the earth. Someone told her gruffly that she'd shut up if she knew what was good for her. Same old shit.

Ollie took Mrs. Dumfries' gun from his pocket and I grabbed his arm. "Don't be crazy."

He shook free. "I know what I'm doing," he said.

He tapped the barrel of the gun on the window, his face set in a nearly masklike expression of distaste. The speed of the creatures' wings increased until they were only a blur—if you hadn't known, you might have believed they weren't winged creatures at all. Then they simply flew away.

Some of the others saw what Ollie had done and got the idea. They used the mop handles to tap on the windows. The things flew away, but came right back. Apparently they had no more brains than your average housefly, either. The near-panic dissolved in a babble of conversation. I heard someone asking someone else what he thought those things would do if they landed on you. That was a question I had no interest in seeing answered.

The tapping on the windows began to die away. Ollie turned toward me and started to say something, but before he could do more than open his mouth, something came out of the fog and snatched one of the crawling things off the glass. I think I screamed. I'm not sure.

It was a flying thing. Beyond that I could not have said for sure. The fog appeared to darken in exactly the way Ollie had described, only the dark smutch didn't fade away; it solidified into something with flapping, leathery wings, an albino-white body, and reddish eyes. It thudded into the glass hard enough to make it shiver. Its beak opened. It scooped the pink thing in and was gone. The whole incident took no more than five seconds. I had a bare final impression of the pink thing wiggling and flapping as it went down the hatch, the way a small fish will wiggle and flap in the beak of a seagull.

Now there was another thud, and yet another. People began screaming again, and there was a stampede toward the back of the store. Then there was a more piercing scream, one of pain, and Ollie said, "Oh my God, that old lady fell down and they just ran over her."

He ran back through the checkout aisle. I turned to follow, and then I saw something that stopped me dead where I was standing.

High up and to my right, one of the lawn-food bags was sliding slowly backward. Tom Smalley was right under it, staring out into the mist through his loophole.

Another of the pink bugs landed on the thick plate glass of the loophole where Ollie and I had been standing. One of the flying things swooped down and grabbed it. The old woman who had been trampled went on screaming in a shrill, cracked voice.

That bag. That sliding bag.

"Smalley!" I shouted. "Look out! Heads up!"

In the general confusion, he never heard me. The bag teetered, then fell. It struck him squarely on the head. He went down hard, catching his jaw on the shelf that ran below the show window.

One of the albino flying things was squirming its way through the jagged hole in the glass. I could hear the soft scraping sound that it made, now that some of the screaming had stopped. Its red eyes glittered in its triangular head, which was slightly cocked to one side. A heavy, hooked beak opened and closed rapaciously. It looked a bit like the paintings of pterodactyls you may have seen in the dinosaur books, more like something out of a lunatic's nightmare.

I grabbed one of the torches and slam-dunked it into a can of charcoal lighter fluid, tipping it over and spilling a pool of the stuff across the floor.

The flying creature paused on top of the lawn-food bags, glaring around, shifting slowly and malignantly from one taloned foot to the other. It was a stupid creature, I am quite sure of that. Twice it tried to spread its wings, which struck the walls and then folded themselves over its hunched back like the wings of a griffin. The third time it tried, it lost its balance and fell clumsily from its perch, still trying to spread its wings. It landed on Tom Smalley's back. One flex of its claws and Tom's shirt ripped wide open. Blood began to flow.

I was there, less than three feet away. My torch was dripping lighter fluid. I was emotionally pumped up to kill it if I could . . . and then realized I had no matches to light it with. I had used the last one lighting a cigar for Mr. McVey an hour ago.

The place was in pandemonium now. People had seen the thing roosting on Smalley's back, something no one in the world had seen before. It darted its head forward at a questing angle, and tore a chunk of meat from the back of Smalley's neck.

I was getting ready to use the torch as a bludgeon when the clothwrapped head of it suddenly blazed alight. Dan Miller was there, holding a Zippo lighter with a Marine emblem on it. His face was as harsh as a rock with horror and fury.

"Kill it," he said hoarsely. "Kill it if you can." Standing beside him was Ollie. He had Mrs. Dumfries'.38 in his hand, but he had no clear shot.

The thing spread its wings and flapped them once—apparently not to fly away but to secure a better hold on its prey—and then its leathery-white, membranous wings enfolded poor Smalley's entire upper body. Then the sounds came—mortal tearing sounds that I cannot bear to describe in any detail.

All of this happened in bare seconds. Then I thrust my torch at the thing. There was the sensation of striking something with no more real substance than a box kite. The next moment the entire creature was blazing. It made a screeching sound and its wings spread; its head jerked and its reddish eyes rolled with what I most sincerely hope was great agony. It took off with a sound like linen bedsheets flapping on a clothesline in a stiff spring breeze. It uttered that rusty shrieking sound again.

Heads turned up to follow its flaming, dying course. I think that nothing in the entire business stands in my memory so strongly as that bird-thing blazing a zigzagging course above the aisles of the Federal Supermarket, dropping charred and smoking bits of itself here and there. It finally crashed into the spaghetti sauces, splattering Ragú and Prince and Prima Salsa everywhere like gouts of blood. It was little more than ash and bone. The smell of its burning was high and sickening. And underlying it like a counterpoint was the thin and acrid stench of the mist, eddying in through the broken place in the glass.

For a moment there was utter silence. We were united in the black wonder of that brightly flaming deathflight. Then someone howled. Others screamed. And from somewhere in the back I could hear my son crying.

A hand grabbed me. It was Bud Brown. His eyes were bulging from their sockets. His lips were drawn back from his false teeth in a snarl. "One of those other things," he said, and pointed.

One of the bugs had come in through the hole and it now perched on a lawn-food bag, housefly wings buzzing—you could hear them; it sounded like a cheap department-store electric fan—eyes bulging from their stalks. Its pink and noxiously plump body was aspirating rapidly.

I moved toward it. My torch was guttering but not yet out. But Mrs. Reppler, the third-grade teacher, beat me to it. She was maybe fifty-five, maybe sixty, rope-thin. Her body had a tough, dried-out look that always makes me think of beef jerky.

She had a can of Raid in each hand like some crazy gunslinger in an existential comedy. She uttered a snarl of anger that would have done credit to a caveman splitting the skull of an enemy. Holding the pressure cans out at the full length of each arm, she pressed the buttons. A thick spray of insect-killer coated the thing. It went into throes of agony, twisting and turning crazily and at last falling from the bags, bouncing off the body of Tom Smalley—who was dead beyond any doubt or question—and finally landing on the floor. Its wings buzzed madly, but they weren't taking it anywhere; they were too heavily coated with Raid. A few moments later the wings slowed, then stopped. It was dead.

You could hear people crying now. And moaning. The old lady who had been trampled was moaning. And you could hear laughter. The laughter of the damned. Mrs. Reppler stood over her kill, her thin chest rising and falling rapidly.

Hatlen and Miller had found one of those dollies that the stockboys use to trundle cases of things around the store, and together they heaved it atop the lawn-food bags, blocking off the wedge-shaped hole in the glass. As a temporary measure, it was a good one.

Amanda Dumfries came forward like a sleepwalker. In one hand she held a plastic floor bucket. In the other she held a whisk broom, still done up in its see-through wrapping. She bent, her eyes still wide and blank, and swept the dead pink thing—bug, slug, whatever it was—into the bucket. You could hear the crackle of the wrapping on the whisk broom as it brushed the floor. She walked over to the OUT door. There were none of the bugs on it. She opened it a little way and threw the bucket out. It landed on its side and rolled back and forth in ever-decreasing arcs. One of the pink things buzzed out of the night, landed on the floor pail, and began to crawl over it.

Amanda burst into tears. I walked over and put an arm around her shoulders.

At one-thirty the following morning I was sitting with my back against the white enamel side of the meat counter in a semidoze. Billy's head was in my lap. He was solidly asleep. Not far away Amanda Dumfries was sleeping with her head pillowed on someone's jacket.

Not long after the flaming death of the bird-thing, Ollie and I had gone back out to the storage area and had gathered up half a dozen of the pads such as the one I'd covered Billy with earlier. Several people were sleeping on these. We had also brought back several heavy crates of oranges and pears, and four of us working together had been able to swing them to the tops of the lawn-food bags in front of the hole in the glass. The bird-creatures would have a tough time shifting one of those crates; they weighed about ninety pounds each.

But the birds and the buglike things the birds ate weren't the only things out there. There was the tentacled thing that had taken Norm. There was the frayed clothesline to think about. There was the unseen thing that had uttered that low, guttural roar to think about. We had heard sounds like it since—sometimes quite distant—but how far was "distant" through the damping effect of the mist? And sometimes they were close enough to shake the building and make it seem as if the ventricles of your heart had suddenly been loaded up with ice water.

Billy started in my lap and moaned. I brushed his hair and he moaned more loudly. Then he seemed to find sleep's less dangerous waters again. My own doze was broken and I was staring wide awake again. Since dark, I had only managed to sleep about ninety minutes, and that had been dream-haunted. In one of the dream fragments it had been the night before again. Billy and Steffy were standing in front of the picture window, looking out at the black and slate-gray waters, out at the silver spinning waterspout that heralded the storm. I tried to get to them, knowing that a strong enough wind could break the window and throw deadly glass darts all the way across the living room. But no matter how I ran, I seemed to get no closer to them. And then a bird rose out of the waterspout, a gigantic scarlet *oiseau de mort* whose prehistoric wingspan darkened the entire lake from west to east. Its beak opened, revealing a maw the size of the Holland Tunnel. And as the bird came to gobble up my wife and son, a low, sinister voice began to whisper over and over again: *The Arrowhead Project . . . the Arrowhead Project . . . the Arrowhead Project . . .*

Not that Billy and I were the only ones sleeping poorly. Others screamed in their sleep, and some went on screaming after they woke up. The beer was disappearing from the cooler at a great rate. Buddy Eagleton had restocked it once from out back with no comment. Mike Hatlen told me the Sominex was gone. Not depleted but totally wiped out. He guessed that some people might have taken six or eight bottles.

"There's some Nytol left," he said. "You want a bottle, David?" I shook my head and thanked him.

And in the last aisle down by Register 5, we had our winos. There were about seven of them, all out-of-staters except for Lou Tattinger, who ran the Pine Tree Car Wash. Lou didn't need any excuse to sniff the cork, as the saying was. The wino brigade was pretty well anesthetized.

Oh yes—there were also six or seven people who had gone crazy.

Crazy isn't the best word; perhaps I just can't think of the proper one. But there were these people who had lapsed into a complete stupor without benefit of beer, wine, or pills. They stared at you with blank and shiny doorknob eyes. The hard cement of reality had come apart in some unimaginable earthquake, and these poor devils had fallen through. In time, some of them might come back. If there was time.

The rest of us had made our own mental compromises, and in some cases I suppose they were fairly odd. Mrs. Reppler, for instance, was convinced the whole thing was a dream—or so she said. And she spoke with some conviction.

I looked over at Amanda. I was developing an uncomfortably strong feeling for her—uncomfortable but not exactly unpleasant. Her eyes were an incredible, brilliant green . . . for a while I had kept an eye on her to see if she was going to take out a pair of contact lenses, but apparently the color was true. I wanted to make love to her. My wife was at home, maybe alive, more probably dead, alone either way, and I loved her; I wanted to get Billy and me back to her more than anything, but I also wanted to screw this lady named Amanda Dumfries. I tried to tell myself it was just the situation we were in, and maybe it was, but that didn't change the wanting.

I dozed in and out, then jerked awake more fully around three. Amanda had shifted into a sort of fetal position, her knees pulled up toward her chest, hands clasped between her thighs. She seemed to be sleeping deeply. Her sweatshirt had pulled up slightly on one side, showing clean white skin. I looked at it and began to get an extremely useless and uncomfortable erection.

I tried to divert my mind to a new track and got thinking about how I had wanted to paint Brent Norton yesterday. No, nothing as important as a painting, but . . . just sit him on a log with my beer in his hand and sketch his sweaty, tired face and the two wings of his carefully processed hair sticking up untidily in the back. It could have been a good picture. It took me twenty years of living with my father to accept the idea that being good could be good enough.

You know what talent is? The curse of expectation. As a kid you have to deal with that, beat it somehow. If you can write, you think God put you on earth to blow Shakespeare away. Of if you can paint, maybe you think—I did—that God put you on earth to blow your father away.

It turned out I wasn't as good as he was. I kept trying to be for longer than I should have, maybe. I had a show in New York and it did poorly—the art critics beat me over the head with my father. A year later I was supporting myself and Steff with the commercial stuff. She was pregnant and I sat down and talked to myself about it. The result of that conversation was a belief that serious art was always going to be a hobby for me, no more.

I did Golden Girl Shampoo ads—the one where the Girl is standing astride her bike, the one where she's playing Frisbee on the beach, the one where she's standing on the balcony of her apartment with a drink in her hand. I've done short-story illustrations for most of the big slicks, but I broke into that field doing fast illustrations for the stories in the sleazier men's magazines. I've done some movie posters. The money comes in. We keep our heads nicely above water.

I had one final show in Bridgton, just last summer. I showed nine canvases that I had painted in five years, and I sold six of them. The one I absolutely would not sell showed the Federal market, by some queer coincidence. The perspective was from the far end of the parking lot. In my picture, the parking lot was empty except for a line of Campbell's Beans and Franks cans, each one larger than the last as they marched toward the viewer's eye. The last one appeared to be about eight feet tall. The picture was titled *Beans and False Perspective*. A man from California who was a top exec in some company that makes tennis balls and rackets and who knows what other sports equipment seemed to want that picture very badly, and would not take no for an answer in spite of the NFS card tucked into the bottom left-hand corner of the spare wooden frame. He began at six hundred dollars and worked his way up to four thousand. He said he wanted it for his study. I would not let him have it, and he went away sorely puzzled. Even so, he didn't quite give up; he left his card in case I changed my mind.

I could have used the money—that was the year we put the addition on the house and bought the four-wheel-drive—but I just couldn't sell it. I couldn't sell it because I felt it was the best painting I had ever done and I wanted it to look at after someone would ask me, with totally unconscious cruelty, when I was going to do something serious.

Then I happened to show it to Ollie Weeks one day last fall. He asked me if he could photograph it and run it as an ad one week, and that was the end of my own false perspective. Ollie had recognized my painting for what it was, and by doing so, he forced me to recognize it, too. A perfectly good piece of slick commercial art. No more. And, thank God, no less.

I let him do it, and then I called the exec at his home in San Luis Obispo and told him he could have the painting for twenty-five hundred if he still wanted it. He did, and I shipped it UPS to the coast. And since then that voice of disappointed expectation—that cheated child's voice that can never be satisfied with such a mild superlative as good—has fallen pretty much silent. And except for a few rumbles—like the sounds of those unseen creatures somewhere out in the foggy night—it has been pretty much silent ever since. Maybe you can tell me—why should the silencing of that childish, demanding voice seem so much like dying?

Around four o'clock Billy woke up—partially, at least—and looked around with bleary, uncomprehending eyes. "Are we still here?"

"Yeah, honey," I said. "We are."

He started to cry with a weak helplessness that was horrible. Amanda woke up and looked at us.

"Hey, kid," she said, and pulled him gently to her. "Everything is going to look a little better come morning."

"No," Billy said. "No it won't. It won't. It won't."

"Shh," she said. Her eyes met mine over his head. "Shh, it's past your bedtime."

"I want my *mother!*"

"Yeah, you do," Amanda said. "Of course you do."

Billy squirmed around in her lap until he could look at me. Which he did for some time. And then slept again.

"Thanks," I said. "He needed you."

"He doesn't even know me."

"That doesn't change it."

"So what do you think?" she asked. Her green eyes held mine steadily. "What do you really think?"

"Ask me in the morning."

"I'm asking you now."

I opened my mouth to answer and then Ollie Weeks materialized out of the gloom like something from a horror tale. He had a flashlight with one of the ladies' blouses over the lens, and he was pointing it toward the ceiling. It made strange shadows on his haggard face. "David," he whispered.

Amanda looked at him, first startled, then scared again.

"Ollie, what is it?" I asked.

"David," he whispered again. Then: "Come on. Please."

"I don't want to leave Billy. He just went to sleep."

"I'll be with him," Amanda said. "You better go." Then, in a lower voice: "Jesus, this is never going to end."

VIII. What Happened to the Soldiers. With Amanda. A Conversation with Dan Miller.

I went with Ollie. He was headed for the storage area. As we passed the cooler, he grabbed a beer.

"Ollie, what is it?"

"I want you to see it."

He pushed through the double doors. They slipped shut behind us with a little backwash of air. It was cold. I didn't like this place, not after what had happened to Norm. A part of my mind insisted on reminding me that there was still a small scrap of dead tentacle lying around someplace.

Ollie let the blouse drop from the lens of his light. He trained it overhead. At first I had an idea that someone had hung a couple of mannequins from one of the heating pipes below the ceiling. That they had hung them on piano wire or something, a kid's Halloween trick.

Then I noticed the feet, dangling about seven inches off the cement floor. There were two piles of kicked-over cartons. I looked up at the faces and a scream began to rise in my throat because they were not the faces of department-store dummies. Both heads were cocked to the side, as if appreciating some horribly funny joke, a joke that had made them laugh until they turned purple.

Their shadows. Their shadows thrown long on the wall behind them. Their tongues. Their protruding tongues.

They were both wearing uniforms. They were the kids I had noticed earlier and had lost track of along the way. The army brats from—

The scream. I could hear it starting in my throat as a moan, rising like a police siren, and then Ollie gripped my arm just above the elbow. "Don't scream, David. No one knows about this but you and me. And that's how I want to keep it."

Somehow I bit it back.

"Those army kids," I managed.

"From the Arrowhead Project," Ollie said. "Sure." Something cold was thrust into my hand. The beer can. "Drink this. You need it."

I drained the can completely dry.

Ollie said, "I came back to see if we had any extra cartridges for that gas grill Mr. McVey has been using. I saw these guys. The way I figure, they must have gotten the nooses ready and stood on top of those two piles of cartons. They must have tied their hands for each other and then balanced each other while they stepped through the length of rope between their wrists. So . . . so that their hands would be behind them, you know. Then—this is the way I figure—they stuck their heads into the nooses and pulled them tight by jerking their heads to one side. Maybe one of them counted to three and they jumped together. I don't know."

"It couldn't be done," I said through a dry mouth. But their hands were tied behind them, all right. I couldn't seem to take my eyes away from that.

"It could. If they wanted to bad enough, David, they could."

"But why?"

"I think you know why. Not any of the tourists, the summer people—like that guy Miller—but there are people from around here who could make a pretty decent guess."

"The Arrowhead Project?"

Ollie said, "I stand by one of those registers all day long and I hear a lot. All this spring I've been hearing things about that damned Arrowhead thing, none of it good. The black ice on the lakes—"

I thought of Bill Giosti leaning in my window, blowing warm alcohol in my face. Not just atoms, but *different* atoms. Now these bodies hanging from that overhead pipe. The cocked heads. The dangling shoes. The tongues protruding like summer sausages.

I realized with fresh horror that new doors of perception were opening up inside. New? Not so. Old doors of perception. The perception of a child who has not yet learned to protect itself by developing the tunnel vision that keeps out ninety percent of the universe. Children see everything their eyes happen upon, hear everything in their ears' range. But if life is the rise of consciousness (as a crewel-work sampler my wife made in high school proclaims), then it is also the reduction of input.

Terror is the widening of perspective and perception. The horror was in knowing I was swimming down to a place most of us leave when we get out of diapers and into training pants. I could see it on Ollie's face, too. When rationality begins to break down, the circuits of the human brain can overload. Axons grow bright and feverish. Hallucinations turn real: the quicksilver puddle at the point where perspective makes parallel lines seem to intersect is really there; the dead walk and talk; a rose begins to sing.

"I've heard stuff from maybe two dozen people," Ollie said. "Justine Robards. Nick Tochai. Ben Michaelson. You can't keep secrets in small towns. Things get out. Sometimes it's like a spring—it just bubbles up out of the earth and no one has an idea where it came from. You overhear something at the library and pass it on, or at the marina in Harrison, Christ knows where else, or why. But all spring and summer I've been hearing Arrowhead Project, Arrowhead Project."

"But these two," I said. "Christ, Ollie, they're just kids."

"There were kids in Nam who used to take ears. I was there. I saw it."

"But . . . what would drive them to do this?"

"I don't know. Maybe they knew something. Maybe they only suspected. They must have known people in here would start asking them questions eventually. If there is an eventually."

"If you're right," I said, "it must be something really bad."

"That storm," Ollie said in his soft, level voice. "Maybe it knocked something loose up there. Maybe there was an accident. They could have been fooling around with anything. Some people claim they were messing with high-intensity lasers and masers. Sometimes I hear fusion power. And suppose . . . suppose they ripped a hole straight through into another dimension?"

"That's hogwash," I said.

"Are they?" Ollie asked, and pointed at the bodies.

"No. The question now is: What do we do?"

"I think we ought to cut them down and hide them," he said promptly. "Put them under a pile of stuff people won't want—dog food, dish detergent, stuff like that. If this gets out, it will only make things worse. That's why I came to you, David. I felt you are the only one I could really trust.''

I muttered, ''It's like the Nazi war criminals killing themselves in their cells after the war was lost.''

''Yeah. I had that same thought.''

We fell silent, and suddenly those soft shuffling noises began outside the steel loading door again—the sound of the tentacles feeling softly across it. We drew together. My flesh was crawling.

''Okay,'' I said.

''We'll make it as quick as we can,'' Ollie said. His sapphire ring glowed mutely as he moved his flashlight. ''I want to get out of here fast.''

I looked up at the ropes. They had used the same sort of clothesline the man in the golf cap had allowed me to tie around his waist. The nooses had sunk into the puffed flesh of their necks, and I wondered again what it could have been to make both of them go through with it. I knew what Ollie meant by saying that if the news of the double suicide got out, it would make things worse. For me it already had—and I wouldn't have believed that possible.

There was a snicking sound. Ollie had opened his knife, a good heavy job made for slitting open cartons. And, of course, cutting rope.

''You or me?'' he asked.

I swallowed. ''One each.''

We did it.

When I got back, Amanda was gone and Mrs. Turman was with Billy. They were both sleeping. I walked down one of the aisles and a voice said: ''Mr. Drayton. David.'' It was Amanda, standing by the stairs to the manager's office, her eyes like emeralds. ''What was it?''

''Nothing,'' I said.

She came over to me. I could smell faint perfume. And oh how I wanted her. ''You liar,'' she said.

''It was nothing. A false alarm.''

''If that's how you want it.'' She took my hand. ''I've just been up to the office. It's empty and there's a lock on the door.'' Her face was perfectly calm, but her eyes were lambent, almost feral, and a pulse beat steadily in her throat.

''I don't—''

"I saw the way you looked at me," she said. "If we need to talk about it, it's no good. The Turman woman is with your son."

"Yes." It came to me that this was a way—maybe not the best one, but a way, nevertheless—to take the curse off what Ollie and I had just done. Not the best way, just the only way.

We went up the narrow flight of stairs and into the office. It was empty, as she had said. And there was a lock on the door. I turned it. In the darkness she was nothing but a shape. I put my arms out, touched her, and pulled her to me. She was trembling. We went down on the floor, first kneeling, kissing, and I cupped one firm breast and could feel the quick thudding of her heart through her sweatshirt. I thought of Steffy telling Billy not to touch the live wires. I thought of the bruise that had been on her hip when she took off the brown dress on our wedding night. I thought of the first time I had seen her, biking across the mall of the University of Maine at Orono, me bound for one of Vincent Hartgen's classes with my portfolio under my arm. And my erection was enormous.

We lay down then, and she said, "Love me, David. Make me warm." When she came, she dug into my back with her nails and called me by a name that wasn't mine. I didn't mind. It made us about even.

When we came down, some sort of creeping dawn had begun. The blackness outside the loopholes went reluctantly to dull gray, then to chrome, then to the bright, featureless, and unsparkling white of a drive-in movie screen. Mike Hatlen was asleep in a folding chair he had scrounged somewhere. Dan Miller sat on the floor a little distance away, eating a Hostess donut. The kind that's powdered with white sugar.

"Sit down, Mr. Drayton," he invited.

I looked around for Amanda, but she was already halfway up the aisle. She didn't look back. Our act of love in the dark already seemed something out of a fantasy, impossible to believe even in this weird daylight. I sat down.

"Have a donut." He held the box out.

I shook my head. "All that white sugar is death. Worse than cigarettes."

That made him laugh a little bit. "In that case, have two."

I was surprised to find a little laughter left inside me—he

had surprised it out, and I liked him for it. I did take two of his donuts. They tasted pretty good. I chased them with a cigarette, although it is not normally my habit to smoke in the mornings.

"I ought to get back to my kid," I said. "He'll be waking up."

Miller nodded. "Those pink bugs," he said. "They're all gone. So are the birds. Hank Vannerman said the last one hit the windows around four. Apparently the . . . the wildlife . . . is a lot more active when it's dark."

"You don't want to tell Brent Norton that," I said. "Or Norm."

He nodded again and didn't say anything for a long time. Then he lit a cigarette of his own and looked at me. "We can't stay here, Drayton," he said.

"There's food. Plenty to drink."

"The supplies don't have anything to do with it, and you know it. What do we do if one of the big beasties out there decides to break in instead of just going bump in the night? Do we try to drive it off with broom handles and charcoal lighter fluid?"

Of course he was right. Perhaps the mist was protecting us in a way. Hiding us. But maybe it wouldn't hide us for long, and there was more to it than that. We had been in the Federal for eighteen hours, more or less, and I could feel a kind of lethargy spreading over me, not much different from the lethargy I've felt on one or two occasions when I've tried to swim too far. There was an urge to play it safe, to just stay put, to take care of Billy *(and maybe to bang Amanda Dumfries in the middle of the night,* a voice murmured), to see if the mist wouldn't just lift, leaving everything as it had been.

I could see it on the other faces as well, and it suddenly occurred to me that there were people now in the Federal who probably wouldn't leave under any circumstance. The very thought of going out the door after all that had happened would freeze them.

Miller had been watching these thoughts cross my face, maybe. He said, "There were about eighty people in here when that damn fog came. From that number you subtract the bag-boy, Norton, and the four people that went out with him, and that man Smalley. That leaves seventy-three."

And subtracting the two soldiers, now resting under a stack of Purina Puppy Chow bags, it made seventy-one.

"Then you subtract the people who have just opted out," he went on. "There are ten or twelve of those. Say ten. That leaves about sixty-three. *But—*" He raised one sugar-powdered finger. "Of those sixty-three, we've got twenty or so that just won't leave. You'd have to drag them out kicking and screaming."

"Which all goes to prove what?"

"That we've got to get out, that's all. And I'm going. Around noon, I think. I'm planning to take as many people as will come. I'd like you and your boy to come along."

"After what happened to Norton?"

"Norton went like a lamb to the slaughter. That doesn't mean I have to, or the people who come with me."

"How can you prevent it? We have exactly one gun."

"And lucky to have that. But if we could make it across the intersection, maybe we could get down to the Sportsman's Exchange on Main Street. They've got more guns there than you could shake a stick at."

"That's one 'if' and one 'maybe' too many."

"Drayton," he said, "it's an iffy situation."

That rolled very smoothly off his tongue, but he didn't have a little boy to watch out for.

"Look, let it pass for now, okay? I didn't get much sleep last night, but I got a chance to think over a few things. Want to hear them?"

"Sure."

He stood up and stretched. "Take a walk over to the window with me."

We went through the checkout lane nearest the bread racks and stood at one of the loopholes. The man who was keeping watch there said, "The bugs are gone."

Miller slapped him on the back. "Go get yourself a coffee-and, fella. I'll keep an eye out."

"Okay. Thanks."

He walked away, and Miller and I stepped up to his loophole. "So tell me what you see out there," he said.

I looked. The litter barrel had been knocked over in the night, probably by one of the swooping bird-things, spilling a trash of papers, cans, and paper shake cups from the Dairy Queen down the road all over the hottop. Beyond that I could see the rank of cars closest to the market fading into whiteness. That was all I could see, and I told him so.

"That blue Chevy pickup is mine," he said. He pointed and I could see just a hint of blue in the mist. "But if you think back to when you pulled in yesterday, you'll remember that the parking lot was pretty jammed, right?"

I glanced back at my Scout and remembered I had only gotten the space close to the market because someone else had been pulling out. I nodded.

Miller said, "Now couple something else with that fact, Drayton. Norton and his four . . . what did you call them?"

"Flat-Earthers."

"Yeah, that's good. Just what they were. They go out, right? Almost the full length of that clothesline. Then we heard those roaring noises, like there was a goddam herd of elephants out there. Right?"

"It didn't sound like elephants," I said. "It sounded like—"

Like something from the primordial ooze was the phrase that came to mind, but I didn't want to say that to Miller, not after he had clapped that guy on the back and told him to go get a coffee-and like the coach jerking a player from the big game. I might have said it to Ollie, but not to Miller. "I don't know what it sounded like," I finished lamely.

"But it sounded *big*."

"Yeah." It had sounded pretty goddam big.

"So how come we didn't hear cars getting bashed around? Screeching metal? Breaking glass?"

"Well, because—" I stopped. He had me. "I don't know."

Miller said, "No way they were out of the parking lot when whatever-it-was hit them. I'll tell you what I think. I think we didn't hear any cars getting around because a lot of them might be gone. Just . . . gone. Fallen into the earth, vaporized, you name it. Strong enough to splinter these beams and twist them out of shape and knock stuff off the shelves. And the town whistle stopped at the same time."

I was trying to visualize half the parking lot gone. Trying to visualize walking out there and just coming to a brand-new drop in the land where the hottop with its neat yellow-lined parking slots left off. A drop, a slope . . . or maybe an out-and-out precipice falling away into the featureless white mist . . .

After a couple of seconds I said, "If you're right, how far do you think you're going to get in your pickup?"

"I wasn't thinking of my truck. I was thinking of your four-wheel-drive."

That was something to chew over, but not now. "What else is on your mind?"

Miller was eager to go on. "The pharmacy next door, that's on my mind. What about that?"

I opened my mouth to say I didn't have the slightest idea what he was talking about, and then shut it with a snap. The Bridgton Pharmacy had been doing business when we drove in yesterday. Not the laundromat, but the drugstore had been wide open, the doors chocked with rubber doorstops to let in a little cool air—the power outage had killed their air conditioning, of course. The door to the pharmacy could be no more than twenty feet from the door of the Federal market. So why—

"Why haven't any of those people turned up over here?" Miller asked for me. "It's been eighteen hours. Aren't they hungry? They're sure not over there eating Dristan and Stayfree Mini-pads."

"There's food," I said. "They're always selling food items on special. Sometimes it's animal crackers, sometimes it's those toaster pastries, all sorts of things. Plus the candy rack."

"I just don't believe they'd stick with stuff like that when there's all kinds of stuff over here."

"What are you getting at?"

"What I'm getting at is that I want to get out but I don't want to be dinner for some refugee from a grade-B horror picture. Four or five of us could go next door and check out the situation in the drugstore. As sort of a trial balloon."

"That's everything?"

"No, there's one other thing."

"What's that?"

"Her," Miller said simply, and jerked his thumb toward one of the middle aisles. "That crazy cunt. That witch."

It was Mrs. Carmody he had jerked his thumb at. She was no longer alone; two women had joined her. From their bright clothes I guessed they were probably tourists or summer people, ladies who had maybe left their families to "just run into town and get a few things" and were now eaten up with worry over their husbands and kids. Ladies eager to grasp at almost any straw. Maybe even the black comfort of a Mrs. Carmody.

Her pantsuit shone out with its same baleful resplendence. She was talking, gesturing, her face hard and grim. The two ladies in their bright clothes (but not as bright as Mrs. Carmody's pantsuit, no, and her gigantic satchel of a purse was still tucked firmly under one doughy arm) were listening raptly.

"She's another reason I want to get out, Drayton. By tonight she'll have six people sitting with her. If those pink bugs and the birds come back tonight, she'll have a whole congregation sitting with her by tomorrow morning. Then we can start worrying about who she'll tell them to sacrifice to make it all better. Maybe me, or you, or that guy Hatlen. Maybe your kid."

"That's idiocy," I said. But was it? The cold chill crawling up my back said not necessarily. Mrs. Carmody's mouth moved and moved. The eyes of the tourist ladies were fixed on her wrinkled lips. Was it idiocy? I thought of the dusty stuffed animals drinking at their looking-glass stream. Mrs. Carmody had power. Even Steff, normally hardheaded and straight-from-the-shoulder, invoked the old lady's name with unease.

That crazy cunt, Miller had called her. *That witch.*

"The people in this market are going through a section-eight experience for sure," Miller said. He gestured at the red-painted beams framing the show-window segments . . . twisted and splintered and buckled out of shape. "Their minds probably feel like those beams look. Mine sure as shit does. I spent half of last night thinking I must have flipped out of my gourd, that I was probably in a straitjacket in Danvers, raving my head off about bugs and dinosaur birds and tentacles and that it would all go away just as soon as the nice orderly came along and shot a wad of Thorazine into my arm." His small face was strained and white. He looked at Mrs. Carmody and then back at me. "I tell you it might happen. As people get flakier, she's going to look better and better to some of them. And I don't want to be around if that happens."

Mrs. Carmody's lips, moving and moving. Her tongue dancing around her old lady's snaggle teeth. She did look like a witch. Put her in a pointy black hat and she would be perfect. What was she saying to her two captured birds in their bright summer plumage?

Arrowhead Project? Black Spring? Abominations from the cellars of the earth? Human sacrifice?

Bullshit.

All the same—

"So what do you say?"

"I'll go this far," I answered him. "We'll try going over to the drug. You, me, Ollie if he wants to go, one or two others. Then we'll talk it over again." Even that gave me the feeling of walking out over an impossible drop on a narrow beam. I wasn't going to help Billy by killing myself. On the other hand, I wasn't going to help him by just sitting on my ass, either. Twenty feet to the drugstore. That wasn't so bad.

"When?" he asked.

"Give me an hour."

"Sure," he said.

IX. The Expedition to the Pharmacy.

I told Mrs. Turman, and I told Amanda, and then I told Billy. He seemed better this morning; he had eaten two donuts and a bowl of Special K for breakfast. Afterward I raced him up and down two of the aisles and even got him giggling a little. Kids are so adaptable that they can scare the living shit right out of you. He was too pale, the flesh under his eyes was still puffed from the tears he had cried in the night, and his face had a horribly *used* look. In a way it had become like an old man's face, as if too much emotional voltage had been running behind it for too long. But he was still alive and still able to laugh . . . at least until he remembered where he was and what was happening.

After the windsprints we sat down with Amanda and Hattie Turman and drank Gatorade from paper cups and I told him I was going over to the drugstore with a few other people.

"I don't want you to," he said immediately, his face clouding.

"It'll be all right, Big Bill. I'll bring you a *Spiderman* comic book."

"I want you to stay *here*." Now his face was not just cloudy; it was thundery. I took his hand. He pulled it away. I took it again.

"Billy, we have to get out of here sooner or later. You see that, don't you?"

"When the fog goes away . . ." But he spoke with no conviction at all. He drank his Gatorade slowly and without relish.

"Billy, it's been almost one whole day now."

"I want Mommy."

"Well, maybe this is the first step on the way to getting back to her."

Mrs. Turman said, "Don't build the boy's hopes up, David."

"What the hell," I snapped at her, "the kid's got to hope for something."

She dropped her eyes. "Yes. I suppose he does."

Billy took no notice of this. "Daddy . . . Daddy, there are things out there. *Things.*"

"Yes, we know that. But a lot of them—not all, but a lot—don't seem to come out until it's nighttime."

"They'll wait," he said. His eyes were huge, centered on mine. "They'll wait in the fog . . . and when you can't get back inside, they'll come to eat you up. Like in the fairy stories." He hugged me with fierce, panicky tightness. "Daddy, please don't go."

I pried his arms loose as gently as I could and told him that I had to. "But I'll be back, Billy."

"All right," he said huskily, but he wouldn't look at me anymore. He didn't believe I would be back. It was on his face, which was no longer thundery but woeful and grieving. I wondered again if I could be doing the right thing, putting myself at risk. Then I happened to glance down the middle aisle and saw Mrs. Carmody there. She had gained a third listener, a man with a grizzled cheek and a mean and rolling bloodshot eye. His haggard brow and shaking hands almost screamed the word hangover. It was none other than your friend and his, Myron LaFleur. The fellow who had felt no compunction at all about sending a boy out to do a man's job.

That crazy cunt. That witch.

I kissed Billy and hugged him hard. Then I walked down to the front of the store—but not down the housewares aisle. I didn't want to fall under her eye.

Three-quarters of the way down, Amanda caught up with me. "Do you really have to do this?" she asked.

"Yes, I think so."

"Forgive me if I say it sounds like so much macho bullshit to me." There were spots of color high on her cheeks and her eyes were greener than ever. She was highly—no, royally—pissed.

I took her arm and recapped my discussion with Dan Miller. The riddle of the cars and the fact that no one from the pharmacy had joined us didn't move her much. The business about Mrs. Carmody did.

"He could be right," she said.

"Do you really believe that?"

"I don't know. There's a poisonous feel to that woman. And if people are frightened badly enough for long enough, they'll turn to anyone that promises a solution."

"But human sacrifice, Amanda?"

"The Aztecs were into it," she said evenly. "Listen, David. You come back. If anything happens . . . *anything* . . . you come back. Cut and run if you have to. Not for me, what happened last night was nice, but that was last night. Come back for your boy."

"Yes. I will."

"I wonder," she said, and now she looked like Billy, haggard and old. It occurred to me that most of us looked that way. But not Mrs. Carmody. Mrs. Carmody looked younger somehow, and more vital. As if she had come into her own. As if . . . as if she were thriving on it.

We didn't get going until 9:30 A.M. Seven of us went: Ollie, Dan Miller, Mike Hatlen, Myron LaFleur's erstwhile buddy Jim (also hungover, but seemingly determined to find some way to atone), Buddy Eagleton, myself. The seventh was Hilda Reppler. Miller and Hatlen tried halfheartedly to talk her out of coming. She would have none of it. I didn't even try. I suspected she might be more competent than any of us, except maybe for Ollie. She was carrying a small canvas shopping basket, and it was loaded with an arsenal of Raid and Black Flag spray cans, all of them uncapped and ready for action. In her free hand she held a Spaulding Jimmy Connors tennis racket from a display of sporting goods in Aisle 2.

"What you gonna do with that, Mrs. Reppler?" Jim asked.

"I don't know," she said. She had a low, raspy, competent voice. "But it feels right in my hand." She looked him over closely, and her eye was cold. "Jim Grondin, isn't it? Didn't I have you in school?"

Jim's lips stretched in an uneasy egg-suck grin. "Yes'm. Me and my sister Pauline."

"Too much to drink last night?"

Jim, who towered over her and probably outweighed her by one hundred pounds, blushed to the roots of his American Legion crewcut. "Aw, no—"

She turned away curtly, cutting him off. "I think we're ready," she said.

All of us had something, although you would have called it an odd assortment of weapons. Ollie had Amanda's gun, Buddy Eagleton had a steel pinchbar from out back somewhere. I had a broom handle.

"Okay," Dan Miller said, raising his voice a bit. "You folks want to listen up a minute?"

A dozen people had drifted down toward the OUT door to see what was going on. They were loosely knotted, and to their right stood Mrs. Carmody and her new friends.

"We're going over to the drugstore to see what the situation is there. Hopefully, we'll be able to bring something back to aid Mrs. Clapham." She was the lady who had been trampled yesterday, when the bugs came. One of her legs had been broken and she was in a great deal of pain.

Miller looked us over. "We're not going to take any chances," he said. "At the first sign of anything threatening, we're going to pop back into the market—"

"And bring all the fiends of hell down on our heads!" Mrs. Carmody cried.

"She's right!" one of the summer ladies seconded. "You'll make them notice us! You'll make them come! Why can't you just leave well enough alone?"

There was a murmur of agreement from some of the people who had gathered to watch us go.

I said, "Lady, is this what you call well enough?"

She dropped her eyes, confused.

Mrs. Carmody marched a step forward. Her eyes were blazing. "You'll die out there, David Drayton! Do you want to make your son an orphan?" She raised her eyes and raked all of us with them. Buddy Eagleton dropped his eyes and simultaneously raised the pinchbar, as if to ward her off.

"All of you will die out there! Haven't you realized that the end of the world has come? The Fiend has been let loose! Star Wormwood blazes and each one of you that steps out that door will be torn apart! And they'll come for those of us who are left, just as this good woman said! Are you people going to let that happen?'' She was appealing to the onlookers now, and a little mutter ran through them. "After what happened to the unbelievers yesterday? It's death! *It's death! It's—''*

A can of peas flew across two of the checkout lanes suddenly and struck Mrs. Carmody on the right breast. She staggered backward with a startled squawk.

Amanda stood forward. "Shut up," she said. "Shut up, you miserable buzzard.''

"She serves the Foul One!'' Mrs. Carmody screamed. A jittery smile hung on her face. "Who did you sleep with last night, missus? Who did you lie down with last night? Mother Carmody sees, oh yes, Mother Carmody sees what others miss.''

But the moment's spell she had created was broken, and Amanda's eyes never wavered.

"Are we going or are we going to stand here all day?'' Mrs. Reppler asked.

And we went. God help us, we went.

Dan Miller was in the lead. Ollie came second, I was last, with Mrs. Reppler in front of me. I was as scared as I've ever been, I think, and the hand wrapped around my broom handle was sweaty-slick.

There was that thin, acrid, and unnatural smell of the mist. By the time I got out the door, Miller and Ollie had already faded into it, and Hatlen, who was third, was nearly out of sight.

Only twenty feet, I kept telling myself. *Only twenty feet.*

Mrs. Reppler walked slowly and firmly ahead of me, her tennis racket swinging lightly from her right hand. To our left was a red cinderblock wall. To our right the first rank of cars, looming out of the mist like ghost ships. Another trash barrel materialized out of the whiteness, and beyond that was a bench where people sometimes sat to wait their turn at the pay phone. *Only twenty feet, Miller's probably there by now, twenty feet is only ten or twelve paces, so—*

"Oh my God!'' Miller screamed. "Oh dear sweet God, look at this!''

Miller had gotten there, all right.

Buddy Eagleton was ahead of Mrs. Reppler and he turned to run, his eyes wide and stary. She batted him lightly in the chest with her tennis racket. "Where do you think *you're* going?" she asked in her tough, slightly raspy voice, and that was all the panic there was.

The rest of us drew up to Miller. I took one glance back over my shoulder and saw that the Federal had been swallowed by the mist. The red cinderblock wall faded to a thin wash pink and then disappeared utterly, probably five feet on the Bridgton Pharmacy side of the OUT door. I felt more isolated, more simply alone, than ever in my life. It was as if I had lost the womb.

The pharmacy had been the scene of a slaughter.

Miller and I, of course, were very close to it—almost on top of it. All the things in the mist operated primarily by sense of smell. It stood to reason. Sight would have been almost completely useless to them. Hearing a little better, but as I've said, the mist had a way of screwing up the acoustics, making things that were close sound distant and—sometimes—things that were far away sound close. The things in the mist followed their truest sense. They followed their noses.

Those of us in the market had been saved by the power outage as much as by anything else. The electric-eye doors wouldn't operate. In a sense, the market had been sealed up when the mist came. But the pharmacy doors . . . they had been chocked open. The power failure had killed their air conditioning and they had opened the doors to let in the breeze. Only something else had come in as well.

A man in a maroon T-shirt lay facedown in the doorway. Or at first I thought his T-shirt was maroon; then I saw a few white patches at the bottom and understood that once it had been all white. The maroon was dried blood. And there was something else wrong with him. I puzzled it over in my mind. Even when Buddy Eagleton turned around and was noisily sick, it didn't come immediately. I guess when something that . . . that *final* happens to someone, your mind rejects it at first . . . unless maybe you're in a war.

His head was gone, that's what it was. His legs were splayed out inside the pharmacy doors, and his head should have been hanging over the low step. But his head just wasn't.

Jim Grondin had had enough. He turned away, his hands

over his mouth, his bloodshot eyes gazing madly into mine. Then he stumbled-staggered back toward the market.

The others took no notice. Miller had stepped inside. Mike Hatlen followed. Mrs. Reppler stationed herself at one side of the double doors with her tennis racket. Ollie stood on the other side with Amanda's gun drawn and pointing at the pavement.

He said quietly, "I seem to be running out of hope, David."

Buddy Eagleton was leaning weakly against the pay-phone stall like someone who has just gotten bad news from home. His broad shoulders shook with the force of his sobs.

"Don't count us out yet," I said to Ollie. I stepped up to the door. I didn't want to go inside, but I had promised my son a comic book.

The Bridgton Pharmacy was a crazy shambles. Paperbacks and magazines were everywhere. There was a *Spiderman* comic and an *Incredible Hulk* almost at my feet, and without thinking, I picked them up and jammed them into my back pocket for Billy. Bottles and boxes lay in the aisles. A hand hung over one of the racks.

Unreality washed over me. The wreckage . . . the *carnage*— that was bad enough. But the place also looked like it had been the scene of some crazy party. It was hung and festooned with what I at first took to be streamers. But they weren't broad and flat; they were more like very thick strings or very thin cables. It struck me that they were almost the same bright white as the mist itself, and a cold chill sketched its way up my back like frost. Not crepe. What? Magazines and books hung dangling in the air from some of them.

Mike Hatlen was prodding a strange black thing with one foot. It was long and bristly. "What the fuck is this?" he asked no one in particular.

And suddenly I knew. I knew what had killed all those unlucky enough to be in the pharmacy when the mist came. The people who had been unlucky enough to get smelled out. *Out*—

"Out," I said. My throat was completely dry, and the word came out like a lint-covered bullet. "Get out of here."

Ollie looked at me. "David . . . ?"

"They're spiderwebs," I said. And then two screams came out of the mist. The first of fear, maybe. The second of pain.

It was Jim. If there were dues to be paid, he was paying them.

"Get out!" I shouted at Mike and Dan Miller.

Then something looped out of the mist. It was impossible to see it against that white background, but I could hear it. It sounded like a bullwhip that had been halfheartedly flicked. And I could see it when it twisted around the thigh of Buddy Eagleton's jeans.

He screamed and grabbed for the first thing handy, which happened to be the telephone. The handset flew the length of its cord and then swung back and forth. *"Oh Jesus that HURTS!"* Buddy screamed.

Ollie grabbed for him, and I saw what was happening. At the same instant I understood why the head of the man in the doorway was missing. The thin white cable that had twisted around Buddy's leg like a silk rope *was sinking into his flesh*. That leg of his jeans had been neatly cut off and was sliding down his leg. A neat, circular incision in his flesh was brimming blood as the cable went deeper.

Ollie pulled him hard. There was a thin snapping sound and Buddy was free. His lips had gone blue with shock.

Mike and Dan were coming, but too slowly. Then Dan ran into several hanging threads and got stuck, exactly like a bug on flypaper. He freed himself with a tremendous jerk, leaving a flap of his shirt hanging from the webbing.

Suddenly the air was full of those languorous bullwhip cracks, and the thin white cables were drifting down all around us. They were coated with the same corrosive substance. I dodged two of them, more by luck than by skill. One landed at my feet and I could hear a faint hiss of bubbling hottop. Another floated out of the air and Mrs. Reppler calmly swung her tennis racket at it. The thread stuck fast, and I heard a high-pitched *twing! twing! twing!* as the corrosive ate through the racket's strings and snapped them. It sounded like someone rapidly plucking the strings of a violin. A moment later a thread wrapped around the upper handle of the racket and it was jerked into the mist.

"Get back!" Ollie screamed.

We got moving. Ollie had an arm around Buddy. Dan Miller and Mike Hatlen were on each side of Mrs. Reppler. The white strands of web continued to drift out of the fog, impossible to see unless your eye could pick them out against the red cinderblock background.

One of them wrapped around Mike Hatlen's left arm. Another whipped around his neck in a series of quick winding-up snaps. His jugular went in a jetting, jumping explosion and he was dragged away, head lolling. One of his Bass loafers fell off and lay there on its side.

Buddy suddenly slumped forward, almost dragging Ollie to his knees. "He's passed out, David. Help me."

I grabbed Buddy around the waist and we pulled him along in a clumsy, stumbling fashion. Even in unconsciousness, Buddy kept his grip on his steel pinchbar. The leg that the strand of web had wrapped around hung away from his body at a terrible angle.

Mrs. Reppler had turned around. "Ware!" she screamed in her rusty voice. "Ware behind you!"

As I started to turn, one of the web-strands floated down on top of Dan Miller's head. His hands beat at it, tore at it.

One of the spiders had come out of the mist from behind us. It was the size of a big dog. It was black with yellow piping. *Racing stripes,* I thought crazily. Its eyes were reddish-purple, like pomegranates. It strutted busily toward us on what might have been as many as twelve or fourteen many-jointed legs—it was no ordinary earthly spider blown up to horror-movie size; it was something totally different, perhaps not really a spider at all. Seeing it, Mike Hatlen would have understood what that bristly black thing he had been prodding at in the pharmacy really was.

It closed in on us, spinning its webbing from an oval-shaped orifice on its upper belly. The strands floated out toward us in what was nearly a fan shape. Looking at this nightmare, so like the death-black spiders brooding over their dead flies and bugs in the shadows of our boathouse, I felt my mind trying to tear completely loose from its moorings. I believe now that it was only the thought of Billy that allowed me to keep any semblance of sanity. I was making some sound. Laughing. Crying. Screaming. I don't know.

But Ollie Weeks was like a rock. He raised Amanda's pistol as calmly as a man on a target range and emptied it in spaced shots into the creature at point-blank range. Whatever hell it came from, it wasn't invulnerable. A black ichor splattered from its body and it made a terrible mewling sound, so low it was more felt than heard, like a bass note from a synthesizer. Then it scuttered back into the mist and was gone. It might have been a phantasm from a horrible drug-dream . . . except for the puddles of sticky black stuff it had left behind.

There was a clang as Buddy finally dropped his steel pinchbar.

"He's dead," Ollie said. "Let him go, David. The fucking thing got his femoral artery, he's dead. Let's get the Christ out of here." His face was once more running with sweat and his eyes bulged from his big round face. One of the web-strands floated easily down on the back of his hand and Ollie swung his arm, snapping it. The strand left a bloody weal.

Mrs. Reppler screamed "Ware!" again, and we turned toward her. Another of them had come out of the mist and had wrapped its legs around Dan Miller in a mad lover's embrace. He was striking at it with his fists. As I bent and picked up Buddy's pinchbar, the spider began to wrap Dan in its deadly thread, and his struggles became a grisly, jittering death dance.

Mrs. Reppler walked toward the spider with a can of Black Flag insect repellent held outstretched in one hand. The spider's legs reached for her. She depressed the button and a cloud of the stuff jetted into one of its sparkling, jewel-like eyes. That low-pitched mewling sound came again. The spider seemed to shudder all over and then it began to lurch backward, hairy legs scratching at the pavement. It dragged Dan's body, bumping and rolling, behind it. Mrs. Reppler threw the can of bug spray at it. It bounced off the spider's body and clattered to the hottop. The spider struck the side of a small sports car hard enough to make it rock on its springs, and then it was gone.

I got to Mrs. Reppler, who was swaying on her feet and dead pale. I put an arm around her. "Thank you, young man," she said. "I feel a bit faint."

"That's okay," I said hoarsely.

"I would have saved him if I could."

"I know that."

Ollie joined us. We ran for the market doors, the threads falling all around us. One lit on Mrs. Reppler's marketing basket and sank into the canvas side. She tussled grimly for what was hers, dragging back on the strap with both hands, but she lost it. It went bumping off into the mist, end over end.

As we reached the IN door, a smaller spider, no bigger than a cocker spaniel puppy, raced out of the fog along the side of the building. It was producing no webbing; perhaps it wasn't mature enough to do so.

As Ollie leaned one beefy shoulder against the door so Mrs. Reppler could go through, I heaved the steel bar at the thing like a javelin and impaled it. It writhed madly, legs scratching at the air, and its red eyes seemed to find mine, and mark me . . .

"David!" Ollie was still holding the door.

I ran in. He followed me.

Pallid, frightened faces stared at us. Seven of us had gone out. Three of us had come back. Ollie leaned against the heavy glass door, barrel chest heaving. He began to reload Amanda's gun. His white assistant manager's shirt was plastered to his body, and large gray sweat-stains had crept out from under his arms.

"What?" someone asked in a low, hoarse voice.

"Spiders," Mrs. Reppler answered grimly. "The dirty bastards snatched my market basket."

Then Billy hurled his way into my arms, crying. I held on to him. Tight.

X. The Spell of Mrs. Carmody.
The Second Night in the Market.
The Final Confrontation.

It was my turn to sleep, and for four hours I remember nothing at all. Amanda told me I talked a lot, and screamed once or twice, but I remember no dreams. When I woke up it was afternoon. I was terribly thirsty. Some of the milk had gone over, but some of it was still okay. I drank a quart.

Amanda came over to where Billy, Mrs. Turman, and I were. The old man who had offered to make a try for the shotgun in the trunk of his car was with her—Cornell, I remembered. Ambrose Cornell.

"How are you, son?" he asked.

"All right." But I was still thirsty and my head ached. Most of all, I was scared. I slipped an arm around Billy and looked from Cornell to Amanda. "What's up?"

Amanda said, "Mr. Cornell is worried about that Mrs. Carmody. So am I."

"Billy why don't you take a walk over here with me?" Hattie asked.

"I don't want to," Billy said.

"Go on, Big Bill," I told him, and he went—reluctantly.

"Now what about Mrs. Carmody?" I asked.

"She's stirrin things up," Cornell said. He looked at me with an old man's grimness. "I think we got to put a stop to it. Just about any way we can."

Amanda said, "There are almost a dozen people with her now. It's like some crazy kind of a church service."

I remembered talking with a writer friend who lived in Otisfield and supported his wife and two kids by raising chickens and turning out one paperback original a year—spy stories. We had gotten talking about the bulge in popularity of books concerning themselves with the supernatural. Gault pointed out that in the forties *Weird Tales* had only been able to pay a pittance, and that in the fifties it went broke. When the machines fail, he had said (while his wife candled eggs and roosters crowed querulously outside), when the technologies fail, when the conventional religious systems fail, people have got to have something. Even a zombie lurching through the night can seem pretty cheerful compared to the existential comedy/horror of the ozone layer dissolving under the combined assault of a million fluorocarbon spray cans of deodorant.

We had been trapped here for twenty-six hours and we hadn't been able to do diddlyshit. Our one expedition outside had resulted in fifty-seven percent losses. It wasn't so surprising that Mrs. Carmody had turned into a growth stock, maybe.

"Has she really got a dozen people?" I asked.

"Well, only eight," Cornell said. "But she never shuts up! It's like those ten-hour speeches Castro used to make. It's a goddam filibuster."

Eight people. Not that many, not even enough to fill up a jury box. But I understood the worry on their faces. It was enough to make them the single largest political force in the market, especially now that Dan and Mike were gone. The thought that the biggest single group in our closed system was listening to her rant on about the pits of hell and the seven vials being opened made me feel pretty damn claustrophobic.

"She's started talking about human sacrifice again," Amanda said. "Bud Brown came over and told her to stop talking that drivel in his store. And two of the men that are with her—one of them was that man Myron LaFleur—told him he was the one who better shut up because it was still a free country. He wouldn't shut up and there was a . . . well, a shoving match, I guess you'd say."

"Brown got a bloody nose," Cornell said. "They mean business."

I said, "Surely not to the point of actually killing someone."

Cornell said softly, "I don't know how far they'll go if that mist doesn't let up. But I don't want to find out. I intend to get out of here."

"Easier said than done." But something had begun to tick over in my mind. *Scent.* That was the key. We had been left pretty much alone in the market. The bugs might have been attracted to the light, as more ordinary bugs were. The birds had simply followed their food supply. But the bigger things had left us alone unless we unbuttoned for some reason. The slaughter in the Bridgton Pharmacy had occurred because the doors had been left chocked open—I was sure of that. The thing or things that had gotten Norton and his party had sounded as big as a house, but it or they hadn't come near the market. And that meant that maybe . . .

Suddenly I wanted to talk to Ollie Weeks. I needed to talk to him.

"I intend to get out or die trying," Cornell said. "I got no plans to spend the rest of the summer in here."

"There have been four suicides," Amanda said suddenly.

"What?" The first thing to cross my mind, in a semiguilty flash, was that the bodies of the soldiers had been discovered.

"Pills," Cornell said shortly. "Me and two or three other guys carried the bodies out back."

I had to stifle a shrill laugh. We had a regular morgue going back there.

"It's thinning out," Cornell said. "I want to get gone."

"You won't make it to your car. Believe me."

"Not even to that first rank? That's closer than the drugstore."

I didn't answer him. Not then.

About an hour later I found Ollie holding up the beer cooler and drinking a Busch. His face was impassive but he also seemed to be watching Mrs. Carmody. She was tireless, apparently. And she was indeed discussing human sacrifice again, only now no one was telling her to shut up. Some of the people who had told her to shut up yesterday were either with her today or at least willing to listen—and the others were outnumbered.

"She could have them talked around to it by tomorrow morning," Ollie remarked. "Maybe not . . . but if she did, who do you think she'd single out for the honor?"

Bud Brown had crossed her. So had Amanda. There was the man who had struck her. And then, of course, there was me.

"Ollie," I said, "I think maybe half a dozen of us could get out of here. I don't know how far we'd get, but I think we could at least get out."

"How?"

I laid it out for him. It was simple enough. If we dashed across to my Scout and piled in, they would get no human scent. At least not with the windows rolled up.

"But suppose they're attracted to some other scent?" Ollie asked. "Exhaust, for instance?"

"Then we'd be cooked," I agreed.

"Motion," he said. "The motion of a car through fog might also draw them, David."

"I don't think so. Not without the scent of prey. I really believe that's the key to getting away."

"But you don't know."

"No, not for sure."

"Where would you want to go?"

"First? Home. To get my wife."

"David—"

"All right. To check. To be *sure.*"

"The things out there could be everyplace, David. They could get you the minute you stepped out of your Scout into your dooryard."

"If that happened, the Scout would be yours. All I'd ask would be that you take care of Billy as well as you could for as long as you could."

Ollie finished his Busch and dropped the can back into the cooler, where it clattered among the empties. The butt of the gun Amanda's husband had given her protruded from his pocket.

"South?" he asked, meeting my eyes.

"Yeah, I would," I said. "Go south and try to get out of the mist. Try like hell."

"How much gas you got?"

"Almost full."

"Have you thought that it might be impossible to get out?"

I had. Suppose what they had been fooling with at the Arrowhead Project had pulled this entire region into another dimension as easily as you or I would turn a sock inside out? "It had crossed my mind," I said, "but the alternative seems to be waiting around to see who Mrs. Carmody taps for the place of honor."

"Were you thinking about today?"

"No, it's afternoon already and those things get active at night. I was thinking about tomorrow, very early."

"Who would you want to take?"

"Me and you and Billy. Hattie Turman. Amanda Dumfries. That old guy Cornell and Mrs. Reppler. Maybe Bud Brown, too. That's eight, but Billy can sit on someone's lap and we can all squash together."

He thought it over. "All right," he said finally. "We'll try. Have you mentioned this to anyone else?"

"No, not yet."

"My advice would be not to, not until about four tomorrow morning. I'll put a couple of bags of groceries under the checkout nearest the door. If we're lucky we can squeak out before anyone knows what's happening." His eyes drifted to Mrs. Carmody again. "If she knew, she might try to stop us."

"You think so?"

Ollie got another beer. "I think so," he said.

That afternoon—yesterday afternoon—passed in a kind of slow motion. Darkness crept in, turning the fog to that dull chrome color again. What world was left outside slowly dissolved to black by eight-thirty.

The pink bugs returned, then the bird-things, swooping into the windows and scooping them up. Something roared occasionally from the dark, and once, shortly before midnight, there was a long, drawn-out *Aaaaa-rooooooo!* that caused people to turn toward the blackness with frightened, searching faces. It was the sort of sound you'd imagine a bull alligator might make in a swamp.

It went pretty much as Miller had predicted. By the small hours, Mrs. Carmody had gained another half a dozen souls. Mr. McVey the butcher was among them, standing with his arms folded, watching her.

She was totally wound up. She seemed to need no sleep. Her sermon, a steady stream of horrors out of Doré, Bosch, and Jonathan Edwards, went on and on, building toward some climax. Her group began to murmur with her, to rock back and forth unconsciously, like true believers at a tent revival. Their eyes were shiny and blank. They were under her spell.

Around 3:00 A.M. (the sermon went on relentlessly, and the people who were not interested had retreated to the back to try to get some sleep) I saw Ollie put a bag of groceries on a shelf under the checkout nearest the OUT door. Half an hour later he put another bag beside it. No one appeared to notice him but me. Billy, Amanda, and Mrs. Turman slept together by the denuded cold-cuts section. I joined them and fell into an uneasy doze.

At four-fifteen by my wristwatch, Ollie shook me awake. Cornell was with him, his eyes gleaming brightly from behind his spectacles.

"It's time, David," Ollie said.

A nervous cramp hit my belly and then passed. I shook Amanda awake. The question of what might happen with both Amanda and Stephanie in the car together passed into my mind, and then passed right out again. Today it would be best to take things just as they came.

Those remarkable green eyes opened and looked into mine. "David?"

"We're going to take a stab at getting out of here. Do you want to come?"

"What are you talking about?"

I started to explain, then woke up Mrs. Turman so I would only have to go through it the once.

"Your theory about scent," Amanda said. "It's really only an educated guess at this point, isn't it?"

"Yes."

"It doesn't matter to me," Hattie said. Her face was white and in spite of the sleep she'd gotten there were large discolored patches under her eyes. "I would do anything—take any chances—just to see the sun again."

Just to see the sun again. A little shiver coursed through me. She had put her finger on a spot that was very close to the center of my own fears, on the sense of almost foregone doom that had gripped me since I had seen Norm dragged out through the loading door. You could only see the sun through the mist as a little silver coin. It was like being on Venus.

It wasn't so much the monstrous creatures that lurked in the mist; my shot with the pinchbar had shown me they were no

Lovecraftian horrors with immortal life but only organic creatures with their own vulnerabilities. It was the mist itself that sapped the strength and robbed the will. *Just to see the sun again.* She was right. That alone would be worth going through a lot of hell.

I smiled at Hattie and she smiled tentatively back.

"Yes," Amanda said. "Me too."

I began to shake Billy awake as gently as I could.

"I'm with you," Mrs. Reppler said briefly.

We were all together by the meat counter, all but Bud Brown. He had thanked us for the invitation and then declined it. He would not leave his place in the market, he said, but added in a remarkably gentle tone of voice that he didn't blame Ollie for doing so.

An unpleasant, sweetish aroma was beginning to drift up from the white enamel case now, a smell that reminded me of the time our freezer went on the fritz while we were spending a week on the Cape. Perhaps, I thought, it was the smell of spoiling meat that had driven Mr. McVey over to Mrs. Carmody's team.

"*—expiation! It's expiation we want to think about now! We have been scourged with whips and scorpions! We have been punished for delving into secrets forbidden by God of old! We have seen the lips of the earth open! We have seen the obscenities of nightmare! The rock will not hide them, the dead tree gives no shelter! And how will it end? What will stop it?*"

"*Expiation!*" shouted good old Myron LaFleur.

"Expiation . . . expiation . . ." They whispered it uncertainly.

"*Let me hear you say it like you mean it!*" Mrs. Carmody shouted. The veins stood out on her neck in bulging cords. Her voice was cracking and hoarse now, but still full of power. And it occurred to me that it was the mist that had given her that power—the power to cloud men's minds, to make a particularly apt pun—just as it had taken away the sun's power from the rest of us. Before, she had been nothing but a mildly eccentric old woman with an antiques store in a town that was lousy with antiques stores. Nothing but an old woman with a few stuffed animals in the back room and a reputation for

(that witch . . . that cunt)

folk medicine. It was said she could find water with an applewood stick, that she could charm warts, and sell you a cream that would fade freckles to shadows of their former selves. I had even heard—was it from old Bill Giosti?—that Mrs. Carmody could be seen (in total confidence) about your love life; that if you were having the bedroom miseries, she could give you a drink that would put the ram back in your rod.

"EXPIATION!" they all cried together.

"Expiation, that's right!" she shouted deliriously. *"It's expiation gonna clear away this fog! Expiation gonna clear off these monsters and abominations! Expiation gonna drop the scales of mist from our eyes and let us see!"* Her voice dropped a notch. *"And what does the Bible say expiation is? What is the only cleanser for sin in the Eye and Mind of God?"*

"Blood."

This time the chill shuddered up through my entire body, cresting at the nape of my neck and making the hairs there stiffen. Mr. McVey had spoken that word, Mr. McVey the butcher who had been cutting meat in Bridgton ever since I was a kid holding my father's talented hand. Mr. McVey taking orders and cutting meat in his stained whites. Mr. McVey, whose acquaintanceship with the knife was long— yes, and with the saw and cleaver as well. Mr. McVey who would understand better than anyone else that the cleanser of the soul flows from the wounds of the body.

"Blood . . ." they whispered.

"Daddy, I'm scared," Billy said. He was clutching my hand tightly, his small face strained and pale.

"Ollie," I said, "why don't we get out of this loony bin?"

"Right on," he said. "Let's go."

We started down the second aisle in a loose group—Ollie, Amanda, Cornell, Mrs. Turman, Mrs. Reppler, Billy, and I. It was a quarter to five in the morning and the mist was beginning to lighten again.

"You and Cornell take the grocery bags," Ollie said to me.

"Okay."

"I'll go first. Your Scout is a four-door, is it?"

"Yeah. It is."

"Okay, I'll open the driver's door and the back door on the same side. Mrs. Dumfries, can you carry Billy?"

She picked him up in her arms.

"Am I too heavy?" Billy asked.

"No, hon."

"Good."

"You and Billy get in front," Ollie went on. "Shove way over. Mrs. Turman in front, in the middle. David, you behind the wheel. The rest of us will—"

"Where did you think you were going?"

It was Mrs. Carmody.

She stood at the head of the checkout line where Ollie had hidden the bags of groceries. Her pantsuit was a yellow scream in the gloom. Her hair frizzed out wildly in all directions, reminding me momentarily of Elsa Lanchester in *The Bride of Frankenstein*. Her eyes blazed. Ten or fifteen people stood behind her, blocking the IN and OUT doors. They had the look of people who had been in car accidents, or who had seen a UFO land, or who had seen a tree pull its roots up and walk.

Billy cringed against Amanda and buried his face against her neck.

"Going out now, Mrs. Carmody," Ollie said. His voice was curiously gentle. "Stand away, please."

"You can't go out. That way is death. Don't you know that by now?"

"No one has interfered with you," I said. "All we want is the same privilege."

She bent and found the bags of groceries unerringly. She must have known what we were planning all along. She pulled them out from the shelf where Ollie had placed them. One ripped open, spilling cans across the floor. She threw the other and it smashed open with the sound of breaking glass. Soda ran fizzing every which way and sprayed off the chrome facing of the next checkout lane.

"These are the sort of people who brought it on!" she shouted. "People who will not bend to the will of the Almighty! Sinners in pride, haughty they are, and stiff-necked! It is from their number that the sacrifice must come! *From their number the blood of expiation!*"

A rising rumble of agreement spurred her on. She was in a frenzy now. Spittle flew from her lips as she screamed at the people crowding up behind her: *"It's the boy we want! Grab him! Take him! It's the boy we want!"*

They surged forward, Myron LaFleur in the lead, his eyes blankly joyous. Mr. McVey was directly behind him, his face blank and stolid.

Amanda faltered backward, holding Billy more tightly. His

arms were wrapped around her neck. She looked at me, terrified. "David, what do I—"

"*Get them both!*" Mrs. Carmody screamed. "*Get his whore, too!*"

She was an apocalypse of yellow and dark joy. Her purse was still over her arm. She began to jump up and down. "*Get the boy, get the whore, get them both, get them all, get—*"

A single sharp report rang out.

Everything froze, as if we were a classroom full of unruly children and the teacher had just stepped back in and shut the door sharply. Myron LaFleur and Mr. McVey stopped where they were, about ten paces away. Myron looked back uncertainly at the butcher. He didn't look back or even seem to realize that LaFleur was there. Mr. McVey had a look I had seen on too many other faces in the last two days. He had gone over. His mind had snapped.

Myron backed up, staring at Ollie Weeks with widening, fearful eyes. His backing-up became a run. He turned the corner of the aisle, skidded on a can, fell down, scrambled up again, and was gone.

Ollie stood in the classic target shooter's position, Amanda's gun clasped in both hands. Mrs. Carmody still stood at the head of the checkout lane. Both of her liver-spotted hands were clasped over her stomach. Blood poured out between her fingers and splashed her yellow slacks.

Her mouth opened and closed. Once. Twice. She was trying to talk. At last she made it.

"*You will all die out there,*" she said, and then she pitched slowly forward. Her purse slithered off her arm, struck the floor, and spilled its contents. A paper-wrapped tube rolled across the distance between us and struck one of my shoes. Without thinking, I bent over and picked it up. It was a half-used package of Rolaids. I threw it down again. I didn't want to touch anything that belonged to her.

The "congregation" was backing away, spreading out, their focus broken. None of them took their eyes from the fallen figure and the dark blood spreading out from beneath her body. "You murdered her!" someone cried out in fear and anger. But no one pointed out that she had been planning something similar for my son.

Ollie was still frozen in his shooter's position, but now his mouth was trembling. I touched him gently. "Ollie, let's go. And thank you."

"I killed her," he said hoarsely. "Damn if I didn't kill her."

"Yes," I said. "That's why I thanked you. Now let's go."

We began to move again.

With no grocery bags to carry—thanks to Mrs. Carmody—I was able to take Billy. We paused for a moment at the door, and Ollie said in a low, strained voice, "I wouldn't have shot her, David. Not if there had been any other way."

"Yeah."

"You believe it?"

"Yeah, I do."

"Then let's go."

We went out.

XI. The End.

Ollie moved fast, the pistol in his right hand. Before Billy and I were more than out the door he was at my Scout, an insubstantial Ollie, like a ghost in a television movie. He opened the driver's door. Then the back door. Then something came out of the mist and cut him nearly in half.

I never got a good look at it, and for that I think I'm grateful. It appeared to be red, the angry color of a cooked lobster. It had claws. It was making a low grunting sound, not much different from the sound we had heard after Norton and his little band of Flat-Earthers went out.

Ollie got off one shot, and then the thing's claws scissored forward and Ollie's body seemed to unhinge in a terrible glut of blood. Amanda's gun fell out of his hand, struck the pavement, and discharged. I caught a nightmare glimpse of huge black lusterless eyes, the size of giant handfuls of sea grapes, and then the thing lurched back into the mist with what remained of Ollie Weeks in its grip. A long, multi-segmented scorpion's body dragged harshly on the paving.

There was an instant of choices. Maybe there always is, no matter how short. Half of me wanted to run back into the market with Billy hugged to my chest. The other half was racing for the Scout, throwing Billy inside, lunging after him. Then Amanda screamed. It was a high, rising sound that seemed to spiral up and up until it was nearly ultrasonic. Billy cringed against me, digging his face against my chest.

One of the spiders had Hattie Turman. It was big. It had knocked her down. Her dress had pulled up over her scrawny knees as it crouched over her, its bristly, spiny legs caressing her shoulders. It began to spin its web.

Mrs. Carmody was right, I thought. *We're going to die out here, we are really going to die out here.*

"Amanda!" I yelled.

No response. She was totally gone. The spider straddled what remained of Billy's babysitter, who had enjoyed jigsaw puzzles and those damned Double-Crostics that no normal person can do without going nuts. Its threads crisscrossed her body, the white strands already turning red as the acid coating sank into her.

Cornell was backing slowly toward the market, his eyes as big as dinner plates behind his specs. Abruptly he turned and ran. He clawed the IN door open and ran inside.

The split in my mind closed as Mrs. Reppler stepped briskly forward and slapped Amanda, first forehand, then backhand. Amanda stopped screaming. I went to her, spun her around to face the Scout, and screamed "GO!" into her face.

She went. Mrs. Reppler brushed past me. She pushed Amanda into the Scout's back seat, got in after her, and slammed the door shut.

I yanked Billy loose and threw him in. As I climbed in myself, one of those spider threads drifted down and lit on my ankle. It burned the way a fishing line pulled rapidly through your closed fist will burn. And it was strong. I gave my foot a hard yank and it broke. I slipped in behind the wheel.

"Shut it, oh shut the door, dear God!" Amanda screamed.

I shut the door. A bare instant later, one of the spiders thumped softly against it. I was only inches from its red, viciously stupid eyes. Its legs, each as thick as my wrist, slipped back and forth across the square bonnet. Amanda screamed ceaselessly, like a firebell.

"Woman, shut your head," Mrs. Reppler told her.

The spider gave up. It could not smell us, ergo we were no longer there. It strutted back into the mist on its unsettling number of legs, became a phantasm, and then was gone.

I looked out the window to make sure it was gone and then opened the door.

"What are you doing?" Amanda screamed, but I knew what I was doing. I like to think Ollie would have done exactly the same thing. I half-stepped, half-leaned out, and got the gun. Something came rapidly toward me, but I never saw it. I pulled back in and slammed the door shut.

Amanda began to sob. Mrs. Reppler put an arm around her and comforted her briskly.

Billy said, "Are we going home, Daddy?"

"Big Bill, we're gonna try."

"Okay," he said quietly.

I checked the gun and then put it into the glove compartment. Ollie had reloaded it after the expedition to the drugstore. The rest of the shells had disappeared with him, but that was all right. He had fired at Mrs. Carmody, he had fired once at the clawed thing, and the gun had discharged once when it hit the ground. There were four of us in the Scout, but if push came right down to shove, I'd find some other way out for myself.

I had a terrible moment when I couldn't find my key ring. I checked all my pockets, came up empty, and then checked them all again, forcing myself to go slowly and calmly. They were in my jeans pocket; they had gotten down under the coins, as keys sometimes will. The Scout started easily. At the confident roar of the engine, Amanda burst into fresh tears.

I sat there, letting it idle, waiting to see what was going to be drawn by the sound of the engine or the smell of the exhaust. Five minutes, the longest five of my life, drifted by. Nothing happened.

"Are we going to sit here or are we going to go?" Mrs. Reppler asked at last.

"Go," I said. I backed out of the slot and put on the low beams.

Some urge—probably a base one—made me cruise past the Federal market as close as I could get. The Scout's right bumper bunted the trash barrel to one side. It was impossible to see in except through the loopholes—all those fertilizer and lawn-food bags made the place look as if it were in the throes of some mad garden sale—but at each loophole there were two or three pale faces, staring out at us.

Then I swung to the left, and the mist closed impenetrably behind us. And what has become of those people I do not know.

I drove back down Kansas Road at five miles an hour, feeling my way. Even with the Scout's headlights and running lights on, it was impossible to see more than seven or ten feet ahead.

The earth had been through some terrible contortion; Miller

had been right about that. In places the road was merely cracked, but in others the ground itself seemed to have caved in, tilting up great slabs of paving. I was able to get over with the help of the four-wheel drive. Thank God for that. But I was terribly afraid that we would soon come to an obstacle that even the four-wheel drive couldn't get us over.

It took me forty minutes to make a drive that usually only took seven or eight. At last the sign that marked our private road loomed out of the mist. Billy, roused at a quarter of five, had fallen solidly asleep inside this car that he knew so well it must have seemed like home to him.

Amanda looked at the road nervously. "Are you really going down there?"

"I'm going to try," I said.

But it was impossible. The storm that had whipped through had loosened a lot of trees, and that weird, twisting drop had finished the job of tumbling them. I was able to crunch over the first two; they were fairly small. Then I came to a hoary old pine lying across the road like an outlaw's barricade. It was still almost a quarter of a mile to the house. Billy slept on beside me, and I put the Scout in Park, put my hands over my eyes, and tried to think what to do next.

Now, as I sit in the Howard Johnson's near Exit 3 of the Maine Turnpike, writing all of this down on HoJo stationery, I suspect that Mrs. Reppler, that tough and capable old broad, could have laid out the essential futility of the situation in a few quick strokes. But she had the kindness to let me think it through for myself.

I couldn't get out. I couldn't leave them. I couldn't even kid myself that all the horror-movie monsters were back at the Federal; when I cracked the window I could hear them in the woods, crashing and blundering around on the steep fall of land they call the Ledges around these parts. The moisture drip-drip-dripped from the overhanging leaves. Overhead the mist darkened momentarily as some nightmarish and half-seen living kite overflew us.

I tried to tell myself—then and now—that if she was very quick, if she buttoned up the house with herself inside, that she had enough food for ten days to two weeks. It only works a little bit. What keeps getting in the way is my last memory of her, wearing her floppy sunhat and gardening gloves, on her way to our little vegetable patch with the mist rolling inexorably across the lake behind her.

It is Billy I have to think about now. Billy, I tell myself. Big Bill, Big Bill . . . I should write it maybe a hundred times on this sheet of paper, like a child condemned to write *I will not throw spitballs in school* as the sunny three-o'clock stillness spills through the windows and the teacher corrects homework papers at her desk and the only sound is her pen, while somewhere, far away, kids pick up teams for scratch baseball.

Anyway, at last I did the only thing I could do. I reversed the Scout carefully back to Kansas Road. Then I cried.

Amanda touched my shoulder timidly. "David, I'm so sorry," she said.

"Yeah," I said, trying to stop the tears and not having much luck. "Yeah, so am I."

I drove to Route 302 and turned left, toward Portland. This road was also cracked and blasted in places, but was, on the whole, more passable than Kansas Road had been. I was worried about the bridges. The face of Maine is cut with running water, and there are bridges everywhere, big and small. But the Naples Causeway was intact, and from there it was plain—if slow—sailing all the way to Portland.

The mist held thick. Once I had to stop, thinking that trees were lying across the road. Then the trees began to move and undulate and I understood they were more tentacles. I stopped, and after a while they drew back. Once a great green thing with an iridescent green body and long transparent wings landed on the hood. It looked like a grossly misshapen dragonfly. It hovered there for a moment, then took wing again and was gone.

Billy woke up about two hours after we had left Kansas Road behind and asked if we had gotten Mommy yet. I told him I hadn't been able to get down our road because of fallen trees.

"Is she all right, Dad?"

"Billy, I don't know. But we'll come back and see."

He didn't cry. He dozed off again instead. I would have rather had his tears. He was sleeping too damn much and I didn't like it.

I began to get a tension headache. It was driving through the fog at a steady five or ten miles an hour that did it, the tension of knowing that anything might come out of it, anything at all—a washout, a landspill, or Ghidra the Three-headed Monster. I think I prayed. I prayed to God that Stephanie was alive and that He wouldn't take my adultery out on her. I prayed to God to let me get Billy to safety because he had been through so much.

Most people had pulled to the side of the road when the mist came, and by noon we were in North Windham. I tried the River Road, but about four miles down, a bridge spanning a small and noisy stream had fallen into the water. I had to reverse for nearly a mile before I found a spot wide enough to turn around. We went to Portland by Route 302 after all.

When we got there, I drove the cutoff to the turnpike. The neat line of tollbooths guarding the access had been turned into vacant-eyed skeletons of smashed Pola-Glas. All of them were empty. In the sliding glass doorway of one was a torn jacket with Maine Turnpike Authority patches on the sleeves. It was drenched with tacky, drying blood. We had not seen a single living person since leaving the Federal.

Mrs. Reppler said, "David, try your radio."

I slapped my forehead in frustration and anger at myself, wondering how I could have been stupid enough to forget the Scout's AM/FM for so long.

"Don't do that," Mrs. Reppler said curtly. "You can't think of everything. If you try, you will go mad and be of no use at all."

I got nothing but a shriek of static all the way across the AM band, and the FM yielded nothing but a smooth and ominous silence.

"Does that mean everything's off the air?" Amanda asked. I knew what she was thinking, maybe. We were far enough south now so that we should have been picking up a selection of strong Boston stations—WRKO, WBZ, WMEX. But if Boston had gone—

"It doesn't mean anything for sure," I said. "That static on the AM band is pure interference. The mist is having a damping effect on radio signals, too."

"Are you sure that's all it is?"

"Yes," I said, not sure at all.

We went south. The mileposts rolled past, counting down

from about forty. When we reached Mile I, we would be at the New Hampshire border. Going on the turnpike was slower; a lot of the drivers hadn't wanted to give up, and there had been rear-end collisions in several places. Several times I had to use the median strip.

At about twenty past one—I was beginning to feel hungry—Billy clutched my arm. "Daddy, what's that? *What's that!*"

A shadow loomed out of the mist, staining it dark. It was as tall as a cliff and coming right at us. I jammed on the brakes. Amanda, who had been catnapping, was thrown forward.

Something came; again, that is all I can say for sure. It may have been the fact that the mist only allowed us to glimpse things briefly, but I think it just as likely that there are certain things that your brain simply disallows. There are things of such darkness and horror—just, I suppose, as there are things of such great beauty—that they will not fit through the puny human doors of perception.

It was six-legged, I know that; its skin was slaty gray that mottled to dark brown in places. Those brown patches reminded me absurdly of the liver spots on Mrs. Carmody's hands. Its skin was deeply wrinkled and grooved, and clinging to it were scores, hundreds, of those pinkish "bugs" with the stalk-eyes. I don't know how big it actually was, but it passed directly over us. One of its gray, wrinkled legs smashed down right beside my window, and Mrs. Reppler said later she could not see the underside of its body, although she craned her neck up to look. She saw only two Cyclopean legs going up and up into the mist like living towers until they were lost to sight.

For the moment it was over the Scout I had an impression of something so big that it might have made a blue whale look the size of a trout—in other words, something so big that it defied the imagination. Then it was gone, sending a seismological series of thuds back. It left tracks in the cement of the Interstate, tracks so deep I could not see the bottoms. Each single track was nearly big enough to drop the Scout into.

For a moment no one spoke. There was no sound but our breathing and the diminishing thud of that great Thing's passage.

Then Billy said, "Was it a dinosaur, Dad? Like the bird that got into the market?"

"I don't think so. I don't think there was ever an animal that big, Billy. At least not on earth."

I thought of the Arrowhead Project and wondered again what crazy damned thing they could have been doing up there.

"Can we go on?" Amanda asked timidly. "It might come back."

Yes, and there might be more up ahead. But there was no point in saying so. We had to go somewhere. I drove on, weaving in and out between those terrible tracks until they veered off the road.

That is what happened. Or nearly all—there is one final thing I'll get to in a moment. But you mustn't expect some neat conclusion. There is no *And they escaped from the mist into the good sunshine of a new day;* or *When we awoke the National Guard had finally arrived;* or even that great old standby: *It was all a dream.*

It is, I suppose, what my father always frowningly called "an Alfred Hitchcock ending," by which he meant a conclusion in ambiguity that allowed the reader or viewer to make up his own mind about how things ended. My father had nothing but contempt for such stories, saying they were "cheap shots."

We got to this Howard Johnson's near Exit 3 as dusk began to close in, making driving a suicidal risk. Before that, we took a chance on the bridge that spans the Saco River. It looked badly twisted out of shape, but in the mist it was impossible to tell if it was whole or not. That particular game we won.

But there's tomorrow to think of, isn't there?

As I write this, it is a quarter to one in the morning, July the twenty-third. The storm that seemed to signal the beginning of it all was only four days ago. Billy is sleeping in the lobby on a mattress that I dragged out for him. Amanda and Mrs. Reppler are close by. I am writing by the light of a big Delco flashlight, and outside the pink bugs are ticking and thumping off the glass. Every now and then there is a louder thud as one of the birds takes one off.

The Scout has enough gas to take us maybe another

ninety miles. The alternative is to try to gas up here; there is an Exxon out on the service island, and although the power is off, I believe I could siphon some up from the tank. But—

But it means being outside.

If we can get gas—here or further along—we'll keep going. I have a destination in mind now, you see. It's that last thing I wanted to tell you about.

I couldn't be sure. That is the thing, the damned thing. It might have been my imagination, nothing but wish fulfillment. And even if not, it is such a long chance. How many miles? How many bridges? How many things that would love to tear up my son and eat him even as he screamed in terror and agony?

The chances are so good that it was nothing but a daydream that I haven't told the others . . . at least, not yet.

In the manager's apartment I found a large battery-operated multiband radio. From the back of it, a flat antenna wire led out through the window. I turned it on, switched over to BAT., fiddled with the tuning dial, with the SQUELCH knob, and still got nothing but static or dead silence.

And then, at the far end of the AM band, just as I was reaching for the knob to turn it off, I thought I heard, or dreamed I heard, one single word.

There was no more. I listened for an hour, but there was no more. If there was that one word, it came through some minute shift in the damping mist, an infinitesimal break that immediately closed again.

One word.

I've got to get some sleep . . . if I can sleep and not be haunted until daybreak by the faces of Ollie Weeks and Mrs. Carmody and Norm the bag-boy . . . and by Steff's face, half-shadowed by the wide brim of her sunhat.

There is a restaurant here, a typical HoJo restaurant with a dining room and a long, horseshoe-shaped lunch counter. I am going to leave these pages on the counter and perhaps someday someone will find them and read them.

One word.

If I only really heard it. If only.

I'm going to bed now. But first I'm going to kiss my son

and whisper two words in his ear. Against the dreams that may come, you know.

Two words that sound a bit alike.

One of them is Hartford.

The other is hope.

Here There Be Tygers

Charles needed to go to the bathroom very badly.

There was no longer any use in trying to fool himself that he could wait for recess. His bladder was screaming at him, and Miss Bird had caught him squirming.

There were three third-grade teachers in the Acorn Street Grammar School. Miss Kinney was young and blond and bouncy and had a boyfriend who picked her up after school in a blue Camaro. Mrs. Trask was shaped like a Moorish pillow and did her hair in braids and laughed boomingly. And there was Miss Bird.

Charles had known he would end up with Miss Bird. He had *known* that. It had been inevitable. Because Miss Bird obviously wanted to destroy him. She did not allow children to go to the basement. The basement, Miss Bird said, was where the boilers were kept, and well-groomed ladies and gentlemen would never go down *there*, because basements were nasty, sooty old things. Young ladies and gentlemen do not go to the basement, she said. They go to the *bathroom*.

Charles squirmed again.

Miss Bird cocked an eye at him. "Charles," she said clearly, still pointing her pointer at Bolivia, "do you need to go to the bathroom?"

Cathy Scott in the seat ahead of him giggled, wisely covering her mouth.

Kenny Griffen sniggered and kicked Charles under his desk.

Charles went bright red.

"Speak up, Charles," Miss Bird said brightly. "Do you need to—" *(urinate she'll say urinate she always does)*

"Yes, Miss Bird."

"Yes, what?"

"I have to go to the base—to the bathroom."

Miss Bird smiled. "Very well, Charles. You may go to the bathroom and urinate. Is that what you need to do? Urinate?"

Charles hung his head, convicted.

"Very well, Charles. You may do so. And next time kindly don't wait to be asked."

General giggles. Miss Bird rapped the board with her pointer.

Charles trudged up the row toward the door, thirty pairs of eyes boring into his back, and every one of those kids, including Cathy Scott, knew that he was going into the bathroom to urinate. The door was at least a football field's length away. Miss Bird did not go on with the lesson but kept her silence until he had opened the door, entered the blessedly empty hall, and shut the door again.

He walked down toward the boys' bathroom

(basement basement basement IF I WANT)

dragging his fingers along the cool tile of the wall, letting them bounce over the thumbtack-stippled bulletin board and slide lightly across the red

(BREAK GLASS IN CASE OF EMERGENCY)

fire-alarm box.

Miss Bird *liked* it. Miss Bird *liked* making him have a red face. In front of Cathy Scott—who *never* needed to go to the basement, was that fair?—and everybody else.

Old b-i-t-c-h, he thought. He spelled because he had decided last year God didn't say it was a sin if you spelled.

He went into the boys' bathroom.

It was very cool inside, with a faint, not unpleasant smell of chlorine hanging pungently in the air. Now, in the middle of the morning, it was clean and deserted, peaceful and quite pleasant, not at all like the smoky, stinky cubicle at the Star Theatre downtown.

The bathroom

(!basement!)

was built like an L, the short side lined with tiny square mirrors and white porcelain washbowls and a paper towel dispenser,

(NIBROC)

the longer side with two urinals and three toilet cubicles.

Charles went around the corner after glancing morosely at his thin, rather pallid face in one of the mirrors.

The tiger was lying down at the far end, just underneath the pebbly-white window. It was a large tiger, with tawny venetian blinds and dark stripes laid across its pelt. It looked up alertly at Charles, and its green eyes narrowed. A kind of silky, purring grunt issued from its mouth. Smooth muscles flexed, and the tiger got to its feet. Its tail switched, making little chinking sounds against the porcelain side of the last urinal.

The tiger looked quite hungry and very vicious.

Charles hurried back the way he had come. The door seemed to take forever to wheeze pneumatically closed behind him, but when it did, he considered himself safe. This door only swung in, and he could not remember ever reading or hearing that tigers are smart enough to open doors.

Charles wiped the back of his hand across his nose. His heart was thumping so hard he could hear it. He still needed to go to the basement, worse than ever.

He squirmed, winced, and pressed a hand against his belly. He *really* had to go to the basement. If he could only be sure no one would come, he could use the girls'. It was right across the hall. Charles looked at it longingly, knowing he would never dare, not in a million years. What if Cathy Scott should come? Or—black horror!—what if *Miss Bird* should come?

Perhaps he had imagined the tiger.

He opened the door wide enough for one eye and peeked in.

The tiger was peeking back from around the angle of the L, its eye a sparkling green. Charles fancied he could see a tiny blue fleck in that deep brilliance, as if the tiger's eye had eaten one of his own. As if—

A hand slid around his neck.

Charles gave a stifled cry and felt his heart and stomach cram up into his throat. For one terrible moment he thought he was going to wet himself.

It was Kenny Griffen, smiling complacently. "Miss Bird sent me after you 'cause you been gone six years. You're in trouble."

"Yeah, but I can't go to the basement," Charles said, feeling faint with the fright Kenny had given him.

"Yer constipated!" Kenny chortled gleefully. "Wait'll I tell *Caaathy!*"

"You better not!" Charles said urgently. "Besides, I'm not. There's a tiger in there."

"What's he doing?" Kenny asked. "Takin a piss?"

"I don't know," Charles said, turning his face to the wall. "I just wish he'd go away." He began to weep.

"Hey," Kenny said, bewildered and a little frightened. "Hey."

"What if I *have* to go? What if I can't help it? Miss Bird'll say—"

"Come on," Kenny said, grabbing his arm in one hand and pushing the door open with the other. "You're making it up."

They were inside before Charles, terrified, could break free and cower back against the door.

"Tiger," Kenny said disgustedly. "Boy, Miss Bird's gonna *kill* you."

"It's around the other side."

Kenny began to walk past the washbowls. "Kitty-kitty-kitty? Kitty?"

"Don't!" Charles hissed.

Kenny disappeared around the corner. "Kitty-kitty? Kitty-kitty? Kit—"

Charles darted out the door again and pressed himself against the wall, waiting, his hands over his mouth and his eyes squinched shut, waiting, waiting for the scream.

There was no scream.

He had no idea how long he stood there, frozen, his bladder bursting. He looked at the door to the boys' basement. It told him nothing. It was just a door.

He wouldn't.

He *couldn't.*

But at last he went in.

The washbowls and the mirrors were neat, and the faint smell of chlorine was unchanged. But there seemed to be a smell under it. A faint, unpleasant smell, like freshly sheared copper.

With groaning (but silent) trepidation, he went to the corner of the L and peeped around.

The tiger was sprawled on the floor, licking its large paws with a long pink tongue. It looked incuriously at Charles. There was a torn piece of shirt caught in one set of claws.

But his need was a white agony now, and he couldn't help it. He *had* to. Charles tiptoed back to the white porcelain basin closest the door.

Miss Bird slammed in just as he was zipping his pants.

"Why, you dirty, filthy little boy," she said almost reflectively.

Charles was keeping a weather eye on the corner. "I'm sorry, Miss Bird . . . the tiger . . . I'm going to clean the sink . . . I'll use soap . . . I swear I will . . ."

"Where's Kenneth?" Miss Bird asked calmly.

"I don't know."

He didn't, really.

"Is he back there?"

"No!" Charles cried.

Miss Bird stalked to the place where the room bent. "Come here, Kenneth. Right this moment."

"Miss Bird—"

But Miss Bird was already around the corner. She meant to pounce. Charles thought Miss Bird was about to find out what pouncing was really all about.

He went out the door again. He got a drink at the drinking fountain. He looked at the American flag hanging over the entrance to the gym. He looked at the bulletin board. Woodsy Owl said GIVE A HOOT, DON'T POLLUTE. Officer Friendly said NEVER RIDE WITH STRANGERS. Charles read everything twice.

Then he went back to the classroom, walked down his row to his seat with his eyes on the floor, and slid into his seat. It was a quarter to eleven. He took out *Roads to Everywhere* and began to read about Bill at the Rodeo.

The Monkey

When Hal Shelburn saw it, when his son Dennis pulled it out of a mouldering Ralston-Purina carton that had been pushed far back under one attic eave, such a feeling of horror and dismay rose in him that for one moment he thought he would scream. He put one fist to his mouth, as if to cram it back . . . and then merely coughed into his fist. Neither Terry nor Dennis noticed, but Petey looked around, momentarily curious.

"Hey, neat," Dennis said respectfully. It was a tone Hal rarely got from the boy anymore himself. Dennis was twelve.

"What is it?" Peter asked. He glanced at his father again before his eyes were dragged back to the thing his big brother had found. "What is it, Daddy?"

"It's a monkey, fartbrains," Dennis said. "Haven't you ever seen a monkey before?"

"Don't call your brother fartbrains," Terry said automatically, and began to examine a box of curtains. The curtains were slimy with mildew and she dropped them quickly. "Uck."

"Can I have it, Daddy?" Petey asked. He was nine.

"What do you mean?" Dennis cried. "*I* found it!"

"Boys, please," Terry said. "I'm getting a headache."

Hal barely heard them. The monkey glimmered up at him from his older son's hands, grinning its old familiar grin. The

160

same grin that had haunted his nightmares as a kid, haunted them until he had—

Outside a cold gust of wind rose, and for a moment lips with no flesh blew a long note through the old, rusty gutter outside. Petey stepped closer to his father, eyes moving uneasily to the rough attic roof through which nailheads poked.

"What was that, Daddy?" he asked as the whistle died to a guttural buzz.

"Just the wind," Hal said, still looking at the monkey. Its cymbals, crescents of brass rather than full circles in the weak light of the one naked bulb, were moveless, perhaps a foot apart, and he added automatically, "Wind can whistle, but it can't carry a tune." Then he realized that was a saying of Uncle Will's, and a goose ran over his grave.

The note came again, the wind coming off Crystal Lake in a long, droning swoop and then wavering in the gutter. Half a dozen small drafts puffed cold October air into Hal's face— God, this place was so much like the back closet of the house in Hartford that they might all have been transported thirty years back in time.

I won't think about that.

But now of course it was all he *could* think about.

In the back closet where I found that goddammed monkey in that same box.

Terry had moved away to examine a wooden crate filled with knickknacks, duck-walking because the pitch of the eaves was so sharp.

"I don't like it," Petey said, and felt for Hal's hand. "Dennis c'n have it if he wants. Can we go, Daddy?"

"Worried about ghosts, chickenguts?" Dennis inquired.

"Dennis, you stop it," Terry said absently. She picked up a waferthin cup with a Chinese pattern. "This is nice. This—"

Hal saw that Dennis had found the wind-up key in the monkey's back. Terror flew through him on dark wings.

"Don't do that!"

It came out more sharply than he had intended, and he had snatched the monkey out of Dennis's hands before he was really aware he had done it. Dennis looked around at him, startled. Terry had also glanced back over her shoulder, and Petey looked up. For a moment they were all silent, and the wind whistled again, very low this time, like an unpleasant invitation.

"I mean, it's probably broken," Hal said.

It used to be broken . . . except when it wanted not to be.

"Well, you didn't have to *grab*," Dennis said.

"Dennis, shut up."

Dennis blinked and for a moment looked almost uneasy. Hal hadn't spoken to him so sharply in a long time. Not since he had lost his job with National Aerodyne in California two years before and they had moved to Texas. Dennis decided not to push it . . . for now. He turned back to the Ralston-Purina carton and began to root through it again, but the other stuff was nothing but junk. Broken toys bleeding springs and stuffings.

The wind was louder now, hooting instead of whistling. The attic began to creak softly, making a noise like footsteps.

"Please, Daddy?" Petey asked, only loud enough for his father to hear.

"Yeah," he said. "Terry, let's go."

"I'm not through with this—"

"I said let's *go*."

It was her turn to look startled.

They had taken two adjoining rooms in a motel. By ten that night the boys were asleep in their room and Terry was asleep in the adults' room. She had taken two Valiums on the ride back from the home place in Casco. To keep her nerves from giving her a migraine. Just lately she took a lot of Valium. It had started around the time National Aerodyne had laid Hal off. For the last two years he had been working for Texas Instruments—it was $4,000 less a year, but it was work. He told Terry they were lucky. She agreed. There were plenty of software architects drawing unemployment, he said. She agreed. The company housing in Arnette was every bit as good as the place in Fresno, he said. She agreed, but he thought her agreement to all of it was a lie.

And he was losing Dennis. He could feel the kid going, achieving a premature escape velocity, so long, Dennis, bye-bye stranger, it was nice sharing this train with you. Terry said she thought the boy was smoking reefer. She smelled it sometimes. You have to talk to him, Hal. And *he* agreed, but so far he had not.

The boys were asleep. Terry was asleep. Hal went into the

bathroom and locked the door and sat down on the closed lid of the john and looked at the monkey.

He hated the way it felt, that soft brown nappy fur, worn bald in spots. He hated its grin—*that monkey grins just like a nigger,* Uncle Will had said once, but it didn't grin like a nigger or like anything human. Its grin was all teeth, and if you wound up the key, the lips would move, the teeth would seem to get bigger, to become vampire teeth, the lips would writhe and the cymbals would bang, stupid monkey, stupid clockwork monkey, stupid, stupid—

He dropped it. His hands were shaking and he dropped it.

The key clicked on the bathroom tile as it struck the floor. The sound seemed very loud in the stillness. It grinned at him with its murky amber eyes, doll's eyes, filled with idiot glee, its brass cymbals poised as if to strike up a march for some band from hell. On the bottom the words MADE IN HONG KONG were stamped.

"You can't be here," he whispered. "I threw you down the well when I was nine."

The monkey grinned up at him.

Outside in the night, a black capful of wind shook the motel.

Hal's brother Bill and Bill's wife Collette met them at Uncle Will's and Aunt Ida's the next day. "Did it ever cross your mind that a death in the family is a really lousy way to renew the family connection?" Bill asked him with a bit of a grin. He had been named for Uncle Will. Will and Bill, champions of the rodayo, Uncle Will used to say, and ruffle Bill's hair. It was one of his sayings . . . like the wind can whistle but it can't carry a tune. Uncle Will had died six years before, and Aunt Ida had lived on here alone, until a stroke had taken her just the previous week. Very sudden, Bill had said when he called long distance to give Hal the news. As if he could know; as if anyone could know. She had died alone.

"Yeah," Hal said. "The thought crossed my mind."

They looked at the place together, the home place where they had finished growing up. Their father, a merchant mariner, had simply disappeared as if from the very face of the earth when they were young; Bill claimed to remember him vaguely, but Hal had no memories of him at all. Their mother had died when Bill was ten and Hal eight. Aunt Ida had brought them here on a Greyhound bus which left from Hartford, and they had been raised here, and gone to college from here. This had been the place they were homesick for. Bill had stayed in Maine and now had a healthy law practice in Portland.

Hal saw that Petey had wandered off toward the blackberry tangles that lay on the eastern side of the house in a mad jumble. "Stay away from there, Petey," he called.

Petey looked back, questioning. Hal felt simple love for the boy rush him . . . and he suddenly thought of the monkey again.

"Why, Dad?"

"The old well's back there someplace," Bill said. "But I'll be damned if I remember just where. Your dad's right, Petey—it's a good place to stay away from. Thorns'll do a job on you. Right, Hal?"

"Right," Hal said automatically. Petey moved away, not looking back, and then started down the embankment toward the small shingle of beach where Dennis was skipping stones over the water. Hal felt something in his chest loosen a little.

Bill might have forgotten where the old well was, but late that afternoon Hal went to it unerringly, shouldering his way through the brambles that tore at his old flannel jacket and hunted for his eyes. He reached it and stood there, breathing hard, looking at the rotted, warped boards that covered it. After a moment's debate, he knelt (his knees fired twin pistol shots) and moved two of the boards aside.

From the bottom of that wet, rock-lined throat a drowning face stared up at him, wide eyes, grimacing mouth. A moan escaped him. It was not loud, except in his heart. There it had been very loud.

It was his own face in the dark water.

Not the monkey's. For a moment he had thought it was the monkey's.

He was shaking. Shaking all over.

I threw it down the well. I threw it down the well, please God don't let me be crazy, I threw it down the well.

The well had gone dry the summer Johnny McCabe died, the year after Bill and Hal came to stay with Uncle Will and Aunt Ida. Uncle Will had borrowed money from the bank to have an artesian well sunk, and the blackberry tangles had grown up around the old dug well. The dry well.

Except the water had come back. Like the monkey.

This time the memory would not be denied. Hal sat there helplessly, letting it come, trying to go with it, to ride it like a surfer riding a monster wave that will crush him if he falls off his board, just trying to get through it so it would be gone again.

He had crept out here with the monkey late that summer, and the blackberries had been out, the smell of them thick and cloying. No one came in here to pick, although Aunt Ida would sometimes stand at the edge of the tangles and pick a cupful of berries into her apron. In here the blackberries had gone past ripe to overripe, some of them were rotting, sweating a thick white fluid like pus, and the crickets sang maddeningly in the high grass underfoot, their endless cry: *Reeeeee*—

The thorns tore at him, brought dots of blood onto his cheeks and bare arms. He made no effort to avoid their sting. He had been blind with terror—so blind that he had come within inches of stumbling onto the rotten boards that covered the well, perhaps within inches of crashing thirty feet to the well's muddy bottom. He had pinwheeled his arms for balance, and more thorns had branded his forearms. It was that memory that had caused him to call Petey back sharply.

That was the day Johnny McCabe died—his best friend. Johnny had been climbing the rungs up to his treehouse in his backyard. The two of them had spent many hours up there that summer, playing pirate, seeing make-believe galleons out on the lake, unlimbering the cannons, reefing the stuns'l (whatever *that* was), preparing to board. Johnny had been climbing up to the treehouse as he had done a thousand times before, and the rung just below the trapdoor in the bottom of the treehouse had snapped off in his hands and Johnny had fallen thirty feet to the ground and had broken his neck and it was the monkey's fault, the monkey, the goddam hateful monkey. When the phone rang, when Aunt Ida's mouth dropped open and then formed an O of horror as her friend Milly from down the road told her the news, when Aunt Ida said, "Come out on the porch, Hal, I have to tell you some bad news—" he had thought with sick horror, *The monkey! What's the monkey done now?*

There had been no reflection of his face trapped at the bottom of the well the day he threw the monkey down, only stone cobbles and the stink of wet mud. He had looked at the monkey lying there on the wiry grass that grew between the blackberry tangles, its cymbals poised, its grinning teeth huge between its splayed lips, its fur rubbed away in balding, mangy patches here and there, its glazed eyes.

"I hate you," he hissed at it. He wrapped his hand around its loathsome body, feeling the nappy fur crinkle. It grinned at him as he held it up in front of his face. "Go on!" he dared it, beginning to cry for the first time that day. He shook it. The poised cymbals trembled minutely. The monkey spoiled everything good. Everything. "Go on, clap them! Clap them!"

The monkey only grinned.

"Go on and clap them!" His voice rose hysterically. *"Fraidycat, fraidycat, go on and clap them! I dare you! DOUBLE DARE YOU!"*

Its brownish-yellow eyes. Its huge gleeful teeth.

He threw it down the well then, mad with grief and terror. He saw it turn over once on its way down, a simian acrobat doing a trick, and the sun glinted one last time on those cymbals. It struck the bottom with a thud, and that must have jogged its clockwork, for suddenly the cymbals *did* begin to beat. Their steady, deliberate, and tinny banging rose to his ears, echoing and fey in the stone throat of the dead well: *jang-jang-jang-jang—*

Hal clapped his hands over his mouth, and for a moment he could see it down there, perhaps only in the eye of imagination . . . lying there in the mud, eyes glaring up at the small circle of his boy's face peering over the lip of the well (as if marking that face forever), lips expanding and contracting around those grinning teeth, cymbals clapping, funny wind-up monkey.

Jang-jang-jang-jang, who's dead? Jang-jang-jang-jang, is it Johnny McCabe, falling with his eyes wide, doing his own acrobatic somersault as he falls through the bright summer vacation air with the splintered rung still held in his hands to strike the ground with a single bitter snapping sound, with blood flying out of his nose and mouth and wide eyes? Is it Johnny, Hal? Or is it you?

Moaning, Hal had shoved the boards across the hole, getting splinters in his hands, not caring, not even aware of them until later. And still he could hear it, even through the boards, muffled now and somehow all the worse for that: it was down there in stone-faced dark, clapping its cymbals and jerking its repulsive body, the sound coming up like sounds heard in a dream.

Jang-jang-jang-jang, who's dead this time?

He fought and battered his way back through the blackberry creepers. Thorns stitched fresh lines of welling blood briskly across his face and burdocks caught in the cuffs of his jeans, and he fell full-length once, his ears still jangling, as if it had followed him. Uncle Will found him later, sitting on an old tire in the garage and sobbing, and he had thought Hal was crying for his dead friend. So he had been; but he had also cried in the aftermath of terror.

He had thrown the monkey down the well in the afternoon. That evening, as twilight crept in through a shimmering mantle of ground-fog, a car moving too fast for the reduced visibility had run down Aunt Ida's Manx cat in the road and gone right on. There had been guts everywhere, Bill had thrown up, but Hal had only turned his face away, his pale, still face, hearing Aunt Ida's sobbing (this on top of the news about the McCabe boy had caused a fit of weeping that was almost hysterics, and it was almost two hours before Uncle Will could calm her completely) as if from miles away. In his heart there was a cold and exultant joy. It hadn't been his turn. It had been Aunt Ida's Manx, not him, not his brother Bill or his Uncle Will (just two champions of the rodayo). And now the monkey was gone, it was down the well, and one scruffy Manx cat with ear mites was not too great a price to pay. If the monkey wanted to clap its hellish cymbals now, let it. It could clap and clash them for the crawling bugs and beetles, the dark things that made their home in the well's stone gullet. It would rot down there. Its loathsome cogs and wheels and springs would rust down there. It would die down there. In the mud and the darkness. Spiders would spin it a shroud.

But . . . it had come back.

Slowly, Hal covered the well again, as he had on that day, and in his ears he heard the phantom echo of the monkey's cymbals: *Jang-jang-jang-jang, who's dead, Hal? Is it Terry?*

Dennis? Is it Petey, Hal? He's your favorite, isn't he? Is it him? Jang-jang-jang—

"Put that *down!*"

Petey flinched and dropped the monkey, and for one nightmare moment Hal thought that would do it, that the jolt would jog its machinery and the cymbals would begin to beat and clash.

"Daddy, you scared me."

"I'm sorry. I just . . . I don't want you to play with that."

The others had gone to see a movie, and he had thought he would beat them back to the motel. But he had stayed at the home place longer than he would have guessed; the old, hateful memories seemed to move in their own eternal time zone.

Terry was sitting near Dennis, watching *The Beverly Hillbillies*. She watched the old, grainy print with a steady, bemused concentration that spoke of a recent Valium pop. Dennis was reading a rock magazine with Culture Club on the cover. Petey had been sitting cross-legged on the carpet goofing with the monkey.

"It doesn't work anyway," Petey said. *Which explains why Dennis let him have it,* Hal thought, and then felt ashamed and angry at himself. He felt this uncontrollable hostility toward Dennis more and more often, but in the aftermath he felt demeaned and tacky . . . helpless.

"No," he said. "It's old. I'm going to throw it away. Give it to me."

He held out his hand and Peter, looking troubled, handed it over.

Dennis said to his mother, "Pop's turning into a friggin schizophrenic."

Hal was across the room even before he knew he was going, the monkey in one hand, grinning as if in approbation. He hauled Dennis out of his chair by the shirt. There was a purring sound as a seam came adrift somewhere. Dennis looked almost comically shocked. His copy of *Rock Wave* fell to the floor.

"Hey!"

"You come with me," Hal said grimly, pulling his son toward the door to the connecting room.

"Hal!" Terry nearly screamed. Petey just goggled.

Hal pulled Dennis through. He slammed the door and then slammed Dennis against the door. Dennis was starting to look scared. "You're getting a mouth problem," Hal said.

"Let *go* of me! You tore my shirt, you—"

Hal slammed the boy against the door again. "Yes," he said. "A real mouth problem. Did you learn that in school? Or back in the smoking area?"

Dennis flushed, his face momentarily ugly with guilt. "I wouldn't be in that shitty school if you didn't get canned!" he burst out.

Hal slammed Dennis against the door again. "I didn't get canned, I got laid off, you know it, and I don't need any of your shit about it. You have problems? Welcome to the world, Dennis. Just don't lay all of them off on me. You're eating. Your ass is covered. You are twelve years old, and at twelve, I don't . . . need any . . . shit from you." He punctuated each phrase by pulling the boy forward until their noses were almost touching and then slamming Dennis back into the door. It was not hard enough to hurt, but Dennis was scared—his father had not laid a hand on him since they moved to Texas—and now he began to cry with a young boy's loud, braying, healthy sobs.

"Go ahead, beat me up!" he yelled at Hal, his face twisted and blotchy. "Beat me up if you want, I know how much you fucking hate me!"

"I don't hate you. I love you a lot, Dennis. But I'm your dad and you're going to show me respect or I'm going to bust you for it."

Dennis tried to pull away. Hal pulled the boy to him and hugged him; Dennis fought for a moment and then put his face against Hal's chest and wept as if exhausted. It was the sort of cry Hal hadn't heard from either of his children in years. He closed his eyes, realizing that he felt exhausted himself.

Terry began to hammer on the other side of the door. "Stop it, Hal! Whatever you're doing to him, stop it!"

"I'm not killing him," Hal said. "Go away, Terry."

"Don't you—"

"It's all right, Mom," Dennis said, muffled against Hal's chest.

He could feel her perplexed silence for a moment, and then she went. Hal looked at his son again.

"I'm sorry I bad-mouthed you, Dad," Dennis said reluctantly.

"Okay. I accept that with thanks. When we get home next week, I'm going to wait two or three days and then I'm going to go through all your drawers, Dennis. If there's something in them you don't want me to see, you better get rid of it."

That flash of guilt again. Dennis lowered his eyes and wiped away snot with the back of his hand.

"Can I go now?" He sounded sullen once more.

"Sure," Hal said, and let him go. *Got to take him camping in the spring, just the two of us. Do some fishing, like Uncle Will used to do with Bill and me. Got to get close to him. Got to try.*

He sat down on the bed in the empty room, and looked at the monkey. *You'll never be close to him again, Hal,* its grin seemed to say. *Count on it. I am back to take care of business, just like you always knew I would be, someday.*

Hal laid the monkey aside and put a hand over his eyes.

That night Hal stood in the bathroom, brushing his teeth, and thought. *It was in the* same *box. How could it be in the* same box?

The toothbrush jabbed upward, hurting his gums. He winced.

He had been four, Bill six, the first time he saw the monkey. Their missing father had bought a house in Hartford, and it had been theirs, free and clear, before he died or fell into a hole in the middle of the world or whatever it had been. Their mother worked as a secretary at Holmes Aircraft, the helicopter plant out in Westville, and a series of sitters came in to stay with the boys, except by then it was just Hal that the sitters had to mind through the day—Bill was in first grade, big school. None of the babysitters stayed for long. They got pregnant and married their boyfriends or got work at Holmes, or Mrs. Shelburn would discover they had been at the cooking sherry or her bottle of brandy which was kept in the sideboard for special occasions. Most were stupid girls who seemed only to want to eat or sleep. None of them wanted to read to Hal as his mother would do.

The sitter that long winter was a huge, sleek black girl named Beulah. She fawned over Hal when Hal's mother was around and sometimes pinched him when she wasn't. Still, Hal had some liking for Beulah, who once in a while would read him a lurid tale from one of her confession or true-detective magazines ("Death Came for the Voluptuous Red-head," Beulah would intone ominously in the dozy daytime silence of the living room, and pop another Reese's peanut butter cup into her mouth while Hal solemnly studied the grainy tabloid pictures and drank milk from his Wish-Cup). The liking made what happened worse.

He found the monkey on a cold, cloudy day in March. Sleet ticked sporadically off the windows, and Beulah was asleep on the couch, a copy of *My Story* tented open on her admirable bosom.

Hal had crept into the back closet to look at his father's things.

The back closet was a storage space that ran the length of the second floor on the left side, extra space that had never been finished off. You got into it by using a small door—a down-the-rabbit-hole sort of door—on Bill's side of the boys' bedroom. They both liked to go in there, even though it was chilly in winter and hot enough in summer to wring a bucket-ful of sweat out of your pores. Long and narrow and some-how snug, the back closet was full of fascinating junk. No matter how much stuff you looked at, you never seemed to be able to look at it all. He and Bill had spent whole Saturday afternoons up here, barely speaking to each other, taking things out of boxes, examining them, turning them over and over so their hands could absorb each unique reality, putting them back. Now Hal wondered if he and Bill hadn't been trying, as best they could, to somehow make contact with their vanished father.

He had been a merchant mariner with a navigator's certifi-cate, and there were stacks of charts in the closet, some marked with neat circles (and the dimple of the compass's swing-point in the center of each). There were twenty vol-umes of something called *Barron's Guide to Navigation*. A set of cockeyed binoculars that made your eyes feel hot and funny if you looked through them too long. There were touristy things from a dozen ports of call—rubber hula-hula dolls, a black cardboard bowler with a torn band that said YOU PICK A GIRL AND I'LL PICCADILLY, a glass globe with a tiny Eiffel Tower inside. There were envelopes with foreign stamps tucked carefully away inside, and foreign coins; there were rock samples from the Hawaiian island of Maui, a glassy black—heavy and somehow ominous—and funny records in foreign languages.

That day, with the sleet ticking hypnotically off the roof just above his head, Hal worked his way all the way down to the far end of the back closet, moved a box aside, and saw another box behind it—a Ralston-Purina box. Looking over the top was a pair of glassy hazel eyes. They gave him a start and he skittered back for a moment, heart thumping, as if he had discovered a deadly pygmy. Then he saw its silence, the glaze in those eyes, and realized it was some sort of toy. He moved forward again and lifted it carefully from the box.

It grinned its ageless, toothy grin in the yellow light, its cymbals held apart.

Delighted, Hal had turned it this way and that, feeling the crinkle of its nappy fur. Its funny grin pleased him. Yet hadn't there been something else? An almost instinctive feeling of disgust that had come and gone almost before he was aware of it? Perhaps it was so, but with an old, old memory like this one, you had to be careful not to believe too much. Old memories could lie. But . . . hadn't he seen that same expression on Petey's face, in the attic of the home place?

He had seen the key set into the small of its back, and turned it. It had turned far too easily; there were no winding-up clicks. Broken, then. Broken, but still neat.

He took it out to play with it.

"Whatchoo got, Hal?" Beulah asked, waking from her nap.

"Nothing," Hal said. "I found it."

He put it up on the shelf on his side of the bedroom. It stood atop his Lassie coloring books, grinning, staring into space, cymbals poised. It was broken, but it grinned nonetheless. That night Hal awakened from some uneasy dream, bladder full, and got up to use the bathroom in the hall. Bill was a breathing lump of covers across the room.

Hal came back, almost asleep again . . . and suddenly the monkey began to beat its cymbals together in the darkness.

Jang-jang-jang-jang—

He came fully awake, as if snapped in the face with a cold, wet towel. His heart gave a staggering leap of surprise, and a tiny, mouselike squeak escaped his throat. He stared at the monkey, eyes wide, lips trembling.

Jang-jang-jang-jang—

Its body rocked and humped on the shelf. Its lips spread and closed, spread and closed, hideously gleeful, revealing huge and carnivorous teeth.

"Stop," Hal whispered.

His brother turned over and uttered a loud, single snore. All else was silent . . . except for the monkey. The cymbals clapped and clashed, and surely it would wake his brother, his mother, the world. It would wake the dead.

Jang-jang-jang-jang—

Hal moved toward it, meaning to stop it somehow, perhaps put his hand between its cymbals until it ran down, and then it stopped on its own. The cymbals came together one last time—*jang!*—and then spread slowly apart to their original position. The brass glimmered in the shadows. The monkey's dirty yellowish teeth grinned.

The house was silent again. His mother turned over in her bed and echoed Bill's single snore. Hal got back into his own bed and pulled the covers up, his heart beating fast, and he thought: *I'll put it back in the closet again tomorrow. I don't want it.*

But the next morning he forgot all about putting the monkey back because his mother didn't go to work. Beulah was dead. Their mother wouldn't tell them exactly what happened. "It was an accident, just a terrible accident," was all she would say. But that afternoon Bill bought a newspaper on his way home from school and smuggled page four up to their room under his shirt. Bill read the article haltingly to Hal while their mother cooked supper in the kitchen, but Hal could read the headline for himself—TWO KILLED IN APARTMENT SHOOT-OUT. Beulah McCaffery, 19, and Sally Tremont, 20, had been shot by Miss McCaffery's boyfriend, Leonard White, 25, following an argument over who was to go out and pick up an order of Chinese food. Miss Tremont had expired at Hartford Receiving. Beulah McCaffery had been pronounced dead at the scene.

It was like Beulah just disappeared into one of her own detective magazines, Hal Shelburn thought, and felt a cold chill race up his spine and then circle his heart. And then he realized the shootings had occurred about the same time the monkey—

"Hal?" It was Terry's voice, sleepy. "Coming to bed?"

He spat toothpaste into the sink and rinsed his mouth. "Yes," he said.

He had put the monkey in his suitcase earlier, and locked it up. They were flying back to Texas in two or three days. But before they went, he would get rid of the damned thing for good.

Somehow.

"You were pretty rough on Dennis this afternoon," Terry said in the dark.

"Dennis has needed somebody to start being rough on him for quite a while now, I think. He's been drifting. I just don't want him to start falling."

"Psychologically, beating the boy isn't a very productive—"

"I didn't *beat* him, Terry—for Christ's sake!"

"—way to assert parental authority—"

"Oh, don't give me any of that encounter-group shit," Hal said angrily.

"I can see you don't want to discuss this." Her voice was cold.

"I told him to get the dope out of the house, too."

"You did?" Now she sounded apprehensive. "How did he take it? What did he say?"

"Come on, Terry! What *could* he say? You're fired?"

"Hal, what's the *matter* with you? You're not like this— what's *wrong?*"

"Nothing," he said, thinking of the monkey locked away in his Samsonite. Would he hear it if it began to clap its cymbals? Yes, he surely would. Muffled, but audible. Clapping doom for someone, as it had for Beulah, Johnny McCabe, Uncle Will's dog Daisy. *Jang-jang-jang,* is it you, Hal? "I've just been under a strain."

"I *hope* that's all it is. Because I don't like you this way."

"No?" And the words escaped before he could stop them: he didn't even want to stop them. "So pop a Valium and everything will look okay again."

He heard her draw breath in and let it out shakily. She began to cry then. He could have comforted her (maybe), but there seemed to be no comfort in him. There was too much terror. It would be better when the monkey was gone again, gone for good. Please God, gone for good.

He lay wakeful until very late, until morning began to gray the air outside. But he thought he knew what to do.

*   *   *

Bill had found the monkey the second time.

That was about a year and a half after Beulah McCaffery had been pronounced Dead at the Scene. It was summer. Hal had just finished kindergarten.

He came in from playing and his mother called, "Wash your hands, Señor, you are feelthy like a peeg." She was on the porch, drinking an iced tea and reading a book. It was her vacation; she had two weeks.

Hal gave his hands a token pass under cold water and printed dirt on the hand towel. "Where's Bill?"

"Upstairs. You tell him to clean his side of the room. It's a mess."

Hal, who enjoyed being the messenger of unpleasant news in such matters, rushed up. Bill was sitting on the floor. The small down-the-rabbit-hole door leading to the back closet was ajar. He had the monkey in his hands.

"That's busted," Hal said immediately.

He was apprehensive, although he barely remembered coming back from the bathroom that night and the monkey suddenly beginning to clap its cymbals. A week or so after that, he had had a bad dream about the monkey and Beulah—he couldn't remember exactly what—and had awakened screaming, thinking for a moment that the soft weight on his chest was the monkey, that he would open his eyes and see it grinning down at him. But of course the soft weight had only been his pillow, clutched with panicky tightness. His mother came in to soothe him with a drink of water and two chalky-orange baby aspirin, those Valiums of childhood's troubled times. She thought it was the fact of Beulah's death that had caused the nightmare. So it was, but not in the way she thought.

He barely remembered any of this now, but the monkey still scared him, particularly its cymbals. And its teeth.

"I know that," Bill said, and tossed the monkey aside. "It's stupid." It landed on Bill's bed, staring up at the ceiling, cymbals poised. Hal did not like to see it there. "You want to go down to Teddy's and get Popsicles?"

"I spent my allowance already," Hal said. "Besides, Mom says you got to clean up your side of the room."

"I can do that later," Bill said. "And I'll loan you a

nickel, if you want." Bill was not above giving Hal an Indian rope burn sometimes, and would occasionally trip him up or punch him for no particular reason, but mostly he was okay.

"Sure," Hal said gratefully. "I'll just put the busted monkey back in the closet first, okay?"

"Nah," Bill said, getting up. "Let's go-go-go."

Hal went. Bill's moods were changeable, and if he paused to put the monkey away, he might lose his Popsicle. They went down to Teddy's and got them, and not just any Popsicles, either, but the rare blueberry ones. Then they went down to the Rec where some kids were getting up a baseball game. Hal was too small to play, but he sat far out in foul territory, sucking his blueberry Popsicle and chasing what the big kids called "Chinese home runs." They didn't get home until almost dark, and their mother whacked Hal for getting the hand towel dirty and whacked Bill for not cleaning up his side of the room, and after supper there was TV, and by the time all of that happened, Hal had forgotten all about the monkey. It somehow found its way up onto *Bill's* shelf, where it stood right next to Bill's autographed picture of Bill Boyd. And there it stayed for nearly two years.

By the time Hal was seven, babysitters had become an extravagance, and Mrs. Shelburn's parting shot each morning was, "Bill, look after your brother."

That day, however, Bill had to stay after school and Hal came home alone, stopping at each corner until he could see absolutely no traffic coming in either direction, and then skittering across, shoulders hunched, like a doughboy crossing no-man's-land. He let himself into the house with the key under the mat and went immediately to the refrigerator for a glass of milk. He got the bottle, and then it slipped through his fingers and crashed to smithereens on the floor, the pieces of glass flying everywhere.

Jang-jang-jang-jang, from upstairs, in their bedroom. *Jang-jang-jang, hi, Hal! Welcome home! And by the way, Hal, is it you? Is it you this time? Are they going to find you Dead at the Scene?*

He stood there, immobile, looking down at the broken glass and the puddle of milk, full of a terror he could not name or understand. It was simply there, seeming to ooze from his pores.

He turned and rushed upstairs to their room. The monkey

stood on Bill's shelf, seeming to stare at him. The monkey had knocked the autographed picture of Bill Boyd facedown onto Bill's bed. The monkey rocked and grinned and beat its cymbals together. Hal approached it slowly, not wanting to, but not able to stay away. Its cymbals jerked apart and crashed together and jerked apart again. As he got closer, he could hear the clockwork running in the monkey's guts.

Abruptly, uttering a cry of revulsion and terror, he swatted it from the shelf as one might swat a bug. It struck Bill's pillow and then fell on the floor, cymbals beating together, *jang-jang-jang,* lips flexing and closing as it lay there on its back in a patch of late April sunshine.

Hal kicked it with one Buster Brown, kicked it as hard as he could, and this time the cry that escaped him was one of fury. The clockwork monkey skittered across the floor, bounced off the wall and lay still. Hal stood staring at it, fists bunched, heart pounding. It grinned saucily back at him, the sun of a burning pinpoint in one glass eye. *Kick me all you want,* it seemed to tell him, *I'm nothing but cogs and clockwork and a worm gear or two, kick me all you feel like, I'm not real, just a funny clockwork monkey is all I am, and who's dead? There's been an explosion at the helicopter plant! What's that rising up into the sky like a big bloody bowling ball with eyes where the finger-holes should be? Is it your mother's head, Hal? Whee! What a ride your mother's head is having! Or down at Brook Street Corner! Looky-here, pard! The car was going too fast! The driver was drunk! There's one Bill less in the world! Could you hear the crunching sound when the wheels ran over his skull and his brains squirted out his ears? Yes? No? Maybe? Don't ask me, I don't know, I can't know, all I know how to do is beat these cymbals together jang-jang-jang, and who's Dead at the Scene, Hal? Your mother? Your brother? Or is it you, Hal? Is it you?*

He rushed at it again, meaning to stomp it, smash it, jump on it until cogs and gears flew and its horrible glass eyes rolled along the floor. But just as he reached it, its cymbals came together once more, very softly . . . *(jang)* . . . as a spring somewhere inside expanded one final, minute notch . . . and a sliver of ice seemed to whisper its way through the walls of his heart, impaling it, stilling its fury and leaving him sick with terror again. The monkey almost seemed to know—how gleeful its grin seemed!

He picked it up, tweezing one of its arms between the thumb and first finger of his right hand, mouth drawn down in a bow of loathing, as if it were a corpse he held. Its mangy fake fur seemed hot and fevered against his skin. He fumbled open the tiny door that led to the back closet and turned on the bulb. The monkey grinned at him as he crawled down the length of the storage area between boxes piled on top of boxes, past the set of navigation books and the photograph albums with their fume of old chemicals and the souvenirs and the old clothes, and Hal thought: *If it begins to clap its cymbals together now and move in my hand, I'll scream, and if I scream, it'll do more than grin, it'll start to laugh, to laugh at me, and then I'll go crazy and they'll find me in here, drooling and laughing crazy, I'll be crazy, oh please dear God, please dear Jesus, don't let me go crazy—*

He reached the far end and clawed two boxes aside, spilling one of them, and jammed the monkey back into the Ralston-Purina box in the farthest corner. And it leaned in there, comfortably, as if home at last, cymbals poised, grinning its simian grin, as if the joke were still on Hal. Hal crawled backward, sweating, hot and cold, all fire and ice, waiting for the cymbals to begin, and when they began, the monkey would leap from its box and scurry beetlelike toward him, clockwork whirring, cymbals clashing madly, and—

—and none of that happened. He turned off the light and slammed the small down-the-rabbit-hole door and leaned on it, panting. At last he began to feel a little better. He went downstairs on rubbery legs, got an empty bag, and began carefully to pick up the jagged shards and splinters of the broken milk bottle, wondering if he was going to cut himself and bleed to death, if that was what the clapping cymbals had meant. But that didn't happen, either. He got a towel and wiped up the milk and then sat down to see if his mother and brother would come home.

His mother came first, asking, "Where's Bill?"

In a low, colorless voice, now sure that Bill must be Dead at some Scene, Hal started to explain about the school play meeting, knowing that, even given a very long meeting, Bill should have been home half an hour ago.

His mother looked at him curiously, started to ask what was wrong, and then the door opened and Bill came in—only it was not Bill at all, not really. This was a ghost-Bill, pale and silent.

"What's wrong?" Mrs. Shelburn exclaimed. "Bill, what's wrong?"

Bill began to cry and they got the story through his tears. There had been a car, he said. He and his friend Charlie Silverman were walking home together after the meeting and the car came around Brook Street Corner too fast and Charlie had frozen, Bill had tugged Charlie's hand once but had lost his grip and the car—

Bill began to bray out loud, hysterical sobs, and his mother hugged him to her, rocking him, and Hal looked out on the porch and saw two policemen standing there. The squad car in which they had conveyed Bill home was standing at the curb. Then he began to cry himself . . . but his tears were tears of relief.

It was Bill's turn to have nightmares now—dreams in which Charlie Silverman died over and over again, knocked out of his Red Ryder cowboy boots and was flipped onto the hood of the rusty Hudson Hornet the drunk had been piloting. Charlie Silverman's head and the Hudson's windshield had met with explosive force. Both had shattered. The drunk driver, who owned a candy store in Milford, suffered a heart attack shortly after being taken into custody (perhaps it was the sight of Charlie Silverman's brains drying on his pants), and his lawyer was quite successful at the trial with his "this man has been punished enough" theme. The drunk was given sixty days (suspended) and lost his privilege to operate a motor vehicle in the state of Connecticut for five years . . . which was about as long as Bill Shelburn's nightmares lasted. The monkey was hidden away again in the back closet. Bill never noticed it was gone from his shelf . . . or if he did, he never said.

Hal felt safe for a while. He even began to forget about the monkey again, or to believe it had only been a bad dream. But when he came home from school on the afternoon his mother died, it was back on his shelf, cymbals poised, grinning down at him.

He approached it slowly, as if from outside himself—as if his own body had been turned into a wind-up toy at the sight of the monkey. He saw his hand reach out and take it down. He felt the nappy fur crinkle under his hand, but the feeling was muffled, mere pressure, as if someone had shot him full of Novocain. He could hear his breathing, quick and dry, like the rattle of wind through straw.

He turned it over and grasped the key and years later he would think that his drugged fascination was like that of a man who puts a six-shooter with one loaded chamber against a closed and jittering eyelid and pulls the trigger.

No don't—let it alone throw it away don't touch it—

He turned the key and in the silence he heard a perfect tiny series of winding-up clicks. When he let the key go, the monkey began to clap its cymbals together and he could feel its body jerking, bend-and-*jerk,* bend-and-*jerk,* as if it were alive, it *was* alive, writhing in his hand like some loathsome pygmy, and the vibration he felt through its balding brown fur was not that of turning cogs but the beating of its heart.

With a groan, Hal dropped the monkey and backed away, fingernails digging into the flesh under his eyes, palms pressed to his mouth. He stumbled over something and nearly lost his balance (then he would have been right down on the floor with it, his bulging blue eyes looking into its glassy hazel ones). He scrambled toward the door, backed through it, slammed it, and leaned against it. Suddenly he bolted for the bathroom and vomited.

It was Mrs. Stukey from the helicopter plant who brought the news and stayed with them those first two endless nights, until Aunt Ida got down from Maine. Their mother had died of a brain embolism in the middle of the afternoon. She had been standing at the water cooler with a cup of water in one hand and had crumpled as if shot, still holding the paper cup in one hand. With the other she had clawed at the water cooler and had pulled the great glass bottle of Poland water down with her. It had shattered . . . but the plant doctor, who came on the run, said later that he believed Mrs. Shelburn was dead before the water had soaked through her dress and her underclothes to wet her skin. The boys were never told any of this, but Hal knew anyway. He dreamed it again and again on the long nights following his mother's death. *You still have trouble gettin to sleep, little brother?* Bill had asked him, and Hal supposed Bill thought all the thrashing and bad dreams had to do with their mother dying so suddenly, and that was right . . . but only partly right. There was the guilt;

the certain, deadly knowledge that he had killed his mother by winding the monkey up on that sunny after-school afternoon.

When Hal finally fell asleep, his sleep must have been deep. When he awoke, it was nearly noon. Petey was sitting cross-legged in a chair across the room, methodically eating an orange section by section and watching a game show on TV.

Hal swung his legs out of bed, feeling as if someone had punched him down into sleep . . . and then punched him back out of it. His head throbbed. "Where's your mom, Petey?"

Petey glanced around. "She and Dennis went shopping. I said I'd hang out here with you. Do you always talk in your sleep, Dad?"

Hal looked at his son cautiously. "No. What did I say?"

"I couldn't make it out. It scared me, a little."

"Well, here I am in my right mind again," Hal said, and managed a small grin. Petey grinned back, and Hal felt simple love for the boy again, an emotion that was bright and strong and uncomplicated. He wondered why he had always been able to feel so good about Petey, to feel he understood Petey and could help him, and why Dennis seemed a window too dark to look through, a mystery in his ways and habits, the sort of boy he could not understand because he had never been that sort of boy. It was too easy to say that the move from California had changed Dennis, or that—

His thoughts froze. The monkey. The monkey was sitting on the windowsill, cymbals poised. Hal felt his heart stop dead in his chest and then suddenly begin to gallop. His vision wavered, and his throbbing head began to ache ferociously.

It had escaped from the suitcase and now stood on the windowsill, grinning at him. *Thought you got rid of me, didn't you? But you've thought that before, haven't you?*

Yes, he thought sickly. Yes, I have.

"Pete, did you take that monkey out of my suitcase?" he asked, knowing the answer already. He had locked the suitcase and had put the key in his overcoat pocket.

Petey glanced at the monkey, and something—Hal thought it was unease—passed over his face. "No," he said. "Mom put it there."

"Mom did?"

"Yeah. She took it from you. She laughed."

"Took it from me? What are you talking about?"

"You had it in bed with you. I was brushing my teeth, but Dennis saw. He laughed, too. He said you looked like a baby with a teddy bear."

Hal looked at the monkey. His mouth was too dry to swallow. He'd had it in *bed* with him? In *bed*? That loathsome fur against his cheek, maybe against his *mouth*, those glaring eyes staring into his sleeping face, those grinning teeth near his neck? *On* his neck? Dear *God*.

He turned abruptly and went to the closet. The Samsonite was there, still locked. The key was still in his overcoat pocket.

Behind him, the TV snapped off. He came out of the closet slowly. Peter was looking at him soberly. "Daddy, I don't like that monkey," he said, his voice almost too low to hear.

"Nor do I," Hal said.

Petey looked at him closely, to see if he was joking, and saw that he was not. He came to his father and hugged him tight. Hal could feel him trembling.

Petey spoke into his ear then, very rapidly, as if afraid he might not have courage enough to say it again . . . or that the monkey might overhear.

"It's like it looks at you. Like it looks at you no matter where you are in the room. And if you go into the other room, it's like it's looking through the wall at you. I kept feeling like it . . . like it wanted me for something."

Petey shuddered. Hal held him tight.

"Like it wanted you to wind it up," Hal said.

Pete nodded violently. "It isn't really broken, is it, Dad?"

"Sometimes it is," Hal said, looking over his son's shoulder at the monkey. "But sometimes it still works."

"I kept wanting to go over there and wind it up. It was so quiet, and I thought, I can't, it'll wake up Daddy, but I still wanted to, and I went over and I . . . I *touched* it and I hate the way it feels . . . but I liked it, too . . . and it was like it was saying, Wind me up, Petey, we'll play, your father isn't going to wake up, he's never going to wake up at all, wind me up, wind me up . . ."

The boy suddenly burst into tears.

"It's bad, I know it is. There's something wrong with it. Can't we throw it out, Daddy? Please?"

The monkey grinned its endless grin at Hal. He could feel Petey's tears between them. Late-morning sun glinted off the monkey's brass cymbals—the light reflected upward and put sun streaks on the motel's plain white stucco ceiling.

"What time did your mother think she and Dennis would be back, Petey?"

"Around one." He swiped at his red eyes with his shirt sleeve, looking embarrassed at his tears. But he wouldn't look at the monkey. "I turned on the TV," he whispered. "And I turned it up loud."

"That was all right, Petey."

How would it have happened? Hal wondered. *Heart attack? An embolism, like my mother? What? It doesn't really matter, does it?*

And on the heels of that, another, colder thought: *Get rid of it, he says. Throw it out. But can it be gotten rid of? Ever?*

The monkey grinned mockingly at him, its cymbals held a foot apart. Did it suddenly come to life on the night Aunt Ida died? he wondered suddenly. Was that the last sound she heard, the muffled *jang-jang-jang* of the monkey beating its cymbals together up in the black attic while the wind whistled along the drainpipe?

"Maybe not so crazy," Hal said slowly to his son. "Go get your flight bag, Petey."

Petey looked at him uncertainly. "What are we going to do?"

Maybe it can be got rid of. Maybe permanently, maybe just for a while . . . a long while or a short while. Maybe it's just going to come back and come back and that's all this is about . . . but maybe I—we—can say good-bye to it for a long time. It took twenty years to come back this time. It took twenty years to get out of the well . . .

"We're going to go for a ride," Hal said. He felt fairly calm, but somehow too heavy inside his skin. Even his eyeballs seemed to have gained weight. "But first I want you to take your flight bag out there by the edge of the parking lot and find three or four good-sized rocks. Put them inside the bag and bring it back to me. Got it?"

Understanding flickered in Petey's eyes. "All right, Daddy."

Hal glanced at his watch. It was nearly 12:15. "Hurry. I want to be gone before your mother gets back."

"Where are we going?"

"To Uncle Will's and Aunt Ida's," Hal said. "To the home place."

Hal went into the bathroom, looked behind the toilet, and got the bowl brush leaning there. He took it back to the window and stood there with it in his hand like a cut-rate magic wand. He looked out at Petey in his melton shirt-jacket, crossing the parking lot with his flight bag, DELTA showing clearly in white letters against a blue field. A fly bumbled in an upper corner of the window, slow and stupid with the end of the warm season. Hal knew how it felt.

He watched Petey hunt up three good-sized rocks and then start back across the parking lot. A car came around the corner of the motel, a car that was moving too fast, much too fast, and without thinking, reaching with the kind of reflex a good shortstop shows going to his right, the hand holding the brush flashed down, as if in a karate chop . . . and stopped.

The cymbals closed soundlessly on his intervening hand, and he felt something in the air. Something like rage.

The car's brakes screamed. Petey flinched back. The driver motioned to him, impatiently, as if what had almost happened was Petey's fault, and Petey ran across the parking lot with his collar flapping and into the motel's rear entrance.

Sweat was running down Hal's chest; he felt it on his forehead like a drizzle of oily rain. The cymbals pressed coldly against his hand, numbing it.

Go on, he thought grimly. *Go on, I can wait all day. Until hell freezes over, if that's what it takes.*

The cymbals drew apart and came to rest. Hal heard one faint *click!* from inside the monkey. He withdrew the brush and looked at it. Some of the white bristles had blackened, as if singed.

The fly bumbled and buzzed, trying to find the cold October sunshine that seemed so close.

Pete came bursting in, breathing quickly, cheeks rosy. "I got three good ones, Dad, I—" He broke off. "Are you all right, Daddy?"

"Fine," Hal said. "Bring the bag over."

Hal hooked the table by the sofa over to the window with his foot, so it stood below the sill, and put the flight bag on it. He spread its mouth open like lips. He could see the stones Petey had collected glimmering inside. He used the toilet-bowl brush to hook the monkey forward. It teetered for a moment and then fell into the bag. There was a faint *jing!* as one of its cymbals struck one of the rocks.

"Dad? Daddy?" Petey sounded frightened. Hal looked around at him. Something was different; something had changed. What was it?

Then he saw the direction of Petey's gaze and he knew. The buzzing of the fly had stopped. It lay dead on the windowsill.

"Did the monkey do that?" Petey whispered.

"Come on," Hal said, zipping the bag shut. "I'll tell you while we ride out to the home place."

"How can we go? Mom and Dennis took the car."

"Don't worry," Hal said, and ruffled Petey's hair.

He showed the desk clerk his driver's license and a twenty-dollar bill. After taking Hal's Texas Instruments digital watch as collateral, the clerk handed Hal the keys to his own car—a battered AMC Gremlin. As they drove east on Route 302 toward Casco, Hal began to talk, haltingly at first, then a little faster. He began by telling Petey that his father had probably brought the monkey home with him from overseas, as a gift for his sons. It wasn't a particularly unique toy—there was nothing strange or valuable about it. There must have been hundreds of thousands of wind-up monkeys in the world, some made in Hong Kong, some in Taiwan, some in Korea. But somewhere along the line—perhaps even in the dark back closet of the house in Connecticut where the two boys had begun their growing up—something had happened to the monkey. Something bad. It might be, Hal said as he tried to coax the clerk's Gremlin up past forty, that some bad things—maybe even most bad things—weren't even really awake and aware of what they were. He left it there because that was probably as much as Petey could understand, but his mind continued on its own course. He thought that most evil might be very much like a monkey full of clockwork that you wind up; the clockwork turns, the cymbals begin to beat, the teeth grin, the stupid glass eyes laugh . . . or appear to laugh. . . .

He told Petey about finding the monkey, but little more—he did not want to terrify his already scared boy any more than he was already. The story thus became disjointed, not really clear, but Petey asked no questions; perhaps he was filling in the blanks for himself, Hal thought, in much the same way that he had dreamed his mother's death over and over, although he had not been there.

Uncle Will and Aunt Ida had both been there for the funeral. Afterward, Uncle Will had gone back to Maine—it was harvesttime—and Aunt Ida had stayed on for two weeks with the boys to neaten up her sister's affairs before bringing them back to Maine. But more than that, she spent the time making herself known to them—they were so stunned by their mother's sudden death that they were nearly comatose. When they couldn't sleep, she was there with warm milk; when Hal woke at three in the morning with nightmares (nightmares in which his mother approached the water cooler without seeing the monkey that floated and bobbed in its cool sapphire depths, grinning and clapping its cymbals, each converging pair of sweeps leaving trails of bubbles behind); she was there when Bill came down with first a fever and then a rash of painful mouth sores and then hives three days after the funeral; she was there. She made herself known to the boys, and before they rode the bus from Hartford to Portland with her, both Bill and Hal had come to her separately and wept on her lap while she held them and rocked them, and the bonding began.

The day before they left Connecticut for good to go "down Maine" (as it was called in those days), the rag-man came in his old rattly truck and picked up the huge pile of useless stuff that Bill and Hal had carried out to the sidewalk from the back closet. When all the junk had been set out by the curb for pickup, Aunt Ida had asked them to go through the back closet again and pick out any souvenirs or remembrances they wanted specially to keep. We just don't have room for it all, boys, she told them, and Hal supposed Bill had taken her at her word and had gone through all those fascinating boxes their father had left behind one final time. Hal did not join his older brother. Hal had lost his taste for the back closet. A terrible idea had come to him during those first two weeks of mourning: perhaps his father hadn't just disappeared, or run away because he had an itchy foot and had discovered marriage wasn't for him.

Maybe the monkey had gotten him.

When he heard the rag-man's truck roaring and farting and backfiring its way down the block, Hal nerved himself, snatched the monkey from his shelf where it had been since the day his mother died (he had not dared to touch it until then, not even to throw it back into the closet), and ran downstairs with it. Neither Bill nor Aunt Ida saw him. Sitting on top of a barrel filled with broken souvenirs and moldy books was the Ralston-Purina carton, filled with similar junk. Hal had slammed the monkey back into the box it had originally come out of, hysterically daring it to begin clapping its cymbals (*go on, go on, I dare you, dare you, DOUBLE DARE YOU*), but the monkey only waited there, leaning back nonchalantly, as if expecting a bus, grinning its awful, knowing grin.

Hal stood by, a small boy in old corduroy pants and scuffed Buster Browns, as the rag-man, an Italian gent who wore a crucifix and whistled through the space in his teeth, began loading boxes and barrels into an ancient truck with wooden stake sides. Hal watched as he lifted both the barrel and the Ralston-Purina box balanced atop it; he watched the monkey disappear into the bed of the truck; he watched as the rag-man climbed back into the cab, blew his nose mightily into the palm of his hand, wiped his hand with a huge red handkerchief, and started the truck's engine with a roar and a blast of oily blue smoke; he watched the truck draw away. And a great weight had dropped away from his heart—he actually felt it go. He had jumped up and down twice, as high as he could jump, his arms spread, palms held out, and if any of the neighbors had seen him, they would have thought it odd almost to the point of blasphemy, perhaps—*why is that boy jumping for joy* (for that was surely what it was; a jump for joy can hardly be disguised), they surely would have asked themselves, *with his mother not even a month in her grave?*

He was doing it because the monkey was gone, gone forever.

Or so he had thought.

Not three months later Aunt Ida had sent him up into the attic to get the boxes of Christmas decorations, and as he crawled around looking for them, getting the knees of his pants dusty, he had suddenly come face to face with it again, and his wonder and terror had been so great that he had to bite sharply into the side of his hand to keep from screaming . . . or fainting dead away. There it was, grinning its toothy grin, cymbals poised a foot apart and ready to clap, leaning nonchalantly back against one corner of a Ralston-Purina carton as if waiting for a bus, seeming to say: *Thought you got rid of me, didn't you? But I'm not that easy to get rid of, Hal. I like you, Hal. We were made for each other, just a boy and his pet monkey, a couple of good old buddies. And somewhere south of here there's a stupid old Italian rag-man lying in a claw-foot tub with his eyeballs bulging and his dentures half-popped out of his mouth, his screaming mouth, a ragman who smells like a burned-out Exide battery. He was saving me for his grandson, Hal, he put me on the bathroom shelf with his soap and his razor and his Burma-Shave and the Philco radio he listened to the Brooklyn Dodgers on, and I started to clap, and one of my cymbals hit that old radio and into the tub it went, and then I came to you, Hal, I worked my way along the country roads at night and the moonlight shone off my teeth at three in the morning and I left many people Dead at many Scenes. I came to you, Hal, I'm your Christmas present, so wind me up, who's dead? Is it Bill? Is it Uncle Will? Is it you, Hal? Is it you?*

Hal had backed away, grimacing madly, eyes rolling, and nearly fell going downstairs. He told Aunt Ida he hadn't been able to find the Christmas decorations—it was the first lie he had ever told her, and she had seen the lie on his face but had not asked him why he had told it, thank God—and later when Bill came in she asked *him* to look and he brought the Christmas decorations down. Later, when they were alone, Bill hissed at him that he was a dummy who couldn't find his own ass with both hands and a flashlight. Hal said nothing. Hal was pale and silent, only picking at his supper. And that night he dreamed of the monkey again, one of its cymbals striking the Philco radio as it babbled out Dean Martin singing Whenna da moon hitta you eye like a big pizza pie *ats-a moray,* the radio tumbling into the bathtub as the monkey grinned and beat its cymbals together with a *JANG* and a *JANG* and a *JANG;* only it wasn't the Italian rag-man who was in the tub when the water turned electric.

It was him.

* * *

Hal and his son scrambled down the embankment behind the home place to the boathouse that jutted out over the water on its old pilings. Hal had the flight bag in his right hand. His throat was dry, his ears were attuned to an unnaturally keen pitch. The bag was very heavy.

Hal set down the flight bag. "Don't touch that," he said. Hal felt in his pocket for the ring of keys Bill had given him and found one neatly labeled B'HOUSE on a scrap of adhesive tape.

The day was clear and cold, windy, the sky a brilliant blue. The leaves of the trees that crowded up to the verge of the lake had gone every bright fall shade from blood red to schoolbus yellow. They talked in the wind. Leaves swirled around Petey's sneakers as he stood anxiously by, and Hal could smell November just downwind, with winter crowding close behind it.

The key turned in the padlock and he pulled the swing doors open. Memory was strong; he didn't even have to look to kick down the wooden block that held the door open. The smell in here was all summer: canvas and bright wood, a lingering lusty warmth.

Uncle Will's rowboat was still here, the oars neatly shipped as if he had last loaded it with his fishing tackle and two six-packs of Black Label yesterday afternoon. Bill and Hal had both gone out fishing with Uncle Will many times, but never together. Uncle Will maintained the boat was too small for three. The red trim, which Uncle Will had touched up each spring, was now faded and peeling, though, and spiders had spun silk in the boat's bow.

Hal laid hold of the boat and pulled it down the ramp to the little shingle of beach. The fishing trips had been one of the best parts of his childhood with Uncle Will and Aunt Ida. He had a feeling that Bill felt much the same. Uncle Will was ordinarily the most taciturn of men, but once he had the boat positioned to his liking, some sixty or seventy yards offshore, lines set and bobbers floating on the water, he would crack a beer for himself and one for Hal (who rarely drank more than half of the one can Uncle Will would allow, always with the ritual admonition from Uncle Will that Aunt Ida must never be told because "she'd shoot me for a stranger if she knew I was givin you boys beer, don't you know"), and wax expansive. He would tell stories, answer questions, rebait Hal's hook when it needed rebaiting; and the boat would drift where the wind and the mild current wanted it to be.

"How come you never go right out to the middle, Uncle Will?" Hal had asked once.

"Look overside there," Uncle Will had answered.

Hal did. He saw the blue water and his fish line going down into black.

"You're looking into the deepest part of Crystal Lake," Uncle Will said, crunching his empty beer can in one hand and selecting a fresh one with the other. "A hundred feet if she's an inch. Amos Culligan's old Studebaker is down there somewhere. Damn fool took it out on the lake one early December, before the ice was made. Lucky to get out of it alive, he was. They'll never get that Stud out, nor see it until Judgment Trump blows. Lake's one deep sonofawhore right here, it is. Big ones are right here, Hal. No need to go out no further. Let's see how your worm looks. Reel that sonofawhore right in."

Hal did, and while Uncle Will put a fresh crawler from the old Crisco tin that served as his bait box on his hook, he stared into the water, fascinated, trying to see Amos Culligan's old Studebaker, all rust and waterweed drifting out of the open driver's side window through which Amos had escaped at the absolute last moment, waterweed festooning the steering wheel like a rotting necklace, waterweed dangling from the rearview mirror and drifting back and forth in the currents like some strange rosary. But he could see only blue shading to black, and there was the shape of Uncle Will's night crawler, the hook hidden inside its knots, hung up there in the middle of things, its own sun-shafted version of reality. Hal had a brief, dizzying vision of being suspended over a mighty gulf, and he had closed his eyes for a moment until the vertigo passed. That day, he seemed to recollect, he had drunk his entire can of beer.

. . . *the deepest part of Crystal Lake . . . a hundred feet if she's an inch.*

He paused a moment, panting, and looked up at Petey, still watching anxiously. "You want some help, Daddy?"

"In a minute."

He had his breath again, and now he pulled the rowboat across the narrow strip of sand to the water, leaving a groove. The paint had peeled, but the boat had been kept under cover and it looked sound.

When he and Uncle Will went out, Uncle Will would pull the boat down the ramp, and when the bow was afloat, he would clamber in, grab an oar to push with and say: "Push me off, Hal . . . this is where you earn your truss!"

"Hand that bag in, Petey, and then give me a push," he said. And, smiling a little, he added: "This is where you earn your truss."

Petey didn't smile back. "Am I coming, Daddy?"

"Not this time. Another time I'll take you out fishing, but . . . not this time."

Petey hesitated. The wind tumbled his brown hair and a few yellow leaves, crisp and dry, wheeled past his shoulders and landed at the edge of the water, bobbing like boats themselves.

"You should have stuffed 'em," he said, low.

"What?" But he thought he understood what Petey had meant.

"Put cotton over the cymbals. Taped it on. So it couldn't . . . make that noise."

Hal suddenly remembered Daisy coming toward him—not walking but lurching—and how, quite suddenly, blood had burst from both of Daisy's eyes in a flood that soaked her ruff and pattered down on the floor of the barn, how she had collapsed on her forepaws . . . and on the still, rainy spring air of that day he had heard the sound, not muffled but curiously clear, coming from the attic of the house fifty feet away: *Jang-jang-jang-jang!*

He had begun to scream hysterically, dropping the armload of wood he had been getting for the fire. He ran for the kitchen to get Uncle Will, who was eating scrambled eggs and toast, his suspenders not even up over his shoulders yet.

She was an old dog, Hal, Uncle Will had said, his face haggard and unhappy—he looked old himself. *She was twelve, and that's old for a dog. You mustn't take on now—old Daisy wouldn't like that.*

Old, the vet had echoed, but he had looked troubled all the same, because dogs don't die of explosive brain hemorrhages, even at twelve ("Like as if someone had stuck a firecracker in her head," Hal overheard the vet saying to Uncle Will as Uncle Will dug a hole in back of the barn not far from the place where he had buried Daisy's mother in 1950; "I never seen the beat of it, Will'').

And later, terrified almost out of his mind but unable to help himself, Hal had crept up to the attic.

Hello, Hal, how you doing? The monkey grinned from its shadowy corner. Its cymbals were poised, a foot or so apart. The sofa cushion Hal had stood on end between them was now all the way across the attic. Something— some force—had thrown it hard enough to split its cover, and stuffing foamed out of it. *Don't worry about Daisy,* the monkey whispered inside his head, its glassy hazel eyes fixed on Hal Shelburn's wide blue ones. *Don't worry about Daisy, she was old, Hal, even the vet said so, and by the way, did you see the blood coming out of her eyes, Hal? Wind me up, Hal. Wind me up, let's play, and who's dead, Hal? Is it you?*

And when he came back to himself he had been crawling toward the monkey as if hypnotized. One hand had been outstretched to grasp the key. He scrambled backward then, and almost fell down the attic stairs in his haste—probably would have if the stairwell had not been so narrow. A little whining noise had been coming from his throat.

Now he sat in the boat, looking at Petey. "Muffling the cymbals doesn't work," he said. "I tried it once."

Petey cast a nervous glance at the flight bag. "What happened, Daddy?"

"Nothing I want to talk about now," Hal said, "and nothing you want to hear about. Come on and give me a push."

Petey bent to it, and the stern of the boat grated along the sand. Hal dug in with an oar, and suddenly that feeling of being tied to the earth was gone and the boat was moving lightly, its own thing again after years in the dark boathouse, rocking on the light waves. Hal unshipped the other oar and clicked the oarlocks shut.

"Be careful, Daddy," Petey said.

"This won't take long," Hal promised, but he looked at the flight bag and wondered.

He began to row, bending to the work. The old, familiar

ache in the small of his back and between his shoulder blades began. The shore receded. Petey was magically eight again, six, a four-year-old standing at the edge of the water. He shaded his eyes with one infant hand.

Hal glanced casually at the shore but would not allow himself to actually study it. It had been nearly fifteen years, and if he studied the shoreline carefully, he would see the changes rather than the similarities and become lost. The sun beat on his neck, and he began to sweat. He looked at the flight bag, and for a moment he lost the bend-and-pull rhythm. The flight bag seemed . . . seemed to be bulging. He began to row faster.

The wind gusted, drying the sweat and cooling his skin. The boat rose and the bow slapped water to either side when it came down. Hadn't the wind freshened, just in the last minute or so? And was Petey calling something? Yes. Hal couldn't make out what it was over the wind. It didn't matter. Getting rid of the monkey for another twenty years—or maybe

(please God forever)

forever—that was what mattered.

The boat reared and came down. He glanced left and saw baby whitecaps. He looked shoreward again and saw Hunter's Point and a collapsed wreck that must have been the Burdons' boathouse when he and Bill were kids. Almost there, then. Almost over the spot where Amos Culligan's famous Studebaker had plunged through the ice one long-ago December. Almost over the deepest part of the lake.

Petey was screaming something; screaming and pointing. Hal still couldn't hear. The rowboat rocked and rolled, flatting off clouds of thin spray to either side of its peeling bow. A tiny rainbow glowed in one, was pulled apart. Sunlight and shadow raced across the lake in shutters and the waves were not mild now; the whitecaps had grown up. His sweat had dried to gooseflesh, and spray had soaked the back of his jacket. He rowed grimly, eyes alternating between the shoreline and the flight bag. The boat rose again, this time so high that for a moment the left oar pawed at air instead of water.

Petey was pointing at the sky, his scream now only a faint, bright runner of sound.

Hal looked over his shoulder.

The lake was a frenzy of waves. It had gone a deadly dark shade of blue sewn with white seams. A shadow raced across the water toward the boat and something in its shape was familiar, so terribly familiar, that Hal looked up and then the scream was there, struggling in his tight throat.

The sun was behind the cloud, turning it into a hunched working shape with two gold-edged crescents held apart. Two holes were torn in one end of the cloud, and sunshine poured through in two shafts.

As the cloud crossed over the boat, the monkey's cymbals, barely muffled by the flight bag, began to beat. *Jang-jang-jang-jang, it's you, Hal, it's finally you, you're over the deepest part of the lake now and it's your turn, your turn, your turn—*

All the necessary shoreline elements had clicked into their places. The rotting bones of Amos Culligan's Studebaker lay somewhere below, this was where the big ones were, this was the place.

Hal shipped the oars to the locks in one quick jerk, leaned forward, unmindful of the wildly rocking boat, and snatched the flight bag. The cymbals made their wild, pagan music; the bag's sides bellowed as if with tenebrous respiration.

"*Right here, you sonofawhore!*" Hal screamed. "*RIGHT HERE!*"

He threw the bag over the side.

It sank fast. For a moment he could see it going down, sides moving, and for that endless moment *he could still hear the cymbals beating.* And for a moment the black waters seemed to clear and he could see down into that terrible gulf of waters to where the big ones lay; there was Amos Culligan's Studebaker, and Hal's mother was behind its slimy wheel, a grinning skeleton with a lake bass staring coldly from one fleshless eye socket. Uncle Will and Aunt Ida lolled beside her, and Aunt Ida's gray hair trailed upward as the bag fell, turning over and over, a few silver bubbles trailing up: *jang-jang-jang-jang . . .*

Hal slammed the oars back into the water, scraping blood from his knuckles *(and ah God the back of Amos Culligan's Studebaker had been full of dead children! Charlie Silverman . . . Johnny McCabe . . .),* and began to bring the boat about.

There was a dry pistol-shot crack between his feet, and

suddenly clear water was welling up between two boards. The boat was old; the wood had shrunk a bit, no doubt; it was just a small leak. But it hadn't been there when he rowed out. He would have sworn to it.

The shore and lake changed places in his view. Petey was at his back now. Overhead, that awful simian cloud was breaking up. Hal began to row. Twenty seconds was enough to convince him he was rowing for his life. He was only a so-so swimmer, and even a great one would have been put to the test in this suddenly angry water.

Two more boards suddenly shrank apart with that pistol-shot sound. More water poured into the boat, dousing his shoes. There were tiny metallic snapping sounds that he realized were nails breaking. One of the oarlocks snapped and flew off into the water—would the swivel itself go next?

The wind now came from his back, as if trying to slow him down or even drive him into the middle of the lake. He was terrified, but he felt a crazy kind of exhilaration through the terror. The monkey was gone for good this time. He knew it somehow. Whatever happened to him, the monkey would not be back to draw a shadow over Dennis's life or Petey's. The monkey was gone, perhaps resting on the roof or the hood of Amos Culligan's Studebaker at the bottom of Crystal Lake. Gone for good.

He rowed, bending forward and rocking back. That cracking, crimping sound came again, and now the rusty Crisco can that had been lying in the bow of the boat was floating in three inches of water. Spray blew in Hal's face. There was a louder snapping sound, and the bow seat fell in two pieces and floated next to the bait box. A board tore off the left side of the boat, and then another, this one at the waterline, tore off at the right. Hal rowed. Breath rasped in his mouth, hot and dry, and then his throat swelled with the coppery taste of exhaustion. His sweaty hair flew.

Now a crack zipped directly up the bottom of the rowboat, zigzagged between his feet, and ran up to the bow. Water gushed in; he was in water up to his ankles, then to the swell of calf. He rowed, but the boat's shoreward movement was sludgy now. He didn't dare look behind him to see how close he was getting.

Another board tore loose. The crack running up the center of the boat grew branches, like a tree. Water flooded in.

Hal began to make the oars sprint, breathing in great failing gasps. He pulled once . . . twice . . . and on the third pull both oar swivels snapped off. He lost one oar, held on to the other. He rose to his feet and began to flail at the water with it. The boat rocked, almost capsized, and spilled him back onto his seat with a thump.

Moments later more boards tore loose, the seat collapsed, and he was lying in the water which filled the bottom of the boat, astounded at its coldness. He tried to get on his knees, desperately thinking: *Petey must not see this, must not see his father drown right in front of his eyes, you're going to swim, dog-paddle if you have to, but do, do something—*

There was another splintering crack—almost a crash—and he was in the water, swimming for the shore as he never had swum in his life . . . and the shore was amazingly close. A minute later he was standing waist-deep in water, not five yards from the beach.

Petey splashed toward him, arms out, screaming and crying and laughing. Hal started toward him and floundered. Petey, chest-deep, floundered.

They caught each other.

Hal, breathing in great winded gasps, nevertheless hoisted the boy into his arms and carried him up to the beach, where both of them sprawled, panting.

"Daddy? Is it gone? That nastybad monkey?"

"Yes. I think it's gone. For good this time."

"The boat fell apart. It just . . . fell apart all around you."

Hal looked at the boards floating loose on the water forty feet out. They bore no resemblance to the tight handmade rowboat he had pulled out of the boathouse.

"It's all right now," Hal said, leaning back on his elbows. He shut his eyes and let the sun warm his face.

"Did you see the cloud?" Petey whispered.

"Yes. But I don't see it now . . . do you?"

They looked at the sky. There were scattered white puffs here and there, but no large dark cloud. It was gone, as he had said.

Hal pulled Petey to his feet. "There'll be towels up at the house. Come on." But he paused, looking at his son. "You were crazy, running out there like that."

Petey looked at him solemnly. "You were brave, Daddy."

"Was I?" The thought of bravery had never crossed his mind. Only his fear. The fear had been too big to see anything else. If anything else had indeed been there. "Come on, Pete."

"What are we going to tell Mom?"

Hal smiled. "I dunno, big guy. We'll think of something."

He paused a moment longer, looking at the boards floating on the water. The lake was calm again, sparkling with small wavelets. Suddenly Hal thought of summer people he didn't even know—a man and his son, perhaps, fishing for the big one. *I've got something, Dad!* the boy screams. *Well reel it up and let's see,* the father says, and coming up from the depths, weeds draggling from its cymbals, grinning its terrible, welcoming grin . . . the monkey.

He shuddered—but those were only things that might be.

"Come on," he said to Petey again, and they walked up the path through the flaming October woods toward the home place.

From The Bridgton News
October 24, 1980

MYSTERY OF THE DEAD FISH
By Betsy Moriarty

HUNDREDS of dead fish were found floating belly-up on Crystal Lake in the neighboring township of Casco late last week. The largest numbers appeared to have died in the vicinity of Hunter's Point, although the lake's currents make this a bit difficult to determine. The dead fish included all types commonly found in these waters— bluegills, pickerel, sunnies, carp, hornpout, brown and rainbow trout, even one landlocked salmon. Fish and Game authorities say they are mystified . . .

Cain Rose Up

Garrish walked out of the bright May sunshine and into the coolness of the dorm. It took his eyes a moment to adjust, and at first Harry the Beaver was just a bodiless voice from the shadows.

"It was a bitch, wasn't it?" the Beaver asked. "Wasn't that one a really truly bitch?"

"Yes," Garrish said. "It was tough."

Now his eyes pulled in the Beaver. He was rubbing a hand across the pimples on his forehead and sweating under his eyes. He was wearing sandals and a 69 T-shirt with a button on the front that said Howdy Doody was a pervert. The Beaver's huge buck teeth loomed in the gloom.

"I was gonna drop it in January," the Beaver said. "I kept telling myself to do it while there was still time. And then add-drop was over and it was either go for it or pick up an incomplete. I think I flunked it, Curt. Honest to God."

The housemother stood in the corner by the mailboxes. She was an extremely tall woman who looked vaguely like Rudolph Valentino. She was trying to push a slip strap back under the sweaty armhole of her dress with one hand while she tacked up a dorm sign-out sheet with the other.

"Tough," Garrish repeated.

"I wanted to bag a few off you but I didn't dare, honest to

199

God, that guy's got eyes like an eagle. You think you got your A all right?"

"I guess maybe I flunked," Garrish said.

The Beaver gaped. "You think you *flunked? You* think you—"

"I'm going to take a shower, okay?"

"Yeah, sure, Curt. Sure. Was that your last test?"

"Yes," Garrish said. "That was my last test."

Garrish crossed the lobby and pushed through the doors and began to climb. The stairwell smelled like an athletic supporter. Same old stairs. His room was on the fifth floor.

Quinn and that other idiot from three, the one with the hairy legs, piled by him, tossing a softball back and forth. A little fella wearing horn-rimmed glasses and a valiantly struggling goatee passed him between four and five, holding a calculus book to his chest like a Bible, his lips moving in a rosary of logarithms. His eyes were blank as blackboards.

Garrish paused and looked after him, wondering if he wouldn't be better off dead, but the little fella was now only a bobbing, disappearing shadow on the wall. It bobbed once more and was gone. Garrish climbed to five and walked down the hall to his room. Pig Pen had left two days ago. Four finals in three days, wham-bam and thank-ya-ma'am. Pig Pen knew how to arrange things. He had left only his pinups, two dirty mismatched sweatsocks, and a ceramic parody of Rodin's *Thinker* perched on a toilet seat.

Garrish put his key in the lock and turned it.

"Curt! Hey, Curt!"

Rollins, the asinine floor-counselor who had sent Jimmy Brody up to visit the Dean of Men for a drinking offense, was coming down the hall and waving at him. He was tall, well-built, crewcut, symmetrical. He looked varnished.

"You all done?" Rollins asked.

"Yeah."

"Don't forget to sweep the floor of the room and fill out the damage report, okay?"

"Yeah."

"I slid a damage report under your door last Thursday, didn't I?"

"Yeah."

"If I'm not in my room, just slide the damage report and the key under the door."

"Okay."

Rollins seized his hand and shook it twice, fast, pumppump. Rollins's palm was dry, the skin grainy. Shaking hands with Rollins was like shaking hands with a fistful of salt.

"Have yourself a good summer, m'man."

"Right."

"Don't work too hard."

"No."

"Use it, but don't abuse it."

"I will and I won't."

Rollins looked momentarily puzzled and then he laughed. "Take care, now." He slapped Garrish's shoulder and then walked back down the hall, pausing once to tell Ron Frane to turn down his stereo. Garrish could see Rollins lying dead in a ditch with maggots in his eyes. Rollins wouldn't care. Neither would the maggots. You either ate the world or the world ate you and it was okay either way.

Garrish stood thoughtfully, watching until Rollins was out of sight, and then he let himself into his room.

With Pig Pen's cyclonic clutter gone it looked barren and sterile. The swirled, heaped, drifted pile that had been Pig Pen's bed was stripped down to the bare—if slightly come-stained—mattress pad. Two *Playboy* gatefolds looked down at him with frozen two-dimensional come-ons.

Not much change in Garrish's half of the room, which had always been barracks-neat. You could drop a quarter on the top blanket of Garrish's bed and it would bounce. All that neat had gotten on Piggy's nerves. He was an English major with a fine turn of phrase. He called Garrish a pigeonholer. The only thing on the wall above Garrish's bed was a huge blow-up of Humphrey Bogart that he had gotten in the college bookstore. Bogie had an automatic pistol in each hand and he was wearing suspenders. Pig Pen said pistols and braces were impotency symbols. Garrish doubted if Bogie had been impotent, although he had never read anything about him.

He went to the closet door, unlocked it, and brought out the big walnut-stocked .352 Magnum that his father, a Methodist minister, had bought him for Christmas. He had bought the telescopic sight himself last March.

You weren't supposed to have guns in your room, not even hunting rifles, but it hadn't been hard. He had signed it out of the university gun storage room the day before with a forged withdrawal slip. He put it in its waterproof leather scabbard, and left it in the woods behind the football field. Then, this morning around three A.M., he just went out and got it and brought it upstairs through the sleeping corridors.

He sat down on the bed with the gun across his knees and wept a little bit. The *Thinker* on the toilet seat was looking at him. Garrish put the gun on his bed, crossed the room, and slapped it off Piggy's table and onto the floor, where it shattered. There was a knock at the door.

Garrish put the rifle under his bed. "Come in."

It was Bailey, standing there in his skivvies. There was a puff of lint in his bellybutton. There was no future for Bailey. Bailey would marry a stupid girl and they would have stupid kids. Later on he would die of cancer or maybe renal failure.

"How was the chem final, Curt?"

"All right."

"I just wondered if I could borrow your notes. I've got it tomorrow."

"I burned them with my trash this morning."

"Oh. Hey, Jesus! Did Piggy go and do that?" He pointed at the remains of the *Thinker*.

"I guess so."

"Why did he want to go and do that? I liked that thing. I was going to buy it off him." Bailey had sharp, ratty little features. His skivvies were thready and saggy-seated. Garrish could see exactly how he would look, dying of emphysema or something in an oxygen tent. How he would look yellow. I could help you, Garrish thought.

"You think he'd mind if I scoffed up those pinups?"

"I guess not."

"Okay." Bailey crossed the room, stepping his bare feet gingerly over the pottery shards, and untacked the Playmates. "That picture of Bogart is really sharp, too. No tits, but, hey! You know?" Bailey peered at Garrish to see if Garrish would smile. When Garrish did not, he said, "I don't suppose you planned on throwing it away, or anything?"

"No. I was just getting ready to take a shower."

"Okay. Have a good summer if I don't see you again, Curt."

"Thanks."

Bailey went back to the door, the seat of his skivvies

flapping. He paused at the door. "Another four-point this semester, Curt?"

"At least."

"Good deal. See you next year."

He went out and closed the door. Garrish sat on the bed for a little while, then took the gun out, stripped it, and cleaned it. He put the muzzle up to his eye and looked at the tiny circle of light at the far end. The barrel was clean. He reintegrated the gun.

In the third drawer of his bureau were three heavy boxes of Winchester ammunition. He laid these on the windowsill. He locked the room's door and went back to the window. He pulled the blinds up.

The mall was bright and green, peppered with strolling students. Quinn and his idiot friend had gotten up a raggle-taggle softball game. They scurried back and forth like crippled ants escaping a broken burrow.

"Let me tell you something," Garrish told Bogie. "God got mad at Cain because Cain had an idea God was a vegetarian. His brother knew better. God made the world in His image, and if you don't eat the world, the world eats you. So Cain says to his brother, 'Why didn't you tell me?' And his brother says, 'Why didn't you listen?' And Cain says, 'Okay, I'm listening now.' So he waxes his brother and says, 'Hey God! You want meat? Here it is! You want roast or ribs or Abelburgers or what?' And God told him to put on his boogie shoes. So . . . what do you think?"

No reply from Bogie.

Garrish put the window up and rested his elbows on the ledge, not letting the barrel of the .352 project out into the sunlight. He looked into the sight.

He was centered on Carlton Memorial women's dormitory across the mall. Carlton was more popularly known as the dog kennels. He put the crosshairs on a big Ford wagon. A blond coed in jeans and a blue shell top was talking to her mother while her father, red-faced and balding, loaded suitcases into the back.

Someone knocked on the door.

Garrish waited.

The knock came again.

"Curt? I'll give you half a rock for the Bogart poster."

Bailey.

Garrish said nothing. The girl and her mother were laughing at something, not knowing there were microbes in their intestines, feeding, dividing, multiplying. The girl's father joined them and they stood in the sunlight together, a family portrait in the crosshairs.

"Damn it all," Bailey said. His feet padded down the hall.

Garrish squeezed the trigger.

The gun kicked hard against his shoulder, the good, padded kick you get when you have seated the gun in exactly the right place. The smiling girl's blond head sheared itself away.

Her mother went on smiling for a moment, and then her hand went to her mouth. She screamed through her hand. Garrish shot through it. Hand and head disappeared in a red spray. The man who had been loading the suitcases broke into a lumbering run.

Garrish tracked him and shot him in the back. He raised his head, looking out of the sight for a moment. Quinn was holding the softball and looking at the blond girl's brains, which were splattered on the NO PARKING sign behind her prone body. Quinn didn't move. All across the mall people stood frozen, like children engaged in a game of statues.

Somebody pounded on the door, then rattled the handle. Bailey again. "Curt? You all right, Curt? I think somebody's—"

"Good drink, good meat, good God, let's eat!" Garrish exclaimed, and shot at Quinn. He pulled instead of squeezing and the shot went wide. Quinn was running. No problem. The second shot took Quinn in the neck and he flew maybe twenty feet.

"Curt Garrish is killing himself!" Bailey was screaming. "Rollins! Rollins! Come quick!"

His footsteps faded down the hall.

Now they were starting to run. Garrish could hear them screaming. Garrish could hear the faint smack-smack sound of their shoes on the walks.

He looked up at Bogie. Bogie held his two guns and looked beyond him. He looked at the shattered remnants of Piggy's *Thinker* and wondered what Piggy was doing today, if he was sleeping or watching TV or eating some great big wonderful meal. Eat the world, Piggy, Garrish thought. You gulp that sucker right down.

"Garrish!" It was Rollins now, pounding on the door. "Open up, Garrish!"

"It's locked," Bailey panted. "He looked lousy, he killed himself, I know it."

Garrish pushed the muzzle out of the window again. A boy in a madras shirt was crouched down behind a bush, scanning the dormitory windows with desperate intensity. He wanted to run for it, Garrish saw, but his legs were frozen.

"Good God, let's eat," Garrish murmured, and began to pull the trigger again.

Mrs. Todd's Shortcut

"**T**here goes the Todd woman," I said.

Homer Buckland watched the little Jaguar go by and nodded. The woman raised her hand to Homer. Homer nodded his big, shaggy head to her but didn't raise his own hand in return. The Todd family had a big summer home on Castle Lake, and Homer had been their caretaker since time out of mind. I had an idea that he disliked Worth Todd's second wife every bit as much as he'd liked 'Phelia Todd, the first one.

This was just about two years ago and we were sitting on a bench in front of Bell's Market, me with an orange soda-pop, Homer with a glass of mineral water. It was October, which is a peaceful time in Castle Rock. Lots of the lake places still get used on the weekends, but the aggressive, boozy summer socializing is over by then and the hunters with their big guns and their expensive nonresident permits pinned to their orange caps haven't started to come into town yet. Crops have been mostly laid by. Nights are cool, good for sleeping, and old joints like mine haven't yet started to complain. In October the sky over the lake is passing fair, with those big white clouds that move so slow; I like how they seem so flat on the bottoms, and how they are a little gray there, like with a shadow of sundown foretold, and I can watch the sun sparkle on the water and not be bored for some space of minutes. It's in October, sitting on the bench in front of Bell's and watching the lake from afar off, that I still wish I was a smoking man.

"She don't drive as fast as 'Phelia," Homer said. "I swan I used to think what an old-fashion name she had for a woman that could put a car through its paces like she could."

Summer people like the Todds are nowhere near as interesting to the year-round residents of small Maine towns as they themselves believe. Year-round folk prefer their own love stories and hate stories and scandals and rumors of scandal. When that textile fellow from Amesbury shot himself, Estonia Corbridge found that after a week or so she couldn't even get invited to lunch on her story of how she found him with the pistol still in one stiffening hand. But folks are still not done talking about Joe Camber, who got killed by his own dog.

Well, it don't matter. It's just that they are different racecourses we run on. Summer people are trotters; us others that don't put on ties to do our week's work are just pacers. Even so there was quite a lot of local interest when Ophelia Todd disappeared back in 1973. Ophelia was a genuinely nice woman, and she had done a lot of things in town. She worked to raise money for the Sloan Library, helped to refurbish the war memorial, and that sort of thing. But *all* the summer people like the idea of raising money. You mention raising money and their eyes light up and commence to gleam. You mention raising money and they can get a committee together and appoint a secretary and keep an agenda. They like that. But you mention *time* (beyond, that is, one big long walloper of a combined cocktail party and committee meeting) and you're out of luck. Time seems to be what summer people mostly set a store by. They lay it by, and if they could put it up in Ball jars like preserves, why, they would. But 'Phelia Todd seemed willing to *spend* time—to do desk duty in the library as well as to raise money for it. When it got down to using scouring pads and elbow grease on the war memorial, 'Phelia was right out there with town women who had lost sons in three different wars, wearing an overall with her hair done up in a kerchief. And when kids needed ferrying to a summer swim program, you'd be as apt to see her as anyone headed down Landing Road with the back of Worth Todd's big shiny pickup full of kids. A good woman. Not a town woman, but a good woman. And when she disappeared, there was concern. Not grieving, exactly, because a disappearance is not exactly like a death. It's not like chopping something off with a cleaver; more like something running down the sink so slow you don't know it's all gone until long after it is.

" 'Twas a Mercedes she drove," Homer said, answering the question I hadn't asked. "Two-seater sportster. Todd got it for her in sixty-four or sixty-five, I guess. You remember her taking the kids to the lake all those years they had Frogs and Tadpoles?"

"Ayuh."

"She'd drive 'em no more than forty, mindful they was in the back. But it chafed her. That woman had lead in her foot and a ball bearing sommers in the back of her ankle."

It used to be that Homer never talked about his summer people. But then his wife died. Five years ago it was. She was plowing a grade and the tractor tipped over on her and Homer was taken bad off about it. He grieved for two years or so and then seemed to feel better. But he was not the same. He seemed waiting for something to happen, waiting for the next thing. You'd pass his neat little house sometimes at dusk and he would be on the porch smoking a pipe with a glass of mineral water on the porch rail and the sunset would be in his eyes and pipe smoke around his head and you'd think—I did, anyway—*Homer is waiting for the next thing*. This bothered me over a wider range of my mind than I liked to admit, and at last I decided it was because if it had been me, I wouldn't have been waiting for the next thing, like a groom who has put on his morning coat and finally has his tie right and is only sitting there on a bed in the upstairs of his house and looking first at himself in the mirror and then at the clock on the mantel and waiting for it to be eleven o'clock so he can get married. If it had been me, I would not have been waiting for the next thing; I would have been waiting for the last thing.

But in that waiting period—which ended when Homer went to Vermont a year later—he sometimes talked about those people. To me, to a few others.

"She never even drove fast with her husband, s'far as I know. But when I drove with her, she made that Mercedes strut."

A fellow pulled in at the pumps and began to fill up his car. The car had a Massachusetts plate.

"It wasn't one of these new sports cars that run on onleaded gasoline and hitch every time you step on it; it was one of the old ones, and the speedometer was calibrated all the way up to a hundred and sixty. It was a funny color of brown and I ast her one time what you called that color and she said it was Champagne. Ain't that *good*, I says, and she laughs fit to split. I like a woman who will laugh when you don't have to point her right at the joke, you know."

The man at the pumps had finished getting his gas.

"Afternoon, gentlemen," he says as he comes up the steps.

"A good day to you," I says, and he went inside.

" 'Phelia was always lookin for a shortcut," Homer went on as if we had never been interrupted. "That woman was mad for a shortcut. I never saw the beat of it. She said if you can save enough distance, you'll save time as well. She said her father swore by that scripture. He was a salesman, always on the road, and she went with him when she could, and he was always lookin for the shortest way. So she got in the habit.

"I ast her one time if it wasn't kinda funny—here she was on the one hand, spendin her time rubbin up that old statue in the Square and takin the little ones to their swimmin lessons instead of playing tennis and swimming and getting boozed up like normal summer people, and on the other hand bein so damn set on savin fifteen minutes between here and Fryeburg that thinkin about it probably kep her up nights. It just seemed to me the two things went against each other's grain, if you see what I mean. She just looks at me and says, 'I like being helpful, Homer. I like driving, too—at least sometimes, when it's a challenge—but I don't like the *time* it takes. It's like mending clothes—sometimes you take tucks and sometimes you let things out. Do you see what I mean?'

" 'I guess so, missus,' I says, kinda dubious.

" 'If sitting behind the wheel of a car was my idea of a really good time *all* the time, I would look for long-cuts,' she says, and that tickled me s'much I had to laugh."

The Massachusetts fellow came out of the store with a six-pack in one hand and some lottery tickets in the other.

"You enjoy your weekend," Homer says.

"I always do," the Massachusetts fellow says. "I only wish I could afford to live here all year round."

"Well, we'll keep it all in good order for when you *can* come," Homer says, and the fellow laughs.

We watched him drive off toward someplace, that Massachusetts plate showing. It was a green one. My Marcy says those are the ones the Massachusetts Motor Registry gives to drivers who ain't had a accident in that strange, angry, fuming state for two years. If you have, she says, you got to have a red one so people know to watch out for you when they see you on the roll.

"They was in-state people, you know, the both of them," Homer said, as if the Massachusetts fellow had reminded him of the fact.

"I guess I did know that," I said.

"The Todds are just about the only birds we got that fly north in the winter. The new one, I don't think she likes flying north too much."

He sipped his mineral water and fell silent a moment, thinking.

"*She* didn't mind it, though," Homer said. "At least, I *judge* she didn't although she used to complain about it something fierce. The complaining was just a way to explain why she was always lookin' for a shortcut."

"And you mean her husband didn't mind her traipsing down every wood-road in tarnation between here and Bangor just so she could see if it was nine-tenths of a mile shorter?"

"He didn't care piss-all," Homer said shortly, and got up, and went in the store. There now, Owens, I told myself, you know it ain't safe to ast him questions when he's yarning, and you went right ahead and ast one, and you have buggered a story that was starting to shape up promising.

I sat there and turned my face up into the sun and after about ten minutes he come out with a boiled egg and sat down. He ate her and I took care not to say nothing and the water on Castle Lake sparkled as blue as something as might be told of in a story about treasure. When Homer had finished his egg and had a sip of mineral water, he went on. I was surprised, but still said nothing. It wouldn't have been wise.

"They had two or three different chunks of rolling iron," he said. "There was the Cadillac, and his truck, and her little Mercedes go-devil. A couple of winters he left the truck, 'case they wanted to come down and do some skiin. Mostly when the summer was over he'd drive the Caddy back up and she'd take her go-devil.''

I nodded but didn't speak. In truth, I was afraid to risk another comment. Later I thought it would have taken a lot of comments to shut Homer Buckland up that day. He had been wanting to tell the story of Mrs. Todd's shortcut for a long time.

''Her little go-devil had a special odometer in it that told you how many miles was in a trip, and every time she set off from Castle Lake to Bangor she'd set it to 000-point-0 and let her clock up to whatever. She had made a game of it, and she used to chafe me with it.''

He paused, thinking that back over.

''No, that ain't right.''

He paused more and faint lines showed up on his forehead like steps on a library ladder.

''She *made* like she made a game of it, but it was a serious business to her. Serious as anything else, anyway.'' He flapped a hand and I think he meant the husband. ''The glovebox of the little go-devil was filled with maps, and there was a few more in the back where there would be a seat in a regular car. Some was gas station maps, and some was pages that had been pulled from the Rand-McNally Road Atlas; she had some maps from Appalachian Trail guidebooks and a whole mess of topographical survey-squares, too. It wasn't her having those maps that made me think it wa'n't a game; it was how she'd drawed lines on all of them, showing routes she'd taken or at least tried to take.

''She'd been stuck a few times, too, and had to get a pull from some farmer with a tractor and chain.

''I was there one day laying tile in the bathroom, sitting there with grout squittering out of every damn crack you could see—I dreamed of nothing but squares and cracks that was bleeding grout that night—and she come stood in the doorway and talked to me about it for quite a while. I used to chafe her about it, but I was also sort of interested, and not just because my brother Franklin used to live down-Bangor and I'd traveled most of the roads she was telling me of. I was interested just because a man like me is always uncommon interested in knowing the shortest way, even if he don't always want to take it. You that way too?''

"Ayuh," I said. There's something powerful about knowing the shortest way, even if you take the longer way because you know your mother-in-law is sitting home. Getting there quick is often for the birds, although no one holding a Massachusetts driver's license seems to know it. But *knowing* how to get there quick—or even knowing how to get there a way that the person sitting beside you don't know . . . that has power.

"Well, she had them roads like a Boy Scout has his knots," Homer said, and smiled his large, sunny grin. "She says, 'Wait a minute, wait a minute,' like a little girl, and I hear her through the wall rummaging through her desk, and then she comes back with a little notebook that looked like she'd had it a good long time. Cover was all rumpled, don't you know, and some of the pages had pulled loose from those little wire rings on one side.

" 'The way Worth goes—the way *most* people go—is Route 97 to Mechanic Falls, then Route 11 to Lewiston, and then the Interstate to Bangor. 156.4 miles.' "

I nodded.

" 'If you want to skip the turnpike—and save some distance—you'd go to Mechanic Falls, Route 11 to Lewiston, Route 202 to Augusta, then up Route 9 through China Lake and Unity and Haven to Bangor. That's 144.9 miles.'

" 'You won't save no time that way, missus,' I says, 'not going through Lewiston *and* Augusta. Although I will admit that drive up the Old Derry Road to Bangor is real pretty.'

" 'Save enough miles and soon enough you'll save time,' she says. 'And I didn't say that's the way I'd go, although I have a good many times; I'm just running down the routes most people use. Do you want me to go on?'

" 'No,' I says, 'just leave me in this cussed bathroom all by myself starin at all these cussed cracks until I start to rave.'

" 'There are four major routes in all,' she says. 'The one by Route 2 is 163.4 miles. I only tried it once. Too long.'

" 'That's the one I'd hosey if my wife called and told me it was leftovers,' I says, kinda low.

" 'What was that?' she says.

" 'Nothin,' I says. 'Talkin to the grout.'

" 'Oh. Well, the fourth—and there aren't too many who know about it, although they are all good roads—paved, anyway—is across Speckled Bird Mountain on 219 to 202 *beyond* Lewiston. Then, if you take Route 19, you can get around Augusta. Then you take the Old Derry Road. That way is just 129.2.'

"I didn't say nothing for a little while and p'raps she thought I was doubting her because she says, a little pert, 'I know it's hard to believe, but it's so.'

"I said I guessed that was about right, and I thought— looking back—it probably was. Because that's the way I'd usually go when I went down to Bangor to see Franklin when he was still alive. I hadn't been that way in years, though. Do you think a man could just—well—forget a road, Dave?''

I allowed it was. The turnpike is easy to think of. After a while it almost fills a man's mind, and you think not how could I get from here to there but how can I get from here to the turnpike ramp that's *closest* to there. And that made me think that maybe there are lots of roads all over that are just going begging; roads with rock walls beside them, real roads with blackberry bushes growing alongside them but nobody to eat the berries but the birds and gravel pits with old rusted chains hanging down in low curves in front of their entryways, the pits themselves as forgotten as a child's old toys with scrumgrass growing up their deserted unremembered sides. Roads that have just been forgot except by the people who live on them and think of the quickest way to get off them and onto the turnpike where you can pass on a hill and not fret over it. We like to joke in Maine that you can't get there from here, but maybe the joke is on us. The truth is there's about a damn thousand ways to do it and man doesn't bother.

Homer continued: "I grouted tile all afternoon in that hot little bathroom and she stood there in the doorway all that time, one foot crossed behind the other, bare-legged, wearin loafers and a khaki-colored skirt and a sweater that was some darker. Hair was drawed back in a hosstail. She must have been thirty-four or -five then, but her face was lit up with what she was tellin me and I swan she looked like a sorority girl home from school on vacation.

"After a while she musta got an idea of how long she'd been there cuttin the air around her mouth because she says, 'I must be boring the hell out of you, Homer.'

" 'Yes'm,' I says, 'you are. I druther you went away and left me to talk to this damn grout.'

" 'Don't be sma'at, Homer,' she says.

" 'No, missus, you ain't borin me,' I says.

"So she smiles and then goes back to it, pagin through her little notebook like a salesman checkin his orders. She had those four main ways—well, really three because she gave up on Route 2 right away—but she must have had forty different other ways that were play-offs on those. Roads with state numbers, roads without, roads with names, roads without. My head fair spun with 'em. And finally she says to me, 'You ready for the blue-ribbon winner, Homer?'

" 'I guess so,' I says.

" 'At least it's the blue-ribbon winner *so far*,' she says. 'Do you know, Homer, that a man wrote an article in *Science Today* in 1923 proving that no man could run a mile in under four minutes? He *proved* it, with all sorts of calculations based on the maximum length of the male thigh-muscles, maximum length of stride, maximum lung capacity, maximum heart-rate, and a whole lot more. I was *taken* with that article! I was so taken that I gave it to Worth and asked him to give it to Professor Murray in the math department at the University of Maine. I wanted those figures checked because I was sure they must have been based on the wrong postulates, or something. Worth probably thought I was being silly—"Ophelia's got a bee in her bonnet" is what he says—but he took them. Well, Professor Murray checked through the man's figures quite carefully . . . and do you know *what*, Homer?'

" 'No, missus.'

" 'Those figures were *right*. The man's criteria were *solid*. He proved, back in 1923, that a man couldn't run a mile in under four minutes. He *proved* that. But people do it all the time, and do you know what that means?'

" 'No, missus,' I said, although I had a glimmer.

" 'It means that no blue ribbon is forever,' she says. 'Someday—if the world doesn't explode itself in the meantime—someone will run a *two*-minute mile in the Olympics. It may take a hundred years or a thousand, but it will happen. Because there is no ultimate blue ribbon. There is zero, and there is eternity, and there is mortality, but there is no *ultimate*.'

"And there she stood, her face clean and scrubbed and

shinin, that darkish hair of hers pulled back from her brow, as if to say 'Just you go ahead and disagree if you can.' But I couldn't. Because I believe something like that. It is much like what the minister means, I think, when he talks about grace.

" 'You ready for the blue-ribbon winner *for now?*' she says.

" 'Ayuh,' I says, and I even stopped groutin for the time bein. I'd reached the tub anyway and there wasn't nothing left but a lot of those frikkin squirrelly little corners. She drawed a deep breath and then spieled it out at me as fast as that auctioneer goes over in Gates Falls when he has been putting the whiskey to himself, and I can't remember it all, but it went something like this."

Homer Buckland shut his eyes for a moment, his big hands lying perfectly still on his long thighs, his face turned up toward the sun. Then he opened his eyes again and for a moment I swan he *looked* like her, yes he did, a seventy-year-old man looking like a woman of thirty-four who was at that moment in her time looking like a college girl of twenty, and I can't remember exactly what *he* said any more than *he* could remember exactly what *she* said, not just because it was complex but because I was so fetched by how he looked sayin it, but it went close enough like this:

" 'You set out Route 97 and then cut up Denton Street to the Old Townhouse Road and that way you get around Castle Rock downtown but back to 97. Nine miles up you can go an old logger's road a mile and a half to Town Road #6, which takes you to Big Anderson Road by Sites' Cider Mill. There's a cut-road the old-timers call Bear Road, and that gets you to 219. Once you're on the far side of Speckled Bird Mountain you grab the Stanhouse Road, turn left onto the Bull Pine Road—there's a swampy patch there but you can spang right through it if you get up enough speed on the gravel—and so you come out on Route 106. 106 cuts through Alton's Plantation to the Old Derry Road—and there's two or three woods roads there that you follow and so come out on Route 3 just beyond Derry Hospital. From there it's only four miles to Route 2 in Etna, and so into Bangor.'

"She paused to get her breath back, then looked at me. 'Do you know how long that is, all told?'

" 'No'm,' I says, thinking it sounds like about a hundred and ninety miles and four bust springs.

" 'It's 116.4 miles,' she says."

I laughed. The laugh was out of me before I thought I wasn't doing myself any favor if I wanted to hear this story to the end. But Homer grinned himself and nodded.

"I know. And *you* know I don't like to argue with anyone, Dave. But there's a difference between having your leg pulled and getting it shook like a damn apple tree.

" 'You don't believe me,' she says.

" 'Well, it's *hard* to believe, missus,' I said.

" 'Leave that grout to dry and I'll show you,' she says. 'You can finish behind the tub tomorrow. Come on, Homer. I'll leave a note for Worth—he may not be back tonight anyway—and you can call your wife! We'll be sitting down to dinner in the Pilot's Grille in'—she looks at her watch—'two hours and forty-five minutes from right now. And if it's a minute longer, I'll buy you a bottle of Irish Mist to take home with you. You see, my dad was right. Save enough miles and you'll save time, even if you have to go through every damn bog and sump in Kennebec County to do it. Now what do you say?'

"She was lookin at me with her brown eyes just like lamps, there was a devilish look in them that said turn your cap around back'rds, Homer, and climb aboard this hoss, I be first and you be second and let the devil take the hindmost, and there was a grin on her face that said the exact same thing, and I tell you, Dave, I wanted to *go*. I didn't even want to top that damn can of grout. And I *certain* sure didn't want to drive that go-devil of hers. I wanted just to sit in it on the shotgun side and watch her get in, see her skirt come up a little, see her pull it down over her knees or not, watch her hair shine."

He trailed off and suddenly let off a sarcastic, choked laugh. That laugh of his sounded like a shotgun loaded with rock salt.

"Just call up Megan and say, 'You know 'Phelia Todd, that woman you're halfway to being so jealous of now you can't see straight and can't ever find a good word to say about her? Well, her and me is going to make this speed-run down to Bangor in that little champagne-colored go-devil Mercedes of hers, so don't wait dinner.'

"Just call her up and say that. Oh *yes*. Oh *ayuh*."

And he laughed again with his hands lying there on his legs just as natural as ever was and I seen something in his face that was almost hateful and after a minute he took his glass of mineral water from the railing there and got outside some of it.

"You didn't go," I said.

"Not *then*."

He laughed, and this laugh was gentler.

"She must have seen something in my face, because it as like she found herself again. She stopped looking like a sorority girl and just looked like 'Phelia Todd again. She looked down at the notebook like she didn't know what it was she had been holding and put it down by her side, almost behind her skirt.

"I says, 'I'd like to do just that thing, missus, but I got to finish up here, and my wife has got a roast on for dinner.'

"She says, 'I understand, Homer—I just got a little carried away. I do that a lot. All the time, Worth says.' Then she kinda straightened up and says, 'But the offer holds, any time you want to go. You can even throw your shoulder to the back end if we get stuck somewhere. Might save me five dollars.' And she laughed.

" 'I'll take you up on it, missus,' I says, and she seen that I meant what I said and wasn't just being polite.

" 'And before you just go believing that a hundred and sixteen miles to Bangor is out of the question, get out your own map and see how many miles it would be as the crow flies.'

"I finished the tiles and went home and ate leftovers—there wa'n't no roast, and I think 'Phelia Todd knew it—and after Megan was in bed, I got out my yardstick and a pen and my Mobil map of the state, and I did what she had told me . . . because it had laid hold of my mind a bit, you see. I drew a straight line and did out the calculations accordin to the scale of miles. I was some surprised. Because if you went from Castle Rock up there to Bangor like one of those little Piper Cubs could fly on a clear day—if you didn't have to mind lakes, or stretches of lumber company woods that was chained off, or bogs, or crossing rivers where there wasn't no bridges, why, it would just be seventy-nine miles, give or take."

I jumped a little.

"Measure it yourself, if you don't believe me," Homer said. "I never knew Maine was so small until I seen that."

He had himself a drink and then looked around at me.

"There come a time the next spring when Megan was away in New Hampshire visiting with her brother. I had to go down to the Todds' house to take off the storm doors and put on the screens, and her little Mercedes go-devil was there. She was down by herself.

"She come to the door and says: 'Homer! Have you come to put on the screen doors?'

"And right off I says: 'No, missus, I come to see if you want to give me a ride down to Bangor the short way.'

"Well, she looked at me with no expression on her face at all, and I thought she had forgotten all about it. I felt my face gettin red, the way it will when you feel you just pulled one hell of a boner. Then, just when I was getting ready to 'pologize, her face busts into that grin again and she says, 'You just stand right there while I get my keys. And don't change your mind, Homer!'

"She come back a minute later with 'em in her hand. 'If we get stuck, you'll see mosquitoes just about the size of dragonflies.'

" 'I've seen 'em as big as English sparrows up in Rangely, missus,' I said, 'and I guess we're both a spot too heavy to be carried off.'

"She laughs. 'Well, I warned you, anyway. Come on, Homer.'

" 'And if we ain't there in two hours and forty-five minutes,' I says, kinda sly, 'you was gonna buy me a bottle of Irish Mist.'

"She looks at me kinda surprised, the driver's door of the go-devil open and one foot inside. 'Hell, Homer,' she says, 'I told you that was the Blue Ribbon for *then*. I've found a way up there that's *shorter*. We'll be there in two and a half hours. Get in here, Homer. We are going to roll.' "

He paused again, hands lying calm on his thighs, his eyes dulling, perhaps seeing that champagne-colored two-seater heading up the Todds' steep driveway.

"She stood the car still at the end of it and says, 'You sure?'

" 'Let her rip,' I says. The ball bearing in her ankle rolled

and that heavy foot come down. I can't tell you nothing much
about whatall happened after that. Except after a while I
couldn't hardly take my eyes off her. There was somethin
wild that crep into her face, Dave—something *wild* and something *free,* and it frightened my heart. She was beautiful, and
I was took with love *for* her, anyone would have been, any
man, anyway, and maybe any woman too, but I was scairt *of*
her too, because she looked like she could kill you if her eye
left the road and fell on you and she decided to love you
back. She was wearin blue jeans and a old white shirt with
the sleeves rolled up—I had a idea she was maybe fixin to
paint somethin on the back deck when I came by—but after
we had been goin for a while seemed like she was dressed in
nothin but all this white billowy stuff like a pitcher in one of
those old gods-and-goddesses books.''

He thought, looking out across the lake, his face very
somber.

''Like the huntress that was supposed to drive the moon
across the sky.''

''Diana?''

''Ayuh. Moon was her go-devil. 'Phelia looked like that to
me and I just tell you fair out that I was stricken in love for
her and never would have made a move, even though I was
some younger then than I am now. I would not have made a
move even had I been twenty, although I suppose I might of
at sixteen, and been killed for it—killed if she looked at me
was the way it felt.

''She was like that woman drivin the moon across the sky,
halfway up over the splashboard with her gossamer stoles all
flyin out behind her in silver cobwebs and her hair streamin
back to show the dark little hollows of her temples, lashin
those horses and tellin me to get along faster and never mind
how they blowed, just faster, faster, *faster.*

''We went down a lot of woods roads—the first two or
three I knew, and after that I didn't know none of them. We
must have been a sight to those trees that had never seen
nothing with a motor in it before but big old pulp-trucks and
snowmobiles; that little go-devil that would most likely have
looked more at home on the Sunset Boulevard than shooting
through those woods, spitting and bulling its way up one hill
and then slamming down the next through those dusty green
bars of afternoon sunlight—she had the top down and I could

smell everything in those woods, and you know what an old fine smell that is, like something which has been mostly left alone and is not much troubled. We went on across corduroy which had been laid over some of the boggiest parts, and black mud squelched up between some of those cut logs and she laughed like a kid. Some of the logs was old and rotted, because there hadn't been nobody down a couple of those roads—except for her, that is—in I'm going to say five or ten years. We was *alone*, except for the birds and whatever animals seen us. The sound of that go-devil's engine, first buzzin along and then windin up high and fierce when she punched in the clutch and shifted down . . . that was the only motor-sound I could hear. And although I knew we had to be close to *someplace* all the time—I mean, these days you always are—I started to feel like we had gone back in time, and there wasn't *nothing*. That if we stopped and I climbed a high tree, I wouldn't see nothing in any direction but woods and woods and more woods. And all the time she's just *hammering* that thing along, her hair all out behind her, smilin, her eyes flashin. So we come out on the Speckled Bird Mountain Road and for a while I known where we were again, and then she turned off and for just a little bit I *thought* I knew, and then I didn't even bother to kid myself no more. We went cut-slam down another woods road, and then we come out—I swear it—on a nice paved road with a sign that said MOTORWAY B. You ever heard of a road in the state of Maine that was called MOTORWAY B?''

"No," I says. "Sounds English."

"Ayuh. *Looked* English. These trees like willows overhung the road. 'Now watch out here, Homer,' she says, 'one of those nearly grabbed me a month ago and gave me an Indian burn.'

"I didn't know what she was talkin about and started to say so, and then I seen that even though there was no wind, the branches of those trees was dippin down—they was *waverin* down. They looked black and wet inside the fuzz of green on them. I couldn't believe what I was seein. Then one of em snatched off my cap and I knew I wasn't asleep. 'Hi!' I shouts. 'Give that back!'

" 'Too late now, Homer,' she says, and laughs. 'There's daylight, just up ahead . . . we're okay.'

"Then another one of em comes down, on her side this

time, and snatches at her—I swear it did. She ducked, and it caught in her hair and pulled a lock of it out. 'Ouch, dammit that *hurts!*' she yells, but she was laughin, too. The car swerved a little when she ducked and I got a look into the woods and holy God, Dave! *Everythin* in there was movin. There was grasses wavin and plants that was all knotted together so it seemed like they made faces, and I seen somethin sittin in a squat on top of a stump, and it looked like a tree-toad, only it was as big as a full-growed cat.

"Then we come out of the shade to the top of a hill and she says, 'There! That was exciting, wasn't it?' as if she was talkin about no more than a walk through the Haunted House at the Fryeburg Fair.

"About five minutes later we swung onto another of her woods roads. I didn't want no more woods right then—I can tell you that for sure—but these were just plain old woods. Half an hour after that, we was pulling into the parking lot of the Pilot's Grille in Bangor. She points to that little odometer for trips and says, 'Take a gander, Homer.' I did, and it said 111.6. 'What do you think now? Do you believe in my shortcut?'

"That wild look had mostly faded out of her, and she was just 'Phelia Todd again. But that other look wasn't entirely gone. It was like she was two women, 'Phelia and Diana, and the part of her that was Diana was so much in control when she was driving the back roads that the part that was 'Phelia didn't have no idea that her shortcut was taking her through places . . . places that ain't on any map of Maine, not even on those survey-squares.

"She says again, 'What do you think of my shortcut, Homer?'

"And I says the first thing to come into my mind, which ain't something you'd usually say to a lady like 'Phelia Todd. 'It's a real piss-cutter, missus,' I says.

"She laughs, just as pleased as punch, and I seen it then, just as clear as glass: She didn't remember none of the funny stuff. Not the willow-branches—except they weren't willows, not at all, not really anything like em, or anything else—that grabbed off m'hat, not that MOTORWAY B sign, or that awful-lookin toad-thing. *She didn't remember none of that funny stuff!* Either I had dreamed it was there or she had dreamed it wasn't. All I knew for sure, Dave, was that we had rolled only a hundred and eleven miles and gotten to Bangor, and that wasn't no daydream; it was right there on the little go-devil's odometer, in black and white.

" 'Well, it is,' she says. 'It *is* a piss-cutter. I only wish I could get Worth to give it a go sometime . . . but he'll never get out of his rut unless someone blasts him out of it, and it would probably take a Titan II missile to do that, because I believe he has built himself a fallout shelter at the bottom of that rut. Come on in, Homer, and let's dump some dinner into you.'

"And she bought me one hell of a dinner, Dave, but I couldn't eat very much of it. I kep thinkin about what the ride back might be like, now that it was drawing down dark. Then, about halfway through the meal, she excused herself and made a telephone call. When she came back she ast me if I would mind drivin the go-devil back to Castle Rock for her. She said she had talked to some woman who was on the same school committee as her, and the woman said they had some kind of problem about somethin or other. She said she'd grab herself a Hertz car if Worth couldn't see her back down. 'Do you mind awfully driving back in the dark?' she ast me.

"She looked at me, kinda smilin, and I knew she remembered *some* of it all right—Christ knows how much, but she remembered enough to know I wouldn't want to try her way after dark, if ever at all . . . although I seen by the light in her eyes that it wouldn't have bothered her a bit.

"So I said it wouldn't bother me, and I finished my meal better than when I started it. It was drawin down dark by the time we was done, and she run us over to the house of the woman she'd called. And when she gets out she looks at me with that same light in her eyes and says, 'Now, you're *sure* you don't want to wait, Homer? I saw a couple of side roads just today, and although I can't find them on my maps, I think they might chop a few miles.'

"I says, 'Well, missus, I would, but at my age the best bed to sleep in is my own, I've found. I'll take your car back and never put a ding in her . . . although I guess I'll probably put on some more miles than you did.'

"Then she laughed, kind of soft, and she give me a kiss. That was the best kiss I ever had in my whole life, Dave. It was just on the cheek, and it was the chaste kiss of a married woman, but it was as ripe as a peach, or like those flowers that open in the dark, and when her lips touched my skin I felt like . . . I don't know exactly what I felt like, because a man can't easily hold on to those things that happened to him with a girl who was ripe when the world was young or how those things felt—I'm talking around what I mean, but I think you understand. Those things all get a red cast to them in your memory and you cannot see through it at all.

" 'You're a sweet man, Homer, and I love you for listening to me and riding with me,' she says. 'Drive safe.'

"Then in she went, to that woman's house. Me, I drove home."

"How did you go?" I asked.

He laughed softly. "By the turnpike, you damned fool," he said, and I never seen so many wrinkles in his face before as I did then.

He sat there, looking into the sky.

"Came the summer she disappeared. I didn't see much of her . . . that was the summer we had the fire, you'll remember, and then the big storm that knocked down all the trees. A busy time for caretakers. Oh, I *thought* about her from time to time, and about that day, and about that kiss, and it started to seem like a dream to me. Like one time, when I was about sixteen and couldn't think about nothing but girls. I was out plowing George Bascomb's west field, the one that looks acrost the lake at the mountains, dreamin about what teenage boys dream of. And I pulled up this rock with the harrow blades, and it split open, and it *bled*. At least, it looked to me like it bled. Red stuff come runnin out of the cleft in the rock and soaked into the soil. And I never told no one but my mother, and I never told her what it meant to me, or what happened to me, although she washed my drawers and maybe she knew. Anyway, she suggested I ought to pray on it. Which I did, but I never got no enlightenment, and after a while something started to suggest to my mind that it had been a dream. It's that way, sometimes. There is holes in the *middle*, Dave. Do you know that?"

"Yes," I says, thinking of one night when I'd seen something. That was in '59, a bad year for us, but my kids didn't know it was a bad year; all they knew was that they wanted to eat just like always. I'd seen a bunch of whitetail in Henry Brugger's back field, and I was out there after dark with a jacklight in August. You can shoot two when they're summer-fat; the second'll come back and sniff at the first as if to say *What the hell? Is it fall already?* and you can pop him like a bowlin pin. You can hack off enough meat to feed yowwens for six weeks and bury what's left. Those are two whitetails the hunters who come in November don't get a shot at, but kids have to eat. Like the man from Massachusetts said, *he'd* like to be able to afford to live here the year around, and all I can say is sometimes you pay for the privilege after dark. So there I was, and I seen this big orange light in the sky; it come down and down, and I stood and watched it with my mouth hung on down to my breastbone and when it hit the lake the whole of it was lit up for a minute a purple-orange that seemed to go right up to the sky in rays. Wasn't nobody ever said nothing to me about that light, and I never said nothing to nobody myself, partly because I was afraid they'd laugh, but also because they'd wonder what the hell I'd been doing out there after dark to start with. And after a while it was like Homer said— it seemed like a dream I had once had, and it didn't signify to me because I couldn't make nothing of it which would turn under my hand. It was like a moonbeam. It didn't have no handle and it didn't have no blade. I couldn't make it work so I left it alone, like a man does when he knows the day is going to come up nevertheless.

"There are *holes* in the middle of things," Homer said, and he sat up straighter, like he was mad. "Right in the damn *middle* of things, not even to the left or right where your p'riph'ral vision is and you could say 'Well, but hell—' They are there and you go around them like you'd go around a pothole in the road that would break an axle. You know? And you forget it. Or like if you are plowin, you can plow a dip. But if there's somethin like a *break* in the earth, where you see darkness, like a cave might be there, you say 'Go around, old hoss. Leave that alone! I got a good shot over here to the left'ards.' Because it wasn't a cave you was lookin for, or some kind of college excitement, but good plowin.

"*Holes* in the *middle* of things."

He fell still a long time then and I let him be still. Didn't have no urge to move him. And at last he says:

"She disappeared in August. I seen her for the first time in early July, and she looked . . ." Homer turned to me and spoke each word with careful, spaced emphasis. "Dave Owens, she looked *gorgeous!* Gorgeous and wild and almost untamed. The little wrinkles I'd started to notice around her eyes all seemed to be gone. Worth Todd, he was at some conference or something in Boston. And she stands there at the edge of the deck—I was out in the middle with my shirt off—and she says, 'Homer, you'll never believe it.'

" 'No, missus, but I'll try,' I says.

" 'I found two new roads,' she says, 'and I got up to Bangor this last time in just sixty-seven miles.'

"I remembered what she said before and I says, 'That's not possible, missus. Beggin your pardon, but I did the mileage on the map myself, and seventy-nine is tops . . . as the crow flies.'

"She laughed, and she looked prettier than ever. Like a goddess in the sun, on one of those hills in a story where there's nothing but green grass and fountains and no puckies to tear at a man's forearms at all. 'That's right,' she says, 'and you can't run a mile in under four minutes. It's been mathematically *proved*.'

" 'It ain't the same,' I says.

" 'It's the same,' she says. 'Fold the map and see how many miles it is then, Homer. It can be a little less than a straight line if you fold it a little, or it can be a lot less if you fold it a lot.'

"I remembered our ride then, the way you remember a dream, and I says, 'Missus, you can fold a map on paper but you can't fold *land*. Or at least you shouldn't ought to try. You want to leave it alone.'

" 'No sir,' she says. 'It's the one thing right now in my life that I won't leave alone, because it's *there*, and it's *mine*.'

"Three weeks later—this would be about two weeks before she disappeared—she give me a call from Bangor. She says, 'Worth has gone to New York, and I am coming down. I've misplaced my damn key, Homer. I'd like you to open the house so I can get in.'

"Well, that call come at eight o'clock, just when it was starting to come down dark. I had a sanwidge and a beer before leaving—about twenty minutes. Then I took a ride down there. All in all, I'd say I was forty-five minutes. When I got down there to the Todds', I seen there was a light on in the pantry I didn't leave on while I was comin down the driveway. I was lookin at that, and I almost run right into her little go-devil. It was parked kind of on a slant, the way a drunk would park it, and it was splashed with muck all the way up to the windows, and there was this stuff stuck in that mud along the body that looked like seaweed . . . only when my lights hit it, it seemed to be *movin*. I parked behind it and got out of my truck. That stuff wasn't seaweed, but it *was* weeds, and it *was* movin . . . kinda slow and sluggish, like it was dyin. I touched a piece of it, and it tried to wrap itself around my hand. It felt nasty and awful. I drug my hand away and wiped it on my pants. I went around to the front of the car. It looked like it had come through about ninety miles of splash and low country. Looked *tired*, it did. Bugs was splashed all over the windshield—only they didn't look like no kind of bugs *I* ever seen before. There was a moth that was about the size of a sparrow, its wings still flappin a little, feeble and dyin. There was things like mosquitoes, only they had real eyes that you could see—and they seemed to be seein *me*. I could hear those weeds scrapin against the body of the go-devil, dyin, tryin to get a hold on somethin. And all I could think was Where in the hell has she been? And how did she get here in only three-quarters of an hour? Then I seen somethin else. There was some kind of a animal half-smashed onto the radiator grille, just under where that Mercedes ornament is—the one that looks kinda like a star looped up into a circle? Now most small animals you kill on the road is bore right under the car, because they are crouching when it hits them, hoping it'll just go over and leave them with their hide still attached to their meat. But every now and then one will jump, not away, but right at the damn car, as if to get in one good bite of whatever the buggardly thing is that's going to kill it—I have known that to happen. This thing had maybe done that. And it looked mean enough to jump a Sherman tank. It looked like something which come of a mating between a woodchuck and a weasel, but there was other stuff thrown in that a body didn't even want to look at. It hurt your eyes, Dave; worse'n that, it hurt your *mind*. Its pelt was matted with blood, and there was claws sprung out of the pads on its feet like a cat's claws, only longer. It had big yellowy eyes, only they was glazed. When I was a kid I had a porcelain marble—a croaker—that looked like that. And teeth. Long thin needle teeth that looked almost like darning needles, stickin out of its mouth. Some of them was sunk right into that steel grillwork. That's why it was still hanging on; it had hung its *own* self on by the teeth. I looked at it and knowed it had a headful of poison just like a rattlesnake, and it jumped at that go-devil when it saw it was about to be run down, tryin to bite it to death. And I wouldn't be the one to try and yonk it offa there because I had cuts on my hands—hay-cuts—and I thought it would kill me as dead as a stone parker if some of that poison seeped into the cuts.

"I went around to the driver's door and opened it. The inside light come on, and I looked at that special odometer that she set for trips . . . and what I seen there was 31.6.

"I looked at that for a bit, and then I went to the back door. She'd forced the screen and broke the glass by the lock so she could get her hand through and let herself in. There was a note that said: 'Dear Homer—got here a little sooner than I thought I would. Found a shortcut, and it is a dilly! You hadn't come yet so I let myself in like a burglar. Worth is coming day after tomorrow. Can you get the screen fixed and the door reglazed by then? Hope so. Things like that always bother him. If I don't come out to say hello, you'll know I'm asleep. The drive was very tiring, but I was here in no time! Ophelia.'

"*Tirin!* I took another look at that bogey-thing hangin offa the grille of her car, and I thought Yessir, it *must* have been tiring. By God, *yes.*"

He paused again, and cracked a restless knuckle.

"I seen her only once more. About a week later. Worth was there, but he was swimmin out in the lake, back and forth, back and forth, like he was sawin wood or signin papers. More like he was signin papers, I guess.

" 'Missus,' I says, 'this ain't my business, but you ought to leave well enough alone. That night you come back and broke the glass of the door to come in, I seen somethin hangin off the front of your car—'

" 'Oh, the chuck! I took care of that,' she says.

" 'Christ!' I says. 'I hope you took some care!'

" 'I wore Worth's gardening gloves,' she said. 'It wasn't anything anyway, Homer, but a jumped-up woodchuck with a little poison in it.'

" 'But missus,' I says, 'where there's woodchucks there's bears. And if that's what the woodchucks look like along your shortcut, what's going to happen to you if a bear shows up?'

"She looked at me, and I seen that other woman in her—that Diana-woman. She says, 'If things are different along those roads, Homer, maybe I am different, too. Look at this.'

"Her hair was done up in a clip at the back, looked sort of like a butterfly and had a stick through it. She let it down. It was the kind of hair that would make a man wonder what it would look like spread out over a pillow. She says, 'It was coming in gray, Homer. Do you see any gray?' And she spread it with her fingers so the sun could shine on it.

" 'No'm,' I says.

"She looks at me, her eyes all a-sparkle, and she says, 'Your wife is a good woman, Homer Buckland, but she has seen me in the store and in the post office, and we've passed the odd word or two, and I have seen her looking at my hair in a kind of satisfied way that only women know. I know what she says, and what she tells her friends . . . that Ophelia Todd has started dyeing her hair. But I have not. I have lost my way looking for a shortcut more than once . . . lost my way . . . and lost my gray.' And she laughed, not like a college girl but like a girl in high school. I admired her and longed for her beauty, but I seen that other beauty in her face as well just then . . . and I felt afraid again. Afraid *for* her, and afraid *of* her.

" 'Missus,' I says, 'you stand to lose more than a little sta'ch in your hair.'

" 'No,' she says. 'I tell you I am different over there . . . I am *all myself* over there. When I am going along that road in my little car I am not Ophelia Todd, Worth Todd's wife who could never carry a child to term, or that woman who tried to write poetry and failed at it, or the woman who sits and takes notes in committee meetings, or anything or anyone else. When I am on that road I am in the heart of myself, and I feel like—'

" *'Diana,'* I said.

"She looked at me kind of funny and kind of surprised, and then she laughed. 'O like some goddess, I suppose,' she said. 'She will do better than most because I am a night person—I love to stay up until my book is done or until the National Anthem comes on the TV, and because I am very pale, like the moon—Worth is always saying I need a tonic, or blood tests or some sort of similar bosh. But in her heart what every woman wants to be is some kind of goddess, I think—men pick up a ruined echo of that thought and try to put them on pedestals (a woman, who will pee down her own leg if she does not squat! it's funny when you stop to think of it)—but what a man senses is not what a woman wants. A woman wants to be in the clear, is all. To stand if she will, or walk . . .' Her eyes turned toward that little go-devil in the driveway, and narrowed. Then she smiled. 'Or to *drive*, Homer. A man will not see that. He thinks a goddess wants to loll on a slope somewhere on the foothills of Olympus and eat fruit, but there is no god or goddess in that. All a woman wants is what a man wants—a woman wants to *drive*.'

" 'Be careful where you drive, missus, is all,' I says, and she laughs and give me a kiss spang in the middle of the forehead.

"She says, 'I will, Homer,' but it didn't mean nothing, and I known it, because she said it like a man who says he'll be careful to his wife or his girl when he knows he won't . . . can't.

"I went back to my truck and waved to her once, and it was a week later that Worth reported her missing. Her and that go-devil both. Todd waited seven years and had her declared legally dead, and then he waited another year for good measure—I'll give the sucker that much—and then he married the second Missus Todd, the one that just went by. And I don't expect you'll believe a single damn word of the whole yarn."

In the sky one of those big flat-bottomed clouds moved enough to disclose the ghost of the moon—half-full and pale as milk. And something in my heart leaped up at the sight, half in fright, half in love.

"I do though," I said. "Every frigging damned word. And even if it ain't true, Homer, it ought to be."

He give me a hug around the neck with his forearm, which is all men can do since the world don't let them kiss but only women, and laughed, and got up.

"Even if it *shouldn't* ought to be, it is," he said. He got his watch out of his pants and looked at it. "I got to go down the road and check on the Scott place. You want to come?"

"I believe I'll sit here for a while," I said, "and think."

He went to the steps, then turned back and looked at me, half-smiling. "I believe she was right," he said. "She *was* different along those roads she found . . . wasn't nothing that would dare touch her. You or me, maybe, but not her.

"And I believe she's young."

Then he got in his truck and set off to check the Scott place.

That was two years ago, and Homer has since gone to Vermont, as I think I told you. One night he come over to see me. His hair was combed, he had a shave, and he smelled of some nice lotion. His face was clear and his eyes were alive. That night he looked sixty instead of seventy, and I was glad for him and I envied him and I hated him a little, too. Arthritis is one buggardly great old fisherman, and that night Homer didn't look like arthritis had any fishhooks sunk into his hands the way they were sunk into mine.

"I'm going," he said.

"Ayuh?"

"Ayuh."

"All right; did you see to forwarding your mail?"

"Don't want none forwarded," he said. "My bills are paid. I am going to make a clean break."

"Well, give me your address. I'll drop you a line from one time to the another, old hoss." Already I could feel loneliness settling over me like a cloak . . . and looking at him, I knew that things were not quite what they seemed.

"Don't have none yet," he said.

"All right," I said. *"Is* it Vermont, Homer?"

"Well," he said, "it'll do for people who want to know."

I almost didn't say it and then I did. "What does she look like now?"

"Like Diana," he said. "But she is kinder."

"I envy you, Homer," I said, and I did.

I stood at the door. It was twilight in that deep part of summer when the fields fill with perfume and Queen Anne's Lace. A full moon was beating a silver track across the lake. He went across my porch and down the steps. A car was standing on the soft shoulder of the road, its engine idling heavy, the way the old ones do that still run full bore straight ahead and damn the torpedoes. Now that I think of it, that car *looked* like a torpedo. It looked beat up some, but as if it could go the ton without breathin hard. He stopped at the foot of my steps and picked something up—it was his gas can, the big one that holds ten gallons. He went down my walk to the passenger side of the car. She leaned over and opened the door. The inside light came on and just for a moment I saw her, long red hair around her face, her forehead shining like a lamp. Shining like the *moon*. He got in and she drove away. I stood out on my porch and watched the taillights of her little go-devil twinkling red in the dark . . . getting smaller and smaller. They were like embers, then they were like flickerflies, and then they were gone.

Vermont, I tell the folks from town, and Vermont they believe, because it's as far as most of them can see inside their heads. Sometimes I almost believe it myself, mostly when I'm tired and done up. Other times I think about them, though—all this October I have done so, it seems, because October is the time when men think mostly about far places and the roads which might get them there. I sit on the bench in front of Bell's Market and think about Homer Buckland and about the beautiful girl who leaned over to open his door when he come down that path with the full red gasoline can in his right hand—she looked like a girl of no more than sixteen, a girl on her learner's permit, and her beauy *was* terrible, but I believe it would no longer kill the man it turned itself on; for a moment her eyes lit on me, I was not killed, although part of me died at her feet.

Olympus must be a glory to the eyes and the heart, and there are those who crave it and those who find a clear way to it, mayhap, but I know Castle Rock like the back of my hand and I could never leave it for no shortcuts where the roads may go; in October the sky over the lake is no glory but it is passing fair, with those big white clouds that move so slow; I sit here on the bench, and think about 'Phelia Todd and Homer Buckland, and I don't necessarily wish I was where they are . . . but I still wish I was a smoking man.

The Jaunt

"This is the last call for Jaunt-701," the pleasant female voice echoed through the Blue Concourse of New York's Port Authority Terminal. The PAT had not changed much in the last three hundred years or so—it was still grungy and a little frightening. The automated female voice was probably the most pleasant thing about it. "This is Jaunt Service to Whitehead City, Mars," the voice continued. "All ticketed passengers should now be in the Blue Concourse sleep lounge. Make sure your validation papers are in order. Thank you."

The upstairs sleep lounge was not at all grungy. It was wall-to-wall carpeted in oyster gray. The walls were an eggshell white and hung with pleasant nonrepresentational prints. A steady, soothing progression of colors met and swirled on the ceiling. There were one hundred couches in the large room, neatly spaced in rows of ten. Five Jaunt attendants circulated, speaking in low, cheery voices and offering glasses of milk. At one side of the room was the entranceway, flanked by armed guards and another Jaunt attendant who was checking the validation papers of a latecomer, a harried-looking businessman with the New York *World-Times* folded under one arm. Directly opposite, the floor dropped away in a trough about five feet wide and perhaps ten feet long; it passed through a doorless opening and looked a bit like a child's slide.

The Oates family lay side by side on four Jaunt couches near the far end of the room. Mark Oates and his wife, Marilys, flanked the two children.

"Daddy, will you tell me about the Jaunt now?" Ricky asked. "You promised."

"Yeah, Dad, you promised," Patricia added, and giggled shrilly for no good reason.

A businessman with a build like a bull glanced over at them and then went back to the folder of papers he was examining as he lay on his back, his spit-shined shoes neatly together. From everywhere came the low murmur of conversation and the rustle of passengers settling down on the Jaunt couches.

Mark glanced over at Marilys Oates and winked. She winked back, but she was almost as nervous as Patty sounded. *Why not?* Mark thought. First Jaunt for all three of them. He and Marilys had discussed the advantages and drawbacks of moving the whole family for the last six months—since he'd gotten notification from Texaco Water that he was being transferred to Whitehead City. Finally they had decided that all of them would go for the two years Mark would be stationed on Mars. He wondered now, looking at Marilys's pale face, if she was regretting the decision.

He glanced at his watch and saw it was still almost half an hour to Jaunt-time. That was enough time to tell the story . . . and he supposed it would take the kids' minds off their nervousness. Who knew, maybe it would even cool Marilys out a little.

"All right," he said. Ricky and Pat were watching him seriously, his son twelve, his daughter nine. He told himself again that Ricky would be deep in the swamp of puberty and his daughter would likely be developing breasts by the time they got back to earth, and again found it difficult to believe. The kids would be going to the tiny Whitehead Combined School with the hundred-odd engineering and oil-company brats that were there; his son might well be going on a geology field trip to Phobos not so many months distant. It was difficult to believe . . . but true.

Who knows? he thought wryly. *Maybe it'll do something about my Jaunt-jumps, too.*

"So far as we know," he began, "the Jaunt was invented about three hundred and twenty years ago, around the year 1987, by a fellow named Victor Carune. He did it as part of a private research project that was funded by some government money . . . . and eventually the government took it over, of course. In the end it came down to either the government or the oil companies. The reason we don't know the exact date is because Carune was something of an eccentric—"

"You mean he was crazy, Dad?" Ricky asked.

"Eccentric means a little bit crazy, dear," Marilys said, and smiled across the children at Mark. She looked a little less nervous now, he thought.

"Oh."

"Anyway, he'd been experimenting with the process for quite some time before he informed the government of what he had," Mark went on, "and he only told them because he was running out of money and they weren't going to re-fund him."

"Your money cheerfully refunded," Pat said, and giggled shrilly again.

"That's right, honey," Mark said, and ruffled her hair gently. At the far end of the room he saw a door slide noiselessly open and two more attendants came out, dressed in the bright red jumpers of the Jaunt Service, pushing a rolling table. On it was a stainless-steel nozzle attached to a rubber hose; beneath the table's skirts, tastefully hidden, Mark knew there were two bottles of gas; in the net bag hooked to the side were one hundred disposable masks. Mark went on talking, not wanting his people to see the representatives of Lethe until they had to. And, if he was given enough time to tell the whole story, they would welcome the gas-passers with open arms.

Considering the alternative.

"Of course, you know that the Jaunt is teleportation, no more or less," he said. "Sometimes in college chemistry and physics they call it the Carune Process, but it's really teleportation, and it was Carune himself—if you can believe the stories—who named it 'the Jaunt.' He was a science-fiction reader, and there's a story by a man named Alfred Bester, *The Stars My Destination* it's called, and this fellow Bester made up the word 'jaunte' for teleportation in it.

Except in his book, you could Jaunt just by thinking about it, and we can't really do that.''

The attendants were fixing a mask to the steel nozzle and handing it to an elderly woman at the far end of the room. She took it, inhaled once, and fell quiet and limp on her couch. Her skirt had pulled up a little, revealing one slack thigh road-mapped with varicose veins. An attendant considerately readjusted it for her while the other pulled off the used mask and affixed a fresh one. It was a process that made Mark think of the plastic glasses in motel rooms. He wished to God that Patty would cool out a little bit; he had seen children who had to be held down, and sometimes they screamed as the rubber mask covered their faces. It was not an abnormal reaction in a child, he supposed, but it was nasty to watch and he didn't want to see it happen to Patty. About Rick he felt more confident.

"I guess you could say the Jaunt came along at the last possible moment," he resumed. He spoke toward Ricky, but reached across and took his daughter's hand. Her fingers closed over his with an immediate panicky tightness. Her palm was cool and sweating lightly. "The world was running out of oil, and most of what was left belonged to the middle-eastern desert peoples, who were committed to using it as a political weapon. They had formed an oil cartel they called OPEC—"

"What's a cartel, Daddy?" Patty asked.

"Well, a monopoly," Mark said.

"Like a club, honey," Marilys said. "And you could only be in that club if you had lots of oil."

"Oh."

"I don't have time to sketch the whole mess in for you," Mark said. "You'll study some of it in school, but it *was* a mess—let's let it go at that. If you owned a car, you could only drive it two days a week, and gasoline cost fifteen oldbucks a gallon—"

"Gosh," Ricky said, "it only costs four cents or so a gallon now, doesn't it, Dad?"

Mark smiled. "That's why we're going where we're going, Rick. There's enough oil on Mars to last almost eight thousand years, and enough on Venus to last another twenty thousand . . . but oil isn't even that important, anymore. Now what we need most of all is—"

"Water!" Patty cried, and the businessman looked up from his papers and smiled at her for a moment.

"That's right," Mark said. "Because in the years between 1960 and 2030, we poisoned most of ours. The first waterlift from the Martian ice-caps was called—"

"Operation Straw." That was Ricky.

"Yes. 2045 or thereabouts. But long before that, the Jaunt was being used to find sources of clean water here on earth. And now water is our major Martian export . . . the oil's strictly a sideline. But it was important then."

The kids nodded.

"The point is, those things were always there, but we were only able to get it because of the Jaunt. When Carune invented his process, the world was slipping into a new dark age. The winter before, over ten thousand people had frozen to death in the United States alone because there wasn't enough energy to heat them."

"Oh, yuck," Patty said matter-of-factly.

Mark glanced to his right and saw the attendants talking to a timid-looking man, persuading him. At last he took the mask and seemed to fall dead on his couch seconds later. *First-timer*, Mark thought. *You can always tell*.

"For Carune, it started with a pencil . . . some keys . . . a wristwatch . . . then some mice. The mice showed him there was a problem . . ."

Victor Carune came back to his laboratory in a stumbling fever of excitement. He thought he knew now how Morse had felt, and Alexander Graham Bell, and Edison . . . but this was bigger than all of them, and twice he had almost wrecked the truck on the way back from the pet shop in New Paltz, where he had spent his last twenty dollars on nine white mice. What he had left in the world was the ninety-three cents in his right front pocket and the eighteen dollars in his savings account . . . but this did not occur to him. And if it had, it certainly would not have bothered him.

The lab was in a renovated barn at the end of a mile-long dirt road off Route 26. It was making the turn onto this road where he had just missed cracking up his Brat pickup truck for the second time. The gas tank was almost empty and there would be no more for ten days to two weeks, but this did not concern him, either. His mind was in a delirious whirl.

What had happened was not totally unexpected, no. One of the reasons the government had funded him even to the paltry tune of twenty thousand a year was because the unrealized possibility had always been there in the field of particle transmission.

But to have it happen like this . . . suddenly . . . with no warning . . . and powered by less electricity than was needed to run a color TV . . . God! *Christ!*

He brought the Brat to a screech-halt in the dirt of the dooryard, grabbed the box on the dirty seat beside him by its grab-handles (on the box were dogs and cats and hamsters and goldfish and the legend I CAME FROM STACKPOLE'S HOUSE OF PETS) and *ran* for the big double doors. From inside the box came the scurry and whisk of his test subjects.

He tried to push one of the big doors open along its track, and when it wouldn't budge, he remembered that he had locked it. Carune uttered a loud "Shit!" and fumbled for his keys. The government commanded that the lab be locked at all times—it was one of the strings they put on their money—but Carune kept forgetting.

He brought his keys out and for a moment simply stared at them, mesmerized, running the ball of his thumb over the notches in the Brat's ignition key. He thought again: *God! Christ!* Then he scrabbled through the keys on the ring for the Yale key that unlocked the barn door.

As the first telephone had been used inadvertently—Bell crying into it, "Watson, come here!" when he spilled some acid on his papers and himself—so the first act of teleportation had occurred by accident. Victor Carune had teleported the first two fingers of his left hand across the fifty-yard width of the barn.

Carune had set up two portals at opposite sides of the barn. On his end was a simple ion gun, available from any electronics supply warehouse for under five hundred dollars. On the other end, standing just beyond the far portal—both of them rectangular and the size of a paperback book—was a cloud chamber. Between them was what appeared to be an opaque shower curtain, except that shower curtains are not made of lead. The idea was to shoot the ions through Portal One and then walk around and watch them streaming across the cloud chamber standing just beyond Portal Two, with the lead shield between to prove they really were being transmitted. Except that, for the last two years, the process had only worked twice, and Carune didn't have the slightest idea why.

As he was setting the ion gun in place, his fingers had slipped through the portal—ordinarily no problem, but this morning his hip had also brushed the toggle switch on the control panel at the left of the portal. He was not aware of what had happened—the machinery gave off only the lowest audible hum—until he felt a tingling sensation in his fingers.

"It was not like an electric shock," Carune wrote in his one and only article on the subject before the government shut him up. The article was published, of all places, in *Popular Mechanics*. He had sold it to them for seven hundred and fifty dollars in a last-ditch effort to keep the Jaunt a matter of private enterprise. "There was none of that unpleasant tingle that one gets if one grasps a frayed lamp cord, for instance. It was more like the sensation one gets if one puts one's hand on the casing of some small machine that is working very hard. The vibration is so fast and light that it is, literally, a tingling sensation.

"Then I looked down at the portal and saw that my index finger was gone on a diagonal slant through the middle knuckle, and my second finger was gone slightly above that. In addition, the nail portion of my third finger had disappeared."

Carune had jerked his hand back instinctively, crying out. He so much expected to see blood, he wrote later, that he actually hallucinated blood for a moment or two. His elbow struck the ion gun and knocked it off the table.

He stood there with his fingers in his mouth, verifying that they were still there, and whole. The thought that he had been working too hard crossed his mind. And then the other thought crossed his mind: the thought that the last set of modifications might have . . . might have done something.

He did not push his fingers back in; in fact, Carune only Jaunted once more in his entire life.

At first, he did nothing. He took a long, aimless walk around the barn, running his hands through his hair, wondering if he should call Carson in New Jersey or perhaps Buffington in Charlotte. Carson wouldn't accept a collect phone call, the cheap ass-kissing bastard, but Buffington probably would. Then an idea struck and he ran across to Portal Two, thinking that if his fingers had actually crossed the barn, there might be some sign of it.

There was not, of course. Portal Two stood atop three stacked Pomona orange crates, looking like nothing so much as one of those toy guillotines missing the blade. On one side of its stainless-steel frame was a plug-in jack, from which a cord ran back to the transmission terminal, which was little more than a particle transformer hooked into a computer feed-line.

Which reminded him—

Carune glanced at his watch and saw it was quarter past eleven. His deal with the government consisted of short money, plus computer time, which was infinitely valuable. His computer tie-in lasted until three o'clock this afternoon, and then it was good-bye until Monday. He had to get moving, had to do something—

"I glanced at the pile of crates again," Carune writes in his *Popular Mechanics* article, "and then I looked at the pads of my fingers. And sure enough, the proof was there. It would not, I thought then, convince anyone but myself; but in the beginning, of course, it is only one's self that one has to convince."

"What was it, Dad?" Ricky asked.

"Yeah!" Patty added. "What?"

Mark grinned a little. They were all hooked now, even Marilys. They had nearly forgotten where they were. From the corner of his eye he could see the Jaunt attendants whisper-wheeling their cart slowly among the Jaunters, putting them to sleep. It was never as rapid a process in the civilian sector as it was in the military, he had discovered; civilians got nervous and wanted to talk it over. The nozzle and the rubber mask were too reminiscent of hospital operating rooms, where the surgeon with his knives lurked somewhere behind the anesthetist with her selection of gases in stainless-steel canisters. Sometimes there was panic, hysteria; and always there were a few who simply lost their nerve. Mark had observed two of these as he spoke to the children: two men who had simply arisen from their couches, walked across to the entryway with no fanfare at all, unpinned the validation papers that had been affixed to their lapels, turned them in, and exited without looking back. Jaunt attendants were under strict instructions not to argue with those who left; there were always standbys, sometimes as many as forty or fifty of them, hoping against hope. As those who simply couldn't take it left, standbys were let in with their own validations pinned to their shirts.

"Carune found two splinters in his index finger," he told the children. "He took them out and put them aside. One was lost, but you can see the other one in the Smithsonian Annex in Washington. It's in a hermetically sealed glass case near the moon rocks the first space travelers brought back from the moon—"

"Our moon, Dad, or one of Mars's?" Ricky asked.

"Ours," Mark said, smiling a little. "Only one manned rocket flight has ever landed on Mars, Ricky, and that was a French expedition somewhere about 2030. Anyway, that's why there happens to be a plain old splinter from an orange crate in the Smithsonian Institution. Because it's the first object that we have that was actually teleported—jaunted—across space."

"What happened then?" Patty asked.

"Well, according to the story, Carune ran . . ."

Carune ran back to Portal One and stood there for a moment, heart thudding, out of breath. *Got to calm down*, he told himself. *Got to think about this. You can't maximize your time if you go off half-cocked.*

Deliberately disregarding the forefront of his mind, which was screaming at him to hurry up and do *something*, he dug his nail-clippers out of his pocket and used the point of the file to dig the splinters out of his index finger. He dropped them onto the white inner sleeve of a Hershey bar he had eaten while tinkering with the transformer and trying to widen its afferent capability (he had apparently succeeded in that beyond his wildest dreams). One rolled off the wrapper and was lost; the other ended up in the Smithsonian Institution, locked in a glass case that was cordoned off with thick velvet ropes and watched vigilantly and eternally by a computer-monitored closed-circuit TV camera.

The splinter extraction finished, Carune felt a little calmer. A pencil. That was as good as anything. He took one from beside the clipboard on the shelf above him and ran it gently into Portal One. It disappeared smoothly, inch by inch, like something in an optical illusion or in a very good magician's trick. The pencil had said EBERHARD FABER NO. 2 on one of its sides, black letters stamped on yellow-painted wood. When he had pushed the pencil in until all but EBERH had disappeared, Carune walked around to the other side of Portal One. He looked in.

He saw the pencil in cut-off view, as if a knife had chopped smoothly through it. Carune felt with his fingers where the rest of the pencil should have been, and of course there was nothing. He ran across the barn to Portal Two, and there was the missing part of the pencil, lying on the top crate. Heart thumping so hard that it seemed to shake his entire chest, Carune grasped the sharpened point of his pencil and pulled it the rest of the way through.

He held it up; he looked at it. Suddenly he took it and wrote IT WORKS! on a piece of barn-board. He wrote it so hard that the lead snapped on the last letter. Carune began to laugh shrilly in the empty barn; to laugh so hard that he startled the sleeping swallows into flight among the high rafters.

"Works!" he shouted, and ran back to Portal One. He was waving his arms, the broken pencil knotted up in one fist. "Works! Works! *Do you hear me, Carson, you prick? It works AND I DID IT!"*

"Mark, watch what you say to the children," Marilys reproached him.

Mark shrugged. "It's what he's supposed to have said."

"Well, can't you do a little selective editing?"

"Dad?" Patty asked. "Is that pencil in the museum, too?"

"Does a bear shit in the woods?" Mark said, and then clapped one hand over his mouth. Both children giggled wildly—but that shrill note was gone from Patty's voice, Mark was glad to hear—and after a moment of trying to look serious, Marilys began to giggle too.

The keys went through next; Carune simply tossed them through the portal. He was beginning to think on track again now, and it seemed to him that the first thing that needed finding out was if the process produced things on the other end exactly as they had been, or if they were in any way changed by the trip.

He saw the keys go through and disappear; at exactly the

same moment he heard them jingle on the crate across the barn. He ran across—really only trotting now—and on the way he paused to shove the lead shower curtain back on its track. He didn't need either it or the ion gun now. Just as well, since the ion gun was smashed beyond repair.

He grabbed the keys, went to the lock the government had forced him to put on the door, and tried the Yale key. It worked perfectly. He tried the house key. It also worked. So did the keys which opened his file cabinets and the one which started the Brat pickup.

Carune pocketed the keys and took off his watch. It was a Seiko quartz LC with a built-in calculator below the digital face—twenty-four tiny buttons that would allow him to do everything from addition to subtraction to square roots. A delicate piece of machinery—and just as important, a chronometer. Carune put it down in front of Portal One and pushed it through with a pencil.

He ran across and grabbed it up. When he put it through, the watch had said 11:31:07. It now said 11:31:49. Very good. Right on the money, only he should have had an assistant over there to peg the fact that there had been no time gain once and forever. Well, no matter. Soon enough the government would have him wading hip-deep in assistants.

He tried the calculator. Two and two still made four, eight divided by four was still two; the square root of eleven was still 3.3166247 . . . and so on.

That was when he decided it was mouse-time.

"What happened with the mice, Dad?" Ricky asked.

Mark hesitated briefly. There would have to be some caution here, if he didn't want to scare his children (not to mention his wife) into hysteria minutes away from their first Jaunt. The major thing was to leave them with the knowledge that everything was all right now, that the problem had been licked.

"As I said, there was a slight problem . . ."

Yes. Horror, lunacy, and death. How's that for a slight problem, kids?

Carune set the box which read I CAME FROM STACKPOLE'S HOUSE OF PETS down on the shelf and glanced at his watch. Damned if he hadn't put the thing on upside down. He turned it around and saw that it was a quarter of two. He had only an hour and a quarter of computer time left. *How the time flies when you're having fun*, he thought, and giggled wildly.

He opened the box, reached in, and pulled out a squeaking white mouse by the tail. He put it down in front of Portal One and said, "Go on, mouse." The mouse promptly ran down the side of the orange crate on which the portal stood and scuttered across the floor.

Cursing, Carune chased it, and managed to actually get one hand on it before it squirmed through a crack between two boards and was gone.

"SHIT!" Carune screamed, and ran back to the box of mice. He was just in time to knock two potential escapees back into the box. He got a second mouse, holding this one around the body (he was by trade a physicist, and the ways of white mice were foreign to him), and slammed the lid of the box back down.

This one he gave the old heave-ho. It clutched at Carune's palm, but to no avail; it went head over ratty little paws through Portal One. Carune heard it immediately land on the crates across the barn.

This time he sprinted, remembering how easily the first mouse had eluded him. He need not have worried. The white mouse merely crouched on the crate, its eyes dull, its sides aspirating weakly. Carune slowed down and approached it carefully; he was not a man used to fooling with mice, but you didn't have to be a forty-year veteran to see something was terribly wrong here.

("The mouse didn't feel so good after it went through," Mark Oates told his children with a wide smile that was only noticeably false to his wife.)

Carune touched the mouse. It was like touching something inert—packed straw or sawdust, perhaps—except for the aspirating sides. The mouse did not look around at Carune; it stared straight ahead. He had thrown in a squirming, very frisky and alive little animal; here was something that seemed to be a living waxwork likeness of a mouse.

Then Carune snapped his fingers in front of the mouse's small pink eyes. It blinked . . . and fell dead on its side.

"So Carune decided to try another mouse," Mark said.

"What happened to the first mouse?" Ricky asked.

Mark produced that wide smile again. "It was retired with full honors," he said.

Carune found a paper bag and put the mouse into it. He would take it to Mosconi, the vet, that evening. Mosconi could dissect it and tell him if its inner works had been rearranged. The government would disapprove his bringing a private citizen into a project which would be classified triple top secret as soon as they knew about it. Tough titty, as the kitty was reputed to have said to the babes who complained about the warmth of the milk. Carune was determined that the Great White Father in Washington would know about this as late in the game as possible. For all the scant help the Great White Father had given him, he could wait. Tough titty.

Then he remembered that Mosconi lived way the hell and gone on the other side of New Paltz, and that there wasn't enough gas in the Brat to get even halfway across town . . . let alone back.

But it was 2:03—he had less than an hour of computer time left. He would worry about the goddam dissection later.

Carune constructed a makeshift chute leading to the entrance of Portal One (really the first Jaunt-Slide, Mark told the children, and Patty found the idea of a Jaunt-Slide for mice deliciously funny) and dropped a fresh white mouse into it. He blocked the end with a large book, and after a few moments of aimless pattering and sniffing, the mouse went through the portal and disappeared.

Carune ran back across the barn.

The mouse was DOA.

There was no blood, no bodily swellings to indicate that a radical change in pressure had ruptured something inside. Carune supposed that oxygen starvation might—

He shook his head impatiently. It took the white mouse only nanoseconds to go through; his own watch had confirmed that time remained a constant in the process, or damn close to it.

The second white mouse joined the first in the paper sack. Carune got a third out (a fourth, if you counted the fortunate mouse that had escaped through the crack), wondering for the first time which would end first—his computer time or his supply of mice.

He held this one firmly around the body and forced its haunches through the portal. Across the room he saw the haunches reappear . . . just the haunches. The disembodied little feet were digging frantically at the rough wood of the crate.

Carune pulled the mouse back. No catatonia here; it bit the webbing between his thumb and forefinger hard enough to bring blood. Carune dropped the mouse hurriedly back into the I CAME FROM STACKPOLE'S HOUSE OF PETS box and used the small bottle of hydrogen peroxide in his lab first-aid kit to disinfect the bite.

He put a Band-Aid over it, then rummaged around until he found a pair of heavy work-gloves. He could feel the time running out, running out, running out. It was 2:11 now.

He got another mouse out and pushed it through backward—all the way. He hurried across to Portal Two. This mouse lived for almost two minutes; it even walked a little, after a fashion. It staggered across the Pomona orange crate, fell on its side, struggled weakly to its feet, and then only squatted there. Carune snapped his fingers near its head and it lurched perhaps four steps further before falling on its side again. The aspiration of its sides slowed . . . slowed . . . stopped. It was dead.

Carune felt a chill.

He went back, got another mouse, and pushed it halfway through headfirst. He saw it reappear at the other end, just the head . . . then the neck and chest. Cautiously, Carune relaxed his grip on the mouse's body, ready to grab if it got frisky. It didn't. The mouse only stood there, half of it on one side of the barn, half on the other.

Carune jogged back to Portal Two.

The mouse was alive, but its pink eyes were glazed and dull. Its whiskers didn't move. Going around to the back of the portal, Carune saw an amazing sight; as he had seen the pencil in cutaway, so now he saw the mouse. He saw the vertebrae of its tiny spine ending abruptly in round white circles; he saw its blood moving through the vessels; he saw the tissue moving gently with the tide of life around its minuscule gullet. If nothing else, he thought (and wrote later in his *Popular Mechanics* article), it would make a wonderful diagnostic tool.

Then he noticed that the tidal movement of the tissues had ceased. The mouse had died.

Carune pulled the mouse out by the snout, not liking the

feel of it, and dropped it into the paper sack with its companions. *Enough with the white mice*, he decided. *The mice die. They die if you put them through all the way, and they die if you put them through halfway headfirst. Put them through halfway butt-first, they stay frisky.*

What the hell is in there?

Sensory input, he thought almost randomly. *When they go through they see something—hear something—touch something—God, maybe even* smell *something—that literally kills them. What?*

He had no idea—but he meant to find out.

Carune still had almost forty minutes before COMLINK pulled the data base out from under him. He unscrewed the thermometer from the wall beside his kitchen door, trotted back to the barn with it, and put it through the portals. The thermometer went in at 83 degrees F; it came out at 83 degrees F. He rummaged through the spare room where he kept a few toys to amuse his grandchildren with; among them he found a packet of balloons. He blew one of them up, tied it off, and batted it through the portal. It came out intact and unharmed—a start down the road toward answering his question about a sudden change in pressure somehow caused by what he was already thinking of as the Jaunting process.

With five minutes to go before the witching hour, he ran into his house, snatched up his goldfish bowl (inside, Percy and Patrick swished their tails and darted about in agitation) and ran back with it. He shoved the goldfish bowl through Portal One.

He hurried across to Portal Two, where his goldfish bowl sat on the crate. Patrick was floating belly-up; Percy swam slowly around near the bottom of the bowl, as if dazed. A moment later he also floated belly-up. Carune was reaching for the goldfish bowl when Percy gave a weak flick of his tail and resumed his lackadaisical swimming. Slowly, he seemed to throw off whatever the effect had been, and by the time Carune got back from Mosconi's Veterinary Clinic that night at nine o'clock, Percy seemed as perky as ever.

Patrick was dead.

Carune fed Percy a double ration of fish food and gave Patrick a hero's burial in the garden.

After the computer had cut him out for the day, Carune decided to hitch a ride over to Mosconi's. Accordingly, he was standing on the shoulder of Route 26 at a quarter of four that afternoon, dressed in jeans and a loud plaid sport coat, his thumb out, a paper bag in his other hand.

Finally, a kid driving a Chevette not much bigger than a sardine can pulled over, and Carune got in. "What you got in the bag, my man?"

"Bunch of dead mice," Carune said. Eventually another car stopped. When the farmer behind the wheel asked about the bag, Carune told him it was a couple of sandwiches.

Mosconi dissected one of the mice on the spot, and agreed to dissect the others later and call Carune on the telephone with the results. The initial result was not very encouraging; so far as Mosconi could tell, the mouse he had opened up was perfectly healthy except for the fact that it was dead.

Depressing.

"Victor Carune was eccentric, but he was no fool," Mark said. The Jaunt attendants were getting close now, and he supposed he would have to hurry up . . . or he would be finishing this in the Wake-Up Room in Whitehead City. "Hitching a ride back home that night—and he had to walk most of the way, so the story goes—he realized that he had maybe solved a third of the energy crisis at one single stroke. All the goods that had to go by train and truck and boat and plane before that day could be Jaunted. You could write a letter to your friend in London or Rome or Senegal, and he could have it the very next day—without an ounce of oil needing to be burned. We take it for granted, but it was a big thing to Carune, believe me. And to everyone else, as well."

"But what happened to the mice, Daddy?" Rick asked.

"That's what Carune kept asking himself," Mark said, "because he also realized that if *people* could use the Jaunt, that would solve almost *all* of the energy crisis. And that we might be able to conquer space. In his *Popular Mechanics* article he said that even the stars could finally be ours. And the metaphor he used was crossing a shallow stream without getting your shoes wet. You'd just get a big rock, and throw it in the stream, then get another rock, stand on the first rock, and throw *that* into the stream, go back and get a third rock, go back to the second rock, throw the third rock into the stream, and keep up like that until you'd made a path of stepping-stones all the way across the stream . . . or in this case, the solar system, or maybe even the galaxy."

"I don't get that at *all*," Patty said.

"That's because you got turkey-turds for brains," Ricky said smugly.

"I do *not*! Daddy, Ricky said—"

"Children, don't," Marilys said gently.

"Carune pretty much foresaw what has happened," Mark said. "Drone rocket ships programmed to land, first on the moon, then on Mars, then on Venus and the outer moons of Jupiter . . . drones really only programmed to do one thing after they landed—"

"Set up a Jaunt station for astronauts," Ricky said.

Mark nodded. "And now there are scientific outposts all over the solar system, and maybe someday, long after we're gone, there will even be another planet for us. There are Jaunt ships on their way to four different star systems with solar systems of their own . . . but it'll be a long, long time before they get there."

"I want to know what happened to the *mice*," Patty said impatiently.

"Well, eventually the government got into it," Mark said. "Carune kept them out as long as he could, but finally they got wind of it and landed on him with both feet. Carune was nominal head of the Jaunt project until he died ten years later, but he was never really in charge of it again."

"Jeez, the poor guy!" Rick said.

"But he got to be a hero," Patricia said. "He's in *all* the history books, just like President Lincoln and President Hart."

I'm sure that's a great comfort to him . . . wherever he is, Mark thought, and then went on, carefully glossing over the rough parts.

The government, which had been pushed to the wall by the escalating energy crisis, did indeed come in with both feet. They wanted the Jaunt on a paying basis as soon as possible— like yesterday. Faced with economic chaos and the increasingly probable picture of anarchy and mass starvation in the 1990's, only last-ditch pleading made them put off announcement of the Jaunt before an exhaustive spectrographic analysis of Jaunted articles could be completed. When the analyses were complete—and showed no changes in the makeup of

Jaunted artifacts—the existence of the Jaunt was announced with international hoopla. Showing intelligence for once (necessity is, after all, the mother of invention), the U.S. government put Young and Rubicam in charge of the pr.

That was where the myth-making around Victor Carune, an elderly, rather peculiar man who showered perhaps twice a week and changed his clothes only when he thought of it, began. Young and Rubicam and the agencies which followed them turned Carune into a combination of Thomas Edison, Eli Whitney, Pecos Bill, and Flash Gordon. The blackly funny part of all this (and Mark Oates did not pass this on to his family) was that Victor Carune might even then have been dead or insane; art imitates life, they say, and Carune would have been familiar with the Robert Heinlein novel about the doubles who stand in for figures in the public eye.

Victor Carune was a problem; a nagging problem that wouldn't go away. He was a loudmouthed foot-dragger, a holdover from the Ecological Sixties—a time when there was still enough energy floating around to allow foot-dragging as a luxury. These, on the other hand, were the Nasty Eighties, with coal clouds befouling the sky and a long section of the California coastline expected to be uninhabitable for perhaps sixty years due to a nuclear "excursion."

Victor Carune remained a problem until about 1991—and then he became a rubber stamp, smiling, quiet, grandfatherly; a figure seen waving from podiums in newsfilms. In 1993, three years before he officially died, he rode in the pace-car at the Tournament of Roses Parade.

Puzzling. And a little ominous.

The results of the announcement of the Jaunt—of working teleportation—on October 19th, 1988, was a hammerstroke of worldwide excitement and economic upheaval. On the world money markets, the battered old American dollar suddenly skyrocketed through the roof. People who had bought gold at eight hundred and six dollars an ounce suddenly found that a pound of gold would bring something less than twelve hundred dollars. In the year between the announcement of the Jaunt and the first working Jaunt-Stations in New York and L.A., the stock market climbed a little over a thousand points. The price of oil dropped only seventy cents a barrel, but by 1994, with Jaunt-Stations crisscrossing the U.S. at the pressure-points of seventy major cities, OPEC had ceased to exist, and the price of oil began to tumble. By 1998, with Stations in most free-world cities and goods routinely Jaunted between Tokyo and Paris, Paris and London, London and New York, New York and Berlin, oil had dropped to fourteen dollars a barrel. By 2006, when people at last began to use the Jaunt on a regular basis, the stock market had leveled off five thousand points above its 1987 levels, oil was selling for six dollars a barrel, and the oil companies had begun to change their names. Texaco became Texaco Oil/Water, and Mobil had become Mobil Hydro-2-Ox.

By 2045, water-prospecting became the big game and oil had become what it had been in 1906: a toy.

"What about the *mice*, Daddy?" Patty asked impatiently. "What happened to the *mice?*"

Mark decided it might be okay now, and he drew the attention of his children to the Jaunt attendants, who were passing gas out only three aisles from them. Rick only nodded, but Patty looked troubled as a lady with a fashionably shaved-and-painted head took a whiff from the rubber mask and fell unconscious.

"Can't Jaunt when you're awake, can you, Dad?" Ricky said.

Mark nodded and smiled reassuringly at Patricia. "Carune understood even before the government got into it," he said.

"How *did* the government get into it, Mark?" Marilys asked.

Mark smiled. "Computer time," he said. "The data base. That was the only thing that Carune couldn't beg, borrow, or steal. The computer handled the actual particulate transmission—billions of pieces of information. It's still the computer, you know, that makes sure you don't come through with your head somewhere in the middle of your stomach."

Marilys shuddered.

"Don't be frightened," he said. "There's never been a screw-up like that, Mare. *Never.*"

"There's always a first time," she muttered.

Mark looked at Ricky. "How did he know?" he asked his son. "How did Carune know you had to be asleep, Rick?"

"When he put the mice in backwards," Rick said slowly, "they were all right. At least as long as he didn't put them *all* in. They were only—well, messed up—when he put them in headfirst. Right?"

"Right," Mark said. The Jaunt attendants were moving in now, wheeling their silent cart of oblivion. He wasn't going to have time to finish after all; perhaps it was just as well. "It didn't take many experiments to clarify what was happening, of course. The Jaunt killed the entire trucking business, kids, but at least it took the pressure off the experimenters—"

Yes. Foot-dragging had become a luxury again, and the tests had gone on for better than twenty years, although Carune's first tests with drugged mice had convinced him that unconscious animals were not subject to what was known forever after as the Organic Effect or, more simply, the Jaunt Effect.

He and Mosconi had drugged several mice, put them through Portal One, retrieved them at the other side, and had waited anxiously for their test subjects to reawaken . . . or to die. They had reawakened, and after a brief recovery period they had taken up their mouse-lives—eating, fucking, playing, and shitting—with no ill effects whatsoever. Those mice became the first of several generations which were studied with great interest. They showed no long-term ill effects; they did not die sooner, their pups were not born with two heads or green fur and neither did these pups show any other long-term effects.

"When did they start with people, Dad?" Rick asked, although he had certainly read this in school. "Tell that part!"

"I wanna know what happened to the *mice!*" Patty said again.

Although the Jaunt attendants had now reached the head of their aisle (they themselves were near the foot), Mark Oates paused a moment to reflect. His daughter, who knew less, had nevertheless listened to her heart and asked the right question. Therefore, it was his son's question he chose to answer.

The first human Jaunters had not been astronauts or test pilots; they were convict volunteers who had not even been screened with any particular interest in their psychological stability. In fact, it was the view of the scientists now in charge (Carune was not one of them; he had become what is commonly called a titular head) that the freakier they were, the better; if a mental spaz could go through and come out all right—or at least, no worse than he or she had been going in—then the process was probably safe for the executives, politicians, and fashion models of the world.

Half a dozen of these volunteers were brought to Province, Vermont (a site which had since become every bit as famous as Kitty Hawk, North Carolina, had once been), gassed, and fed through the portals exactly two hand-miles apart, one by one.

Mark told his children this, because of course all six of the volunteers came back just fine and feeling perky, thank you. He did not tell them about the purported *seventh* volunteer. This figure, who might have been real, or myth, or (most probably) a combination of the two, even had a name: Rudy Foggia. Foggia was supposed to have been a convicted murderer, sentenced to death in the state of Florida for the murders of four old people at a Sarasota bridge party. According to the apocrypha, the combined forces of the Central Intelligence Agency and the Effa Bee Eye had come to Foggia with a unique, one-time, take-it-or-leave-it, absolutely-not-to-be-repeated offer. Take the Jaunt wide awake. Come through okay and we put your pardon, signed by Governor Thurgood, in your hand. Out you walk, free to follow the One True Cross or to off a few more old folks playing bridge in their yellow pants and white shoes. Come through dead or insane, tough titty. As the kitty was purported to have said. What do you say?

Foggia, who understood that Florida was one state that really meant business about the death penalty and whose lawyer had told him that he was in all probability the next to ride Old Sparky, said okay.

Enough scientists to fill a jury box (with four or five left over as alternates) were present on the Great Day in the summer of 2007, but if the Foggia story was true—and Mark Oates believed it probably was—he doubted if it had been any of the scientists who talked. More likely it had been one of the guards who had flown with Foggia from Raiford to Montpelier and then escorted him from Montpelier to Province in an armored truck.

"If I come through this alive," Foggia is reported to have said, "I want a chicken dinner before I blow this joint." He then stepped through Portal One and reappeared at Portal Two immediately.

He came through alive, but Rudy Foggia was in no condition to eat his chicken dinner. In the space it took to Jaunt across the two miles (pegged at 0.000000000067 of a second by computer), Foggia's hair had turned snow white. His face had not changed in any physical way—it was not lined or jowly or wasted—but it gave the impression of great, almost incredible age. Foggia shuffled out of the portal, his eyes bulging blankly, his mouth twitching, his hands splayed out in front of him. Presently he began to drool. The scientists who had gathered around drew away from him and no, Mark really doubted if any of them had talked; they knew about the rats, after all, and the guinea pigs, and the hamsters; any animal, in fact, with more brains than your average flatworm. They must have felt a bit like those German scientists who tried to impregnate Jewish women with the sperm of German shepherds.

"What happened?" one of the scientists shouted (is reputed to have shouted). It was the only question Foggia had a chance to answer.

"It's eternity in there," he said, and dropped dead of what was diagnosed as a massive heart attack.

The scientists foregathered there were left with his corpse (which was neatly taken care of by the CIA and the Effa Bee Eye) and that strange and awful dying declaration: *It's eternity in there.*

"Daddy, I want to know what happened to the *mice*," Patty repeated. The only reason she had a chance to ask again was because the man in the expensive suit and the Eterna-Shine shoes had developed into something of a problem for the Jaunt attendants. He didn't really want to take the gas, and was disguising it with a lot of bluff, bully-boy talk. The attendants were doing their job as well as they could—smiling, cajoling, persuading—but it had slowed them down.

Mark sighed. He had opened the subject—only as a way of distracting his children from the pre-Jaunt festivities, it was true, but he *had* opened it—and now he supposed he would have to close it as truthfully as he could without alarming them or upsetting them.

He would not tell them, for instance, about C. K. Summers's

book, *The Politics of the Jaunt,* which contained one section called "The Jaunt Under the Rose," a compendium of the more believable rumors about the Jaunt. The story of Rudy Foggia, he of the bridgeclub murders and the uneaten chicken dinner, was in there. There were also case histories of some other thirty (or more . . . or less . . . or who knows) volunteers, scapegoats, or madmen who had Jaunted wide awake over the last three hundred years. Most of them arrived at the other end dead. The rest were hopelessly insane. In some cases, the act of reemerging had actually seemed to shock them to death.

Summers's section of Jaunt rumors and apocrypha contained other unsettling intelligence as well: the Jaunt had apparently been used several times as a murder weapon. In the most famous (and only documented) case, which had occurred a mere thirty years ago, a Jaunt researcher named Lester Michaelson had tied up his wife with their daughter's plexiplast Dreamropes and pushed her, screaming, through the Jaunt portal at Silver City, Nevada. But before doing it, Michaelson had pushed the Nil button on his Jaunt board, erasing each and every one of the hundreds of thousands of possible portals through which Mrs. Michaelson might have emerged—anywhere from neighboring Reno to the experimental Jaunt-Station on Io, one of the Jovian moons. So there was Mrs. Michaelson, Jaunting forever somewhere out there in the ozone. Michaelson's lawyer, after Michaelson had been held sane and able to stand trial for what he had done (within the narrow limits of the law, perhaps he was sane, but in any practical sense, Lester Michaelson was just as mad as a hatter), had offered a novel defense: his client could not be tried for murder because no one could prove conclusively that Mrs. Michaelson was dead.

This had raised the terrible specter of the woman, discorporeal but somehow still sentient, screaming in limbo . . . forever. Michaelson was convicted and executed.

In addition, Summers suggested, the Jaunt had been used by various tinpot dictators to get rid of political dissidents and political adversaries; some thought that the Mafia had their own illegal Jaunt-Stations, tied into the central Jaunt computer through their CIA connections. It was suggested that the Mafia used the Jaunt's Nil capability to get rid of bodies which, unlike that of the unfortunate Mrs. Michaelson, were already dead. Seen in that light, the Jaunt became the ultimate Jimmy Hoffa machine, ever so much better than the local gravel pit or quarry.

All of this had led to Summers's conclusions and theories about the Jaunt; and that, of course, led back to Patty's persistent question about the mice.

"Well," Mark said slowly, as his wife signaled with her eyes for him to be careful, "even now no one really knows, Patty. But all the experiments with animals—including the mice—seemed to lead to the conclusion that while the Jaunt is almost instantaneous *physically*, it takes a long, *long* time mentally."

"I don't get it," Patty said glumly. "I knew I wouldn't."

But Ricky was looking at his father thoughtfully. "They went on thinking," he said. "The test animals. And so would we, if we didn't get knocked out."

"Yes," Mark said. "That's what we believe now."

Something was dawning in Ricky's eyes. Fright? Excitement? "It isn't just teleportation, is it, Dad? It's some kind of time-warp."

It's eternity in there, Mark thought.

"In a way," he said. "But that's a comic-book phrase—it sounds good but doesn't really mean anything, Rick. It seems to revolve around the idea of consciousness, and the fact that consciousness doesn't particulate—it remains whole and constant. It also retains some screwy sense of time. But we don't know how pure consciousness would measure time, or even if that concept has any meaning to pure mind. We can't even conceive what pure mind might be."

Mark fell silent, troubled by his son's eyes, which were suddenly so sharp and curious. *He understands but he doesn't understand,* Mark thought. Your mind can be your best friend; it can keep you amused even when there's nothing to read, nothing to do. But it can turn on you when it's left with no input for too long. It can turn on you, which means that it turns on itself, savages itself, perhaps consumes itself in an unthinkable act of auto-cannibalism. How long in there, in terms of years? 0.000000000067 seconds for the body to Jaunt, but how long for the unparticulated consciousness? A hundred years? A thousand? A million? A billion? How long alone with your thoughts in an endless field of white? And then, when a billion eternities have passed, the crashing return of light and form and body. Who wouldn't go insane?

"Ricky—" he began, but the Jaunt attendants had arrived with their cart.

"Are you ready?" one asked.

Mark nodded.

"Daddy, I'm scared," Patty said in a thin voice. "Will it hurt?"

"No, honey, of course it won't hurt," Mark said, and his voice was calm enough, but his heart was beating a little fast—it always did, although this would be something like his twenty-fifth Jaunt. "I'll go first and you'll see how easy it is."

The Jaunt attendant looked at him questioningly. Mark nodded and made a smile. The mask descended. Mark took it in his own hands and breathed deep of the dark.

The first thing he became aware of was the hard black Martian sky as seen through the top of the dome which surrounded Whitehead City. It was night here, and the stars sprawled with a fiery brilliance undreamed of on earth.

The second thing he became aware of was some sort of disturbance in the recovery room—mutters, then shouts, then a shrill scream. *Oh dear God, that's Marilys!* he thought, and struggled up from his Jaunt couch, fighting the waves of dizziness.

There was another scream, and he saw Jaunt attendants running toward their couches, their bright red jumpers flying around their knees. Marilys staggered toward him, pointing. She screamed again and then collapsed on the floor, sending an unoccupied Jaunt couch rolling slowly down the aisle with one weakly clutching hand.

But Mark had already followed the direction of her pointing finger. He had seen. It hadn't been fright in Ricky's eyes; it had been excitement. He should have known, because he knew Ricky—Ricky, who had fallen out of the highest crotch of the tree in their backyard in Schenectady when he was only seven, who had broken his arm (and was lucky that had been all he'd broken); Ricky who dared to go faster and further on his Slideboard than any other kid in the neighborhood; Ricky who was first to take any dare. Ricky and fear were not well acquainted.

Until now.

Beside Ricky, his sister still mercifully slept. The thing that had been his son bounced and writhed on its Jaunt couch, a twelve-year-old boy with a snow-white fall of hair and eyes which were incredibly ancient, the corneas gone a sickly yellow. Here was a creature older than time masquerading as a boy; and yet it bounced and writhed with a kind of horrid, obscene glee, and at its choked, lunatic cackles the Jaunt attendants drew back in terror. Some of them fled, although they had been trained to cope with just such an unthinkable eventuality.

The old-young legs twitched and quivered. Claw hands beat and twisted and danced on the air; abruptly they descended and the thing that had been his son began to claw at its face.

"Longer than you think, Dad!" it cackled. "Longer than you think! Held my breath when they gave me the gas! Wanted to see! I saw! I saw! Longer than you think!"

Cackling and screeching, the thing on the Jaunt couch suddenly clawed its own eyes out. Blood gouted. The recovery room was an aviary of screaming voices now.

"Longer than you think, Dad! I saw! I saw! Long Jaunt! Longer than you think—"

It said other things before the Jaunt attendants were finally able to bear it away, rolling its couch swiftly away as it screamed and clawed at the eyes that had seen the unseeable forever and ever; it said other things, and then it began to scream, but Mark Oates didn't hear it because by then he was screaming himself.

The Wedding Gig

In the year 1927 we were playing jazz in a speakeasy just south of Morgan, Illinois, a town seventy miles from Chicago. It was real hick country, not another big town for twenty miles in any direction. But there were a lot of farmboys with a hankering for something stronger than Moxie after a hot day in the field, and a lot of would-be jazz-babies out stepping with their drugstore-cowboy boyfriends. There were also some married men (you always know them, friend; they might as well be wearing signs) coming far out of their way to be where no one would recognize them while they cut a rug with their not-quite-legit lassies.

That was when jazz was jazz, not noise. We had a five-man combination—drums, cornet, trombone, piano, trumpet—and we were pretty good. That was still three years before we made our first record and four years before talkies.

We were playing "Bamboo Bay" when this big fellow walked in, wearing a white suit and smoking a pipe with more squiggles in it than a French horn. The whole band was a little tight by that time but everyone in the crowd was absolutely blind and really ramping the joint. They were in a good mood, though; there hadn't been a single fight all night. All of us guys were sweating rivers and Tommy Englander, the guy who ran the place, kept sending up rye as smooth as a varnished plank. Englander was a good joe to work for, and he liked our sound. Of course that made him aces in my book.

The guy in the white suit sat down at the bar and I forgot him. We finished up the set with "Aunt Hagar's Blues," which was a tune that passed for racy out in the boondocks back then, and got a good round of applause. Manny had a big grin on his face when he put his trumpet down, and I clapped him on the back as we left the bandstand. There was a lonely-looking girl in a green evening gown who had been giving me the eye all night. She was a redhead, and I've always been partial to those. I got a signal from her eyes and the tilt of her head, so I started weaving through the crowd to see if she wanted a drink.

I was halfway there when the man in the white suit stepped in front of me. Up close he looked like a pretty tough egg. His hair was bristling up in the back in spite of what smelled like a whole bottle of Wildroot Creme Oil and he had the flat, oddly shiny eyes that some deep-sea fish have.

"Want to talk to you outside," he said.

The redhead looked away with a small pout.

"It can wait," I said. "Let me by."

"My name is Scollay. Mike Scollay."

I knew the name. Mike Scollay was a small-time racketeer from Shytown who paid for his beer and skittles by running booze in from Canada. The high-tension stuff that started out where the men wear skirts and play bagpipes. When they aren't tending the vats, that is. His picture had been in the paper a few times. The last time had been when some other dancehall Dan tried to gun him down.

"You're pretty far from Chicago, my friend," I said.

"I brought some chaperones," he said, "don't worry. Outside."

The redhead took another look. I pointed at Scollay and shrugged. She sniffed and turned her back.

"There," I said. "You queered that."

"Bimbos like that are a penny a bushel in Chi," he said.

"I didn't *want* a bushel."

"Outside."

I followed him out. The air was cool on my skin after the smoky atmosphere of the club, sweet with fresh-cut alfalfa. The stars were out, soft and flickering. The hoods were out, too, but they didn't look soft, and the only things flickering were their cigarettes.

"I got a job for you," Scollay said.

"Is that so."

"Pays two C's. Split it with the band or hold back a hundred for yourself."

"What is it?"

"A gig, what else? My sis is tying the knot. I want you to play for the reception. She likes Dixieland. Two of my boys say you play good Dixieland."

I told you Englander was good to work for. He was paying us eighty bucks a week. This guy was offering over twice that for one gig.

"It's from five to eight, next Friday," Scollay said. "At the Sons of Erin Hall on Grover Street."

"It's too much," I said. "How come?"

"There's two reasons," Scollay said. He puffed on his pipe. It looked out of place in the middle of that yegg's face. He should have had a Lucky Strike Green dangling from that mouth, or maybe a Sweet Caporal. The Cigarette of Bums. With the pipe he didn't look like a bum. The pipe made him look sad and funny.

"Two reasons," he repeated. "Maybe you heard the Greek tried to rub me out."

"I saw your picture in the paper," I said. "You were the guy trying to crawl into the sidewalk."

"Smart guy," he growled, but with no real force. "I'm getting too big for him. The Greek is getting old. He thinks small. He ought to be back in the old country, drinking olive oil and looking at the Pacific."

"I think it's the Aegean," I said.

"I don't give a tin shit if it's Lake Huron," he said. "Point is, he don't want to be old. He still wants to get me. He don't know the coming thing when he sees it."

"That's you."

"You're fucking-A."

"In other words, you're paying two C's because our last number might be arranged for Enfield rifle accompaniment."

Anger flashed in his face, but there was something else there, as well. I didn't know what it was then, but I think I do now. I think it was sorrow. "Buddy Gee, I got the best protection money can buy. If anyone funny sticks his nose in, he won't get a chance to sniff twice.''

''What's the other thing?''

He spoke softly. ''My sister's marrying an Italian.''

''A good Catholic like you,'' I sneered softly.

The anger flashed again, white-hot, and for a minute I thought I'd pushed him too far. ''A good *mick!* A good old shanty-Irish mick, sonny, and you better not forget it!'' To that he added, almost too low to be heard, ''Even if I did lose most of my hair, it was red.''

I started to say something, but he didn't give me the chance. He swung me around and pressed his face down until our noses almost touched. I have never seen such anger and humiliation and rage and determination in a man's face. You never see that look on a white face these days, how it is to be hurt and made to feel small. All that love and hate. But I saw it on his face that night and knew I could crack wise a few more times and get my ass killed.

''She's fat,'' he half-whispered, and I could smell checker-berry mints on his breath. ''A lot of people have been laughing at me while my back was turned. They don't do it when I can see them, though, I'll tell you that, Mr. Cornet Player. Because maybe this dago was all she could get. But you're not gonna laugh at me or her or the dago. And nobody else is, either. Because you're gonna play too loud. No one is going to laugh at my sis.''

''We never laugh when we play our gigs. Makes it too hard to pucker.''

That relieved the tension. He laughed—a short, barking laugh. ''You be there, ready to play at five. The Sons of Erin on Grover Street. I'll pay your expenses both ways, too.''

He wasn't asking. I felt railroaded into the decision, but he wasn't giving me time to talk it over. He was already striding away, and one of his chaperones was holding open the back door of a Packard coupé.

They drove away. I stayed out awhile longer and had a smoke. The evening was soft and fine and Scollay seemed more and more like something I might have dreamed. I was just wishing we could bring the bandstand out to the parking lot and play when Biff tapped me on the shoulder.

''Time,'' he said.

''Okay.''

We went back in. The redhead had picked up some salt-and-pepper sailor who looked twice her age. I don't know what a member of the U.S. Navy was doing in Illinois, but as far as I was concerned, she could have him if her taste was that bad. I didn't feel so good. The rye had gone to my head, and Scollay seemed a lot more real in here, where the fumes of what he and his kind sold were strong enough to float on.

"We had a request for 'Camptown Races,' " Charlie said.

"Forget it," I said curtly. "We don't play that nigger stuff till after midnight."

I could see Billy-Boy stiffen as he was sitting down to the piano, and then his face was smooth again. I could have kicked myself around the block, but, goddammit, a man can't shift gears on his mouth overnight, or in a year, or maybe even in ten. In those days nigger was a word I hated and kept saying.

I went over to him. "I'm sorry, Bill—I haven't been myself tonight."

"Sure," he said, but his eyes looked over my shoulder and I knew my apology wasn't accepted. That was bad, but I'll tell you what was worse—knowing he was disappointed in me.

I told them about the gig during our next break, being square with them about the money and how Scollay was a hoodlum (although I didn't tell them about the other hood who was out to get him). I also told them that Scollay's sister was fat and Scollay was sensitive about it. Anyone who cracked any jokes about inland barges might wind up with a third breather-hole, somewhat above the other two.

I kept looking at Billy-Boy Williams while I talked, but you could read nothing on the cat's face. It would be easier trying to figure out what a walnut was thinking by reading the wrinkles on the shell. Billy-Boy was the best piano player we ever had, and we were all sorry about the little ways it got taken out on him as we traveled from one place to another. In the south was the worst, of course—Jim Crow car, nigger heaven at the movies, stuff like that—but it wasn't that great in the north, either. But what could I do? Huh? You go on and tell me. In those days you lived with those differences.

*   *   *

We turned up at the Sons of Erin Hall on Friday at four o'clock, an hour before. We drove up in the special Ford truck Biff and Manny and me put together. The back end was all enclosed with canvas, and there were two cots bolted on the floor. We even had an electric hotplate that ran off the battery, and the band's name was painted on the outside.

The day was just right—a ham-and-egger if you ever saw one, with little white summer clouds casting shadows on the fields. But once we got into the city it was hot and kind of grim, full of the hustle and bustle you got out of touch with in a place like Morgan. By the time we got to the hall my clothes were sticking to me and I needed to visit the comfort station. I could have used a shot of Tommy Englander's rye, too.

The Sons of Erin was a big wooden building, affiliated with the church where Scollay's sis was getting married. You know the sort of place I mean if you ever took the Wafer, I guess—CYO meetings on Tuesdays, bingo on Wednesdays, and a sociable for the kids on Saturday nights.

We trooped up the walk, each of us carrying his instrument in one hand and some part of Biff's drum-kit in the other. A thin lady with no breastworks to speak of was directing traffic inside. Two sweating men were hanging crepe paper. There was a bandstand at the front of the hall, and over it was a banner and a couple of big pink paper wedding bells. The tinsel lettering on the banner said BEST ALWAYS MAUREEN AND RICO.

Maureen and Rico. Damned if I couldn't see why Scollay was so wound up. Maureen and Rico. Stone the crows.

The thin lady swooped down on us. She looked like she had a lot to say so I beat her to punch. "We're the band," I said.

"The band?" She blinked at our instruments distrustfully. "Oh. I was hoping you were the caterers."

I smiled as if caterers always carried snare drums and trombone cases.

"You can—" she began, but just then a ruff-tuff-creampuff of about nineteen strolled over. A cigarette was dangling from the corner of his mouth, but so far as I could see it wasn't doing a thing for his image except making his left eye water.

"Open that shit up," he said.

Charlie and Biff looked at me. I shrugged. We opened our cases and he looked at the horns. Seeing nothing that looked like you could load it and fire it, he wandered back to his corner and sat down on a folding chair.

"You can set your things up right away," the thin lady went on, as if she had never been interrupted. "There's a piano in the other room. I'll have my men wheel it in when we're done putting up our decorations."

Biff was already lugging his drum-kit up on to the little stage.

"I thought you were the caterers," she repeated in a distraught way. "Mr. Scollay ordered a wedding cake and there are hors d'oeuvres and roasts of beef and—"

"They'll be here, ma'am," I said. "They get payment on delivery."

"—two roasts of pork and a capon and Mr. Scollay will be just *furious* if—" She saw one of her men pausing to light a cigarette just below a dangling streamer of crepe and shrieked, *"HENRY!"* The man jumped as if he had been shot. I escaped to the bandstand.

We were all set up by a quarter of five. Charlie, the trombone player, was wah-wahing away into a mute and Biff was loosening up his wrists. The caterers had arrived at 4:20 and Miss Gibson (that was the thin lady's name; she made a business out of such affairs) almost threw herself on them.

Four long tables had been set up and covered with white linen, and four black women in caps and aprons were setting places. The cake had been wheeled into the middle of the room for everyone to gasp over. It was six layers high, with a little bride and groom standing on top.

I walked outside to grab a fag and just about halfway through it I heard them coming—tooting away and raising a racket. I stayed where I was until I saw the lead car coming around the corner of the block below the church, then I snubbed my smoke and went inside.

"They're coming," I told Miss Gibson.

She went white and actually swayed on her heels. There was a lady that should have taken up a different profession—interior decoration, maybe, or library science. "The tomato juice!" she screamed. "Bring in the tomato juice!"

I went back to the bandstand and we got ready. We had

played gigs like this before—what combo hasn't?—and when the doors opened, we swung into a ragtime version of "The Wedding March" that I had arranged myself. If you think that sounds sort of like a lemonade cocktail I have to agree with you, but most receptions we played for just ate it up, and this one was no different. Everybody clapped and yelled and whistled, then started gassing amongst themselves. But I could tell by the way some of them were tapping their feet while they talked that we were getting through. We were on—I thought it was going to be a good gig. I know everything they say about the Irish, and most of it's true, but, hot damn! they can't not have a good time once they are set up for it.

All the same, I have to admit I almost blew the whole number when the groom and the blushing bride walked in. Scollay, dressed in a morning coat and striped trousers, shot me a hard look, and don't think I didn't see it. I managed to keep a poker face, and the rest of the band did, too—no one so much as missed a note. Lucky for us. The wedding party, which looked as if it were made up almost entirely of Scollay's goons and their molls, were wise already. They had to be, if they'd been at the church. But I'd only heard faint rumblings, you might say.

You've heard about Jack Sprat and his wife. Well, this was a hundred times worse. Scollay's sister had the red hair he was losing, and it was long and curly. But not that pretty auburn shade you may be imagining. No, this was County Cork red—bright as a carrot and kinky as a bedspring. Her natural complexion was curd-white but she was wearing almost too many freckles to tell. And had Scollay said she was fat? Brother, that was like saying you could buy a few things in Macy's. She was a human dinosaur—three hundred and fifty pounds if she was one. It had all gone to her bosom and hips and butt and thighs, like it usually does on fat girls, making what should be sexy grotesque and sort of frightening instead. Some fat girls have pathetically pretty faces, but Scollay's sis didn't even have that. Her eyes were too close together, her mouth was too big, and she had jug-ears. Then there were the freckles. Even thin she would have been ugly enough to stop a clock—hell, a whole show-window of them.

That alone wouldn't have made anybody laugh, unless they were stupid or just poison-mean. It was when you added the groom, Rico, to the picture that you wanted to laugh until you cried. He could have put on a top hat and still stood in the top half of her shadow. He looked like he might have weighed ninety pounds or so, soaking wet. He was skinny as a rail, his complexion darkly olive. When he grinned around nervously, his teeth looked like a picket fence in a slum neighborhood.

We kept right on playing.

Scollay roared: "The bride and the groom! God give 'em every happiness!" *And if God don't,* his thundering brow proclaimed, *you folks here better—at least today.*

Everyone shouted their approval and applauded. We finished our number with a flourish, and that brought another round. Scollay's sister Maureen smiled. God, her mouth was big. Rico simpered.

For a while everyone just walked around, eating cheese and cold cuts on crackers and drinking Scollay's best bootleg Scotch. I had three shots myself between numbers, and it put Tommy Englander's rye in the shade.

Scollay began to look happier, too—a little, anyway.

He cruised by the bandstand once and said, "You guys play pretty good." Coming from a music lover like him, I reckoned that was a real compliment.

Just before everyone sat down to the meal, Maureen came up herself. She was even uglier up close, and her white gown (there must have been enough white satin wrapped around that mama to cover three beds) wasn't helping her at all. She asked us if we could play "Roses of Picardy" like Red Nichols and His Five Pennies, because, she said, it was her very favorite song. Fat and ugly she was, but hoity-toity she was not—unlike some of the two-bitters who'd been dropping by to make requests. We played it, but not very well. Still, she gave us a sweet smile that was almost enough to make her pretty, and she applauded when it was done.

They sat down to dinner around 6:15, and Miss Gibson's hired help rolled the chow to them. They fell to like a bunch of animals, which was not entirely surprising, and kept knocking back that high-tension booze the whole time. I couldn't help watching the way Maureen was eating. I tried to look away, but my eye kept wandering back, as if to make sure it was seeing what it *thought* it was seeing. The rest of them were packing it in, but she made them look like old ladies in a tearoom. She had no more time for sweet smiles or listening to "Roses of Picardy"; you could have stuck a sign in front of her that said WOMAN WORKING. That lady didn't need a knife and fork; she needed a steam shovel and a conveyor belt. It was sad to watch her. And Rico (you could just see his chin over the table where the bride was sitting, and a pair of brown eyes as shy as a deer's) kept handing her things, never changing that nervous simper.

We took a twenty-minute break while the cake-cutting ceremony was going on, and Miss Gibson herself fed us in the kitchen. It was hot as blazes with the cookstove on, and none of us was too hungry. The gig had started out feeling right and now it felt wrong. I could see it on my band's faces . . . on Miss Gibson's, too, for that matter.

By the time we returned to the bandstand, the drinking had begun in earnest. Tough-looking guys staggered around with silly grins on their mugs or stood in corners haggling over racing forms. Some couples wanted to Charleston, so we played "Aunt Hagar's Blues" (those goons ate it up) and "I'm Gonna Charleston Back to Charleston" and some other numbers like that. Jazz-baby stuff. The debs rocked around the floor, flashing their rolled hose and shaking their fingers beside their faces and yelling voe-doe-dee-oh-doe, a phrase that makes me feel like sicking up my supper to this very day. It was getting dark out. The screens had fallen off some of the windows and moths came in and flitted around the light fixtures in clouds. And, as the song says, the band played on. The bride and groom stood on the sidelines—neither of them seemed interested in slipping away early—almost completely neglected. Even Scollay seemed to have forgotten about them. He was pretty drunk.

It was almost 8:00 when the little fellow crept in. I spotted him immediately because he was sober and he looked scared; scared as a nearsighted cat in a dog pound. He walked up to Scollay, who was talking with some floozie right by the bandstand, and tapped him on the shoulder. Scollay wheeled around, and I heard every word they said. Believe me, I wish I hadn't.

"Who the hell are you?" Scollay asked rudely.

"My name is Demetrius," the fellow said. "Demetrius Katzenos. I come from the Greek."

Motion on the floor came to a dead stop. Jacket buttons were freed, and hands stole out of sight under lapels. I saw

Manny looking nervous. Hell, I didn't feel so calm myself. We kept on playing though, you bet.

"Is that right," Scollay said quietly, almost reflectively.

The guy burst out, "I didn't want to come, Mr. Scollay! The Greek, he has my wife. He say he kill her if I doan give you his message!"

"What message?" Scollay growled. The thunderclouds were back on his forehead.

"He say—" The guy paused with an agonized expression. His throat worked as if the words were physical things, caught in there and choking him. "He say to tell you your sister is one fat pig. He say . . . he say . . . ." His eyes rolled wildly at Scollay's still expression. I shot a look at Maureen. She looked as if she had been slapped. "He say she got an itch. He say if a fat woman got an itch on her back, she buy a back-scratcher. He say if a woman got an itch in her parts, she buy a man."

Maureen gave a great strangled cry and ran out, weeping. The floor shook. Rico pattered after her, his face bewildered. He was wringing his hands.

Scollay had grown so red his cheeks were actually purple. I half-expected—maybe more than half-expected—his brains to just blow out his ears. I saw that same look of mad agony I had seen in the dark outside Englander's. Maybe he was just a cheap hood, but I felt sorry for him. You would have, too.

When he spoke his voice was very quiet—almost mild.

"Is there more?"

The little Greek man quailed. His voice was splintery with anguish. "Please doan kill me, Mr. Scollay! My wife—the Greek, he got my wife! I doan *want* to say these thing! He got my wife, my woman—"

"I ain't going to hurt you," Scollay said, quieter still. "Just tell me the rest."

"He say the whole town laughing at you."

We had stopped playing and there was dead silence for a second. Then Scollay turned his eyes to the ceiling. Both of his hands were shaking and held out clenched in front of him. He was holding them in fists so tight that it seemed I could see his hamstrings standing out right through his shirt.

"*ALL RIGHT!*" he screamed. "*ALL RIGHT!*"

He broke for the door. Two of his men tried to stop him, tried to tell him it was suicide, just what the Greek wanted, but Scollay was like a crazy man. He knocked them down and rushed out into the black summer night.

In the dead quiet that followed, all I could hear was the messenger's tortured breathing and somewhere out back, the soft sobbing of the bride.

Just about then the young kid who had braced us when we came in uttered a curse and made for the door. He was the only one.

Before he could even get under the big paper shamrock hung in the foyer, automobile tires screeched on the pavement and engines revved up—a lot of engines. It sounded like Memorial Day at the Brickyard out there.

"Oh dear-to-Jaysus!" the kid screamed from the doorway. "It's a fucking caravan! *Get down, boss! Get down! Get down—*"

The night exploded with gunfire. It was like World War I out there for maybe a minute, maybe two. Bullets stitched across the open door of the hall, and one of the hanging light-globes overhead exploded. Outside the night was bright with Winchester fireworks. Then the cars howled away. One of the molls was brushing broken glass out of her bobbed hair.

Now that the danger was over, the rest of the goons rushed out. The door to the kitchen banged open and Maureen ran through again. Everything she had was jiggling. Her face was more puffy than ever. Rico came in her wake like a bewildered valet. They went out the door.

Miss Gibson appeared in the empty hall, her eyes wide and shocked. The little man who had started all the trouble with his singing telegram had powdered.

"It was shooting," Miss Gibson murmured. "What happened?"

"I think the Greek just cooled the paymaster," Biff said.

She looked at me, bewildered, but before I could translate Billy-Boy said in his soft, polite voice: "He means that Mr. Scollay just got rubbed out, Miz Gibson."

Miss Gibson stared at him, her eyes getting wider and wider, and then she fainted dead away. I felt a little like fainting myself.

Just then, from outside, came the most anguished scream I have ever heard, then or since. That unholy caterwauling just went on and on. You didn't have to peek out the door to know who was tearing her heart out in the street, keening over her dead brother even while the cops and newshawks were on their way.

"Let's blow," I muttered. "Quick."

We had it packed in before five minutes had passed. Some of the goons came back inside, but they were too drunk and too scared to notice the likes of us.

We went out the back, each of us carrying part of Biff's drum-kit. Quite a parade we must have made, walking up the street, for anyone who saw us. I led the way with my horn case tucked under my arm and a cymbal in each hand. The boys stood on the corner at the end of the block while I went back for the truck. The cops hadn't shown yet. The big girl was still crouched over the body of her brother in the middle of the street, wailing like a banshee while her tiny groom ran around her like a moon orbiting a big planet.

I drove down to the corner and the boys threw everything in the back, willy-nilly. Then we hauled ass out of there. We averaged forty-five miles an hour all the way back to Morgan, back roads or not, and either Scollay's goons must never have bothered to tip the cops to us, or else the cops didn't care, because we never heard from them.

We never got the two hundred bucks, either.

She came into Tommy Englander's about ten days later, a fat Irish girl in a black mourning dress. The black didn't look any better than the white satin.

Englander must have known who she was (her picture had been in the Chicago papers, next to Scollay's) because he showed her to a table himself and shushed a couple of drunks at the bar who had been snickering at her.

I felt badly for her, like I feel for Billy-Boy sometimes. It's tough to be on the outside. You don't have to be out there to know, although I'd have to agree that you can't know just what it's like. And she had been very sweet, the little I had talked to her.

When the break came, I went over to her table.

"I'm sorry about your brother," I said awkwardly. "I know he really cared for you, and—"

"I might as well have fired those guns myself," she said. She was looking down at her hands, and now that I noticed them I saw that they were really her best feature, small and comely. "Everything that little man said was true."

"Oh, say now," I replied—a *non sequitur* if ever there was one, but what else was there to say? I was sorry I'd come over, she talked so strangely. As if she was all alone, and crazy.

"I'm not going to divorce him, though," she went on. "I'd kill myself first, and damn my soul to hell."

"Don't talk that way," I said.

"Haven't you ever wanted to kill yourself?" she asked, looking at me passionately. "Doesn't it make you feel like that when people use you badly and then laugh at you? Or did no one ever do it to you? You may *say* so, but you'll pardon me if I don't believe it. Do you know what it feels like to eat and eat and hate yourself for it and then eat more? Do you know what it feels like to kill your own brother because you are *fat?*"

People were turning to look, and the drunks were sniggering again.

"I'm sorry," she whispered.

I wanted to tell her I was sorry, too. I wanted to tell her . . . oh, anything at all, I reckon, that would make her feel better. Holler down to where she was, inside all that flab. But I couldn't think of a single thing.

So I just said, "I have to go. We have to play another set."

"Of course," she said softly. "Of course you must . . . or they'll start to laugh at *you*. But why I came was—will you play 'Roses of Picardy'? I thought you played it very nicely at the reception. Will you do that?"

"Sure," I said. "Be glad to."

And we did. But she left halfway through the number, and since it was sort of schmaltzy for a place like Englander's, we dropped it and swung into a ragtime version of "The Varsity Drag." That one always tore them up. I drank too much the rest of the evening and by closing I had forgotten all about her. Well, almost.

Leaving for the night, it came to me. What I should have told her. Life goes on—that's what I should have said. That's what you say to people when a loved one dies. But, thinking it over, I was glad I didn't. Because maybe that was what she was afraid of.

*   *   *

Of course now everyone knows about Maureen Romano and her husband Rico, who survives her as the taxpayers' guest in the Illinois State Penitentiary. How she took over Scollay's two-bit organization and turned it into a Prohibition empire that rivaled Capone's. How she wiped out two other North Side gang leaders and swallowed their operations. How she had the Greek brought before her and supposedly killed him by sticking a piece of piano wire through his left eye and into his brain as he knelt in front of her, blubbering and pleading for his life. Rico, the bewildered valet, became her first lieutenant, and was responsible for a dozen gangland hits himself.

I followed Maureen's exploits from the West Coast, where we were making some pretty successful records. Without Billy-Boy, though. He formed a band of his own not long after we left Englander's, an all-black combination that played Dixieland and ragtime. They did real well down south, and I was glad for them. It was just as well. Lots of places wouldn't even audition us with a Negro in the group.

But I was telling you about Maureen. She made great news copy, and not just because she was a kind of Ma Barker with brains, although that was part of it. She was *awful* big and she was *awful* bad, and Americans from coast to coast felt a strange sort of affection for her. When she died of a heart attack in 1933, some of the papers said she weighed five hundred pounds. I doubt it, though. No one gets that big, do they?

Anyway, *her* funeral made the front pages. It was more than you could say for her brother, who never got past page four in his whole miserable career. It took ten pallbearers to carry her coffin. There was a picture of them toting it in one of the tabloids. It was a horrible picture to look at. Her coffin was the size of a meat locker—which, in a way, I suppose it was.

Rico wasn't bright enough to hold things together by himself, and he fell for assault with intent to kill the very next year.

I've never been able to get her out of my mind, or the agonized, hangdog way Scollay had looked that first night when he talked about her. But I cannot feel too sorry for her, looking back. Fat people can always stop eating. Guys like Billy-Boy Williams can only stop breathing. I still don't see any way I could have helped either of them, but I *do* feel sort of bad every now and then. Probably just because I've gotten a lot older and don't sleep as well as I did when I was a kid. That's all it is, isn't it?

Isn't it?

Paranoid: A Chant

I can't go out no more.
There's a man by the door
in a raincoat
smoking a cigarette.

But

I've put him in my diary
and the mailers are all lined up
on the bed, bloody in the glow
of the bar sign next door.

He knows that if I die
(or even drop out of sight)
the diary goes and everyone knows
the CIA's in Virginia.

500 mailers bought from
500 drug counters each one different
and 500 notebooks
with 500 pages in every one.

I am prepared.

*   *   *

I can see him from up here.
His cigarette winks from just
above his trenchcoat collar
and somewhere there's a man on a subway
sitting under a Black Velvet ad thinking my name.

Men have discussed me in back rooms.
If the phone rings there's only dead breath.
In the bar across the street a snubnose
revolver has changed hands in the men's room.
Each bullet has my name on it.
My name is written in back files
and looked up in newspaper morgues.

My mother's been investigated;
thank God she's dead.

They have writing samples
and examine the back loops of pees
and the crosses of tees.

My brother's with them, did I tell you?
His wife is Russian and he
keeps asking me to fill out forms.
I have it in my diary.
Listen—
    listen
      do listen:
        you must listen.

In the rain, at the bus stop,
black crows with black umbrellas
pretend to look at their watches, but
it's not raining. Their eyes are silver dollars.
Some are scholars in the pay of the FBI
most are the foreigners who pour through
our streets. I fooled them
got off the bus at 25th and Lex
where a cabby watched me over his newspaper.

In the room above me an old woman
has put an electric suction cup on her floor.

It sends out rays through my light fixture
and now I write in the dark
by the bar sign's glow.
I tell you I *know*.

They sent me a dog with brown spots
and a radio cobweb in its nose.
I drowned it in the sink and wrote it up
in folder GAMMA.

I don't look in the mailbox anymore.
The greeting cards are letter-bombs.

(Step away! Goddam you!
Step away, I know tall people!
I tell you I know *very* tall people!)

The luncheonette is laid with talking floors
and the waitress says it was salt but I know arsenic
when it's put before me. And the yellow taste of mustard
to mask the bitter odor of almonds.

I have seen strange lights in the sky.
Last night a dark man with no face crawled through nine miles
of sewer to surface in my toilet, listening
for phone calls through the cheap wood with
chrome ears.
I tell you, man, I *hear*.

I saw his muddy handprints
on the porcelain.

I don't answer the phone now,
have I told you that?

They are planning to flood the earth with sludge.
They are planning break-ins.

They have got physicians
advocating weird sex positions.
They are making addictive laxatives
and suppositories that burn.

They know how to put out the sun
with blowguns.

I pack myself in ice—have I told you that?
It obviates their infrascopes.
I know chants and I wear charms.
You may think you have me but I could destroy you
any second now.

Any second now.

Any second now.

Would you like some coffee, my love?

Did I tell you I can't go out no more?
There's a man by the door
in a raincoat.

The Raft

It was forty miles from Horlicks University in Pittsburgh to Cascade Lake, and although dark comes early to that part of the world in October and although they didn't get going until six o'clock, there was still a little light in the sky when they got there. They had come in Deke's Camaro. Deke didn't waste any time when he was sober. After a couple of beers, he made that Camaro walk and talk.

He had hardly brought the car to a stop at the pole fence between the parking lot and the beach before he was out and pulling off his shirt. His eyes were scanning the water for the raft. Randy got out of the shotgun seat, a little reluctantly. This had been his idea, true enough, but he had never expected Deke to take it seriously. The girls were moving around in the back seat, getting ready to get out.

Deke's eyes scanned the water restlessly, side to side (*sniper's eyes*, Randy thought uncomfortably), and then fixed on a point.

"It's there!" he shouted, slapping the hood of the Camaro. "Just like you said, Randy! Hot damn! Last one in's a rotten egg!"

"Deke—" Randy began, resetting his glasses on his nose, but that was all he bothered with, because Deke was vaulting the fence and running down the beach, not looking back at Randy or Rachel or LaVerne, only looking out at the raft, which was anchored about fifty yards out on the lake.

Randy looked around, as if to apologize to the girls for getting them into this, but they were looking at Deke—Rachel looking at him was all right, Rachel was Deke's girl, but LaVerne was looking at him too and Randy felt a hot momentary spark of jealousy that got him moving. He peeled off his own sweatshirt, dropped it beside Deke's, and hopped the fence.

"Randy!" LaVerne called, and he only pulled his arm forward through the gray twilit October air in a come-on gesture, hating himself a little for doing it—she was unsure now, perhaps ready to cry it off. The idea of an October swim in the deserted lake wasn't just part of a comfortable, well-lighted bull-session in the apartment he and Deke shared anymore. He liked her, but Deke was stronger. And damned if she didn't have the hots for Deke, and damned if it wasn't irritating.

Deke unbuckled his jeans, still running, and pushed them off his lean hips. He somehow got out of them all the way without stopping, a feat Randy could not have duplicated in a thousand years. Deke ran on, now only wearing bikini briefs, the muscles in his back and buttocks working gorgeously. Randy was more than aware of his own skinny shanks as he dropped his Levi's and clumsily shook them free of his feet—with Deke it was ballet, with him burlesque.

Deke hit the water and bellowed, "Cold! Mother of Jesus!"

Randy hesitated, but only in his mind, where things took longer—*that water's forty-five degrees, fifty at most,* his mind told him. *Your heart could stop.* He was pre-med, he knew that was true . . . but in the physical world he didn't hesitate at all. He leaped it, and for a moment his heart *did* stop, or seemed to; his breath clogged in his throat and he had to force a gasp of air into his lungs as all his submerged skin went numb. *This is crazy,* he thought, and then: *But it was your idea, Pancho.* He began to stroke after Deke.

The two girls looked at each other for a moment. LaVerne shrugged and grinned. "If they can, we can," she said, stripping off her Lacoste shirt to reveal an almost transparent bra. "Aren't girls supposed to have an extra layer of fat?"

Then she was over the fence and running for the water, unbuttoning her cords. After a moment Rachel followed her, much as Randy had followed Deke.

*   *   *

The girls had come over to the apartment at midafternoon —on Tuesdays a one-o'clock was the latest class any of them had. Deke's monthly allotment had come in—one of the football-mad alums (the players called them "angels") saw that he got two hundred a month in cash—and there was a case of beer in the fridge and a new Night Ranger album on Randy's battered stereo. The four of them set about getting pleasantly oiled. After a while the talk had turned to the end of the long Indian summer they had been enjoying. The radio was predicting flurries for Wednesday. LaVerne had advanced the opinion that weathermen predicting snow flurries in October should be shot, and no one had disagreed.

Rachel said that summers had seemed to last forever when she was a girl, but now that she was an adult ("a doddering senile nineteen," Deke joked, and she kicked his ankle), they got shorter every year. "It seemed like I spent my life out at Cascade Lake," she said, crossing the decayed kitchen linoleum to the icebox. She peered in, found an Iron City Light hiding behind a stack of blue Tupperware storage boxes (the one in the middle contained some nearly prehistoric chili which was now thickly festooned with mold—Randy was a good student and Deke was a good football player, but neither of them was worth a fart in a noisemaker when it came to housekeeping), and appropriated it. "I can still remember the first time I managed to swim all the way out to the raft. I stayed there for damn near two hours, scared to swim back."

She sat down next to Deke, who put an arm around her. She smiled, remembering, and Randy suddenly thought she looked like someone famous or semi-famous. He couldn't quite place the resemblance. It would come to him later, under less pleasant circumstances.

"Finally my brother had to swim out and tow me back on an inner tube. God, he was mad. And I had a sunburn like you wouldn't believe."

"The raft's still out there," Randy said, mostly to say something. He was aware that LaVerne had been looking at Deke again; just lately it seemed like she looked at Deke a lot.

But now she looked at him. "It's almost *Halloween*, Randy. Cascade Beach has been closed since Labor Day."

"Raft's probably still out there, though," Randy said. "We were on the other side of the lake on a geology field trip about three weeks ago and I saw it then. It looked like . . ." He shrugged. " . . . a little bit of summer that somebody forgot to clean up and put away in the closet until next year."

He thought they would laugh at that, but no one did—not even Deke.

"Just because it was there last year doesn't mean it's still there," LaVerne said.

"I mentioned it to a guy," Randy said, finishing his own beer. "Billy DeLois, do you remember him, Deke?"

Deke nodded. "Played second string until he got hurt."

"Yeah, I guess so. Anyway, he comes from out that way, and he said the guys who own the beach never take it in until the lake's almost ready to freeze. Just lazy—at least, that's what he said. He said that some year they'd wait too long and it would get ice-locked."

He fell silent, remembering how the raft had looked, anchored out there on the lake—a square of bright white wood in all that bright blue autumn water. He remembered how the sound of the barrels under it—that buoyant *clunk-clunk* sound—had drifted up to them. The sound was soft, but sounds carried well on the still air around the lake. There had been that sound and the sound of crows squabbling over the remnants of some farmer's harvested garden.

"Snow tomorrow," Rachel said, getting up as Deke's hand wandered almost absently down to the upper swell of her breast. She went to the window and looked out. "What a bummer."

"I'll tell you what," Randy said, "let's go on out to Cascade Lake. We'll swim out to the raft, say good-bye to summer, and then swim back."

If he hadn't been half-loaded he never would have made the suggestion, and he certainly didn't expect anyone to take it seriously. But Deke jumped on it.

"All right! Awesome, Pancho! Fooking *awesome!*" La-Verne jumped and spilled her beer. But she smiled—the smile made Randy a little uneasy. "Let's do it!"

"Deke, you're crazy," Rachel said, also smiling—but her smile looked a little tentative, a little worried.

"No, I'm going to do it," Deke said, going for his coat, and with a mixture of dismay and excitement, Randy noted Deke's grin—reckless and a little crazy. The two of them had been rooming together for three years now—the Jock and the

Brain, Cisco and Pancho, Batman and Robin—and Randy recognized that grin. Deke wasn't kidding; he meant to do it. In his head he was already halfway there.

Forget it, Cisco—not me. The words rose to his lips, but before he could say them LaVerne was on her feet, the same cheerful, loony look in her own eyes (or maybe it was just too much beer). "I'm up for it!"

"Then let's go!" Deke looked at Randy. "Whatchoo say, Pancho?"

He had looked at Rachel for a moment then, and saw something almost frantic in her eyes—as far as he himself was concerned, Deke and LaVerne could go out to Cascade Lake together and plow the back forty all night; he would not be delighted with the knowledge that they were boffing each other's brains out, yet neither would he be surprised. But that look in the other girl's eyes, that haunted look—

"Ohhh, *Ceesco!*" Randy cried.

"Ohhhh, *Pancho!*" Deke cried back, delighted.

They slapped palms.

Randy was halfway to the raft when he saw the black patch on the water. It was beyond the raft and to the left of it, more out toward the middle of the lake. Five minutes later the light would have failed too much for him to tell it was anything more than a shadow . . . if he had seen it at all. *Oil slick?* he thought, still pulling hard through the water, faintly aware of the girls splashing behind him. But what would an oil slick be doing on an October-deserted lake? And it was oddly circular, small, surely no more than five feet in diameter—

"*Whoooo!*" Deke shouted again, and Randy looked toward him. Deke was climbing the ladder on the side of the raft, shaking off water like a dog. "Howya doon, Pancho?"

"Okay!" he called back, pulling harder. It really wasn't as bad as he had thought it might be, not once you got in and got moving. His body tingled with warmth and now his motor was in overdrive. He could feel his heart putting out good revs, heating him from the inside out. His folks had a place on Cape Cod, and the water there was worse than this in mid-July.

"You think it's bad now, Pancho, wait'll you get out!" Deke yelled gleefully. He was hopping up and down, making the raft rock, rubbing his body.

Randy forgot about the oil slick until his hands actually grasped the rough, white-painted wood of the ladder on the shore side. Then he saw it again. It was a little closer. A round dark patch on the water, like a big mole, rising and falling on the mild waves. When he had first seen it the patch had been maybe forty yards from the raft. Now it was only half that distance.

How can that be? How—

Then he came out of the water and the cold air bit his skin, bit it even harder than the water had when he first dived in. "Ohhhhhh, *shit!*" He yelled, laughing, shivering in his Jockey shorts.

"Pancho, you ees some kine of beeg asshole," Deke said happily. He pulled Randy up. "Cold enough for you? You sober yet?"

"I'm sober! I'm sober!" He began to jump around as Deke had done, clapping his arms across his chest and stomach in an X. They turned to look at the girls.

Rachel had pulled ahead of LaVerne, who was doing something that looked like a dog paddle performed by a dog with bad instincts.

"You ladies okay?" Deke bellowed.

"Go to hell, Macho City!" LaVerne called, and Deke broke up again.

Randy glanced to the side and saw that odd dark circular patch was even closer—ten yards now, and still coming. It floated on the water, round and regular, like the top of a large steel drum, but the limber way it rode the swells made it clear that it was not the surface of a solid object. Fear, directionless but powerful, suddenly seized him.

"*Swim!*" he shouted at the girls, and bent down to grasp Rachel's hand as she reached the ladder. He hauled her up. She bumped her knee hard—he heard the thud clearly.

"Ow! *Hey!* What—"

LaVerne was still ten feet away. Randy glanced to the side again and saw the round thing nuzzle the offside of the raft. The thing was as dark as oil, but he was sure it wasn't oil—too dark, too thick, too *even.*

"Randy, that *hurt!* What are you doing, being fun—"

"LaVerne! *Swim!*" Now it wasn't just fear; now it was terror.

LaVerne looked up, maybe not hearing the terror but at

least hearing the urgency. She looked puzzled but she dog-paddled faster, closing the distance to the ladder.

"Randy, what's wrong with you?" Deke asked.

Randy looked to the side again and saw the thing fold itself around the raft's square corner. For a moment it looked like a Pac-Man image with its mouth open to eat electronic cookies. Then it slipped all the way around the corner and began to slide along the raft, one of its edges now straight.

"Help me get her up!" Randy grunted to Deke, and reached for her hand. "Quick!"

Deke shrugged good-naturedly and reached for LaVerne's other hand. They pulled her up and onto the raft's board surface bare seconds before the black thing slid by the ladder, its sides dimpling as it slipped past the ladder's uprights.

"Randy, have you gone crazy?" LaVerne was out of breath, a little frightened. Her nipples were clearly visible through the bra. They stood out in cold hard points.

"That thing," Randy said, pointing. "Deke? What is it?"

Deke spotted it. It had reached the left-hand corner of the raft. It drifted off a little to one side, reassuming its round shape. It simply floated there. The four of them looked at it.

"Oil slick, I guess," Deke said.

"You really racked my knee," Rachel said, glancing at the dark thing on the water and then back at Randy. "You—"

"It's not an oil slick," Randy said. "Did you ever see a round oil slick? That thing looks like a checker."

"I never saw an oil slick at all," Deke replied. He was talking to Randy but he was looking at LaVerne. LaVerne's panties were almost as transparent as her bra, the delta of her sex sculpted neatly in silk, each buttock a taut crescent. "I don't even believe in them. I'm from Missouri."

"I'm going to bruise," Rachel said, but the anger had gone out of her voice. She had seen Deke looking at LaVerne.

"*God,* I'm cold," LaVerne said. She shivered prettily.

"It went for the girls," Randy said.

"Come on, Pancho. I thought you said you got sober."

"It went for the girls," he repeated stubbornly, and thought: *No one knows we're here. No one at all.*

"Have *you* ever seen an oil slick, Pancho?" He had put his arm around LaVerne's bare shoulders in the same almost-absent way that he had touched Rachel's breast earlier that day. He wasn't touching LaVerne's breast—not yet, anyway—

but his hand was close. Randy found he didn't care much, one way or another. That black, circular patch on the water. He cared about that.

"I saw one on the Cape, four years ago," he said. "We all pulled birds out of the surf and tried to clean them off—"

"Ecological, Pancho," Deke said approvingly. "Mucho ecological, I theenk."

Randy said, "It was just this big, sticky mess all over the water. In streaks and big smears. It didn't look like that. It wasn't, you know, *compact.*"

It looked like an accident, he wanted to say. *That thing doesn't look like an accident; it looks like it's on purpose.*

"I want to go back now," Rachel said. She was still looking at Deke and LaVerne. Randy saw dull hurt in her face. He doubted if she knew it showed.

"So go," LaVerne said. There was a look on her face—*the clarity of absolute triumph,* Randy thought, and if the thought seemed pretentious, it also seemed exactly right. The expression was not aimed precisely at Rachel . . . but neither was LaVerne trying to hide it from the other girl.

She moved a step closer to Deke; a step was all there was. Now their hips touched lightly. For one brief moment Randy's attention passed from the thing floating on the water and focused on LaVerne with an almost exquisite hate. Although he had never hit a girl, in that one moment he could have hit her with real pleasure. Not because he loved her (he had been a little infatuated with her, yes, and more than a little horny for her, yes, and a lot jealous when she had begun to come on to Deke back at the apartment, oh yes, but he wouldn't have brought a girl he actually *loved* within fifteen miles of Deke in the first place), but because he knew that expression on Rachel's face—how that expression felt inside.

"I'm afraid," Rachel said.

"Of an *oil slick?*" LaVerne asked incredulously, and then laughed. The urge to hit her swept over Randy again—to just swing a big roundhouse open-handed blow through the air, to wipe that look of half-assed hauteur from her face and leave a mark on her cheek that would bruise in the shape of a hand.

"Let's see you swim back, then," Randy said.

LaVerne smiled indulgently at him. "I'm not ready to go," she said, as if explaining to a child. She looked up at the sky, then at Deke. "I want to watch the stars come out."

Rachel was a short girl, pretty, but in a gamine, slightly insecure way that made Randy think of New York girls—you saw them hurrying to work in the morning, wearing their smartly tailored skirts with slits in the front or up one side, wearing that same look of slightly neurotic prettiness. Rachel's eyes always sparkled, but it was hard to tell if it was good cheer that lent them that lively look or just free-floating anxiety.

Deke's tastes usually ran more to tall girls with dark hair and sleepy sloe eyes, and Randy saw it was now over between Deke and Rachel—whatever there had been, something simple and maybe a little boring on his part, something deep and complicated and probably painful on hers. It was over, so cleanly and suddenly that Randy almost heard the snap: a sound like dry kindling broken over a knee.

He was a shy boy, but he moved to Rachel now and put an arm around her. She glanced up at him briefly, her face unhappy but grateful for his gesture, and he was glad he had improved the situation for her a little. That similarity bobbed into his mind again. Something in her face, her looks—

He first associated it with TV game shows, then with commercials for crackers or wafers or some damn thing. It came to him then—she looked like Sandy Duncan, the actress who had played in the revival of *Peter Pan* on Broadway.

"What is that thing?" she asked. "Randy? What is it?"

"I don't know."

He glanced at Deke and saw Deke looking at him with that familiar smile that was more loving familiarity than contempt . . . but the contempt was there, too. Maybe Deke didn't even know it, but it was. The expression said *Here goes ole worry-wart Randy, pissing in his didies again*. It was supposed to make Randy mumble an addition—*It's probably nothing, Don't worry about it, It'll go away*. Something like that. He didn't. Let Deke smile. The black patch on the water scared him. That was the truth.

Rachel stepped away from Randy and knelt prettily on the corner of the raft closest to the thing, and for a moment she triggered an even clearer memory-association: the girl on the White Rock labels. *Sandy Duncan on the White Rock labels*, his mind amended. Her hair, a close-cropped, slightly coarse blond, lay wetly against her finely shaped skull. He could see goosebumps on her shoulder blades above the white band of her bra.

"Don't fall in, Rache," LaVerne said with bright malice.

"Quit it, LaVerne," Deke said, still smiling.

Randy looked from them, standing in the middle of the raft with their arms loosely around each other's waists, hips touching lightly, and back at Rachel. Alarm raced down his spine and out through his nerves like fire. The black patch had halved the distance between it and the corner of the raft where Rachel was kneeling and looking at it. It had been six or eight feet away before. Now the distance was three feet or less. And he saw a strange look in her eyes, a round blankness that seemed queerly like the round blankness of the thing in the water.

Now it's Sandy Duncan sitting on a White Rock label and pretending to be hypnotized by the rich delicious flavor of Nabisco Honey Grahams, he thought idiotically, feeling his heart speed up as it had in the water, and he called out, "Get away from there, Rachel!"

Then everything happened very fast—things happened with the rapidity of fireworks going off. And yet he saw and heard each thing with perfect, hellish clarity. Each thing seemed caught in its own little capsule.

LaVerne laughed—on the quad in a bright afternoon hour it might have sounded like any college girl's laugh, but out here in the growing dark it sounded like the arid cackle of a witch making magic in a pot.

"Rachel, maybe you better get b—" Deke said, but she interrupted him, almost surely for the first time in her life, and indubitably for the last.

"It has colors!" she cried in a voice of utter, trembling wonder. Her eyes stared at the black patch on the water with blank rapture, and for just a moment Randy thought he saw what she was talking about—colors, yeah, colors, swirling in rich, inward-turning spirals. Then they were gone, and there was only dull, lusterless black again. "Such beautiful colors!"

"Rachel!"

She reached for it—out and down—her white arm, marbled with gooseflesh, her hand, held out to it, meaning to touch; he saw she had bitten her nails ragged.

"Ra—"

He sensed the raft tilt in the water as Deke moved toward

them. He reached for Rachel at the same time, meaning to pull her back, dimly aware that he didn't want Deke to be the one to do it.

Then Rachel's hand touched the water—her forefinger only, sending out one delicate ripple in a ring—and the black patch surged over it. Randy heard her gasp in air, and suddenly the blankness left her eyes. What replaced it was agony.

The black, viscous substance ran up her arm like mud . . . and under it, Randy saw her skin dissolving. She opened her mouth and screamed. At the same moment she began to tilt outward. She waved her other hand blindly at Randy and he grabbed for it. Their fingers brushed. Her eyes met his, and she still looked hellishly like Sandy Duncan. Then she fell outward and splashed into the water.

The black thing flowed over the spot where she had landed.

"What happened?" LaVerne was screaming behind them. *"What happened? Did she fall in? What happened to her?"*

Randy made as if to dive in after her and Deke pushed him backwards with casual force. "No," he said in a frightened voice that was utterly unlike Deke.

All three of them saw her flail to the surface. Her arms came up, waving—no, not arms. One arm. The other was covered with a black membrane that hung in flaps and folds from something red and knitted with tendons, something that looked a little like a rolled roast of beef.

"Help!" Rachel screamed. Her eyes glared at them, away from them, at them, away—her eyes were like lanterns being waved aimlessly in the dark. She beat the water into a froth. *"Help it hurts please help it hurts IT HURTS IT HURRRRR—"*

Randy had fallen when Deke pushed him. Now he got up from the boards of the raft and stumbled forward again, unable to ignore that voice. He tried to jump in and Deke grabbed him, wrapping his big arms around Randy's thin chest.

"No, she's dead," he whispered harshly. "Christ, can't you see that? She's *dead,* Pancho."

Thick blackness suddenly poured across Rachel's face like a drape, and her screams were first muffled and then cut off entirely. Now the black stuff seemed to bind her in crisscrossing ropes. Randy could see it sinking into her like acid, and when her jugular vein gave way in a dark, pumping jet, he saw the thing send out a pseudopod after the escaping blood.

He could not believe what he was seeing, could not understand it . . . but there was no doubt, no sensation of losing his mind, no belief that he was dreaming or hallucinating.

LaVerne was screaming. Randy turned to look at her just in time to see her slap a hand melodramatically over her eyes like a silent movie heroine. He thought he would laugh and tell her this, but found he could not make a sound.

He looked back at Rachel. Rachel was almost not there anymore.

Her struggles had weakened to the point where they were really no more than spasms. The blackness oozed over her—*bigger now*, Randy thought, *it's bigger, no question about it*—with mute, muscular power. He saw her hand beat at it; saw the hand become stuck, as if in molasses or on flypaper; saw it consumed. Now there was a sense of her form only, not in the water but in the black thing, not turning but being turned, the form becoming less recognizable, a white flash—*bone*, he thought sickly, and turned away, vomiting helplessly over the side of the raft.

LaVerne was still screaming. Then there was a dull *whap!* and she stopped screaming and began to snivel.

He hit her, Randy thought. *I was going to do that, remember?*

He stepped back, wiping his mouth, feeling weak and ill. And scared. So scared he could think with only one tiny wedge of his mind. Soon he would begin to scream himself. Then Deke would have to slap him, Deke wouldn't panic, oh no, Deke was hero material for sure. *You gotta be a football hero . . . to get along with the beautiful girls*, his mind sang cheerfully. Then he could hear Deke talking to him, and he looked up at the sky, trying to clear his head, trying desperately to put away the vision of Rachel's form becoming blobbish and inhuman as that black thing ate her, not wanting Deke to slap him the way he had slapped LaVerne.

He looked up at the sky and saw the first stars shining up there—the shape of the Dipper already clear as the last white light faded out of the west. It was nearly seven-thirty.

"Oh Ceeesco," he managed. "We are in beeg trouble thees time, I theeenk."

"What is it?" His hand fell on Randy's shoulder, gripping and twisting painfully. "It ate her, did you see that? It *ate* her, it fucking *ate her up!* What *is* it?"

"I don't know. Didn't you hear me before?"

"You're *supposed* to know, you're a fucking brain-ball, you take all the fucking science courses!" Now Deke was almost screaming himself, and that helped Randy get a little more control.

"There's nothing like that in any science book I ever read," Randy told him. "The last time I saw anything like that was the Halloween Shock-Show down at the Rialto when I was twelve."

The thing had regained its round shape now. It floated on the water ten feet from the raft.

"It's bigger," LaVerne moaned.

When Randy had first seen it, he had guessed its diameter at about five feet. Now it had to be at least eight feet across.

"It's bigger because it ate Rachel!" LaVerne cried, and began to scream again.

"Stop that or I'm going to break your jaw," Deke said, and she stopped—not all at once, but winding down the way a record does when somebody turns off the juice without taking the needle off the disc. Her eyes were huge things.

Deke looked back at Randy. "You all right, Pancho?"

"I don't know. I guess so."

"My man." Deke tried to smile, and Randy saw with some alarm that he was succeeding—was some part of Deke enjoying this? "You don't have any idea at all what it might be?"

Randy shook his head. Maybe it was an oil slick, after all . . . or had been, until something had happened to it. Maybe cosmic rays had hit it in a certain way. Or maybe Arthur Godfrey had pissed atomic Bisquick all over it, who knew? Who *could* know?

"Can we swim past it, do you think?" Deke persisted, shaking Randy's shoulder.

"No!" LaVerne shrieked.

"Stop it or I'm gonna smoke you, LaVerne," Deke said, raising his voice again. "I'm not kidding."

"You saw how fast it took Rachel," Randy said.

"Maybe it was hungry then," Deke answered. "But maybe now it's full."

Randy thought of Rachel kneeling there on the corner of the raft, so still and pretty in her bra and panties, and felt his gorge rise again.

"You try it," he said to Deke.

Deke grinned humorlessly. "Oh Pancho."

"Oh Ceesco."

"I want to go home," LaVerne said in a furtive whisper. "Okay?"

Neither of them replied.

"So we wait for it to go away," Deke said. "It came, it'll go away."

"Maybe," Randy said.

Deke looked at him, his face full of a fierce concentration in the gloom. "Maybe? What's this maybe shit?"

"We came, and it came. I saw it come—like it smelled us. If it's full, like you say, it'll go. I guess. If it still wants chow—" He shrugged.

Deke stood thoughtfully, head bent. His short hair was still dripping a little.

"We wait," he said. "Let it eat fish."

Fifteen minutes passed. They didn't talk. It got colder. It was maybe fifty degrees and all three of them were in their underwear. After the first ten minutes, Randy could hear the brisk, intermittent clickety-click of his teeth. LaVerne had tried to move next to Deke, but he pushed her away—gently but firmly enough.

"Let me be for now," he said.

So she sat down, arms crossed over her breasts, hands cupping her elbows, shivering. She looked at Randy, her eyes telling him he could come back, put his arm around her, it was okay now.

He looked away instead, back at the dark circle on the water. It just floated there, not coming any closer, but not going away, either. He looked toward the shore and there was the beach, a ghostly white crescent that seemed to float. The trees behind it made a dark, bulking horizon line. He thought he could see Deke's Camaro, but he wasn't sure.

"We just picked up and went," Deke said.

"That's right," Randy said.

"Didn't tell anyone."

"No."

"So no one knows we're here."

"No."

"Stop it!" LaVerne shouted. "Stop it, you're scaring me!"

''Shut your pie-hole,'' Deke said absently, and Randy laughed in spite of himself—no matter how many times Deke said that, it always slew him. ''If we have to spend the night out here, we do. Somebody'll hear us yelling tomorrow. We're hardly in the middle of the Australian Outback, are we, Randy?''

Randy said nothing.

''Are we?''

''You know where we are,'' Randy said. ''You know as well as I do. We turned off Route 41, we came up eight miles of back road—''

''Cottages every fifty feet—''

''Summer cottages. This is October. They're empty, the whole bucking funch of them. We got here and you had to drive around the damn gate, NO TRESPASSING signs every fifty feet—''

''So? A caretaker—'' Deke was sounding a little pissed now, a little off-balance. A little scared? For the first time tonight, for the first time this month, this year, maybe for the first time in his whole life? Now there was an awesome thought—Deke loses his fear-cherry. Randy was not sure it was happening, but he thought maybe it was . . . and he took a perverse pleasure in it.

''Nothing to steal, nothing to vandalize,'' he said. ''If there's a caretaker, he probably pops by here on a bimonthly basis.''

''Hunters—''

''Next month, yeah,'' Randy said, and shut his mouth with a snap. He had also succeeded in scaring himself.

''Maybe it'll leave us alone,'' LaVerne said. Her lips made a pathetic, loose little smile. ''Maybe it'll just . . . you know . . . leave us alone.''

Deke said, ''Maybe pigs will—''

''It's moving,'' Randy said.

LaVerne leaped to her feet. Deke came to where Randy was and for a moment the raft tilted, scaring Randy's heart into a gallop and making LaVerne scream again. Then Deke stepped back a little and the raft stabilized, with the left front corner (as they faced the shoreline) dipped down slightly more than the rest of the raft.

It came with an oily, frightening speed, and as it did, Randy saw the colors Rachel had seen—fantastic reds and yellows and blues spiraling across an ebony surface like limp plastic or dark, lithe Naugahyde. It rose and fell with the waves and that changed the colors, made them swirl and blend. Randy realized he was going to fall over, fall right into it, he could feel himself tilting out—

With the last of his strength he brought his right fist up into his own nose—the gesture of a man stifling a cough, only a little high and a lot hard. His nose flared with pain, he felt blood run warmly down his face, and then he was able to step back, crying out: "Don't look at it! Deke! Don't look right at it, the colors make you loopy!"

"It's trying to get under the raft," Deke said grimly. "What's this shit, Pancho?"

Randy looked—he looked very carefully. He saw the thing nuzzling the side of the raft, flattening to a shape like half a pizza. For a moment it seemed to be piling up there, thickening, and he had an alarming vision of it piling up enough to run onto the surface of the raft.

Then it squeezed under. He thought he heard a noise for a moment—a rough noise, like a roll of canvas being pulled through a narrow window—but that might have only been nerves.

"Did it go under?" LaVerne said, and there was something oddly nonchalant about her tone, as if she were trying with all her might to be conversational, but she was screaming, too. "Did it go under the raft? Is it under us?"

"Yes," Deke said. He looked at Randy. "I'm going to swim for it right now," he said. "If it's under there I've got a good chance."

"No!" LaVerne screamed. "No, don't leave us here, don't—"

"I'm fast," Deke said, looking at Randy, ignoring LaVerne completely. "But I've got to go while it's under there."

Randy's mind felt as if it was whizzing along at Mach two—in a greasy, nauseating way it was exhilarating, like the last few seconds before you puke into the slipstream of a cheap carnival ride. There was time to hear the barrels under the raft clunking hollowly together, time to hear the leaves on the trees beyond the beach rattling dryly in a little puff of wind, time to wonder why it had gone under the raft.

"Yes," he said to Deke. "But I don't think you'll make it."

"I'll make it," Deke said, and started toward the edge of the raft.

He got two steps and then stopped.

His breath had been speeding up, his brain getting his heart and lungs ready to swim the fastest fifty yards of his life and now his breath stopped like the rest of him, simply stopped in the middle of an inhale. He turned his head, and Randy saw the cords in his neck stand out.

"Panch—" he said in an amazed, choked voice, and then he began to scream.

He screamed with amazing force, great baritone bellows that splintered up toward wild soprano levels. They were loud enough to echo back from the shore in ghostly half-notes. At first Randy thought he was just screaming, and then he realized it was a word—no, two words, the same two words over and over: *"My foot!"* Deke was screaming. *"My foot! My foot! My foot!"*

Randy looked down. Deke's foot had taken on an odd sunken look. The reason was obvious, but Randy's mind refused to accept it at first—it was too impossible, too insanely grotesque. As he watched, Deke's foot was being pulled down between two of the boards that made up the surface of the raft.

Then he saw the dark shine of the black thing beyond the heel and the toes, dark shine alive with swirling, malevolent colors.

The thing had his foot (*"My foot!"* Deke screamed, as if to confirm this elementary deduction. *"My foot, oh my foot, my FOOOOOOT!"*). He had stepped on one of the cracks between the boards (*step on a crack, break yer mother's back*, Randy's mind gibbered), and the thing had been down there. The thing had—

"Pull!" he screamed back suddenly. *"Pull, Deke, goddammit, PULL!"*

"What's happening?" LaVerne hollered, and Randy realized dimly that she wasn't just shaking his shoulder; she had sunk her spade-shaped fingernails into him like claws. She was going to be absolutely no help at all. He drove an elbow into her stomach. She made a barking, coughing noise and sat down on her fanny. He leaped to Deke and grabbed one of Deke's arms.

It was as hard as Carrara marble, every muscle standing out

like the rib of a sculpted dinosaur skeleton. Pulling Deke was like trying to pull a big tree out of the ground by the roots. Deke's eyes were turned up toward the royal purple of the post-dusk sky, glazed and unbelieving, and still he screamed, screamed, screamed.

Randy looked down and saw that Deke's foot had now disappeared into the crack between the boards up to the ankle. That crack was perhaps only a quarter of an inch wide, surely no more than half an inch, but his foot had gone into it. Blood ran across the white boards in thick dark tendrils. Black stuff like heated plastic pulsed up and down in the crack, up and down, like a heart beating.

Got to get him out. Got to get him out quick or we're never gonna get him out at all . . . hold on, Cisco, please hold on . . .

LaVerne got to her feet and backed away from the gnarled, screaming Deke-tree in the center of the raft which floated at anchor under the October stars on Cascade Lake. She was shaking her head numbly, her arms crossed over her belly where Randy's elbow had gotten her.

Deke leaned hard against him, arms groping stupidly. Randy looked down and saw blood gushing from Deke's shin, which now tapered the way a sharpened pencil tapers to a point—only the point here was white, not black, the point was a bone, barely visible.

The black stuff surged up again, sucking, eating.

Deke wailed.

Never going to play football on that foot again, WHAT foot, ha-ha, and he pulled Deke with all his might and it was still like pulling at a rooted tree.

Deke lurched again and now he uttered a long, drilling shriek that made Randy fall back, shrieking himself, hands covering his ears. Blood burst from the pores of Deke's calf and shin; his kneecap had taken on a purple, bulging look as it tried to absorb the tremendous pressure being put on it as the black thing hauled Deke's leg down through the narrow crack inch by inch.

Can't help him. How strong it must be! Can't help him now, I'm sorry, Deke, so sorry—

"Hold me, Randy," LaVerne screamed, clutching at him everywhere, digging her face into his chest. Her face was so hot it seemed to sizzle. "Hold me, please, won't you hold me—"

This time, he did.

It was only later that a terrible realization came to Randy: the two of them could almost surely have swum ashore while the black thing was busy with Deke—and if LaVerne refused to try it, he could have done it himself. The keys to the Camaro were in Deke's jeans, lying on the beach. He could have done it . . . but the realization that he could have never came to him until too late.

Deke died just as his thigh began to disappear into the narrow crack between the boards. He had stopped shrieking minutes before. Since then he had uttered only thick, syrupy grunts. Then those stopped, too. When he fainted, falling forward, Randy heard whatever remained of the femur in his right leg splinter in a greenstick fracture.

A moment later Deke raised his head, looked around groggily, and opened his mouth. Randy thought he meant to scream again. Instead, he voided a great jet of blood, so thick it was almost solid. Both Randy and LaVerne were splattered with its warmth and she began to scream again, hoarsely now.

"*Oooog!*" she cried, her face twisted in half-mad revulsion. "*Oooog!* Blood! *Ooooog,* blood! *Blood!*" She rubbed at herself and only succeeded in smearing it around.

Blood was pouring from Deke's eyes, coming with such force that they had bugged out almost comically with the force of the hemorrhage. Randy thought: *Talk about vitality! Christ, LOOK at that! He's like a goddammed human fire hydrant! God! God! God!*

Blood streamed from both of Deke's ears. His face was a hideous purple turnip, swelled shapeless with the hydrostatic pressure of some unbelievable reversal; it was the face of a man being clutched in a bear hug of monstrous and unknowable force.

And then, mercifully, it was over.

Deke collapsed forward again, his hair hanging down on the raft's bloody boards, and Randy saw with sickish amazement that even Deke's scalp had bled.

Sounds from under the raft. Sucking sounds.

That was when it occurred to his tottering, overloaded mind that he could swim for it and stand a good chance of making it. But LaVerne had gotten heavy in his arms, ominously heavy; he looked at her slack face, rolled back an eyelid to disclose only white, and knew that she had not fainted but fallen into a state of shock-unconsciousness.

Randy looked at the surface of the raft. He could lay her down, of course, but the boards were only a foot across. There was a diving board platform attached to the raft in the summertime, but that, at least, had been taken down and stored somewhere. Nothing left but the surface of the raft itself, fourteen boards, each a foot wide and twenty feet long. No way to put her down without laying her unconscious body across any number of those cracks.

Step on a crack, break your mother's back.

Shut up.

And then, tenebrously, his mind whispered: *Do it anyway. Put her down and swim for it.*

But he did not, could not. An awful guilt rose in him at the thought. He held her, feeling the soft, steady drag on his arms and back. She was a big girl.

Deke went down.

Randy held LaVerne in his aching arms and watched it happen. He did not want to, and for long seconds that might even have been minutes he turned his face away entirely; but his eyes always wandered back.

With Deke dead, it seemed to go faster.

The rest of his right leg disappeared, his left leg stretching out further and further until Deke looked like a one-legged ballet dancer doing an impossible split. There was the wishbone crack of his pelvis, and then, as Deke's stomach began to swell ominously with new pressure, Randy looked away for a long time, trying not to hear the wet sounds, trying to concentrate on the pain in his arms. He could maybe bring her around, he thought, but for the time being it was better to have the throbbing pain in his arms and shoulders. It gave him something to think about.

From behind him came a sound like strong teeth crunching up a mouthful of candy jawbreakers. When he looked back, Deke's ribs were collapsing into the crack. His arms were up and out, and he looked like an obscene parody of Richard Nixon giving the V-for-victory sign that had driven demonstrators wild in the sixties and seventies.

His eyes were open. His tongue had popped out at Randy.

Randy looked away again, out across the lake. *Look for*

lights, he told himself. He knew there were no lights over there, but he told himself that anyway. *Look for lights over there, somebody's got to be staying the week in his place, fall foliage, shouldn't miss it, bring your Nikon, folks back home are going to love the slides.*

When he looked back, Deke's arms were straight up. He wasn't Nixon anymore; now he was a football ref signaling that the extra point had been good.

Deke's head appeared to be sitting on the boards.

His eyes were still open.

His tongue was still sticking out.

"Oh Ceesco," Randy muttered, and looked away again. His arms and shoulders were shrieking now, but still he held her in his arms. He looked at the far side of the lake. The far side of the lake was dark. Stars unrolled across the black sky, a spill of cold milk somehow suspended high in the air.

Minutes passed. *He'll be gone now. You can look now. Okay, yeah, all right. But don't look. Just to be safe, don't look. Agreed? Agreed. Most definitely. So say we all and so say all of us.*

So he looked anyway and was just in time to see Deke's fingers being pulled down. They were moving—probably the motion of the water under the raft was being transmitted to the unknowable thing which had caught Deke, and that motion was then being transmitted to Deke's fingers. Probably, probably. But it looked to Randy as if Deke was waving to him. The Cisco Kid was waving adiós. For the first time he felt his mind give a sickening wrench—it seemed to cant the way the raft itself had canted when all four of them had stood on the same side. It righted itself, but Randy suddenly understood that madness—real lunacy—was perhaps not far away at all.

Deke's football ring—All-Conference, 1981—slid slowly up the third finger of his right hand. The starlight rimmed the gold and played in the minute gutters between the engraved numbers, 19 on one side of the reddish stone, 81 on the other. The ring slid off his finger. The ring was a little too big to fit down through the crack, and of course it wouldn't squeeze.

It lay there. It was all that was left of Deke now. Deke was gone. No more dark-haired girls with sloe eyes, no more flicking Randy's bare rump with a wet towel when Randy came out of the shower, no more breakaway runs from midfield with fans rising to their feet in the bleachers and cheerleaders turning hysterical cartwheels along the sidelines. No more fast rides after dark in the Camaro with Thin Lizzy blaring "The Boys Are Back in Town" out of the tape deck. No more Cisco Kid.

There was that faint rasping noise again—a roll of canvas being pulled slowly through a slit of a window.

Randy was standing with his bare feet on the boards. He looked down and saw the cracks on either side of both feet suddenly filled with slick darkness. His eyes bulged. He thought of the way the blood had come spraying from Deke's mouth in an almost solid rope, the way Deke's eyes had bugged out as if on springs as hemorrhages caused by hydrostatic pressure pulped his brain.

It smells me. It knows I'm here. Can it come up? Can it get up through the cracks? Can it? Can it?

He stared down, unaware of LaVerne's limp weight now, fascinated by the enormity of the question, wondering what the stuff would feel like when it flowed over his feet, when it hooked into him.

The black shininess humped up almost to the edge of the cracks (Randy rose on tiptoes without being at all aware he was doing it), and then it went down. That canvasy slithering resumed. And suddenly Randy saw it on the water again, a great dark mole, now perhaps fifteen feet across. It rose and fell with the mild wavelets, rose and fell, rose and fell, and when Randy began to see the colors pulsing evenly across it, he tore his eyes away.

He put LaVerne down, and as soon as his muscles unlocked, his arms began to shake wildly. He let them shake. He knelt beside her, her hair spread across the white boards in an irregular dark fan. He knelt and watched that dark mole on the water, ready to yank her up again if it showed any signs of moving.

He began to slap her lightly, first one cheek and then the other, back and forth, like a second trying to bring a fighter around. LaVerne didn't want to come around. LaVerne did not want to pass Go and collect two hundred dollars or take a ride on the Reading. LaVerne had seen enough. But Randy couldn't guard her all night, lifting her like a canvas sack every time that thing moved (and you couldn't look at the thing too long; that was another thing). He had learned a trick, though. He hadn't learned it in college. He had learned it from a friend of his older brother's. This friend had been a paramedic in Nam, and he knew all sorts of tricks—how to catch head lice off a human scalp and make them race in a matchbox, how to cut cocaine with baby laxative, how to sew up deep cuts with ordinary needle and thread. One day they had been talking about ways to bring abysmally drunken folks around so these abysmally drunken people wouldn't puke down their own throats and die, as Bon Scott, the lead singer of AC/DC, had done.

"You want to bring someone around in a hurry?" the friend with the catalogue of interesting tricks had said. "Try this." And he told Randy the trick which Randy now used.

He leaned over and bit LaVerne's earlobe as hard as he could.

Hot, bitter blood squirted into his mouth. LaVerne's eye-lids flew up like windowshades. She screamed in a hoarse, growling voice and struck out at him. Randy looked up and saw the far side of the thing only; the rest of it was already under the raft. It had moved with eerie, horrible, silent speed.

He jerked LaVerne up again, his muscles screaming protest, trying to knot into charley horses. She was beating at his face. One of her hands struck his sensitive nose and he saw red stars.

"Quit it!" he shouted, shuffling his feet onto the boards. "Quit it, you bitch, it's under us again, quit it or I'll fucking drop you, I swear to God I will!"

Her arms immediately stopped flailing at him and closed quietly around his neck in a drowner's grip. Her eyes looked white in the swimming starlight.

"Stop it!" She didn't. "Stop it, LaVerne, you're choking me!"

Tighter. Panic flared in his mind. The hollow clunk of the barrels had taken on a duller, muffled note—it was the thing underneath, he supposed.

"I can't breathe!"

The hold loosened a little.

"Now listen. I'm going to put you down. It's all right if you—"

But *put you down* was all she had heard. Her arms tightened in that deadly grip again. His right hand was on her back. He hooked it into a claw and raked at her. She kicked her legs, mewling harshly, and for a moment he almost lost his balance. She felt it. Fright rather than pain made her stop struggling.

"Stand on the boards."

"No!" Her air puffed a hot desert wind against his cheek.

"It can't get you if you stand on the boards."

"No, don't put me down, it'll get me, I know it will, I know—"

He raked at her back again. She screamed in anger and pain and fear. "You get down or I'll drop you, LaVerne."

He lowered her slowly and carefully, both of them breathing in sharp little whines—oboe and flute. Her feet touched the boards. She jerked her legs up as if the boards were hot.

"Put them *down!*" He hissed at her. "I'm not Deke, I can't hold you all night!"

"Deke—"

"Dead."

Her feet touched the boards. Little by little he let go of her. They faced each other like dancers. He could see her waiting for its first touch. Her mouth gaped like the mouth of a goldfish.

"Randy," she whispered. "Where is it?"

"Under. Look down."

She did. He did. They saw the blackness stuffing the cracks, stuffing them almost all the way across the raft now. Randy sensed its eagerness, and thought she did, too.

"Randy, please—"

"Shhhh."

They stood there.

Randy had forgotten to strip off his watch when he ran into the water, and now he marked off fifteen minutes. At a quarter past eight, the black thing slid out from under the raft again. It drew about fifteen feet off and then stopped as it had before.

"I'm going to sit down," he said.

"No!"

"I'm tired," he said. "I'm going to sit down and you're going to watch it. Just remember to keep looking away. Then I'll get up and you sit down. We go like that. Here." He gave her his watch. "Fifteen-minute shifts."

"It ate Deke," she whispered.

"Yes."

"What is it?"

"I don't know."

"I'm cold."

"Me too."

"Hold me, then."

"I've held you enough."

She subsided.

Sitting down was heaven; not having to watch the thing was bliss. He watched LaVerne instead, making sure that her eyes kept shifting away from the thing on the water.

"What are we going to do, Randy?"

He thought.

"Wait," he said.

At the end of fifteen minutes he stood up and let her first sit and then lie down for half an hour. Then he got her on her feet again and she stood for fifteen minutes. They went back and forth. At a quarter of ten, a cold rind of moon rose and beat a path across the water. At ten-thirty, a shrill, lonely cry rose, echoing across the water, and LaVerne shrieked.

"Shut up," he said. "It's just a loon."

"I'm freezing, Randy—I'm numb all over."

"I can't do anything about it."

"Hold me," she said. "You've got to. We'll hold each other. We can both sit down and watch it together."

He debated, but the cold sinking into his own flesh was now bone-deep, and that decided him. "Okay."

They sat together, arms wrapped around each other, and something happened—natural or perverse, it happened. He felt himself stiffening. One of his hands found her breast, cupped in damp nylon, and squeezed. She made a sighing noise, and her hand stole to the crotch of his underpants.

He slid his other hand down and found a place where there was some heat. He pushed her down on her back.

"No," she said, but the hand in his crotch began to move faster.

"I can see it," he said. His heartbeat had sped up again, pushing blood faster, pushing warmth toward the surface of his chilled bare skin. "I can watch it."

She murmured something, and he felt elastic slide down his hips to his upper thighs. He watched it. He slid upward, forward, into her. Warmth. God, she was warm there, at least. She made a guttural noise and her fingers grabbed at his cold, clenched buttocks.

He watched it. It wasn't moving. He watched it. He watched it closely. The tactile sensations were incredible, fantastic. He was not experienced, but neither was he a virgin; he had made love with three girls and it had never been like this. She moaned and began to lift her hips. The raft rocked gently, like the world's hardest waterbed. The barrels underneath murmured hollowly.

He watched it. The colors began to swirl—slowly now, sensuously, not threatening; he watched it and he watched the colors. His eyes were wide. The colors were in his eyes. He wasn't cold now; he was hot now, hot the way you got your first day back on the beach in early June, when you could feel the sun tightening your winter-white skin, reddening it, giving it some

(colors)

color, some tint. First day at the beach, first day of summer, drag out the Beach Boys oldies, drag out the Ramones. The Ramones were telling you that Sheena is a punk rocker, the Ramones were telling you that you can hitch a ride to Rockaway Beach, the sand, the beach, the colors

(moving it's starting to move)

and the feel of summer, the texture; Gary U.S. Bonds, school is out and I can root for the Yankees from the bleachers, girls in bikinis on the beach, the beach, the beach, oh do you love do you love

(love)

the beach do you love

(love I love)

firm breasts fragrant with Coppertone oil, and if the bottom of the bikini was small enough you might see some

(hair her hair HER HAIR IS IN THE OH GOD IN THE WATER HER HAIR)

He pulled back suddenly, trying to pull her up, but the thing moved with oily speed and tangled itself in her hair like a webbing of thick black glue and when he pulled her up she was already screaming and she was heavy with it; it came out of the water in a twisting, gruesome membrane that rolled with flaring nuclear colors—scarlet-vermilion, flaring emerald, sullen ocher.

It flowed down over LaVerne's face in a tide, obliterating it.

Her feet kicked and drummed. The thing twisted and moved where her face had been. Blood ran down her neck in streams. Screaming, not hearing himself scream, Randy ran at her, put his foot against her hip, and shoved. She went flopping and tumbling over the side, her legs like alabaster in the moonlight. For a few endless moments the water frothed and splashed against the side of the raft, as if someone had hooked the world's largest bass in there and it was fighting like hell.

Randy screamed. He screamed. And then, for variety, he screamed some more.

Some half an hour later, long after the frantic splashing and struggling had ended, the loons began to scream back.

That night was forever.

The sky began to lighten in the east around a quarter to five, and he felt a sluggish rise in his spirit. It was momentary; as false as the dawn. He stood on the boards, his eyes half closed, his chin on his chest. He had been sitting on the boards until an hour ago, and had been suddenly awakened—without even knowing until then that he had fallen asleep, that was the scary part—by that unspeakable hissing-canvas sound. He leaped to his feet bare seconds before the blackness began to suck eagerly for him between the boards. His breath whined in and out; he bit at his lip, making it bleed.

Asleep, you were asleep, you asshole!

The thing had oozed out from under again half an hour later, but he hadn't sat down again. He was afraid to sit down, afraid he would go to sleep and that this time his mind wouldn't trip him awake in time.

His feet were still planted squarely on the boards as a stronger light, real dawn this time, filled the east and the first morning birds began to sing. The sun came up, and by six o'clock the day was bright enough for him to be able to see the beach. Deke's Camaro, bright yellow, was right where Deke had parked it, nose in to the pole fence. A bright litter of shirts and sweaters and four pairs of jeans were twisted into little shapes along the beach. The sight of them filled him with fresh horror when he thought his capacity for horror must surely be exhausted. He could see *his* jeans, one leg pulled inside out, the pocket showing. His jeans looked so *safe* lying there on the sand; just waiting for him to come along and pull the inside-out leg back through so it was right, grasping the pocket as he did so the change wouldn't fall out. He could almost feel them whispering up his legs, could feel himself buttoning the brass button above the fly—

(do you love yes I love)

He looked left and there it was, black, round as a checker, floating lightly. Colors began to swirl across its hide and he looked away quickly.

"Go home," he croaked. "Go home or go to California and find a Roger Corman movie to audition for."

A plane droned somewhere far away, and he fell into a dozing fantasy: *We are reported missing, the four of us. The search spreads outward from Horlicks. A farmer remembers being passed by a yellow Camaro "going like a bat out of hell." The search centers in the Cascade Lake area. Private pilots volunteer to do a quick aerial search, and one guy, buzzing the lake in his Beechcraft Twin Bonanza, sees a kid standing naked on the raft, one kid, one survivor, one—*

He caught himself on the edge of toppling over and brought his fist into his nose again, screaming at the pain.

The black thing arrowed at the raft immediately and squeezed underneath—it could hear, perhaps, or sense . . . or *something*.

Randy waited.

This time it was forty-five minutes before it came out.

His mind slowly orbited in the growing light.

(do you love yes I love rooting for the Yankees   and Cat-
fish   do you love the Catfish yes I love the
      (Route 66 remember the Corvette George Maharis in the
Corvette Martin Milner in the Corvette do you love the Corvette
      (yes I love the Corvette
      (I love do you love
      (so hot the sun is like a burning glass it was in her hair and
it's the light I remember best the light the summer light
      (the summer light of)

afternoon.

Randy was crying.

He was crying because something new had been added now—every time he tried to sit down, the thing slid under the raft. It wasn't entirely stupid, then; it had either sensed or figured out that it could get at him while he was sitting down.

"Go away," Randy wept at the great black mole floating on the water. Fifty yards away, mockingly close, a squirrel was scampering back and forth on the hood of Deke's Camaro. "Go away, please, go anywhere, but leave me alone. I don't love you."

The thing didn't move. Colors began to swirl across its visible surface.

(you do *you* do *love me)*

Randy tore his eyes away and looked at the beach, looked for rescue, but there was no one there, no one at all. His jeans still lay there, one leg inside out, the white lining of one pocket showing. They no longer looked to him as if someone was going to pick them up. They looked like relics.

He thought: *If I had a gun, I would kill myself now.*

He stood on the raft.

The sun went down.

Three hours later, the moon came up.

Not long after that, the loons began to scream.

Not long after *that*, Randy turned and looked at the black thing on the water. He could not kill himself, but perhaps the thing could fix it so there was no pain; perhaps that was what the colors were for.

(do you do you do you love)

He looked for it and it was there, floating, riding the waves.

"Sing with me," Randy croaked. "I can root for the Yankees from the bleachers . . . I don't have to worry 'bout teachers . . . I'm so glad that school is out . . . I am gonna . . . sing and shout."

The colors began to form and twist. This time Randy did not look away.

He whispered, "Do you love?"

Somewhere, far across the empty lake, a loon screamed.

Word Processor
of the Gods

At first glance it looked like a Wang word processor—it had a Wang keyboard and a Wang casing. It was only on second glance that Richard Hagstrom saw that the casing had been split open (and not gently, either; it looked to him as if the job had been done with a hacksaw blade) to admit a slightly larger IBM cathode tube. The archive discs which had come with this odd mongrel were not floppy at all; they were as hard as the 45's Richard had listened to as a kid.

"What in the name of *God* is that?" Lina asked as he and Mr. Nordhoff lugged it over to his study piece by piece. Mr. Nordhoff had lived next door to Richard Hagstrom's brother's family . . . Roger, Belinda, and their boy, Jonathan.

"Something Jon built," Richard said. "Meant for me to have it, Mr. Nordhoff says. It looks like a word processor."

"Oh yeah," Nordhoff said. He would not see his sixties again and he was badly out of breath. "That's what he said it was, the poor kid . . . think we could set it down for a minute, Mr. Hagstrom? I'm pooped."

"You bet," Richard said, and then called to his son, Seth, who was tooling odd, atonal chords out of his Fender guitar downstairs—the room Richard had envisioned as a "family room" when he had first paneled it had become his son's "rehearsal hall" instead.

307

"Seth!" he yelled. "Come give us a hand!"

Downstairs, Seth just went on warping chords out of the Fender. Richard looked at Mr. Nordhoff and shrugged, ashamed and unable to hide it. Nordhoff shrugged back as if to say *Kids! Who expects anything better from them these days?* Except they both knew that Jon—poor doomed Jon Hagstrom, his crazy brother's son—had been better.

"You were good to help me with this," Richard said.

Nordhoff shrugged. "What else has an old man got to do with his time? And I guess it was the least I could do for Jonny. He used to cut my lawn gratis, do you know that? I wanted to pay him, but the kid wouldn't take it. He was quite a boy." Nordhoff was still out of breath. "Do you think I could have a glass of water, Mr. Hagstrom?"

"You bet." He got it himself when his wife didn't move from the kitchen table, where she was reading a bodice-ripper paperback and eating a Twinkie. "Seth!" he yelled again. "Come on up here and help us, okay?"

But Seth just went on playing muffled and rather sour bar chords on the Fender for which Richard was still paying.

He invited Nordhoff to stay for supper, but Nordhoff refused politely. Richard nodded, embarrassed again but perhaps hiding it a little better this time. *What's a nice guy like you doing with a family like that?* his friend Bernie Epstein had asked him once, and Richard had only been able to shake his head, feeling the same dull embarrassment he was feeling now. He *was* a nice guy. And yet somehow this was what he had come out with—an overweight, sullen wife who felt cheated out of the good things in life, who felt that she had backed the losing horse (but who would never come right out and say so), and an uncommunicative fifteen-year-old son who was doing marginal work in the same school where Richard taught . . . a son who played weird chords on the guitar morning, noon and night (mostly night) and who seemed to think that would somehow be enough to get him through.

"Well, what about a beer?" Richard asked. He was reluctant to let Nordhoff go— he wanted to hear more about Jon.

"A beer would taste awful good," Nordhoff said, and Richard nodded gratefully.

"Fine," he said, and went back to get them a couple of Buds.

* * *

His study was in a small shedlike building that stood apart from the house—like the family room, he had fixed it up himself. But unlike the family room, this was a place he thought of as his own—a place where he could shut out the stranger he had married and the stranger she had given birth to.

Lina did not, of course, approve of him having his own place, but she had not been able to stop it—it was one of the few little victories he had managed over her. He supposed that in a way she *had* backed a losing horse—when they had gotten married sixteen years before, they had both believed he would write wonderful, lucrative novels and they would both soon be driving around in Mercedes-Benzes. But the one novel he had published had not been lucrative, and the critics had been quick to point out that it wasn't very wonderful, either. Lina had seen things the critics' way, and that had been the beginning of their drifting apart.

So the high school teaching job which both of them had seen as only a stepping-stone on their way to fame, glory, and riches, had now been their major source of income for the last fifteen years—one helluva long stepping-stone, he sometimes thought. But he had never quite let go of his dream. He wrote short stories and the occasional article. He was a member in good standing of the Authors Guild. He brought in about $5,000 in additional income with his typewriter each year, and no matter how much Lina might grouse about it, that rated him his own study . . . especially since she refused to work.

"You've got a nice place here," Nordhoff said, looking around the small room with the mixture of old-fashioned prints on the walls. The mongrel word processor sat on the desk with the CPU tucked underneath. Richard's old Olivetti electric had been put aside for the time being on top of one of the filing cabinets.

"It serves the purpose," Richard said. He nodded at the word processor. "You don't suppose that thing really works, do you? Jon was only fourteen."

"Looks funny, doesn't it?"

"It sure does," Richard agreed.

Nordhoff laughed. "You don't know the half of it," he said. "I peeked down into the back of the video unit. Some of the wires are stamped IBM, and some are stamped Radio Shack. There's most of a Western Electric telephone in there. And believe it or not, there's a small motor from an Erector Set.'' He sipped his beer and said in a kind of afterthought: "Fifteen. He just turned fifteen. A couple of days before the accident.'' He paused and said it again, looking down at his bottle of beer. "Fifteen.'' He didn't say it loudly.

"Erector Set?'' Richard blinked at the old man.

"That's right. Erector Set puts out an electric model kit. Jon had one of them, since he was . . . oh, maybe six. I gave it to him for Christmas one year. He was crazy for gadgets even then. Any kind of gadget would do him, and did that little box of Erector Set motors tickle him? I guess it did. He kept it for almost ten years. Not many kids do that, Mr. Hagstrom.''

"No,'' Richard said, thinking of the boxes of Seth's toys he had lugged out over the years—discarded, forgotten, or wantonly broken. He glanced at the word processor. "It doesn't work, then.''

"I wouldn't bet on that until you try it,'' Nordhoff said. "The kid was damn near an electrical genius.''

"That's sort of pushing it, I think. I know he was good with gadgets, and he won the State Science Fair when he was in the sixth grade—''

"Competing against kids who were much older—high school seniors some of them,'' Nordhoff said. "Or that's what his mother said.''

"It's true. We were all very proud of him.'' Which wasn't exactly true. Richard had been proud, and Jon's mother had been proud; the boy's father didn't give a shit at all. "But Science Fair projects and building your very own hybrid word-cruncher—'' He shrugged.

Nordhoff set his beer down. "There was a kid back in the fifties,'' he said, "who made an atom smasher out of two soup cans and about five dollars' worth of electrical equipment. Jon told me about that. And he said there was a kid out in some hick town in New Mexico who discovered tachyons—negative particles that are supposed to travel backwards through time—in 1954. A kid in Waterbury, Connecticut—eleven years old—who made a pipe-bomb out of the celluloid he scraped off the backs of a deck of playing cards. He blew up an empty doghouse with it. Kids're funny sometimes. The supersmart ones in particular. You might be surprised.''

"Maybe. Maybe I will be."

"He was a fine boy, regardless."

"You loved him a little, didn't you?"

"Mr. Hagstrom," Nordhoff said, "I loved him a lot. He was a genuinely all-right kid."

And Richard thought how strange it was—his brother, who had been an utter shit since the age of six, had gotten a fine woman and a fine bright son. He himself, who had always tried to be gentle and good (whatever "good" meant in this crazy world), had married Lina, who had developed into a silent, piggy woman, and had gotten Seth by her. Looking at Nordhoff's honest, tired face, he found himself wondering exactly how that had happened and how much of it had been his own fault, a natural result of his own quiet weakness.

"Yes," Richard said. "He was, wasn't he?"

"Wouldn't surprise me if it worked," Nordhoff said. "Wouldn't surprise me at all."

After Nordhoff had gone, Richard Hagstrom plugged the word processor in and turned it on. There was a hum, and he waited to see if the letters IBM would come up on the face of the screen. They did not. Instead, eerily, like a voice from the grave, these words swam up, green ghosts, from the darkness:

HAPPY BIRTHDAY, UNCLE RICHARD! JON.

"Christ," Richard whispered, sitting down hard. The accident that had killed his brother, his wife, and their son had happened two weeks before—they had been coming back from some sort of day trip and Roger had been drunk. Being drunk was a perfectly ordinary occurrence in the life of Roger Hagstrom. But this time his luck had simply run out and he had driven his dusty old van off the edge of a ninety-foot drop. It had crashed and burned. *Jon was fourteen—no, fifteen. Just turned fifteen a couple of days before the accident, the old man said. Another three years and he would have gotten free of that hulking, stupid bear. His birthday . . . and mine coming up soon.*

A week from today. The word processor had been Jon's birthday present for him.

That made it worse, somehow. Richard could not have said precisely how, or why, but it did. He reached out to turn off the screen and then withdrew his hand.

Some kid made an atom smasher out of two soup cans and five dollars' worth of auto electrical parts.

Yeah, and the New York City sewer system is full of alligators and the U.S. Air Force has the body of an alien on ice somewhere in Nebraska. Tell me a few more. It's bullshit. But maybe that's something I don't want to know for sure.

He got up, went around to the back of the VDT, and looked through the slots. Yes, it was as Nordhoff had said. Wires stamped RADIO SHACK MADE IN TAIWAN. Wires stamped WESTERN ELECTRIC and WESTREX and ERECTOR SET, with the little circled trademark r. And he saw something else, something Nordhoff had either missed or hadn't wanted to mention. There was a Lionel Train transformer in there, wired up like the Bride of Frankenstein.

"Christ," he said, laughing but suddenly near tears. "Christ, Jonny, what did you think you were doing?"

But he knew that, too. He had dreamed and talked about owning a word processor for years, and when Lina's laughter became too sarcastic to bear, he had talked about it to Jon. "I could write faster, rewrite faster, and submit more," he remembered telling Jon last summer—the boy had looked at him seriously, his light blue eyes, intelligent but always so carefully wary, magnified behind his glasses. "It would be great . . . really great."

"Then why don't you get one, Uncle Rich?"

"They don't exactly give them away," Richard had said, smiling. "The Radio Shack model starts at around three grand. From there you can work yourself up into the eighteen-thousand-dollar range."

"Well, maybe I'll build you one sometime," Jon had said.

"Maybe you just will," Richard had said, clapping him on the back. And until Nordhoff had called, he had thought no more about it.

Wires from hobby-shop electrical models.

A Lionel Train transformer.

Christ.

He went around to the front again, meaning to turn it off, as if to actually try to write something on it and fail would somehow defile what his earnest, fragile

(doomed)

nephew had intended.

Instead, he pushed the EXECUTE button on the board. A funny little chill scraped across his spine as he did it—EXECUTE was a funny word to use, when you thought of it. It wasn't a word he associated with writing; it was a word he associated with gas chambers and electric chairs . . . and, perhaps, with dusty old vans plunging off the sides of roads.

EXECUTE.

The CPU was humming louder than any he had ever heard on the occasions when he had window-shopped word processors; it was, in fact, almost roaring. *What's in the memory-box, Jon?* he wondered. *Bed springs? Train transformers all in a row? Soup cans?* He thought again of Jon's eyes, of his still and delicate face. Was it strange, maybe even sick, to be jealous of another man's son?

But he should have been mine. I knew it . . . and I think he knew it, too. And then there was Belinda, Roger's wife. Belinda who wore sunglasses too often on cloudy days. The big ones, because those bruises around the eyes have a nasty way of spreading. But he looked at her sometimes, sitting there still and watchful in the loud umbrella of Roger's laughter, and he thought almost the exact same thing: *She should have been mine.*

It was a terrifying thought, because they had both known Belinda in high school and had both dated her. He and Roger had been two years apart in age and Belinda had been perfectly between them, a year older than Richard and a year younger than Roger. Richard had actually been the first to date the girl who would grow up to become Jon's mother. Then Roger had stepped in, Roger who was older and bigger, Roger who always got what he wanted, Roger who would hurt you if you tried to stand in his way.

I got scared. I got scared and I let her get away. Was it as simple as that? Dear God help me, I think it was. I'd like to have it a different way, but perhaps it's best not to lie to yourself about such things as cowardice. And shame.

And if those things were true—if Lina and Seth had somehow belonged with his no-good of a brother and if Belinda and Jon had somehow belonged with him, what did that prove? And exactly how was a thinking person supposed to deal with such an absurdly balanced screw-up? Did you laugh? Did you scream? Did you shoot yourself for a yellow dog?

Wouldn't surprise me if it worked. Wouldn't surprise me at all.

EXECUTE.

His fingers moved swiftly over the keys. He looked at the screen and saw these letters floating green on the surface of the screen:

MY BROTHER WAS A WORTHLESS DRUNK.

They floated there and Richard suddenly thought of a toy he had had when he was a kid. It was called a Magic Eight-Ball. You asked it a question that could be answered yes or no and then you turned the Magic Eight-Ball over to see what it had to say on the subject—its phony yet somehow entrancingly mysterious responses included such things as IT IS ALMOST CERTAIN, I WOULD NOT PLAN ON IT, and ASK AGAIN LATER.

Roger had been jealous of that toy, and finally, after bullying Richard into giving it to him one day, Roger had thrown it onto the sidewalk as hard as he could, breaking it. Then he had laughed. Sitting here now, listening to the strangely choppy roar from the CPU cabinet Jon had jury-rigged, Richard remembered how he had collapsed to the sidewalk, weeping, unable to believe his brother had done such a thing.

"*Bawl*-baby, *bawl*-baby, look at the baby *bawl*," Roger had taunted him. "It wasn't nothing but a cheap, shitty toy anyway, Richie. Lookit there, nothing in it but a bunch of little signs and a lot of water."

"*I'M TELLING!*" Richard had shrieked at the top of his lungs. His head felt hot. His sinuses were stuffed shut with tears of outrage. "*I'M TELLING ON YOU, ROGER! I'M TELLING MOM!*"

"You tell and I'll break your arm," Roger said, and in his chilling grin Richard had seen he meant it. He had not told.

MY BROTHER WAS A WORTHLESS DRUNK.

Well, weirdly put together or not, it screen-printed. Whether it would store information in the CPU still remained to be seen, but Jon's mating of a Wang board to an IBM screen had actually worked. Just coincidentally it called up some pretty crappy memories, but he didn't suppose that was Jon's fault.

He looked around his office, and his eyes happened to fix on the one picture in here that he hadn't picked and didn't like. It was a studio portrait of Lina, her Christmas present to him two years ago. *I want you to hang it in your study,* she'd said, and so of course he had done just that. It was, he supposed, her way of keeping an eye on him even when she wasn't here. *Don't forget me, Richard. I'm here. Maybe I backed the wrong horse, but I'm still here. And you better remember it.*

The studio portrait with its unnatural tints went oddly with the amiable mixture of prints by Whistler, Homer, and N. C. Wyeth. Lina's eyes were half-lidded, the heavy Cupid's bow of her mouth composed in something that was not quite a smile. *Still here, Richard,* her mouth said to him. *And don't you forget it.*

He typed:

MY WIFE'S PHOTOGRAPH HANGS ON THE WEST WALL OF MY STUDY.

He looked at the words and liked them no more than he liked the picture itself. He punched the DELETE button. The words vanished. Now there was nothing at all on the screen but the steadily pulsing cursor.

He looked up at the wall and saw that his wife's picture had also vanished.

He sat there for a very long time—it felt that way, at least—looking at the wall where the picture had been. What finally brought him out of his daze of utter unbelieving shock was the smell from the CPU—a smell he remembered from his childhood as clearly as he remembered the Magic Eight-Ball Roger had broken because it wasn't his. The smell was essence of electric train transformer. When you smelled that you were supposed to turn the thing off so it could cool down.

And so he would.

In a minute.

He got up and walked over to the wall on legs which felt numb. He ran his fingers over the Armstrong paneling. The picture had been here, yes, *right here*. But it was gone now, and the hook it had hung on was gone, and there was no hole where he had screwed the hook into the paneling.

Gone.

The world abruptly went gray and he staggered backwards, thinking dimly that he was going to faint. He held on grimly until the world swam back into focus.

He looked from the blank place on the wall where Lina's picture had been to the word processor his dead nephew had cobbled together.

You might be surprised, he heard Nordhoff saying in his

mind. *You might be surprised, you might be surprised, oh
yes, if some kid in the fifties could discover particles that
travel backwards through time, you might be surprised what
your genius of a nephew could do with a bunch of discarded
word processor elements and some wires and electrical com-
ponents. You might be so surprised that you'll feel as if you're
going insane.*

The transformer smell was richer, stronger now, and he
could see wisps of smoke rising from the vents in the screen
housing. The noise from the CPU was louder, too. It was
time to turn it off—smart as Jon had been, he apparently
hadn't had time to work out all the bugs in the crazy thing.

But had he known it would do this?

Feeling like a figment of his own imagination, Richard sat
down in front of the screen again and typed:

MY WIFE'S PICTURE IS ON THE WALL.

He looked at this for a moment, looked back at the keyboard, and then hit the EXECUTE key.

He looked at the wall.

Lina's picture was back, right where it had always been.

"Jesus," he whispered. "Jesus Christ."

He rubbed a hand up his cheek, looked at the keyboard
(blank again now except for the cursor), and then typed:

MY FLOOR IS BARE.

He then touched the INSERT button and typed:

EXCEPT FOR TWELVE TWENTY-DOLLAR GOLD PIECES IN A SMALL
COTTON SACK.

He pressed EXECUTE.

He looked at the floor, where there was now a small white
cotton sack with a drawstring top. WELLS FARGO was stenciled
on the bag in faded black ink.

"Dear Jesus," he heard himself saying in a voice that
wasn't his. "Dear Jesus, dear good Jesus—"

He might have gone on invoking the Savior's name for
minutes or hours if the word processor had not started beep-
ing at him steadily. Flashing across the top of the screen was
the word OVERLOAD.

Richard turned off everything in a hurry and left his study
as if all the devils of hell were after him.

But before he went he scooped up the small drawstring
sack and put it in his pants pocket.

*   *   *

When he called Nordhoff that evening, a cold November wind was playing tuneless bagpipes in the trees outside. Seth's group was downstairs, murdering a Bob Seger tune. Lina was out at Our Lady of Perpetual Sorrows, playing bingo.

"Does the machine work?" Nordhoff asked.

"It works, all right," Richard said. He reached into his pocket and brought out a coin. It was heavy—heavier than a Rolex watch. An eagle's stern profile was embossed on one side, along with the date 1871. "It works in ways you wouldn't believe."

"I might," Nordhoff said evenly. "He was a very bright boy, and he loved you very much, Mr. Hagstrom. But be careful. A boy is only a boy, bright or otherwise, and love can be misdirected. Do you take my meaning?"

Richard didn't take his meaning at all. He felt hot and feverish. That day's paper had listed the current market price of gold at $514 an ounce. The coins had weighed out at an average of 4.5 ounces each on his postal scale. At the current market rate that added up to $27,756. And he guessed that was perhaps only a quarter of what he could realize for those coins if he sold them *as* coins.

"Mr. Nordhoff, could you come over here? Now? Tonight?"

"No," Nordhoff said. "No, I don't think I want to do that, Mr. Hagstrom. I think this ought to stay between you and Jon."

"But—"

"Just remember what I said. For Christ's sake, be careful." There was a small click and Nordhoff was gone.

He found himself out in his study again half an hour later, looking at the word processor. He touched the ON/OFF key but didn't turn it on just yet. The second time Nordhoff said it, Richard had heard it. *For Christ's sake, be careful.* Yes. He would have to be careful. A machine that could do such a thing—

How *could* a machine do such a thing?

He had no idea . . . but in a way, that made the whole crazy thing easier to accept. He was an English teacher and sometime writer, not a technician, and he had a long history of not understanding how things worked: phonographs, gasoline engines, telephones, televisions, the flushing mechanism in his toilet. His life had been a history of understanding operations rather than principles. Was there any difference here, except in degree?

He turned the machine on. As before it said: HAPPY BIRTHDAY, UNCLE RICHARD! JON. He pushed EXECUTE and the message from his nephew disappeared.

This machine is not going to work for long, he thought suddenly. He felt sure that Jon must have still been working on it when he died, confident that there was time, Uncle Richard's birthday wasn't for three weeks, after all—

But time had run out for Jon, and so this totally amazing word processor, which could apparently insert new things or delete old things from the real world, smelled like a frying train transformer and started to smoke after a few minutes. Jon hadn't had a chance to perfect it. He had been—

Confident that there was time?

But that was wrong. That was *all* wrong. Richard knew it. Jon's still, watchful face, the sober eyes behind the thick spectacles . . . there was no confidence there, no belief in the comforts of time. What was the word that had occurred to him earlier that day? *Doomed.* It wasn't just a *good* word for Jon; it was the *right* word. That sense of doom had hung about the boy so palpably that there had been times when Richard had wanted to hug him, to tell him to lighten up a little bit, that sometimes there were happy endings and the good didn't always die young.

Then he thought of Roger throwing his Magic Eight-Ball at the sidewalk, throwing it just as hard as he could; he heard the plastic splinter and saw the Eight-Ball's magic fluid—just water after all—running down the sidewalk. And this picture merged with a picture of Roger's mongrel van, HAGSTROM'S WHOLESALE DELIVERIES written on the side, plunging over the edge of some dusty, crumbling cliff out in the country, hitting dead squat on its nose with a noise that was, like Roger himself, no big deal. He saw—although he didn't want to—the face of his brother's wife disintegrate into blood and bone. He saw Jon burning in the wreck, screaming, turning black.

No confidence, no real hope. He had always exuded a sense of time running out. And in the end he had turned out to be right.

"What does that mean?" Richard muttered, looking at the blank screen.

How would the Magic Eight-Ball have answered that? ASK AGAIN LATER? OUTCOME IS MURKY? Or perhaps IT IS CERTAINLY SO?

The noise coming from the CPU was getting louder again, and more quickly than this afternoon. Already he could smell the train transformer Jon had lodged in the machinery behind the screen getting hot.

Magic dream machine.

Word processor of the gods.

Was that what it was? Was that what Jon had intended to give his uncle for his birthday? The space-age equivalent of a magic lamp or a wishing well?

He heard the back door of the house bang open and then the voices of Seth and the other members of Seth's band. The voices were too loud, too raucous. They had either been drinking or smoking dope.

"Where's your old man, Seth?" he heard one of them ask.

"Goofing off in his study, like usual, I guess," Seth said. "I think he—" The wind rose again then, blurring the rest, but not blurring their vicious tribal laughter.

Richard sat listening to them, his head cocked a little to one side, and suddenly he typed:

MY SON IS SETH ROBERT HAGSTROM.

His finger hovered over the DELETE button.

What are you doing? his mind screamed at him. *Can you be serious? Do you intend to murder your own son?*

"He must do somethin in there," one of the others said.

"He's a goddam dimwit," Seth answered. "You ask my mother sometime. She'll tell you. He—"

I'm not going to murder him. I'm going to . . . to DELETE him.

His finger stabbed down on the button.

"—ain't never done nothing but—"

The words MY SON IS SETH ROBERT HAGSTROM vanished from the screen.

Outside, Seth's words vanished with them.

There was no sound out there now but the cold November wind, blowing grim advertisements for winter.

Richard turned off the word processor and went outside. The driveway was empty. The group's lead guitarist, Norm somebody, drove a monstrous and somehow sinister old LTD station wagon in which the group carried their equipment to their infrequent gigs. It was not parked in the driveway now. Perhaps it was somewhere in the world, tooling down some highway or parked in the parking lot of some greasy hamburger hangout, and Norm was also somewhere in the world, as was Davey, the bassist, whose eyes were frighteningly blank and who wore a safety pin dangling from one earlobe, as was the drummer, who had no front teeth. They were somewhere in the world, somewhere, but not here, because Seth wasn't here, Seth had never been here.

Seth had been DELETED.

"I have no son," Richard muttered. How many times had he read that melodramatic phrase in bad novels? A hundred? Two hundred? It had never rung true to him. But here it was true. Now it was true. Oh yes.

The wind gusted, and Richard was suddenly seized by a vicious stomach cramp that doubled him over, gasping. He passed explosive wind.

When the cramps passed, he walked into the house.

The first thing he noticed was that Seth's ratty tennis shoes—he had four pairs of them and refused to throw any of them out—were gone from the front hall. He went to the stairway banister and ran his thumb over a section of it. At age ten (old enough to know better, but Lina had refused to allow Richard to lay a hand on the boy in spite of that), Seth had carved his initials deeply into the wood of that banister, wood which Richard had labored over for almost one whole summer. He had sanded and filled and revarnished, but the ghost of those initials had remained.

They were gone now.

Upstairs. Seth's room. It was neat and clean and unlived-in, dry and devoid of personality. It might as well have had a sign on the doorknob reading GUEST ROOM.

Downstairs. And it was here that Richard lingered the longest. The snarls of wire were gone; the amplifiers and microphones were gone; the litter of tape recorder parts that Seth was always going to "fix up" were gone (he did not have Jon's hands or concentration). Instead the room bore the deep (if not particularly pleasant) stamp of Lina's personality— heavy, florid furniture and saccharin velvet tapestries (one depicting a Last Supper at which Christ looked like Wayne Newton, another showing deer against a sunset Alaskan skyline), a glaring rug as bright as arterial blood. There was no longer the faintest sense that a boy named Seth Hagstrom had once inhabited this room. This room, or any of the other rooms in the house.

Richard was still standing at the foot of the stairs and looking around when he heard a car pull into the driveway.

Lina, he thought, and felt a surge of almost frantic guilt. *It's Lina, back from bingo, and what's she going to say when she sees that Seth is gone? What . . . what . . .*

Murderer! he heard her screaming. *You murdered my boy!*

But he hadn't murdered Seth.

"I DELETED him," he muttered, and went upstairs to meet her in the kitchen.

Lina was fatter.

He had sent a woman off to bingo who weighed a hundred and eighty pounds or so. The woman who came back in weighed at least three hundred, perhaps more; she had to twist slightly sideways to get in through the back door. Elephantine hips and thighs rippled in tidal motions beneath polyester slacks the color of overripe green olives. Her skin, merely sallow three hours ago, was now sickly and pale. Although he was no doctor, Richard thought he cold read serious liver damage or incipient heart disease in that skin. Her heavy-lidded eyes regarded Richard with a steady, even contempt.

She was carrying the frozen corpse of a huge turkey in one of her flabby hands. It twisted and turned within its cellophane wrapper like the body of a bizarre suicide.

"What are you staring at, Richard?" she asked.

You, Lina. I'm staring at you. Because this is how you turned out in a world where we had no children. This is how you turned out in a world where there was no object for your love—poisoned as your love might be. This is how Lina looks in a world where everything comes in and nothing at all goes out. You, Lina. That's what I'm staring at. You.

"That bird, Lina," he managed finally. "That's one of the biggest damn turkeys I've ever seen."

"Well don't just stand there looking at it, idiot! Help me with it!"

He took the turkey and put it on the counter, feeling its waves of cheerless cold. It sounded like a block of wood.

"Not *there!*" she cried impatiently, and gestured toward the pantry. "It's not going to fit in there! Put it in the freezer!"

"Sorry," he murmured. They had never had a freezer before. Never in the world where there had been a Seth.

He took the turkey into the pantry, where a long Amana freezer sat under cold white fluorescent tubes like a cold white coffin. He put it inside along with the cryogenically preserved corpses of other birds and beasts and then went back into the kitchen. Lina had taken the jar of Reese's peanut butter cups from the cupboard and was eating them methodically, one after the other.

"It was the Thanksgiving bingo," she said. "We had it this week instead of next because next week Father Phillips has to go in hospital and have his gall-bladder out. I won the coverall." She smiled. A brown mixture of chocolate and peanut butter dripped and ran from her teeth.

"Lina," he said, "are you ever sorry we never had children?"

She looked at him as if he had gone utterly crazy. "What in the name of God would I want a rug-monkey for?" she asked. She shoved the jar of peanut butter cups, now reduced by half, back into the cupboard. "I'm going to bed. Are you coming, or are you going back out there and moon over your typewriter some more?"

"I'll go out for a little while more, I think," he said. His voice was surprisingly steady. "I won't be long."

"Does that gadget work?"

"What—" Then he understood and he felt another flash of guilt. She knew about the word processor, of course she did. Seth's DELETION had not affected Roger and the track that Roger's family had been on. "Oh. Oh, no. It doesn't do anything."

She nodded, satisfied. "That nephew of yours. Head always in the clouds. Just like you, Richard. If you weren't such a mouse, I'd wonder if maybe you'd been putting it where you hadn't ought to have been putting it about fifteen years ago." She laughed a coarse, surprisingly powerful laugh— the laugh of an aging, cynical bawd—and for a moment he almost leaped at her. Then he felt a smile surface on his own lips—a smile as thin and white and cold as the Amana freezer that had replaced Seth on this new track.

"I won't be long," he said. "I just want to note down a few things."

"Why don't you write a Nobel Prize-winning short story, or something?" she asked indifferently. The hall floorboards creaked and muttered as she swayed her huge way toward the stairs. "We still owe the optometrist for my reading glasses and we're a payment behind on the Betamax. Why don't you make us some damn money?"

"Well," Richard said, "I don't know, Lina. But I've got some good ideas tonight. I really do."

She turned to look at him, seemed about to say something sarcastic—something about how none of his good ideas had put them on easy street but she had stuck with him anyway—and then didn't. Perhaps something about his smile deterred her. She went upstairs. Richard stood below, listening to her thundering tread. He could feel sweat on his forehead. He felt simultaneously sick and exhilarated.

He turned and went back out to his study.

This time when he turned the unit on, the CPU did not hum or roar; it began to make an uneven howling noise. That hot train transformer smell came almost immediately from the housing behind the screen, and as soon as he pushed the EXECUTE button, erasing the HAPPY BIRTHDAY, UNCLE RICHARD! message, the unit began to smoke.

Not much time, he thought. *No . . . that's not right. No time at all. Jon knew it, and now I know it, too.*

The choices came down to two: Bring Seth back with the INSERT button (he was sure he could do it; it would be as easy as creating the Spanish doubloons had been) or finish the job.

The smell was getting thicker, more urgent. In a few moments, surely no more, the screen would start blinking its OVERLOAD message.

He typed:

MY WIFE IS ADELINA MABEL WARREN HAGSTROM.

He punched the DELETE button.

He typed:

I AM A MAN WHO LIVES ALONE.

Now the word began to blink steadily in the upper right-hand corner of the screen: OVERLOAD OVERLOAD OVERLOAD.

Please. Please let me finish. Please, please, please . . .

The smoke coming from the vents in the video cabinet was

thicker and grayer now. He looked down at the screaming CPU and saw that smoke was also coming from its vents . . . and down in that smoke he could see a sullen red spark of fire.

Magic Eight-Ball, will I be healthy, wealthy, or wise? Or will I live alone and perhaps kill myself in sorrow? Is there time enough?

CANNOT SEE NOW. TRY AGAIN LATER.

Except there *was* no later.

He struck the INSERT button and the screen went dark, except for the constant OVERLOAD message, which was now blinking at a frantic, stuttery rate.

He typed:

EXCEPT FOR MY WIFE, BELINDA, AND MY SON, JONATHAN.

Please. Please.

He hit the EXECUTE button.

The screen went blank. For what seemed like ages it remained blank, except for OVERLOAD, which was now blinking so fast that, except for a faint shadow, it seemed to remain constant, like a computer executing a closed loop of command. Something inside the CPU popped and sizzled, and Richard groaned.

Then green letters appeared on the screen, floating mystically on the black:

I AM A MAN WHO LIVES ALONE EXCEPT FOR MY WIFE, BELINDA, AND MY SON, JONATHAN.

He hit the EXECUTE button twice.

Now, he thought. *Now I will type: ALL THE BUGS IN THIS WORD PROCESSOR WERE FULLY WORKED OUT BEFORE MR. NORDHOFF BROUGHT IT OVER HERE. Or I'll type: I HAVE IDEAS FOR AT LEAST TWENTY BEST-SELLING NOVELS. Or I'll type: MY FAMILY AND I ARE GOING TO LIVE HAPPILY EVER AFTER. Or I'll type—*

But he typed nothing. His fingers hovered stupidly over the keys as he felt—literally *felt*—all the circuits in his brain jam up like cars grid-locked into the worst Manhattan traffic jam in the history of internal combustion.

The screen suddenly filled up with the word:

LOADOVERLOADOVERLOADOVERLOADOVERLOADOVERLOADOVER-LOAD

There was another pop, and then an explosion from the CPU. Flames belched out of the cabinet and then died away.

Richard leaned back in his chair, shielding his face in case the screen should implode. It didn't. It only went dark.

He sat there, looking at the darkness of the screen.

CANNOT TELL FOR SURE. ASK AGAIN LATER.

"Dad?"

He swiveled around in his chair, heart pounding so hard he felt that it might actually tear itself out of his chest.

Jon stood there, Jon Hagstrom, and his face was the same but somehow different—the difference was subtle but noticeable. Perhaps, Richard thought, the difference was the difference in paternity between two brothers. Or perhaps it was simply that that wary, watching expression was gone from the eyes, slightly overmagnified by thick spectacles (wire-rims now, he noticed, not the ugly industrial horn-rims that Roger had always gotten the boy because they were fifteen bucks cheaper).

Maybe it was something even simpler: that look of doom was gone from the boy's eyes.

"Jon?" he said hoarsely, wondering if he had actually wanted something more than this. Had he? It seemed ridiculous, but he supposed he had. He supposed people always did. "Jon, it's you, isn't it?"

"Who else would it be?" He nodded toward the word processor. "You didn't hurt yourself when that baby went to data heaven, did you?"

Richard smiled. "No. I'm fine."

Jon nodded. "I'm sorry it didn't work. I don't know what ever possessed me to use all those cruddy parts." He shook his head. "Honest to God I don't. It's like I *had* to. Kid's stuff."

"Well," Richard said, joining his son and putting an arm around his shoulders, "you'll do better next time, maybe."

"Maybe. Or I might try something else."

"That might be just as well."

"Mom said she had cocoa for you, if you wanted it."

"I do," Richard said, and the two of them walked together from the study to a house into which no frozen turkey won in a bingo coverall game had ever come. "A cup of cocoa would go down just fine right now."

"I'll cannibalize anything worth cannibalizing out of that thing tomorrow and then take it to the dump," Jon said.

Richard nodded. "Delete it from our lives," he said, and they went into the house and the smell of hot cocoa, laughing together.

The Man Who
Would Not
Shake Hands

Stevens served drinks, and soon after eight o'clock on that bitter winter night, most of us retired with them to the library. For a time no one said anything; the only sounds were the crackle of the fire in the hearth, the dim click of billiard balls, and, from outside, the shriek of the wind. Yet it was warm enough in here, at 249B East 35th.

I remember that David Adley was on my right that night, and Emlyn McCarron, who had once given us a frightening story about a woman who had given birth under unusual circumstances, was on my left. Beyond him was Johanssen, with his *Wall Street Journal* folded in his lap.

Stevens came in with a small white packet and handed it to George Gregson without so much as a pause. Stevens is the perfect butler in spite of his faint Brooklyn accent (or maybe *because* of it), but his greatest attribute, so far as I am concerned, is that he always knows to whom the packet must go if no one asks for it.

George took it without protest and sat for a moment in his high wing chair, looking into the fireplace, which is big enough to broil a good-sized ox. I saw his eyes flick momentarily to the inscription chiseled into the keystone: IT IS THE TALE, NOT HE WHO TELLS IT.

He tore the packet open with his old, trembling fingers and tossed the contents into the fire. For a moment the flames turned into a rainbow, and there was murmured laughter. I turned and saw Stevens standing far back in the shadows by the foyer door. His hands were crossed behind his back. His face was carefully blank.

I suppose we all jumped a little when his scratchy, almost querulous voice broke the silence; I know that I did.

"I once saw a man murdered right in this room," George Gregson said, "although no juror would have convicted the killer. Yet, at the end of the business, he convicted himself—and served as his own executioner!"

There was a pause while he lit his pipe. Smoke drifted around his seamed face in a blue raft, and he shook the wooden match out with the slow, declamatory gestures of a man whose joints hurt him badly. He threw the stick into the fireplace, where it landed on the ashy remains of the packet. He watched the flames char the wood. His sharp blue eyes brooded beneath their bushy salt-and-pepper brows. His nose was large and hooked, his lips thin and firm, his shoulders hunched almost to the back of his skull.

"Don't tease us, George!" growled Peter Andrews. "Bring it on!"

"No fear. Be patient." And we all had to wait until he had his pipe fired to his complete satisfaction. When a fine bed of coals had been laid in the large briar bowl, George folded his large, slightly palsied hands over one knee and said:

"Very well, then. I'm eighty-five and what I'm going to tell you occurred when I was twenty or thereabouts. It was 1919, at any rate, and I was just back from the Great War. My fiancée had died five months earlier, of influenza. She was only nineteen, and I fear I drank and played cards a great deal more than I should. She had been waiting for two years, you understand, and during that period I received a letter faithfully each week. Perhaps you may understand why I indulged myself so heavily. I had no religious beliefs, finding the general tenets and theories of Christianity rather comic in the trenches, and I had no family to support me. And so I can say with truth that the good friends who saw me through my time of trial rarely left me. There were fifty-three of them (more than most people have!): fifty-two cards and a bottle of Cutty Sark whiskey. I had taken up residence in the very rooms I inhabit now, on Brennan Street. But they were much cheaper then, and there were considerably fewer medicine bottles and pills and nostrums cluttering the shelves. Yet I spent most of my time here, at 249B, for there was almost always a poker game to be found.''

David Adley interrupted, and although he was smiling, I don't think he was joking at all. "And was Stevens here back then, George?''

George looked around at the butler. "Was it you, Stevens, or was it your father?''

Stevens allowed himself the merest ghost of a smile. "As 1919 was over sixty-five years ago, sir, it was my grandfather, I must allow.''

"Yours is a post that runs in the family, we must take it,'' Adley mused.

"As you take it, sir,'' Stevens replied gently.

"Now that I think back on it,'' George said, "there is a remarkable resemblance between you and your . . . did you say grandfather, Stevens?''

"Yes, sir, so I said.''

"If you and he were put side by side, I'd be hard put to tell which was which . . . but that's neither here nor there, is it?''

"No, sir.''

"I was in the game room—right through that same little door over there—playing patience the first and only time I met Henry Brower. There were four of us who were ready to sit down and play poker; we only wanted a fifth to make the evening go. When Jason Davidson told me that George Oxley, our usual fifth, had broken his leg and was laid up in bed with a cast at the end of a damned pulley contraption, it seemed that we should have no game that night. I was contemplating the prospect of finishing the evening with nothing to take my mind off my own thoughts but patience and a mind-blotting quantity of whiskey when the fellow across the room said in a calm and pleasant voice, 'If you gentlemen have been speaking of poker, I would very much enjoy picking up a hand, if you have no particular objections.'

"He had been buried behind a copy of the New York *World* until then, so that when I looked over I was seeing him for the first time. He was a young man with an old face, if you take my meaning. Some of the marks I saw on his face I had begun to see stamped on my own since the death of Rosalie. Some—but not all. Although the fellow could have been no older than twenty-eight from his hair and hands and manner of walking, his face seemed marked with experience and his eyes, which were very dark, seemed more than sad; they seemed almost haunted. He was quite good-looking, with a short, clipped mustache and darkish blond hair. He wore a good-looking brown suit and his top collar button had been loosened. 'My name is Henry Brower,' he said.

"Davidson immediately rushed across the room to shake hands; in fact, he acted as though he might actually snatch Brower's hand out of Brower's lap. An odd thing happened: Brower dropped his paper and held both hands up and out of reach. The expression on his face was one of horror.

"Davidson halted, quite confused, more bewildered than angry. He was only twenty-two himself—God, how young we all were in those days—and a bit of a puppy.

" 'Excuse me,' Brower said with complete gravity, 'but I never shake hands!'

"Davidson blinked. 'Never?' he said. 'How very peculiar. Why in the world not?' Well, I've told you that he was a bit of a puppy. Brower took it in the best possible way, with an open (yet rather troubled) smile.

" 'I've just come back from Bombay,' he said. 'It's a strange, crowded, filthy place, full of disease and pestilence. The vultures strut and preen on the very city walls by the thousands. I was there on a trade mission for two years, and I seem to have picked up a horror of our Western custom of handshaking. I know I'm foolish and impolite, and yet I cannot seem to bring myself to it. So if you would be so very good as to let me off with no hard feelings . . .'

" 'Only on one condition,' Davidson said with a smile.

" 'What would that be?'

" 'Only that you draw up to the table and share a tumbler of George's whiskey while I go for Baker and French and Jack Wilden.'

"Brower smiled at him, nodded, and put his paper away. Davidson made a brash circled thumb-and-finger, and chased away to get the others. Brower and I drew up to the green-felted table, and when I offered him a drink he declined with thanks and ordered his own bottle. I suspected it might have something to do with his odd fetish and said nothing. I have known men whose horror of germs and disease stretched that far and even further . . . and so may many of you."

There were nods of agreement.

" 'It's good to be here,' Brower told me reflectively. 'I've shunned any kind of companionship since I returned from my post. It's not good for a man to be alone, you know. I think that, even for the most self-sufficient of men, being isolated from the flow of humanity must be the worst form of torture!' He said this with a queer kind of emphasis, and I nodded. I had experienced such loneliness in the trenches, usually at night. I experienced it again, more keenly, after learning of Rosalie's death. I found myself warming to him in spite of his self-professed eccentricity.

" 'Bombay must have been a fascinating place,' I said.

" 'Fascinating . . . and terrible! There are things over there which are undreamed of in our philosophy. Their reaction to motorcars is amusing: the children shrink from them as they go by and then follow them for blocks. They find the airplane terrifying and incomprehensible. Of course, we Americans view these contraptions with complete equanimity—even complacency!—but I assure you that my reaction was exactly the same as theirs when I first observed a street-corner beggar swallow an entire packet of steel needles and then pull them, one by one, from the open sores at the end of his fingers. Yet here is something that natives of that part of the world take utterly for granted.

" 'Perhaps,' he added somberly, 'the two cultures were never intended to mix, but to keep their separate wonders to themselves. For an American such as you or I to swallow a packet of needles would result in a slow, horrible death. And as for the motorcar . . .' He trailed off, and a bleak, shadowed expression came to his face.

"I was about to speak when Stevens the Elder appeared with Brower's bottle of Scotch, and directly following him, Davidson and the others.

"Davidson prefaced the introductions by saying, 'I've told them all of your little fetish, Henry, so you needn't fear for a thing. This is Darrel Baker, the fearsome-looking fellow with the beard is Andrew French, and last but not least, Jack Wilden. George Gregson you already know.'

"Brower smiled and nodded at all of them in lieu of shaking hands. Poker chips and three fresh decks of cards were produced, money was changed for markers, and the game began.

"We played for better than six hours, and I won perhaps

two hundred dollars. Darrel Baker, who was not a particularly good player, lost about eight hundred (not that *he* would ever feel the pinch; his father owned three of the largest shoe factories in New England), and the rest had split Baker's losses with me about evenly. Davidson was a few dollars up and Brower a few down; yet for Brower to be near even was no mean feat, for he had had astoundingly bad cards for most of the evening. He was adroit at both the traditional five-card draw and the newer seven-card-stud variety of the game, and I thought that several times he had won money on cool bluffs that I myself would have hesitated to try.

"I did notice one thing: although he drank quite heavily—by the time French prepared to deal the last hand, he had polished off almost an entire bottle of Scotch—his speech did not slur at all, his card-playing skill never faltered, and his odd fixation about the touching of hands never flagged. When he won a pot, he never touched it if someone had markers or change or if someone had 'gone light' and still had chips to contribute. Once, when Davidson placed his glass rather close to his elbow, Brower flinched back abruptly, almost spilling his own drink. Baker looked surprised, but Davidson passed it off with a remark.

"Jack Wilden had commented a few moments earlier that he had a drive to Albany staring him in the face later that morning, and once more around the table would do for him. So the deal came to French, and he called seven-card stud.

"I can remember that final hand as clearly as my own name, although I should be pressed to describe what I had for lunch yesterday or whom I ate it with. The mysteries of age, I suppose, and yet I think that if any of you other fellows had been there you might remember it as well.

"I was dealt two hearts down and one up. I can't speak for Wilden or French, but young Davidson had the ace of hearts and Brower the ten of spades. Davidson bet two dollars—five was our limit—and the cards went round again. I drew a heart to make four, Brower drew a jack of spades to go with his ten. Davidson had caught a trey which did not seem to improve his hand, yet he threw three dollars into the pot. 'Last hand,' he said merrily. 'Drop it in, boys! There's a lady who would like to go out on the town with me tomorrow night!'

"I don't suppose I would have believed a fortune-teller if

he had told me how often that remark would come back to haunt me at odd moments, right down to this day.

"French dealt our third round of up cards. I got no help with my flush, but Baker, who was the big loser, paired up something—kings, I think. Brower had gotten a deuce of diamonds that did not seem to help anything. Baker bet the limit on his pair, and Davidson promptly raised him five. Everyone stayed in the game, and our last up card came around the table. I drew the king of hearts to fill up my flush, Baker drew a third to his pair, and Davidson got a second ace that fairly made his eyes sparkle. Brower got a queen of clubs, and for the life of me I couldn't see why he remained in. His cards looked as bad as any he had folded that night.

"The bettings began to get a little steep. Baker bet five, Davidson raised five, Brower called. Jack Wilden said, 'Somehow I don't think my pair is quite good enough,' and threw in his hand. I called the ten and raised another five. Baker called and raised again.

"Well, I needn't bore you with a raise-by-raise description. I'll only say that there was a three-raise limit per man, and Baker, Davidson, and I each took three raises of five dollars. Brower merely called each bet and raise, being careful to wait until all hands were clear of the pot before throwing his money in. And there was a lot of money in there—slightly better than two hundred dollars—as French dealt us our last card facedown.

"There was a pause as we all looked, although it meant nothing to me; I had my hand, and from what I could see on the table it was good. Baker threw in five, Davidson raised, and we waited to see what Brower would do. His face was slightly flushed with alcohol, he had removed his tie and unbuttoned a second shirt button, but he seemed quite calm. 'I call . . . and raise five,' he said.

"I blinked a little, for I had fully expected him to fold. Still, the cards I held told me I must play to win, and so I raised five. We played with no limit to the number of raises a player could make on the last card, and so the pot grew marvelously. I stopped first, being content simply to call in view of the full house I had become more and more sure someone must be holding. Baker stopped next, blinking warily from Davidson's pair of aces to Brower's mystifying junk hand. Baker was not the best of card players, but he was good enough to sense something in the wind.

"Between them, Davidson and Brower raised at least ten more times, perhaps more. Baker and I were carried along, unwilling to cast away our large investments. The four of us had run out of chips, and greenbacks now lay in a drift over the huge sprawl of markers.

" 'Well,' Davidson said, following Brower's latest raise, 'I believe I'll simply call. If you've been running a bluff, Henry, it's been a fine one. But I have you beaten and Jack's got a long trip ahead of him tomorrow.' And with that he put a five-dollar bill on top of the pile and said, 'I call.'

"I don't know about the others, but I felt a distinct sense of relief that had little to do with the large sum of money I had put into the pot. The game had been becoming cutthroat, and while Baker and I could afford to lose, if it came to that, Jase Davidson could not. He was currently at loose ends, living on a trust fund—not a large one—left him by his aunt. And Brower—how well could he stand the loss? Remember, gentlemen, that by this time there was better than a thousand dollars on the table."

George paused here. His pipe had gone out.

"Well, what happened?" Adley leaned forward. "Don't tease us, George. You've got us all on the edge of our chairs. Push us off or settle us back in."

"Be patient," George said, unperturbed. He produced another match, scratched it on the sole of his shoe, and puffed at his pipe. We waited intently, without speaking. Outside, the wind screeched and hooted around the eaves.

When the pipe was aglow and things seemed set to rights, George continued:

"As you know, the rules of poker state that the man who has been called should show first. But Baker was too anxious to end the tension; he pulled out one of his three down cards and turned it over to show four kings.

" 'That does me,' I said. 'A flush.'

" 'I have you,' Davidson said to Baker, and showed two of his down cards. Two aces, to make four. 'Damn well played.' And he began to pull in the huge pot.

" 'Wait!' Brower said. He did not reach out and touch Davidson's hand as most would have done, but his voice was enough. Davidson paused to look and his mouth fell—actually *fell* open as if all the muscles there had turned to water. Brower had turned over *all three* of his down cards, to reveal a straight flush, from the eight to the queen. 'I believe this beats your aces?' Brower said politely.

"Davidson went red, then white. 'Yes,' he said slowly, as if discovering the fact for the first time. 'Yes, it does.'

"I would give a great deal to know Davidson's motivation for what came next. He knew of Brower's extreme aversion to being touched; the man had showed it in a hundred different ways that night. It may have been that Davidson simply forgot it in his desire to show Brower (and all of us) that he could cut his losses and take even such a grave reversal in a sportsmanlike way. I've told you that he was something of a puppy, and such a gesture would probably have been in his character. But puppies can also nip when they are provoked. They aren't killers—a puppy won't go for the throat; but many a man has had his fingers stitched to pay for teasing a little dog too long with a slipper or a rubber bone. That would also be a part of Davidson's character, as I remember him.

"I would, as I can say, give a great deal to know . . . but the results are all that matter, I suppose.

"When Davidson took his hands away from the pot, Brower reached over to rake it in. At that instant, Davidson's face lit up with a kind of ruddy good fellowship, and he plucked Brower's hand from the table and wrung it firmly. 'Brilliant playing, Henry, simply brilliant. I don't believe I ever—'

"Brower cut him off with a high, womanish scream that was frightful in the deserted silence of the game room, and jerked away. Chips and currency cascaded every which way as the table tottered and nearly fell over.

"We were all immobilized with the sudden turn of events, and quite unable to move. Brower staggered away from the table, holding his hand out in front of him like a masculine version of Lady Macbeth. He was as white as a corpse, and the stark terror on his face is beyond my powers of description. I felt a bolt of horror go through me such as I had never experienced before or since, not even when they brought me the telegram with the news of Rosalie's death.

"Then he began to moan. It was a hollow, awful sound, cryptlike. I remember thinking, *Why, the man's quite insane;* and then he said the queerest thing: 'The switch . . . I've left

the switch on in the motorcar . . . O God, I am so *sorry!'*
And he fled up the stairs toward the main lobby.

"I was the first to come out of it. I lurched out of my chair
and chased after him, leaving Baker and Wilden and Davidson sitting around the huge pot of money Brower had won.
They looked like graven Inca statues guarding a tribal treasure.

"The front door was still swinging to and fro, and when I
dashed out into the street I saw Brower at once, standing on
the edge of the sidewalk and looking vainly for a taxi. When
he saw me he cringed so miserably that I could not help
feeling pity intermixed with wonder.

" 'Here,' I said, 'wait! I'm sorry for what Davidson did
and I'm sure he didn't mean it; all the same, if you must go
because of it, you must. But you've left a great deal of money
behind and you shall have it.'

" 'I should never have come,' he groaned. 'But I was so
desperate for any kind of human fellowship that I . . . I . . .'
Without thinking, I reached out to touch him—the most
elemental gesture of one human being to another when he is
grief-stricken—but Brower shrank away from me and cried,
'Don't touch me! Isn't one enough? O God, why don't I just
die?'

"His eye suddenly lit feverishly on a stray dog with slat-
thin sides and mangy, chewed fur that was making its way up
the other side of the deserted, early-morning street. The cur's
tongue hung out and it walked with a wary, three-legged
limp. It was looking, I suppose, for garbage cans to tip over
and forage in.

" 'That could be me over there,' he said reflectively, as if
to himself. 'Shunned by everyone, forced to walk alone and
venture out only after every other living thing is safe behind
locked doors. Pariah dog!'

" 'Come now,' I said, a little sternly, for such talk smacked
more than a little of the melodramatic. 'You've had some
kind of nasty shock and obviously something has happened to
put your nerves in a bad state, but in the War I saw a
thousand things which—'

" 'You don't believe me, do you?' he asked. 'You think
I'm in the grip of some sort of hysteria, don't you?'

" 'Old man, I really don't know what you might be
gripping or what might be gripping you, but I *do* know that if
we continue to stand out here in the damp night air, we'll

both *catch* the grippe. Now if you'd care to step back inside with me—only as far as the foyer, if you'd like—I'll ask Stevens to—'

"His eyes were wild enough to make me acutely uneasy. There was no light of sanity left in them, and he reminded me of nothing so much as the battle-fatigued psychotics I had seen carried away in carts from the front lines: husks of men with awful, blank eyes like potholes to hell, mumbling and gibbering.

" 'Would you care to see how one outcast responds to another?' he asked me, taking no notice of what I had been saying at all. 'Watch, then, and see what I've learned in strange ports of call!'

"And he suddenly raised his voice and said imperiously, 'Dog!'

"The dog raised his head, looked at him with wary, rolling eyes (one glittered with rabid wildness; the other was filmed by a cataract), and suddenly changed direction and came limpingly, reluctantly, across the street to where Brower stood.

"It did not want to come; that much was obvious. It whined and growled and tucked its mangy rope of a tail between its legs; but it was drawn to him nonetheless. It came right up to Brower's feet, and then lay upon its belly, whining and crouching and shuddering. Its emaciated sides went in and out like a bellows, and its good eye rolled horribly in its socket.

"Brower uttered a hideous, despairing laugh that I still hear in my dreams, and squatted by it. 'There,' he said. 'You see? It knows me as one of its kind . . . and knows what I bring it!' He reached for the dog and the cur uttered a snarling, lugubrious howl. It bared its teeth.

" 'Don't!' I cried sharply. 'He'll bite!'

"Brower took no notice. In the glow of the streetlight his face was livid, hideous, the eyes black holes burnt in parchment. 'Nonsense,' he crooned. 'Nonsense. I only want to shake hands with him . . . as your friend shook with me!' And suddenly he seized the dog's paw and shook it. The dog made a horrible howling noise, but made no move to bite him.

"Suddenly Brower stood up. His eyes seemed to have cleared somewhat, and except for his excessive pallor, he might have again been the man who had offered courteously to pick up a hand with us earlier the night before.

" 'I'm leaving now,' he said quietly. 'Please apologize to your friends and tell them I'm sorry to have acted like such a fool. Perhaps I'll have a chance to . . . redeem myself another time.'

" 'It's we who owe you the apology,' I said. 'And have you forgotten the money? It's better than a thousand dollars.'

" 'O yes! The money!' And his mouth curved in one of the bitterest smiles I have ever seen.

" 'Never mind coming into the lobby,' I said. 'If you will promise to wait right here, I'll bring it. Will you do that?'

" 'Yes,' he said. 'If you wish, I'll do that.' And he looked reflectively down at the dog whining at his feet. 'Perhaps he would like to come to my lodgings with me and have a square meal for once in his miserable life.' And the bitter smile reappeared.

"I left him then, before he could reconsider, and went downstairs. Someone—probably Jack Wilden; he always had an orderly mind—had changed all the markers for greenbacks and had stacked the money neatly in the center of the green felt. None of them spoke to me as I gathered it up. Baker and Jack Wilden were smoking wordlessly; Jason Davidson was hanging his head and looking at his feet. His face was a picture of misery and shame. I touched him on the shoulder as I went back to the stairs and he looked at me gratefully.

"When I reached the street again, it was utterly deserted. Brower had gone. I stood there with a wad of greenbacks in each hand, looking vainly either way, but nothing moved. I called once, tentatively, in case he should be standing in the shadows someplace near, but there was no response. Then I happened to look down. The stray dog was still there, but his days of foraging in trash cans were over. He was quite dead. The fleas and ticks were leaving his body in marching columns. I stepped back, revolted and yet also filled with a species of odd, dreamy terror. I had a premonition that I was not yet through with Henry Brower, and so I wasn't; but I never saw him again."

The fire in the grate had died to guttering flames and cold had begun to creep out of the shadows, but no one moved or spoke while George lit his pipe again. He sighed and re-crossed his legs, making the old joints crackle, and resumed.

"Needless to say, the others who had taken part in the game were unanimous in opinion: we must find Brower and give him his money. I suppose some would think we were insane to feel so, but that was a more honorable age. Davidson was in an awful funk when he left; I tried to draw him aside and offer him a good word or two, but he only shook his head and shuffled out. I let him go. Things would look different to him after a night's sleep, and we could go looking for Brower together. Wilden was going out of town, and Baker had 'social rounds' to make. It would be a good way for Davidson to gain back a little self-respect, I thought.

"But when I went round to his apartment the next morning, I found him not yet up. I might have awakened him, but he was a young fellow and I decided to let him sleep the morning away while I spaded up a few elementary facts.

"I called here first, and talked to Stevens's—" He turned toward Stevens and raised an eyebrow.

"Grandfather, sir," Stevens said.

"Thank you."

"You're welcome, sir, I'm sure."

"I talked to Stevens's grandfather. I spoke to him in the very spot where Stevens himself now stands, in fact. He said that Raymond Greer, a fellow I knew slightly, had spoken for Brower. Greer was with the city trade commission, and I immediately went to his office in the Flatiron Building. I found him in, and he spoke to me immediately.

"When I told him what had happened the night before, his face became filled with a confusion of pity, gloom, and fear.

" 'Poor old Henry!' he exclaimed. 'I knew it was coming to this, but I never suspected it would arrive so quickly.'

" 'What?' I asked.

" 'His breakdown,' Greer said. 'It stems from his year in Bombay, and I suppose no one but Henry will ever know the whole story. But I'll tell you what I can.'

"The story that Greer unfolded to me in his office that day increased both my sympathy and understanding. Henry Brower, it appeared, had been unluckily involved in a real tragedy. And, as in all classic tragedies of the stage, it had stemmed from a fatal flaw—in Brower's case, forgetfulness.

"As a member of the trade-commission group in Bombay, he had enjoyed the use of a motorcar, a relative rarity there. Greer said that Brower took an almost childish pleasure in driving it through the narrow streets and byways of the city, scaring up chickens in great, gabbling flocks and making the women and men fall on their knees to their heathen gods. He drove it everywhere, attracting great attention and huge crowds of ragged children that followed him about but always hung back when he offered them a ride in the marvelous device, which he constantly did. The auto was a Model-A Ford with a truck body, and one of the earliest cars able to start not only by a crank but by the touch of a button. I ask you to remember that.

"One day Brower took the auto far across the city to visit one of the high poobahs of that place concerning possible consignments of jute rope. He attracted his usual notice as the Ford machine growled and backfired through the streets, sounding like an artillery barrage in progress—and, of course, the children followed.

"Brower was to take dinner with the jute manufacturer, an affair of great ceremony and formality, and they were only halfway through the second course, seated on an open-air terrace above the teeming street below, when the familiar racketing, coughing roar of the car began below them, accompanied by screams and shrieks.

"One of the more adventurous boys—and the son of an obscure holy man—had crept into the cab of the auto, convinced that whatever dragon there was under the iron hood could not be roused without the white man behind the wheel. And Brower, intent upon the coming negotiations, had left the switch on and the spark retarded.

"One can imagine the boy growing more daring before the eyes of his peers as he touched the mirror, waggled the wheel, and made mock tooting noises. Each time he thumbed his nose at the dragon under the hood, the awe in the faces of the others must have grown.

"His foot must have been pressed down on the clutch, perhaps for support, when he pushed the starter button. The engine was hot; it caught fire immediately. The boy, in his extreme terror, would have reacted by removing his foot from the clutch immediately, preparatory to jumping out. Had the car been older or in poorer condition, it would have stalled. But Brower cared for it scrupulously, and it leaped forward in a series of bucking, roaring jerks. Brower was just in time to see this as he rushed from the jute manufacturer's house.

"The boy's fatal mistake must have been little more than an accident. Perhaps, in his flailings to get out, an elbow accidentally struck the throttle. Perhaps he pulled it with the panicky hope that this was how the white man choked the dragon back into sleep. However it happened . . . it happened. The auto gained suicidal speed and charged down the crowded, roiling street, bumping over bundles and bales, crushing the wicker cages of the animal vendor, smashing a flower cart to splinters. It roared straight downhill toward the street's turning, leaped over the curb, crashed into a stone wall and exploded in a ball of flame.''

George switched his briar from one side of his mouth to the other.

"This was all Greer could tell me, because it was all Brower had told him that made any sense. The rest was a kind of deranged harangue on the folly of two such disparate cultures ever mixing. The dead boy's father evidently confronted Brower before he was recalled and flung a slaughtered chicken at him. There was a curse. At this point, Greer gave me a smile which said that we were both men of the world, lit a cigarette, and remarked, 'There's always a curse when a thing of this sort happens. The miserable heathens must keep up appearances at all costs. It's their bread and butter.'

" 'What was the curse?' I wondered.

" 'I should have thought you would have guessed,' said Greer. 'The wallah told him that a man who would practice sorcery on a small child should become a pariah, an outcast. Then he told Brower that any living thing he touched with his hands would die. Forever and forever, amen.' Greer chuckled.

" 'Brower believed it?'

"Greer believed he did. 'You must remember that the man had suffered a dreadful shock. And now, from what you tell me, his obsession is worsening rather than curing itself.'

" 'Can you tell me his address?'

"Greer hunted through his files, and finally came up with a listing. 'I don't guarantee that you'll find him there,' he said. 'People have been naturally reluctant to hire him, and I understand he hasn't a great deal of money.'

"I felt a pang of guilt at this, but said nothing. Greer struck me as a little too pompous, a little too smug, to deserve what little information I had on Henry Brower. But as I rose, something prompted me to say, 'I saw Brower shake hands with a mangy street cur last night. Fifteen minutes later the dog was dead.'

" 'Really? How interesting.' He raised his eyebrows as if the remark had no bearing on anything we had been discussing.

"I rose to take my leave and was about to shake Greer's hand when the secretary opened his office door. 'Pardon me, but you are Mr. Gregson?'

"I told her I was.

" 'A man named Baker has just called. He's asked you to come to twenty-three Nineteenth Street immediately.'

"It gave me quite a nasty start, because I had already been there once that day—it was Jason Davidson's address. When I left Greer's office, he was just settling back with his pipe and *The Wall Street Journal*. I never saw him again, and don't count it any great loss. I was filled with a very specific dread—the kind that will nevertheless not quite crystallize into an actual fear with a fixed object, because it is too awful, too unbelievable to actually be considered."

Here I interrupted his narrative. "Good God, George! You're not going to tell us he was dead?"

"Quite dead," George agreed. "I arrived almost simultaneously with the coroner. His death was listed as a coronary thrombosis. He was short of his twenty-third birthday by sixteen days.

"In the days that followed, I tried to tell myself that it was all a nasty coincidence, best forgotten. I did not sleep well, even with the help of my good friend Mr. Cutty Sark. I told myself that the thing to do was divide that night's last pot between the three of us and forget that Henry Brower had ever stepped into our lives. But I could not. I drew a cashier's check for the sum instead, and went to the address that Greer had given me, which was in Harlem.

"He was not there. His forwarding address was a place on the East Side, a slightly less-well-off neighborhood of nonetheless respectable brownstones. He had left those lodgings a full month before the poker game, and the new address was in the East Village, an area of ramshackle tenements.

"The building superintendent, a scrawny man with a huge black mastiff snarling at his knee, told me that Brower had moved out on April third—the day after our game. I asked for a forwarding address and he threw back his head and emitted a screaming gobble that apparently served him in the place of laughter.

" 'The only forradin' address they gives when they leave

here is Hell, boss. But sometimes they stops in the Bowery on their way there.'

"The Bowery was then what it is only believed to be by out-of-towners now: the home of the homeless, the last stop for the faceless men who only care for another bottle of cheap wine or another shot of the white powder that brings long dreams. I went there. In those days there were dozens of flophouses, a few benevolent missions that took drunks in for the night, and hundreds of alleys where a man might hide an old, louse-ridden mattress. I saw scores of men, all of them little more than shells, eaten by drink and drugs. No names were known or used. When a man has sunk to a final basement level, his liver rotted by wood alcohol, his nose an open, festering sore from the constant sniffing of cocaine and potash, his fingers destroyed by frostbite, his teeth rotted to black stubs—a man no longer has a use for a name. But I described Henry Brower to every man I saw, with no response. Bartenders shook their heads and shrugged. The others just looked at the ground and kept walking.

"I didn't find him that day, or the next, or the next. Two weeks went by, and then I talked to a man who said a fellow like that had been in Devarney's Rooms three nights before.

"I walked there; it was only two blocks from the area I had been covering. The man at the desk was a scabrous ancient with a peeling bald skull and rheumy, glittering eyes. Rooms were advertised in the flyspecked window facing the street at a dime a night. I went through my description of Brower, the old fellow nodding all the way through it. When I had finished, he said:

" 'I know him, young meester. Know him well. But I can't quite recall . . . I think ever s'much better with a dollar in front of me.'

"I produced a dollar and he made it disappear neat as a button, arthritis notwithstanding.

" 'He was here, young meester, but he's gone.'

" 'Do you know where?'

" 'I can't quite recall,' the desk clerk said. 'I might, howsomever, with a dollar in front of me.'

"I produced a second bill, which he made disappear as neatly as he had the first. At this, something seemed to strike him as being deliciously funny, and a rasping, tubercular cough came out of his chest.

" 'You've had your amusement,' I said, 'and been well paid for it as well. Now, do you know where this man is?'

"The old man laughed gleefully again. 'Yes—Potter's Field is his new residence; eternity's the length of his lease; and he's got the Devil for a roommate. How do you like *them* apples, young meester? He must've died sometime yesterday morning, for when I found him at noon he was still warm and toasty. Sitting bolt upright by the winder, he was. I'd gone up to either have his dime against the dark or show him the door. As it turned out, the city showed him six feet of earth.' This caused another unpleasant outburst of senile glee.

" 'Was there anything unusual?' I asked, not quite daring to examine the import of my own question. 'Anything out of the ordinary?'

" 'I seem to recall somethin' . . . Let me see . . .'

"I produced a dollar to aid his memory, but this time it did not produce laughter, although it disappeared with the same speed.

" 'Yes, there was something passin odd about it,' the old man said. 'I've called the city hack for enough of them to know. Bleedin Jesus, ain't I! I've found 'em hangin from the hook on the door, found 'em dead in bed, found 'em out on the fire escape in January with a bottle between their knees frozen just as blue as the Atlantic. I even found one fella that drowned in the washstand, although that was over thirty years ago. But this fella—sittin bolt upright in his brown suit, just like some swell from uptown, with his hair all combed. Had hold of his right wrist with his left hand, he did. I've seen all kinds, but he's the only one I ever seen that died shakin his own hand.'

"I left and walked all the way to the docks, and the old man's last words seemed to play over and over again in my brain like a phonograph record that has gotten stuck in one groove. *He's the only one I ever seen that died shakin his own hand.*

"I walked down to the end of one of the piers, out to where the dirty gray water lapped the encrusted pilings. And then I ripped that cashier's check into a thousand pieces and threw it into the water."

George Gregson shifted and cleared his throat. The fire had burned down to reluctant embers, and cold was creeping into the deserted game room. The tables and chairs seemed spectral and unreal, like furnishings glimpsed in a dream where past and present merge. The flames rimmed the letters cut into the fireplace keystone with dull orange light: IT IS THE TALE, NOT HE WHO TELLS IT.

"I only saw him once, and once was enough; I've never forgotten. But it did serve to bring me out of my own time of mourning, for any man who can walk among his fellows is not wholly alone.

"If you'll bring me my coat, Stevens, I believe I'll toddle along home—I've stayed far past my usual bedtime."

And when Stevens had brought it, George smiled and pointed at a small mole just below the left corner of Stevens's mouth. "The resemblance really *is* remarkable, you know—your grandfather had a mole in that exact same place."

Stevens smiled but made no reply. George left, and the rest of us slipped out soon after.

Beachworld

FedShip ASN/29 fell out of the sky and crashed. After a while two men slipped from its cloven skull like brains. They walked a little way and then stood, helmets beneath their arms, and looked at where they had finished up.

It was a beach in no need of an ocean—it was its own ocean, a sculpted sea of sand, a black-and-white-snapshot sea frozen forever in troughs and crests and more troughs and crests.

Dunes.

Shallow ones, steep ones, smooth ones, corrugated ones. Knifecrested dunes, plane-crested dunes, irregularly crested dunes that resembled dunes piled on dunes—dune-dominoes.

Dunes. But no ocean.

The valleys which were the troughs between these dunes snaked in mazy black rat-runs. If one looked at those twisting lines long enough, they might seem to spell words—black words hovering over the white dunes.

"Fuck," Shapiro said.

"Bend over," Rand said.

Shapiro started to spit, then thought better of it. Looking at all that sand made him think better of it. This was not the time to go wasting moisture, perhaps. Half-buried in the sand, ASN/29 didn't look like a dying bird anymore; it looked like a gourd that had broken open and disclosed rot

345

inside. There had been a fire. The starboard fuel-pods had all exploded.

"Too bad about Grimes," Shapiro said.

"Yeah." Rand's eyes were still roaming the sand sea, out to the limiting line of the horizon and then coming back again.

It *was* too bad about Grimes. Grimes was dead. Grimes was now nothing but large chunks and small chunks in the aft storage compartment. Shapiro had looked in and thought: *It looks like God decided to eat Grimes, found out he didn't taste good, and sicked him up again*. That had been too much for Shapiro's own stomach. That, and the sight of Grimes's teeth scattered across the floor of the storage compartment.

Shapiro now waited for Rand to say something intelligent, but Rand was quiet. Rand's eyes tracked over the dunes, traced the clockspring windings of the deep troughs between.

"Hey!" Shapiro said at last. "What do we do? Grimes is dead; you're in command. What do we do?"

"Do?" Rand's eyes moved back and forth, back and forth, over the stillness of the dunes. A dry, steady wind ruffled the rubberized collar of the Environmental Protection suit. "If you don't have a volleyball, I don't know."

"What are you talking about?"

"Isn't that what you're supposed to do on the beach?" Rand asked. "Play volleyball?"

Shapiro had been scared in space many times, and close to panic when the fire broke out; now, looking at Rand, he heard a rumor of fear too large to comprehend.

"It's big," Rand said dreamily, and for one moment Shapiro thought that Rand was speaking of Shapiro's own fear. "One hell of a big beach. Something like this could go on forever. You could walk a hundred miles with your surfboard under your arm and still be where you started, almost, with nothing behind you but six or seven footprints. And if you stood in the same place for five minutes, the last six or seven would be gone, too."

"Did you get a topographical compscan before we came down?" Rand was in shock, he decided. Rand was in shock but Rand was not crazy. He could give Rand a pill if he had to. And if Rand continued to spin his wheels, he could give him a shot. "Did you get a look at—"

Rand looked at him briefly. "What?"

The green places. That had been what he was going to say.
It sounded like a quote from Psalms, and he couldn't say it.
The wind made a silver chime in his mouth.

"What?" Rand asked again.

"Compscan! *Compscan!*" Shapiro screamed. "You ever
hear of a compscan, dronehead? What's this place like? Where's
the ocean at the end of the fucking *beach?* Where's the lakes?
Where's the nearest greenbelt? Which direction? Where does
the beach end?"

"End? Oh. I grok you. It never ends. No greenbelts, no ice
caps. No oceans. This is a beach in search of an ocean, mate.
Dunes and dunes and dunes, and they never end."

"But what'll we do for water?"

"Nothing we can do."

"The ship . . . it's beyond repair!"

"No shit, Sherlock."

Shapiro fell quiet. It was now either be quiet or become
hysterical. He had a feeling—almost a certainty—that if he
became hysterical, Rand would just go on looking at the
dunes until Shapiro worked it out, or until he didn't.

What did you call a beach that never ended? Why, you
called it a desert! Biggest motherfucking desert in the universe, wasn't that right?

In his head he heard Rand respond: *No shit, Sherlock.*

Shapiro stood for some time beside Rand, waiting for the
man to wake up, to *do* something. After a while his patience
ran out. He began to slide and stumble back down the flank
of the dune they had climbed to look around. He could feel
the sand sucking against his boots. *Want to suck you down,
Bill,* his mind imagined the sand saying. In his mind it was
the dry, arid voice of a woman who was old but still terribly
strong. *Want to suck you right down here and give you a
great . . . big . . . hug.*

That made him think about how they used to take turns
letting the others bury them up to their necks at the beach
when he was a kid. Then it had been fun—now it scared him.
So he turned that voice off—this was no time for memory
lane, Christ, no—and walked through the sand with short,
sharp kicking strides, trying unconsciously to mar the symmetrical perfection of its slope and surface.

"Where are you going?" Rand's voice for the first time
held a note of awareness and concern.

"The beacon," Shapiro said. "I'm going to turn it on. We were on a mapped lane of travel. It'll be picked up, vectored. It's a question of time. I know the odds are shitty, but maybe somebody will come before—"

"The beacon's smashed to hell," Rand said. "It happened when we came down."

"Maybe it can be fixed," Shapiro called back over his shoulder. As he ducked through the hatchway he felt better in spite of the smells—fried wiring and a bitter whiff of Freon gas. He told himself he felt better because he had thought of the beacon. No matter how paltry, the beacon offered some hope. But it wasn't the thought of the beacon that had lifted his spirits; if Rand said it was broken, it was probably most righteously broken. But he could no longer see the dunes— could no longer see that big, never-ending beach.

That was what made him feel better.

When he got to the top of the first dune again, struggling and panting, his temples pounding with the dry heat, Rand was still there, still staring and staring and staring. An hour had gone by. The sun stood directly above them. Rand's face was wet with perspiration. Jewels of it nestled in his eyebrows. Droplets ran down his cheeks like tears. More droplets ran down the cords of his neck and into the neck of his EP suit like drops of colorless oil running into the guts of a pretty good android.

Dronehead I called him, Shapiro thought with a little shudder. *Christ, that's what he looks like—not an android but a dronehead who just took a neck-shot with a very big needle.*

And Rand had been wrong after all.

"Rand?"

No answer.

"The beacon wasn't broken." There was a flicker in Rand's eyes. Then they went blank again, staring out at the mountains of sand. Frozen, Shapiro had first thought them, but he supposed they moved. The wind was constant. They would move. Over a period of decades and centuries, they would . . . well, would *walk*. Wasn't that what they called dunes on a beach? Walking dunes? He seemed to remember that from his childhood. Or school. Or someplace, and what in the hell did it matter?

Now he saw a delicate rill of sand slip down the flank of one of them. As if it heard

(heard what I was thinking)

Fresh sweat on the back of his neck. All right, he was getting a touch of the whim-whams. Who wouldn't? This was a tight place they were in, very tight. And Rand seemed not to know it . . . or not to care.

"It had some sand in it, and the warbler was cracked, but there must have been sixty of those in Grimes's odds-and-ends box."

Is he even hearing me?

"I don't know how the sand got in it—it was right where it was supposed to be, in the storage compartment behind the bunk, three closed hatches between it and the outside, but—"

"Oh, sand spreads. Gets into everything. Remember going to the beach when you were a kid, Bill? You'd come home and your mother would yell at you because there was sand everywhere? Sand in the couch, sand on the kitchen table, sand down the foot of your bed? Beach sand is very . . ." He gestured vaguely, and then that dreamy, unsettling smile resurfaced. ". . . ubiquitous."

"—but it didn't hurt it any," Shapiro continued. "The emergency power output system is ticking over and I plugged the beacon into it. I put on the earphones for a minute and asked for an equivalency reading at fifty parsecs. Sounds like a power saw. It's better than we could have hoped."

"No one's going to come. Not even the Beach Boys. The Beach Boys have all been dead for eight thousand years. Welcome to Surf City, Bill. Surf City *sans* surf."

Shapiro stared out at the dunes. He wondered how long the sand had been here. A trillion years? A quintillion? Had there been life here once? Maybe even something with intelligence? Rivers? Green places? Oceans to make it a real beach instead of a desert?

Shapiro stood next to Rand and thought about it. The steady wind ruffled his hair. And quite suddenly he was sure all those things had been, and he could picture how they must have ended.

The slow retreat of the cities as their waterways and outlying areas were first speckled, then dusted, finally drifted and choked by the creeping sand.

He could see the shiny brown alluvial fans of mud, sleek as sealskins at first but growing duller and duller in color as they spread further and further out from the mouths of the rivers—

out and out until they met each other. He could see sleek sealskin mud becoming reed-infested swamp, then gray, gritty till, finally shifting white sand.

He could see mountains shortening like sharpened pencils, their snow melting as the rising sand brought warm thermal updrafts against them; he could see the last few crags pointing at the sky like the fingertips of men buried alive; he could see them covered and immediately forgotten by the profoundly idiotic dunes.

What had Rand called them?

Ubiquitous.

If you just had a vision, Billy-boy, it was a pretty goddam dreadful one.

Oh, but no, it wasn't. It wasn't dreadful; it was peaceful. It was as quiet as a nap on a Sunday afternoon. What was more peaceful than the beach?

He shook these thoughts away. It helped to look back toward the ship.

"There isn't going to be any cavalry," Rand said. "The sand will cover us and after a while we'll be the sand and the sand will be us. Surf City with no surf—can you catch that wave, Bill?"

And Shapiro was scared because he *could* catch it. You couldn't see all those dunes without getting it.

"Fucking dronehead asshole," he said. He went back to the ship.

And hid from the beach.

Sunset finally came. The time when, at the beach—any *real* beach—you were supposed to put away the volleyball and put on your sweats and get out the weenies and the beer. Not time to start necking yet, but almost. Time to look *forward* to the necking.

Weenies and beer had not been a part of ASN/29's stores. Shapiro spent the afternoon carefully bottling all of the ship's water. He used a porta-vac to suck up that which had run out of the ruptured veins in the ship's supply system and puddled on the floor. He got the small bit left in the bottom of the shattered hydraulic system's water tank. He did not over-look even the small cylinder in the guts of the air-purification system which circulated air in the storage areas.

Finally, he went into Grimes's cabin.

Grimes had kept goldfish in a circular tank constructed especially for weightless conditions. The tank was built of impact-resistant clear-polymer plastic, and had survived the crash easily. The goldfish—like their owner—had not been impact-resistant. They floated in a dull orange clump at the top of the ball, which had come to rest under Grimes's bunk, along with three pairs of very dirty underwear and half a dozen porno holograph-cubes.

He held the globe aquarium for a moment, looking fixedly into it. "Alas, poor Yorick, I knew him well," he said suddenly, and laughed a screaming, distracted laugh. Then he got the net Grimes kept in his lockbin and dipped it into the tank. He removed the fish and then wondered what to do with them. After a moment he took them to Grimes's bed and raised his pillow.

There was sand underneath.

He put the fish there regardless, then carefully poured the water into the jerrican he was using as a catcher. It would all have to be purified, but even if the purifiers hadn't been working, he thought that in another couple of days he wouldn't balk at drinking aquarium water just because it might have a few loose scales and a little goldfish shit in it.

He purified the water, divided it, and took Rand's share back up the side of the dune. Rand was right where he had been, as if he had never moved.

"Rand. I brought you your share of the water." He unzipped the pouch on the front of Rand's EP suit and slipped the flat plastic flask inside. He was about to press the zip-strip closed with his thumbnail when Rand brushed his hand away. He took the flask out. Stenciled on the front was ASN/CLASS SHIP'S SUPPLIES STORAGE FLASK CL. #23196755 STERILE WHEN SEAL IS UNBROKEN. The seal was broken now, of course; Shapiro had had to fill the bottle up.

"I purified—"

Rand opened his fingers. The flask fell into the sand with a soft plop. "Don't want it."

"Don't . . . Rand, what's wrong with you? Jesus Christ, will you *stop* it?"

Rand did not reply.

Shapiro bent over and picked up storage flask #23196755. He brushed off the grains of sand clinging to the sides as if they were huge, swollen germs.

"What's *wrong* with you?" Shapiro repeated. "Is it shock? Do you think that's what it is? Because I can give you a pill . . . or a shot. But it's getting to me, I don't mind telling you. You just standing out here looking at the next forty miles of nothing! It's *sand*! Just *sand*!"

"It's a beach," Rand said dreamily. "Want to make a sand castle?"

"Okay, good," Shapiro said. "I'm going to go get a needle and an amp of Yellowjack. If you want to act like a goddam dronehead, I'll treat you like one."

"If you try to inject me with something, you better be quiet when you sneak up behind me," Rand said mildly. "Otherwise, I'll break your arm."

He could do it, too. Shapiro, the astrogator, weighed a hundred and forty pounds and stood five-five. Physical combat was not his specialty. He grunted an oath and turned away, back to the ship, holding Rand's flask.

"I think it's alive," Rand said. "I'm actually pretty sure of it."

Shapiro looked back at him and then out at the dunes. The sunset had given them a gold filigree at their smooth, sweeping caps, a filigree that shaded delicately down to the blackest ebony in the troughs; on the next dune, ebony shaded back to gold. Gold to black. Black to gold. Gold to black and black to gold and gold to—

Shapiro blinked his eyes rapidly, and rubbed a hand over them.

"I have several times felt this particular dune move under my feet," Rand told Shapiro. "It moves very gracefully. It is like feeling the tide. I can smell its smell on the air, and the smell is like salt."

"You're crazy," Shapiro said. He was so terrified that he felt as if his brains had turned to glass.

Rand did not reply. Rand's eyes searched the dunes, which went from gold to black to gold to black in the sunset.

Shapiro went back to the ship.

Rand stayed on the dune all night, and all the next day.

Shapiro looked out and saw him. Rand had taken off his EP suit, and the sand had almost covered it. Only one sleeve stuck out, forlorn and supplicating. The sand above and below it reminded Shapiro of a pair of lips sucking with a toothless greed at a tender morsel. Shapiro felt a crazy desire to pelt up the side of the dune and rescue Rand's EP suit.

He did not.

He sat in his cabin and waited for the rescue ship. The smell of Freon had dissipated. It was replaced by the even less desirable smell of Grimes decaying.

The rescue ship did not come that day or that night or on the third day.

Sand somehow appeared in Shapiro's cabin, although the hatchway was closed and the seal still appeared perfectly tight. He sucked the little puddles of sand up with the porta-vac as he had sucked up puddles of spilled water on that first day.

He was very thirsty all the time. His flask was nearly empty already.

He thought he had begun to smell salt on the air; in his sleep he heard the sound of gulls.

And he could hear the sand.

The steady wind was moving the first dune closer to the ship. His cabin was still okay—thanks to the porta-vac—but the sand was already taking over the rest. Mini-dunes had reached through the blown locks and laid hold of ASN/29. It sifted in tendrils and membranes through the vents. There was a drift in one of the blown tanks.

Shapiro's face grew gaunt and pebbly with beard shadow.

Near sunset of the third day, he climbed up the dune to check on Rand. He thought about taking a hypodermic, then rejected it. It was a lot more than shock; he knew that now. Rand was insane. It would be best if he died quickly. And it looked as if that was exactly what was going to happen.

Shapiro was gaunt; Rand was emaciated. His body was a scrawny stick. His legs, formerly rich and thick with iron-pumper's muscle, were now slack and droopy. The skin hung on them like loose socks that keep falling down. He was wearing only his undershorts, and they were red nylon, and they looked absurdly like a ball-hugger bathing suit. A light beard had begun to grow on his face, fuzzing his hollow cheeks and chin. His beard was the color of beach sand. His hair, formerly a listless brown shade, had bleached out to a near blond. It hung over his forehead. Only his eyes, peering through the fringe of his hair with bright blue intensity, still lived fully. They studied the beach

(the dunes goddammit the DUNES)
relentlessly.

Now Shapiro saw a bad thing. It was a very bad thing indeed. He saw that Rand's face was turning into a sand dune. His beard and his hair were choking his skin.

"You," Shapiro said, "are going to die. If you don't come down to the ship and drink, you are going to die."

Rand said nothing.

"Is that what you *want?*"

Nothing. There was the vacuous snuffle of the wind, but no more. Shapiro observed that the creases of Rand's neck were filling up with sand.

"The only thing I *want,*" Rand said in a faint, faraway voice like the wind, "is my Beach Boys tapes. They're in my cabin."

"Fuck you!" Shapiro said furiously. "But do you know what I hope? I hope a ship comes before you die. I want to see you holler and scream when they pull you away from your precious goddam beach. I want to see what happens then!"

"Beach'll get you, too," Rand said. His voice was empty and rattling, like wind inside a split gourd—a gourd which has been left in a field at the end of October's last harvest. "Take a listen, Bill. Listen to the *wave.*"

Rand cocked his head. His mouth, half-open, revealed his tongue. It was as shriveled as a dry sponge.

Shapiro heard something.

He heard the dunes. They sang songs of Sunday afternoon at the beach—naps on the beach with no dreams. Long naps. Mindless peace. The sound of crying gulls. Shifting, thoughtless particles. Walking dunes. He heard . . . and was drawn. Drawn toward the dunes.

"You hear it," Rand said.

Shapiro reached into his nose and dug with two fingers until it bled. Then he could close his eyes; his thoughts came slowly and clumsily together. His heart was racing.

I was almost like Rand. Jesus! . . . it almost had me!

He opened his eyes again and saw that Rand had become a conch shell on a long deserted beach, straining forward toward all the mysteries of an undead sea, staring out at the dunes and the dunes and the dunes.

No more, Shapiro moaned inside himself.

Oh, but listen to this wave, the dunes whispered back.

Against his better judgment, Shapiro listened.

Then his better judgment ceased to exist.

Shapiro thought: *I could hear better if I sat down.*

He sat down at Rand's feet and put his heels on his thighs like a Yaqui Indian and listened.

He heard the Beach Boys and the Beach Boys were singing about fun, fun, fun. He heard them singing that the girls on the beach were all within reach. He heard—

—a hollow sighing of the wind, not in his ear but in the canyon between right brain and left brain—he heard that sighing somewhere in the blackness which is spanned only by the suspension bridge of the corpus callosum, which connects conscious thought to the infinite. He felt no hunger, no thirst, no heat, no fear. He heard only the voice in the emptiness.

And a ship came.

It came swooping out of the sky, afterburners scratching a long orange track from right to left. Thunder belted the delta-wave topography, and several dunes collapsed like bullet-path brain damage. The thunder ripped Billy Shapiro's head open and for a moment he was torn both ways, *ripped,* torn down the middle—

Then he was up on his feet.

"Ship!" he screamed. *"Holy fuck! Ship! Ship! SHIP!"*

It was a belt trader, dirty and buggered by five hundred—or five thousand—years of clan service. It surfed through the air, banged crudely upright, skidded. The captain blew jets and fused sand into black glass. Shapiro cheered the wound.

Rand looked around like a man awaking from a deep dream.

"Tell it to go away, Billy."

"You don't understand." Shapiro was shambling around, shaking his fists in the air. "You'll be all right—"

He broke toward the dirty trader in big, leaping strides, like a kangaroo running from a ground fire. The sand clutched at him. Shapiro kicked it away. Fuck you, sand. I got a honey back in Hansonville. Sand never had no honey. Beach never had no hard-on.

The trader's hull split. A gangplank popped out like a tongue. A man strode down it behind three sampler androids and a guy built into treads that was surely the captain. He wore a beret with a clan symbol on it, anyway.

One of the androids waved a sampler wand at him. Shapiro batted it away. He fell on his knees in front of the captain and embraced the treads which had replaced the captain's dead legs.

"The dunes . . . Rand . . . no water . . . alive . . . hypnotized him . . . dronehead world . . . I . . . thank God . . ."

A steel tentacle whipped around Shapiro and yanked him away on his gut. Dry sand whispered underneath him like laughter.

"It's okay," the captain said. *"Bey-at shel! Me! Me! Gat!"*

The android dropped Shapiro and backed away, clittering distractedly to itself.

"All this way for a fucking Fed!" the captain exclaimed bitterly.

Shapiro wept. It hurt, not just in his head, but in his liver.

"Dud! *Gee-yat! Gat!* Water-for-him-Cry!"

The man who had been in the lead tossed him a nippled low-grav bottle. Shapiro upended it and sucked greedily, spilling crystal-cold water into his mouth, down his chin, in dribbles that darkened his tunic, which had bleached to the color of bone. He choked, vomited, then drank again.

Dud and the captain watched him closely. The androids clittered.

At last Shapiro wiped his mouth and sat up. He felt both sick and well.

"You Shapiro?" the captain asked.

Shapiro nodded.

"Clan affiliation?"

"None."

"ASN number?"

"29."

"Crew?"

"Three. One dead. The other—Rand—up there." He pointed but did not look.

The captain's face did not change. Dud's face did.

"The beach got him," Shapiro said. He saw their questioning, veiled looks. "Shock . . . maybe. He seems hypnotized. He keeps talking about the . . . the Beach Boys . . . never mind, you wouldn't know. He wouldn't drink or eat. He's bad off."

"Dud. Take one of the andies and get him down from there." He shook his head. "Fed ship, Christ. No salvage."

Dud nodded. A few moments later he was scrambling up the side of the dune with one of the andies. The andy looked like a twenty-year-old surfer who might make dope money on the side servicing bored widows, but his stride gave him away even more than the segmented tentacles which grew from his armpits. The stride, common to all androids, was the slow, reflective, almost painful stride of an aging English butler with hemorrhoids.

There was a buzz from the captain's dashboard.

"I'm here."

"This is Gomez, Cap. We got a situation here. Compscan and surface telemetry show us a very unstable surface. There's no bedrock that we can targ. We're resting on our own burn, and right now that may be the hardest thing on the whole planet. Trouble is, the burn itself is starting to settle."

"Recommendation?"

"We ought to get out."

"When?"

"Five minutes ago."

"You're a laugh riot, Gomez."

The captain punched a button and the communicator went out.

Shapiro's eyes were rolling. "Look, never mind Rand. He's had it."

"I'm taking you both back," the captain said. "I got no salvage, but the Federation ought to pay something for the two of you . . . not that either of you are worth much, as far as I can see. He's crazy and you're chickenshit."

"No . . . you don't understand. You—"

The captain's cunning yellow eyes gleamed.

"You got any contra?" he asked.

"Captain . . . look . . . please—"

"Because if you do, there's no sense just leaving it here. Tell me what it is and where it is. I'll split seventy-thirty. Standard salvor's fee. Couldn't do any better than that, hey? You—"

The burn suddenly tilted beneath them. Quite noticeably tilted. A horn somewhere inside the trader began to blat with muffled regularity. The communicator on the captain's dashboard went off again.

"There!" Shapiro screamed. *"There, do you see what you're up against? You want to talk about contraband now? WE HAVE GOT TO GET THE FUCK OUT OF HERE!"*

"Shut up, handsome, or I'll have one of these guys sedate you," the captain said. His voice was serene but his eyes had changed. He thumbed the communicator.

"Cap, I got ten degrees of tilt and we're getting more. The elevator's going down, but it's going on an angle. We've still got time, but not much. The ship's going to fall over."

"The struts will hold her."

"No, sir. Begging the captain's pardon, they won't."

"Start firing sequences, Gomez."

"Thank you, sir." The relief in Gomez's voice was unmistakable.

Dud and the android were coming back down the flank of the dune. Rand wasn't with them. The andy fell further and further behind. And now a strange thing happened. The andy fell over on its face. The captain frowned. It did not fall as an andy is supposed to fall—which is to say, like a human being, more or less. It was as if someone had pushed over a mannequin in a department store. It fell over like that. Thump, and a little tan cloud of sand puffed up from around it.

Dud went back and knelt by it. The andy's legs were still moving as if it dreamed, in the 1.5 million Freon-cooled micro-circuits that made up its mind, that it still walked. But the leg movements were slow and cracking. They stopped. Smoke began to come out of its pores and its tentacles shivered in the sand. It was gruesomely like watching a human die. A deep grinding came from inside it: *Graaaagggg!*

"Full of sand," Shapiro whispered. "It's got Beach Boys religion."

The captain glanced at him impatiently. "Don't be ridiculous, man. That thing could walk through a sandstorm and not get a grain inside it."

"Not on *this* world."

The burn settled again. The trader was now clearly canted. There was a low groan as the struts took more weight.

"Leave it!" the captain bawled at Dud. "Leave it, leave it! *Gee-yat! Come-me-for-Cry!*"

Dud came, leaving the andy to walk face-down in the sand.

"What a balls-up," the captain muttered.

He and Dud engaged in a conversation spoken entirely in a rapid pidgin dialect which Shapiro was able to follow to some degree. Dud told the captain that Rand had refused to come. The andy had tried to grab Rand, but with no force. Even then it was moving jerkily, and strange grating sounds were coming from inside it. Also, it had begun to recite a combination of galactic strip-mining coordinates and a catalogue of the captain's folk-music tapes. Dud himself had then closed with Rand. They had struggled briefly. The captain told Dud that if Dud had allowed a man who had been standing three days in the hot sun to get the better of him, that maybe he ought to get another First.

Dud's face darkened with embarrassment, but his grave, concerned look never faltered. He slowly turned his head, revealing four deep furrows in his cheek. They were welling slowly.

"Him-gat big indics," Dud said. *"Strong-for-Cry. Him-gat for umby."*

"Umby-him for-Cry?" The captain was looking at Dud sternly.

Dud nodded. *"Umby. Beyat-shel. Umby-for-Cry."*

Shapiro had been frowning, conning his tired, frightened mind for that word. Now it came. *Umby.* It meant crazy. *He's strong, for Christ's sake. Strong because he's crazy. He's got big ways, big force. Because he's crazy.*

Big ways . . . or maybe it meant big waves. He wasn't sure. Either way it came to the same.

Umby.

The ground shifted underneath them again, and sand blew across Shapiro's boots.

From behind them came the hollow *ka-thud, ka-thud, ka-thud* of the breather-tubes opening. Shapiro thought it one of the most lovely sounds he had ever heard in his life.

The captain sat deep in thought, a weird centaur whose lower half was treads and plates instead of horse. Then he looked up and thumbed the communicator.

"Gomez, send Excellent Montoya down here with a tranquilizer gun."

"Acknowledged."

The captain looked at Shapiro. "Now, on top of everything else, I've lost an android worth your salary for the next ten years. I'm pissed off. I mean to have your buddy."

"Captain." Shapiro could not help licking his lips. He knew this was a very ill-chosen thing to do. He did not want to appear mad, hysterical, or craven, and the captain had apparently decided he was all three. Licking his lips like that would only add to the impression . . . but he simply couldn't help himself. "Captain, I cannot impress on you too strongly the need to get off this world as soon as poss—"

"Can it, dronehead," the captain said, not unkindly.

A thin scream rose from the top of the nearest dune.

"Don't touch me! Don't come near me! Leave me alone! All of you!"

"Big indics gat umby," Dud said gravely.

"Ma-him, yeah-mon," the captain returned, and then turned to Shapiro. "He really *is* bad off, isn't he?"

Shapiro shuddered. "You don't know. You just—"

The burn settled again. The struts were groaning louder than ever. The communicator crackled. Gomez's voice was thin, a little unsteady.

"We have to get out of here right now, Cap!"

"All right." A brown man appeared on the gangway. He held a long pistol in one gloved hand. The captain pointed at Rand. *"Ma-him, for-Cry. Can?"*

Excellent Montoya, unperturbed by the tilting earth that was not earth but only sand fused to glass (and there were deep cracks running through it now, Shapiro saw), unbothered by the groaning struts or the eerie sight of an android that now appeared to be digging its own grave with its feet, studied Rand's thin figure for a moment.

"Can," he said.

"Gat! Gat-for-Cry!" The captain spat to one side. "Shoot his pecker off, I don't care," he said. "Just as long as he's still breathing when we ship."

Excellent Montoya raised the pistol. The gesture was apparently two-thirds casual and one-third careless, but Shapiro, even in his state of near-panic, noted the way Montoya's head tilted to one side as he lined the barrel up. Like many in the clans, the gun would be nearly a part of him, like pointing his own finger.

There was a hollow *fooh!* as he squeezed the trigger and the tranquilizer dart blew out of the barrel.

A hand reached out of the dune and clawed it down.

It was a large brown hand, wavery, made of sand. It simply reached up, in defiance of the wind, and smothered the momentary glitter of the dart. Then the sand fell back with a heavy *thrrrrap*. No hand. Impossible to believe there *had* been. But they had all seen it.

"Giddy-hump," the captain said in an almost conversational voice.

Excellent Montoya fell on his knees. *"Aidy-May-for-Cry, bit-gat come! Saw-hoh got belly-gat-for-Cry!—"*

Numbly, Shapiro realized Montoya was saying a rosary in pidgin.

Up on the dune, Rand was jumping up and down, shaking his fists at the sky, screeching thinly in triumph.

A hand. It was a HAND. He's right; it's alive, alive, alive—

"Indic!" the captain said sharply to Montoya. *"Cannit! Gat!"*

Montoya shut up. His eyes touched on the capering figure of Rand and then he looked away. His face was full of superstitious horror nearly medieval in quality.

"Okay," the captain said. "I've had enough. I quit. We're going."

He shoved two buttons on his dashboard. The motor that should have swiveled him neatly around so he faced up the gangplank again did not hum; it squealed and grated. The captain cursed. The burn shifted again.

"Captain!" Gomez. In a panic.

The captain slammed in another button and the treads began to move backward up the gangplank.

"Guide me," the captain said to Shapiro. "I got no fucking rearview mirror. It was a hand, wasn't it?"

"Yes."

"I want to get out of here," the captain said. "It's been fourteen years since I had a cock, but right now I feel like I'm pissing myself."

Thrrap! A dune suddenly collapsed over the gangway. Only it wasn't a dune; it was an arm.

"Fuck, oh fuck," the captain said.

On his dune, Rand capered and screeched.

Now the threads of the captain's lower half began to grind. The mini-tank of which the captain's head and shoulders were the turret now began to judder backward.

"What—"

The treads locked. Sand splurted out from between them.

"Pick me up!" the captain bawled to the two remaining androids. *"Now! RIGHT NOW!"*

Their tentacles curled around the tread sprockets as they

picked him up—he looked ridiculously like a faculty member about to be tossed in a blanket by a bunch of roughhousing fraternity boys. He was thumbing the communicator.

"Gomez! Final firing sequence! Now! Now!"

The dune at the foot of the gangplank shifted. Became a hand. A large brown hand that began to scrabble up the incline.

Shrieking, Shapiro bolted from that hand.

Cursing, the captain was carried away from it.

The gangplank was pulled up. The hand fell off and became sand again. The hatchway irised closed. The engines howled. No time for a couch; no time for anything like that. Shapiro dropped into a crash-fold position on the bulkhead and was promptly smashed flat by the acceleration. Before unconsciousness washed over him, it seemed he could feel sand grasping at the trader with muscular brown arms, straining to hold them down—

Then they were up and away.

Rand watched them go. He was sitting down. When the track of the trader's jets was at last gone from the sky, he turned his eyes out to the placid endlessness of the dunes.

"We got a '34 wagon and we call it a woody," he croaked to the empty, moving sand. "It ain't very cherry; it's an oldy but a goody."

Slowly, reflectively, he began to cram handful after handful of sand into his mouth. He swallowed . . . swallowed . . . swallowed. Soon his belly was a swollen barrel and sand began to drift over his legs.

The Reaper's Image

"We moved it last year, and quite an operation it was, too," Mr. Carlin said as they mounted the stairs. "Had to move it by hand, of course. No other way. We insured it against accident with Lloyd's before we even took it out of the case in the drawing room. Only firm that would insure for the sum we had in mind."

Spangler said nothing. The man was a fool. Johnson Spangler had learned a long time ago that the only way to talk to a fool was to ignore him.

"Insured it for a quarter of a million dollars," Mr. Carlin resumed when they reached the second-floor landing. His mouth quirked in a half-bitter, half-humorous line. "And a pretty penny it cost, too." He was a little man, not quite fat, with rimless glasses and a tanned bald head that shone like a varnished volleyball. A suit of armor, guarding the mahogany shadows of the second-floor corridor, stared at them impassively.

It was a long corridor, and Spangler eyed the walls and hangings with a cool professional eye. Samuel Claggert had bought in copious quantities, but he had not bought well. Like so many of the self-made industry emperors of the late 1800's, he had been little more than a pawnshop rooter masquerading in collector's clothing, a connoisseur of canvas monstrosities, trashy novels and poetry collections in ex-

363

pensive cowhide bindings, and atrocious pieces of sculpture, all of which he considered Art.

Up here the walls were hung—festooned was perhaps a better word—with imitation Moroccan drapes, numberless (and, no doubt, anonymous) madonnas holding numberless haloed babes while numberless angels flitted hither and thither in the background, grotesque scrolled candelabra, and one monstrous and obscenely ornate chandelier surmounted by a salaciously grinning nymphet.

Of course the old pirate had come up with a few interesting items; the law of averages demanded it. And if the Samuel Claggert Memorial Private Museum (Guided Tours on the Hour—Admission $1.00 Adults, $.50 Children—nauseating) was 98 percent blatant junk, there was always that other two percent, things like the Coombs long rifle over the hearth in the kitchen, the strange little *camera obscura* in the parlor, and of course the—

"The Delver looking-glass was removed from downstairs after a rather unfortunate . . . incident," Mr. Carlin said abruptly, motivated apparently by a ghastly glaring portrait of no one in particular at the base of the next staircase. "There had been others—harsh words, wild statements—but this was an attempt to actually *destroy* the mirror. The woman, a Miss Sandra Bates, came in with a rock in her pocket. Fortunately her aim was bad and she only cracked a corner of the case. The mirror was unharmed. The Bates girl had a brother—"

"No need to give me the dollar tour," Spangler said quietly. "I'm conversant with the history of the Delver glass."

"Fascinating, isn't it?" Carlin cast him an odd, oblique look. "There was that English duchess in 1709 . . . and the Pennsylvania rug merchant in 1746 . . . not to mention—"

"I'm conversant with the history," Spangler repeated quietly. "It's the workmanship I'm interested in. And then, of course, there's the question of authenticity—"

"Authenticity!" Mr. Carlin chuckled, a dry sound, as if bones had stirred in a cupboard below the stairs. "It's been examined by experts, Mr. Spangler."

"So was the Lemlier Stradivarius."

"So true," Mr. Carlin said with a sigh. "But no Stradivarius ever had quite the . . . the unsettling effect of the Delver glass."

"Yes, quite," Spangler said in his softly contemptuous

voice. He understood now that there would be no stopping Carlin; he had a mind which was perfectly in tune with the age. "Quite."

They climbed the third and fourth flights in silence. As they drew closer to the roof of the rambling structure, it became oppressively hot in the dark upper galleries. With the heat came a creeping stench that Spangler knew well, for he had spent all his adult life working in it—a smell of long-dead flies in shadowy corners, of wet rot and creeping wood lice behind the plaster. The smell of age. It was a smell common only to museums and mausoleums. He imagined much the same smell might arise from the grave of a virginal young girl, forty years dead.

Up here the relics were piled helter-skelter in true junk-shop profusion; Mr. Carlin led Spangler through a maze of statuary, frame-splintered portraits, pompous gold-plated birdcages, the dismembered skeleton of an ancient tandem bicycle. He led him to the far wall where a stepladder had been set up beneath a trapdoor in the ceiling. A dusty padlock hung from the trap.

Off to the left, an imitation Adonis stared at them pitilessly with blank pupilless eyes. One arm was outstretched, and a yellow sign hung on the wrist which read: ABSOLUTELY NO ADMITTANCE.

Mr. Carlin produced a key ring from his jacket pocket, selected a key, and mounted the stepladder. He paused on the third rung, his bald head gleaming faintly in the shadows. "I don't like that mirror," he said. "I never did. I'm afraid to look into it. I'm afraid I might look into it one day and see . . . what the rest of them saw."

"They saw nothing but themselves," Spangler said.

Mr. Carlin began to speak, stopped, shook his head, and fumbled above him, craning his neck to fit the key properly into the lock. "Should be replaced," he muttered. "It's—damn!" The lock sprung suddenly and swung out of the hasp. Mr. Carlin made a fumbling grab for it and almost fell off the ladder. Spangler caught it deftly and looked up at him. He was clinging shakily to the top of the stepladder, face white in the brown semidarkness.

"You *are* nervous about it, aren't you?" Spangler said in a mildly wondering tone.

Mr. Carlin said nothing. He seemed paralyzed.

"Come down," Spangler said. "Please. Before you fall."

Carlin descended the ladder slowly, clinging to each rung like a man tottering over a bottomless chasm. When his feet touched the floor he began to babble, as if the floor contained some current that had turned him on, like an electric light.

"A quarter of a million," he said. "A quarter of a million dollars' worth of insurance to take that . . . *thing* from down there to up here. That goddam *thing*. They had to rig a special block and tackle to get it into the gable storeroom up there. And I was hoping—almost praying—that someone's fingers would be slippery . . . that the rope would be the wrong test . . . that the thing would fall and be shattered into a million pieces—"

"Facts," Spangler said. "Facts, Carlin. Not cheap paperback novels, not cheap tabloid stories or equally cheap horror movies. *Facts.* Number one: John Delver was an English craftsman of Norman descent who made mirrors in what we call the Elizabethan period of England's history. He lived and died uneventfully. No pentacles scrawled on the floor for the housekeeper to rub out, no sulfur-smelling documents with a splotch of blood on the dotted line. Number two: His mirrors have become collector's items due principally to fine craftsmanship and to the fact that a form of crystal was used that has a mildly magnifying and distorting effect upon the eye of the beholder—a rather distinctive trademark. Number three: Only five Delvers remain in existence to our present knowledge—two of them in America. They are priceless. Number four: This Delver and one other that was destroyed in the London Blitz have gained a rather spurious reputation due largely to falsehood, exaggeration, and coincidence—"

"Fact number five," Mr. Carlin said. "You're a supercilious bastard, aren't you?"

Spangler looked with mild detestation at the blind-eyed Adonis.

"I was guiding the tour that Sandra Bates's brother was a part of when he got his look into your precious Delver mirror, Spangler. He was perhaps sixteen, part of a high-school group. I was going through the history of the glass and had just got to the part *you* would appreciate—extolling the flawless craftsmanship, the perfection of the glass itself—when the boy raised his hand. 'But what about that black splotch in the upper left-hand corner?' he asked. 'That looks like a mistake.'

"And one of his friends asked him what he meant, so the Bates boy started to tell him, then stopped. He looked at the mirror very closely, pushing right up to the red velvet guard-rope around the case—*then he looked behind him as if what he had seen had been the reflection of someone—of someone in black—standing at his shoulder*. 'It looked like a man,' he said. 'But I couldn't see the face. It's gone now.' And that was all."

"Go on," Spangler said. "You're itching to tell me it was the Reaper—I believe that is the common explanation, isn't it? That occasional chosen people see the Reaper's image in the glass? Get it out of your system, man. The *National Enquirer* would love it! Tell me about the horrific consequences and defy me to explain it. Was he later hit by a car? Did he jump out of a window? What?"

Mr. Carlin chuckled a forlorn little chuckle. "You should know better, Spangler. Haven't you told me twice that you are . . . ah . . . conversant with the history of the DeIver glass. There *were* no horrific consequences. There never have been. That's why the DeIver glass isn't Sunday-supplementized like the Koh-i-noor Diamond or the curse on King Tut's tomb. It's mundane compared to those. You think I'm a fool, don't you?"

"Yes," Spangler said. "Can we go up now?"

"Certainly," Mr. Carlin said passionately. He climbed the ladder and pushed the trapdoor. There was a clickety-clackety-bump as it was drawn up into the shadows by a counterweight, and then Mr. Carlin disappeared into the shadows. Spangler followed. The blind Adonis stared unknowingly after them.

The gable room was explosively hot, lit only by one cobwebby, many-angled window that filtered the hard outside light into a dirty milky glow. The looking-glass was propped at an angle to the light, catching most of it and reflecting a pearly patch onto the far wall. It had been bolted securely into a wooden frame. Mr. Carlin was not looking at it. Quite studiously not looking at it.

"You haven't even put a dustcloth over it," Spangler said, visibly angered for the first time.

"I think of it as an eye," Mr. Carlin said. His voice was still drained, perfectly empty. "If it's left open, always open, perhaps it will go blind."

Spangler paid no attention. He took off his jacket, folded the buttons carefully in, and with infinite gentleness he wiped the dust from the convex surface of the glass itself. Then he stood back and looked at it.

It was genuine. There was no doubt about it, never had been, really. It was a perfect example of Delver's particular genius. The cluttered room behind him, his own reflection, Carlin's half-turned figure—they were all clear, sharp, almost three-dimensional. The faint magnifying effect of the glass gave everything a slightly curved effect that added an almost fourth-dimensional distortion. It was—

His thought broke off, and he felt another wave of anger.

"Carlin."

Carlin said nothing.

"Carlin, you damned fool, I thought you said that girl didn't harm the mirror!"

No answer.

Spangler stared at him icily in the glass. "There is a piece of friction tape in the upper left-hand corner. Did she crack it? For God's sake, man, speak up!"

"You're seeing the Reaper," Carlin said. His voice was deadly and without passion. "There's no friction tape on the mirror. Put your hand over it . . . dear God."

Spangler wrapped the upper sleeve of his coat carefully around his hand, reached out, and pressed it gently against the mirror. "You see? Nothing supernatural. It's gone. My hand covers it."

"Covers it? Can you feel the tape? Why don't you pull it off?"

Spangler took his hand away carefully and looked into the glass. Everything in it seemed a little more distorted; the room's odd angles seemed to yaw crazily as if on the verge of sliding off into some unseen eternity. There was no dark spot in the mirror. It was flawless. He felt a sudden unhealthy dread rise in him and despised himself for feeling it.

"It looked like him, didn't it?" Mr. Carlin asked. His face was very pale, and he was looking directly at the floor. A muscle twitched spasmodically in his neck. "Admit it, Spangler. It looked like a hooded figure standing behind you, didn't it?"

"It looked like friction tape masking a short crack," Spangler said very firmly. "Nothing more, nothing less—"

"The Bates boy was very husky," Carlin said rapidly. His words seemed to drop into the hot, still atmosphere like stones into dark water. "Like a football player. He was wearing a letter sweater and dark green chinos. We were halfway to the upper-half exhibits when—"

"The heat is making me feel ill," Spangler said a little unsteadily. He had taken out a handkerchief and was wiping his neck. His eyes searched the convex surface of the mirror in small, jerky movements.

"When he said he wanted a drink of water . . . a drink of water, for God's sake!"

Carlin turned and stared wildly at Spangler. "How was I to know? How was I to know?"

"Is there a lavatory? I think I'm going to—"

"His sweater . . . I just caught a glimpse of his sweater going down the stairs . . . then . . ."

"—be sick."

Carlin shook his head, as if to clear it, and looked at the floor again. "Of course. Third door on your left, second floor, as you go toward the stairs." He looked up appealingly. "How was I to *know*?"

But Spangler had already stepped down onto the ladder. It rocked under his weight and for a moment Carlin thought—hoped—that he would fall. He didn't. Through the open square in the floor Carlin watched him descend, holding his mouth lightly with one hand.

"Spangler—?"

But he was gone.

Carlin listened to his footfalls fade to echoes, then die away. When they were gone, he shivered violently. He tried to move his own feet to the trapdoor, but they were frozen. Just that last, hurried glimpse of the boy's sweater . . . God! . . .

It was as if huge invisible hands were pulling his head, forcing it up. Not wanting to look, Carlin stared into the glimmering depths of the DeIver looking-glass.

There was nothing there.

The room was reflected back to him faithfully, its dusty confines transmuted into glimmering infinity. A snatch of a half-remembered Tennyson poem occurred to him, and he muttered it aloud: " ' "I am half-sick of shadows," said the Lady of Shalott . . .' "

And still he could not look away, and the breathing still-ness held him. From around one corner of the mirror a moth-eaten buffalo head peered at him with flat obsidian eyes.

The boy had wanted a drink of water and the fountain was in the first-floor lobby. He had gone downstairs and—

And had never come back.

Ever.

Anywhere.

Like the duchess who had paused after primping before her glass for a *soirée* and decided to go back into the sitting room for her pearls. Like the rug-merchant who had gone for a carriage ride and had left behind him only an empty carriage and two closemouthed horses.

And the Delver glass had been in New York from 1897 until 1920, had been there when Judge Crater—

Carlin stared as if hypnotized into the shallow depths of the mirror. Below, the blind-eyed Adonis kept watch.

He waited for Spangler much like the Bates family must have waited for their son, much like the duchess's husband must have waited for his wife to return from the sitting room. He stared into the mirror and waited.

And waited.

And waited.

Nona

Do you love?

I hear her voice saying this—sometimes I still hear it. In my dreams.

Do you love?

Yes, I answer. *Yes—and true love will never die.*

Then I wake up screaming.

I don't know how to explain it, even now. I can't tell you why I did those things. I couldn't do it at the trial, either. And there are a lot of people here who ask me about it. There's a psychiatrist who does. But I am silent. My lips are sealed. Except here in my cell. Here I am not silent. I wake up screaming.

In the dream I see her walking toward me. She is wearing a white gown, almost transparent, and her expression is one of mingled desire and triumph. She comes to me across a dark room with a stone floor and I smell dry October roses. Her arms are held open and I go to her with mine out to enfold her.

I feel dread, revulsion, unutterable longing. Dread and revulsion because I know what this place is, longing because I love her. I will always love her. There are times when I wish there were still a death penalty in this state. A short walk down a dim corridor, a straightbacked chair fitted with a steel skullcap, clamps . . . then one quick jolt and I would be with her.

As we come together in the dream my fear grows, but it is impossible for me to draw back from her. My hands press against the smooth plane of her back, her skin near under silk. She smiles with those deep, black eyes. Her head tilts up to mine and her lips part, ready to be kissed.

That's when she changes, shrivels. Her hair grows coarse and matted, melting from black to an ugly brown that spills down over the creamy whiteness of her cheeks. The eyes shrink and go beady. The whites disappear and she is glaring at me with tiny eyes like two polished pieces of jet. The mouth becomes a maw through which crooked yellow teeth protrude.

I try to scream. I try to wake up.

I can't. I'm caught again. I'll always be caught.

I am in the grip of a huge, noisome graveyard rat. Lights sway in front of my eyes. October roses. Somewhere a dead bell is chanting.

"Do you love?" this thing whispers. "Do you love?" The smell of roses is its breath as it swoops toward me, dead flowers in a charnel house.

"Yes," I tell the rat-thing. "Yes—and true love will never die." Then I do scream, and I am awake.

They think what we did together drove me crazy. But my mind is still working in some way or other, and I've never stopped looking for the answers. I still want to know how it was, and what it was.

They've let me have paper and a pen with a felt tip. I'm going to write everything down. Maybe I'll answer some of their questions and maybe while I'm doing that I can answer some of my own. And when I'm done, there's something else. Something they *don't* know I have. Something I took. It's here under my mattress. A knife from the prison dining hall.

I'll have to start by telling you about Augusta.

As I write this it is night, a fine August night poked through with blazing stars. I can see them through the mesh of my window, which overlooks the exercise yard and a slice of sky I can block out with two fingers. It's hot, and I'm naked except for my shorts. I can hear the soft summer sound of frogs and crickets. But I can bring back winter just by closing my eyes. The bitter cold of that night, the bleakness, the hard, unfriendly lights of a city that was not my city. It was the fourteenth of February.

See, I remember everything.

And look at my arms—covered with sweat, they've pulled into gooseflesh.

Augusta . . .

When I got to Augusta I was more dead than alive, it was that cold. I had picked a fine day to say good-bye to the college scene and hitchhike west; it looked like I might freeze to death before I got out of the state.

A cop had kicked me off the interstate ramp and threatened to bust me if he caught me thumbing there again. I was almost tempted to wisemouth him and let him do it. The flat, four-lane stretch of highway had been like an airport landing strip, the wind whooping and pushing membranes of powdery snow skirling along the concrete. And to the anonymous Them behind their Saf-T-Glas windshields, everyone standing in the breakdown lane on a dark night is either a rapist or a murderer, and if he's got long hair you can throw in child molester and faggot on top.

I tried it awhile on the access road, but it was no good. And along about a quarter of eight I realized that if I didn't get someplace warm quick, I was going to pass out.

I walked a mile and a half before I found a combination diner and diesel stop on 202 just inside the city limits. JOE'S GOOD EATS, the neon said. There were three big rigs parked in the crushed-stone parking lot, and one new sedan. There was a wilted Christmas wreath on the door that nobody had bothered to take down, and next to it a thermometer showing just five degrees of mercury above big zero. I had nothing to cover my ears but my hair, and my rawhide gloves were falling apart. The tips of my fingers felt like pieces of furniture.

I opened the door and went in.

The heat was the first thing that struck me, warm and good. Next a hillbilly song on the juke, the unmistakable voice of Merle Haggard: "We don't let our hair grow long and shaggy, like the hippies out in San Francisco do."

The third thing that struck me was The Eye. You know about The Eye once you let your hair get down below the lobes of your ears. Right then people know you don't belong to the Lions, Elks, or the VFW. You know about The Eye, but you never get used to it.

Right now the people giving me The Eye were four truckers in one booth, two more at the counter, a pair of old ladies wearing cheap fur coats and blue rinses, the short-order cook, and a gawky kid with soapsuds on his hands. There was a girl sitting at the far end of the counter, but all she was looking at was the bottom of her coffee cup.

She was the fourth thing that struck me.

I'm old enough to know there's no such thing as love at first sight. It's just something Rodgers and Hammerstein thought up one day to rhyme with moon and June. It's for kids holding hands at the Prom, right?

But looking at her made me feel something. You can laugh, but you wouldn't have if you'd seen her. She was almost unbearably beautiful. I knew without a doubt that everybody else in Joe's knew that the same as me. Just like I knew she had been getting The Eye before I came in. She had coal-colored hair, so black that it seemed nearly blue under the fluorescents. It fell freely over the shoulders of her scuffed tan coat. Her skin was cream-white, with just the faintest blooded touch lingering beneath the skin—the cold she had brought in with her. Dark, sooty lashes. Solemn eyes that slanted up the tiniest bit at the corners. A full and mobile mouth below a straight, patrician nose. I couldn't tell what her body looked like. I didn't care. You wouldn't, either. All she needed was that face, that hair, that *look*. She was exquisite. That's the only word we have for her in English.

Nona.

I sat two stools down from her, and the short-order cook came over and looked at me. "What?"

"Black coffee, please."

He went to get it. From behind me someone said: "Well I guess Christ came back, just like my mamma always said He would."

The gawky dishwasher laughed, a quick yuk-yuk sound. The truckers at the counter joined in.

The short-order cook brought me my coffee back, jarred it down on the counter and spilled some on the thawing meat of my hand. I jerked it back.

"Sorry," he said indifferently.

"He's gonna heal it hisself," one of the truckers in the booth called over.

The blue-rinse twins paid their checks and hurried out. One of the knights of the road sauntered over to the juke and put another dime in. Johnny Cash began to sing "A Boy Named Sue." I blew on my coffee.

Someone tugged at my sleeve. I turned my head and there she was—she'd moved over to the empty stool. Looking at that face close up was almost blinding. I spilled some more of my coffee.

"I'm sorry." Her voice was low, almost atonal.

"My fault. I can't feel what I'm doing yet."

"I—"

She stopped, seemingly at a loss. I suddenly realized that she was scared. I felt my first reaction to her swim over me again—to protect her and take care of her, make her not afraid. "I need a ride," she finished in a rush. "I didn't dare ask any of them." She made a barely perceptible gesture toward the truckers in the booth.

How can I make you understand that I would have given anything—*anything*—to be able to tell her, *Sure, finish your coffee, I'm parked right outside*. It sounds crazy to say I felt that way after half a dozen words out of her mouth, and the same number out of mine, but I did. Looking at her was like looking at the Mona Lisa or the Venus de Milo come to breathing life. And there was another feeling. It was as if a sudden, powerful light had been turned on in the confused darkness of my mind. It would make it easier if I could say she was a pickup and I was a fast man with the ladies, quick with a funny line and lots of patter, but she wasn't and I wasn't. All I knew was I didn't have what she needed and it tore me up.

"I'm thumbing," I told her. "A cop kicked me off the interstate and I only came here to get out of the cold. I'm sorry."

"Are you from the university?"

"I was. I quit before they could fire me."

"Are you going home?"

"No home to go to. I was a state ward. I got to school on a scholarship. I blew it. Now I don't know where I'm going." My life story in five sentences. I guess it made me feel depressed.

She laughed—the sound made me run hot and cold. "We're cats out of the same bag, I guess."

I *thought* she said cats. I *thought* so. Then. But I've had time to think, in here, and more and more it seems to me that she might have said *rats*. *Rats* out of the same bag. Yes. And they are not the same, are they?

I was about to make my best conversational shot—something witty like "Is that so?"—when a hand came down on my shoulder.

I turned around. It was one of the truckers from the booth. He had blond stubble on his chin and there was a wooden kitchen match poking out of his mouth. He smelled of engine oil and looked like something out of a Steve Ditko drawing.

"I think you're done with that coffee," he said. His lips parted around the match in a grin. He had a lot of very white teeth.

"What?"

"You stinking the place up, fella. You *are* a fella, aren't you? Kind of hard to tell."

"You aren't any rose yourself," I said. "What's that after-shave, handsome? *Eau de Crankcase?*"

He gave me a hard shot across the side of the face with his open hand. I saw little black dots.

"Don't fight in here," the short-order cook said. "If you're going to scramble him, do it outside."

"Come on, you goddammed commie," the trucker said.

This is the spot where the girl is supposed to say something like "Unhand him" or "You brute." She wasn't saying anything. She was watching both of us with feverish intensity. It was scary. I think it was the first time I'd noticed how huge her eyes really were.

"Do I have to sock you again?"

"No. Come on, shitheels."

I don't know how that jumped out of me. I don't like to fight. I'm not a good fighter. I'm an even worse name-caller. But I was angry, just then. It came up on me all at once that I wanted to kill him.

Maybe he got a mental whiff of it. For just a second a shade of uncertainty flicked over his face, an unconscious wondering if maybe he hadn't picked the wrong hippie. Then it was gone. He wasn't going to back off from some long-haired elitist effeminate snob who used the flag to wipe his ass with—at least not in front of his buddies. Not a big ole truck-driving son-of-a-gun like him.

The anger pounded over me again. *Faggot? Faggot?* I felt out of control, and it was good to feel that way. My tongue was thick in my mouth. My stomach was a slab.

We walked across to the door, and my buddy's buddies almost broke their backs getting up to watch the fun.

Nona? I thought of her, but only in an absent, back-of-my-mind way. I knew Nona would be there. Nona would take care of me. I knew it the same way I knew it would be cold outside. It was strange to know that about a girl I had only met five minutes before. Strange, but I didn't think about that until later. My mind was taken up—no, almost blotted out—by the heavy cloud of rage. I felt homicidal.

The cold was so clear and so clean that it felt as if we were cutting it with our bodies like knives. The frosted gravel of the parking lot gritted harshly under his heavy boots and under my shoes. The moon, full and bloated, looked down on us with a vapid eye. It was faintly ringed, suggesting bad weather on the way. The sky was as black as a night in hell. We left tiny dwarfed shadows behind our feet in the monochrome glare of a single sodium light set high on a pole beyond the parked rigs. Our breath plumed the air in short bursts. The trucker turned to me, his gloved fists balled.

"Okay, you son-of-a-bitch," he said.

I seemed to be swelling—my whole body seemed to be swelling. Somehow, numbly, I knew that my intellect was about to be eclipsed by an invisible something that I had never suspected might be in me. It was terrifying—but at the same time I welcomed it, desired it, lusted for it. In that last instant of coherent thought it seemed that my body had become a stone pyramid or a cyclone that could sweep everything in front of it like colored pick-up sticks. The trucker seemed small, puny, insignificant. I laughed at him. I laughed, and the sound was as black and as bleak as that moonstruck sky overhead.

He came at me swinging his fists. I batted down his right, took his left on the side of my face without feeling it, and then kicked him in the guts. The air barfed out of him in a white cloud. He tried to back away, holding himself and coughing.

I ran around in back of him, still laughing like some

farmer's dog barking at the moon, and I had pounded him three times before he could make even a quarter turn—the neck, the shoulder, one red ear.

He made a yowling noise, and one of his flailing hands brushed my nose. The fury that had taken me over mushroomed and I kicked him again, bringing my foot up high and hard, like a punter. He screamed into the night and I heard a rib snap. He folded up and I jumped him.

At the trial one of the other truck drivers testified I was like a wild animal. And I was. I can't remember much of it, but I can remember that, snarling and growling at him like a wild dog.

I straddled him, grabbed double handfuls of his greasy hair, and began to rub his face into the gravel. In the flat glare of the sodium light his blood seemed black, like beetle's blood.

"Jesus, stop it!" somebody yelled.

Hands grabbed my shoulders and pulled me off. I saw whirling faces and I struck at them.

The trucker was trying to creep away. His face was a staring mask of blood from which his dazed eyes peered. I began to kick him, dodging away from the others, grunting with satisfaction each time I connected on him.

He was beyond fighting back. All he knew was to try to get away. Each time I kicked him his eyes would squeeze closed, like the eyes of a tortoise, and he would halt. Then he would start to crawl again. He looked stupid. I decided I was going to kill him. I was going to kick him to death. Then I would kill the rest of them—all but Nona.

I kicked him again and he flopped over on his back and looked up at me dazedly.

"Uncle," he croaked. "I cry Uncle. Please. Please—"

I knelt down beside him, feeling the gravel bite into my knees through my thin jeans.

"Here you are, handsome," I whispered. "Here's your uncle."

I hooked my hands onto his throat.

Three of them jumped me all at once and knocked me off him. I got up, still grinning, and started toward them. They backed away, three big men, all of them scared green.

And it clicked off.

Just like that it clicked off and it was just me, standing in the parking lot of Joe's Good Eats, breathing hard and feeling sick and horrified.

I turned and looked back toward the diner. The girl was there; her beautiful features were lit with triumph. She raised one fist to shoulder height in salute like the one those black guys gave at the Olympics that time.

I turned back to the man on the ground. He was still trying to crawl away, and when I approached him his eyeballs rolled fearfully.

"Don't you touch him!" one of his friends cried.

I looked at them, confused. "I'm sorry . . . I didn't mean to . . . to hurt him so bad. Let me help—"

"You get out of here, that's what you do," the short-order cook said. He was standing in front of Nona at the foot of the steps, clutching a greasy spatula in one hand. "I'm calling the cops."

"Hey, man, he was the guy who *started* it! He—"

"Don't give me any of your lip, you lousy queer," he said, backing up. "All I know is you just about killed that guy. I'm calling the cops!" He dashed back inside.

"Okay," I said to nobody in particular. "Okay, that's good, okay."

I had left my rawhide gloves inside, but it didn't seem like a good idea to go back in and get them. I put my hands in my pockets and started to walk back to the interstate access road. I figured my chances of hitching a ride before the cops picked me up were about one in ten. My ears were freezing and I felt sick to my stomach. Some purty night.

"Wait! Hey, wait!"

I turned around. It was her, running to catch up with me, her hair flying out behind her.

"You were wonderful!" she said. "Wonderful!"

"I hurt him bad," I said dully. "I never did anything like that before."

"I wish you'd killed him!"

I blinked at her in the frosty light.

"You should have heard the things they were saying about me before you came in. Laughing in that big, brave, dirty way—haw, haw, lookit the little girl out so long after dark. Where you going, honey? Need a lift? I'll give you a ride if you'll give me a ride. *Damn!*"

She glared back over her shoulder as if she could strike

them dead with a sudden bolt from her dark eyes. Then she turned them on me, and again it seemed like that searchlight had been turned on in my mind. "My name's Nona. I'm coming with you."

"Where? To jail?" I tugged at my hair with both hands. "With this, the first guy who gives us a ride is apt to be a state cop. That cook meant what he said about calling them."

"I'll hitch. You stand behind me. They'll stop for me. They stop for a girl, if she's pretty."

I couldn't argue with her about that and didn't want to. Love at first sight? Maybe not. But it was something. Can you get that wave?

"Here," she said, "you forgot these." She held out my gloves.

She hadn't gone back inside, and that meant she'd had them all along. She'd known she was coming with me. It gave me an eerie feeling. I put on my gloves and we walked up the access road to the turnpike ramp.

She was right about the ride. We got one with the first car that swung onto the ramp.

We didn't say anything else while we waited, but it seemed as if we did. I won't give you a load of bull about ESP and that stuff; you know what I'm talking about. You've felt it yourself if you've ever been with someone you were really close to, or if you've taken one of those drugs with initials for a name. You don't have to talk. Communication seems to shift over to some high-frequency emotional band. A twist of the hand does it all. We were strangers. I only knew her first name and now that I think back I don't believe I ever told her mine at all. But we were doing it. It wasn't love. I hate to keep repeating that, but I feel I have to. I wouldn't dirty that word with whatever we had—not after what we did, not after Castle Rock, not after the dreams.

A high, wailing shriek filled the cold silence of the night, rising and falling.

"That's an ambulance I think," I said.

"Yes."

Silence again. The moon's light was fading behind a thickening membrane of cloud. I thought the ring around the moon hadn't lied; we would have snow before the night was over.

Lights poked over the hill.

I stood behind her without having to be told. She brushed her hair back and raised that beautiful face. As I watched the car signal for the entrance ramp I was swept with a feeling of unreality—it was unreal that this beautiful girl had elected to come with me, it was unreal that I had beaten a man to the point where an ambulance had to be called for him, it was unreal to think I might be in jail by morning. Unreal. I felt caught in a spiderweb. But who was the spider?

Nona put out her thumb. The car, a Chevrolet sedan, went by us and I thought it was going to keep right on going. Then the taillights flashed and Nona grabbed my hand. "Come on, we got a ride!" She grinned at me with childish delight and I grinned back at her.

The guy was reaching enthusiastically across the seat to open the door for her. When the dome light flashed on I could see him—a fairly big man in an expensive camel's hair coat, graying around the edges of his hat, prosperous features softened by years of good meals. A businessman or a salesman. Alone. When he saw me he did a double take, but it was a second or two too late to put the car back in gear and haul ass. And it was easier for him this way. Later he could fib himself into believing he had seen both of us, that he was a truly good-hearted soul giving a young couple a break.

"Cold night," he said as Nona slid in beside him and I got in beside her.

"It certainly is," Nona said sweetly. "Thank you!"

"Yeah," I said. "Thanks."

"Don't mention it." And we were off, leaving sirens, busted-up truckers, and Joe's Good Eats behind us.

I had gotten kicked off the interstate at seven-thirty. It was only eight-thirty then. It's amazing how much you can do in a short time, or how much can be done to you.

We were approaching the yellow flashing lights that signal the Augusta toll station.

"How far are you going?" the driver asked.

That was a stumper. I had been hoping to make it as far as Kittery and crash with an acquaintance who was teaching school there. It still seemed as good an answer as any and I was opening my mouth to give it when Nona said:

"We're going to Castle Rock. It's a small town just south and west of Lewiston-Auburn."

Castle Rock. That made me feel strange. Once upon a time

I had been on pretty good terms with Castle Rock. But that was before Ace Merrill messed me up.

The guy brought his car to a stop, took a toll ticket, and then we were on our way again.

"I'm only going as far as Gardiner, myself," he said, lying smoothly. "One exit up. But that's a start for you."

"It sure is," Nona said, just as sweetly as before. "It was nice of you to stop on such a cold night." And while she was saying it I was getting her anger on that high emotional wavelength, naked and full of venom. It scared me, the way ticking from a wrapped package might scare me.

"My name's Blanchette," he said. "Norman Blanchette." He waved his hand in our direction to be shaken.

"Cheryl Craig," Nona said, taking it daintily.

I took her cue and gave him a false name. "Pleasure," I mumbled.

His hand was soft and flabby. It felt like a hot-water bottle in the shape of a hand. The thought sickened me. It sickened me that we had been forced to beg a ride with this patronizing man who thought he had seen a chance to pick up a pretty girl hitching all by herself, a girl who might or might not agree to an hour spent in a motel room in return for enough cash to buy a bus ticket. It sickened me to know that if I had been alone this man who had just offered me his flabby, hot hand would have zipped by without a second look. It sickened me to know he would drop us at the Gardiner exit, cross over, and then dart right back on the interstate, bypassing us on the southbound ramp without a look, congratulating himself on how smoothly he had solved an annoying situation. Everything about him sickened me. The porky droop of his jowls, the slicked-back wigs of his hair, the smell of his cologne.

And what right did he have? What right?

The sickness curdled, and the flowers of rage began to bloom again. The headlights of his prosperous Impala sedan cut the night with smooth ease, and my rage wanted to reach out and strangle everything that he was set in among—the kind of music I knew he would listen to as he lay back in his La-Z-Boy recliner with the evening paper in his hot-water-bottle hands, the rinse his wife would use in her hair, the Underalls I knew she would wear, the kids always sent off to the movies or off to school or off to camp—as long as they were off somewhere—his snobbish friends and the drunken parties they would attend with them.

But his cologne—that was the worst. It filled the car with sweet, sickish scent. It smelled like the perfumed disinfectant they use in a slaughterhouse at the end of each shift.

The car ripped through the night with Norman Blanchette holding the wheel with his bloated hands. His manicured nails gleamed softly in the lights from the instrument panel. I wanted to crack a wing window and get away from that cloying smell. No, more—I wanted to crank the whole window down and stick my head out into the cold air, wallow in chilled freshness—but I was frozen, frozen in the dumb maw of my wordless, inexpressible hate.

That was when Nona put the nail file into my hand.

When I was three I got a bad case of the flu and had to go to the hospital. While I was there, my dad fell asleep smoking in bed and the house burned down with my folks and my older brother Drake in it. I have their pictures. They look like actors in an old 1958 American International horror movie, faces you don't know like those of the big stars, more like Elisha Cook, Jr., and Mara Corday and some child actor you can't quite remember—Brandon de Wilde, maybe.

I had no relatives to go to and so I was sent to a home in Portland for five years. Then I became a state ward. That means a family takes you in and the state pays them thirty dollars a month for your keep. I don't think there was ever a state ward who acquired a taste for lobster. Usually a couple will take two or three wards—not because the milk of human kindness flows in their veins but as a business investment. They feed you. They take the thirty the state gives them and they feed you. If a kid is fed up he can earn his keep doing chores around the place. That thirty turns into forty, fifty, maybe sixty-five bucks. Capitalism as it applies to the unhomed. Greatest country in the world, right?

My "folks" were named Hollis and they lived in Harlow, across the river from Castle Rock. They had a three-story farmhouse with fourteen rooms. There was coal heat in the kitchen that got upstairs any way it could. In January you went to bed with three quilts over you and still weren't sure if your feet were on when you woke in the morning. You had to put them on the floor where you could look at them to be sure. Mrs. Hollis was fat. Mr. Hollis was skimpy and rarely spoke. He wore a red-and-black hunting cap all year round. The house was a helter-skelter mess of white-elephant furniture, rummage-sale stuff, moldy mattresses, dogs, cats, and automotive parts laid on newspaper. I had three "brothers," all of them wards. We had a nodding acquaintance, like co-travelers on a three-day bus trip.

I made good grades in school and went out for spring baseball when I was a high-school sophomore. Hollis was yapping after me to quit, but I stuck with it until the thing with Ace Merrill happened. Then I didn't want to go anymore, not with my face all puffed out and cut, not with the stories Betsy Malenfant was telling around. So I quit the team, and Hollis got me a job jerking sodas in the local drugstore.

In February of my junior year I took the College Boards, paying for them with the twelve bucks I had socked away in my mattress. I got accepted at the university with a small scholarship and a good work-study job in the library. The expression on the Hollises' faces when I showed them the financial-aid papers is the best memory of my life.

One of my "brothers," Curt, ran away. I couldn't have done that. I was too passive to take a step like that. I would have been back after two hours on the road. School was the only way out for me, and I took it.

The last thing Mrs. Hollis said when I left was, "You send us something when you can." I never saw either of them again. I made good grades my freshman year and got a job that summer working full-time in the library. I sent them a Christmas card that first year, but that was the only one.

In the first semester of my sophomore year I fell in love. It was the biggest thing that had ever happened to me. Pretty? She would have knocked you back two steps. To this day I have no idea what she saw in me. I don't even know if she loved me or not. I think she did at first. After that I was just a habit that's hard to break, like smoking or driving with your elbow poked out the window. She held me for a while, maybe not wanting to break the habit. Maybe she held me for wonder, or maybe it was just her vanity. Good boy, roll over, sit up, fetch the paper. Here's a kiss good night. It doesn't matter. For a while it was love, then it was like love, then it was over.

I slept with her twice, both times after other things had taken over for love. That fed the habit for a little while. Then she came back from the Thanksgiving break and said she was in love with a Delta Tau Delta who came from her hometown. I tried to get her back and almost made it once, but she had something she hadn't had before—perspective.

Whatever I had been building up all those years since the fire wiped out the B-movie actors who had once been my family, that broke it down. That guy's pin on her blouse.

After that, I was on-again-off-again with three or four girls who were willing to sleep with me. I could blame it on my childhood, say I never had good sexual models, but that wasn't it. I'd never had any trouble with the girl. Only now that the girl was gone.

I started being afraid of girls, a little. And it wasn't so much the ones I was impotent with as the ones I wasn't, the ones I could make it with. They made me uneasy. I kept asking myself where they were hiding whatever axes they liked to grind and when they were going to let me have it. I'm not so strange at that. You show me a married man or a man with a steady woman, and I'll show you someone who is asking himself (maybe only in the early hours of the morning or on Friday afternoon when she's off buying groceries), *What is she doing when I'm not around? What does she really think of me?* And maybe most of all, *How much of me has she got? How much is left?* Once I started thinking about those things, I thought about them all the time.

I started to drink and my grades took a nose dive. During semester break I got a letter saying that if they didn't improve in six weeks, my second-semester scholarship check would be withheld. I and some guys I hung around with got drunk and stayed drunk for the whole holiday. On the last day we went to a whorehouse and I operated just fine. It was too dark to see faces.

My grades stayed about the same. I called the girl once and cried over the telephone. She cried too, and in a way I think that pleased her. I didn't hate her then and I don't now. But she scared me. She scared me plenty.

On February 9 I got a letter from the dean of Arts and Sciences saying I was flunking two or three courses in my major field. On February 13 I got a hesitant sort of letter from the girl. She wanted everything to be all right between us.

She was planning to marry the guy from Delta Tau Delta in July or August, and I could be invited if I wanted to be. That was almost funny. What could I give her for a wedding gift? My heart with a red ribbon tied around it? My head? My cock?

On the fourteenth, Valentine's Day, I decided it was time for a change of scene. Nona came next, but you know about that.

You have to understand how she was to me if this is to do any good at all. She was more beautiful than the girl, but that wasn't it. Good looks are cheap in a wealthy country. It was the her inside. She was sexy, but the sexiness that came from her was somehow plantlike—blind sex, a kind of clinging, not-to-be-denied sex that is not so important because it is as instinctual as photosynthesis. Not like an animal but like a plant. You get that wave? I knew we would make love, that we would make it as men and women do, but that our joining would be as blunt and remote and meaningless as ivy clinging its way up a trellis in the August sun.

The sex was important only because it was unimportant.

I think—no, I'm sure—that violence was the real motive force. The violence was real and not just a dream. It was as big and as fast and as hard as Ace Merrill's '52 Ford. The violence of Joe's Good Eats, the violence of Norman Blanchette. And there was even something blind and vegetative about that. Maybe she was only a clinging vine after all, because the Venus flytrap is a species of vine, but that plant is carnivorous and will make animal motion when a fly or a bit of raw meat is placed in its jaws. And it was all real. The sporulating vine may only dream that it fornicates, but I am sure the Venus flytrap tastes that fly, relishes its diminishing struggle as its jaws close around it.

The last part was my own passivity. I could not fill up the hole in my life. Not the hole left by the girl when she said good-bye—I don't want to lay this at her door—but the hole that had always been there, the dark, confused swirling that never stopped down in the middle of me. Nona filled that hole. She made me move and act.

She made me noble.

Now maybe you understand a little of it. Why I dream of her. Why the fascination remains in spite of the remorse and the revulsion. Why I hate her. Why I fear her. And why even now I still love her.

It was eight miles from the Augusta ramp to Gardiner and we did it in a few short minutes. I grasped the nail file woodenly at my side and watched the green reflectorized sign—KEEP RIGHT FOR EXIT 14—twinkle up out of the night. The moon was gone and it had begun to spit snow.

"Wish I were going farther," Blanchette said.

"That's all right," Nona said warmly, and I could feel her fury buzzing and burrowing into the meat under my skull like a drill bit. "Just drop us at the top of the ramp."

He drove up, observing the ramp speed of thirty miles an hour. I knew what I was going to do. It felt as if my legs had turned to warm lead.

The top of the ramp was lit by one overhead light. To the left I could see the lights of Gardiner against the thickening cloud cover. To the right, nothing but blackness. There was no traffic coming either way along the access road.

I got out. Nona slid across the seat, giving Norman Blanchette a final smile. I wasn't worried. She was quarterbacking the play.

Blanchette was smiling an infuriating porky smile, relieved at being rid of us. "Well, good ni—"

"Oh my purse! Don't drive off with my purse!"

"I'll get it," I told her. I leaned back into the car. Blanchette saw what I had in my hand, and the porky smile on his face froze solid.

Now lights showed on the hill, but it was too late to stop. Nothing could have stopped me. I picked up Nona's purse with my left hand. With my right I plunged the steel nail file into Blanchette's throat. He bleated once.

I got out of the car. Nona was waving the oncoming vehicle down. I couldn't see what it was in the dark and snow; all I could make out were the two bright circles of its headlamps. I crouched behind Blanchette's car, peeking through the back windows.

The voices were almost lost in the filling throat of the wind.

" . . . trouble, lady?"

" . . . father . . . wind . . . had a heart attack! Will you . . ."

I scurried around the trunk of Norman Blanchette's Impala, bent over. I could see them now. Nona's slender silhouette and a taller form. They appeared to be standing by a pickup truck. They turned and approached the driver's-side window of the Chevy, where Norman Blanchette was slumped over the wheel with Nona's file in his throat. The driver of the pickup was a young kid in what looked like an Air Force parka. He leaned inside. I came up behind him.

"Jesus, lady!" he said. "There's blood on this guy! What—"

I hooked my right elbow around his throat and grabbed my right wrist with my left hand. I pulled him up hard. His head connected with the top of the door and made a hollow *thock!* He went limp in my arms.

I could have stopped then. He hadn't gotten a good look at Nona, hadn't seen me at all. I could have stopped. But he was a busybody, a meddler, somebody else in our way, trying to hurt us. I was tired of being hurt. I strangled him.

When it was done I looked up and saw Nona spotlighted in the conflicting lights of the car and the truck, her face a grotesque rictus of hate, love, triumph, and joy. She held her arms out to me and I went into them. We kissed. Her mouth was cold but her tongue was warm. I plunged both hands into the secret hollows of her hair, and the wind screamed around us.

"Now fix it," she said. "Before someone else comes."

I fixed it. It was a slipshod job, but I knew that was all we needed. A little more time. After that it wouldn't matter. We would be safe.

The kid's body was light. I picked him up in both arms, carried him across the road, and threw him into the gully beyond the guardrails. His body tumbled loosely all the way to the bottom, head over heels, like the ragbag man Mr. Hollis had me put out in the cornfield every July. I went back to get Blanchette.

He was heavier, and bleeding like a stuck pig. I tried to pick him up, staggered three steps backward, and then he slipped out of my arms and fell onto the road. I turned him over. The new snow had stuck to his face, turning it into a skier's mask.

I bent over, grabbed him under the arms, and dragged him to the gully. His feet left trailing grooves behind him. I threw him over and watched him slide down the embankment on his back, his arms up over his head. His eyes were wide open, staring raptly at the snowflakes falling into them. If the snow kept coming, they would both be just two vague humps by the time the plows came by.

I went back across the road. Nona had already climbed into the pickup truck without having to be told which vehicle we would use. I could see the pallid smear of her face, the dark holes of her eyes, but that was all. I got into Blanchette's car, sitting in the streaks of his blood that had gathered on the nubby vinyl seat cover, and drove it onto the shoulder. I turned off the headlights, put on the four-way flashers, and got out. To anyone passing by, it would look like a motorist who had engine trouble and then walked into town to find a garage. I was very pleased with my improvisation. It was as if I had been murdering people all my life. I trotted back to the idling truck, got in behind the wheel, and pointed it toward the turnpike entrance ramp.

She sat next to me, not touching but close. When she moved I could sometimes feel a strand of her hair on my neck. It was like being touched with a tiny electrode. Once I had to put my hand out and feel her leg, to make sure she was real. She laughed quietly. It was all real. The wind howled around the windows, driving snow in great, flapping gusts.

We ran south.

Just across the bridge from Harlow as you go up 126 toward Castle Heights, you come up on a huge renovated farm that goes under the laughable title of the Castle Rock Youth League. They have twelve lanes of candlepin bowling with cranky automatic pinsetters that usually take the last three days of the week off, a few ancient pinball machines, a juke featuring the greatest hits of 1957, three Brunswick pool tables, and a Coke-and-chips counter where you also rent bowling shoes that look like they might have just come off the feet of dead winos. The name of the place is laughable because most of the Castle Rock youth head up to the drive-in at Jay Hill at night or go to the stock-car races at Oxford Plains. The people who do hang out there are mostly toughies from Gretna, Harlow, and the Rock itself. The average is one fight per evening in the parking lot.

I started hanging out there when I was a high-school sophomore. One of my acquaintances, Bill Kennedy, was working there three nights a week and if there was nobody waiting for a table he'd let me shoot some pool for free. It wasn't much, but it was better than going back to the Hollises' house.

That's where I met Ace Merrill. Nobody much doubted that he was the toughest guy in three towns. He drove a chopped and channeled '52 Ford, and it was rumored that he could push it all the way to 130 if he had to. He'd come in like a king, his hair greased back and glistening in a perfect duck's-ass pompadour, shoot a few games of double-bank for a dime a ball (Was he good? You guess.), buy Betsy a Coke when she came in, and then they'd leave. You could almost hear a reluctant sigh of relief from those present when the scarred front door wheezed shut. Nobody ever went out in the parking lot with Ace Merrill.

Nobody, that is, but me.

Betsy Malenfant was his girl, the prettiest girl in Castle Rock, I guess. I don't think she was terrifically bright, but that didn't matter when you got a look at her. She had the most flawless complexion I had ever seen, and it didn't come out of a cosmetic bottle, either. Hair as black as coal, dark eyes, generous mouth, a body that just wouldn't quit—and she didn't mind showing it off. Who was going to drag her out back and try to stoke her locomotive while Ace was around? Nobody sane, that's who.

I fell hard for her. Not like the girl and not like Nona, even though Betsy did look like a younger version of her, but it was just as desperate and just as serious in its way. If you've ever had the worst case of puppy love going around, you know how I felt. She was seventeen, two years older than I.

I started going down there more and more often, even nights when Billy wasn't on, just to catch a glimpse of her. I felt like a birdwatcher, except it was a desperate kind of game for me. I'd go back home, lie to the Hollises about where I'd been, and climb up to my room. I'd write long, passionate letters to her, telling her everything I'd like to do to her, and then tear them up. Study halls at school I'd dream about asking her to marry me so we could run away to Mexico together.

She must have tumbled to what was happening, and it must have flattered her a little, because she was nice to me when Ace wasn't around. She'd come over and talk to me, let me buy her a Coke, sit on a stool, and kind of rub her leg against mine. It drove me crazy.

One night in early November I was just mooning around, shooting a little pool with Bill, waiting for her to come in. The place was deserted because it wasn't even eight o'clock yet, and a lonesome wind was snuffling around outside, threatening winter.

"You better lay off," Bill said, shooting the nine straight into the corner.

"Lay off what?"

"You know."

"No I don't." I scratched and Billy added a ball to the table. He ran six and while he was running them I went over to put a dime in the juke.

"Betsy Malenfant." He lined up the one carefully and sent it walking up the rail. "Charlie Hogan was telling Ace about the way you been sniffing around her. Charlie thought it was really funny, her being older and all, but Ace wasn't laughing."

"She's nothing to me," I said through paper lips.

"She better not be," Bill said, and then a couple of guys came in and he went over to the counter and gave them a cue ball.

Ace came in around nine and he was alone. He'd never taken any notice of me before, and I'd just about forgotten what Billy said. When you're invisible you get to thinking you're invulnerable. I was playing pinball and I was pretty involved. I didn't even notice the place get quiet as people stopped bowling or shooting pool. The next thing I knew, somebody had thrown me right across the pinball machine. I landed on the floor in a heap. I got up feeling scared and sick. He had tilted the machine, wiping out my three replays. He was standing there and looking at me with not a strand of hair out of place, his garrison jacket half unzipped.

"You stop messing around," he said softly, "or I'm going to change your face."

He went out. Everybody was looking at me and I wanted to sink right down through the floor until I saw there was a kind of grudging admiration on most of their faces. So I brushed myself off, unconcerned, and put another dime in the pinball machine. The TILT light went out. A couple of guys came over and clapped me on the back before they went out, not saying anything.

At eleven, when the place closed, Billy offered me a ride home.

"You're going to take a fall if you don't watch out."

"Don't worry about me," I said.

He didn't answer.

Two or three nights later Betsy came in by herself around seven. There was one other kid there, this weird little four-eyes named Vern Tessio, who flunked out of school a couple of years before. I hardly noticed him. He was even more invisible than I was.

She came right over to where I was shooting, close enough so I could smell the clean-soap smell on her skin. It made me feel dizzy.

"I heard about what Ace did to you," she said. "I'm not supposed to talk to you anymore and I'm not going to, but I've got something to make it all better." She kissed me. Then she went out, before I could even get my tongue down from the roof of my mouth. I went back to my game in a daze. I didn't even see Tessio when he went out to spread the word. I couldn't see anything but her dark, dark eyes.

So later that night I ended up in the parking lot with Ace Merrill, and he beat the living Jesus out of me. It was cold, bitterly cold, and at the end I began to sob, not caring who was watching or listening, which by then was everybody. The single sodium arc lamp looked down on all of it mercilessly. I didn't even land a punch on him.

"Okay," he said, squatting down next to me. He wasn't even breathing hard. He took a switchblade out of his pocket and pressed the chrome button. Seven inches of moon-drenched silver sprang into the world. "This is what you get next time. I'll carve my name on your balls." Then he got up, gave me one last kick, and left. I just lay there for maybe ten minutes, shivering on the hard-packed dirt. No one came to help me up or pat me on the back, not even Bill. Betsy didn't show up to make it all better.

Finally I got up by myself and hitchhiked home. I told Mrs. Hollis I'd hitched a ride with a drunk and he drove off the road. I never went back to the bowling alley again.

I understand that Ace dropped Betsy not long after, and from then on she went downhill at a rapidly increasing rate of speed—like a pulp truck with no brakes. She picked up a case of the clap on the way. Billy said he saw her one night in the

Manoir up in Lewiston, hustling guys for drinks. She had lost most of her teeth, and her nose had been broken somewhere along the line, he said. He said I would never recognize her. By then I didn't much care one way or the other.

The pickup had no snow tires, and before we got to the Lewiston exit I had begun to skid around in the new powder. It took us over forty-five minutes to make the twenty-two miles.

The man at the Lewiston exit point took my toll card and my sixty cents. "Slippery traveling?"

Neither of us answered him. We were getting close to where we wanted to go now. If I hadn't had that odd kind of wordless contact with her, I would have been able to tell just by the way she sat on the dusty seat of the pickup, her hands folded tightly over her purse, those eyes fixed straight ahead on the road with fierce intensity. I felt a shudder work through me.

We took Route 136. There weren't many cars on the road; the wind was freshening and the snow was coming down harder than ever. On the other side of Harlow Village we passed a big Buick Riviera that had slewed around sideways and climbed the curb. Its fourway flashers were going and I had a ghostly double image of Norman Blanchette's Impala. It would be drifted in with snow now, nothing but a ghostly lump in the darkness.

The Buick's driver tried to flag me down but I went by him without slowing, spraying him with slush. My wipers were clogging with snow and I reached out and snapped at the one on my side. Some of the snow loosened and I could see a little better.

Harlow was a ghost town, everything dark and closed. I signaled right to go over the bridge into Castle Rock. The rear wheels wanted to slide out from under me, but I handled the skid. Up ahead and across the river I could see the dark shadow that was the Castle Rock Youth League building. It looked shut up and lonely. I felt suddenly sorry, sorry that there had been so much pain. And death. That was when Nona spoke for the first time since the Gardiner exit.

"There's a policeman behind you."

"Is he—?"

"No. His flasher is off."

But it made me nervous and maybe that's why it happened. Route 136 makes a ninety-degree turn on the Harlow side of the river and then it's straight across the bridge into Castle Rock. I made the first turn, but there was ice on the Rock side.

"Damn—"

The rear end of the truck flirted around and before I could steer clear, it had smashed into one of the heavy steel bridge stanchions. We went sliding all the way around like kids on a Flexible Flyer, and the next thing I saw was the bright headlights of the police car behind us. He put on his brakes—I could see the red reflections in the falling snow—but the ice got him, too. He plowed right into us. There was a grinding, jarring shock as we went into the supporting girders again. I was jolted into Nona's lap, and even in that confused split second I had time to relish the smooth firmness of her thigh. Then everything stopped. *Now* the cop had his flasher on. It sent blue, revolving shadows chasing across the hood of the truck and the snowy steel crosswork of the Harlow-Castle Rock bridge. The dome light inside the cruiser came on as the cop got out.

If he hadn't been behind us it wouldn't have happened. That thought was playing over and over in my mind, like a phonograph needle stuck in a single flawed groove. I was grinning a strained, frozen grin into the dark as I groped on the floor of the truck's cab for something to hit him with.

There was an open toolbox. I came up with a socket wrench and laid it on the seat between Nona and me. The cop leaned in the window, his face changing like a devil's in the light from his flasher.

"Traveling a little fast for the conditions, weren't you, guy?"

"Following a little close, weren't you?" I asked. "For the conditions?"

He might have flushed. It was hard to tell in the flickering light.

"Are you lipping off to me, son?"

"I am if you're trying to pin the dents in your cruiser on me."

"Let's see your driver's license and your registration."

I got out my wallet and handed him my license.

"Registration?"

"It's my brother's truck. He carries the registration in his wallet."

"That right?" He looked at me hard, trying to stare me down. When he saw it would take a while, he looked past me at Nona. I could have ripped his eyes out for what I saw in them. "What's your name?"

"Cheryl Craig, sir."

"What are you doing riding around in his brother's pickup in the middle of a snowstorm, Cheryl?"

"We're going to see my uncle."

"In the Rock."

"That's right, yes."

"I don't know any Craigs in Castle Rock."

"His name is Emonds. On Bowen Hill."

"That right?" He walked around to the back of the truck to look at the plate. I opened the door and leaned out. He was writing it down. He came back while I was still leaning out, spotlighted from the waist up in the glare of his headlights. "I'm going to . . . What's that all over you, boy?"

I didn't have to look down to know what was all over me. I used to think that leaning out like that was just absentmindedness, but writing all of this has changed my mind. I don't think it was absentminded at all. I think I wanted him to see it. I held on to the socket wrench.

"What do you mean?"

He came two steps closer. "You're hurt—cut yourself, looks like. Better—"

I swung at him. His hat had been knocked off in the crash and his head was bare. I hit him dead on, just above the forehead. I've never forgotten the sound that made, like a pound of butter falling onto a hard floor.

"Hurry," Nona said. She put a calm hand on my neck. It was very cool, like air in a root cellar. My foster mother had a root cellar.

Funny I should remember that. She sent me down there for vegetables in the winter. She canned them herself. Not in real cans, of course, but in thick Mason jars with those rubber sealers that go under the lid.

I went down there one day to get a jar of waxed beans for our supper. The preserves were all in boxes, neatly marked in Mrs. Hollis's hand. I remember that she always misspelled raspberry, and that used to fill me with a secret superiority.

On this day I went past the boxes marked "razberry" and into the corner where she kept the beans. It was cool and dark. The walls were plain dark earth and in wet weather they exuded moisture in trickling, crooked streams. The smell was a secret, dark effluvium composed of living things and earth and stored vegetables, a smell remarkably like that of a woman's private parts. There was an old, shattered printing press in one corner that had been there ever since I came, and sometimes I used to play with it and pretend I could get it going again. I loved the root cellar. In those days—I was nine or ten—the root cellar was my favorite place. Mrs. Hollis refused to set foot in it, and it was against her husband's dignity to go down and fetch up vegetables. So I went there and smelled that peculiar secret earthy smell and enjoyed the privacy of its womblike confinement. It was lit by one cob-webby bulb that Mr. Hollis had strung, probably before the Boer War. Sometimes I wiggled my hands and made huge, elongated rabbits on the wall.

I got the beans and was about to go back when I heard a rustling movement under one of the old boxes. I went over and lifted it up.

There was a brown rat beneath it, lying on its side. It rolled its head up at me and stared. Its sides were heaving violently and it bared its teeth. It was the biggest rat I had ever seen, and I leaned closer. It was in the act of giving birth. Two of its young, hairless and blind, were already nursing at its belly. Another was halfway into the world.

The mother glared at me helplessly, ready to bite. I wanted to kill it, kill all of them, squash them, but I couldn't. It was the most horrible thing I'd ever seen. As I watched, a small brown spider—a daddy longlegs, I think—crawled rapidly across the floor. The mother snatched it up and ate it.

I fled. Halfway up the stairs I fell and broke the jar of beans. Mrs. Hollis thrashed me, and I never went into the root cellar again unless I had to.

I stood looking down at the cop, remembering.

"Hurry," Nona said again.

He was much lighter than Norman Blanchette had been, or perhaps my adrenaline was just flowing more freely. I gathered him up in both arms and carried him over to the edge of the bridge. I could barely make out the falls downstream, and upstream the GS&WM railroad trestle was only a gaunt shadow, like a scaffold. The night wind whooped and screamed, and the snow beat against my face. For a moment I held the cop against my chest like a sleeping newborn child, and then I remembered what he really was and threw him over the side and down into the darkness.

We went back to the truck and got in, but it wouldn't start. I cranked the engine until I could smell the sweetish aroma of gas from the flooded carb, and then stopped.

"Come on," I said.

We went to the cruiser. The front seat was littered with violation tags, forms, two clipboards. The shortwave under the dash crackled and sputtered.

"Unit Four, come in, Four. Do you copy?"

I reached under and turned it off, banging my knuckles on something as I searched for the right toggle switch. It was a shotgun, pump action. Probably the cop's personal property. I unclipped it and handed it to Nona. She put it on her lap. I backed the cruiser up. It was dented but otherwise not hurt. It had snow tires and they bit nicely once we got over the ice that had done the damage.

Then we were in Castle Rock. The houses, except for an occasional shanty trailer set back from the road, had disappeared. The road itself hadn't been plowed yet and there were no tracks except the ones we were leaving behind us. Monolithic fir trees, weighted with snow, towered all around us, and they made me feel tiny and insignificant, just some tiny morsel caught in the throat of this night. It was now after ten o'clock.

I didn't see much of college social life during my freshman year at the university. I studied hard and worked in the library shelving books and repairing bindings and learning how to catalogue. In the spring there was JV baseball.

Near the end of the academic year, just before finals, there was a dance at the gym. I was at loose ends, studied up for my first two tests, and I wandered down. I had the buck admission, so I went in.

It was dark and crowded and sweaty and frantic as only a college social before the ax of finals can be. There was sex in the air. You didn't have to smell it; you could almost reach out and grab it in both hands, like a wet piece of heavy cloth.

You knew that love was going to be made later on, or what passes for love. People were going to make it under bleachers and in the steam plant parking lot and in apartments and dormitory rooms. It was going to be made by desperate man/boys with the draft one step behind them and by pretty coeds who were going to drop out this year and go home and start a family. It would be made with tears and laughter, drunk and sober, stiffly and with no inhibition. But mostly it would be made quickly.

There were a few stags, but not many. It wasn't a night you needed to go anyplace stag. I drifted down by the raised bandstand. As I got closer to the sound, the beat, the music got to be a palpable thing. The group had a half circle of five-foot amplifiers behind them, and you could feel your eardrums flapping in and out with the bass signature.

I leaned up against the wall and watched. The dancers moved in prescribed patterns (as if they were trios instead of couples, the third invisible but between, being humped from the front and back), feet moving through the sawdust that had been sprinkled over the varnished floor. I didn't see anybody I knew and I began to feel lonely, but pleasantly so. I was at that stage of the evening where you fantasize that everyone is looking at you, the romantic stranger, out of the corners of their eyes.

About a half hour later I went out and got a Coke in the lobby. When I went back in somebody had started a circle dance and I was pulled in, my arms around the shoulders of two girls I had never seen before. We went around and around. There were maybe two hundred people in the circle and it covered half the gym floor. Then part of it collapsed and twenty or thirty people formed another circle in the middle of the first and started to go around the other way. It made me feel dizzy. I saw a girl who looked like Betsy Malenfant, but I knew that was a fantasy. When I looked for her again I couldn't see her or anyone who looked like her.

When the thing finally broke up I felt weak and not at all well. I made my way back over to the bleachers and sat down. The music was too loud, the air too greasy. My mind kept pitching and yawing. I could hear my heartbeat in my head, the way you do after you throw the biggest drunk of your life.

I used to think what happened next happened because I was

tired and a little nauseated from going around and around, but as I said before, all this writing has brought everything into sharper focus. I can't believe that anymore.

I looked up at them again, all the beautiful, hurrying people in the semidarkness. It seemed to me that all the men looked terrified, their faces elongated into grotesque, slow-motion masks. It was understandable. The women—coeds in their sweaters, short skirts, their bell-bottoms—were all turning into rats. At first it didn't frighten me. I even chuckled. I knew what I was seeing was some kind of hallucination, and for a while I could watch it almost clinically.

Then some girl stood on tiptoe to kiss her fellow, and that was too much. Hairy, twisted face with black buckshot eyes reaching up, mouth spreading to reveal teeth . . .

I left.

I stood in the lobby for a moment, half distracted. There was a bathroom down the hall, but I went past it and up the stairs.

The locker room was on the third floor and I had to run the last flight. I pulled the door open and ran for one of the bathroom stalls. I threw up amid the mixed smells of liniment, sweaty uniforms, oiled leather. The music was far away down there, the silence up here virginal. I felt comforted.

We had to come to a stop sign at Southwest Bend. The memory of the dance had left me excited for a reason I didn't understand. I began to shake.

She looked at me, smiling with her dark eyes. "Now?"

I couldn't answer her. I was shaking too badly for that. She nodded slowly, for me.

I drove onto a spur of Route 7 that must have been a logging road in the summertime. I didn't drive in too deeply because I was afraid of getting stuck. I popped off the headlights and flecks of snow began to gather silently on the windshield.

"Do you love?" she asked, almost kindly.

Some kind of sound kept escaping me, being dragged out of me. I think it must have been a close oral counterpart to the thoughts of a rabbit caught in a snare.

"Here," she said. "Right here."

It was ecstasy.

*   *   *

We almost didn't get back onto the main road. The snow-plow had gone by, orange lights winking and flashing in the night, throwing up a huge wall of snow in our way.

There was a shovel in the trunk of the police car. It took me half an hour to dig out, and by then it was almost midnight. She turned on the police radio while I was doing it, and it told us what we had to know. The bodies of Blanchette and the kid from the pickup truck had been found. They suspected that we had taken the cruiser. The cop's name had been Essegian, and that's a funny name. There used to be a major-league ballplayer named Essegian—I think he played for the Dodgers. Maybe I had killed one of his relatives. It didn't bother me to know the cop's name. He had been following too close and he had gotten in our way.

We drove back onto the main road.

I could feel her excitement, high and hot and burning. I stopped long enough to clear the windshield with my arm and then we were going again.

We went through west Castle Rock and I knew without having to be told where to turn. A snow-crusted sign said it was Stackpole Road.

The plow had not been here, but one vehicle had been through before us. The tracks of its tires were still freshly cut in the blowing, restless snow.

A mile, then less than a mile. Her fierce eagerness, her need, came to me and I began to feel jumpy again. We came around a curve and there was the power truck, bright orange body and warning flashers pulsing the color of blood. It was blocking the road.

You can't imagine her rage—our rage, really—because now, after what happened, we were really one. You can't imagine the sweeping feeling of intense paranoia, the conviction that every hand was now turned against us.

There were two of them. One was a bending shadow in the darkness ahead. The other was holding a flashlight. He came toward us, his light bobbing like a lurid eye. And there was more than hate. There was fear—fear that it was all going to be snatched away from us at the last moment.

He was yelling, and I cranked down my window.

"You can't get through here! Go on back by the Bowen Road! We got a live line down here! You can't—"

I got out of the car, lifted the shotgun, and gave him both

barrels. He was flung back against the orange truck and I staggered back against the cruiser. He slipped down an inch at a time, staring at me incredulously, and then he fell into the snow.

"Are there more shells?" I asked Nona.

"Yes." She gave them to me. I broke the shotgun, ejected the spent cartridges, and put in new ones.

The guy's buddy had straightened up and was watching incredulously. He shouted something at me that was lost in the wind. It sounded like a question but it didn't matter. I was going to kill him. I walked toward him and he just stood there, looking at me. He didn't move, even when I raised the shotgun. I don't think he had any conception of what was happening. I think he thought it was a dream.

I fired one barrel and was low. A great flurry of snow exploded up, coating him. Then he bellowed a great terrified scream and ran, taking one gigantic bound over the fallen power cable in the road. I fired the other barrel and missed again. Then he was gone into the dark and I could forget him. He wasn't in our way anymore. I went back to the cruiser.

"We'll have to walk," I said.

We walked past the fallen body, stepped over the spitting power line, and walked up the road, following the widely spaced tracks of the fleeing man. Some of the drifts were almost up to her knees, but she was always a little ahead of me. We were both panting.

We came over a hill and descended into a narrow dip. On one side was a leaning, deserted shed with glassless windows. She stopped and gripped my arm.

"There," she said, and pointed across to the other side. Her grip was strong and painful even through my coat. Her face was set in a glaring, triumphant rictus. "There. There."

It was a graveyard.

We slipped and stumbled up the banking and clambered over a snow-covered stone wall. I had been here too, of course. My real mother had come from Castle Rock, and although she and my father had never lived there, this was where the family plot had been. It was a gift to my mother from her parents, who had lived and died in Castle Rock. During the thing with Betsy I had come here often to read the poems of John Keats and Percy Shelley. I suppose you think that was a silly, sophomoric thing to do, but I don't. Not even now. I felt close to them, comforted. After Ace Merrill beat me up I never went there again. Not until Nona led me there.

I slipped and fell in the loose powder, twisting my ankle. I got up and walked on it, using the shotgun as a crutch. The silence was infinite and unbelievable. The snow fell in soft, straight lines, mounding atop the leaning stones and crosses, burying all but the tips of the corroded flagholders that would only hold flags on Memorial Day and Veterans Day. The silence was unholy in its immensity, and for the first time I felt terror.

She led me toward a stone building set into the rise of the hill at the back of the cemetery. A vault. A snow-whited sepulcher. She had a key. I knew she would have a key, and she did.

She blew the snow away from the door's flange and found the keyhole. The sound of the turning tumblers seemed to scratch across the darkness. She leaned on the door and it swung inward.

The odor that came out at us was as cool as autumn, as cool as the air in the Hollis root cellar. I could see in only a little way. There were dead leaves on the stone floor. She entered, paused, looked back over her shoulder at me.

"No," I said.

"Do you *love?*" she asked, and laughed at me.

I stood in the darkness, feeling everything begin to run together—past, present, future. *I* wanted to run, run screaming, run fast enough to take back everything I had done.

Nona stood there looking at me, the most beautiful girl in the world, the only thing that had ever been mine. She made a gesture with her hands on her body. I'm not going to tell you what it was. You would know it if you saw it.

I went in. She closed the door.

It was dark but I could see perfectly well. The place was alight with a slowly running green fire. It ran over the walls and snaked across the leaf-littered floor in tongues. There was a bier in the center of the vault, but it was empty. Withered rose petals were scattered across it like an ancient bridal offering. She beckoned to me, then pointed to the small door at the rear. Small, unmarked door. I dreaded it. I think I knew then. She had used me and laughed at me. Now she would destroy me.

But I couldn't stop. I went to that door because I had to. The mental telegraph was still working at what I felt was glee—a terrible, insane glee—and triumph. My hand trembled toward the door. It was coated with green fire.

I opened the door and saw what was there.

It was the girl, my girl. Dead. Her eyes stared vacantly into that October vault, into my own eyes. She smelled of stolen kisses. She was naked and she had been ripped open from throat to crotch, her whole body turned into a womb. And something lived in there. The rats. I could not see them but I could hear them, rustling inside her. I knew that in a moment her dry mouth would open and she would ask me if I loved. I backed away, my whole body numb, my brain floating on a dark cloud.

I turned to Nona. She was laughing, holding her arms out to me. And with a sudden blaze of understanding I knew, I knew, I knew. The last test. The last final. I had passed it and *I was free!*

I turned back to the doorway and of course it was nothing but an empty stone closet with dead leaves on the floor.

I went to Nona. I went to my life.

Her arms reached around my neck and I pulled her against me. That was when she began to change, to ripple and run like wax. The great dark eyes became small and beady. The hair coarsened, went brown. The nose shortened, the nostrils dilated. Her body lumped and hunched against me.

I was being embraced by a rat.

"Do you love?" it squealed. "Do you love, do you love?" Her lipless mouth stretched upward for mine.

I didn't scream. There were no screams left. I doubt if I will ever scream again.

It's so hot in here.

I don't mind the heat, not really. I like to sweat if I can shower. I've always thought of sweat as a good thing, a *masculine* thing, but sometimes, in the heat, there are bugs that bite—spiders, for instance. Did you know that the female spiders sting and eat their mates? They do, right after copulation.

Also, I've heard scurryings in the walls. I don't like that.

I've given myself writer's cramp, and the felt tip of the pen is all soft and mushy. But I'm done now. And things look different. It doesn't seem the same anymore at all.

Do you realize that for a while they almost had me believing that I did all those horrible things myself? Those men from the truck stop, the guy from the power truck who got away. They said I was alone. I was alone when they found me, almost frozen to death in that graveyard by the stones that mark my father, my mother, my brother Drake. But that only means she left, you can see that. Any fool could. But I'm glad she got away. Truly I am. But you must realize she was with me all the time, every step of the way.

I'm going to kill myself now. It will be much better. I'm tired of all the guilt and agony and bad dreams, and also I don't like the noises in the walls. Anybody could be in there. Or anything.

I'm not crazy. I know that and trust that you do, too. If you say you *aren't* crazy that's supposed to mean you are, but I am beyond all those little games. She was with me, she was real. I love her. True love will never die. That's how I signed all my letters to Betsy, the ones I tore up.

But Nona was the only one I ever really loved.

It's so hot in here. And I don't like the sounds in the walls.

Do you love?

Yes, I love.

And true love will never die.

For Owen

Walking to school you ask me
what other schools have grades.

I get as far as Fruit Street and your eyes go away.

As we walk under these yellow trees
you have your army lunch box under one arm and your
short legs, dressed in combat fatigues,
make your shadow into a scissors
that cuts nothing on the sidewalk.

You tell me suddenly that all the students there are fruits.

Everyone picks on the blueberries because they are so small.
The bananas, you say, are patrol boys.
In your eyes I see homerooms of oranges,
assemblies of apples.

All, you say, have arms and legs

and the watermelons are often tardy.
They waddle, and they are fat.
"Like me," you say.

          *   *   *

I could tell you things but better not.

That watermelon children cannot tie their own shoes;
the plums do it for them.
Or how I steal your face—
steal it, steal it, and wear it for my own.
It wears out fast on my face.

It's the stretching that does it.
I could tell you that dying's an art
and I am learning fast.
In that school I think you have already
picked up your own pencil
and begun to write your name.

Between now and then I suppose we could
someday play you truant and drive over to Fruit Street
and I could park in a rain of these October leaves
and we could watch a banana escort the last tardy watermelon
through those tall doors.

Survivor Type

Sooner or later the question comes up in every *medical student's career. How much shock-trauma can the patient stand? Different instructors answer the question in different ways, but cut to its base level, the answer is always another question:* How badly does the patient want to survive?

January 26

Two days since the storm washed me up. I paced the island off just this morning. Some island! It is 190 paces wide at its thickest point, and 267 paces long from tip to tip.

So far as I can tell, there is nothing on it to eat.

My name is Richard Pine. This is my diary. If I'm found (*when*), I can destroy this easily enough. There is no shortage of matches. Matches and heroin. Plenty of both. Neither of them worth doodlysquat here, ha-ha. So I will write. It will pass the time, anyway.

If I'm to tell the whole truth—and why not? I sure have the time!—I'll have to start by saying I was born Richard Pinzetti, in New York's Little Italy. My father was an Old World guinea. I wanted to be a surgeon. My father would laugh, call me crazy, and tell me to get him another glass of wine. He died of cancer when he was forty-six. I was glad.

I played football in high school. I was the best damn football player my school ever produced. Quarterback. I made

All-City my last two years. I hated football. But if you're a poor wop from the projects and you want to go to college, sports are your only ticket. So I played, and I got my athletic scholarship.

In college I only played ball until my grades were good enough to get a full academic scholarship. Pre-med. My father died six weeks before graduation. Good deal. Do you think I wanted to walk across that stage and get my diploma and look down and see that fat greaseball sitting there? Does a hen want a flag? I got into a fraternity, too. It wasn't one of the good ones, not with a name like Pinzetti, but a fraternity all the same.

Why am I writing this? It's almost funny. No, I take that back. It *is* funny. The great Dr. Pine, sitting on a rock in his pajama bottoms and a T-shirt, sitting on an island almost small enough to spit across, writing his life story. Am I hungry! Never mind, I'll write my goddam life story if I want to. At least it keeps my mind off my stomach. Sort of.

I changed my name to Pine before I started med school. My mother said I was breaking her heart. What heart? The day after my old man was in the ground, she was out hustling that Jew grocer down at the end of the block. For someone who loved the name so much, she was in one hell of a hurry to change her copy of it to Steinbrunner.

Surgery was all I ever wanted. Ever since high school. Even then I was wrapping my hands before every game and soaking them afterward. If you want to be a surgeon, you have to take care of your hands. Some of the kids used to rag me about it, call me chickenshit. I never fought them. Playing football was risk enough. But there were ways. The one that got on my case the most was Howie Plotsky, a big dumb bohunk with zits all over his face. I had a paper route, and I was selling the numbers along with the papers. I had a little coming in lots of ways. You get to know people, you listen, you make connections. You have to, when you're hustling the street. Any asshole knows how to die. The thing to learn is how to survive, you know what I mean? So I paid the biggest kid in school, Ricky Brazzi, ten bucks to make Howie Plotsky's mouth disappear. Make it disappear, I said. I will pay you a dollar for every tooth you bring me. Rico brought me three teeth wrapped up in a paper towel. He dislocated two of his knuckles doing the job, so you see the kind of trouble I could have got into.

In med school while the other suckers were running themselves ragged trying to bone up—no pun intended, ha-ha—between waiting tables or selling neckties or buffing floors, I kept the rackets going. Football pools, basketball pools, a little policy. I stayed on good terms with the old neighborhood. And I got through school just fine.

I didn't get into pushing until I was doing my residency. I was working in one of the biggest hospitals in New York City. At first it was just prescription blanks. I'd sell a tablet of a hundred blanks to some guy from the neighborhood, and he'd forge the names of forty or fifty different doctors on them, using writing samples I'd also sell him. The guy would turn around and peddle the blanks on the street for ten or twenty dollars apiece. The speed freaks and the nodders loved it.

And after a while I found out just how much of a balls-up the hospital drug room was in. Nobody knew what was coming in or going out. There were people lugging the goodies out by the double handfuls. Not me. I was always careful. I never got into trouble until I got careless—and unlucky. But I'm going to land on my feet. I always do.

Can't write any more now. My wrist's tired and the pencil's dull. I don't know why I'm bothering, anyway. Somebody'll probably pick me up soon.

January 27

The boat drifted away last night and sank in about ten feet of water off the north side of the island. Who gives a rip? The bottom was like Swiss cheese after coming over the reef anyway. I'd already taken off anything that was worth taking. Four gallons of water. A sewing kit. A first-aid kit. This book I'm writing in, which is supposed to be a lifeboat inspection log. That's a laugh. Whoever heard of a lifeboat with no FOOD on it? The last report written in here is August 8, 1970. Oh, yes, two knives, one dull and one fairly sharp, one combination fork and spoon. I'll use them when I eat my supper tonight. Roast rock. Ha-ha. Well, I did get my pencil sharpened.

When I get off this pile of guano-splattered rock, I'm going to sue the bloody hell out of Paradise Lines, Inc. That alone is worth living for. And I am going to live. I'm going to get out of this. Make no mistake about it. I am going to get out of this.

(later)

When I was making my inventory, I forgot one thing: two kilos of pure heroin, worth about $350,000, New York street value. Here it's worth el zilcho. Sort of funny, isn't it? Ha-ha!

January 28

Well, I've eaten—if you want to call that eating. There was a gull perched on one of the rocks at the center of the island. The rocks are all jumbled up into a kind of mini-mountain there—all covered with birdshit, too. I got a chunk of stone that just fitted into my hand and climbed up as close to it as I dared. It just stood there on its rock, watching me with its bright black eyes. I'm surprised that the rumbling of my stomach didn't scare it off.

I threw the rock as hard as I could and hit it broadside. It let out a loud squawk and tried to fly away, but I'd broken its right wing. I scrambled up after it and it hopped away. I could see the blood trickling over its white feathers. The son of a bitch led me a merry chase; once, on the other side of the central rockpile, I got my foot caught in a hole between two rocks and nearly fractured my ankle.

It began to tire at last, and I finally caught it on the east side of the island. It was actually trying to get into the water and paddle away. I caught a handful of its tailfeathers and it turned around and pecked me. Then I had one hand around its feet. I got my other hand on its miserable neck and broke it. The sound gave me great satisfaction. Lunch is served, you know? Ha! Ha!

I carried it back to my "camp," but even before I plucked and gutted it, I used iodine to swab the laceration its beak had made. Birds carry all sorts of germs, and the last thing I need now is an infection.

The operation on the gull went quite smoothly. I could not cook it, alas. Absolutely no vegetation or driftwood on the island and the boat has sunk. So I ate it raw. My stomach wanted to regurgitate it immediately. I sympathized but could not allow it. I counted backward until the nausea passed. It almost always works.

Can you imagine that bird, almost breaking my ankle and then pecking me? If I catch another one tomorrow, I'll torture it. I let this one off too easily. Even as I write, I am able to glance down at its severed head on the sand. Its black eyes, even with the death-glaze on them, seem to be mocking me.

Do gulls have brains in any quantity?

Are they edible?

January 29

No chow today. One gull landed near the top of the rockpile but flew off before I could get close enough to "throw it a forward pass," ha-ha! I've started a beard. Itches like hell. If the gull comes back and I get it, I'm going to cut its eyes out before I kill it.

I was one hell of a surgeon, as I believe I may have said. They drummed me out. It's a laugh, really; they all do it, and they're so bloody sanctimonious when someone gets caught at it. Screw you, Jack, I got mine. The Second Oath of Hippocrates and Hypocrites.

I had enough socked away from my adventures as an intern and a resident (that's supposed to be like an officer and a gentleman according to the Oath of Hypocrites, but don't you believe it) to set myself up in practice on Park Avenue. A good thing for me, too; I had no rich daddy or established patron, as so many of my "colleagues" did. By the time my shingle was out, my father was nine years in his pauper's grave. My mother died the year before my license to practice was revoked.

It was a kickback thing. I had a deal going with half a dozen East Side pharmacists, with two drug supply houses, and with at least twenty other doctors. Patients were sent to me and I sent patients. I performed operations and prescribed the correct post-op drugs. Not all the operations were necessary, but I never performed one against a patient's will. And I never had a patient look down at what was written on the prescrip blank and say, "I don't want this." Listen: they'd have a hysterectomy in 1965 or a partial thyroid in 1970, and still be taking painkillers five or ten years later, if you'd let them. Sometimes I did. I wasn't the only one, you know. They could afford the habit. And sometimes a patient would have trouble sleeping after minor surgery. Or trouble getting diet pills. Or Librium. It could all be arranged. Ha! Yes! If they hadn't gotten it from me, they would have gotten it from someone else.

Then the tax people got to Lowenthal. That sheep. They waved five years in his face and he coughed up half a dozen names. One of them was mine. They watched me for a while, and by the time they landed, I was worth a lot more than five years. There were a few other deals, including the prescription blanks, which I hadn't given up entirely. It's funny, I didn't really need that stuff anymore, but it was a habit. Hard to give up that extra sugar.

Well, I knew some people. I pulled some strings. And I threw a couple of people to the wolves. Nobody I liked, though. Everyone I gave to the feds was a real son of a bitch.

Christ, I'm hungry.

January 30

No gulls today. Reminds me of the signs you'd sometimes see on the pushcarts back in the neighborhood. NO TOMATOES TODAY. I walked out into the water up to my waist with the sharp knife in my hand. I stood completely still in that one place with the sun beating down on me for four hours. Twice I thought I was going to faint, but I counted backward until it passed. I didn't see one fish. Not one.

January 31

Killed another gull, the same way I did the first. I was too hungry to torture it the way I had been promising myself. I gutted and ate it. Squeezed the tripes and then ate them, too. It's strange how you can feel your vitality surge back. I was beginning to get scared there, for a while. Lying in the shade of the big central rockpile, I'd think I was hearing voices. My father. My mother. My ex-wife. And worst of all the big Chink who sold me the heroin in Saigon. He had a lisp, possibly from a partially cleft palate.

"Go ahead," his voice came out of nowhere. "Go ahead and thnort a little. You won't notith how hungry you are then. It'h beautiful . . ." But I've never done dope, not even sleeping pills.

Lowenthal killed himself, did I tell you that? That sheep.

He hanged himself in what used to be his office. The way I look at it, he did the world a favor.

I wanted my shingle back. Some of the people I talked to said it could be done—but it would cost big money. More grease than I'd ever dreamed of. I had $40,000 in a safe-deposit box. I decided I'd have to take a chance and try to turn it over. Double or triple it.

So I went to see Ronnie Hanelli. Ronnie and I played football together in college, and when his kid brother decided on internal med, I helped him get a residency. Ronnie himself was in pre-law, how's that for funny? On the block when we were growing up we called him Ronnie the Enforcer because he umped all the stickball games and reffed the hockey. If you didn't like his calls, you had your choice—you could keep your mouth shut or you could eat knuckles. The Puerto Ricans called him *Ronniewop*. All one word like that. *Ronniewop*. Used to tickle him. And that guy went to college, and then to law school, and he breezed through his bar exam the first time he took it, and then he set up shop in the old neighborhood, right over the Fish Bowl Bar. I close my eyes and I can still see him cruising down the block in that white Continental of his. The biggest fucking loan shark in the city.

I knew Ronnie would have something for me. "It's dangerous," he said. "But you could always take care of yourself. And if you can get the stuff back in, I'll introduce you to a couple of fellows. One of them is a state representative."

He gave me two names over there. One of them was the big Chink, Henry Li-Tsu. The other was a Vietnamese named Solom Ngo. A chemist. For a fee he would test the Chink's product. The Chink was known to play "jokes" from time to time. The "jokes" were plastic bags filled with talcum powder, with drain cleaner, with cornstarch. Ronnie said that one day Li-Tsu's little jokes would get him killed.

February 1

There was a plane. It flew right across the island. I tried to climb to the top of the rockpile and wave to it. My foot went into a hole. The same damn hole I got it stuck in the day I killed the first bird, I think. I've fractured my ankle, compound fracture. It went like a gunshot. The pain was unbelievable. I screamed and lost my balance, pinwheeling my arms like a madman, but I went down and hit my head and everything went black. I didn't wake up until dusk. I lost some blood where I hit my head. My ankle had swelled up like a tire, and I'd got myself a very nasty sunburn. I think if there had been another hour of sun, it would have blistered.

Dragged myself back here and spent last night shivering and crying with frustration. I disinfected the head wound, which is just above the right temporal lobe, and bandaged it as well as I could. Just a superficial scalp wound plus minor concussion, I think, but my ankle . . . it's a bad break, involved in two places, possibly three.

How will I chase the birds now?

It had to be a plane looking for survivors from the *Callas*. In the dark and the storm, the lifeboat must have carried miles from where it sank. They may not be back this way.

God, my ankle hurts so bad.

February 2

I made a sign on the small white shingle of a beach on the island's south side, where the lifeboat grounded. It took me all day, with pauses to rest in the shade. Even so, I fainted twice. At a guess, I'd say I've lost 25 lbs, mostly from dehydration. But now, from where I sit, I can see the four letters it took me all day to spell out; dark rocks against the white sand, they say HELP in characters four feet high. Another plane won't miss me.

If there is another plane.

My foot throbs constantly. There is swelling still and ominous discoloration around the double break. Discoloration seems to have advanced. Binding it tightly with my shirt alleviates the worst of the pain, but it's still bad enough so that I faint rather than sleep.

I have begun to think I may have to amputate.

February 3

Swelling and discoloration worse still. I'll wait until tomorrow. If the operation does become necessary, I believe I can carry it through. I have matches for sterilizing the sharp knife, I have needle and thread from the sewing kit. My shirt for a bandage.

I even have two kilos of "painkiller," although hardly of the type I used to prescribe. But they would have taken it if they could have gotten it. You bet. Those old blue-haired ladies would have snorted Glade air freshener if they thought it would have gotten them high. Believe it!

February 4

I've decided to amputate my foot. No food four days now. If I wait any longer, I run the risk of fainting from combined shock and hunger in the middle of the operation and bleeding to death. And as wretched as I am, I still want to live. I remember what Mockridge used to say in Basic Anatomy. Old Mockie, we used to call him. Sooner or later, he'd say, the question comes up in every medical student's career: How much shock-trauma can the patient stand? And he'd whack his pointer at his chart of the human body, hitting the liver, the kidneys, the heart, the spleen, the intestines. Cut to its base level, gentlemen, he'd say, the answer is always another question: How badly does the patient want to survive?

I think I can bring it off.

I really do.

I suppose I'm writing to put off the inevitable, but it did occur to me that I haven't finished the story of how I came to be here. Perhaps I should tie up that loose end in case the operation does go badly. It will only take a few minutes, and I'm sure there will be enough daylight left for the operation, for, according to my Pulsar, it's only nine past nine in the morning. Ha!

I flew to Saigon as a tourist. Does that sound strange? It shouldn't. There are still thousands of people who visit there every year in spite of Nixon's war. There are people who go to see car wrecks and cockfights, too.

My Chinese friend had the merchandise. I took it to Ngo, who pronounced it very high-grade stuff. He told me that Li-Tsu had played one of his jokes four months ago and that his wife had been blown up when she turned on the ignition of her Opel. Since then there had been no more jokes.

I stayed in Saigon for three weeks; I had booked passage back to San Francisco on a cruise ship, the *Callas*. First cabin. Getting on board with the merchandise was no trouble; for a fee Ngo arranged for two customs officials to simply wave me on after running through my suitcases. The merchandise was in an airline flight bag, which they never even looked at.

"Getting through U.S. customs will be much more difficult," Ngo told me. "That, however, is your problem."

I had no intention of taking the merchandise through U.S. customs. Ronnie Hanelli had arranged for a skin diver who would do a certain rather tricky job for $3,000. I was to meet him (two days ago, now that I think of it) in a San Francisco flophouse called the St. Regis Hotel. The plan was to put the merchandise in a waterproof can. Attached to the top was a timer and a packet of red dye. Just before we docked, the canister was to be thrown overboard—but not by me, of course.

I was still looking for a cook or a steward who could use a little extra cash and who was smart enough—or stupid enough—to keep his mouth closed afterward, when the *Callas* sank.

I don't know how or why. It was storming, but the ship seemed to be handling that well enough. Around eight o'clock on the evening of the 23rd, there was an explosion somewhere belowdecks. I was in the lounge at the time, and the *Callas* began to list almost immediately. To the left . . . do they call that "port" or "starboard"?

People were screaming and running in every direction. Bottles were falling off the backbar and shattering on the floor. A man staggered up from one of the lower levels, his shirt burned off, his skin barbecued. The loudspeaker started telling people to go to the lifeboat stations they had been assigned during the drill at the beginning of the cruise. The passengers went right on running hither and yon. Very few of them had bothered to show up during the lifeboat drill. I not only showed up, I came early—I wanted to be in the front row, you see, so I would have an unobstructed view of everything. I always pay close attention when the matter concerns my own skin.

I went down to my stateroom, got the heroin bags, and put one in each of my front pockets. Then I went to Lifeboat Station 8. As I went up the stairwell to the main deck there were two more explosions and the boat began to list even more severely.

Topside, everything was confusion. I saw a screeching woman with a baby in her arms run past me, gaining speed as she sprinted down the slippery, canting deck. She hit the rail with her thighs, and flipped outward. I saw her do two midair somersaults and part of a third before I lost sight of her. There was a middle-aged man sitting in the center of the shuffleboard court and pulling his hair. Another man in cook's whites, horribly burned about his face and hands, was stumbling from place to place and screaming, "HELP ME! CAN'T SEE! HELP ME! CAN'T SEE!"

The panic was almost total: it had run from the passengers to the crew like a disease. You must remember that the time elapsed from the first explosion to the actual sinking of the *Callas* was only about twenty minutes. Some of the lifeboat stations were clogged with screaming passengers, while others were absolutely empty. Mine, on the listing side of the ship, was almost deserted. There was no one there but myself and a common sailor with a pimply, pallid face.

"Let's get this buckety-bottomed old whore in the water," he said, his eyes rolling crazily in their sockets. "This bloody tub is going straight to the bottom."

The lifeboat gear is simple enough to operate, but in his fumbling nervousness, he got his side of the block and tackle tangled. The boat dropped six feet and then hung up, the bow two feet lower than the stern.

I was coming around to help him when he began to scream. He'd succeeded in untangling the snarl and had gotten his hand caught at the same time. The whizzing rope smoked over his open palm, flaying off skin, and he was jerked over the side.

I tossed the rope ladder overboard, hurried down it, and unclipped the lifeboat from the lowering ropes. Then I rowed, something I had occasionally done for pleasure on trips to my friends' summer houses, something I was now doing for my life. I knew that if I didn't get far enough away from the dying *Callas* before she sank, she would pull me down with her.

Just five minutes later she went. I hadn't escaped the suction entirely; I had to row madly just to stay in the same place. She went under very quickly. There were still people clinging to the rail of her bow and screaming. They looked like a bunch of monkeys.

The storm worsened. I lost one oar but managed to keep the other. I spent that whole night in a kind of dream, first bailing, then grabbing the oar and paddling wildly to get the boat's prow into the next bulking wave.

Sometime before dawn on the 24th, the waves began to strengthen behind me. The boat rushed forward. It was terrifying but at the same time exhilarating. Suddenly most of the planking was ripped out from under my feet, but before the lifeboat could sink it was dumped on this godforsaken pile of rocks. I don't even know where I am; have no idea at all. Navigation not my strong point, ha-ha.

But I know what I have to do. This may be the last entry, but somehow I think I'll make it. Haven't I always? And they are really doing marvelous things with prosthetics these days. I can get along with one foot quite nicely.

It's time to see if I'm as good as I think I am. Luck.

February 5
Did it.

The pain was the part I was most worried about. I can stand pain, but I thought that in my weakened condition, a combination of hunger and agony might force unconsciousness before I could finish.

But the heroin solved that quite nicely.

I opened one of the bags and sniffed two healthy pinches from the surface of a flat rock—first the right nostril, then the left. It was like sniffing up some beautifully numbing ice that spread through the brain from the bottom up. I aspirated the heroin as soon as I finished writing in this diary yesterday— that was at 9:45. The next time I checked my watch the shadows had moved, leaving me partially in the sun, and the time was 12:41. I had nodded off. I had never dreamed that it could be so beautiful, and I can't understand why I was so scornful before. The pain, the terror, the misery . . . they all disappear, leaving only a calm euphoria.

It was in this state that I operated.

There was, indeed, a great deal of pain, most of it in the early part of the operation. But the pain seemed disconnected from me, like somebody else's pain. It bothered me, but it was also quite interesting. Can you understand that? If you've used a strong morphine-based drug yourself, perhaps you can. It does more than dull pain. It induces a state of mind. A serenity. I can understand why people get hooked on it, although "hooked" seems an awfully strong word, used most commonly, of course, by those who have never tried it.

About halfway through, the pain started to become a more personal thing. Waves of faintness washed over me. I looked longingly at the open bag of white powder, but forced myself to look away. If I went on the nod again, I'd bleed to death as surely as if I'd fainted. I counted backward from a hundred instead.

Loss of blood was the most critical factor. As a surgeon, I was vitally aware of that. Not a drop could be spilled unnecessarily. If a patient hemorrhages during an operation in a hospital, you can give him blood. I had no such supplies. What was lost—and by the time I had finished, the sand beneath my leg was dark with it—was lost until my own internal factory could resupply. I had no clamps, no hemostats, no surgical thread.

I began the operation at exactly 12:45. I finished at 1:50, and immediately dosed myself with heroin, a bigger dose than before. I nodded into a gray, painless world and remained there until nearly five o'clock. When I came out of it, the sun was nearing the western horizon, beating a track of gold across the blue Pacific toward me. I've never seen anything so beautiful . . . all the pain was paid for in that one instant. An hour later I snorted a bit more, so as to fully enjoy and appreciate the sunset.

Shortly after dark I—

I—

Wait. Haven't I told you I'd had nothing to eat *for four days?* And that the only help I could look to in the matter of replenishing my sapped vitality was my own body? Above all, haven't I told you, over and over, that survival is a business of the mind? The superior mind? I won't justify myself by saying you would have done the same thing. First of all, you're probably not a surgeon. Even if you knew the mechanics of amputation, you might have botched the job so badly you would have bled to death anyway. And even if you had lived through the operation and the shock-trauma, the thought might never have entered your preconditioned head. Never mind. No one has to know. My last act before leaving the island will be to destroy this book.

I was very careful.

I washed it thoroughly before I ate it.

February 7

Pain from the stump has been bad—excruciating from time to time. But I think the deep-seated itch as the healing process begins has been worse. I've been thinking this afternoon of all the patients that have babbled to me that they couldn't stand the horrible, unscratchable itch of mending flesh. And I would smile and tell them they would feel better tomorrow, privately thinking what whiners they were, what jellyfish, what ungrateful babies. Now I understand. Several times I've come close to ripping the shirt bandage off the stump and scratching at it, digging my fingers into the soft raw flesh, pulling out the rough stitches, letting the blood gout onto the sand, anything, anything, to be rid of that maddening horrible *itch*.

At those times I count backward from one hundred. And snort heroin.

I have no idea how much I've taken into my system, but I do know I've been "stoned" almost continually since the operation. It depresses hunger, you know. I'm hardly aware of being hungry at all. There is a faint, faraway gnawing in my belly, and that's all. It could easily be ignored. I can't do that, though. Heroin has no measurable caloric value. I've been testing myself, crawling from place to place, measuring my energy. It's ebbing.

Dear God, I hope not, but . . . another operation may be necessary.

(later)

Another plane flew over. Too high to do me any good; all I could see was the contrail etching itself across the sky. I waved anyway. Waved and screamed at it. When it was gone I wept.

Getting too dark to see now. Food. I've been thinking about all kinds of food. My mother's lasagna. Garlic bread. Escargots. Lobster. Prime ribs. Peach melba. London broil. The huge slice of pound cake and the scoop of homemade vanilla ice cream they give you for dessert in Mother Crunch on First Avenue. Hot pretzels baked salmon baked Alaska baked ham with pineapple rings. Onion rings. Onion dip with potato chips cold iced tea in long long sips french fries make you smack your lips.

100, 99, 98, 97, 96, 95, 94

God God God

February 8

Another gull landed on the rockpile this morning. A huge fat one. I was sitting in the shade of my rock, what I think of as my camp, my bandaged stump propped up. I began to salivate as soon as the gull landed. Just like one of Pavlov's dogs. Drooling helplessly, like a baby. Like a baby.

I picked up a chunk of stone large enough to fit my hand nicely and began to crawl toward it. Fourth quarter. We're down by three. Third and long yardage. Pinzetti drops back to pass (Pine, I mean, *Pine*). I didn't have much hope. I was sure it would fly off. But I had to try. If I could get it, a bird as plump and insolent as that one, I could postpone a second operation indefinitely. I crawled toward it, my stump hitting a rock from time to time and sending stars of pain through my whole body, and waited for it to fly off.

It didn't. It just strutted back and forth, its meaty breast thrown out like some avian general reviewing troops. Every now and then it would look at me with its small, nasty black eyes and I would freeze like a stone and count backward from one hundred until it began to pace back and forth again. Every time it fluttered its wings, my stomach filled up with ice. I continued to drool. I couldn't help it. I was drooling like a baby.

I don't know how long I stalked it. An hour? Two? And the closer I got, the harder my heart pounded and the tastier that gull looked. It almost seemed to be teasing me, and I began to believe that as soon as I got in throwing range it would fly off. My arms and legs were beginning to tremble. My mouth was dry. The stump was twanging viciously. I think now that I must have been having withdrawal pains. But so soon? I've been using the stuff less than a week!

Never mind. I need it. There's plenty left, plenty. If I have to take the cure later on when I get back to the States, I'll check into the best clinic in California and do it with a smile. That's not the problem right now, is it?

When I did get in range, I didn't want to throw the rock. I became insanely sure that I would miss, probably by feet. I had to get closer. So I continued to crawl up the rockpile, my head thrown back, the sweat pouring off my wasted, scarecrow body. My teeth have begun to rot, did I tell you that? If I were a superstitious man, I'd say it was because I ate—

Ha! We know better, don't we?

I stopped again. I was much closer to it than I had been to either of the other gulls. I still couldn't bring myself to commit. I clutched the rock until my fingers ached and still I couldn't throw it. Because I knew exactly what it would mean if I missed.

I don't care if I use all the merchandise! I'll sue the ass off them! I'll be in clover for the rest of my life! *My long long life!*

I think I would have crawled right up to it without throwing if it hadn't finally taken wing. I would have crept up and strangled it. But it spread its wings and took off. I screamed at it and reared up on my knees and threw my rock with all my strength. And I hit it!

The bird gave a strangled squawk and fell back on the other side of the rockpile. Gibbering and laughing, unmindful now of striking the stump or opening the wound, I crawled over the top and to the other side. I lost my balance and banged my head. I didn't even notice it, not then, although it has raised a pretty nasty lump. All I could think of was the bird and how I had hit it, fantastic luck, even on the wing I had hit it!

It was flopping down toward the beach on the other side, one wing broken, its underbody red with blood. I crawled as fast as I could, but it crawled faster yet. Race of the cripples! Ha! Ha! I might have gotten it—I was closing the distance—except for my hands. I have to take good care of my hands. I may need them again. In spite of my care, the palms were scraped by the time we reached the narrow shingle of beach, and I'd shattered the face of my Pulsar watch against a rough spine of rock.

The gull flopped into the water, squawking noisomely, and I clutched at it. I got a handful of tailfeathers, which came off in my fist. Then I fell in, inhaling water, snorting and choking.

I crawled in further. I even tried to swim after it. The bandage came off my stump. I began to go under. I just managed to get back to the beach, shaking with exhaustion, racked with pain, weeping and screaming, cursing the gull. It floated there for a long time, always further and further out. I seem to remember begging it to come back at one point. But when it went out over the reef, I think it was dead.

It isn't fair.

It took me almost an hour to crawl back around to my camp. I've snorted a large amount of heroin, but even so I'm bitterly angry at the gull. If I wasn't going to get it, why did it have to tease me so? Why didn't it just fly off?

February 9

I've amputated my left foot and have bandaged it with my pants. Strange. All through the operation I was drooling. Drooooling. Just like when I saw the gull. Drooling help-lessly. But I made myself wait until after dark. I just counted backward from one hundred . . . twenty or thirty times! Ha! Ha!

Then . . .

I kept telling myself: Cold roast beef. Cold roast beef. Cold roast beef.

February 11 (?)

Rain the last two days. And high winds. I managed to move some rocks from the central pile, enough to make a hole I could crawl into. Found one small spider. Pinched it between my fingers before he could get away and ate him up. Very nice. Juicy. Thought to myself that the rocks over me might fall and bury me alive. Didn't care.

Spent the whole storm stoned. Maybe it rained three days instead of two. Or only one. But I think it got dark twice. I love to nod off. No pain or itching then. I know I'm going to survive this. It can't be a person can go through something like this for nothing.

There was a priest at Holy Family when I was a kid, a little runty guy, and he used to love to talk about hell and mortal sins. He had a real hobbyhorse on them. You can't get back from a mortal sin, that was his view. I dreamed about him last night, Father Hailley in his black bathrobe, and his whiskey nose, shaking his finger at me and saying, "Shame on you, Richard Pinzetti . . . a mortal sin . . . damt to hell, boy . . . damt to hell . . ."

I laughed at him. If this place isn't hell, what is? And the only mortal sin is giving up.

Half of the time I'm delirious; the rest of the time my stumps itch and the dampness makes them ache horribly.

But I won't give up. I swear. Not for nothing. Not all this for nothing.

February 12

Sun is out again, a beautiful day. I hope they're freezing their asses off in the neighborhood.

It's been a good day for me, as good as any day gets on this island. The fever I had while it was storming seems to have dropped. I was weak and shivering when I crawled out of my burrow, but after lying on the hot sand in the sunshine for two or three hours, I began to feel almost human again.

Crawled around to the south side and found several pieces of driftwood cast up by the storm, including several boards from my lifeboat. There was kelp and seaweed on some of the boards. I ate it. Tasted awful. Like eating a vinyl shower curtain. But I felt so much stronger this afternoon.

I pulled the wood up as far as I could so it would dry. I've still got a whole tube of waterproof matches. The wood will make a signal fire if someone comes soon. A cooking fire if not. I'm going to snort up now.

February 13

Found a crab. Killed it and roasted it over a small fire. Tonight I could almost believe in God again.

Feb 14

I just noticed this morning that the storm washed away most of the rocks in my HELP sign. But the storm ended . . . three days ago? Have I really been that stoned? I'll have to watch it, cut down the dosage. What if a ship went by while I was nodding?

I made the letters again, but it took me most of the day and now I'm exhausted. Looked for a crab where I found the other, but nothing. Cut my hands on several of the rocks I used for the sign, but disinfected them promptly with iodine in spite of my weariness. Have to take care of my hands. No matter what.

Feb 15

A gull landed on the tip of the rockpile today. Flew away before I could get in range. I wished it into hell, where it could peck out Father Hailley's bloodshot little eyes through eternity.

Ha! Ha!
Ha! Ha!
Ha

Feb 17(?)

Took off my right leg at the knee, but lost a lot of blood. Pain excruciating in spite of heroin. Shock-trauma would have killed a lesser man. Let me answer with a question: How badly does the patient want to survive? *How badly does the patient want to live?*

Hands trembling. If they are betraying me, I'm through. They have no right to betray me. No right at all. I've taken care of them all their lives. Pampered them. They better not. Or they'll be sorry.

At least I'm not hungry.

One of the boards from the lifeboat had split down the middle. One end came to a point. I used that. I was drooling but I made myself wait. And then I got thinking of . . . oh, barbecues we used to have. That place Will Hammersmith had on Long Island, with a barbecue pit big enough to roast a whole pig in. We'd be sitting on the porch in the dusk with big drinks in our hands, talking about surgical techniques or golf scores or something. And the breeze would pick up and drift the sweet smell of roasting pork over to us. Judas Iscariot, the sweet smell of roasting pork.

Feb?

Took the other leg at the knee. Sleepy all day. "Doctor was this operation necessary?" Haha. Shaky hands, like an old man. Hate them. Blood under the fingernails. Scabs. Remember that model in med school with the glass belly? I feel like that. Only I don't want to look. No way no how. I remember Dom used to say that. Waltz up to you on the street corner in his Hiway Outlaws club jacket. You'd say Dom how'd you make out with her? And Dom would say no way no how. Shee. Old Dom. I wish I'd stayed right in the neighborhood. This sucks so bad as Dom would say. haha.

But I understand, you know, that with the proper therapy, and prosthetics, I could be as good as new. I could come back here and tell people "This. Is where it. Happened."

Hahaha!

February 23 (?)

Found a dead fish. Rotten and stinking. Ate it anyway. Wanted to puke, wouldn't let myself. *I will survive.* So lovely stoned, the sunsets.

February

Don't dare but have to. But how can I tie off the femoral artery that high up? It's as big as a fucking turnpike up there.

Must, somehow. I've marked across the top of the thigh, the part that is still meaty. I made the mark with this pencil.

I wish I could stop drooling.

Fe
You . . . deserve . . . a break today . . . sooo . . . get up
and get away . . . to McDonald's . . . two all-beef patties
. . . special sauce . . . lettuce . . . pickles . . . onions . . .
on a . . . sesame seed bun . . .
Dee . . . deedee . . . dundadee . . .

Febba
Looked at my face in the water today. Nothing but a
skin-covered skull. Am I insane yet? I must be. I'm a monster
now, a freak. Nothing left below the groin. Just a freak. A
head attached to a torso dragging itself along the sand by the
elbows. A crab. A *stoned* crab. Isn't that what they call
themselves now? Hey man I'm just a poor stoned crab can
you spare me a dime.
Hahahaha
They say you are what you eat and if so I HAVEN'T CHANGED
A BIT! Dear God shock-trauma shock-trauma THERE IS NO SUCH
THING AS SHOCK-TRAUMA
HA

Fe/4O?
Dreaming about my father. When he was drunk he lost all
his English. Not that he had anything worth saying anyway.
Fucking dipstick. I was so glad to get out of your house
Daddy you fucking greaseball dipstick nothing cipher zilcho
zero. I knew I'd made it. I walked away from you, didn't I? I
walked on my hands.
But there's nothing left for them to cut off. Yesterday I
took my earlobes

left hand washes the right don't let your left hand know
what your right hands doing one potato two potato three
potato four we got a refrigerator with a store-more door
hahaha.
Who cares. this hand or that. good food good meat good
God let's eat.

lady fingers they taste just like lady fingers

Uncle Otto's Truck

It's a great relief to write this down.

I haven't slept well since I found my Uncle Otto dead and there have been times when I have really wondered if I have gone insane—or if I will. In a way it would all have been more merciful if I did not have the actual object here in my study, where I can look at it, or pick it up and heft it if I should want to. I don't want to do that; I don't want to touch that thing. But sometimes I do.

If I hadn't taken it away from his little one-room house when I fled from it, I could begin persuading myself it was all only an hallucination—a figment of an overworked and overstimulated brain. But it is there. It has weight. It can be hefted in the hand.

It all happened, you see.

Most of you reading this memoir will not believe that, not unless something like it has happened to you. I find that the matter of your belief and my relief are mutually exclusive, however, and so I will gladly tell the tale anyway. Believe what you want.

Any tale of grue should have a provenance or a secret. Mine has both. Let me begin with the provenance—by telling you how my Uncle Otto, who was rich by the standards of Castle County, happened to spend the last twenty years of his life in a one-room house with no plumbing on a back road in a small town.

Otto was born in 1905, the eldest of the five Schenck children. My father, born in 1920, was the youngest. I was the youngest of my father's children, born in 1955, and so Uncle Otto always seemed very old to me.

Like many industrious Germans, my grandfather and grandmother came to America with some money. My grandfather settled in Derry because of the lumber industry, which he knew something about. He did well, and his children were born into comfortable circumstances.

My grandfather died in 1925. Uncle Otto, then twenty, was the only child to receive a full inheritance. He moved to Castle Rock and began to speculate in real estate. In the next five years he made a lot of money dealing in wood and in land. He bought a large house on Castle Hill, had servants, and enjoyed his status as a young, relatively handsome (the qualifier "relatively" because he wore spectacles), extremely eligible bachelor. No one thought him odd. That came later.

He was hurt in the crash of '29—not as badly as some, but hurt is hurt. He held on to his big Castle Hill house until 1933, then sold it because a great tract of woodland had come on the market at a distress sale price and he wanted it desperately. The land belonged to the New England Paper Company.

New England Paper still exists today, and if you wanted to purchase shares in it, I would tell you to go right ahead. But in 1933 the company was offering huge chunks of land at fire-sale prices in a last-ditch effort to stay afloat.

How much land in the tract my uncle was after? That original, fabulous deed has been lost, and accounts differ . . . but by *all* accounts, it was better than four thousand acres. Most of it was in Castle Rock, but it sprawled into Waterford and Harlow, as well. When the deal was broken down, New England Paper was offering it for about two dollars and fifty cents an acre . . . *if* the purchaser would take it all.

That was a total price of about ten thousand dollars. Uncle Otto couldn't swing it, and so he took a partner—a Yankee named George McCutcheon. You probably know the names Schenck and McCutcheon if you live in New England; the company was bought out long ago, but there are still Schenck and McCutcheon hardware stores in forty New England cities, and Schenck and McCutcheon lumberyards from Central Falls to Derry.

McCutcheon was a burly man with a great black beard. Like my Uncle Otto, he wore spectacles. Also like Uncle Otto, he had inherited a sum of money. It must have been a fairish sum, because he and Uncle Otto together swung the purchase of that tract with no further trouble. Both of them were pirates under the skin and they got on well enough together. Their partnership lasted for twenty-two years—until the year I was born, in fact—and prosperity was all they knew.

But it all began with the purchase of those four thousand acres, and they explored them in McCutcheon's truck, cruising the woods roads and the pulper's tracks, grinding along in first gear for the most part, shuddering over washboards and splashing through washouts, McCutcheon at the wheel part of the time, my Uncle Otto at the wheel the rest of the time, two young men who had become New England land barons in the dark depths of the big Depression.

I don't know where McCutcheon came by that truck. It was a Cresswell, if it matters—a breed which no longer exists. It had a huge cab, painted bright red, wide running boards, and an electric starter, but if the starter ever failed, it could be cranked—although the crank could just as easily kick back and break your shoulder, if the man cranking wasn't careful. The bed was twenty feet long with stake sides, but what I remember best about that truck was its snout. Like the cab, it was red as blood. To get at the engine, you had to lift out two steel panels, one on either side. The radiator was as high as a grown man's chest. It was an ugly, monstrous thing.

McCutcheon's truck broke down and was repaired, broke down again and was repaired again. When the Cresswell finally gave up, it gave up in spectacular fashion. It went like the wonderful one-hoss shay in the Holmes poem.

McCutcheon and Uncle Otto were coming up the Black Henry Road one day in 1953, and by Uncle Otto's own admission both of them were "shithouse drunk." Uncle Otto downshifted to first in order to get up Trinity Hill. *That* went fine, but, drunk as he was, he never thought to shift up again coming down the far side. The Cresswell's tired old engine overheated. Neither Uncle Otto nor McCutcheon saw the needle go over the red mark by the letter H on the right side of the dial. At the bottom of the hill, there was an explosion that blew the engine-compartment's folding sides out like red dragon's wings. The radiator cap rocketed into the summer sky. Steam plumed up like Old Faithful. Oil went in a gusher, drenching the windshield. Uncle Otto cramped down on the brake pedal but the Cresswell had developed a bad habit of shooting brake fluid over the last year or so and the pedal just sank to the mat. He couldn't see where he was driving and he ran off the road, first into a ditch and then out of it. If the Cresswell had stalled, all still might have been well. But the engine continued to run and it blew first one piston and then two more, like firecrackers on the Fourth of July. One of them, Uncle Otto said, zinged right through his door, which had flopped open. The hole was big enough to put a fist through. They came to rest in a field full of August golden-rod. They would have had a fine view of the White Mountains if the windshield hadn't been covered with Diamond Gem Oil.

That was the last roundup for McCutcheon's Cresswell; it never moved from that field again. Not that there was any squawk from the landlord; the two of them owned it, of course. Considerably sobered by the experience, the two men got out to examine the damage. Neither was a mechanic, but you didn't have to be to see that the wound was mortal. Uncle Otto was stricken—or so he told my father—and offered to pay for the truck. George McCutcheon told him not to be a fool. McCutcheon was, in fact, in a kind of ecstasy. He had taken one look at the field, at the view of the mountains, and had decided this was the place where he would build his retirement home. He told Uncle Otto just that, in tones one usually saves for a religious conversion. They walked back to the road together and hooked a ride into Castle Rock with the Cushman Bakery truck, which happened to be passing. McCutcheon told my father that it had been God's hand at work—he had been looking for just the perfect place, and there it had been all the time, in that field they passed three and four times a week, with never a spared glance. The hand of God, he reiterated, never knowing that he would die in that field two years later, crushed under the front end of his own truck—the truck which became Uncle Otto's truck when he died.

McCutcheon had Billy Dodd hook his wrecker up to the Cresswell and drag it around so it faced the road. So he could look at it, he said, every time he went by, and know that when Dodd hooked up to it again and dragged it away for good, it would be so that the construction men could come and dig him a cellar-hole. He was something of a sentimentalist, but he was not a man to let sentiment stand in the way of making a dollar. When a pulper named Baker came by a year later and offered to buy the Cresswell's wheels, tires and all, because they were the right size to fit his rig, McCutcheon took the man's twenty dollars like a flash. This was a man, remember, who was then worth a million dollars. He also told Baker to block the truck up aright smart. He said he didn't want to go past it and see it sitting in the field hip-deep in hay and timothy and goldenrod, like some old derelict. Baker did it. A year later the Cresswell rolled off the blocks and crushed McCutcheon to death. The old-timers told the story with relish, always ending by saying that they hoped old Georgie McCutcheon had enjoyed the twenty dollars he got for those wheels.

I grew up in Castle Rock. By the time I was born my father had worked for Schenck and McCutcheon almost ten years, and the truck, which had become Uncle Otto's along with everything else McCutcheon owned, was a landmark in my life. My mother shopped at Warren's in Bridgton, and the Black Henry Road was the way you got there. So every time we went, there was the truck, standing in that field with the White Mountains behind it. It was no longer blocked up—Uncle Otto said that one accident was enough—but just the thought of what had happened was enough to give a small boy in knee-pants a shiver.

It was there in the summer; in the fall with oak and elm trees blazing on the three edges of the field like torches; in the winter with drifts sometimes all the way up and over its bug-eyed headlights, so that it looked like a mastodon struggling in white quicksand; in the spring, when the field was a quagmire of March-mud and you wondered that it just didn't sink into the earth. If not for the underlying backbone of good Maine rock, it might well have done just that. Through all the seasons and years, it was there.

I was even in it, once. My father pulled over to the side of the road one day when we were on our way to the Fryeburg Fair, took me by the hand and led me out to the field. That would have been 1960 or 1961, I suppose. I was frightened of the truck. I had heard the stories of how it had slithered forward and crushed my uncle's partner. I had heard these tales in the barbershop, sitting quiet as a mouse behind a *Life* magazine I couldn't read, listening to the men talk about how he had been crushed, and about how they hoped old Georgie had enjoyed his twenty dollars for those wheels. One of them—it might have been Billy Dodd, crazy Frank's father—said McCutcheon had looked like "a pumpkin that got squot by a tractor wheel." That haunted my thoughts for months . . . but my father, of course, had no idea of that.

My father just thought I might like to sit in the cab of that old truck; he had seen the way I looked at it every time we passed, mistaking my dread for admiration, I suppose.

I remember the goldenrod, its bright yellow dulled by the October chill. I remember the gray taste of the air, a little bitter, a little sharp, and the silvery look of the dead grass. I remember the *whisssht-whissht* of our footfalls. But what I remember best is the truck looming up, getting bigger and bigger—the toothy snarl of its radiator, the bloody red of its paint, the bleary gaze of the windshield. I remember fear sweeping over me in a wave colder and grayer than the taste of the air as my father put his hands in my armpits and lifted me into the cab, saying, "Drive her to Portland, Quentin . . . go to her!" I remember the air sweeping past my face as I went up and up, and then its clean taste was replaced by the smells of ancient Diamond Gem Oil, cracked leather, mouse-droppings, and . . . I swear it . . . blood. I remember trying not to cry as my father stood grinning up at me, convinced he was giving me one hell of a thrill (and so he was, but not the way he thought). It came to me with perfect certainty that he would walk away then, or at least turn his back, and that the truck would just eat me—eat me alive. And what it spat out would look chewed and broken and . . . and sort of exploded. Like a pumpkin that got squot by a tractor wheel.

I began to cry and my father, who was the best of men, took me down and soothed me and carried me back to the car.

He carried me up in his arms, over his shoulder, and I looked at the receding truck, standing there in the field, its huge radiator looming, the dark round hole where the crank was supposed to go looking like a horridly misplaced eye socket, and I wanted to tell him I had smelled blood, and that's why I had cried. I couldn't think of a way to do it. I suppose he wouldn't have believed me anyway.

As a five-year-old who still believed in Santy Claus and the Tooth Fairy and the Allamagoosalum, I also believed that the bad, scary feelings which swamped me when my father boosted me into the cab of the truck *came* from the truck. It took twenty-two years for me to decide it wasn't the Cresswell that had murdered George McCutcheon; my Uncle Otto had done that.

The Cresswell was a landmark in my life, but it belonged to the whole area's consciousness, as well. If you were giving someone directions on how to get from Bridgton to Castle Rock, you told them they'd know they were going right if they saw a big old red truck sitting off to the left in a hayfield three miles or so after the turn from 11. You often saw tourists parked on the soft shoulder (and sometimes they got stuck there, which was always good for a laugh), taking pictures of the White Mountains with Uncle Otto's truck in the foreground for picturesque perspective—for a long time my father called the Cresswell "the Trinity Hill Memorial Tourist Truck," but after a while he stopped. By then Uncle Otto's obsession with it had gotten too strong for it to be funny.

So much for the provenance. Now for the secret.

That he killed McCutcheon is the one thing of which I am absolutely sure. "Squot him like a pumpkin," the barbershop sages said. One of them added: "I bet he was down in front o' that truck, prayin like one o' them greaseball Ay-rabs prayin to Arlah. I can just pitcher him that way. They was tetched, y'know, t'both of them. Just lookit the way Otto Schenck ended up, if you don't believe me. Right across the road in that little house he thought the town was gonna take for a school, and just as crazy as a shithouse rat."

This was greeted with nods and wise looks, because by *then* they thought Uncle Otto was odd, all right—oh, ayuh!

—but there wasn't a one of the barbershop sages who considered that image—McCutcheon down on his knees in front of the truck "like one o' them greaseball Ay-rabs prayin to Arlah"—suspicious as well as eccentric.

Gossip is always a hot item in a small town; people are condemned as thieves, adulterers, poachers, and cheats on the flimsiest evidence and the wildest deductions. Often, I think, the talk gets started out of no more than boredom. I think what keeps this from being actually nasty—which is how most novelists have depicted small towns, from Nathaniel Hawthorne to Grace Metalious—is that most party-line, grocery-store, and barbershop gossip is oddly naive—it is as if these people expect meanness and shallowness, will even invent it if it is not there, but that real and conscious evil may be beyond their conception, even when it floats right before their faces like a magic carpet from one o' those greaseball Ay-rab fairy tales.

How do I know he did it? you ask. Simply because he was with McCutcheon that day? No. Because of the truck. The Cresswell. When his obsession began to overtake him, he went to live across from it in that tiny house . . . even though, in the last few years of his life, he was deathly afraid of the truck beached across the road.

I think Uncle Otto got McCutcheon out into the field where the Cresswell was blocked up by getting McCutcheon to talk about his house plans. McCutcheon was always eager to talk about his house and his approaching retirement. The partners had been made a good offer by a much larger company—I won't mention the name, but if I did you would know it—and McCutcheon wanted to take it. Uncle Otto didn't. There had been a quiet struggle going on between them over the offer since the spring. I think that disagreement was the reason Uncle Otto decided to get rid of his partner.

I think that my uncle might have prepared for the moment by doing two things: first, undermining the blocks holding the truck up, and second, planting something on the ground or perhaps in it, directly in front of the truck, where McCutcheon would see it.

What sort of thing? I don't know. Something bright. A diamond? Nothing more than a chunk of broken glass? It doesn't matter. It winks and flashes in the sun. Maybe McCutcheon sees it. If not, you can be sure Uncle Otto points it out. *What's that?* he asks, pointing. *Dunno*, McCutcheon says, and hurries over to take a look-see.

McCutcheon falls on his knees in front of the Cresswell, just like one o' them greaseball Ay-rabs prayin to Arlah, trying to work the object out of the ground, while my uncle strolls casually around to the back of the truck. One good shove and down it came, crushing McCutcheon flat. Squotting him like a pumpkin.

I suspect there may have been too much pirate in him to have died easily. In my imagination I see him lying pinned beneath the Cresswell's tilted snout, blood streaming from his nose and mouth and ears, his face paper-white, his eyes dark, pleading with my uncle to get help, to get help fast. Pleading . . . then begging . . . and finally cursing my uncle, promising him he would get him, kill him, finish him . . . and my uncle standing there, watching, hands in his pockets, until it was over.

It wasn't long after McCutcheon's death that my uncle began to do things that were first described by the barbershop sages as odd . . . then as queer . . . then as "damn peculiar." The things which finally caused him to be deemed, in the pungent barbershop argot, "as crazy as a shithouse rat" came in the fullness of time—but there seemed little doubt in anyone's mind that his peculiarities began right around the time George McCutcheon died.

In 1965, Uncle Otto had a small one-room house built across from the truck. There was a lot of talk about what old Otto Schenck might be up to out there on the Black Henry by Trinity Hill, but the surprise was total when Uncle Otto finished the little building off by having Chuckie Barger slap on a coat of bright red paint and then announcing it was a gift to the town—a fine new schoolhouse, he said, and all he asked was that they name it after his late partner.

Castle Rock's selectmen were flabbergasted. So was everyone else. Most everyone in the Rock had gone to such a one-room school (or thought they had, which comes down to almost the same thing). But all of the one-room schools were gone from Castle Rock by 1965. The very last of them, the Castle Ridge School, had closed the year before. It's now Steve's Pizzaville out on Route 117. By then the town had a glass-and-cinderblock grammar school on the far side of the common and a fine new high school on Carbine Street. As a result of his eccentric offer, Uncle Otto made it all the way from "odd" to "damn peculiar" in one jump.

The selectmen sent him a letter (not one of them quite dared to go see him in person) thanking him kindly, and hoping he would remember the town in the future, but declining the little schoolhouse on the grounds that the educational needs of the town's children were already well provided for. Uncle Otto flew into a towering rage. Remember the town in the future? he stormed to my father. He would remember them, all right, but not the way they wanted. *He* hadn't fallen off a hay truck yesterday. *He* knew a hawk from a handsaw. And if they wanted to get into a pissing contest with him, he said, they were going to find he could piss like a polecat that had just drunk a keg of beer.

"So what now?" my father asked him. They were sitting at the kitchen table in our house. My mother had taken her sewing upstairs. She said she didn't like Uncle Otto; she said he smelled like a man who took a bath once a month, whether he needed one or not—"and him a rich man," she would always add with a sniff. I think his smell really did offend her but I also think she was frightened of him. By 1965, Uncle Otto had begun to *look* damn peculiar as well as act that way. He went around dressed in green workman's pants held up by suspenders, a thermal underwear shirt, and big yellow workshoes. His eyes had begun to roll in strange directions as he spoke.

"Huh?"

"What are you going to do with the place now?"

"Live in the son of a bitch," Uncle Otto snapped, and that's what he did.

The story of his later years doesn't need much telling. He suffered the dreary sort of madness that one often sees written up in cheap tabloid newspapers. *Millionaire Dies of Malnutrition in Tenement Apartment. Bag Lady Was Rich, Bank Records Reveal. Forgotten Bank Tycoon Dies in Seclusion.*

He moved into the little red house—in later years it faded to a dull, washed-out pink—the very next week. Nothing my father said could talk him out of it. A year afterward, he sold the business I believe he had murdered to keep. His eccentricities had multiplied, but his business sense had not deserted him, and he realized a handsome profit—*staggering* might actually be a better word.

So there was my Uncle Otto, worth perhaps as much as seven millions of dollars, living in that tiny little house on the Black Henry Road. His town house was locked up and shuttered. He had by then progressed beyond "damned peculiar" to "crazy as a shithouse rat." The next progression is expressed in a flatter, less colorful, but more ominous phrase: "dangerous, maybe." That one is often followed by committal.

In his own way, Uncle Otto became as much a fixture as the truck across the road, although I doubt if any tourists ever wanted to take *his* picture. He had grown a beard, which came more yellow than white, as if infected by the nicotine of his cigarettes. He had gotten very fat. His jowls sagged down into wrinkly dewlaps creased with dirt. Folks often saw him standing in the doorway of his peculiar little house, just standing there motionlessly, looking out at the road, and across it.

Looking at the truck—*his* truck.

When Uncle Otto stopped coming to town, it was my father who made sure that he didn't starve to death. He brought him groceries every week, and paid for them out of his own pocket, because Uncle Otto never paid him back—never thought of it, I suppose. Dad died two years before Uncle Otto, whose money ended up going to the University of Maine Forestry Department. I understand they were delighted. Considering the amount, they should have been.

After I got my driver's license in 1972, I often took the weekly groceries out. At first Uncle Otto regarded me with narrow suspicion, but after a while he began to thaw. It was three years later, in 1975, when he told me for the first time that the truck was creeping toward the house.

I was attending the University of Maine myself by then, but I was home for the summer and had fallen into my old habit of taking Uncle Otto his weekly groceries. He sat at his table, smoking, watching me put the canned goods away and listening to me chatter. I thought he might have forgotten who I was; sometimes he did that . . . or pretended to. And once he had turned my blood cold by calling "That you, George?" out the window as I walked up to the house.

On that particular day in July of 1975, he broke into

whatever trivial conversation I was making to ask with harsh abruptness: "What do you make of yonder truck, Quentin?"

That abruptness startled an honest answer out of me: "I wet my pants in the cab of that truck when I was five," I said. "I think if I got up in it now I'd wet them again."

Uncle Otto laughed long and loud. I turned and gazed at him with wonder. I could not remember ever hearing him laugh before. It ended in a long coughing fit that turned his cheeks a bright red. Then he looked at me, his eyes glittering.

"Gettin closer, Quent," he said.

"What, Uncle Otto?" I asked. I thought he had made one of his puzzling leaps from one subject to another—maybe he meant Christmas was getting closer, or the Millennium, or the return of Christ the King.

"That buggardly truck," he said, looking at me in a still, narrow, confidential way that I didn't much like. "Gettin closer every year."

"It is?" I asked cautiously, thinking that here was a new and particularly unpleasant idea. I glanced out at the Cresswell, standing across the road with hay all around it and the White Mountains behind it . . . and for one crazy minute it actually *did* seem closer. Then I blinked and the illusion went away. The truck was right where it had always been, of course.

"Oh, ayuh," he said. "Gets a little closer every year."

"Gee, maybe you need glasses. I can't see any difference at all, Uncle Otto."

" 'Course you can't!" he snapped. "Can't see the hour hand move on your wristwatch, either, can you? Buggardly thing moves too slow to see . . . unless you watch it all the time. Just the way I watch that truck." He winked at me, and I shivered.

"Why would it move?" I asked.

"It wants me, that's why," he said. "Got me in mind all the while, that truck does. One day it'll bust right in here, and that'll be the end. It'll run me down just like it did Mac, and that'll be the end."

This scared me quite badly—his reasonable tone was what scared me the most, I think. And the way the young commonly respond to fright is to crack wise or become flippant. "Ought to move back to your house in town if it bothers you, Uncle Otto," I said, and you never would have known from my tone that my back was ridged with gooseflesh.

He looked at me . . . and then at the truck across the road. "Can't, Quentin," he said. "Sometimes a man just has to stay in one place and wait for it to come to him."

"Wait for what, Uncle Otto?" I asked, although I thought he must mean the truck.

"Fate," he said, and winked again . . . but he looked frightened.

My father fell ill in 1979 with the kidney disease which seemed to be improving just days before it finally killed him. Over a number of hospital visits in the fall of that year, my father and I talked about Uncle Otto. My dad had some suspicions about what might really have happened in 1955— mild ones that became the foundation of my more serious ones. My father had no idea how serious or how deep Uncle Otto's obsession with the truck had become. I did. He stood in his doorway almost all day long, looking at it. Looking at it like a man watching his watch to see the hour hand move.

By 1981 Uncle Otto had lost his few remaining marbles. A poorer man would have been put away years before, but millions in the bank can forgive a lot of craziness in a small town—particularly if enough people think there might be something in the crazy fellow's will for the municipality. Even so, by 1981 people had begun talking seriously about having Uncle Otto put away for his own good. That flat, deadly phrase, "dangerous, maybe," had begun to supersede "crazy as a shithouse rat." He had taken to wandering out to urinate by the side of the road instead of walking back into the woods where his privy was. Sometimes he shook his fist at the Cresswell while he relieved himself, and more than one person passing in his or her car thought Uncle Otto was shaking his fist at *them*.

The truck with the scenic White Mountains in the background was one thing; Uncle Otto pissing by the side of the road with his suspenders hanging down by his knees was something else entirely. *That* was no tourist attraction.

I was by then wearing a business suit more often than the blue jeans that had seen me through college when I took Uncle Otto his weekly groceries—but I still took them. I also tried to persuade him that he had to stop doing his duty by the side of the road, at least in the summertime, when anyone from Michigan, Missouri, or Florida who just happened to be happening by could see him.

I never got through to him. He couldn't be concerned with such minor things when he had the truck to worry about. His concern with the Cresswell had become a mania. He now claimed it was on his side of the road—right in his yard, as a matter of fact.

"I woke up last night around three and there it was, right outside the window, Quentin," he said. "I seen it there, moonlight shinin off the windshield, not six feet from where I was layin, and my heart almost stopped. It almost *stopped*, Quentin."

I took him outside and pointed out that the Cresswell was right where it had always been, across the road in the field where McCutcheon had planned to build. It did no good.

"That's just what you *see*, boy," he said with a wild and infinite contempt, a cigarette shaking in one hand, his eyeballs rolling. "That's just what you *see*."

"Uncle Otto," I said, attempting a witticism, "what you see is what you get."

It was as if he hadn't heard.

"Bugger almost got me," he whispered. I felt a chill. He didn't *look* crazy. Miserable, yes, and terrified, certainly . . . but not crazy. For a moment I remembered my father boosting me into the cab of that truck. I remembered smelling oil and leather . . . and blood. "It almost got me," he repeated.

And three weeks later, it did.

I was the one who found him. It was Wednesday night, and I had gone out with two bags of groceries in the back seat, as I did almost every Wednesday night. It was a hot, muggy evening. Every now and then thunder rumbled distantly. I remember feeling nervous as I rolled up the Black Henry Road in my Pontiac, somehow sure something was going to happen, but trying to convince myself it was just low barometric pressure.

I came around the last corner, and just as my uncle's little house came into view, I had the oddest hallucination—for a moment I thought that damned truck really *was* in his dooryard, big and hulking with its red paint and its rotten stake sides. I went for the brake pedal, but before my foot ever came down on it I blinked and the illusion was gone. But I knew that Uncle Otto was dead. No trumpets, no flashing lights; just that simple knowledge, like knowing where the furniture is in a familiar room.

I pulled into his dooryard in a hurry and got out, heading for the house without bothering to get the groceries.

The door was open—he never locked it. I asked him about that once and he explained to me, patiently, the way you would explain a patently obvious fact to a simpleton, that locking the door would not keep the Cresswell out.

He was lying on his bed, which was to the left of the one room—his kitchen area being to the right. He lay there in his green pants and his thermal underwear shirt, his eyes open and glassy. I don't believe he had been dead more than two hours. There were no flies and no smell, although it had been a brutally hot day.

"Uncle Otto?" I spoke quietly, not expecting an answer—you don't lie on your bed with your eyes open and bugging out like that just for the hell of it. If I felt anything, it was relief. It was over.

"Uncle Otto?" I approached him. "Uncle—"

I stopped, seeing for the first time how strangely misshapen his lower face looked—how swelled and twisted. Seeing for the first time how his eyes were not just staring but actually *glaring* from their sockets. But they were not looking toward the doorway or at the ceiling. They were twisted toward the little window above his bed.

I woke up last night around three and there it was, right outside my window, Quentin. It almost got me.

Squot him like a pumpkin, I heard one of the barbershop sages saying as I sat pretending to read a *Life* magazine and smelling the aromas of Vitalis and Wildroot Creme Oil.

Almost got me, Quentin.

There was a smell in here—not barbershop, and not just the stink of a dirty old man.

It smelled oily, like a garage.

"Uncle Otto?" I whispered, and as I walked toward the bed where he lay I seemed to feel myself shrinking, not just in size but in years . . . becoming twenty again, fifteen, ten, eight, six . . . and finally five. I saw my trembling small hand stretch out toward his swelled face. As my hand touched him, cupping his face, I looked up, and the window was filled with the glaring windshield of the Cresswell—and although it was only for a moment, I would swear on a Bible *that* was no hallucination. The Cresswell was there, in the window, less than six feet from me.

I had placed my fingers on one of Uncle Otto's cheeks, my thumb on the other, wanting to investigate that strange swelling, I suppose. When I first saw the truck in the window, my hand tried to tighten into a fist, forgetting that it was cupped loosely around the corpse's lower face.

In that instant the truck disappeared from the window like smoke—or like the ghost I suppose it was. In the same instant I heard an awful *squirting* noise. Hot liquid filled my hand. I looked down, feeling not just yielding flesh and wetness but something hard and angled. I looked down, and saw, and that was when I began to scream. Oil was pouring out of Uncle Otto's mouth and nose. Oil was leaking from the corners of his eyes like tears. Diamond Gem Oil—the recycled stuff you can buy in a five-gallon plastic container, the stuff McCutcheon had always run in the Cresswell.

But it wasn't *just* oil; there was something sticking out of his mouth.

I kept screaming but for a while I was unable to move, unable to take my oily hand from his face, unable to take my eyes from that big greasy thing sticking out of his mouth—the thing that had so distorted the shape of his face.

At last my paralysis broke and I fled from the house, still screaming. I ran across the dooryard to my Pontiac, flung myself in, and screamed out of there. The groceries meant for Uncle Otto tumbled off the back seat and onto the floor. The eggs broke.

It was something of a wonder that I didn't kill myself in the first two miles—I looked down at the speedometer and saw I was doing better than seventy. I pulled over and took deep breaths until I had myself under some kind of control. I began to realize that I simply could not leave Uncle Otto as I had found him; it would raise too many questions. I would have to go back.

And, I must admit, a certain hellish curiosity had come over me. I wish now that it hadn't, or that I had withstood it; in fact, I wish now I had let them go ahead and ask their questions. But I *did* go back. I stood outside his door for some five minutes—I stood in about the same place and in much the same position where he had stood so often and so long, looking at that truck. I stood there and came to this conclusion: the truck across the road had shifted position, ever so slightly.

Then I went inside.

The first few flies were circling and buzzing around his face. I could see oily prints on his cheeks: thumb on his left, three fingers on his right. I looked nervously at the window where I had seen the Cresswell looming . . . and then I walked over to his bed. I took out my handkerchief and wiped my fingerprints away. Then I reached forward and opened Uncle Otto's mouth.

What fell out was a Champion spark plug—one of the old Maxi-Duty kind, nearly as big as a circus strongman's fist.

I took it with me. Now I wish I hadn't done that, but of course I was in shock. It would all have been more merciful if I didn't have the actual object here in my study where I can look at it, or pick it up and heft it if I should want to—the 1920's-vintage spark plug that fell out of Uncle Otto's mouth.

If it wasn't there, if I hadn't taken it away from his little one-room house when I fled from it the second time, I could perhaps begin the business of persuading myself that all of it—not just coming around the turn and seeing the Cresswell pressed against the side of the little house like a huge red hound, but *all* of it—was only an hallucination. But it is there; it catches the light. It is real. It has weight. *The truck is getting closer every year,* he said, and it seems now that he was right . . . but even Uncle Otto had no idea how close the Cresswell could get.

The town verdict was that Uncle Otto had killed himself by swallowing oil, and it was a nine days' wonder in Castle Rock. Carl Durkin, the town undertaker and not the most closemouthed of men, said that when the docs opened him up to do the autopsy, they found more than three quarts of oil in him . . . and not just in his stomach, either. It had suffused his whole system. What everyone in town wanted to know was: what had he done with the plastic jug? For none was ever found.

As I said, most of you reading this memoir won't believe it . . . at least, not unless something like it has happened to you. But the truck is still out there in its field . . . and for whatever it is worth, it all *happened.*

Morning Deliveries (Milkman #1)

The dawn washed slowly down Culver Street.

To anyone awake inside, the night was still black, but dawn had actually been tiptoeing around for almost half an hour. In the big maple on the corner of Culver and Balfour Avenue, a red squirrel blinked and turned its insomniac's stare on the sleeping houses. Halfway down the block a sparrow alighted in the Mackenzies' birdbath and fluttered pearly drops about itself. An ant bumbled along the gutter and happened upon a tiny crumb of chocolate in a discarded candy wrapper.

The night breeze that had rustled leaves and billowed curtains now packed up. The maple on the corner gave a last rustly shiver and was still, waiting for the full overture that would follow this quiet prologue.

A band of faint light tinged the eastern sky. The darksome whippoorwill went off duty and the chickadees came to tentative life, still hesitant, as if afraid to greet the day on their own.

The squirrel disappeared into a puckered hole in the fork of the maple.

The sparrow fluttered to the lip of the birdbath and paused.

The ant also paused over his treasure like a librarian ruminating over a folio edition.

Culver Street trembled silently on the sunlit edge of the

444

planet—that moving straightedge astronomers call the terminator.

A sound grew quietly out of the silence, swelling unobtrusively until it seemed it had always been there, hidden under the greater noises of the night so lately passed. It grew, took on clarity, and became the decorously muffled motor of a milk truck.

It turned from Balfour onto Culver. It was a fine, beige-colored truck with red lettering on the sides. The squirrel popped out of the puckered mouth of its hole like a tongue, checked on the truck, and then spied a likely-looking bit of nest fodder. It hurried down the trunk headfirst after it. The sparrow took wing. The ant took what chocolate it could manage and headed for its hill.

The chickadees began to sing more loudly.

On the next block, a dog barked.

The letters on the sides of the milk truck read: CRAMER'S DAIRY. There was a picture of a bottle of milk, and below that: MORNING DELIVERIES OUR SPECIALTY!

The milkman wore a blue-gray uniform and a cocked hat. Written over the pocket in gold thread was a name: SPIKE. He was whistling over the comfortable rattle of bottles in ice behind him.

He pulled the truck in to the curb at the Mackenzies' house, took his milk case from the floor beside him, and swung out onto the sidewalk. He paused for a moment to sniff the air, fresh and new and infinitely mysterious, and then he strode strongly up the walk to the door.

A small square of white paper was held to the mailbox by a magnet that looked like a tomato. Spike read what was written there closely and slowly, as one might read a message he had found in an old bottle crusted with salt.

> 1 qt. milk
> 1 econ cream
> 1 ornge jce
> Thanks
>
> Nella M.

Spike the milkman looked at his hand case thoughtfully, set it down, and from it produced the milk and cream. He inspected the sheet again, lifted the tomato-magnet to make sure he had not missed a period, comma, or dash which would change the complexion of things, nodded, replaced the magnet, picked up his case, and went back to the truck.

The back of the milk truck was damp and black and cool. There was a sunken, buggy smell in its air. It mixed uneasily with the smell of dairy products. The orange juice was behind the deadly nightshade. He pulled a carton out of the ice, nodded again, and went back up the walk. He put the carton of juice down with the milk and cream and went back to his truck.

Not too far away, the five-o'clock whistle blew at the industrial laundry where Spike's old friend Rocky worked. He thought of Rocky starting up his laundry wheels in the steamy, gasping heat, and smiled. Perhaps he would see Rocky later. Perhaps tonight . . . when deliveries were done.

Spike started the truck and drove on. A little transistor radio hung on an imitation leather strap from a bloodstained meathook which curved down from the cab's ceiling. He turned it on and quiet music counterpointed his engine as he drove up to the McCarthy house.

Mrs. McCarthy's note was where it always was, wedged into the letter slot. It was brief and to the point:

Chocolate

Spike took out his pen, scrawled *Delivery Made* across it, and pushed it through the letter slot. Then he went back to the truck. The chocolate milk was stacked in two coolers at the very back, handy to the rear doors, because it was a very big seller in June. The milkman glanced at the coolers, then reached over them and took one of the empty chocolate milk cartons he kept in the far corner. The carton was of course brown, and a happy youngster cavorted above printed matter which informed the consumer that this was CRAMER'S DAIRY DRINK   WHOLESOME AND DELICIOUS   SERVE HOT OR COLD KIDS LOVE IT!

He set the empty carton on top of a case of milk. Then he brushed aside ice-chips until he could see the mayonnaise jar. He grabbed it and looked inside. The tarantula moved, but sluggishly. The cold had doped it. Spike unscrewed the lid of the jar and tipped it over the opened carton. The tarantula made a feeble effort to scramble back up the slick glass side of the jar, and succeeded not at all. It fell into the empty chocolate milk carton with a fat plop. The milkman carefully reclosed the carton, put it in his carrier, and dashed up the McCarthys' walk. Spiders were his favorite, and spiders were his *best*, even if he did say so himself. A day when he could deliver a spider was a happy day for Spike.

As he made his way slowly up Culver, the symphony of the dawn continued. The pearly band in the east gave way to a deepening flush of pink, first barely discernible, then rapidly brightening to a scarlet which began almost immediately to fade toward summer blue. The first rays of sunlight, pretty as a drawing in a child's Sunday-school workbook, now waited in the wings.

At the Webbers' house Spike left a bottle of all-purpose cream filled with an acid gel. At the Jenners' he left five quarts of milk. Growing boys there. He had never seen them, but there was a treehouse out back, and sometimes there were bikes and ball bats left in the yard. At the Collinses' two quarts of milk and a carton of yogurt. At Miss Ordway's a carton of eggnog that had been spiked with belladonna.

Down the block a door slammed. Mr. Webber, who had to go all the way into the city, opened the slatted carport door and went inside, swinging his briefcase. The milkman waited for the waspy sound of his little Saab starting up and smiled when he heard it. *Variety is the spice of life*, Spike's mother— God rest her soul!—had been fond of saying, *but we are Irish, and the Irish prefer to take their 'taters plain. Be regular in all ways, Spike, and you will be happy.* And it was just as true as could be, he had found as he rolled down the road of life in his neat beige milk truck.

Only three houses left now.

At the Kincaids' he found a note which read "Nothing today, thanks" and left a capped milk bottle which *looked* empty but contained a deadly cyanide gas. At the Walkers' he left two quarts of milk and a pint of whipping cream.

By the time he reached the Mertons' at the end of the block, rays of sunlight were shining through the trees and dappling the faded hopscotch grid on the sidewalk which passed the Mertons' yard.

Spike bent, picked up what looked like a pretty damned good hopscotching rock—flat on one side—and tossed it. The pebble landed on a line. He shook his head, grinned, and went up the walk, whistling.

The light breeze brought him the smell of industrial laundry soap, making him think again of Rocky. He was surer all the time that he would be seeing Rocky. Tonight.

Here the note was pinned in the Mertons' newspaper holder:

Cancel

Spike opened the door and went in.

The house was crypt-cold and without furniture. Barren it was, stripped to the walls. Even the stove in the kitchen was gone; there was a brighter square of linoleum where it had stood.

In the living room, every scrap of wallpaper had been removed from the walls. The globe was gone from the overhead light. The bulb had been fused black. A huge splotch of drying blood covered part of one wall. It looked like a psychiatrist's inkblot. In the center of it a crater had been gouged deeply into the plaster. There was a matted clump of hair in this crater, and a few splinters of bone.

The milkman nodded, went back out, and stood on the porch for a moment. It would be a fine day. The sky was already bluer than a baby's eye, and patched with guileless little fair-weather clouds . . . the ones baseball players call "angels."

He pulled the note from the newspaper holder and crumpled it into a ball. He put it in the left front pocket of his white milkman's pants.

He went back to his truck, kicking the stone from the hopscotch grid into the gutter. The milk truck rattled around the corner and was gone.

The day brightened.

A boy banged out of a house, grinned up at the sky, and brought in the milk.

Big Wheels: A Tale of The Laundry Game (Milkman #2)

Rocky and Leo, both drunk as the last lords of creation, cruised slowly down Culver Street and then out along Balfour Avenue toward Crescent. They were ensconced in Rocky's 1957 Chrysler. Between them, balanced with drunken care on the monstrous hump of the Chrysler's driveshaft, sat a case of Iron City beer. It was their second case of the evening—the evening had actually begun at four in the afternoon, which was punch-out time at the laundry.

"Shit on a shingle!" Rocky said, stopping at the red blinker-light above the intersection of Balfour Avenue and Highway 99. He did not look for traffic in either direction, but did cast a sly glance behind them. A half-full can of I.C., emblazoned with a colorful picture of Terry Bradshaw, rested against his crotch. He took a swig and then turned left on 99. The universal joint made a thick grunting sound as they started chuggingly off in second gear. The Chrysler had lost its first gear some two months ago.

"Gimme a shingle and I'll shit on it," Leo said obligingly.

"What time is it?"

Leo held up his watch until it was almost touching the tip of his cigarette and then puffed madly until he could get a reading. "Almost eight."

"Shit on a shingle!" They passed a sign which read PITTSBURGH 44.

449

"Nobody is going to inspect this here Detroit honey," Leo said. "Nobody in his right mind, at least."

Rocky fetched third gear. The universal moaned to itself, and the Chrysler began to have the automotive equivalent of a *petit mal* epileptic seizure. The spasm eventually passed, and the speedometer climbed tiredly to forty. It hung there precariously.

When they reached the intersection of Highway 99 and Devon Stream Road (Devon Stream formed the border between the townships of Crescent and Devon for some eight miles), Rocky turned onto the latter almost upon a whim—although perhaps even then some memory of ole Stiff Socks had begun to stir deep down in what passed for Rocky's subconscious.

He and Leo had been driving more or less at random since leaving work. It was the last day of June, and the inspection sticker on Rocky's Chrysler would become invalid at exactly 12:01 A.M. tomorrow. Four hours from right now. *Less* than four hours from right now. Rocky found this eventuality almost too painful to contemplate, and Leo didn't care. It was not his car. Also, he had drunk enough Iron City beer to reach a state of deep cerebral paralysis.

Devon Road wound through the only heavily wooded area of Crescent. Great bunches of elms and oaks crowded in on both sides, lush and alive and full of moving shadows as night began to close over southwestern Pennsylvania. The area was known, in fact, as The Devon Woods. It had attained capital-letter status after the torture-murder of a young girl and her boyfriend in 1968. The couple had been parking out here and were found in the boyfriend's 1959 Mercury. The Merc had real leather seats and a large chrome hood ornament. The occupants had been found in the back seat. Also in the front seat, the trunk, and the glove compartment. The killer had never been found.

"Jughumper better not stall out here," Rocky said. "We're ninety miles from noplace."

"Bunk." This interesting word had risen lately to the top forty of Leo's vocabulary. "There's town, right over there."

Rocky sighed and sipped from his can of beer. The glow was not really town, but the kid was close enough to make argument worthless. It was the new shopping center. Those high-intensity arc sodium lights really threw a glare. While looking in that direction, Rocky drove the car over to the left side of the road, looped back, almost went into the right-hand ditch, and finally got back in his lane again.

"Whoops," he said.

Leo burped and gurgled.

They had been working together at the New Adams Laundry since September, when Leo had been hired as Rocky's washroom helper. Leo was a rodent-featured young man of twenty-two who looked as if he might have quite a lot of jail-time in his future. He claimed he was saving twenty dollars a week from his pay to buy a used Kawasaki motorcycle. He said he was going west on this bike when cold weather came. Leo had held a grand total of twelve jobs since he and the world of academics had parted company at the minimum age of sixteen. He liked the laundry fine. Rocky was teaching him the various wash cycles, and Leo believed he was finally Learning a Skill which would come in handy when he reached Flagstaff.

Rocky, an older hand, had been at New Adams for fourteen years. His hands, ghostlike and bleached as he handled the steering wheel, proved it. He had done a four-month bit for carrying a concealed weapon in 1970. His wife, then puffily pregnant with their third child, announced 1) that it was not his, Rocky's, child but the milkman's child; and 2) that she wanted a divorce, on grounds of mental cruelty.

Two things about this situation had driven Rocky to carry a concealed weapon: 1) he had been cuckolded; and 2) he had been cuckolded by the fa chrissakes *milkman,* a trout-eyed long-haired piece of work named Spike Milligan. Spike drove for Cramer's Dairy.

The milkman, for God's sweet sake! The *milkman,* and could you die? Could you just fucking flop down into the gutter and *die?* Even to Rocky, who had never progressed much beyond reading the Fleer's Funnies that came wrapped around the bubble gum he chewed indefatigably at work, the situation had sonorous classical overtones.

As a result, he had duly informed his wife of two facts: 1) no divorce; and 2) he was going to let a large amount of daylight into Spike Milligan. He had purchased a .32-caliber pistol some ten years ago, which he used occasionally to shoot at bottles, tin cans, and small dogs. He left his house on Oak Street that morning and headed for the dairy, hoping to catch Spike when he finished his morning deliveries.

Rocky stopped at the Four Corners Tavern on the way to have a few beers—six, eight, maybe twenty. It was hard to remember. While he was drinking, his wife called the cops. They were waiting for him on the corner of Oak and Balfour. Rocky was searched, and one of the cops plucked the .32 from his waistband.

"I think you are going away for a while, my friend," the cop who found the gun told him, and that was just what Rocky did. He spent the next four months washing sheets and pillowcases for the State of Pennsylvania. During this period his wife got a Nevada divorce, and when Rocky got out of the slam she was living with Spike Milligan in a Dakin Street apartment house with a pink flamingo on the front lawn. In addition to his two older children (Rocky still more or less assumed they were his), the couple were now possessed of an infant who was every bit as trout-eyed as his daddy. They were also possessed of fifteen dollars a week in alimony.

"Rocky, I think I'm gettin carsick," Leo said. "Couldn't we just pull over and drink?"

"I gotta get a sticker on my wheels," Rocky said. "This is important. A man's no good without his wheels."

"Nobody in his right mind is gonna inspect this—I told you that. It ain't got no turn signals."

"They blink if I step on the brake at the same time, and anybody who don't step on his brakes when he's makin a turn is lookin to do a rollover."

"Window on this side's cracked."

"I'll roll it down."

"What if the inspectionist asks you to roll it up so he can check it?"

"I'll burn that bridge when I come to it," Rocky said coolly. He tossed his beer can out and got a refill. This new one had Franco Harris on it. Apparently the Iron City company was playing the Steelers' Greatest Hits this summer. He popped the top. Beer splurted.

"Wish I had a woman," Leo said, looking into the dark. He smiled strangely.

"If you had a woman, you'd never get out west. What a woman does is keep a man from getting any further west. That's how they operate. That is their mission. Dint you tell me you wanted to go out west?"

"Yeah, and I'm going, too."

"You'll *never* go," Rocky said. "Pretty soon you'll have a woman. Next you'll have abalone. *Alimony*. You know. Women always lead up to alimony. Cars are better. Stick to cars."

"Pretty hard to screw a car."

"You'd be surprised," Rocky said, and giggled.

The woods had begun to straggle away into new dwellings. Lights twinkled up on the left and Rocky suddenly slammed on the brakes. The brake lights and turn signals both went on at once; it was a home wiring job. Leo lurched forward, spilling beer on the seat. "What? What?"

"Look," Rocky said. "I think I know that fella."

There was a tumorous, ramshackle garage and Citgo filling station on the left side of the road. The sign in front said:

BOB'S GAS & SERVICE
BOB DRISCOLL, PROP.
FRONT END ALIGNMENT OUR SPECIALTY
DEFEND YOUR GOD-GIVEN RIGHT TO BEAR ARMS!

And, at the very bottom:

STATE INSPECTION STATION #72

"Nobody in his right mind—" Leo began again.

"It's Bobby Driscoll!" Rocky cried. "Me an Bobby Driscoll went to school together! We got it knocked! Bet your fur!"

He pulled in unevenly, headlights illuminating the open door of the garage bay. He popped the clutch and roared toward it. A stoop-shouldered man in a green coverall ran out, making frantic stopping gestures.

"Thass Bob!" Rocky yelled exultantly. *"Heyyy, Stiff Socks!"*

They ran into the side of the garage. The Chrysler had another seizure, *grand mal* this time. A small yellow flame appeared at the end of the sagging tailpipe, followed by a puff of blue smoke. The car stalled gratefully. Leo lurched forward, spilling more beer. Rocky keyed the engine and backed off for another try.

Bob Driscoll ran over, profanity spilling out of his mouth in colorful streamers. He was waving his arms. *"—the hell you think you're doing, you goddam sonofa—"*

"Bobby!" Rocky yelled, his delight nearly orgasmic. "Hey Stiff Socks! Whatchoo say, buddy?"

Bob peered in through Rocky's window. He had a twisted, tired face that was mostly hidden in the shadow thrown by the bill of his cap. "Who called me Stiff Socks?"

"Me!" Rocky fairly screamed. "It's *me*, you ole finger-diddler! It's your old buddy!"

"Who in the hell—"

"Johnny Rockwell! You gone blind as well as foolish?"

Cautiously: "Rocky?"

"Yeah, you sombitch!"

"Christ Jesus." Slow, unwilling pleasure seeped across Bob's face. "I ain't seen you since . . . well . . . since the Catamounts game, anyway—"

"Shoosh! Wa'n't that some hot ticket?" Rocky slapped his thigh, sending up a gusher of Iron City. Leo burped.

"Sure it was. Only time we ever won our class. Even then we couldn't seem to win the championship. Say, you beat hell out of the side of my garage, Rocky. You—"

"Yeah, same ole Stiff Socks. Same old guy. You ain't changed even a hair." Rocky belatedly peeked as far under the visor of the baseball cap as he could see, hoping this was true. It appeared, however, that ole Stiff Socks had gone either partially or completely bald. "Jesus! Ain't it somethin, runnin into you like this! Did you finally marry Marcy Drew?"

"Hell, yeah. Back in '70. Where were you?"

"Jail, most probably. Lissen, muhfuh, can you inspect this baby?"

Caution again: "You mean your car?"

Rocky cackled. "No—my ole hogleg! *Sure*, my car! Canya?"

Bob opened his mouth to say no.

"This here's an old friend of mine. Leo Edwards. Leo, wantcha to meet the only basketball player from Crescent High who dint change his sweatsocks for four years."

"Pleesdameetcha," Leo said, doing his duty just as his mother had instructed on one of the occasions when that lady was sober.

Rocky cackled. "Want a beer, Stiffy?"

Bob opened his mouth to say no.

"Here's the little crab-catcher!" Rocky exclaimed. He popped the top. The beer, crazied up by the headlong run into the side of Bob Driscoll's garage, boiled over the top and down Rocky's wrist. Rocky shoved it into Bob's hand. Bob sipped quickly, to keep his own hand from being flooded.

"Rocky, we close at—"

"Just a second, just a second, lemme back up. I got somethin crazy here."

Rocky dragged the gearshift lever up into reverse, popped the clutch, skinned a gas pump, and then drove the Chrysler jerkily inside. He was out in a minute, shaking Bob's free hand like a politician. Bob looked dazed. Leo sat in the car, tipping a fresh beer. He was also farting. A lot of beer always made him fart.

"Hey!" Rocky said, staggering around a pile of rusty hubcaps. "You member Diana Rucklehouse?"

"Sure do," Bob said. An unwilling grin came to his mouth. "She was the one with the—" He cupped his hands in front of his chest.

Rocky howled. "Thass *her!* You *got* it, muhfuh! She still in town?"

"I think she moved to—"

"Figures," Rocky said. "The ones who don't stay always move. You can put a sticker on this pig, cantcha?"

"Well, my wife said she'd wait supper and we close at—"

"Jesus, it'd sure put a help on me if you could. I'd sure preciate it. I could do some personal laundry for your wife. Thass what I do. Wash. At New Adams."

"And I am learning," Leo said, and farted again.

"Wash her dainties, whatever you want. Whatchoo say, Bobby?"

"Well, I s'pose I could look her over."

"Sure," Rocky said, clapping Bob on the back and winking at Leo. "Same ole Stiff Socks. What a guy!"

"Yeah," Bob said, sighing. He pulled on his beer, his oily fingers mostly obscuring Mean Joe Green's face. "You beat hell out of your bumper, Rocky."

"Give it some class. Goddam car *needs* some class. But it's one big motherfuckin set of wheels, you know what I mean?"

"Yeah, I guess—"

"Hey! Wantcha to meet the guy I work with! Leo, this is the only basketball player from—"

"You introduced us already," Bob said with a soft, despairing smile.

"Howdy doody," Leo said. He fumbled for another can of Iron City. Silvery lines like railroad tracks glimpsed at high noon on a hot clear day were beginning to trace their way across his field of vision.

"—Crescent High who dint change his—"

"Want to show me your headlights, Rocky?" Bob asked.

"Sure. Great lights. Halogen or nitrogen or some fucking gen. They got class. Pop those little crab-catchers right the fuck on, Leo."

Leo turned on the windshield wipers.

"That's good," Bob said patiently. He took a big swallow of beer. "Now how about the lights?"

Leo popped on the headlights.

"High beam?"

Leo tapped for the dimmer switch with his left foot. He was pretty sure it was down there someplace, and finally he happened upon it. The high beams threw Rocky and Bob into sharp relief, like exhibits in a police lineup.

"Fucking nitrogen headlights, what'd I tell you?" Rocky cried, and then cackled. "Goddam, Bobby! Seein you is better than gettin a check in the mail!"

"How about the turn signals?" Bob asked.

Leo smiled vaguely at Bob and did nothing.

"Better let me do it," Rocky said. He bumped his head a good one as he got in behind the wheel. "The kid don't feel too good, I don't think." He cramped down on the brake at the same time he flicked up the turn-blinker.

"Okay," Bob said, "but does it work without the brake?"

"Does it say anyplace in the motor-vehicle-inspection manual that it *hasta?*" Rocky asked craftily.

Bob sighed. His wife was waiting dinner. His wife had large floppy breasts and blond hair that was black at the roots. His wife was partial to Donuts by the Dozen, a product sold at the local Giant Eagle store. When his wife came to the garage on Thursday nights for her bingo money her hair was usually done up in large green rollers under a green chiffon scarf. This made her head look like a futuristic AM/FM radio. Once, near three in the morning, he had wakened and looked at her slack paper face in the soulless graveyard glare of the streetlight outside their bedroom window. He had thought how easy it could be—just jackknife over on top of her, just drive a knee into her gut so she would lose her air and be unable to scream, just screw both hands around her neck. Then just put her in the tub and whack her into prime cuts and mail her away someplace to Robert Driscoll, c/o General Delivery. Any old place. Lima, Indiana. North Pole, New Hampshire. Intercourse, Pennsylvania. Kunkle, Iowa. Any old place. It could be done. God knew it had been done in the past.

"No," he told Rocky, "I guess it doesn't say anyplace in the regs that they have to work on their own. Exactly. In so many words." He upended the can and the rest of the beer gurgled down his throat. It was warm in the garage and he had had no supper. He could feel the beer rise immediately into his mind.

"Hey, Stiff Socks just came up empty!" Rocky said. "Hand up a brew, Leo."

"No, Rocky, I really . . ."

Leo, who was seeing none too well, finally happened on a can. "Want a wide receiver?" he asked, and passed the can to Rocky. Rocky handed it to Bob, whose demurrals petered out as he held the can's cold actuality in his hand. It bore the smiling face of Lynn Swann. He opened it. Leo farted homily to close the transaction.

All of them drank from football-player cans for a moment.

"Horn work?" Bob finally asked, breaking the silence apologetically.

"Sure." Rocky hit the ring with his elbow. It emitted a feeble squeak. "Battery's a little low, though."

They drank in silence.

"That goddam rat was as big as a cocker spaniel!" Leo exclaimed.

"Kid's carrying quite a load," Rocky explained.

Bob thought about it. "Yuh," he said.

This struck Rocky's funnybone and he cackled through a mouthful of beer. A little trickled out of his nose, and this made Bob laugh. It did Rocky good to hear him, because Bob had looked like one sad sack when they had rolled in.

They drank in silence awhile more.

"Diana Rucklehouse," Bob said meditatively.

Rocky sniggered.

Bob chuckled and held his hands out in front of his chest.

Rocky laughed and held his own out even further.

Bob guffawed. "You member that picture of Ursula Andress that Tinker Johnson pasted on ole lady Freemantle's bulletin board?"

Rocky howled. "And he drawed on those two big old jahoobies—"

"—and she just about had a heart-attack—"

"You two can laugh," Leo said morosely, and farted.

Bob blinked at him. "Huh?"

"Laugh," Leo said. "I said *you* two can *laugh*. Neither of you has got a *hole* in your back."

"Don't lissen to him," Rocky said (a trifle uneasily). "Kid's got a skinful."

"You got a hole in your back?" Bob asked Leo.

"The laundry," Leo said, smiling. "We got these big washers, see? Only we call 'em wheels. They're laundry wheels. That's *why* we call 'em wheels. I load 'em, I pull 'em, I load'em again. Put the shit in dirty, take the shit out clean. That's what I do, and I do it with class." He looked at Bob with insane confidence. "Got a hole in my back from doing it, though."

"Yeah?" Bob was looking at Leo with fascination. Rocky shifted uneasily.

"There's a hole in the *roof*," Leo said. "Right over the third wheel. They're round, see, so we call 'em wheels. When it rains, the water comes down. Drop drop drop. Each drop hits me—whap!—in the back. Now I got a hole there. Like this." He made a shallow curve with one hand. "Wanna see?"

"He don't want to see any such *deformity!*" Rocky shouted. "We're talkin about old times here and there ain't no effing hole in your back *anyway!*"

"I wanna see it," Bob said.

"They're round so we call it the laundry," Leo said.

Rocky smiled and clapped Leo on the shoulder. "No more of this talk or you could be walking home, my good little buddy. Now why don't you hand me up my namesake if there's one left?"

Leo peered down into the carton of beer, and after a while he handed up a can with Rocky Blier on it.

"Atta way to go!" Rocky said, cheerful again.

The entire case was gone an hour later, and Rocky sent Leo stumbling up the road to Pauline's Superette for more. Leo's eyes were ferret-red by this time, and his shirt had come untucked. He was trying with myopic concentration to get his

Camels out of his rolled-up shirt sleeve. Bob was in the bathroom, urinating and singing the school song.

"Doan wanna walk up there," Leo muttered.

"Yeah, but you're too fucking drunk to drive."

Leo walked in a drunken semicircle, still trying to coax his cigarettes out of his shirt sleeve. " 'Z dark. And cold."

"You wanna get a sticker on that car or not?" Rocky hissed at him. He had begun to see weird things at the edges of his vision. The most persistent was a huge bug wrapped in spider-silk in the far corner.

Leo looked at him with his scarlet eyes. "Ain't my car," he said with bogus cunning.

"And you'll never ride in it again, neither, if you don't go and get that beer," Rocky said. He glanced fearfully at the dead bug in the corner. "You just try me and see if I'm kidding."

"Okay," Leo whined. "Okay, you don't have to get pissy about it."

He walked off the road twice on his way up to the corner and once on the way back. When he finally achieved the warmth and light of the garage again, both of them were singing the school song. Bob had managed, by hook or by crook, to get the Chrysler up on the lift. He was wandering around underneath it, peering at the rusty exhaust system.

"There's some holes in your stray' pipe," he said.

"Ain no stray pipes under there," Rocky said. They both found this spit-sprayingly funny.

"Beer's here!" Leo announced, put the case down, sat on a wheel rim, and fell immediately into a half-doze. He had swallowed three himself on the way back to lighten the load.

Rocky handed Bob a beer and held one himself.

"Race? Just like ole times?"

"Sure," Bob said. He smiled tightly. In his mind's eye he could see himself in the cockpit of a low-to-the-ground, streamlined Formula One racer, one hand resting cockily on the wheel as he waited for the drop of the flag, the other touching his lucky piece—the hood ornament from a '59 Mercury. He had forgotten Rocky's straight pipe and his blowsy wife with her transistorized hair curlers.

They opened their beers and chugged them. It was a dead heat; both dropped their cans to the cracked concrete and raised their middle fingers at the same time. Their belches echoed off the walls like rifle shots.

"Just like ole times," Bob said, sounding forlorn. *"Nothing's* just like ole times, Rocky."

"I know it," Rocky agreed. He struggled for a deep, luminous thought and found it. "We're gettin older by the day, Stiffy."

Bob sighed and belched again. Leo farted in the corner and began to hum "Get Off My Cloud."

"Try again?" Rocky asked, handing Bob another beer.

"Mi' as well," Bob said; "mi' jus' as well, Rocky m'boy."

The case Leo had brought back was gone by midnight, and the new inspection was affixed on the left side of Rocky's windshield at a slightly crazy angle. Rocky had made out the pertinent information himself before slapping the sticker on, working carefully to copy over the numbers from the tattered and greasy registration he had finally found in the glove compartment. He *had* to work carefully, because he was seeing triple. Bob sat cross-legged on the floor like a yoga master, a half-empty can of I.C. in front of him. He was staring fixedly at nothing.

"Well, you sure saved my life, Bob," Rocky said. He kicked Leo in the ribs to wake him up. Leo grunted and whoofed. His lids flickered briefly, closed, then flew open wide when Rocky footed him again.

"We home yet, Rocky? We—"

"You just shake her easy, Bobby," Rocky cried cheerfully. He hooked his fingers into Leo's armpit and yanked. Leo came to his feet, screaming. Rocky half-carried him around the Chrysler and shoved him into the passenger seat. "We'll stop back and do her again sometime."

"Those were the days," Bob said. He had grown wet-eyed. "Since then everything just gets worse and worse, you know it?"

"I know it," Rocky said. "Everything has been refitted and beshitted. But you just keep your thumb on it, and don't do anything I wouldn't d—"

"My wife ain't laid me in a year and a half," Bob said, but the words were blanketed by the coughing misfire of Rocky's engine. Bob got to his feet and watched the Chrysler back out of the bay, taking a little wood from the left side of the door.

Leo hung out the window, smiling like an idiot saint. "Come by the laundry sometime, skinner. I'll show you the hole in my back. I'll show you my wheels! I'll show y—" Rocky's arm suddenly shot out like a vaudeville hook and pulled him into the dimness.

"Bye, fella!" Rocky yelled.

The Chrysler did a drunken slalom around the three gas-pump islands and bucketed off into the night. Bob watched until the taillights were only flickerflies and then walked carefully back inside the garage. On his cluttered workbench was a chrome ornament from some old car. He began to play with it, and soon he was crying cheap tears for the old days. Later, some time after three in the morning, he strangled his wife and then burned down the house to make it look like an accident.

"Jesus," Rocky said to Leo as Bob's garage shrank to a point of white light behind them. "How about that? Ole Stiffy." Rocky had reached that stage of drunkenness where every part of himself seemed gone except for a tiny, glowing coal of sobriety somewhere deep in the middle of his mind.

Leo did not reply. In the pale green light thrown by the dashboard instruments, he looked like the dormouse at Alice's tea party.

"He was really bombarded," Rocky went on. He drove on the left side of the road for a while and then the Chrysler wandered back. "Good thing for you—he prob'ly won't remember what you tole him. Another time it could be different. How many times do I have to tell you? You got to shut up about this idea that you got a fucking hole in your back."

"You *know* I got a hole in my back."

"Well, so what?"

"It's *my* hole, that's so what. And I'll talk about *my* hole whenever I—"

He looked around suddenly.

"Truck behind us. Just pulled out of that side road. No lights."

Rocky looked up into the rearview mirror. Yes, the truck was there, and its shape was distinctive. It was a milk truck. He didn't have to read CRAMER'S DAIRY on the side to know whose it was, either.

"It's Spike," Rocky said fearfully. "It's Spike Milligan! Jesus, I thought he only made *morning* deliveries!"

"Who?"

Rocky didn't answer. A tight, drunk grin spread over his lower face. It did not touch his eyes, which were now huge and red, like spirit lamps.

He suddenly floored the Chrysler, which belched blue oil smoke and reluctantly creaked its way up to sixty.

"Hey! You're too drunk to go this fast! You're . . ." Leo paused vaguely, seeming to lose track of his message. The trees and houses raced by them, vague blurs in the graveyard of twelve-fifteen. They blew by a stop sign and flew over a large bump, leaving the road for a moment afterwards. When they came down, the low-hung muffler struck a spark on the asphalt. In the back, cans clinked and rattled. The faces of Pittsburgh Steeler players rolled back and forth, sometimes in the light, sometimes in shadow.

"I was *fooling!*" Leo said wildly. "There ain't no truck!"

"It's him and he kills people!" Rocky screamed. "I seen his bug back in the garage! God *damn!*"

They roared up Southern Hill on the wrong side of the road. A station wagon coming in the other direction skidded crazily over the gravel shoulder and down into the ditch getting out of their way. Leo looked behind him. The road was empty.

"Rocky—"

"*Come and get me, Spike!*" Rocky screamed. "*You just come on and get me!*"

The Chrysler had reached eighty, a speed which Rocky in a more sober frame of mind would not have believed possible. They came around the turn which leads onto the Johnson Flat Road, smoke spurting up from Rocky's bald tires. The Chrysler screamed into the night like a ghost, lights searching the empty road ahead.

Suddenly a 1959 Mercury roared at them out of the dark, straddling the center line. Rocky screamed and threw his hands up in front of his face. Leo had just time to see the Mercury was missing its hood ornament before the crash came.

Half a mile behind, lights flickered on at a side crossing, and a milk truck with CRAMER'S DAIRY written on the side pulled out and began to move toward the pillar of flame and the twisted blackening hulks in the center of the road. It moved at a sedate speed. The transistor dangling by its strap from the meathook played rhythm and blues.

"That's it," Spike said. "Now we're going over to Bob Driscoll's house. He thinks he's got gasoline out in his garage, but I'm not sure he does. This has been one very long day, wouldn't you agree?" But when he turned around, the back of the truck was empty. Even the bug was gone.

Gramma

George's mother went to the door, hesitated there, came back, and tousled George's hair. "I don't want you to worry," she said. "You'll be all right. Gramma, too."

"Sure, I'll be okay. Tell Buddy to lay chilly."

"Pardon me?"

George smiled. "To stay cool."

"Oh. Very funny." She smiled back at him, a distracted, going-in-six-directions-at-once smile. "George, are you sure—"

"I'll be *fine.*"

Are you sure what? Are you sure you're not scared to be alone with Gramma? Was that what she was going to ask?

If it was, the answer is no. After all, it wasn't like he was six anymore, when they had first come here to Maine to take care of Gramma, and he had cried with terror whenever Gramma held out her heavy arms toward him from her white vinyl chair that always smelled of the poached eggs she ate and the sweet bland powder George's mom rubbed into her flabby, wrinkled skin; she held out her white-elephant arms, wanting him to come to her and be hugged to that huge and heavy old white-elephant body: Buddy had gone to her, had been enfolded in Gramma's blind embrace, and Buddy had come out alive . . . but Buddy was two years older.

Now Buddy had broken his leg and was at the CMG Hospital in Lewiston.

"You've got the doctor's number if something *should* go wrong. Which it won't. Right?"

"Sure," he said, and swallowed something dry in his throat. He smiled. Did the smile look okay? Sure. Sure it did. He wasn't scared of Gramma anymore. After all, he wasn't *six* anymore. Mom was going up to the hospital to see Buddy and he was just going to stay here and lay chilly. Hang out with Gramma awhile. No problem.

Mom went to the door again, hesitated again, and came back again, smiling that distracted, going-six-ways-at-once smile. "If she wakes up and calls for her tea—"

"I know," George said, seeing how scared and worried she was underneath that distracted smile. She was worried about Buddy, Buddy and his dumb *Pony League,* the coach had called and said Buddy had been hurt in a play at the plate, and the first George had known of it (he was just home from school and sitting at the table eating some cookies and having a glass of Nestlé's Quik) was when his mother gave a funny little gasp and said, *Hurt? Buddy? How bad?*

"I know *all* that stuff, Mom. I got it knocked. Negative perspiration. Go on, now."

"You're a good boy, George. Don't be scared. You're not scared of Gramma anymore, are you?"

"Huh-uh," George said. He smiled. The smile felt pretty good; the smile of a fellow who was laying chilly with negative perspiration on his brow, the smile of a fellow who Had It Knocked, the smile of a fellow who was most definitely not six anymore. He swallowed. It was a great smile, but beyond it, down in the darkness behind his smile, was one very dry throat. It felt as if his throat was lined with mitten-wool. "Tell Buddy I'm sorry he broke his leg."

"I will," she said, and went to the door again. Four-o'clock sunshine slanted in through the window. "Thank God we took the sports insurance, Georgie. I don't know what we'd do if we didn't have it."

"Tell him I hope he tagged the sucker out."

She smiled her distracted smile, a woman of just past fifty with two late sons, one thirteen, one eleven, and no man. This time she opened the door, and a cool whisper of October came in through the sheds.

"And remember, Dr. Arlinder—"

"Sure," he said. "You better go or his leg'll be fixed by the time you get there."

"She'll probably sleep the whole time," Mom said. "I love you, Georgie. You're a good son." She closed the door on that.

George went to the window and watched her hurry to the old '69 Dodge that burned too much gas and oil, digging the keys from her purse. Now that she was out of the house and didn't know George was looking at her, the distracted smile fell away and she only looked distracted—distracted and sick with worry about Buddy. George felt bad for her. He didn't waste any similar feelings on Buddy, who liked to get him down and sit on top of him with a knee on each of George's shoulders and tap a spoon in the middle of George's forehead until he just about went crazy (Buddy called it the Spoon Torture of the Heathen Chinee and laughed like a madman and sometimes went on doing it until George cried), Buddy who sometimes gave him the Indian Rope Burn so hard that little drops of blood would appear on George's forearm, sitting on top of the pores like dew on blades of grass at dawn, Buddy who had listened so sympathetically when George had one night whispered in the dark of their bedroom that he liked Heather MacArdle and who the next morning ran across the schoolyard screaming *GEORGE AND HEATHER UP IN A TREE, KAY-EYE-ESS-ESS-EYE-EN-GEE! FIRSE COMES LOVE AN THEN COMES MARRITCH! HERE COMES HEATHER WITH A BABY CARRITCH!* like a runaway fire engine. Broken legs did not keep older brothers like Buddy down for long, but George was rather looking forward to the quiet as long as this one did. *Let's see you give me the Spoon Torture of the Heathen Chinee with your leg in a cast, Buddy. Sure, kid—EVERY day.*

The Dodge backed out of the driveway and paused while his mother looked both ways, although nothing would be coming; nothing ever was. His mother would have a two-mile ride over washboards and ruts before she even got to tar, and it was nineteen miles to Lewiston after that.

She backed all the way out and drove away. For a moment dust hung in the bright October afternoon air, and then it began to settle.

He was alone in the house.

With Gramma.

He swallowed.

Hey! Negative perspiration! Just lay chilly, right?

"Right," George said in a low voice, and walked across the small, sunwashed kitchen. He was a towheaded, good-looking boy with a spray of freckles across his nose and cheeks and a look of good humor in his darkish gray eyes.

Buddy's accident had occurred while he had been playing in the Pony League championship game this October 5th. George's Pee Wee League team, the Tigers, had been knocked out of their tournament on the first day, two Saturdays ago *(What a bunch of babies!* Buddy had exulted as George walked tearfully off the field. *What a bunch of PUSSIES!)* . . . and now Buddy had broken his leg. If Mom wasn't so worried and scared, George would have been almost happy.

There was a phone on the wall, and next to it was a note-minder board with a grease pencil hanging beside it. In the upper corner of the board was a cheerful country Gramma, her cheeks rosy, her white hair done up in a bun; a cartoon Gramma who was pointing at the board. There was a comic-strip balloon coming out of the cheerful country Gramma's mouth and she was saying, "REMEMBER *THIS*, SONNY!" Written on the board in his mother's sprawling hand was *Dr. Arlinder, 681-4330*. Mom hadn't written the number there just today, because she had to go to Buddy; it had been there almost three weeks now, because Gramma was having her "bad spells" again.

George picked up the phone and listened.

"—so I told her, I said, 'Mabel, if he treats you like that—' "

He put it down again. Henrietta Dodd. Henrietta was always on the phone, and if it was in the afternoon you could always hear the soap opera stories going on in the background. One night after she had a glass of wine with Gramma (since she started having the "bad spells" again, Dr. Arlinder said Gramma couldn't have the wine with her supper, so Mom didn't either—George was sorry, because the wine made Mom sort of giggly and she would tell stories about her girlhood), Mom had said that every time Henrietta Dodd opened her mouth, all her guts fell out. Buddy and George laughed wildly, and Mom put a hand to her mouth and said *Don't you EVER tell anyone I said that,* and then *she* began to laugh too, all three of them sitting at the supper table laughing, and at last the racket had awakened Gramma, who slept more and more, and she began to cry *Ruth! Ruth! ROO-OOOTH!* in that high, querulous voice of hers, and Mom had stopped laughing and went into her room.

Today Henrietta Dodd could talk all she wanted, as far as George was concerned. He just wanted to make sure the phone was working. Two weeks ago there had been a bad storm, and since then it went out sometimes.

He found himself looking at the cheery cartoon Gramma again, and wondered what it would be like to have a Gramma like that. *His* Gramma was huge and fat and blind; the hypertension had made her senile as well. Sometimes, when she had her "bad spells," she would (as Mom put it) "act out the Tartar," calling for people who weren't there, holding conversations with total emptiness, mumbling strange words that made no sense. On one occasion when she was doing this last, Mom had turned white and had gone in and told her to shut up, shut up, *shut up!* George remembered that occasion very well, not only because it was the only time Mom had ever actually *yelled* at Gramma, but because it was the next day that someone discovered that the Birches cemetery out on the Maple Sugar Road had been vandalized—gravestones knocked over, the old nineteenth-century gates pulled down, and one or two of the graves actually dug up—or something. *Desecrated* was the word Mr. Burdon, the principal, had used the next day when he convened all eight grades for Assembly and lectured the whole school on Malicious Mischief and how some things Just Weren't Funny. Going home that night, George had asked Buddy what *desecrated* meant, and Buddy said it meant digging up graves and pissing on the coffins, but George didn't believe that . . . unless it was late. And dark.

Gramma was noisy when she had her "bad spells," but mostly she just lay in the bed she had taken to three years before, a fat slug wearing rubber pants and diapers under her flannel nightgown, her face runneled with cracks and wrinkles, her eyes empty and blind—faded blue irises floating atop yellowed corneas.

At first Gramma hadn't been totally blind. But she had been *going* blind, and she had to have a person at each elbow to help her totter from her white vinyl egg-and-baby-powder-smelling chair to her bed or the bathroom. In those days, five years ago, Gramma had weighed well over two hundred pounds.

She had held out her arms and Buddy, then eight, had gone to her. George had hung back. And cried.

But I'm not scared now, he told himself, moving across the kitchen in his Keds. *Not a bit. She's just an old lady who has "bad spells" sometimes.*

He filled the teakettle with water and put it on a cold burner. He got a teacup and put one of Gramma's special herb tea bags into it. In case she should wake up and want a cup. He hoped like mad that she wouldn't, because then he would have to crank up the hospital bed and sit next to her and give her the tea a sip at a time, watching the toothless mouth fold itself over the rim of the cup, and listen to the slurping sounds as she took the tea into her dank, dying guts. Sometimes she slipped sideways on the bed and you had to pull her back over and her flesh was *soft,* kind of *jiggly,* as if it was filled with hot water, and her blind eyes would look at you . . .

George licked his lips and walked toward the kitchen table again. His last cookie and half a glass of Quik still stood there, but he didn't want them anymore. He looked at his schoolbooks, covered with Castle Rock Cougars bookcovers, without enthusiasm.

He ought to go in and check on her.

He didn't want to.

He swallowed and his throat still felt as if it was lined with mittenwool.

I'm not afraid of Gramma, he thought. *If she held out her arms I'd go right to her and let her hug me because she's just an old lady. She's senile and that's why she has "bad spells." That's all. Let her hug me and not cry. Just like Buddy.*

He crossed the short entryway to Gramma's room, face set as if for bad medicine, lips pressed together so tightly they were white. He looked in, and there lay Gramma, her yellow-white hair spread around her in a corona, sleeping, her toothless mouth hung open, chest rising under the coverlet so slowly you almost couldn't see it, so slowly that you had to look at her for a while just to make sure she wasn't dead.

Oh God, what if she dies on me while Mom's up to the hospital?

She won't. She won't.

Yeah, but what if she does?

She won't, so stop being a pussy.

One of Gramma's yellow, melted-looking hands moved slowly on the coverlet: her long nails dragged across the sheet and made a minute scratching sound. George drew back quickly, his heart pounding.

Cool as a moose, numbhead, see? Laying chilly.

He went back into the kitchen to see if his mother had been gone only an hour, or perhaps an hour and a half—if the latter, he could start reasonably waiting for her to come back. He looked at the clock and was astounded to see that not even twenty minutes had passed. Mom wouldn't even be *into* the city yet, let alone on her way back out of it! He stood still, listening to the silence. Faintly, he could hear the hum of the refrigerator and the electric clock. The snuffle of the afternoon breeze around the corners of the little house. And then—at the very edge of audibility—the faint, rasping susurrus of skin over cloth . . . Gramma's wrinkled, tallowy hand moving on the coverlet.

He prayed in a single gust of mental breath:

PleaseGoddon'tletherwakeupuntilMomcomeshomeforJesus'-sakeAmen.

He sat down and finished his cookie, drank his Quik. He thought of turning on the TV and watching something, but he was afraid the sound would wake up Gramma and that high, querulous, not-to-be-denied voice would begin calling *Roo-OOTH! RUTH! BRING ME M'TEA! TEA! ROOO-OOOOOTH!*

He slicked his dry tongue over his drier lips and told himself not to be such a pussy. She was an old lady stuck in bed, it wasn't as if she could get up and hurt him, and she was eighty-three years old, she wasn't going to die this afternoon.

George walked over and picked up the phone again.

"—that same day! And she even *knew* he was married! Gorry, I hate these cheap little corner-walkers that think they're so smart! So at Grange I said—"

George guessed that Henrietta was on the phone with Cora Simard. Henrietta hung on the phone most afternoons from one until six with first *Ryan's Hope* and then *One Life to Live* and then *All My Children* and then *As the World Turns* and then *Search for Tomorrow* and then God knew what other ones playing in the background, and Cora Simard was one of her most faithful telephone correspondents, and a lot of what they talked about was 1) who was going to be having a Tupperware party or an Amway party and what the refreshments were apt to be, 2) cheap little corner-walkers, and 3) what they had said to various people at 3-a) the Grange, 3-b) the monthly church fair, or 3-c) K of P Hall Beano.

''—that if I ever saw her up that way again, I guess I could be a good citizen and call—''

He put the phone back in its cradle. He and Buddy made fun of Cora when they went past her house just like all the other kids—she was fat and sloppy and gossipy and they would chant, *Cora-Cora from Bora-Bora, ate a dog turd and wanted more-a!* and Mom would have killed them *both* if she had known that, but now George was glad she and Henrietta Dodd were on the phone. They could talk all afternoon, for all George cared. He didn't mind Cora, anyway. Once he had fallen down in front of her house and scraped his knee— Buddy had been chasing him—and Cora had put a Band-Aid on the scrape and gave them each a cookie, talking all the time. George had felt ashamed for all the times he had said the rhyme about the dog turd and the rest of it.

George crossed to the sideboard and took down his reading book. He held it for a moment, then put it back. He had read all the stories in it already, although school had only been going a month. He read better than Buddy, although Buddy was better at sports. *Won't be better for a while,* he thought with momentary good cheer, *not with a broken leg.*

He took down his history book, sat down at the kitchen table, and began to read about how Cornwallis had surrendered up his sword at Yorktown. His thoughts wouldn't stay on it. He got up, went through the entryway again. The yellow hand was still. Gramma slept, her face a gray, sagging circle against the pillow, a dying sun surrounded by the wild yellowish-white corona of her hair. To George she didn't look anything like people who were old and getting ready to die were supposed to look. She didn't look peaceful, like a sunset. She looked crazy, and . . .

(and dangerous)

. . . yes, okay, and *dangerous*—like an ancient she-bear that might have one more good swipe left in her claws.

George remembered well enough how they had come to Castle Rock to take care of Gramma when Granpa died. Until then Mom had been working in the Stratford Laundry in Stratford, Connecticut. Granpa was three or four years younger than Gramma, a carpenter by trade, and he had worked right up until the day of his death. It had been a heart attack.

Even then Gramma had been getting senile, having her "bad spells." She had always been a trial to her family, Gramma had. She was a volcanic woman who had taught school for fifteen years, between having babies and getting in fights with the Congregational Church she and Granpa and their nine children went to. Mom said that Granpa and Gramma quit the Congregational Church in Scarborough at the same time Gramma decided to quit teaching, but once, about a year ago, when Aunt Flo was up for a visit from her home in Salt Lake City, George and Buddy, listening at the register as Mom and her sister sat up late, talking, heard quite a different story. Granpa and Gramma had been kicked out of the church and Gramma had been fired off her job because she did something wrong. It was something about *books*. Why or how someone could get fired from their job and kicked out of the church just because of *books*, George didn't understand, and when he and Buddy crawled back into their twin beds under the eave, George asked.

There's all kinds of books, Señor El-Stupido, Buddy whispered.

Yeah, but what kind?

How should I know? Go to sleep!

Silence. George thought it through.

Buddy?

What! An irritated hiss.

Why did Mom tell us Gramma quit the church and her job?

Because it's a skeleton in the closet, that's why! Now go to sleep!

But he hadn't gone to sleep, not for a long time. His eyes kept straying to the closet door, dimly outlined in moonlight, and he kept wondering what he would do if the door swung open, revealing a skeleton inside, all grinning tombstone teeth and cistern eye sockets and parrot-cage ribs; white moonlight skating delirious and almost blue on whiter bone. Would he scream? What had Buddy meant, *a skeleton in the closet?* What did skeletons have to do with books? At last he had slipped into sleep without even knowing it and had dreamed he was six again, and Gramma was holding out her arms, her blind eyes searching for him; Gramma's reedy, querulous voice was saying, *Where's the little one, Ruth? Why's he crying? I only want to put him in the closet . . . with the skeleton.*

George had puzzled over these matters long and long, and finally, about a month after Aunt Flo had departed, he went to his mother and told her he had heard her and Aunt Flo talking. He knew what a skeleton in the closet meant by then, because he had asked Mrs. Redenbacher at school. She said it meant having a scandal in the family, and a scandal was something that made people talk a lot. *Like Cora Simard talks a lot?* George had asked Mrs. Redenbacher, and Mrs. Redenbacher's face had worked strangely and her lips had quivered and she had said, *That's not nice, George, but . . . yes, something like that.*

When he asked Mom, her face had gotten very still, and her hands had paused over the solitaire clockface of cards she had been laying out.

Do you think that's a good thing for you to be doing, Georgie? Do you and your brother make a habit of eavesdropping over the register?

George, then only nine, had hung his head.

We like Aunt Flo, Mom. We wanted to listen to her a little longer.

This was the truth.

Was it Buddy's idea?

It had been, but George wasn't going to tell her *that*. He didn't want to go walking around with his head on backwards, which might happen if Buddy found out he had tattled.

No, mine.

Mom had sat silent for a long time, and then she slowly began laying her cards out again. *Maybe it's time you did know,* she had said. *Lying's worse than eavesdropping, I guess, and we all lie to our children about Gramma. And we lie to ourselves too, I guess. Most of the time, we do.* And then she spoke with a sudden, vicious bitterness that was like acid squirting out between her front teeth—he felt that her words were so hot they would have burned his face if he hadn't recoiled. *Except for me. I have to live with her, and I can no longer afford the luxury of lies.*

So his Mom told him that after Granpa and Gramma had gotten married, they had had a baby that was born dead, and a year later they had another baby, and *that* was born dead too, and the doctor told Gramma she would never be able to carry a child to term and all she could do was keep on having babies that were dead or babies that died as soon as they sucked air. That would go on, he said, until one of them died inside her too long before her body could shove it out and it would rot in there and kill her, too.

The doctor told her that.

Not long after, the *books* began.

Books about how to have babies?

But Mom didn't—or wouldn't—say what kind of books they were, or where Gramma got them, or how she *knew* to get them. Gramma got pregnant again, and this time the baby wasn't born dead and the baby didn't die after a breath or two; this time the baby was fine, and that was George's Uncle Larson. And after that, Gramma kept getting pregnant and having babies. Once, Mom said, Granpa had tried to make her get rid of the books to see if they could do it without them (or even if they couldn't, maybe Granpa figured they had enough yowwens by then so it wouldn't matter) and Gramma wouldn't. George asked his mother why and she said: "I think that by then having the books was as important to her as having the babies."

"I don't get it," George said.

"Well," George's mother said, "I'm not sure I do, either . . . I was very small, remember. All I know for sure is that those books got a hold over her. She said there would be no more talk about it and there wasn't, either. Because Gramma wore the pants in our family."

George closed his history book with a snap. He looked at the clock and saw that it was nearly five o'clock. His stomach was grumbling softly. He realized suddenly, and with something very like horror, that if Mom wasn't home by six or so, Gramma would wake up and start hollering for her supper. Mom had forgotten to give him instructions about that, probably because she was so upset about Buddy's leg. He supposed he could make Gramma one of her special frozen dinners. They were special because Gramma was on a saltfree diet. She also had about a thousand different kinds of pills.

As for himself, he could heat up what was left of last

night's macaroni and cheese. ıf he poured a lot of catsup on it, it would be pretty good.

He got the macaroni and cheese out of the fridge, spooned it into a pan, and put the pan on the burner next to the teakettle, which was still waiting in case Gramma woke up and wanted what she sometimes called "a cuppa cheer." George started to get himself a glass of milk, paused, and picked up the telephone again.

"—and I couldn't even believe my eyes when . . . " Henrietta Dodd's voice broke off and then rose shrilly: "Who keeps listening in on this line, I'd like to know!"

George put the phone back on the hook in a hurry, his face burning.

She doesn't know it's you, stupe. There's six parties on the line!

All the same, it was wrong to eavesdrop, even if it was just to hear another voice when you were alone in the house, alone except for Gramma, the fat thing sleeping in the hospital bed in the other room; even when it seemed almost *necessary* to hear another human voice because your Mom was in Lewiston and it was going to be dark soon and Gramma was in the other room and Gramma looked like

(yes oh yes she did)

a she-bear that might have just one more murderous swipe left in her old clotted claws.

George went and got the milk.

Mom herself had been born in 1930, followed by Aunt Flo in 1932, and then Uncle Franklin in 1934. Uncle Franklin had died in 1948, of a burst appendix, and Mom sometimes still got teary about that, and carried his picture. She had liked Frank the best of all her brothers and sisters, and she said there was no need for him to die that way, of peritonitis. She said that God had played dirty when He took Frank.

George looked out the window over the sink. The light was more golden now, low over the hill. The shadow of their back shed stretched all the way across the lawn. If Buddy hadn't broken his dumb *leg,* Mom would be here now, making chili or something (plus Gramma's salt-free dinner), and they would all be talking and laughing and maybe they'd play some gin rummy later on.

George flicked on the kitchen light, even though it really wasn't dark enough for it yet. Then he turned on LO HEAT under his macaroni. His thoughts kept returning to Gramma, sitting in her white vinyl chair like a big fat worm in a dress, her corona of hair every crazy whichway on the shoulders of her pink rayon robe, holding out her arms for him to come, him shrinking back against his Mom, bawling.

Send him to me, Ruth. I want to hug him.

He's a little frightened, Momma. He'll come in time. But his mother sounded frightened, too.

Frightened? Mom?

George stopped, thinking. Was that true? Buddy said your memory could play tricks on you. Had she really sounded frightened?

Yes. She had.

Gramma's voice rising peremptorily: *Don't coddle the boy, Ruth! Send him over here; I want to give him a hug.*

No. He's crying.

And as Gramma lowered her heavy arms from which the flesh hung in great, doughlike gobbets, a sly, senile smile had overspread her face and she had said: *Does he really look like Franklin, Ruth? I remember you saying he favored Frank.*

Slowly, George stirred the macaroni and cheese and catsup. He hadn't remembered the incident so clearly before. Maybe it was the silence that had made him remember. The silence, and being alone with Gramma.

So Gramma had her babies and taught school, and the doctors were properly dumbfounded, and Granpa carpentered and generally got more and more prosperous, finding work even in the depths of the Depression, and at last people began to talk, Mom said.

What did they say? George asked.

Nothing important, Mom said, but she suddenly swept her cards together. *They said your Gramma and Granpa were too lucky for ordinary folks, that's all.* And it was just after that that the books had been found. Mom wouldn't say more than that, except that the school board had found some and that a hired man had found some more. There had been a big scandal. Granpa and Gramma had moved to Buxton and that was the end of it.

The children had grown up and had children of their own,

making aunts and uncles of each other; Mom had gotten married and moved to New York with Dad (who George could not even remember). Buddy had been born, and then they had moved to Stratford and in 1969 George had been born, and in 1971 Dad had been hit and killed by a car driven by the Drunk Man Who Had to Go to Jail.

When Granpa had his heart attack there had been a great many letters back and forth among the aunts and uncles. They didn't want to put the old lady in a nursing home. And she didn't want to *go* to a home. If Gramma didn't want to do a thing like that, it might be better to accede to her wishes. The old lady wanted to go to one of them and live out the rest of her years with that child. But they were all married, and none of them had spouses who felt like sharing their home with a senile and often unpleasant old woman. All were married, that was, except Ruth.

The letters flew back and forth, and at last George's Mom had given in. She quit her job and came to Maine to take care of the old lady. The others had chipped together to buy a small house in outer Castle View, where property values were low. Each month they would send her a check, so she could ''do'' for the old lady and for her boys.

What's happened is my brothers and sisters have turned me into a sharecropper, George could remember her saying once, and he didn't know for sure what that meant, but she had sounded bitter when she said it, like it was a joke that didn't come out smooth in a laugh but instead stuck in her throat like a bone. George knew (because Buddy had told him) that Mom had finally given in because everyone in the big, far-flung family had assured her that Gramma couldn't possibly last long. She had too many things wrong with her—high blood pressure, uremic poisoning, obesity, heart palpitations—to last long. It would be eight months, Aunt Flo and Aunt Stephanie and Uncle George (after whom George had been named) all said; a year at the most. But now it had been five years, and George called that lasting pretty long.

She had lasted pretty long, all right. Like a she-bear in hibernation, waiting for . . . what?

(you know how to deal with her best Ruth you know how to shut her up)

George, on his way to the fridge to check the directions on

one of Gramma's special salt-free dinners, stopped. Stopped cold. Where had that come from? That voice speaking inside his head?

Suddenly his belly and chest broke out in gooseflesh. He reached inside his shirt and touched one of his nipples. It was like a little pebble, and he took his finger away in a hurry.

Uncle George. His "namesake uncle," who worked for Sperry-Rand in New York. It had been his voice. He had said that when he and his family came up for Christmas two—no, three—years ago.

She's more dangerous now that she's senile.
George, be quiet. The boys are around somewhere.

George stood by the refrigerator, one hand on the cold chrome handle, thinking, remembering, looking out into the growing dark. Buddy *hadn't* been around that day. Buddy was already outside, because Buddy had wanted the good sled, that was why; they were going sliding on Joe Camber's hill and the other sled had a buckled runner. So Buddy was outside and here was George, hunting through the boot-and-sock box in the entryway, looking for a pair of heavy socks that matched, and was it *his* fault his mother and Uncle George were talking in the kitchen? George didn't think so. Was it George's fault that God hadn't struck him deaf, or, lacking the extremity of that measure, at least located the conversation elsewhere in the house? George didn't believe that, either. As his mother had pointed out on more than one occasion (usually after a glass of wine or two), God sometimes played dirty.

You know what I mean, Uncle George said.

His wife and his three girls had gone over to Gates Falls to do some last-minute Christmas shopping, and Uncle George was pretty much in the bag, just like the Drunk Man Who Had to Go to Jail. George could tell by the way his uncle slurred his words.

You remember what happened to Franklin when he crossed her.

George, be quiet, or I'll pour the rest of your beer right down the sink!

Well, she didn't really mean to do it. Her tongue just got away from her. Peritonitis—

George, shut up!

Maybe, George remembered thinking vaguely, *God isn't the only one who plays dirty.*

Now he broke the hold of these old memories and looked in the freezer and took out one of Gramma's dinners. Veal. With peas on the side. You had to preheat the oven and then bake it for forty minutes at 300 degrees. Easy. He was all set. The tea was ready on the stove if Gramma wanted that. He could make tea, or he could make dinner in short order if Gramma woke up and yelled for it. Tea or dinner, he was a regular two-gun Sam. Dr. Arlinder's number was on the board, in case of an emergency. Everything was cool. So what was he worried about?

He had never been left alone with Gramma, that was what he was worried about.

Send the boy to me, Ruth. Send him over here.

No. He's crying.

She's more dangerous now . . . you know what I mean.

We all lie to our children about Gramma.

Neither he nor Buddy. Neither of them had ever been left alone with Gramma. Until now.

Suddenly George's mouth went dry. He went to the sink and got a drink of water. He felt . . . funny. These thoughts. These memories. Why was his brain dragging them all up now?

He felt as if someone had dumped all the pieces to a puzzle in front of him and that he couldn't quite put them together. And maybe it was *good* he couldn't put them together, because the finished picture might be, well, sort of boogery. It might—

From the other room, where Gramma lived all her days and nights, a choking, rattling, gargling noise suddenly arose.

A whistling gasp was sucked into George as he pulled breath. He turned toward Gramma's room and discovered his shoes were tightly nailed to the linoleum floor. His heart was spike-iron in his chest. His eyes were wide and bulging. *Go now*, his brain told his feet, and his feet saluted and said *Not at all, sir!*

Gramma had never made a noise like that before.

Gramma had *never* made a noise like that before.

It arose again, a choking sound, low and then descending

lower, becoming an insectile buzz before it died out altogether. George was able to move at last. He walked toward the entryway that separated the kitchen from Gramma's room. He crossed it and looked into her room, his heart slamming. Now his throat was *choked* with wool mittens; it would be impossible to swallow past them.

Gramma was still sleeping and it was all right, that was his first thought; it had only been some weird *sound,* after all; maybe she made it all the time when he and Buddy were in school. Just a snore. Gramma was fine. Sleeping.

That was his first thought. Then he noticed that the yellow hand that had been on the coverlet was now dangling limply over the side of the bed, the long nails almost but not quite touching the floor. And her mouth was open, as wrinkled and caved-in as an orifice dug into a rotten piece of fruit.

Timidly, hesitantly, George approached her.

He stood by her side for a long time, looking down at her, not daring to touch her. The imperceptible rise and fall of the coverlet appeared to have ceased.

Appeared.

That was the key word. *Appeared.*

But that's just because you are spooked, Georgie. You're just being Señor El-Stupido, like Buddy says—it's a game. Your brain's playing tricks on your eyes, she's breathing just fine, she's—

"Gramma?" he said, and all that came out was a whisper. He cleared his throat and jumped back, frightened of the sound. But his voice was a little louder. "Gramma? You want your tea now? Gramma?"

Nothing.

The eyes were closed.

The mouth was open.

The hand hung.

Outside, the setting sun shone golden-red through the trees.

He saw her in a positive fullness then; saw her with that childish and brilliantly unhoused eye of unformed immature reflection, not here, not now, not in bed, but sitting in the white vinyl chair, holding out her arms, her face at the same time stupid and triumphant. He found himself remembering one of the "bad spells" when Gramma began to shout, as if in a foreign language—*Gyaagin! Gyaagin! Hastur degryon Yos-soth-oth!*—and Mom had sent them outside, had screamed

"*Just GO!*" at Buddy when Buddy stopped at the box in the entry to hunt for his gloves, and Buddy had looked back over his shoulder, so scared he was walleyed with it because their mom *never* shouted, and they had both gone out and stood in the driveway, not talking, their hands stuffed in their pockets for warmth, wondering what was happening.

Later, Mom had called them in for supper as if nothing had happened.

(you know how to deal with her best Ruth you know how to shut her up)

George had not thought of that particular "bad spell" from that day to this. Except now, looking at Gramma, who was sleeping so strangely in her crank-up hospital bed, it occurred to him with dawning horror that it was the next day they had learned that Mrs. Harham, who lived up the road and sometimes visited Gramma, had died in her sleep that night.

Gramma's "bad spells."

Spells.

Witches were supposed to be able to cast spells. That's what made them witches, wasn't it? Poisoned apples. Princes into toads. Gingerbread houses. Abracadabra. Presto-chango. *Spells*.

Spilled-out pieces of an unknown puzzle flying together in George's mind, as if by magic.

Magic, George thought, and groaned.

What was the picture? It was Gramma, of course, Gramma and her *books,* Gramma who had been driven out of town, Gramma who hadn't been able to have babies and then had been able to, Gramma who had been driven out of the *church* as well as out of town. The picture was Gramma, yellow and fat and wrinkled and sluglike, her toothless mouth curved into a sunken grin, her faded, blind eyes somehow sly and cunning; and on her head was a black, conical hat sprinkled with silver stars and glittering Babylonian crescents; at her feet were slinking black cats with eyes as yellow as urine, and the smells were pork and blindness, pork and burning, ancient stars and candles as dark as the earth in which coffins lay; he heard words spoken from ancient books, and each word was like a stone and each sentence like a crypt reared in some stinking boneyard and every paragraph like a nightmare caravan of the plague-dead taken to a place of burning; his eye was the eye of a child and in that moment it opened wide in startled understanding on blackness.

Gramma had been a witch, just like the Wicked Witch in the *Wizard of Oz*. And now she was dead. That gargling sound, George thought with increasing horror. That gargling, snoring sound had been a . . . a . . . a *"death rattle."*

"Gramma?" he whispered, and crazily he thought: *Ding-dong, the wicked witch is dead.*

No response. He held his cupped hand in front of Gramma's mouth. There was no breeze stirring around inside Gramma. It was dead calm and slack sails and no wake widening behind the keel. Some of his fright began to recede now, and George tried to think. He remembered Uncle Fred showing him how to wet a finger and test the wind, and now he licked his entire palm and held it in front of Gramma's mouth.

Still nothing.

He started for the phone to call Dr. Arlinder, and then stopped. Suppose he called the doctor and she really wasn't dead at all? He'd be in dutch for sure.

Take her pulse.

He stopped in the doorway, looking doubtfully back at that dangling hand. The sleeve of Gramma's nightie had pulled up, exposing her wrist. But that was no good. Once, after a visit to the doctor when the nurse had pressed her finger to his wrist to take his pulse, George had tried it and hadn't been able to find anything. As far as his own unskilled fingers could tell, he was dead.

Besides, he didn't really want to . . . well . . . to *touch* Gramma. Even if she was dead. *Especially* if she was dead.

George stood in the entryway, looking from Gramma's still, bedridden form to the phone on the wall beside Dr. Arlinder's number, and back to Gramma again. He would just have to call. He would—

—get a mirror!

Sure! When you breathed on a mirror, it got cloudy. He had seen a doctor check an unconscious person that way once in a movie. There was a bathroom connecting with Gramma's room and now George hurried in and got Gramma's vanity mirror. One side of it was regular, the other side magnified, so you could see to pluck out hairs and do stuff like that.

George took it back to Gramma's bed and held one side of the mirror until it was almost touching Gramma's open, gaping mouth. He held it there while he counted to sixty, watching Gramma the whole time. Nothing changed. He was sure she was dead even before he took the mirror away from her mouth and observed its surface, which was perfectly clear and unclouded.

Gramma was dead.

George realized with relief and some surprise that he could feel sorry for her now. Maybe she had been a witch. Maybe not. Maybe she had only *thought* she was a witch. However it had been, she was gone now. He realized with an adult's comprehension that questions of concrete reality became not unimportant but less *vital* when they were examined in the mute bland face of mortal remains. He realized this with an adult's comprehension and accepted with an adult's relief. This was a passing footprint, the shape of a shoe, in his mind. So are all the child's adult impressions; it is only in later years that the child realizes that he was being *made; formed;* shaped by random experiences; all that remains *in the instant* beyond the footprint is that bitter gunpowder smell which is the ignition of an idea beyond a child's given years.

He returned the mirror to the bathroom, then went back through her room, glancing at the body on his way by. The setting sun had painted the old dead face with barbaric, orange-red colors, and George looked away quickly.

He went through the entry and crossed the kitchen to the telephone, determined to do everything right. Already in his mind he saw a certain advantage over Buddy; whenever Buddy started to tease him, he would simply say: *I was all by myself in the house when Gramma died, and I did everything right.*

Call Dr. Arlinder, that was first. Call him and say, "My Gramma just died. Can you tell me what I should do? Cover her up or something?"

No.

"I *think* my Gramma just died."

Yes. Yes, that was better. Nobody thought a little kid knew anything anyway, so that was better.

Or how about:

"I'm pretty sure my Gramma just died—"

Sure! That was best of all.

And tell about the mirror and the death rattle and all. And

the doctor would come right away, and when he was done examining Gramma he would say, "*I pronounce you dead, Gramma,*" and then say to George, "*You laid extremely chilly in a tough situation, George. I want to congratulate you.*" And George would say something appropriately modest.

George looked at Dr. Arlinder's number and took a couple of slow deep breaths before grabbing the phone. His heart was beating fast, but that painful spike-iron thud was gone now. Gramma had died. The worst had happened, and somehow it wasn't as bad as waiting for her to start bellowing for Mom to bring her tea.

The phone was dead.

He listened to the blankness, his mouth still formed around the words *I'm sorry, Missus Dodd, but this is George Bruckner and I have to call the doctor for my Gramma.* No voices. No dial tone. Just dead blankness. Like the dead blankness in the bed in there.

Gramma is—

—is—

(oh she is)

Gramma is laying chilly.

Gooseflesh again, painful and marbling. His eyes fixed on the Pyrex teakettle on the stove, the cup on the counter with the herbal tea bag in it. No more tea for Gramma. Not ever.

(laying so chilly)

George shuddered.

He stuttered his finger up and down on the Princess phone's cutoff button, but the phone was dead. Just as dead as—

(just as chilly as)

He slammed the handset down hard and the bell tinged faintly inside and he picked it up in a hurry to see if that meant it had magically gone right again. But there was nothing, and this time he put it back slowly.

His heart was thudding harder again.

I'm alone in this house with her dead body.

He crossed the kitchen slowly, stood by the table for a minute, and then turned on the light. It was getting dark in the house. Soon the sun would be gone; night would be here.

Wait. That's all I got to do. Just wait until Mom gets back. This is better, really. If the phone went out, it's better that she just died instead of maybe having a fit or something, foaming at the mouth, maybe falling out of bed—

Ah, that was bad. He could have done very nicely without *that* horse-pucky.

Like being alone in the dark and thinking of dead things that were still lively—seeing shapes in the shadows on the walls and thinking of death, thinking of the dead, those things, the way they would stink and the way they would move toward you in the black: thinking this: thinking that: thinking of bugs turning in flesh: burrowing in flesh: eyes that moved in the dark. Yeah. That most of all. Thinking of eyes that moved in the dark and the creak of floorboards as something came across the room through the zebra-stripes of shadows from the light outside. Yeah.

In the dark your thoughts had a perfect circularity, and no matter what you tried to think of—flowers or Jesus or baseball or winning the gold in the 440 at the Olympics—it somehow led back to the form in the shadows with the claws and the unblinking eyes.

"Shittabrick!" he hissed, and suddenly slapped his own face. And hard. He was giving himself the whimwhams, it was time to stop it. He wasn't six anymore. She was dead, that was all, dead. There was no more thought inside her now than there was in a marble or a floorboard or a doorknob or a radio dial or—

And a strong alien unprepared-for voice, perhaps only the unforgiving unbidden voice of simple survival, inside him cried: *Shut up Georgie and get about your goddam business!*

Yeah, okay. Okay, but—

He went back to the door of her bedroom to make sure.

There lay Gramma, one hand out of bed and touching the floor, her mouth hinged agape. Gramma was part of the furniture now. You could put her hand back in bed or pull her hair or pop a water glass into her mouth or put earphones on her head and play Chuck Berry into them full-tilt boogie and it would be all the same to her. Gramma was, as Buddy sometimes said, out of it. Gramma had had the course.

A sudden low and rhythmic thudding noise began, not far to George's left, and he started, a little yipping cry escaping him. It was the storm door, which Buddy had put on just last week. Just the storm door, unlatched and thudding back and forth in the freshening breeze.

George opened the inside door, leaned out, and caught the storm door as it swung back. The wind—it wasn't a breeze but a wind—caught his hair and riffled it. He latched the door firmly and wondered where the wind had come from all of a sudden. When Mom left it had been almost dead calm. But when Mom had left it had been bright daylight and now it was dusk.

George glanced in at Gramma again and then went back and tried the phone again. Still dead. He sat down, got up, and began to walk back and forth through the kitchen, pacing, trying to think.

An hour later it was full dark.

The phone was still out. George supposed the wind, which had now risen to a near-gale, had knocked down some of the lines, probably out by the Beaver Bog, where the trees grew everywhere in a helter-skelter of deadfalls and swampwater. The phone dinged occasionally, ghostly and far, but the line remained blank. Outside the wind moaned along the eaves of the small house and George reckoned he would have a story to tell at the next Boy Scout Camporee, all right . . . just sitting in the house alone with his dead Gramma and the phone out and the wind pushing rafts of clouds fast across the sky, clouds that were black on top and the color of dead tallow, the color of Gramma's claw-hands, underneath.

It was, as Buddy also sometimes said, a Classic.

He wished he was telling it now, with the actuality of the thing safely behind him. He sat at the kitchen table, his history book open in front of him, jumping at every sound . . . and now that the wind was up, there were a lot of sounds as the house creaked in all its unoiled secret forgotten joints.

She'll be home pretty quick. She'll be home and then everything will be okay. Everything
(you never covered her)
will be all r
(never covered her face)

George jerked as if someone had spoken aloud and stared wide-eyed across the kitchen at the useless telephone. You were supposed to pull the sheet up over the dead person's face. It was in all the movies.

Hell with that! I'm not going in there!

No! And no reason why he should! *Mom* could cover her face when she got home! Or *Dr. Arlinder* when he came! Or the *undertaker!*

Someone, anyone, but him.

No reason why he should.

It was nothing to him, and nothing to Gramma.

Buddy's voice in his head:

If you weren't scared, how come you didn't dare to cover her face?

It was nothing to me.

Fraidycat!

Nothing to Gramma, either.

CHICKEN-GUTS fraidycat!

Sitting at the table in front of his unread history book, considering it, George began to see that if he *didn't* pull the counterpane up over Gramma's face, he couldn't claim to have done everything right, and thus Buddy would have a leg (no matter how shaky) to stand on.

Now he saw himself telling the spooky story of Gramma's death at the Camporee fire before taps, just getting to the comforting conclusion where Mom's headlights swept into the driveway—the reappearance of the grown-up, both reestablishing and reconfirming the concept of Order—and suddenly, from the shadows, a dark figure arises, and a pine-knot in the fire explodes and George can see it's Buddy there in the shadows, saying: *If you was so brave, chickenguts, how come you didn't dare to cover up HER FACE?*

George stood up, reminding himself that Gramma was *out of it,* that Gramma was *wasted,* that Gramma was *laying chilly.* He could put her hand back in bed, stuff a tea bag up her nose, put on earphones playing Chuck Berry full blast, etc., etc., and none of it would put a buzz under Gramma, because that was what being dead was *about,* nobody could put a buzz under a dead person, a dead person was the ultimate laid-back cool, and the rest of it was just dreams, ineluctable and apocalyptic and feverish dreams about closet doors swinging open in the dead mouth of midnight, just dreams about moonlight skating a delirious blue on the bones of disinterred skeletons, just—

He whispered, "Stop it, can't you? Stop being so—"

(gross)

He steeled himself. He was going to go in there and pull the coverlet up over her face, and take away Buddy's last leg to stand on. He would administer the few simple rituals of Gramma's death perfectly. He would cover her face and then—his face lit at the symbolism of this—he would put away her unused tea bag and her unused cup. Yes.

He went in, each step a conscious act. Gramma's room was dark, her body a vague hump in the bed, and he fumbled madly for the light switch, not finding it for what seemed to be an eternity. At last it clicked up, flooding the room with low yellow light from the cut-glass fixture overhead.

Gramma lay there, hand dangling, mouth open. George regarded her, dimly aware that little pearls of sweat now clung to his forehead, and wondered if his responsibility in the matter could possibly extend to picking up that cooling hand and putting it back in bed with the rest of Gramma. He decided it did not. Her hand could have fallen out of bed any old time. That was too much. He couldn't touch her. Everything else, but not that.

Slowly, as if moving through some thick fluid instead of air, George approached Gramma. He stood over her, looking down. Gramma was yellow. Part of it was the light, filtered through the old fixture, but not all.

Breathing through his mouth, his breath rasping audibly, George grasped the coverlet and pulled it up over Gramma's face. He let go of it and it slipped just a little, revealing her hairline and the yellow creased parchment of her brow. Steeling himself, he grasped it again, keeping his hands far to one side and the other of her head so he wouldn't have to touch her, even through the cloth, and pulled it up again. This time it stayed. It was satisfactory. Some of the fear went out of George. He had *buried* her. Yes, that was why you covered the dead person up, and why it was right: it was like *burying* them. It was a statement.

He looked at the hand dangling down, unburied, and discovered now that he could touch it, he could tuck it under and bury it with the rest of Gramma.

He bent, grasped the cool hand, and lifted it.

The hand twisted in his and clutched his wrist.

George screamed. He staggered backward, screaming in the empty house, screaming against the sound of the wind reaving the eaves, screaming against the sound of the house's creaking joints. He backed away, pulling Gramma's body askew under the coverlet, and the hand thudded back down, twisting, turning, snatching at the air . . . and then relaxing to limpness again.

I'm all right, it was nothing, it was nothing but a reflex.

George nodded in perfect understanding, and then he remembered again how her hand had turned, clutching his, and he shrieked. His eyes bulged in their sockets. His hair stood out, perfectly on end, in a cone. His heart was a runaway stamping-press in his chest. The world tilted crazily, came back to the level, and then just went on moving until it was tilted the other way. Every time rational thought started to come back, panic goosed him again. He whirled, wanting only to get out of the room to some other room—or even three or four miles down the road, if that was what it took—where he could get all of this under control. So he whirled and ran full tilt into the wall, missing the open doorway by a good two feet.

He rebounded and fell to the floor, his head singing with a sharp, cutting pain that sliced keenly through the panic. He touched his nose and his hand came back bloody. Fresh drops spotted his shirt. He scrambled to his feet and looked around wildly.

The hand dangled against the floor as it had before, but Gramma's body was not askew; it also was as it had been.

He had imagined the whole thing. He had come into the room, and all the rest of it had been no more than a mind-movie.

No.

But the pain had cleared his head. Dead people didn't grab your wrist. Dead was dead. When you were dead they could use you for a hat rack or stuff you in a tractor tire and roll you downhill or et cetera, et cetera, et cetera. When you were dead you might be acted *upon* (by, say, little boys trying to put dead dangling hands back into bed), but your days of *acting* upon—so to speak—were over.

Unless you're a witch. Unless you pick your time to die when no one's around but one little kid, because it's best that way, you can . . . can . . .

Can what?

Nothing. It was stupid. He had imagined the whole thing because he had been scared and that was all there was to it. He wiped his nose with his forearm and winced at the pain. There was a bloody smear on the skin of his inner forearm.

He wasn't going to go near her again, that was all. Reality or hallucination, he wasn't going to mess with Gramma. The bright flare of panic was gone, but he was still miserably scared, near tears, shaky at the sight of his own blood, only wanting his mother to come home and take charge.

George backed out of the room, through the entry, and into the kitchen. He drew a long, shuddery breath and let it out. He wanted a wet rag for his nose, and suddenly he felt like he was going to vomit. He went over to the sink and ran cold water. He bent and got a rag from the basin under the sink—a piece of one of Gramma's old diapers—and ran it under the cold tap, snuffling up blood as he did so. He soaked the old soft cotton diaper-square until his hand was numb, then turned off the tap and wrung it out.

He was putting it to his nose when her voice spoke from the other room.

"Come here, boy," Gramma called in a dead buzzing voice. "Come in here—*Gramma wants to hug you.*"

George tried to scream and no sound came out. No sound at all. But there were sounds in the other room. Sounds that he heard when Mom was in there, giving Gramma her bed-bath, lifting her bulk, dropping it, turning it, dropping it again.

Only those sounds now seemed to have a slightly different and yet utterly specific meaning—it sounded as though Gramma was trying to . . . to get out of bed.

"Boy! Come in here, boy! Right NOW! Step to it!"

With horror he saw that his feet were answering that command. He told them to stop and they just went on, left foot, right foot, hay foot, straw foot, over the linoleum; his brain was a terrified prisoner inside his body—a hostage in a tower.

She IS a witch, she's a witch and she's having one of her "bad spells," oh yeah, it's a "spell" all right, and it's bad, it's REALLY bad, oh God oh Jesus help me help me help me—

George walked across the kitchen and through the entryway and into Gramma's room and yes, she hadn't just *tried* to get out of bed, she *was* out, she was sitting in the white vinyl chair where she hadn't sat for four years, since she got too heavy to walk and too senile to know where she was, anyway.

But Gramma didn't look senile now.

Her face was sagging and doughy, but the senility was gone—if it had ever really been there at all, and not just a mask she wore to lull small boys and tired husbandless women. Now Gramma's face gleamed with fell intelligence—it gleamed like an old, stinking wax candle. Her eyes drooped in her face, lackluster and dead. Her chest was not moving. Her nightie had pulled up, exposing elephantine thighs. The coverlet of her deathbed was thrown back.

Gramma held her huge arms out to him.

"I want to hug you, Georgie," that flat and buzzing deadvoice said. *"Don't be a scared old crybaby. Let your Gramma hug you."*

George cringed back, trying to resist that almost insurmountable pull. Outside, the wind shrieked and roared. George's face was long and twisted with the extremity of his fright; the face of a woodcut caught and shut up in an ancient book.

George began to walk toward her. He couldn't help himself. Step by dragging step toward those outstretched arms. *He would show Buddy that he wasn't scared of Gramma, either. He would go to Gramma and be hugged because he wasn't a crybaby fraidycat. He would go to Gramma now.*

He was almost within the circle of her arms when the window to his left crashed inward and suddenly a wind-blown branch was in the room with them, autumn leaves still clinging to it. The river of wind flooded the room, blowing over Gramma's pictures, whipping her nightgown and her hair.

Now George could scream. He stumbled backward out of her grip and Gramma made a cheated hissing sound, her lips pulling back over smooth old gums; her thick, wrinkled hands clapped uselessly together on moving air.

George's feet tangled together and he fell down. Gramma began to rise from the white vinyl chair, a tottering pile of flesh; she began to stagger toward him. George found he couldn't get up; the strength had deserted his legs. He began to crawl backward, whimpering. Gramma came on, slowly but relentlessly, dead and yet alive, and suddenly George understood what the hug would mean; the puzzle was complete in his mind and somehow he found his feet just as Gramma's hand closed on his shirt. It ripped up the side, and for one moment he felt her cold flesh against his skin before fleeing into the kitchen again.

He would run into the night. Anything other than being hugged by the witch, his Gramma. Because when his mother came back she would find Gramma dead and George alive, oh yes . . . but George would have developed a sudden taste for herbal tea.

He looked back over his shoulder and saw Gramma's grotesque, misshapen shadow rising on the wall as she came through the entryway.

And at that moment the telephone rang, shrilly and stridently.

George seized it without even thinking and screamed into it; screamed for someone to come, to please come. He screamed these things silently; not a sound escaped his locked throat.

Gramma tottered into the kitchen in her pink nightie. Her whitish-yellow hair blew wildly around her face, and one of her horn combs hung askew against her wrinkled neck.

Gramma was grinning.

"Ruth?" It was Aunt Flo's voice, almost lost in the whistling windtunnel of a bad long-distance connection. "Ruth, are you there?" It was Aunt Flo in Minnesota, over two thousand miles away.

"Help me!" George screamed into the phone, and what came out was a tiny, hissing whistle, as if he had blown into a harmonica full of dead reeds.

Gramma tottered across the linoleum, holding her arms out for him. Her hands snapped shut and then open and then shut again. Gramma wanted her hug; she had been waiting for that hug for five years.

"Ruth, can you hear me? It's been storming here, it just started, and I . . . I got scared. Ruth, I can't hear you—"

"Gramma," George moaned into the telephone. Now she was almost upon him.

"George?" Aunt Flo's voice suddenly sharpened; became almost a shriek. "George, is that *you?*"

He began to back away from Gramma, and suddenly realized that he had stupidly backed away from the door and into the corner formed by the kitchen cabinets and the sink. The horror was complete. As her shadow fell over him, the paralysis broke and he screamed into the phone, screamed it over and over again: *"Gramma! Gramma! Gramma!"*

Gramma's cold hands touched his throat. Her muddy, ancient eyes locked on his, draining his will.

Faintly, dimly, as if across many years as well as many miles, he heard Aunt Flo say: "Tell her to lie down, George, tell her to lie down and be still. Tell her she must do it in your name and the name of her father. The name of her taken father is *Hastur*. His name is power in her ear, George—tell her *Lie down in the Name of Hastur—tell her—"*

The old, wrinkled hand tore the telephone from George's nerveless grip. There was a taut pop as the cord pulled out of the phone. George collapsed in the corner and Gramma bent down, a huge heap of flesh above him, blotting out the light.

George screamed: *"Lie down! Be still! Hastur's name! Hastur! Lie down! Be still!"*

Her hands closed around his neck—

"You gotta do it! Aunt Flo said you did! In *my* name! In your *Father's* name! Lie down! Be sti—"

—and squeezed.

When the lights finally splashed into the driveway an hour later, George was sitting at the table in front of his unread history book. He got up and walked to the back door and opened it. To his left, the Princess phone hung in its cradle, its useless cord looped around it.

His mother came in, a leaf clinging to the collar of her coat. "Such a wind," she said. "Was everything all—George? *George, what happened?"*

The blood fell from Mom's face in a single, shocked rush, turning her a horrible clown-white.

"Gramma," he said. "Gramma died. Gramma died, Mommy." And he began to cry.

She swept him into her arms and then staggered back against the wall, as if this act of hugging had robbed the last of her strength. "Did . . . did anything happen?" she asked. *"George, did anything else happen?"*

"The wind knocked a tree branch through her window," George said.

She pushed him away, looked at his shocked, slack face for a moment, and then stumbled into Gramma's room. She was in there for perhaps four minutes. When she came back, she was holding a red tatter of cloth. It was a bit of George's shirt.

"I took this out of her hand," Mom whispered.

"I don't want to talk about it," George said. "Call Aunt Flo, if you want. I'm tired. I want to go to bed."

She made as if to stop him, but didn't. He went up to the room he shared with Buddy and opened the hot-air register so he could hear what his mother did next. She wasn't going to talk to Aunt Flo, not tonight, because the telephone cord had pulled out; not tomorrow, because shortly before Mom had come home, George had spoken a short series of words, some of them bastardized Latin, some only pre-Druidic grunts, and over two thousand miles away Aunt Flo had dropped dead of a massive brain hemorrhage. It was amazing how those words came back. How *everything* came back.

George undressed and lay down naked on his bed. He put his hands behind his head and looked up into the darkness. Slowly, slowly, a sunken and rather horrible grin surfaced on his face.

Things were going to be different around here from now on.

Very different.

Buddy, for instance. George could hardly wait until Buddy came home from the hospital and started in with the Spoon Torture of the Heathen Chinee or an Indian Rope Burn or something like that. George supposed he would have to let Buddy get away with it—at least in the daytime, when people could see—but when night came and they were alone in this room, in the dark, with the door closed . . .

George began to laugh soundlessly.

As Buddy always said, it was going to be a Classic.

The Ballad of the Flexible Bullet

The barbecue was over. It had been a good one; drinks, charcoaled T-bones, rare, a green salad and Meg's special dressing. They had started at five. Now it was eight-thirty and almost dusk—the time when a big party is just starting to get rowdy. But they weren't a big party. There were just the five of them: the agent and his wife, the celebrated young writer and *his* wife, and the magazine editor, who was in his early sixties and looked older. The editor stuck to Fresca. The agent had told the young writer before the editor arrived that there had once been a drinking problem there. It was gone now, and so was the editor's wife . . . which was why they were five instead of six.

Instead of getting rowdy, an introspective mood fell over them as it started to get dark in the young writer's backyard, which fronted the lake. The young writer's first novel had been well reviewed and had sold a lot of copies. He was a lucky young man, and to his credit he knew it.

The conversation had turned with playful gruesomeness from the young writer's early success to other writers who had made their marks early and had then committed suicide. Ross Lockridge was touched upon, and Tom Hagen. The agent's wife mentioned Sylvia Plath and Anne Sexton, and the young writer said that he didn't think Plath qualified as a *successful* writer. She had not committed suicide because of

495

success, he said; she had gained success because she had committed suicide. The agent smiled.

"Please, couldn't we talk about something else?" the young writer's wife asked, a little nervously.

Ignoring her, the agent said, "And madness. There have been those who have gone mad because of success." The agent had the mild but nonetheless rolling tones of an actor offstage.

The writer's wife was about to protest again—she knew that her husband not only liked to talk about these things so he could joke about them, and he wanted to joke about them because he thought about them too much—when the magazine editor spoke up. What he said was so odd she forgot to protest.

"Madness is a flexible bullet."

The agent's wife looked startled. The young writer leaned forward quizzically. He said, "That sounds familiar—"

"Sure," the editor said. "That phrase, the image, 'flexible bullet,' is Marianne Moore's. She used it to describe some car or other. I've always thought it described the condition of madness very well. Madness is a kind of mental suicide. Don't the doctors say now that the only way to truly measure death is by the death of the mind? Madness is a kind of flexible bullet to the brain."

The young writer's wife hopped up. "Anybody want another drink?" She had no takers.

"Well, I do, if we're going to talk about this," she said, and went off to make herself one.

The editor said: "I had a story submitted to me once, when I was working over at *Logan's*. Of course it's gone the way of *Collier's* and *The Saturday Evening Post* now, but we outlasted both of them." He said this with a trace of pride. "We published thirty-six short stories a year, or more, and every year four or five of them would be in somebody's collection of the year's best. And people *read* them. Anyway, the name of this story was 'The Ballad of the Flexible Bullet,' and it was written by a man named Reg Thorpe. A young man about this young man's age, and about as successful."

"He wrote *Underworld Figures*, didn't he?" the agent's wife asked.

"Yes. Amazing track record for a first novel. Great reviews, lovely sales in hardcover and paperback, Literary Guild, everything. Even the movie was pretty good, although not as good as the book. Nowhere near.''

"I loved that book,'' the author's wife said, lured back into the conversation against her better judgment. She had the surprised, pleased look of someone who has just recalled something which has been out of mind for too long. "Has he written anything since then? I read *Underworld Figures* back in college and that was . . . well, too long ago to think about.''

"You haven't aged a day since then,'' the agent's wife said warmly, although privately she thought the young writer's wife was wearing a too-small halter and a too-tight pair of shorts.

"No, he hasn't written anything since then,'' the editor said. "Except for this one short story I was telling you about. He killed himself. Went crazy and killed himself.''

"Oh,'' the young writer's wife said limply. Back to *that*.

"Was the short story published?'' the young writer asked.

"No, but not because the author went crazy and killed himself. It never got into print because the *editor* went crazy and *almost* killed himself.''

The agent suddenly got up to freshen his own drink, which hardly need freshening. He knew that the editor had had a nervous breakdown in the summer of 1969, not long before *Logan's* had drowned in a sea of red ink.

"I was the editor,'' the editor informed the rest of them. "In a sense we went crazy together, Reg Thorpe and I, even though I was in New York, he was out in Omaha, and we never even met. His book had been out about six months and he had moved out there 'to get his head together,' as the phrase was then. And I happen to know this side of the story because I see his wife occasionally when she's in New York. She paints, and quite well. She's a lucky girl. He almost took her with him.''

The agent came back and sat down. "I'm starting to remember some of this now,'' he said. "It wasn't just his wife, was it? He shot a couple of other people, one of them a kid.''

"That's right,'' the editor said. "It was the kid that finally set him off.''

"The *kid* set him off?" the agent's wife asked. "What do you mean?"

But the editor's face said he would not be drawn; he would talk, but not be questioned.

"I know my side of the story because I lived it," the magazine editor said. "I'm lucky, too. Damned lucky. It's an interesting thing about those who try to kill themselves by pointing a gun at their heads and pulling the trigger. You'd think it would be the foolproof method, better than pills or slashing the wrists, but it isn't. When you shoot yourself in the head, you just can't tell what's going to happen. The slug may ricochet off the skull and kill someone else. It may follow the skull's curve all the way around and come out on the other side. It may lodge in the brain and blind you and leave you alive. One man may shoot himself in the forehead with a .38 and wake up in the hospital. Another may shoot himself in the forehead with a .22 and wake up in hell . . . if there is such a place. I tend to believe it's here on earth, possibly in New Jersey."

The writer's wife laughed rather shrilly.

"The only foolproof suicide method is to step off a very high building, and that's a way out that only the extraordinarily dedicated ever take. So damned messy, isn't it?

"But my point is simply this: When you shoot yourself with a flexible bullet, you really don't know what the outcome is going to be. In my case, I went off a bridge and woke up on a trash-littered embankment with a trucker whapping me on the back and pumping my arms up and down like he had only twenty-four hours to get in shape and he had mistaken me for a rowing machine. For Reg, the bullet was lethal. He . . . But I'm telling you a story I have no idea if you want to hear."

He looked around at them questioningly in the gathering gloom. The agent and the agent's wife glanced at each other uncertainly, and the writer's wife was about to say she thought they'd had enough gloomy talk when her husband said, "I'd like to hear it. If you don't mind telling it for personal reasons, I mean."

"I never have told it," the editor said, "but not for personal reasons. Perhaps I never had the correct listeners."

"Then tell away," the writer said.

"Paul—" His wife put her hand on his shoulder. "Don't you think—"

"Not now, Meg."

The editor said:

"The story came in over the transom, and at that time *Logan's* no longer read unsolicited scripts. When they came in, a girl would just put them into return envelopes with a note that said 'Due to increasing costs and the increasing inability of the editorial staff to cope with a steadily increasing number of submissions, *Logan's* no longer reads unsolicited manuscripts. We wish you the best of luck in placing your work elsewhere.' Isn't that a lovely bunch of gobbledegook? It's not easy to use the word 'increasing' three times in one sentence, but they did it."

"And if there was no return postage, the story went into the wastebasket," the writer said. "Right?"

"Oh, absolutely. No pity in the naked city."

An odd expression of unease flitted across the writer's face. It was the expression of a man who is in a tiger pit where dozens of better men have been clawed to pieces. So far this man hasn't seen a single tiger. But he has a feeling that they are there, and that their claws are still sharp.

"Anyway," the editor said, taking out his cigarette case, "this story came in, and the girl in the mailroom took it out, paper-clipped the form rejection to the first page, and was getting ready to put it in the return envelope when she glanced at the author's name. Well, she had read *Underworld Figures*. That fall, everybody had read it, or was reading it, or was on the library waiting list, or checking the drugstore racks for the paperback."

The writer's wife, who had seen the momentary unease on her husband's face, took his hand. He smiled at her. The editor snapped a gold Ronson to his cigarette, and in the growing dark they could all see how haggard his face was— the loose, crocodile-skinned pouches under the eyes, the runneled cheeks, the old man's jut of chin emerging out of that late-middle-aged face like the prow of a ship. That ship, the writer thought, is called old age. No one particularly wants to cruise on it, but the staterooms are full. The gangholds too, for that matter.

The lighter winked out, and the editor puffed his cigarette meditatively.

"The girl in the mailroom who read that story and passed it on instead of sending it back is now a full editor at G. P. Putnam's Sons. Her name doesn't matter; what matters is that on the great graph of life, this girl's vector crossed Reg Thorpe's in the mailroom of *Logan's* magazine. Hers was going up and his was going down. She sent the story to her boss and her boss sent it to me. I read it and loved it. It was really too long, but I could see where he could pare five hundred words off it with no sweat. And that would be plenty."

"What was it about?" the writer asked.

"You shouldn't even have to ask," the editor said. "It fits so beautifully into the total context."

"About going crazy?"

"Yes, indeed. What's the first thing they teach you in your first college creative-writing course? Write about what you know. Reg Thorpe knew about going crazy, because he was engaged in going there. The story probably appealed to me because I was also going there. Now you could say—if you were an editor—that the one thing the American reading public doesn't need foisted on them is another story about Going Mad Stylishly in America, subtopic A, Nobody Talks to Each Other Anymore. A popular theme in twentieth-century literature. All the greats have taken a hack at it and all the hacks have taken an ax to it. But this story was funny. I mean, it was really hilarious.

"I hadn't read anything like it before and I haven't since. The closest would be some of F. Scott Fitzgerald's stories . . . and *Gatsby*. The fellow in Thorpe's story was going crazy, but he was doing it in a very funny way. You kept grinning, and there were a couple of places in this story—the place where the hero dumps the lime Jell-O on the fat girl's head is the best—where you laugh right out loud. But they're jittery laughs, you know. You laugh and then you want to look over your shoulder to see what heard you. The opposing lines of tension in that story were really extraordinary. The more you laughed, the more nervous you got. And the more nervous you got, the more you laughed . . . right up to the point where the hero goes home from the party given in his honor and kills his wife and baby daughter."

"What's the plot?" the agent asked.

"No," the editor said, "that doesn't matter. It was just a

story about a young man gradually losing his struggle to cope with success. It's better left vague. A detailed plot synopsis would only be boring. They always are.

"Anyway, I wrote him a letter. It said this: 'Dear Reg Thorpe, I've just read "The Ballad of the Flexible Bullet" and I think it's great. I'd like to publish it in *Logan's* early next year, if that fits. Does $800 sound okay? Payment on acceptance. More or less.' New paragraph."

The editor indented the evening air with his cigarette.

" 'The story runs a little long, and I'd like you to shorten it by about five hundred words, if you could. I would settle for a two-hundred-word cut, if it comes to that. We can always drop a cartoon.' Paragraph. 'Call, if you want.' My signature. And off the letter went, to Omaha."

"And you remember it, word for word like that?" the writer's wife asked.

"I kept all the correspondence in a special file," the editor said. "His letters, carbons of mine back. There was quite a stack of it by the end, including three or four pieces of correspondence from Jane Thorpe, his wife. I've read the file over quite often. No good, of course. Trying to understand the flexible bullet is like trying to understand how a Möbius strip can have only one side. That's just the way things are in this best-of-all-possible worlds. Yes, I know it all word for word, or almost. Some people have the Declaration of Independence by heart."

"Bet he called you the next day," the agent said, grinning. "Collect."

"No, he didn't call. Shortly after *Underworld Figures*, Thorpe stopped using the telephone altogether. His wife told me that. When they moved to Omaha from New York, they didn't even have a phone put in the new house. He had decided, you see, that the telephone system didn't really run on electricity but on radium. He thought it was one of the two or three best-kept secrets in the history of the modern world. He claimed—to his wife—that all the radium was responsible for the growing cancer rate, not cigarettes or automobile emissions or industrial pollution. Each telephone had a small radium crystal in the handset, and every time you used the phone, you shot your head full of radiation."

"Yuh, he was crazy," the writer said, and they all laughed.

"He wrote instead," the editor said, flicking his cigarette

in the direction of the lake. "His letter said this: 'Dear Henry Wilson (or just Henry, if I may), Your letter was both exciting and gratifying. My wife was, if anything, more pleased than I. The money is fine . . . although in all honesty I must say that the idea of being published in *Logan's* at all seems like more than adequate compensation (but I'll take it, I'll take it). I've looked over your cuts, and they seem fine. I think they'll improve the story as well as clear space for those cartoons. All best wishes, Reg Thorpe.'"

"Under his signature was a funny little drawing . . . more like a doodle. An eye in a pyramid, like the one on the back of the dollar bill. But instead of Novus Ordo Seclorum on the banner beneath, there were these words: Fornit Some Fornus.''

"Either Latin or Groucho Marx," the agent's wife said.

"Just part of Reg Thorpe's growing eccentricity," the editor said. "His wife told me that Reg had come to believe in 'little people,' sort of like elves or fairies. The Fornits. They were luck-elves, and he thought one of them lived in his typewriter."

"Oh my Lord," the writer's wife said.

"According to Thorpe, each Fornit has a small device, like a flitgun, full of . . . good-luck dust, I guess you'd call it. And the good-luck dust—"

"—is called fornus," the writer finished. He was grinning broadly.

"Yes. And his wife thought it quite funny, too. At first. In fact, she thought at first—Thorpe had conceived the Fornits two years before, while he was drafting *Underworld Figures*— that it was just Reg, having her on. And maybe at first he was. It seems to have progressed from a whimsy to a superstition to an outright belief. It was . . . a flexible fantasy. But hard in the end. Very hard."

They were all silent. The grins had faded.

"The Fornits had their funny side," the editor said. "Thorpe's typewriter started going to the shop a lot near the end of their stay in New York, and it was even a more frequent thing when they moved to Omaha. He had a loaner while it was being fixed for the first time out there. The dealership manager called a few days after Reg got his own machine back to tell him he was going to send a bill for cleaning the loaner as well as Thorpe's own machine."

"What was the trouble?" the agent's wife asked.

"I think I know," the writer's wife said.

"It was full of food," the editor said. "Tiny bits of cake and cookies. There was peanut butter smeared on the platens of the keys themselves. Reg was feeding the Fornit in his typewriter. He also 'fed' the loaner, on the off chance that the Fornit had made the switch."

"Boy," the writer said.

"I knew none of these things then, you understand. For the nonce, I wrote back to him and told him how pleased I was. My secretary typed the letter and brought it in for my signature, and then she had to go out for something. I signed it and she wasn't back. And then—for no real reason at all—I put the same doodle below my name. Pyramid. Eye. And 'Fornit Some Fornus.' Crazy. The secretary saw it and asked me if I wanted it sent out that way. I shrugged and told her to go ahead.

"Two days later Jane Thorpe called me. She told me that my letter had excited Reg a great deal. Reg thought he had found a kindred soul . . . someone else who knew about the Fornits. You see what a crazy situation it was getting to be? As far as I knew at that point, a Fornit could have been anything from a lefthanded monkey wrench to a Polish steak knife. Ditto fornus. I explained to Jane that I had merely copied Reg's own design. She wanted to know why. I slipped the question, although the answer would have been because I was very drunk when I signed the letter."

He paused, and an uncomfortable silence fell on the back lawn area. People looked at the sky, the lake, the trees, although they were no more interesting now than they had been a minute or two before.

"I had been drinking all my adult life, and it's impossible for me to say when it began to get out of control. In the professional sense I was on top of the bottle until nearly the very end. I would begin drinking at lunch and come back to the office *el blotto*. I functioned perfectly well there, however. It was the drinks after work—first on the train, then at home—that pushed me over the functional point.

"My wife and I had been having problems that were unrelated to the drinking, but the drinking made the other problems worse. For a long time she had been preparing to leave, and a week before the Reg Thorpe story came in, she did it.

"I was trying to deal with that when the Thorpe story came in. I was drinking too much. And to top it all off, I was having—well, I guess now it's fashionable to call it a mid-life crisis. All I knew at the time was that I was as depressed about my professional life as I was about my personal one. I was coming to grips—or trying to—with a growing feeling that editing mass-market stories that would end up being read by nervous dental patients, housewives at lunchtime, and an occasional bored college student was not exactly a noble occupation. I was coming to grips—again, trying to, all of us at *Logan's* were at that time—with the idea that in another six months, or ten, or fourteen, there might not be any *Logan's*.

"Into this dull autumnal landscape of middle-aged angst comes a very good story by a very good writer, a funny, energetic look at the mechanics of going crazy. It was like a bright ray of sun. I know it sounds strange to say that about a story that ends with the protagonist killing his wife and infant child, but you ask any editor what real joy is, and he'll tell you it's the great story or novel you didn't expect, landing on your desk like a big Christmas present. Look, you all know that Shirley Jackson story, 'The Lottery.' It ends on one of the most downbeat notes you can imagine. I mean, they take a nice lady out and stone her to death. Her son and daughter participate in her murder, for Christ's sake. But it was a great piece of storytelling . . . and I bet the editor at the *New Yorker* who read the story first went home that night whistling.

"What I'm trying to say is the Thorpe story was the best thing in my life right then. The one good thing. And from what his wife told me on the phone that day, my acceptance of that story was the one good thing that had happened to him lately. The author-editor relationship is always mutual parasitism, but in the case of Reg and me, that parasitism was heightened to an unnatural degree."

"Let's go back to Jane Thorpe," the writer's wife said.

"Yes, I did sort of leave her on a side-track, didn't I? She was angry about the Fornit business. At first, I told her I had simply doodled that eye-and-pyramid symbol under my signature, with no knowledge of what it might be, and apologized for whatever I'd done.

"She got over her anger and spilled everything to me. She'd been getting more and more anxious, and she had no one at all to talk to. Her folks were dead, and all her friends were back in New York. Reg wouldn't allow anyone at all in the house. They were tax people, he said, or FBI, or CIA. Not long after they moved to Omaha, a little girl came to the door selling Girl Scout cookies. Reg yelled at her, told her to get the hell out, he knew why she was there, and so on. Jane tried to reason with him. She pointed out that the girl had only been ten years old. Reg told her that the tax people had no souls, no consciences. And besides, he said, the little girl might have been an android. Androids wouldn't be subject to the child-labor laws. He wouldn't put it past the tax people to send an android Girl Scout full of radium crystals to find out if he was keeping any secrets . . . and to shoot him full of cancer rays in the meantime.''

"Good Lord,'' the agent's wife said.

"She'd been waiting for a friendly voice and mine was the first. I got the Girl Scout story, I found out about the care and feeding of Fornits, about fornus, about how Reg refused to use a telephone. She was talking to me from a pay booth in a drugstore five blocks over. She told me that she was afraid it wasn't really tax men or FBI or CIA Reg was worried about. She thought he was really afraid that *They*—some hulking, anonymous group that hated Reg, was jealous of Reg, would stop at nothing to get Reg—had found out about his Fornit and wanted to kill it. If the Fornit was dead, there would be no more novels, no more short stories, nothing. You see? The essence of insanity. *They* were out to get him. In the end, not even the IRS, which had given him the very devil of a time over the income *Underworld Figures* generated, would serve as the boogeyman. In the end it was just *They*. The perfect paranoid fantasy. *They* wanted to kill his Fornit.''

"My God, what did you say to her?'' the agent asked.

"I tried to reassure her,'' the editor said. "There I was, freshly returned from a five-martini lunch, talking to this terrified woman who was standing in a drugstore phone booth in Omaha, trying to tell her it was all right, not to worry that her husband believed that the phones were full of radium crystals, that a bunch of anonymous people were sending android Girl Scouts to get the goods on him, not to worry that her husband had disconnected his talent from his mentality to such a degree that he could believe there was an elf living in his typewriter.

"I don't believe I was very convincing.

"She asked me—no, begged me—to work with Reg on his story, to see that it got published. She did everything but come out and say that 'The Flexible Bullet' was Reg's last contact to what we laughingly call reality.

"I asked her what I should do if Reg mentioned Fornits again. 'Humor him,' she said. Her exact words—humor him. And then she hung up.

"There was a letter in the mail from Reg the next day— five pages, typed, single-spaced. The first paragraph was about the story. The second draft was getting on well, he said. He thought he would be able to shave seven hundred words from the original ten thousand five hundred, bringing the final down to a tight nine thousand eight.

"The rest of the letter was about Fornits and fornus. His own observations, and questions . . . dozens of questions."

"Observations?" The writer leaned forward. "He was actually seeing them, then?"

"No," the editor said. "Not seeing them in an actual sense, but in another way . . . I suppose he was. You know, astronomers knew Pluto was there long before they had a telescope powerful enough to see it. They knew all about it by studying the planet Neptune's orbit. Reg was observing the Fornits in that way. They liked to eat at night, he said, had I noticed that? He fed them at all hours of the day, but he noticed that most of it disappeared after eight P.M."

"Hallucination?" the writer asked.

"No," the editor said. "His wife simply cleared as much of the food out of the typewriter as she could when Reg went out for his evening walk. And he went out every evening at nine o'clock."

"I'd say she had quite a nerve getting after you," the agent grunted. He shifted his large bulk in the lawn chair. "She was feeding the man's fantasy herself."

"You don't understand why she called and why she was so upset," the editor said quietly. He looked at the writer's wife. "But I'll bet you do, Meg."

"Maybe," she said, and gave her husband an uncomfortable sideways look. "She wasn't mad because you were feeding his fantasy. She was afraid you might upset it."

"Bravo." The editor lit a fresh cigarette. "And she removed the food for the same reason. If the food continued to accumulate in the typewriter, Reg would make the logical assumption, proceeding directly from his own decidedly illogical premise. Namely, that his Fornit had either died or left. Hence, no more fornus. Hence, no more writing. Hence . . .''

The editor let the word drift away on cigarette smoke and then resumed:

"He thought that Fornits were probably nocturnal. They didn't like loud noises—he had noticed that he hadn't been able to write on mornings after noisy parties—they hated the TV, they hated free electricity, they hated radium. Reg had sold their TV to Goodwill for twenty dollars, he said, and his wristwatch with the radium dial was long gone. Then the questions. How did I know about Fornits? Was it possible that I had one in residence? If so, what did I think about this, this, and that? I don't need to be more specific, I think. If you've ever gotten a dog of a particular breed and can recollect the questions you asked about its care and feeding, you'll know most of the questions Reg asked me. One little doodle below my signature was all it took to open Pandora's box.''

"What did you write back?" the agent asked.

The editor said slowly, "That's where the trouble really began. For both of us. Jane had said, 'Humor him,' so that's what I did. Unfortunately, I rather overdid it. I answered his letter at home, and I was very drunk. The apartment seemed much too empty. It had a stale smell—cigarette smoke, not enough airing. Things were going to seed with Sandra gone. The dropcloth on the couch all wrinkled. Dirty dishes in the sink, that sort of thing. The middle-aged man unprepared for domesticity.

"I sat there with a sheet of my personal stationery rolled into the typewriter and I thought: *I need a Fornit. In fact, I need a dozen of them to dust this damn lonely house with fornus from end to end.* In that instant I was drunk enough to envy Reg Thorpe his delusion.

"I said I had a Fornit, of course. I told Reg that mine was remarkably similar to his in its characteristics. Nocturnal. Hated loud noises, but seemed to enjoy Bach and Brahms . . . I often did my best work after an evening of listening to them, I said. I had found my Fornit had a decided taste for Kirschner's bologna . . . had Reg ever tried it? I simply left little scraps of it near the Scripto I always carried—my editorial blue pencil, if you like—and it was almost always gone in the morning. Unless, as Reg said, it had been noisy the night before. I told him I was glad to know about radium, even though I didn't have a glow-in-the-dark wristwatch. I told him my Fornit had been with me since college. I got so carried away with my own invention that I wrote nearly six pages. At the end I added a paragraph about the story, a very perfunctory thing, and signed it.''

"And below your signature—?" the agent's wife asked.

"Sure. Fornit Some Fornus." He paused. "You can't see it in the dark, but I'm blushing. I was so goddammed drunk, so goddammed *smug* . . . I might have had second thoughts in the cold light of dawn, but by then it was too late.''

"You'd mailed it the night before?" the writer murmured.

"So I did. And then, for a week and a half, I held my breath and waited. One day the manuscript came in, addressed to me, no covering letter. The cuts were as we had discussed them, and I thought that the story was letter-perfect, but the manuscript was . . . well, I put it in my briefcase, took it home, and retyped it myself. It was covered with weird yellow stains. I thought . . .''

"Urine?" the agent's wife asked.

"Yes, that's what I thought. But it wasn't. And when I got home, there was a letter in my mailbox from Reg. Ten pages this time. In the course of the letter the yellow stains were accounted for. He hadn't been able to find Kirschner's bologna, so had tried Jordan's.

"He said they loved it. Especially with mustard.

"I had been quite sober that day. But his letter combined with those pitiful mustard stains ground right into the pages of his manuscript sent me directly to the liquor cabinet. Do not pass go, do not collect two hundred dollars. Go directly to drunk.''

"What else did the letter say?" the agent's wife asked. She had grown more and more fascinated with the tale, and was now leaning over her not inconsiderable belly in a posture that reminded the writer's wife of Snoopy standing on his doghouse and pretending to be a vulture.

"Only two lines about the story this time. All credit thrown to the Fornit . . . and to me. The bologna had really been a fantastic idea. Rackne loved it, and as a consequence—''

"Rackne?" the author asked.

"That was the Fornit's name," the editor said. "Rackne. As a consequence of the bologna, Rackne had really gotten behind in the rewrite. The rest of the letter was a paranoid chant. You have never seen such stuff in your life.''

"Reg and Rackne . . . a marriage made in heaven," the writer's wife said, and giggled nervously.

"Oh, not at all," the editor said. "Theirs was a working relationship. And Rackne was male."

"Well, tell us about the letter."

"That's one I don't have by heart. It's just as well for you that I don't. Even abnormality grows tiresome after a while. The mailman was CIA. The paperboy was FBI; Reg had seen a silenced revolver in his sack of papers. The people next door were spies of some sort; they had surveillance equipment in their van. He no longer dared to go down to the corner store for supplies because the proprietor was an android. He had suspected it before, he said, but now he was sure. He had seen the wires crisscrossing under the man's scalp, where he was beginning to go bald. And the radium count in his house was way up; at night he could see a dull, greenish glow in the rooms.

"His letter finished this way: 'I hope you'll write back and apprise me of your own situation (and that of your Fornit) as regards *enemies*, Henry. I believe that reaching you has been an occurrence that transcends coincidence. I would call it a life-ring from (God? Providence? Fate? supply your own term) at the last possible instant.

'' 'It is not possible for a man to stand alone for long against a thousand *enemies*. And to discover, at last, that one is *not* alone . . . is it too much to say that the commonality of our experience stands between myself and total destruction? Perhaps not. I must know: are the *enemies* after your Fornit as they are after Rackne? If so, how are you coping? If not, do you have any idea *why not?* I repeat, *I must know.*'

"The letter was signed with the Fornit Some Fornus doodle beneath, and then a P.S. Just one sentence. But lethal. The P.S. said: 'Sometimes I wonder about my wife.'

"I read the letter through three times. In the process, I killed an entire bottle of Black Velvet. I began to consider options on how to answer his letter. It was a cry for help from a drowning man, that was pretty obvious. The story had held him together for a while, but now the story was done. Now he was depending on me to hold him together. Which was perfectly reasonable, since I'd brought the whole thing on myself.

"I walked up and down the house, through all the empty rooms. And I started to unplug things. I was very drunk, remember, and heavy drinking opens unexpected avenues of suggestibility. Which is why editors and lawyers are willing to spring for three drinks before talking contract at lunch."

The agent brayed laughter, but the mood remained tight and tense and uncomfortable.

"And please keep in mind that Reg Thorpe was one hell of a writer. He was absolutely convinced of the things he was saying. FBI. CIA. IRS. *They. The enemies.* Some writers possess a very rare gift for cooling their prose the more passionately they feel their subject. Steinbeck had it, so did Hemingway, and Reg Thorpe had that same talent. When you entered his world, everything began to seem very logical. You began to think it very likely, once you accepted the basic Fornit premise, that the paperboy *did* have a silenced .38 in his bag of papers. That the college kids next door with the van might indeed be KGB agents with death-capsules in wax molars, on a do-or-die mission to kill or capture Rackne.

"Of course, I didn't accept the basic premise. But it seemed so hard to think. And I unplugged things. First the color TV, because everybody knows that they really do give off radiation. At *Logan's* we had published an article by a perfectly reputable scientist suggesting that the radiation given off by the household color television was interrupting human brainwaves just enough to alter them minutely but permanently. This scientist suggested that it might be the reason for declining college-board scores, literacy tests, and grammar-school development of arithmetical skills. After all, who sits closer to the TV than a little kid?

"So I unplugged the TV, and it really did seem to clarify my thoughts. In fact, it made it so much better that I unplugged the radio, the toaster, the washing machine, the dryer. Then I remembered the microwave oven, and I unplugged that. I felt a real sense of relief when that fucking thing's teeth were pulled. It was one of the early ones, about the size of a house, and it probably really *was* dangerous. Shielding on them's better these days.

"It occurred to me just how many things we have in any ordinary middle-class house that plug into the wall. An image occurred to me of this nasty electrical octopus, its tentacles consisting of electrical cables, all snaking into the walls, all connected with wires outside, and all the wires leading to power stations run by the government.

"There was a curious doubling in my mind as I did those things," the editor went on, after pausing for a sip of his Fresca. "Essentially, I was responding to a superstitious impulse. There are plenty of people who won't walk under ladders or open an umbrella in the house. There are basketball players who cross themselves before taking foul shots and baseball players who change their socks when they're in a slump. I think it's the rational mind playing a bad stereo accompaniment with the irrational subconscious. Forced to define 'irrational subconscious,' I would say that it is a small padded room inside all of us, where the only furnishing is a small card table, and the only thing on the card table is a revolver loaded with flexible bullets.

"When you change course on the sidewalk to avoid the ladder or step out of your apartment into the rain with your furled umbrella, part of your integrated self peels off and steps into that room and picks the gun up off the table. You may be aware of two conflicting thoughts: *Walking under a ladder is harmless,* and *Not walking under a ladder is also harmless.* But as soon as the ladder is behind you—or as soon as the umbrella is open—you're back together again."

The writer said, "That's very interesting. Take it a step further for me, if you don't mind. When does that irrational part actually stop fooling with the gun and put it up to its temple?"

The editor said, "When the person in question starts writing letters to the op-ed page of the paper demanding that all the ladders be taken down because walking under them is dangerous."

There was a laugh.

"Having taken it that far, I suppose we ought to finish. The irrational self has actually fired the flexible bullet into the brain when the person begins tearing around town, knocking ladders over and maybe injuring the people that were working on them. It is not certifiable behavior to walk around ladders rather than under them. It is not certifiable behavior to write letters to the paper saying that New York City went broke because of all the people callously walking under workmen's ladders. But it is certifiable to start knocking over ladders."

"Because it's overt," the writer muttered.

The agent said, "You know, you've got something there, Henry. I've got this thing about not lighting three cigarettes on a match. I don't know how I got it, but I did. Then I read somewhere that it came from the trench warfare in World War I. It seems that the German sharpshooters would wait for the Tommies to start lighting each other's cigarettes. On the first light, you got the range. On the second one, you got the windage. And on the third one, you blew the guy's head off. But knowing all that didn't make any difference. I still can't light three on a match. One part of me says it doesn't matter if I light a dozen cigarettes on one match. But the other part—this very ominous voice, like an interior Boris Karloff—says '*Ohhhh, if you dooo . . .*' "

"But all madness isn't superstitious, is it?" the writer's wife asked timidly.

"Isn't it?" the editor replied. "Jeanne d'Arc heard voices from heaven. Some people think they are possessed by demons. Others see gremlins . . . or devils . . . or Fornits. The terms we use for madness suggest superstition in some form or other. Mania . . . abnormality . . . irrationality . . . lunacy . . . insanity. For the mad person, reality has skewed. The whole person begins to reintegrate in that small room where the pistol is.

"But the rational part of me was still very much there. Bloody, bruised, indignant, and rather frightened, but still on the job. Saying: 'Oh, that's all right. Tomorrow when you sober up, you can plug everything back in, thank God. Play your games if you have to. But no more than this. No further than this.'

"That rational voice was right to be frightened. There's something in us that is very much attracted to madness. Everyone who looks off the edge of a tall building has felt at least a faint, morbid urge to jump. And anyone who has ever put a loaded pistol up to his head . . ."

"Ugh, don't," the writer's wife said. "Please."

"All right," the editor said. "My point is just this: even the most well-adjusted person is holding on to his or her sanity by a greased rope. I really believe that. The rationality circuits are shoddily built into the human animal.

"With the plugs pulled, I went into my study, wrote Reg Thorpe a letter, put it in an envelope, stamped it, took it out and mailed it. I don't actually remember doing any of these things. I was too drunk. But I deduce that I did them because when I got up the next morning, the carbon was still by my typewriter, along with the stamps and the box of envelopes. The letter was about what you'd expect from a drunk. What it boiled down to was this: the enemies were drawn by electricity as well as by the Fornits themselves. Get rid of the electricity and you got rid of the enemies. At the bottom I had written, 'The electricity is fucking up your thinking about these things, Reg. Interference with brainwaves. Does your wife have a blender?' ''

''In effect, you had started writing letters to the paper,'' the writer said.

''Yes. I wrote that letter on a Friday night. On Saturday morning I got up around eleven, hung over and only blurrily aware of what sort of mischief I'd been up to the night before. Great pangs of shame as I plugged everything back in. Greater pangs of shame—and fear—when I saw what I'd written to Reg. I looked all over the house for the original to that letter, hoping like hell I hadn't mailed it. But I had. And the way I got through that day was by making a resolution to take my lumps like a man and go on the wagon. Sure I was.

''The following Wednesday there was a letter from Reg. One page, handwritten. Fornit Some Fornus doodles all over it. In the center, just this: 'You were right. Thank you, thank you, thank you. Reg. You were right. Everything is fine now. Reg. Thanks a lot. Reg. Fornit is fine. Reg. Thanks. Reg.' ''

''Oh, my,'' the writer's wife said.

''Bet his wife was mad,'' the agent's wife said.

''But she wasn't. Because it worked.''

''Worked?'' the agent said.

''He got my letter in the Monday-morning post. Monday afternoon he went down to the local power-company office and told them to cut his power off. Jane Thorpe, of course, was hysterical. Her range ran on electricity, she did indeed have a blender, a sewing machine, a washer-dryer combination . . . well, you understand. On Monday evening I'm sure she was ready to have my head on a plate.

''But it was Reg's behavior that made her decide I was a miracle worker instead of a lunatic. He sat her down in the living room and talked to her quite rationally. He said that he knew he'd been acting in a peculiar fashion. He knew that she'd been worried. He told her that he felt much better with the power off, and that he would be glad to help her through any inconvenience that it caused. And then he suggested that they go next door and say hello.''

"Not to the KGB agents with the radium in their van?" the writer asked.

"Yes, to them. Jane was totally floored. She agreed to go over with him but she told me that she was girding herself up for a really nasty scene. Accusations, threats, hysteria. She had begun to consider leaving Reg if he wouldn't get help for his problem. She told me that Wednesday morning on the phone that she had made herself a promise: the power was the next-to-the-last straw. One more thing, and she was going to leave for New York. She was becoming afraid, you see. The thing had worsened by such degrees as to be nearly imperceptible, and she loved him, but even for her it had gotten as far as it could go. She had decided that if Reg said one strange word to the students next door, she was going to break up housekeeping. I found out much later that she had already asked some very circumspect questions about the procedure in Nebraska to effect an involuntary committal.''

"The poor woman," the writer's wife murmured.

"But the evening was a smashing success," the editor said. "Reg was at his most charming . . . and according to Jane, that was very charming indeed. She hadn't seen him so much on in three years. The sullenness, the secretiveness, they were gone. The nervous tics. The involuntary jump and look over his shoulder whenever a door opened. He had a beer and talked about all the topics that were current back in those dim dead days: the war, the possibilities of a volunteer army, the riots in the cities, the pot laws.

"The fact that he had written *Underworld Figures* came up, and they were . . . 'author-struck' was the way Jane put it. Three of the four had read it, and you can bet the odd one wasn't going to linger any on his way to the library.''

The writer laughed and nodded. He knew about that bit.

"So," the editor said, "we leave Reg Thorpe and his wife for just a little while, without electrical power but happier than they've been in a good long time—"

"Good thing he didn't have an IBM typewriter," the agent said.

"—and return to Ye Editor. Two weeks have gone by. Summer is ending. Ye Editor has, of course, fallen off the wagon any number of times, but has managed on the whole to remain pretty respectable. The days have gone their appointed rounds. At Cape Kennedy, they are getting ready to put a man on the moon. The new issue of *Logan's,* with John Lindsay on the cover, is out on the stands, and selling miserably, as usual. I had put in a purchase order for a short story called 'The Ballad of the Flexible Bullet,' by Reg Thorpe, first serial rights, proposed publication January 1970, proposed purchase price $800, which was standard then for a *Logan's* lead story.

"I got a buzz from my superior, Jim Dohegan. Could I come up and see him? I trotted into his office at ten in the morning, looking and feeling my very best. It didn't occur to me until later that Janey Morrison, his secretary, looked like a wake in progress.

"I sat down and asked Jim what I could do for him, or vice versa. I won't say the Reg Thorpe name hadn't entered my mind; having the story was a tremendous coup for *Logan's,* and I suspected a few congratulations were in order. So you can imagine how dumbfounded I was when he slid two purchase orders across the desk at me. The Thorpe story, and a John Updike novella we had scheduled as the February fiction lead. RETURN stamped across both.

"I looked at the revoked purchase orders. I looked at Jimmy. I couldn't make any of it out. I really couldn't get my brains to work over what it meant. There was a block in there. I looked around and I saw his hot plate. Janey brought it in for him every morning when she came to work and plugged it in so he could have fresh coffee when he wanted it. That had been the drill at *Logan's* for three years or more. And that morning all I could think of was, *if that thing was unplugged, I could think. I know if that thing was unplugged, I could put this together.*

"I said, 'What is this, Jim?'

" 'I'm sorry as hell to have to be the one to tell you this, Henry,' he said. *'Logan's* isn't going to be publishing any more fiction as of January 1970.' "

The editor paused to get a cigarette, but his pack was empty. "Does anyone have a cigarette?"

The writer's wife gave him a Salem.

"Thank you, Meg."

He lit it, shook out the match, and dragged deep. The coal glowed mellowly in the dark.

"Well," he said, "I'm sure Jim thought I was crazy. I said, 'Do you mind?' and leaned over and pulled the plug on his hot plate.

"His mouth dropped open and he said, 'What the hell, Henry?'

" 'It's hard for me to think with things like that going,' I said. 'Interference.' And it really seemed to be true, because with the plug pulled, I was able to see the situation a great deal more clearly. 'Does this mean I'm pinked?' I asked him.

" 'I don't know,' he said. 'That's up to Sam and the board. I just don't know, Henry.'

"There were a lot of things I could have said. I guess what Jimmy was expecting was a passionate plea for my job. You know that saying, 'He had his ass out to the wind'? . . . I maintain that you don't understand the meaning of that phrase until you're the head of a suddenly nonexistent department.

"But I didn't plead my cause or the cause of fiction at *Logan's*. I pleaded for Reg Thorpe's story. First I said that we could move it up over the deadline—put it in the December issue.

"Jimmy said, 'Come on, Henry, the December ish is locked up. You know that. And we're talking ten thousand words here.'

" 'Nine-thousand-eight,' I said.

" 'And a full-page illo,' he said. 'Forget it.'

" 'Well, we'll scrap the art,' I said. 'Listen, Jimmy, it's a great story, maybe the best fiction we've had in the last five years.'

"Jimmy said, 'I read it, Henry. I know it's a great story. But we just can't do it. Not in December. It's Christmas, for God's sake, and you want to put a story about a guy who kills his wife and kid under the Christmas trees of America? You must be—' He stopped right there, but I saw him glance over at his hot plate. He might as well have said it out loud, you know?"

The writer nodded slowly, his eyes never leaving the dark shadow that was the editor's face.

"I started to get a headache. A very small headache at first. It was getting hard to think again. I remembered that Janey Morrison had an electric pencil sharpener on her desk. There were all those fluorescents in Jim's office. The heaters. The vending machines in the concession down the hall. When you stopped to think of it, the whole fucking building ran on electricity; it was a wonder that anyone could get anything done. That was when the idea began to creep in, I think. The idea that *Logan's* was going broke because no one could think straight. And the reason no one could think straight was because we were all cooped up in this highrise building that ran on electricity. Our brainwaves were completely messed up. I remember thinking that if you could have gotten a doctor in there with one of those EEG machines, they'd get some awfully weird graphs. Full of those big, spiky alpha waves that characterize malignant tumors in the forebrain.

"Just thinking about those things made my headache worse. But I gave it one more try. I asked him if he would at least ask Sam Vadar, the editor-in-chief, to let the story stand in the January issue. As *Logan's* fiction valedictory, if necessary. The final *Logan's* short story.

"Jimmy was fiddling with a pencil and nodding. He said, 'I'll bring it up, but you know it's not going to fly. We've got a story by a one-shot novelist and we've got a story by John Updike that's just as good . . . maybe better . . . and—'

" *'The Updike story is not better!'* I said.

" 'Well, Jesus, Henry, you don't have to shout—'

" *'I am not shouting!'* I shouted.

"He looked at me for a long time. My headache was quite bad by then. I could hear the fluorescents buzzing away. They sounded like a bunch of flies caught in a bottle. It was a really hateful sound. And I thought I could hear Janey running her electric pencil sharpener. *They're doing it on purpose,* I thought. *They want to mess me up. They know I can't think of the right things to say while those things are running, so . . . so . . .*

"Jim was saying something about bringing it up at the next editorial meeting, suggesting that instead of an arbitrary cut-off date they publish all the stories which I had verbally contracted for . . . although . . .

"I got up, went across the room, and shut off the lights.

" 'What did you do that for?' Jimmy asked.

" 'You know why I did it,' I said. 'You ought to get out of here, Jimmy, before there's nothing left of you.'

"He got up and came over to me. 'I think you ought to take the rest of the day off, Henry,' he said. 'Go home. Rest. I know you've been under a strain lately. I want you to know

I'll do the best I can on this. I feel as strongly as you do . . . well, almost as strongly. But you ought to just go home and put your feet up and watch some TV.'

" 'TV,' I said, and laughed. It was the funniest thing I'd ever heard. 'Jimmy,' I said. 'You tell Sam Vadar something else for me.'

" 'What's that, Henry?'

" 'Tell him he needs a Fornit. This whole outfit. One Fornit? A dozen of them.'

" 'A Fornit,' he said, nodding. 'Okay, Henry. I'll be sure to tell him that.'

"My headache was very bad. I could hardly even see. Somewhere in the back of my mind I was already wondering how I was going to tell Reg and wondering how Reg was going to take it.

" 'I'll put in the purchase order myself, if I can find out who to send it to,' I said. 'Reg might have some ideas. A dozen Fornits. Get them to dust this place with fornus from end to end. Shut off the fucking power, all of it.' I was walking around his office and Jimmy was staring at me with his mouth open. 'Shut off all the power, Jimmy, you tell them that. Tell Sam that. No one can think with all that electrical interference, am I right?'

" 'You're right, Henry, one hundred percent. You just go on home and get some rest, okay? Take a nap or something.'

" 'And Fornits. They don't like all that interference. Radium, electricity, it's all the same thing. Feed them bologna. Cake. Peanut butter. Can we get requisitions for that stuff?' My headache was this black ball of pain behind my eyes. I was seeing two of Jimmy, two of everything. All of a sudden I needed a drink. If there was no fornus, and the rational side of my mind assured me there was not, then a drink was the only thing in the world that would get me right.

" 'Sure, we can get the requisitions,' he said.

" 'You don't believe any of this, do you, Jimmy?' I asked.

" 'Sure I do. It's okay. You just want to go home and rest a little while.'

" 'You don't believe it now,' I said, 'but maybe you will when this rag goes into bankruptcy. How in the name of God can you believe you're making rational decisions when you're sitting less than fifteen yards from a bunch of Coke machines and candy machines and sandwich machines?' Then I really had a terrible thought. *'And a microwave oven!'* I screamed at him. *'They got a microwave oven to heat the sandwiches up in!'*

"He started to say something, but I didn't pay any attention. I ran out. Thinking of that microwave oven explained everything. I had to get away from it. That was what made the headache so bad. I remember seeing Janey and Kate Younger from the ad department and Mert Strong from publicity in the outer office, all of them staring at me. They must have heard me shouting.

"My office was on the floor just below. I took the stairs. I went into my office, turned off all the lights, and got my briefcase. I took the elevator down to the lobby, but I put my briefcase between my feet and poked my fingers in my ears. I also remember the other three or four people in the elevator looking at me rather strangely." The editor uttered a dry chuckle. "They were scared. So to speak. Cooped up in a little moving box with an obvious madman, you would have been scared, too."

"Oh, surely, *that's* a little strong," the agent's wife said.

"Not at all. Madness has to start *somewhere*. If this story's *about* anything—if events in one's own life can ever be said to be *about* anything—then this is a story about the genesis of insanity. Madness has to start somewhere, and it has to go somewhere. Like a road. Or a bullet from the barrel of a gun. I was still miles behind Reg Thorpe, but I was over the line. You bet.

"I had to go somewhere, so I went to Four Fathers, a bar on Forty-ninth. I remember picking that bar specifically because there was no juke and no color TV and not many lights. I remember ordering the first drink. After that I don't remember anything until I woke up the next day in my bed at home. There was puke on the floor and a very large cigarette burn in the sheet over me. In my stupor I had apparently escaped dying in one of two extremely nasty ways—choking or burning. Not that I probably would have felt either."

"Jesus," the agent said, almost respectfully.

"It was a blackout," the editor said. "The first real bona fide blackout of my life—but they're always a sign of the end, and you never have very many. One way or the other, you never have very many. But any alcoholic will tell you that a blackout isn't the same as *passing* out. It would save a lot of trouble if it was. No, when an alky blacks out, he keeps *doing* things. An alky in a blackout is a busy little devil. Sort of like a malign Fornit. He'll call up his ex-wife and abuse her over the phone, or drive his car the wrong way on the turnpike and wipe out a carload of kids. He'll quit his job, rob a market, give away his wedding ring. Busy little devils.

"What *I* had done, apparently, was to come home and write a letter. Only this one wasn't to Reg. It was to me. And *I* didn't write it—at least, according to the *letter* I didn't."

"Who did?" the writer's wife asked.

"Bellis."

"Who's Bellis?"

"His Fornit," the writer said almost absently. His eyes were shadowy and faraway.

"Yes, that's right," the editor said, not looking a bit surprised. He made the letter in the sweet night air for them again, indenting at the proper points with his finger.

" 'Hello from Bellis. I am sorry for your problems, my friend, but would like to point out at the start that you are not the only one with problems. This is no easy job for me. I can dust your damned machine with fornus from now unto forever, but moving the KEYS is supposed to be your job. That's what God made big people FOR. So I sympathize, but that's all of the sympathy you get.

" 'I understand your worry about Reg Thorpe. I worry not about Thorpe but my brother, Rackne. Thorpe worries about what will happen to him if Rackne leaves, but only because he is selfish. The curse of serving writers is that they are *all* selfish. He worries not about what will happen to Rackne if THORPE leaves. Or goes *el bonzo seco*. Those things have apparently never crossed his oh-so-sensitive mind. But, luckily for us, all our unfortunate problems have the same short-term solution, and so I strain my arms and my tiny body to give it to you, my drunken friend. YOU may wonder about long-term solutions; I assure you there are none. All wounds are mortal. Take what's given. You sometimes get a little slack in the rope but the rope always has an end. So what. Bless the slack and don't waste breath cursing the drop. A grateful heart knows that in the end we all swing.

" 'You must pay him for the story yourself. But not with a personal check. Thorpe's mental problems are severe and perhaps dangerous but this in no way indicates stupiddity.' "

The editor stopped here and spelled: *S-t-u-p-i-d-d-i-t-y*. Then he went on. " 'If you give him a personal check he'll crack wise in about nine seconds.

" 'Withdraw eight hundred and some few-odd dollars from your personal account and have your bank open a new account for you in the name Arvin Publishing, Inc. Make sure they understand you want checks that look businesslike— nothing with cute dogs or canyon vistas on them. Find a friend, someone you can trust, and list him as co-drawer. When the checks arrive, make one for eight hundred dollars and have the co-drawer sign the check. Send the check to Reg Thorpe. That will cover your ass for the time being.

" 'Over and out.' It was signed 'Bellis.' Not in holograph. In type."

"Whew," the writer said again.

"When I got up the first thing I noticed was the typewriter. It looked like somebody had made it up as a ghost-typewriter in a cheap movie. The day before it was an old black office Underwood. When I got up—with a head that felt about the size of North Dakota—it was a sort of gray. The last few sentences of the letter were clumped up and faded. I took one look and figured my faithful old Underwood was probably finished. I took a taste and went out into the kitchen. There was an open bag of confectioner's sugar on the counter with a scoop in it. There was confectioner's sugar everywhere between the kitchen and the little den where I did my work in those days."

"Feeding your Fornit," the writer said. "Bellis had a sweet tooth. You thought so, anyway."

"Yes. But even as sick and hung over as I was, I knew perfectly well who the Fornit was."

He ticked off the points on his fingers.

"First, Bellis was my mother's maiden name.

"Second, that phrase *el bonzo seco*. It was a private phrase my brother and I used to use to mean crazy. Back when we were kids.

"Third, and in a way most damning, was that spelling of the word 'stupidity.' It's one of those words I habitually misspell. I had an almost screamingly literate writer once who used to spell 'refrigerator' with a d—'refridgerator'—no matter how many times the copy editors blooped it. And for this guy, who had a doctoral degree from Princeton, 'ugly' was always going to be 'ughly.' ''

The writer's wife uttered a sudden laugh—it was both embarrassed and cheerful. ''I do that.''

''All I'm saying is that a man's misspellings—or a woman's—are his literary fingerprints. Ask any copy editor who has done the same writer a few times.

''No, Bellis was me and I was Bellis. Yet the advice was damned good advice. In fact, I thought it was *great* advice. But here's something else—the subconscious leaves its fingerprints, but there's a stranger down there, too. A hell of a weird guy who knows a hell of a lot. I'd never seen that phrase 'co-drawer' in my life, to the best of my knowledge . . . but there it was, and it was a good one, and I found out some time later that banks actually use it.

''I picked up the phone to call a friend of mine, and this bolt of pain—incredible!—went through my head. I thought of Reg Thorpe and his radium and put the phone down in a hurry. I went to see the friend in person after I'd taken a shower and gotten a shave and had checked myself about nine times in the mirror to make sure my appearance approximated how a rational human being is supposed to look. Even so, he asked me a lot of questions and looked me over pretty closely. So I guess there must have been a few signs that a shower, a shave, and a good dose of Listerine couldn't hide. He wasn't in the biz, and that was a help. News has a way of traveling, you know. In the biz. So to speak. Also, if he'd been in the biz, he would have known Arvin Publishing, Inc., was responsible for *Logan's* and would have wondered just what sort of scam I was trying to pull. But he wasn't, he didn't, and I was able to tell him it was a self-publishing venture I was interested in since *Logan's* had apparently decided to eighty-six the fiction department.''

''Did he ask you why you were calling it Arvin Publishing?'' the writer asked.

''Yes.''

''What did you tell him?''

''I told him,'' the editor said, smiling a wintry smile, ''that Arvin was my mother's maiden name.''

There was a little pause, and then the editor resumed; he spoke almost uninterrupted to the end.

''So I began waiting for the printed checks, of which I

wanted exactly one. I exercised to pass the time. You know—pick up the glass, flex the elbow, empty the glass, flex the elbow again. Until all that exercise wears you out and you just sort of fall forward with your head on the table. Other things happened, but those were the ones that really occupied my mind—the waiting and the flexing. As I remember. I have to reiterate that, because I was drunk a lot of the time, and for every single thing I remember, there are probably fifty or sixty I don't.

"I quit my job—that caused a sigh of relief all around, I'm sure. From them because they didn't have to perform the existential task of firing me for craziness from a department that was no longer in existence, me because I didn't think I could ever face that building again—the elevator, the fluorescents, the phones, the thought of all that waiting electricity.

"I wrote Reg Thorpe and his wife a couple of letters each during that three-week period. I remember doing hers, but not his—like the letter from Bellis, I wrote those letters in black-out periods. But I hewed to my old work habits when I was blotto, just as I hewed to my old misspellings. I never failed to use a carbon . . . and when I came to the next morning, the carbons were lying around. It was like reading letters from a stranger.

"Not that the letters were crazy. Not at all. The one where I finished up with the P.S. about the blender was a lot worse. These letters seemed . . . almost reasonable."

He stopped and shook his head, slowly and wearily.

"Poor Jane Thorpe. Not that things *appeared* to be all that bad at their end. It must have seemed to her that her husband's editor was doing a very skillful—and humane—job of humoring him out of his deepening depression. The question of whether or not it's a good idea to humor a person who has been entertaining all sorts of paranoid fantasies—fantasies which almost led in one case to an actual assault on a little girl—probably occurred to her; if so, she chose to ignore the negative aspects, because she was humoring him, too. Nor have I ever blamed her for it—he wasn't just a meal ticket, some nag that was to be worked and humored, humored and worked until he was ready for the knacker's shop; she loved the guy. In her own special way, Jane Thorpe was a great lady. And after living with Reg from the Early Times to the High Times and finally to the Crazy Times, I think she would have agreed with Bellis about blessing the slack and not wasting your breath cursing the drop. Of course, the more slack you get, the harder you snap when you finally fetch up at the end . . . but even that quick snap can be a blessing, I reckon—who wants to strangle?

"I had return letters from both of them in that short period—remarkably sunny letters . . . although there was a strange, almost final quality to that sunlight. It seemed as if . . . well, never mind the cheap philosophy. If I can think of what I mean, I'll say it. Let it go for now.

"He was playing hearts with the kids next door every night, and by the time the leaves started to fall, they thought Reg Thorpe was just about God come down to earth. When they weren't playing cards or tossing a Frisbee they were talking literature, with Reg gently rallying them through their paces. He'd gotten a puppy from the local animal shelter and walked it every morning and night, meeting other people on the block the way you do when you walk your mutt. People who'd decided the Thorpes were really very peculiar people now began to change their minds. When Jane suggested that, without electrical appliances, she could really use a little house help, Reg agreed at once. She was flabbergasted by his cheery acceptance of the idea. It wasn't a question of money—after *Underworld Figures* they were rolling in dough—it was a question, Jane figured, of *they*. *They* were everywhere, that was Reg's scripture, and what better agent for *they* than a cleaning woman that went everywhere in your house, looked under beds and in closets and probably in desk drawers as well, if they weren't locked and then nailed shut for good measure.

"But he told her to go right ahead, told her he felt like an insensitive clod not to've thought of it earlier, even though—she made a point of telling me this—he was doing most of the heavy chores, such as the hand-washing, himself. He only made one small request: that the woman not be allowed to come into his study.

"Best of all, most encouraging of all from Jane's standpoint, was the fact that Reg had gone back to work, this time on a new novel. She had read the first three chapters and thought they were marvelous. All of this, she said, had begun when I had accepted 'The Ballad of the Flexible Bullet' for

Logan's—the period before that had been dead low ebb. And she blessed me for it.

"I am sure she really meant that last, but her blessing seemed to have no great warmth, and the sunniness of her letter was marred somehow—here we are, back to *that*. The sunshine in her letter was like sunshine on a day when you see those mackerel-scale clouds that mean it's going to rain like hell soon.

"All this good news—hearts and dog and cleaning woman and new novel—and yet she was too intelligent to really believe he was getting well again . . . or so I believed, even in my own fog. Reg had been exhibiting symptoms of psychosis. Psychosis is like lung cancer in one way—neither one of them clears up on its own, although both cancer patients and lunatics may have their good days.

"May I borrow another cigarette, dear?"

The writer's wife gave him one.

"After all," he resumed, bringing out the Ronson, "the signs of his *idée fixe* were all around her. No phone; no electricity. He'd put Reynolds Wrap over all of the switchplates. He was putting food in his typewriter as regularly as he put it into the new puppy's dish. The students next door thought he was a great guy, but the students next door didn't see Reg putting on rubber gloves to pick up the newspaper off the front stoop in the morning because of his radiation fears. They didn't hear him moaning in his sleep, or have to soothe him when he woke up screaming with dreadful nightmares he couldn't remember.

"You, my dear"—he turned toward the writer's wife— "have been wondering why she stuck with him. Although you haven't said as much, it's been on your mind. Am I right?"

She nodded.

"Yes. And I'm not going to offer a long motivational thesis—the convenient thing about stories that are true is that you only need to say *this is what happened* and let people worry for themselves about the why. Generally, nobody ever knows why things happen anyway . . . particularly the ones who say they do.

"But in terms of Jane Thorpe's own selective perception, things *had* gotten one hell of a lot better. She interviewed a middle-aged black woman about the cleaning job, and brought herself to speak as frankly as she could about her husband's idiosyncrasies. The woman, Gertrude Rulin by name, laughed and said she'd done for people who were a whole lot stranger. Jane spent the first week of the Rulin woman's employ pretty much the way she'd spent that first visit with the young people next door—waiting for some crazy outburst. But Reg charmed her as completely as he'd charmed the kids, talking to her about her church work, her husband, and her youngest son, Jimmy, who, according to Gertrude, made Dennis the Menace look like the biggest bore in the first grade. She'd had eleven children in all, but there was a nine-year gap between Jimmy and his next oldest sib. He made things hard on her.

"Reg seemed to be getting well . . . at least, if you looked at things a certain way he did. But he was just as crazy as ever, of course, and so was I. Madness may well be a sort of flexible bullet, but any ballistics expert worth his salt will tell you no two bullets are exactly the same. Reg's one letter to me talked a little bit about his new novel, and then passed directly to Fornits. Fornits in general, Rackne in particular. He speculated on whether *they* actually wanted to kill Fornits, or—he thought this more likely—capture them alive and study them. He closed by saying, 'Both my appetite and my outlook on life have improved immeasurably since we began our correspondence, Henry. Appreciate it all. Affectionately yours, Reg.' And a P.S. below inquiring casually if an illustrator had been assigned to do his story. That caused a guilty pang or two and a quick trip to the liquor cabinet on my part.

"Reg was into Fornits; I was into wires.

"My answering letter mentioned Fornits only in passing—by then I really *was* humoring the man, at least on that subject; an elf with my mother's maiden name and my own bad spelling habits didn't interest me a whole hell of a lot.

"What had come to interest me more and more was the subject of electricity, and microwaves, and RF waves, and RF interference from small appliances, and low-level radiation, and Christ knows what else. I went to the library and took out books on the subject; I bought books on the subject. There was a lot of scary stuff in them . . . and of course that was just the sort of stuff I was looking for.

"I had my phone taken out and my electricity turned off. It helped for a while, but one night when I was staggering in the door drunk with a bottle of Black Velvet in my hand and another one in my topcoat pocket, I saw this little red eye peeping down at me from the ceiling. God, for a minute I thought I was going to have a heart attack. It looked like a bug up there at first . . . a great big dark bug with one glowing eye.

"I had a Coleman gas lantern and I lit it. Saw what it was at once. Only instead of relieving me, it made me feel worse. As soon as I got a good look at it, it seemed I could feel large, clear bursts of pain going through my head—like radio waves. For a moment it was as if my eyes had rotated in their sockets and I could look into my own brain and see cells in there smoking, going black, dying. It was a smoke detector—a gadget which was even newer than microwave ovens back in 1969.

"I bolted out of the apartment and went downstairs—I was on the fifth floor but by then I was always taking the stairs—and hammered on the super's door. I told him I wanted that thing out of there, wanted it out of there *right away*, wanted it out of there *tonight*, wanted it out of there *within the hour*. He looked at me as though I had gone completely—you should pardon the expression—*bonzo seco,* and I can understand that now. That smoke detector was supposed to make me feel *good,* it was supposed to make me *safe.* Now, of course, they're the law, but back then it was a Great Leap Forward, paid for by the building tenants' association.

"He removed it—it didn't take long—but the look in his eyes was not lost upon me, and I could, in some limited way, understand his feelings. I needed a shave, I stank of whiskey, my hair was sticking up all over my head, my topcoat was dirty. He would know I no longer went to work; that I'd had my television taken away; that my phone and electrical service had been voluntarily interrupted. He thought I was crazy.

"I may have been crazy but—like Reg—I was not stupid. I turned on the charm. Editors have got to have a certain amount, you know. And I greased the skids with a ten-dollar bill. Finally I was able to smooth things over, but I knew from the way people were looking at me in the next couple of weeks—my last two weeks in the building, as things turned out—that the story had traveled. The fact that no members of the tenants' association approached me to make wounded noises about my ingratitude was particularly telling. I suppose they thought I might take after them with a steak knife.

"All of that was very secondary in my thoughts that evening, however. I sat in the glow of the Coleman lantern, the only light in the three rooms except for all the electricity in Manhattan that came through the windows. I sat with a bottle in one hand, a cigarette in the other, looking at the plate in the ceiling where the smoke detector with its single red eye—an eye which was so unobtrusive in the daytime that I had never even noticed it—had been. I thought of the undeniable fact that, although I'd had all the electricity turned off in my place, there had been that one live item . . . and where there was one, there might be more.

"Even if there wasn't, the whole building was rotten with wires—it was filled with wires the way a man dying of cancer is filled with evil cells and rotting organs. Closing my eyes I could see all those wires in the darkness of their conduits, glowing with a sort of green nether light And beyond them, the entire city. One wire, almost harmless in itself, running to a switchplate . . . the wire behind the switchplate a little thicker, leading down through a conduit to the basement where it joined a still thicker wire . . . that one leading down under the street to a whole *bundle* of wires, only those wires so thick that they were really cables.

"When I got Jane Thorpe's letter mentioning the tinfoil, part of my mind recognized that she saw it as a sign of Reg's craziness, and that part knew I would have to respond as if my *whole* mind thought she was right. The other part of my mind—by far the largest part now—thought: 'What a marvelous idea!' and I covered my own switchplates in identical fashion the very next day. I was the man, remember, that was supposed to be helping Reg Thorpe. In a desperate sort of way it's actually quite funny.

"I determined that night to leave Manhattan. There was an old family place in the Adirondacks I could go to, and that sounded fine to me. The one thing keeping me in the city was Reg Thorpe's story. If 'The Ballad of the Flexible Bullet' was Reg's life-ring in a sea of madness, it was mine, too—I wanted to place it in a good magazine. With that done, I could get the hell out.

"So that's where the not-so-famous Wilson-Thorpe correspondence stood just before the shit hit the fan. We were like a couple of dying drug addicts comparing the relative merits of heroin and 'ludes. Reg had Fornits in his typewriter, I had Fornits in the walls, and both of us had Fornits in our heads.

"And there was *they*. Don't forget *they*. I hadn't been flogging the story around for long before deciding *they* included every magazine fiction editor in New York—not that there were many by the fall of 1969. If you'd grouped them together, you could have killed the whole bunch of them with one shotgun shell, and before long I started to feel that was a damned good idea.

"It took about five years before I could see it from their perspective. I'd upset the super, and he was just a guy who saw me when the heat was screwed up and when it was time for his Christmas tip. These other guys . . . well, the irony was just that a lot of them really *were* my friends. Jared Baker was the assistant fiction editor at *Esquire* in those days, and Jared and I were in the same rifle company during World War II, for instance. These guys weren't just uneasy after sampling the new improved Henry Wilson. They were appalled. If I'd just sent the story around with a pleasant covering letter explaining the situation—my version of it, anyway—I probably would have sold the Thorpe story almost right away. But oh no, that wasn't good enough. Not for this story. I was going to see that this story got the *personal treatment*. So I went from door to door with it, a stinking, grizzled ex-editor with shaking hands and red eyes and a big old bruise on his left cheekbone from where he ran into the bathroom door on the way to the can in the dark two nights before. I might as well have been wearing a sign reading BELLEVUE-BOUND.

"Nor did I want to talk to these guys in their offices. In fact, I could not. The time had long since passed when I could get into an elevator and ride it up forty floors. So I met them like pushers meet junkies—in parks, on steps, or in the case of Jared Baker, in a Burger Heaven on Forty-ninth Street. Jared at least would have been delighted to buy me a decent meal, but the time had passed, you understand, when any self-respecting *maître d'* would have let me in a restaurant where they serve business people."

The agent winced.

"I got perfunctory promises to read the story, followed by concerned questions about how I was, how much I was drinking. I remember—hazily—trying to tell a couple of them about how electricity and radiation leaks were fucking up everyone's thinking, and when Andy Rivers, who edited fiction for *American Crossings,* suggested I ought to get some help, I told him *he* was the one who ought to get some help.

" 'You see those people out there on the street?' I said. We were standing in Washington Square Park. 'Half of them, maybe even three-quarters of them, have got brain tumors. I wouldn't sell you Thorpe's story on a bet, Andy. Hell, you couldn't understand it in this city. Your brain's in the electric chair and you don't even know it.'

"I had a copy of the story in my hand, rolled up like a newspaper. I whacked him on the nose with it, the way you'd whack a dog for piddling in the corner. Then I walked off. I remember him yelling for me to come back, something about having a cup of coffee and talking it over some more, and then I passed a discount record store with loudspeakers blasting heavy metal onto the sidewalk and banks of snowy-cold fluorescent lights inside, and I lost his voice in a kind of deep buzzing sound inside my head. I remember thinking two things—I had to get out of the city soon, very soon, or I would be nursing a brain tumor of my own, and I had to get a drink right away.

"That night when I got back to my apartment I found a note under the door. It said *We want you out of here, you crazy-bird.* I threw it away without so much as a second thought. We veteran crazy-birds have more important things to worry about than anonymous notes from fellow tenants.

"I was thinking over what I'd said to Andy Rivers about Reg's story. The more I thought about it—and the more drinks I had—the more sense it made. 'Flexible Bullet' was funny, and on the surface it was easy to follow . . . but below that surface level it was surprisingly complex. Did I really think another editor in the city could grasp the story on all levels? Maybe once, but did I still think so now that my eyes had been opened? Did I really think there was room for appreciation and understanding in a place that was wired up like a terrorist's bomb? God, loose volts were leaking out everywhere.

"I read the paper while there was still enough daylight to do so, trying to forget the whole wretched business for a while, and there on page one of the *Times* there was a story about how radioactive material from nuclear-power plants kept disappearing—the article went on to theorize that enough of that stuff in the right hands could quite easily be used to make a very dirty nuclear weapon.

"I sat there at the kitchen table as the sun went down, and in my mind's eye I could see *them* panning for plutonium dust like 1849 miners panning for gold. Only *they* didn't want to blow up the city with it, oh no. *They* just wanted to sprinkle it around and fuck up everyone's minds. They were the bad Fornits, and all that radioactive dust was bad-luck fornus. The worst bad-luck fornus of all time.

"I decided I didn't want to sell Reg's story after all—at least, not in New York. I'd get out of the city just as soon as the checks I'd ordered arrived. When I was upstate, I could start sending it around to the out-of-town literary magazines. *Sewanee Review* would be a good place to start, I reckoned, or maybe *Iowa Review*. I could explain to Reg later. Reg would understand. That seemed to solve the whole problem, so I took a drink to celebrate. And then the drink took a drink. And then the drink took the man. So to speak. I blacked out. I only had one more blackout left in me, as it happened.

"The next day my Arvin Company checks came. I typed one of them up and went to see my friend, the 'co-drawer.' There was another one of those tiresome cross-examinations, but this time I kept my temper. I wanted that signature. Finally, I got it. I went to a business supply store and had them make up an Arvin Company letter-stamp while I waited. I stamped a return address on a business envelope, typed Reg's address (the confectioner's sugar was out of my machine but the keys still had a tendency to stick), and added a brief personal note, saying that no check to an author had ever given me more personal pleasure . . . and that was true. Still is. It was almost an hour before I could bring myself to mail it—I just couldn't get over how *official* it looked. You never would have known that a smelly drunk who hadn't changed his underwear in about ten days had put *that* one together."

He paused, crushed out his cigarette, looked at his watch. Then, oddly like a conductor announcing a train's arrival in some city of importance, he said, "We have reached the inexplicable.

"This is the point in my story which most interested the two psychiatrists and various mental caseworkers with whom I was associated over the next thirty months of my life. It was the only part of it they really wanted me to recant, as a sign that I was getting well again. As one of them put it, 'This is the only part of your story which cannot be explicated as faulty induction . . . once, that is, your sense of logic has been mended.' Finally I *did* recant, because I knew—even if they didn't—that I *was* getting well, and I was damned anxious to get out of the sanitarium. I thought if I didn't get out fairly soon, I'd go crazy all over again. So I recanted— Galileo did, too, when they held his feet to the fire—but I have never recanted in my own mind. I don't say that what I'm about to tell you really happened; I only say I still *believe* it happened. That's a small qualification, but to me it's crucial.

"So, my friends, the inexplicable:

"I spent the next two days preparing to move upstate. The idea of driving the car didn't disturb me at all, by the way. I had read as a kid that the inside of a car is one of the safest places to be during an electrical storm, because the rubber tires serve as near-perfect insulators. I was actually looking forward to getting in my old Chevrolet, cranking up all the windows, and driving out of the city, which I had begun to see as a sink of lightning. Nevertheless, part of my preparations included removing the bulb in the dome light, taping over the socket, and turning the headlight knob all the way to the left to kill the dashlights.

"When I came in on the last night I meant to spend in the apartment, the place was empty except for the kitchen table, the bed, and my typewriter in the den. The typewriter was sitting on the floor. I had no intention of taking it with me—it had too many bad associations, and besides, the keys were going to stick forever. Let the next tenant have it, I thought—it, and Bellis, too.

"It was just sunset, and the place was a funny color. I was pretty drunk, and I had another bottle in my topcoat pocket against the watches of the night. I started across the den, meaning to go into the bedroom, I suppose. There I would sit on the bed and think about wires and electricity and free radiation and drink until I was drunk enough to go to sleep.

"What I called the den was really the living room. I made

it my workplace because it had the nicest light in the whole apartment—a big westward-facing window that looked all the way to the horizon. That's something close to the Miracle of the Loaves and Fishes in a fifth-floor Manhattan apartment, but the line of sight was there. I didn't question it; I just enjoyed it. That room was filled with a clear, lovely light even on rainy days.

"But the quality of the light that evening was eerie. The sunset had filled the room with a red glow. Furnace light. Empty, the room seemed too big. My heels made flat echoes on the hardwood floor.

"The typewriter sat in the middle of the floor, and I was just going around it when I saw there was a ragged scrap of paper stuck under the roller—that gave me a start, because I knew there had been no paper in the machine when I went out for the last time to get the fresh bottle.

"I looked around, wondering if there was someone—some intruder—in the place with me. Except it wasn't really intruders, or burglars, or junkies, I was thinking of . . . it was ghosts.

"I saw a ragged blank place on the wall to the left of the bedroom door. I at least understood where the paper in the typewriter had come from. Someone had simply torn off a ragged piece of the old wallpaper.

"I was still looking at this when I heard a single small clear noise—*clack!*—from behind me. I jumped and whirled around with my heart knocking in my throat. I was terrified, but I knew what that sound was just the same—there was no question at all. You work with words all your life and you know the sound of a typewriter platen hitting paper, even in a deserted room at dusk, where there is no one to strike the key."

They looked at him in the dark, their faces blurred white circles, saying nothing, slightly huddled together now. The writer's wife was holding one of the writer's hands tightly in both of her own.

"I felt . . . outside myself. Unreal. Perhaps this is always the way one feels when one arrives at the point of the inexplicable. I walked slowly over to the typewriter. My heart was pounding madly up there in my throat, but I felt mentally calm . . . icy, even.

"*Clack!* Another platen popped up. I saw it this time—the key was in the third row from the top, on the left.

"I got down on my knees very slowly, and then all the muscles in my legs seemed to go slack and I half-swooned the rest of the way down until I was sitting there in front of the typewriter with my dirty London Fog topcoat spread around me like the skirt of a girl who has made her very deepest curtsy. The typewriter clacked twice more, fast, paused, then clacked again. Each *clack* made the same kind of flat echo my footfalls had made on the floor.

"The wallpaper had been rolled into the machine so that the side with the dried glue on it was facing out. The letters were ripply and bumpy, but I could read them: *rackn,* it said. Then it clacked again and the word was *rackne.*

"Then—" He cleared his throat and grinned a little. "Even all these years later this is hard to tell . . . to just say right out. Okay. The simple fact, with no icing on it, is this. I saw a hand come out of the typewriter. An incredibly tiny hand. It came out from between the keys B and N in the bottom row, curled itself into a fist, and hammered down on the space bar. The machine jumped a space—very fast, like a hiccough—and the hand drew back down inside."

The agent's wife giggled shrilly.

"Can it, Marsha," the agent said softly, and she did.

"The clacks began to come a little faster," the editor went on, "and after a while I fancied I could hear the creature that was shoving the key arms up gasping, the way anyone will gasp when he is working hard, coming closer and closer to his physical limit. After a while the machine was hardly printing at all, and most of the keys were filled with that old gluey stuff, but I could read the impressions. It got out *rackne is d* and then the *y* key stuck to the glue. I looked at it for a moment and then I reached out one finger and freed it. I don't know if it—Bellis—could have freed it himself. I think not. But I didn't want to see it . . . him . . . try. Just the fist was enough to have me tottering on the brink. If I saw the elf entire, so to speak, I think I really would have gone crazy. And there was no question of getting up to run. All the strength had gone out of my legs.

"*Clack-clack-clack,* those tiny grunts and sobs of effort, and after every word that pallid ink- and dirt-streaked fist would come out between the B and the N and hammer down on the space bar. I don't know exactly how long it went on. Seven minutes, maybe. Maybe ten. Or maybe forever.

"Finally the clacks stopped, and I realized I couldn't hear him breathing anymore. Maybe he fainted . . . maybe he just gave up and went away . . . or maybe he died. Had a heart attack or something. All I really know for sure is that the message was not finished. It read, completely in lowercase: *rackne is dying its the little boy jimmy thorpe doesn't know tell thorpe rackne is dying the little boy jimmy is killing rackne bel* . . . and that was all.

"I found the strength to get to my feet then, and I left the room. I walked in great big tippy-toe steps, as if I thought it had gone to sleep and if I made any of those flat echoey noises on the bare wood it would wake up and the typing would start again . . . and I thought if it did, the first *clack* would start me screaming. And then I would just go on until my heart or my head burst.

"My Chevy was in the parking lot down the street, all gassed and loaded and ready to go. I got in behind the wheel and remembered the bottle in my topcoat pocket. My hands were shaking so badly that I dropped it, but it landed on the seat and didn't break.

"I remembered the blackouts, and, my friends, right then a blackout was exactly what I wanted, and exactly what I got. I remember taking the first drink from the neck of the bottle, and the second. I remember turning the key over to accessory and getting Frank Sinatra on the radio singing 'That Old Black Magic,' which seemed fitting enough. Under the circumstances. So to speak. I remember singing along, and having a few more drinks. I was in the back row of the lot, and I could see the traffic light on the corner going through its paces. I kept thinking of those flat clacking sounds in the empty room, and the fading red light in the den. I kept thinking of those puffing sounds, as if some body-building elf had hung fishing sinkers on the ends of a Q-Tip and was doing bench presses inside my old typewriter. I kept seeing the pebbly surface on the back side of that torn scrap of wallpaper. My mind kept wanting to examine what must have gone on before I came back to the apartment . . . kept wanting to see it—him—Bellis—jumping up, grabbing the loose edge of the wallpaper by the door to the bedroom because it was the only thing left in the room approximating

paper—hanging on—finally tearing it loose and carrying it
back to the typewriter on its—on *his*—head like the leaf of a
nipa palm. I kept trying to imagine how he—it—could ever
have run it into the typewriter. And none of that was blacking
out so I kept drinking and Frank Sinatra stopped and there
was an ad for Crazy Eddie's and then Sarah Vaughan came
on singing 'I'm Gonna Sit Right Down and Write Myself a
Letter' and that was something *else* I could relate to since I'd
done just that recently or at least I'd *thought* I had up until
tonight when something happened to give me cause to rethink
my position on that matter so to speak and I sang along with
good old Sarah Soul and right about then I must have achieved
escape velocity because in the middle of the second chorus
with no lag at all I was puking my guts out while somebody
first thumped my back with his palms and then lifted my
elbows behind me and put them down and then thumped my
back with his palms again. That was the trucker. Every time
he thumped I'd feel a great clot of liquid rise up in my throat
and get ready to go back down except then.he'd lift my
elbows and every time he lifted my elbows I'd puke again,
and most of it wasn't even Black Velvet but river water.
When I was able to lift my head enough to look around it was
six o'clock in the evening three days later and I was lying on
the bank of the Jackson River in western Pennsylvania, about
sixty miles north of Pittsburgh. My Chevy was sticking out of
the river, rear end up. I could still read the McCarthy sticker
on the bumper.

"Is there another Fresca, love? My throat's dry as hell."

The writer's wife fetched him one silently, and when she
handed it to him she impulsively bent and kissed his wrinkled, alligator-hide cheek. He smiled, and his eyes sparkled
in the dim light. She was, however, a good and kindly
woman, and the sparkle did not in any way fool her. It was
never merriness which made eyes sparkle that way.

"Thank you, Meg."

He drank deeply, coughed, waved away the offer of a
cigarette.

"I've had enough of those for the evening. I'm going to
quit them entirely. In my next incarnation. So to speak.

"The rest of my own tale really needs no telling. It would
have against it the only sin that any tale can ever really be
guilty of—it's predictable. They fished something like forty

bottles of Black Velvet out of my car, a good many of them empty. I was babbling about elves, and electricity, and Fornits, and plutonium miners, and fornus, and I seemed utterly insane to them, and that of course is exactly what I was.

"Now here's what happend in Omaha while I was driving around—according to the gas credit slips in the Chevy's glove compartment—five northeastern states. All of this, you understand, was information I obtained from Jane Thorpe over a long and painful period of correspondence, which culminated in a face-to-face meeting in New Haven, where she now lives, shortly after I was dismissed from the sanitarium as a reward for finally recanting. At the end of that meeting we wept in each other's arms, and that was when I began to believe that there could be a real life for me—perhaps even happiness—again.

"That day, around three o'clock in the afternoon, there was a knock at the door of the Thorpe home. It was a telegraph boy. The telegram was from me—the last item of our unfortunate correspondence. It read: REG   HAVE RELIABLE INFORMATION THAT RACKNE IS DYING   IT'S THE LITTLE BOY ACCORDING TO BELLIS   BELLIS SAYS THE BOY'S NAME IS JIMMY   FORNIT SOME FORNUS   HENRY.

"In case that marvelous Howard Baker question of *What did he know and when did he know it?* has gone through your mind, I can tell you that I knew Jane had hired a cleaning woman; I didn't know—except through Bellis—that she had a li'l-devil son named Jimmy. I suppose you'll have to take my word for that, although in all fairness I have to add that the shrinks who worked on my case over the next two and a half years never did.

"When the telegram came, Jane was at the grocery store. She found it, after Reg was dead, in one of his back pockets. The time of transmission and delivery were both noted on it, along with the added line *No telephone/Deliver original.* Jane said that although the telegram was only a day old, it had been so much handled that it looked as if he'd had it for a month.

"In a way, that telegram, those twenty-six words, was the real flexible bullet, and I fired it directly into Reg Thorpe's brain all the way from Paterson, New Jersey, and I was so fucking drunk I don't even remember doing it.

"During the last two weeks of his life, ⌐eg had fallen into a pattern that seemed normality itself. He got up at six, made breakfast for himself and his wife, then wrote for an hour. Around eight o'clock he would lock his study and take the dog for a long, leisurely walk around the neighborhood. He was very forthcoming on these walks, stopping to chat with anyone who wanted to chat with him, tying the pooch outside a nearby café to have a midmorning cup of coffee, then rambling on again. He rarely got back to the house before noon. On many days it was twelve-thirty or one o'clock. Part of this was an effort to escape the garrulous Gertrude Rulin, Jane believed, because his pattern hadn't really begun to solidify until a couple of days after she started working for them.

"He would eat a light lunch, lie down for an hour or so, then get up and write for two or three hours. In the evenings he would sometimes go next door to visit with the young people, either with Jane or alone; sometimes he and Jane took in a movie, or just sat in the living room and read. They turned in early, Reg usually a while before Jane. She wrote there was very little sex, and what there was of it was unsuccessful for both of them. 'But sex isn't as important for most women,' she said, 'and Reg was working full-out again, and that was a reasonable substitute for him. I would say that, under the circumstances, those last two weeks were the happiest in the last five years.' I damn near cried when I read that.

"I didn't know anything about Jimmy, but Reg did. Reg knew everything except for the most important fact—that Jimmy had started coming to work with his mother.

"How furious he must have been when he got my telegram and began to realize! Here *they* were, after all. And apparently his own wife was one of *them*, because *she* was in the house when Gertrude and Jimmy were there, and she had never said a thing to Reg about Jimmy. What was it he had written to me in that earlier letter? 'Sometimes I wonder about my wife.'

"When she arrived home on that day the telegram came, she found Reg gone. There was a note on the kitchen table which said, 'Love—I've gone down to the bookstore. Back by suppertime.' This seemed perfectly fine to Jane . . . but if Jane had known about my telegram, the very normality of that note would have scared the hell out of her, I think. She would have understood that Reg believed she had changed sides.

"Reg didn't go near any bookstore. He went to Littlejohn's Gun Emporium downtown. He bought a .45 automatic and two thousand rounds of ammunition. He would have bought an AK-70 if Littlejohn's had been allowed to sell them. He meant to protect his Fornit, you see. From Jimmy, from Gertrude, from Jane. From *them*.

"Everything went according to established routine the next morning. She remembered thinking he was wearing an awfully heavy sweater for such a warm fall day, but that was all. The sweater, of course, was because of the gun. He went out to walk the dog with the .45 stuffed into the waistband of his chinos.

"Except the restaurant where he usually got his morning coffee was as far as he went, and he went directly there, with no lingering or conversation along the way. He took the pup around to the loading area, tied its leash to a railing, and then went back toward his house by way of backyards.

"He knew the schedule of the young people next door very well; knew they would all be out. He knew where they kept their spare key. He let himself in, went upstairs, and watched his own house.

"At eight-forty he saw Gertrude Rulin arrive. And Gertrude wasn't alone. There was indeed a small boy with her. Jimmy Rulin's boisterous first-grade behavior convinced the teacher and the school guidance counselor almost at once that everyone (except maybe Jimmy's mother, who could have used a rest from Jimmy) would be better off if he waited another year. Jimmy was stuck with repeating kindergarten, and he had afternoon sessions for the first half of the year. The two day-care centers in her area were full, and she couldn't change to afternoons for the Thorpes because she had another cleaning job on the other side of town from two to four.

"The upshot of everything was Jane's reluctant agreement that Gertrude could bring Jimmy with her until she was able to make other arrangements. Or until Reg found out, as he was sure to do.

"She thought Reg *might* not mind—he had been so sweetly reasonable about everything lately. On the other hand, he might have a fit. If that happened, other arrangements would *have* to be made. Gertrude said she understood. And for heaven's sake, Jane added, the boy was not to touch any of Reg's things. Gertrude said for sure not; the mister's study door was locked and would stay locked.

"Thorpe must have crossed between the two yards like a sniper crossing no-man's-land. He saw Gertrude and Jane washing bed linen in the kitchen. He didn't see the boy. He moved along the side of the house. No one in the dining room. No one in the bedroom. And then, in the study, where Reg had morbidly expected to see him, there Jimmy was. The kid's face was hot with excitement, and Reg surely must have believed that here was a bona fide agent of *they* at last.

"The boy was holding some sort of death-ray in his hand, it was pointed at the desk . . . and from inside his typewriter, Reg could hear Rackne screaming.

"You may think I'm attributing subjective data to a man who's now dead—or, to be more blunt, making stuff up. But I'm not. In the kitchen, both Jane and Gertrude heard the distinctive warbling sound of Jimmy's plastic space blaster . . . he'd been shooting it around the house ever since he started coming with his mother, and Jane hoped daily that its batteries would go dead. There was no mistaking the sound. No mistaking the place it was coming from, either—Reg's study.

"The kid really *was* Dennis the Menace material, you know—if there was a room in the house where he wasn't supposed to go, that was the one place he *had* to go, or die of curiosity. It didn't take him long to discover that Jane kept a key to Reg's study on the dining-room mantel, either. Had he been in there before? I think so. Jane said she remembered giving the boy an orange three or four days before, and later, when she was clearing out the house, she found orange peels under the little studio sofa in that room. Reg didn't eat oranges—claimed he was allergic to them.

"Jane dropped the sheet she was washing back into the sink and rushed into the bedroom. She heard the loud *wah-wah-wah* of the space blaster, and she heard Jimmy, yelling: *'I'll getcha! You can't run! I can seeya through the GLASS!'* And . . . she said . . . she said that she heard something screaming. A high, despairing sound, she said, so full of pain it was almost insupportable.

" 'When I heard that,' she said, 'I knew that I would have to leave Reg no matter *what* happened, because all the old wives' tales were true . . . madness was catching. Because it was Rackne I was hearing; somehow that rotten little kid was shooting Rackne, killing it with a two-dollar space-gun from Kresge's.

" 'The study door was standing open, the key in it. Later on that day I saw one of the dining-room chairs standing by the mantel, with Jimmy's sneaker prints all over the seat. He was bent over Reg's typewriter table. He—Reg—had an old office model with glass inserts in the sides. Jimmy had the muzzle of his blaster pressed against one of those and was shooting it into the typewriter. *Wah-wah-wah-wah,* and purple pulses of light shooting out of the typewriter, and suddenly I could understand everything Reg had ever said about electricity, because although that thing ran on nothing more than harmless old C or D cells, it really did feel as if there were waves of poison coming out of that gun and rolling through my head and frying my brains.

" ' *"I seeya in there!"* Jimmy was screaming, and his face was filled with a small boy's glee—it was both beautiful and somehow gruesome. *"You can't run away from Captain Future! You're dead, alien!"* And that screaming . . . getting weaker . . . smaller . . .

" ' *"Jimmy, you stop it!"* I yelled.

" 'He jumped. I'd startled him. He turned around . . . looked at me . . . stuck out his tongue . . . and then pushed the blaster against the glass panel and started shooting again. *Wah-wah-wah,* and that rotten purple light.

" 'Gertrude was coming down the hall, yelling for him to stop, to get out of there, that he was going to get the whipping of his life . . . and then the front door burst open and Reg came up the hall, bellowing. I got one good look at him and understood that he was insane. The gun was in his hand.

" ' *"Don't you shoot my baby!"* Gertrude screamed when she saw him, and reached out to grapple with him. Reg simply clubbed her aside.

" 'Jimmy didn't even seem to realize any of this was going on—he just went on shooting the space blaster into the typewriter. I could see that purple light pulsing in the blackness between the keys, and it looked like one of those electrical arcs they tell you not to look at without a pair of special goggles because otherwise it might boil your retinas and make you blind.

" 'Reg came in, shoving past me, knocking me over.

" ' "*RACKNE!*" he screamed. "*YOU'RE KILLING RACKNE!*"

" 'And even as Reg was rushing across the room, apparently planning to kill that child,' Jane told me, 'I had time to wonder just how many times he *had* been in that room, shooting that gun into the typewriter when his mother and I were maybe upstairs changing beds or in the backyard hanging clothes where we couldn't hear the *wah-wah-wah* . . . where we couldn't hear that thing . . . the Fornit . . . inside, screaming.

" 'Jimmy didn't stop even when Reg came bursting in— just kept shooting into the typewriter as if he knew it was his last chance, and since then I have wondered if perhaps Reg wasn't right about *they,* too—only maybe *they* just sort of float around, and every now and then they dive into a person's head like someone doing a double-gainer into a swimming pool and *they* get that somebody to do the dirty work and then check out again, and the guy *they* were in says, "Huh? Me? Did *what?*"

" 'And in the second before Reg got there, the screaming from inside the typewriter turned into a brief, drilling shriek—and I saw blood splatter all over the inside of that glass insert, as if whatever was in there had finally just exploded, the way they say a live animal will explode if you put it in a microwave oven. I know how crazy it sounds, but I *saw* that blood—it hit the glass in a blot and then started to run.

" ' "Got it," Jimmy said, highly satisfied. "Got—"

" 'Then Reg threw him all the way across the room. He hit the wall. The gun was jarred out of his hand, hit the floor, and broke. It was nothing but plastic and Eveready batteries, of course.

" 'Reg looked into the typewriter, and he screamed. Not a scream of pain or fury, although there was fury in it—mostly it was a scream of grief. He turned toward the boy then. Jimmy had fallen to the floor, and whatever he *had* been—if he ever *was* anything more than just a mischievous little boy—now he was just a six-year-old in terror. Reg pointed the gun at him, and that's all I remember.' "

The editor finished his soda and put the can carefully aside.

"Gertrude Rulin and Jimmy Rulin remember enough to make up for the lack," he said. "Jane called out, *'Reg, NO!'* and when he looked around at her, she got to her feet and grappled with him. He shot her, shattering her left elbow, but she didn't let go. As she continued to grapple with him, Gertrude called to her son, and Jimmy ran to her.

"Reg pushed Jane away and shot her again. This bullet tore along the left side of her skull. Even an eighth of an inch to the right and he would have killed her. There is little doubt of that, and none at all that, if not for Jane Thorpe's intervention, he would have surely killed Jimmy Rulin and quite possibly the boy's mother as well.

"He *did* shoot the boy—as Jimmy ran into his mother's arms just outside the door. The bullet entered Jimmy's left buttock on a downward course. It exited from his upper-left thigh, missing the bone, and passed through Gertrude Rulin's shin. There was a lot of blood, but no major damage done to either.

"Gertrude slammed the study door and carried her screaming, bleeding son down the hallway and out the front door."

The editor paused again, thoughtfully.

"Jane was either unconscious by that time or she has deliberately chosen to forget what happened next. Reg sat down in his office chair and put the muzzle of the .45 against the center of his forehead. He pulled the trigger. The bullet did not pass through his brain and leave him a living vegetable, nor did it travel in a semicircle around his skull and exit harmlessly on the far side. The fantasy was flexible, but the final bullet was as hard as it could be. He fell forward across the typewriter, dead.

"When the police broke in, they found him that way; Jane was sitting in a far corner, semiconscious.

"The typewriter was covered with blood, presumably filled with blood as well; head wounds are very, very messy.

"All of the blood was Type O.

"Reg Thorpe's type.

"And that, ladies and gentlemen, is my story; I can tell no more." Indeed, the editor's voice had been reduced to little more than a husky whisper.

There was none of the usual post-party chatter, or even the awkwardly bright conversation people sometimes use to cover a cocktail-party indiscretion of some moment, or to at least disguise the fact that things had at some point become much more serious than a dinner-party situation usually warranted.

But as the writer saw the editor to his car, he was unable to forbear one final question. "The story," he said. "What happened to the story?"

"You mean Reg's—"

" 'The Ballad of the Flexible Bullet,' that's right. The story that caused it all. *That* was the real flexible bullet—for you, if not for him. What in the hell happened to this story that was so goddam great?"

The editor opened the door of his car; it was a small blue Chevette with a sticker on the back bumper which read FRIENDS DON'T LET FRIENDS DRIVE DRUNK. "No, it was never published. If Reg had a carbon copy, he destroyed it following my receipt and acceptance of the tale—considering his paranoid feelings about *they,* that would have been very much in character.

"I had his original plus three photocopies with me when I went into the Jackson River. All four in a cardboard carton. If I'd put that carton in the trunk, I would have the story now, because the rear end of my car never went under—even if it had, the pages could have been dried out. But I wanted it close to me, so I put it in the front, on the driver's side. The windows were open when I went into the water. The pages . . . I assume they just floated away and were carried out to sea. I'd rather believe that than believe they rotted along with the rest of the trash at the bottom of that river, or were eaten by catfish, or something even less aesthetically pleasing. To believe they were carried out to sea is more romantic, and slightly more unlikely, but in matters of what I choose to believe, I find I can still be flexible.

"So to speak."

The editor got into his small car and drove away. The writer stood and watched until the taillights had winked out, and then turned around. Meg was there, standing at the head of their walk in the darkness, smiling a little tentatively at him. Her arms were crossed tightly across her bosom, although the night was warm.

"We're the last two," she said. "Want to go in?"

"Sure."

Halfway up the walk she stopped and said: "There are no Fornits in your typewriter, are there, Paul?"

And the writer, who had sometimes—often—wondered exactly where the words *did* come from, said bravely: "Absolutely not."

They went inside arm in arm and closed the door against the night.

The Reach

"The Reach was wider in those days," Stella Flanders told her great-grandchildren in the last summer of her life, the summer before she began to see ghosts. The children looked at her with wide, silent eyes, and her son, Alden, turned from his seat on the porch where he was whittling. It was Sunday, and Alden wouldn't take his boat out on Sundays no matter how high the price of lobster was.

"What do you mean, Gram?" Tommy asked, but the old woman did not answer. She only sat in her rocker by the cold stove, her slippers bumping placidly on the floor.

Tommy asked his mother: "What does she mean?"

Lois only shook her head, smiled, and sent them out with pots to pick berries.

Stella thought: She's forgot. Or did she ever know?

The Reach had been wider in those days. If anyone knew it was so, that person was Stella Flanders. She had been born in 1884, she was the oldest resident of Goat Island, and she had never once in her life been to the mainland.

Do you love? This question had begun to plague her, and she did not even know what it meant.

Fall set in, a cold fall without the necessary rain to bring a really fine color to the trees, either on Goat or on Raccoon

546

Head across the Reach. The wind blew long, cold notes that fall, and Stella felt each note resonate in her heart.

On November 19, when the first flurries came swirling down out of a sky the color of white chrome, Stella celebrated her birthday. Most of the village turned out. Hattie Stoddard came, whose mother had died of pleurisy in 1954 and whose father had been lost with the *Dancer* in 1941. Richard and Mary Dodge came, Richard moving slowly up the path on his cane, his arthritis riding him like an invisible passenger. Sarah Havelock came, of course; Sarah's mother Annabelle had been Stella's best friend. They had gone to the island school together, grades one to eight, and Annabelle had married Tommy Frane, who had pulled her hair in the fifth grade and made her cry, just as Stella had married Bill Flanders, who had once knocked all of her schoolbooks out of her arms and into the mud (but she had managed not to cry). Now both Annabelle and Tommy were gone and Sarah was the only one of their seven children still on the island. *Her* husband, George Havelock, who had been known to everyone as Big George, had died a nasty death over on the mainland in 1967, the year there was no fishing. An ax had slipped in Big George's hand, there had been blood—too much of it! —and an island funeral three days later. And when Sarah came in to Stella's party and cried, "Happy birthday, Gram!" Stella hugged her tight and closed her eyes

(do you do you love?)

but she did not cry.

There was a tremendous birthday cake. Hattie had made it with her best friend, Vera Spruce. The assembled company bellowed out "Happy Birthday to You" in a combined voice that was loud enough to drown out the wind . . . for a little while, anyway. Even Alden sang, who in the normal course of events would sing only "Onward, Christian Soldiers" and the doxology in church and would mouth the words of all the rest with his head hunched and his big old jug ears just as red as tomatoes. There were ninety-five candles on Stella's cake, and even over the singing she heard the wind, although her hearing was not what it once had been.

She thought the wind was calling her name.

"I was not the only one," she would have told Lois's children if she could. *"In my day there were many that lived*

*and died on the island. There was no mail boat in those days;
Bull Symes used to bring the mail when there was mail. There
was no ferry, either. If you had business on the Head, your
man took you in the lobster boat. So far as I know, there
wasn't a flushing toilet on the island until 1946. 'Twas Bull's
boy Harold that put in the first one the year after the heart
attack carried Bull off while he was out dragging traps. I
remember seeing them bring Bull home. I remember that they
brought him up wrapped in a tarpaulin, and how one of his
green boots poked out. I remember . . ."*

And they would say: "What, Gram? What do you remember?"

How would she answer them? Was there more?

On the first day of winter, a month or so after the birthday
party, Stella opened the back door to get stovewood and
discovered a dead sparrow on the back stoop. She bent down
carefully, picked it up by one foot, and looked at it.

"Frozen," she announced, and something inside her spoke
another word. It had been forty years since she had seen a
frozen bird—1938. The year the Reach had frozen.

Shuddering, pulling her coat closer, she threw the dead
sparrow in the old rusty incinerator as she went by it. The day
was cold. The sky was a clear, deep blue. On the night of her
birthday four inches of snow had fallen, had melted, and no
more had come since then. "Got to come soon," Larry
McKeen down at the Goat Island Store said sagely, as if
daring winter to stay away.

Stella got to the woodpile, picked herself an armload and
carried it back to the house. Her shadow, crisp and clean,
followed her.

As she reached the back door, where the sparrow had
fallen, Bill spoke to her—but the cancer had taken Bill twelve
years before. "Stella," Bill said, and she saw his shadow fall
beside her, longer but just as clear-cut, the shadow-bill of his
shadow-cap twisted jauntily off to one side just as he had
always worn it. Stella felt a scream lodged in her throat. It
was too large to touch her lips.

"Stella," he said again, "when you comin cross to the
mainland? We'll get Norm Jolley's old Ford and go down to
Bean's in Freeport just for a lark. What do you say?"

She wheeled, almost dropping her wood, and there was no

one there. Just the dooryard sloping down to the hill, then the wild white grass, and beyond all, at the edge of everything, clear-cut and somehow magnified, the Reach . . . and the mainland beyond it.

"Gram, what's the Reach?" Lona might have asked . . . although she never had. And she would have given them the answer any fisherman knew by rote: a Reach is a body of water between two bodies of land, a body of water which is open at either end. The old lobsterman's joke went like this: know how to read y'compass when the fog comes, boys; between Jonesport and London there's a mighty long Reach.

"Reach is the water between the island and the mainland," she might have amplified, giving them molasses cookies and hot tea laced with sugar. "I know that much. I know it as well as my husband's name . . . and how he used to wear his hat."

"Gram?" Lona would say. "How come you never been across the Reach?"

"Honey," she would say, "I never saw any reason to go."

In January, two months after the birthday party, the Reach froze for the first time since 1938. The radio warned islanders and main-landers alike not to trust the ice, but Stewie McClelland and Russell Bowie took Stewie's Bombardier Skiddoo out anyway after a long afternoon spent drinking Apple Zapple wine, and sure enough, the skiddoo went into the Reach. Stewie managed to crawl out (although he lost one foot to frostbite). The Reach took Russell Bowie and carried him away.

That January 25 there was a memorial service for Russell. Stella went on her son Alden's arm, and he mouthed the words to the hymns and boomed out the doxology in his great tuneless voice before the benediction. Stella sat afterward with Sarah Havelock and Hattie Stoddard and Vera Spruce in the glow of the wood fire in the town-hall basement. A going-away party for Russell was being held, complete with Za-Rex punch and nice little cream-cheese sandwiches cut into triangles. The men, of course, kept wandering out back for a nip of something a bit stronger than Za-Rex. Russell Bowie's new widow sat red-eyed and stunned beside Ewell

McCracken, the minister. She was seven months big with child—it would be her fifth—and Stella, half-dozing in the heat of the woodstove, thought: *She'll be crossing the Reach soon enough, I guess. She'll move to Freeport or Lewiston and go for a waitress, I guess.*

She looked around at Vera and Hattie, to see what the discussion was.

"No, I didn't hear," Hattie said. "What *did* Freddy say?"

They were talking about Freddy Dinsmore, the oldest man on the island (two years younger'n me, though, Stella thought with some satisfaction), who had sold out his store to Larry McKeen in 1960 and now lived on his retirement.

"Said he'd never seen such a winter," Vera said, taking out her knitting. "He says it is going to make people sick."

Sarah Havelock looked at Stella, and asked if Stella had ever seen such a winter. There had been no snow since that first little bit; the ground lay crisp and bare and brown. The day before, Stella had walked thirty paces into the back field, holding her right hand level at the height of her thigh, and the grass there had snapped in a neat row with a sound like breaking glass.

"No," Stella said. "The Reach froze in '38, but there was snow that year. Do you remember Bull Symes, Hattie?"

Hattie laughed. "I think I still have the black-and-blue he gave me on my sit-upon at the New Year's party in '53. He pinched me *that* hard. What about him?"

"Bull and my own man walked across to the mainland that year," Stella said. "That February of 1938. Strapped on snowshoes, walked across to Dorrit's Tavern on the Head, had them each a shot of whiskey, and walked back. They asked me to come along. They were like two little boys off to the sliding with a toboggan between them."

They were looking at her, touched by the wonder of it. Even Vera was looking at her wide-eyed, and Vera had surely heard the tale before. If you believed the stories, Bull and Vera had once played some house together, although it was hard, looking at Vera now, to believe she had ever been so young.

"And you didn't go?" Sarah asked, perhaps seeing the reach of the Reach in her mind's eye, so white it was almost blue in the heatless winter sunshine, the sparkle of the snow crystals, the mainland drawing closer, walking across, yes, walking across the ocean just like Jesus-out-of-the-boat, leaving the island for the one and only time in your life on *foot*—

"No," Stella said. Suddenly she wished she had brought her own knitting. "I didn't go with them."

"Why *not*?" Hattie asked, almost indignantly.

"It was washday," Stella almost snapped, and then Missy Bowie, Russell's widow, broke into loud, braying sobs. Stella looked over and there sat Bill Flanders in his red-and-black-checked jacket, hat cocked to one side, smoking a Herbert Tareyton with another tucked behind his ear for later. She felt her heart leap into her chest and choke between beats.

She made a noise, but just then a knot popped like a rifle shot in the stove, and neither of the other ladies heard.

"Poor *thing*," Sarah nearly cooed.

"Well shut of that good-for-nothing," Hattie grunted. She searched for the grim depth of the truth concerning the departed Russell Bowie and found it: "Little more than a tramp for pay, that man. She's well out of *that* two-hoss trace."

Stella barely heard these things. There sat Bill, close enough to the Reverend McCracken to have tweaked his nose if he so had a mind; he looked no more than forty, his eyes barely marked by the crow's-feet that had later sunk so deep, wearing his flannel pants and his gum-rubber boots with the gray wool socks folded neatly down over the tops.

"We're waitin on you, Stel," he said. "You come on across and see the mainland. You won't need no snowshoes this year."

There he sat in the town-hall basement, big as Billy-be-damned, and then another knot exploded in the stove and he was gone. And the Reverend McCracken went on comforting Missy Bowie as if nothing had happened.

That night Vera called up Annie Phillips on the phone, and in the course of the conversation mentioned to Annie that Stella Flanders didn't look well, not at all well.

"Alden would have a scratch of a job getting her off-island if she took sick," Annie said. Annie liked Alden because her own son Toby had told her Alden would take nothing stronger than beer. Annie was strictly temperance, herself.

"Wouldn't get her off 'tall unless she was in a coma," Vera said, pronouncing the word in the downeast fashion: *comer*. "When Stella says 'Frog,' Alden jumps. Alden ain't but half-bright, you know. Stella pretty much runs him."

"Oh, ayuh?" Annie said.

Just then there was a metallic crackling sound on the line.

Vera could hear Annie Phillips for a moment longer—not the words, just the sound of her voice going on behind the crackling—and then there was nothing. The wind had gusted up high and the phone lines had gone down, maybe into Godlin's Pond or maybe down by Borrow's Cove, where they went into the Reach sheathed in rubber. It was possible that they had gone down on the other side, on the Head . . . and some might even have said (only half-joking) that Russell Bowie had reached up a cold hand to snap the cable, just for the hell of it.

Not 700 feet away Stella Flanders lay under her puzzle-quilt and listened to the dubious music of Alden's snores in the other room. She listened to Alden so she wouldn't have to listen to the wind . . . but she heard the wind anyway, oh yes, coming across the frozen expanse of the Reach, a mile and a half of water that was now overplated with ice, ice with lobsters down below, and groupers, and perhaps the twisting, dancing body of Russell Bowie, who used to come each April with his old Rogers rototiller and turn her garden.

Who'll turn the earth this April? she wondered as she lay cold and curled under her puzzle-quilt. And as a dream in a dream, her voice answered her voice: *Do you love?* The wind gusted, rattling the storm window. It seemed that the storm window was talking to her, but she turned her face away from its words. And did not cry.

"But Gram," Lona would press (she never gave up, not that one, she was like her mom, and her grandmother before her), "you still haven't told why you never went across."

"Why, child, I have always had everything I wanted right here on Goat."

"But it's so small. We live in Portland. There's buses, Gram!"

"I see enough of what goes on in cities on the TV. I guess I'll stay where I am."

Hal was younger, but somehow more intuitive; he would not press her as his sister might, but his question would go closer to the heart of things: "You never wanted to go across, Gram? Never?"

And she would lean toward him, and take his small hands, and tell him how her mother and father had come to the island shortly after they were married, and how Bull Symes's grandfather had taken Stella's father as a 'prentice on his boat. She would tell him how her mother had conceived four times but one of her babies had miscarried and another had died a week after birth—she would have left the island if they could have saved it at the mainland hospital, but of course it was over before that was even thought of.

She would tell them that Bill had delivered Jane, their grandmother, but not that when it was over he had gone into the bathroom and first puked and then wept like a hysterical woman who had her monthlies p'ticularly bad. Jane, of course, had left the island at fourteen to go to high school; girls didn't get married at fourteen anymore, and when Stella saw her go off in the boat with Bradley Maxwell, whose job it had been to ferry the kids back and forth that month, she knew in her heart that Jane was gone for good, although she would come back for a while. She would tell them that Alden had come along ten years later, after they had given up, and as if to make up for his tardiness, here was Alden still, a lifelong bachelor, and in some ways Stella was grateful for that because Alden was not terribly bright and there are plenty of women willing to take advantage of a man with a slow brain and a good heart (although she would not tell the children that last, either).

She would say: "Louis and Margaret Godlin begat Stella Godlin, who became Stella Flanders; Bill and Stella Flanders begat Jane and Alden Flanders and Jane Flanders became Jane Wakefield; Richard and Jane Wakefield begat Lois Wakefield, who became Lois Perrault; David and Lois Perrault begat Lona and Hal. Those are your names, children: you are Godlin-Flanders-Wakefield-Perrault. Your blood is in the stones of this island, and I stay here because the mainland is too far to reach. Yes, I love; I have loved, anyway, or at least tried to love, but memory is so wide and so deep, and I cannot cross. Godlin-Flanders-Wakefield-Perrault . . ."

That was the coldest February since the National Weather Service began keeping records, and by the middle of the month the ice covering the Reach was safe. Snowmobiles buzzed and whined and sometimes turned over when they climbed the ice-heaves wrong. Children tried to skate, found the ice too bumpy to be any fun, and went back to Godlin's Pond on the far side of the hill, but not before little Justin

McCracken, the minister's son, caught his skate in a fissure and broke his ankle. They took him over to the hospital on the mainland where a doctor who owned a Corvette told him, "Son, it's going to be as good as new."

Freddy Dinsmore died very suddenly just three days after Justin McCracken broke his ankle. He caught the flu late in January, would not have the doctor, told everyone it was "Just a cold from goin out to get the mail without m'scarf," took to his bed, and died before anyone could take him across to the mainland and hook him up to all those machines they have waiting for guys like Freddy. His son George, a tosspot of the first water even at the advanced age (for tosspots, anyway) of sixty-eight, found Freddy with a copy of the *Bangor Daily News* in one hand and his Remington, unloaded, near the other. Apparently he had been thinking of cleaning it just before he died. George Dinsmore went on a three-week toot, said toot financed by someone who knew that George would have his old dad's insurance money coming. Hattie Stoddard went around telling anyone who would listen that old George Dinsmore was a sin and a disgrace, no better than a tramp for pay.

There was a lot of flu around. The school closed for two weeks that February instead of the usual one because so many pupils were out sick. "No snow breeds germs," Sarah Havelock said.

Near the end of the month, just as people were beginning to look forward to the false comfort of March, Alden Flanders caught the flu himself. He walked around with it for nearly a week and then took to his bed with a fever of a hundred and one. Like Freddy, he refused to have the doctor, and Stella stewed and fretted and worried. Alden was not as old as Freddy, but that May he would turn sixty.

The snow came at last. Six inches on Valentine's Day, another six on the twentieth, and a foot in a good old norther on the leap, February 29. The snow lay white and strange between the cove and the mainland, like a sheep's meadow where there had been only gray and surging water at this time of year since time out of mind. Several people walked across to the mainland and back. No snowshoes were necessary this year because the snow had frozen to a firm, glittery crust. They might take a knock of whiskey, too, Stella thought, but they would not take it at Dorrit's. Dorrit's had burned down in 1958.

And she saw Bill all four times. Once he told her: "Y'ought to come soon, Stella. We'll go steppin. What do you say?"

She could say nothing. Her fist was crammed deep into her mouth.

"Everything I ever wanted or needed was here," she *would tell them. "We had the radio and now we have the television, and that's all I want of the world beyond the Reach. I had my garden year in and year out. And lobster? Why, we always used to have a pot of lobster stew on the back of the stove and we used to take it off and put it behind the door in the pantry when the minister came calling so he wouldn't see we were eating 'poor man's soup.'*

"I have seen good weather and bad, and if there were times when I wondered what it might be like to actually be in the Sears store instead of ordering from the catalogue, or to go into one of those Shaw's markets I see on TV instead of buying at the store here or sending Alden across for something special like a Christmas capon or an Easter ham . . . or if I ever wanted, just once, to stand on Congress Street in Portland and watch all the people in their cars and on the sidewalks, more people in a single look than there are on the whole island these days . . . if I ever wanted those things, then I wanted this more. I am not strange. I am not peculiar, or even very eccentric for a woman of my years. My mother sometimes used to say, 'All the difference in the world is between work and want,' and I believe that to my very soul. I believe it is better to plow deep than wide.

"This is my place, and I love it."

One day in middle March, with the sky as white and lowering as a loss of memory, Stella Flanders sat in her kitchen for the last time, laced up her boots over her skinny calves for the last time, and wrapped her bright red woolen scarf (a Christmas present from Hattie three Christmases past) around her neck for the last time. She wore a suit of Alden's long underwear under her dress. The waist of the drawers came up to just below the limp vestiges of her breasts, the shirt almost down to her knees.

Outside, the wind was picking up again, and the radio said there would be snow by afternoon. She put on her coat and her gloves. After a moment of debate, she put a pair of

Alden's gloves on over her own. Alden had recovered from the flu, and this morning he and Harley Blood were over rehanging a storm door for Missy Bowie, who had had a girl. Stella had seen it, and the unfortunate little mite looked just like her father.

She stood at the window for a moment, looking out at the Reach, and Bill was there as she had suspected he might be, standing about halfway between the island and the Head, standing on the Reach just like Jesus-out-of-the-boat, beckoning to her, seeming to tell her by gesture that the time was late if she ever intended to step a foot on the mainland in this life.

"If it's what you want, Bill," she fretted in the silence. "God knows I don't."

But the wind spoke other words. She did want to. She wanted to have this adventure. It had been a painful winter for her—the arthritis which came and went irregularly was back with a vengeance, flaring the joints of her fingers and knees with red fire and blue ice. One of her eyes had gotten dim and blurry (and just the other day Sarah had mentioned—with some unease—that the firespot that had been there since Stella was sixty or so now seemed to be growing by leaps and bounds). Worst of all, the deep, griping pain in her stomach had returned, and two mornings before she had gotten up at five o'clock, worked her way along the exquisitely cold floor into the bathroom, and had spat a great wad of bright red blood into the toilet bowl. This morning there had been some more of it, foul-tasting stuff, coppery and shuddersome.

The stomach pain had come and gone over the last five years, sometimes better, sometimes worse, and she had known almost from the beginning that it must be cancer. It had taken her mother and father and her mother's father as well. None of them had lived past seventy, and so she supposed she had beat the tables those insurance fellows kept by a carpenter's yard.

"You eat like a horse," Alden told her, grinning, not long after the pains had begun and she had first observed the blood in her morning stool. "Don't you know that old fogies like you are supposed to be peckish?"

"Get on or I'll swat ye!" Stella had answered, raising a hand to her gray-haired son, who ducked, mock-cringed, and cried: "Don't, Ma! I take it back!"

Yes, she had eaten hearty, not because she wanted to, but

because she believed (as many of her generation did), that if you fed the cancer it would leave you alone. And perhaps it worked, at least for a while; the blood in her stools came and went, and there were long periods when it wasn't there at all. Alden got used to her taking second helpings (and thirds, when the pain was particularly bad), but she never gained a pound.

Now it seemed the cancer had finally gotten around to what the froggies called the *pièce de résistance*.

She started out the door and saw Alden's hat, the one with the fur-lined ear flaps, hanging on one of the pegs in the entry. She put it on—the bill came all the way down to her shaggy salt-and-pepper eyebrows—and then looked around one last time to see if she had forgotten anything. The stove was low, and Alden had left the draw open too much again— she told him and told him, but that was one thing he was just never going to get straight.

"Alden, you'll burn an extra quarter-cord a winter when I'm gone," she muttered, and opened the stove. She looked in and a tight, dismayed gasp escaped her. She slammed the door shut and adjusted the draw with trembling fingers. For a moment—just a moment—she had seen her old friend Annabelle Frane in the coals. It was her face to the life, even down to the mole on her cheek.

And had Annabelle winked at her?

She thought of leaving Alden a note to explain where she had gone, but she thought perhaps Alden would understand, in his own slow way.

Still writing notes in her head—*Since the first day of winter I have been seeing your father and he says dying isn't so bad; at least I think that's it*—Stella stepped out into the white day.

The wind shook her and she had to reset Alden's cap on her head before the wind could steal it for a joke and cartwheel it away. The cold seemed to find every chink in her clothing and twist into her; damp March cold with wet snow on its mind.

She set off down the hill toward the cove, being careful to walk on the cinders and clinkers that George Dinsmore had spread. Once George had gotten a job driving plow for the town of Raccoon Head, but during the big blow of '77 he had gotten smashed on rye whiskey and had driven the plow smack through not one, not two, but three power poles. There had been no lights over the Head for five days. Stella remembered now how strange it had been, looking across the Reach and seeing only blackness. A body got used to seeing that brave little nestle of lights. Now George worked on the island, and since there was no plow, he didn't get into much hurt.

As she passed Russell Bowie's house, she saw Missy, pale as milk, looking out at her. Stella waved. Missy waved back.

She would tell them this:

"On the island we always watched out for our own. When Gerd Henreid broke the blood vessel in his chest that time, we had covered-dish suppers one whole summer to pay for his operation in Boston—and Gerd came back alive, thank God. When George Dinsmore ran down those power poles and the Hydro slapped a lien on his home, it was seen to that the Hydro had their money and George had enough of a job to keep him in cigarettes and booze . . . why not? He was good for nothing else when his workday was done, although when he was on the clock he would work like a dray-horse. That one time he got into trouble was because it was at night, and night was always George's drinking time. His father kept him fed, at least. Now Missy Bowie's alone with another baby. Maybe she'll stay here and take her welfare and ADC money here, and most likely it won't be enough, but she'll get the help she needs. Probably she'll go, but if she stays she'll not starve . . . and listen, Lona and Hal: if she stays, she may be able to keep something of this small world with the little Reach on one side and the big Reach on the other, something it would be too easy to lose hustling hash in Lewiston or donuts in Portland or drinks at the Nashville North in Bangor. And I am old enough not to beat around the bush about what that something might be: a way of being and a way of living—a feeling."

They had watched out for their own in other ways as well, but she would not tell them that. The children would not understand, nor would Lois and David, although Jane had known the truth. There was Norman and Ettie Wilson's baby that was born a mongoloid, its poor dear little feet turned in, its bald skull lumpy and cratered, its fingers webbed together as if it had dreamed too long and too deep while swimming that interior Reach; Reverend McCracken had come and baptized the baby, and a day later Mary Dodge came, who *even at that time had midwived over a hundred babies, and Norman took Ettie down the hill to see Frank Child's new boat and although she could barely walk, Ettie went with no complaint, although she had stopped in the door to look back at Mary Dodge, who was sitting calmly by the idiot baby's crib and knitting. Mary had looked up at her and when their eyes met, Ettie burst into tears. "Come on," Norman had said, upset. "Come on, Ettie, come on." And when they came back an hour later the baby was dead, one of those crib-deaths, wasn't it merciful he didn't suffer. And many years before that, before the war, during the Depression, three little girls had been molested coming home from school, not badly molested, at least not where you could see the scar of the hurt, and they all told about a man who offered to show them a deck of cards he had with a different kind of dog on each one. He would show them this wonderful deck of cards, the man said, if the little girls would come into the bushes with him, and once in the bushes this man said, "But you have to touch this first." One of the little girls was Gert Symes, who would go on to be voted Maine's Teacher of the Year in 1978, for her work at Brunswick High. And Gert, then only five years old, told her father that the man had some fingers gone on one hand. One of the other little girls agreed that this was so. The third remembered nothing. Stella remembered Alden going out one thundery day that summer without telling her where he was going, although she asked. Watching from the window, she had seen Alden meet Bull Symes at the bottom of the path, and then Freddy Dinsmore had joined them and down at the cove she saw her own husband, whom she had sent out that morning just as usual, with his dinner pail under his arm. More men joined them, and when they finally moved off she counted just one under a dozen. The Reverend McCracken's predecessor had been among them. And that evening a fellow named Daniels was found at the foot of Slyder's Point, where the rocks poke out of the surf like the fangs of a dragon that drowned with its mouth open. This Daniels was a fellow Big George Havelock had hired to help him put new sills under his house and a new engine in his Model A truck. From New Hampshire he was, and he was a sweet-talker who had found other odd jobs to do when the work at the Havelocks' was done . . . and in church, he could carry a tune! Apparently, they said, Daniels had been walking up on top of Slyder's Point and had slipped, tumbling all the way to the bottom. His neck was broken and his head was bashed in. As he had no people that anyone knew of, he was buried on the island, and the Reverend McCracken's predecessor gave the graveyard eulogy, saying as how this Daniels had been a hard worker and a good help even though he was two fingers shy on his right hand. Then he read the benediction and the graveside group had gone back to the town-hall basement where they drank Za-Rex punch and ate cream-cheese sandwiches, and Stella never asked her men where they had gone on the day Daniels fell from the top of Slyder's Point.*

"Children," she would tell them, "we always watched out for our own. We had to, for the Reach was wider in those days and when the wind roared and the surf pounded and the dark came early, why, we felt very small—no more than dust motes in the mind of God. So it was natural for us to join hands, one with the other.

"We joined hands, children, and if there were times when we wondered what it was all for, or if there was ary such a thing as love at all, it was only because we had heard the wind and the waters on long winter nights, and we were afraid.

"No, I've never felt I needed to leave the island. My life was here. The Reach was wider in those days."

Stella reached the cove. She looked right and left, the wind blowing her dress out behind her like a flag. If anyone had been there she would have walked further down and taken her chance on the tumbled rocks, although they were glazed with ice. But no one was there and she walked out along the pier, past the old Symes boathouse. She reached the end and stood there for a moment, head held up, the wind blowing past the padded flaps of Alden's hat in a muffled flood.

Bill was out there, beckoning. Beyond him, beyond the Reach, she could see the Congo Church over there on the Head, its spire almost invisible against the white sky.

Grunting, she sat down on the end of the pier and then stepped onto the snow crust below. Her boots sank a little; not much. She set Alden's cap again—how the wind wanted to tear it off!—and began to walk toward Bill. She thought once that she would look back, but she did not. She didn't believe her heart could stand that.

She walked, her boots crunching into the crust, and listened to the faint thud and give of the ice. There was Bill, further back now but still beckoning. She coughed, spat blood onto the white snow that covered the ice. Now the Reach spread wide on either side and she could, for the first time in her life, read the "Stanton's Bait and Boat" sign over there without Alden's binoculars. She could see the cars passing to and fro on the Head's main street and thought with real wonder: *They can go as far as they want . . . Portland . . . Boston . . . New York City. Imagine!* And she could almost do it, could almost imagine a road that simply rolled on and on, the boundaries of the world knocked wide.

A snowflake skirled past her eyes. Another. A third. Soon it was snowing lightly and she walked through a pleasant world of shifting bright white; she saw Raccoon Head through a gauzy curtain that sometimes almost cleared. She reached up to set Alden's cap again and snow puffed off the bill into her eyes. The wind twisted fresh snow up in filmy shapes, and in one of them she saw Carl Abersham, who had gone down with Hattie Stoddard's husband on the *Dancer*.

Soon, however, the brightness began to dull as the snow came harder. The Head's main street dimmed, dimmed, and at last was gone. For a time longer she could make out the cross atop the church, and then that faded out too, like a false dream. Last to go was that bright yellow-and-black sign reading "Stanton's Bait and Boat," where you could also get engine oil, flypaper, Italian sandwiches, and Budweiser to go.

Then Stella walked in a world that was totally without color, a gray-white dream of snow. *Just like Jesus-out-of-the-boat*, she thought, and at last she looked back but now the island was gone, too. She could see her tracks going back, losing definition until only the faint half-circles of her heels could be seen . . . and then nothing. Nothing at all.

She thought: *It's a whiteout. You got to be careful, Stella, or you'll never get to the mainland. You'll just walk around in a big circle until you're worn out and then you'll freeze to death out here.*

She remembered Bill telling her once that when you were lost in the woods, you had to pretend that the leg which was on the same side of your body as your smart hand was lame. Otherwise that smart leg would begin to lead you and you'd walk in a circle and not even realize it until you came around to your backtrail again. Stella didn't believe she could afford to have that happen to her. Snow today, tonight, and tomorrow, the radio had said, and in a whiteout such as this, she would not even know if she came around to her backtrail, for the wind and the fresh snow would erase it long before she could return to it.

Her hands were leaving her in spite of the two pairs of gloves she wore, and her feet had been gone for some time. In a way, this was almost a relief. The numbness at least shut the mouth of her clamoring arthritis.

Stella began to limp now, making her left leg work harder. The arthritis in her knees had not gone to sleep, and soon they were screaming at her. Her white hair flew out behind her. Her lips had drawn back from her teeth (she still had her own, all save four) and she looked straight ahead, waiting for that yellow-and-black sign to materialize out of the flying whiteness.

It did not happen.

Sometime later, she noticed that the day's bright whiteness had begun to dull to a more uniform gray. The snow fell heavier and thicker than ever. Her feet were still planted on the crust but now she was walking through five inches of fresh snow. She looked at her watch, but it had stopped. Stella realized she must have forgotten to wind it that morning for the first time in twenty or thirty years. Or had it just stopped for good? It had been her mother's and she had sent it with Alden twice to the Head, where Mr. Dostie had first marveled over it and then cleaned it. Her watch, at least, had been to the mainland.

She fell down for the first time some fifteen minutes after she began to notice the day's growing grayness. For a moment she remained on her hands and knees, thinking it would be so easy just to stay here, to curl up and listen to the wind, and then the determination that had brought her through so much reasserted itself and she got up, grimacing. She stood in the wind, looking straight ahead, willing her eyes to see . . . but they saw nothing.

Be dark soon.

Well, she had gone wrong. She had slipped off to one side or the other. Otherwise she would have reached the mainland by now. Yet she didn't believe she had gone so far wrong that she was walking parallel to the mainland or even back in the direction of Goat. An interior navigator in her head whispered that she had overcompensated and slipped off to the left. She believed she was still approaching the mainland but was now on a costly diagonal.

That navigator wanted her to turn right, but she would not do that. Instead, she moved straight on again, but stopped the artificial limp. A spasm of coughing shook her, and she spat bright red into the snow.

Ten minutes later (the gray was now deep indeed, and she found herself in the weird twilight of a heavy snowstorm) she fell again, tried to get up, failed at first, and finally managed to gain her feet. She stood swaying in the snow, barely able to remain upright in the wind, waves of faintness rushing through her head, making her feel alternately heavy and light.

Perhaps not all the roaring she heard in her ears was the wind, but it surely was the wind that finally succeeded in prying Alden's hat from her head. She made a grab for it, but the wind danced it easily out of her reach and she saw it only for a moment, flipping gaily over and over into the darkening gray, a bright spot of orange. It struck the snow, rolled, rose again, was gone. Now her hair flew around her head freely.

"It's all right, Stella," Bill said. "You can wear mine."

She gasped and looked around in the white. Her gloved hands had gone instinctively to her bosom, and she felt sharp fingernails scratch at her heart.

She saw nothing but shifting membranes of snow—and then, moving out of that evening's gray throat, the wind screaming through it like the voice of a devil in a snowy tunnel, came her husband. He was at first only moving colors in the snow: red, black, dark green, lighter green; then these colors resolved themselves into a flannel jacket with a flapping collar, flannel pants, and green boots. He was holding his hat out to her in a gesture that appeared almost absurdly courtly, and his face was Bill's face, unmarked by the cancer that had taken him (had that been all she was afraid of? that a wasted shadow of her husband would come to her, a scrawny concentration-camp figure with the skin pulled taut and shiny over the cheekbones and the eyes sunken deep in the sockets?) and she felt a surge of relief.

"Bill? Is that really you?"

"Course."

"Bill," she said again, and took a glad step toward him. Her legs betrayed her and she thought she would fall, fall

right through him—he was, after all, a ghost—but he caught
her in arms as strong and as competent as those that had
carried her over the threshold of the house that she had shared
only with Alden in these latter years. He supported her, and a
moment later she felt the cap pulled firmly onto her head.

"Is it really you?" she asked again, looking up into his
face, at the crow's-feet around his eyes which hadn't sunk
deep yet, at the spill of snow on the shoulders of his checked
hunting jacket, at his lively brown hair.

"It's me," he said. "It's all of us."

He half-turned with her and she saw the others coming out
of the snow that the wind drove across the Reach in the
gathering darkness. A cry, half joy, half fear, came from her
mouth as she saw Madeline Stoddard, Hattie's mother, in a
blue dress that swung in the wind like a bell, and holding her
hand was Hattie's dad, not a mouldering skeleton somewhere
on the bottom with the *Dancer,* but whole and young. And
there, behind those two—

"Annabelle!" she cried. "Annabelle Frane, is it you?"

It *was* Annabelle; even in this snowy gloom Stella recognized the yellow dress Annabelle had worn to Stella's own
wedding, and as she struggled toward her dead friend, holding Bill's arm, she thought that she could smell roses.

"Annabelle!"

"We're almost there now, dear," Annabelle said, taking
her other arm. The yellow dress, which had been considered
Daring in its day (but, to Annabelle's credit and to everyone
else's relief, not quite a Scandal), left her shoulders bare, but
Annabelle did not seem to feel the cold. Her hair, a soft, dark
auburn, blew long in the wind. "Only a little further."

She took Stella's other arm and they moved forward again.
Other figures came out of the snowy night (for it *was* night
now). Stella recognized many of them, but not all. Tommy
Frane had joined Annabelle; Big George Havelock, who had
died a dog's death in the woods, walked behind Bill; there
was the fellow who had kept the lighthouse on the Head for
most of twenty years and who used to come over to the island
during the cribbage tournament Freddy Dinsmore held every
February—Stella could almost but not quite remember his name.
And there was Freddy himself! Walking off to one side of
Freddy, by himself and looking bewildered, was Russell Bowie.

"Look, Stella," Bill said, and she saw black rising out of

the gloom like the splintered prows of many ships. It was not ships, it was split and fissured rock. They had reached the Head. They had crossed the Reach.

She heard voices, but was not sure they actually spoke:

Take my hand, Stella—

(do you)

Take my hand, Bill—

(oh do you do you)

Annabelle . . . Freddy . . . Russell . . . John . . . Ettie . . . Frank . . . take my hand, take my hand . . . my hand . . .

(do you love)

"Will you take my hand, Stella?" a new voice asked.

She looked around and there was Bull Symes. He was smiling kindly at her and yet she felt a kind of terror in her at what was in his eyes and for a moment she drew away, clutching Bill's hand on her other side the tighter.

"Is it—"

"Time?" Bull asked. "Oh, ayuh, Stella, I guess so. But it don't hurt. At least, I never heard so. All that's before."

She burst into tears suddenly—all the tears she had never wept—and put her hand in Bull's hand. "Yes," she said, "yes I will, yes I did, yes I do."

They stood in a circle in the storm, the dead of Goat Island, and the wind screamed around them, driving its packet of snow, and some kind of song burst from her. It went up into the wind and the wind carried it away. They all sang then, as children will sing in their high, sweet voices as a summer evening draws down to summer night. They sang, and Stella felt herself going to them and with them, finally across the Reach. There was a bit of pain, but not much; losing her maidenhead had been worse. They stood in a circle in the night. The snow blew around them and they sang. They sang, and—

—and Alden could not tell David and Lois, but in the summer after Stella died, when the children came out for their annual two weeks, he told Lona and Hal. He told them that during the great storms of winter the wind seems to sing with almost human voices, and that sometimes it seemed to him he could almost make out the words: "Praise God from whom all blessings flow/Praise Him, ye creatures here below . . ."

But he did not tell them (imagine slow, unimaginative Alden Flanders saying such things aloud, even to the chil-

dren!) that sometimes he would hear that sound and feel cold even by the stove; that he would put his whittling aside, or the trap he had meant to mend, thinking that the wind sang in all the voices of those who were dead and gone . . . that they stood somewhere out on the Reach and sang as children do. He seemed to hear their voices and on these nights he sometimes slept and dreamed that he was singing the doxology, unseen and unheard, at his own funeral.

There are things that can never be told, and there are things, not exactly secret, that are not discussed. They had found Stella frozen to death on the mainland a day after the storm had blown itself out. She was sitting on a natural chair of rock about one hundred yards south of the Raccoon Head town limits, frozen just as neat as you please. The doctor who owned the Corvette said that he was frankly amazed. It would have been a walk of over four miles, and the autopsy required by law in the case of an unattended, unusual death had shown an advanced cancerous condition—in truth, the old woman had been riddled with it. Was Alden to tell David and Lois that the cap on her head had not been his? Larry McKeen had recognized that cap. So had John Bensohn. He had seen it in their eyes, and he supposed they had seen it in his. He had not lived long enough to forget his dead father's cap, the look of its bill or the places where the visor had been broken.

"These are things made for thinking on slowly," he would have told the children if he had known how. "Things to be thought on at length, while the hands do their work and the coffee sits in a solid china mug nearby. They are questions of Reach, maybe: do the dead sing? And do they love the living?"

On the nights after Lona and Hal had gone back with their parents to the mainland in Al Curry's boat, the children standing astern and waving good-bye, Alden considered that question, and others, and the matter of his father's cap.

Do the dead sing? Do they love?

On those long nights alone, with his mother Stella Flanders at long last in her grave, it often seemed to Alden that they did both.

Notes

Not everyone is interested in where short stories come from, and that is perfectly proper—you don't have to understand the internal-combustion engine to drive a car, and you don't need to know the circumstances which surrounded the making of a story to get a bit of pleasure from it. Engines interest mechanics; the creation of stories interests academics, fans, and snoops (the first and the last are almost synonymous, but never mind). I've included a few notes here on a few of the stories—such things as I thought might interest the casual reader. But if you're even more casual than that, I assure you that you can close the book without a qualm—you won't be missing much.

"The Mist"—This was written in the summer of 1976, for an anthology of new stories being put together by my agent, Kirby McCauley. McCauley had created another book of this sort, called *Frights,* two or three years previous. That book was a paperback. This one was to be a hardcover and much more ambitious in scope. It was called *Dark Forces.* Kirby wanted a story from me, and he pursued that story with doggedness, determination . . . and a kind of gentle diplomacy that is, I think, the hallmark of a really good agent.

I couldn't think of a thing. The harder I thought, the more easily nothing came. I began to think that maybe the short-story machine in my head was temporarily or permanently broken. Then came the storm, which was much as described in this story. At the height of it there was indeed a waterspout on Long Lake in Bridgton, where we were living at the time, and I did insist that my family come downstairs with me for a while (although my wife's name is Tabitha—Stephanie is her sister's name). The trip to the market the next day was also much as described in the story, although I was spared the company of such an odious creature as Norton—in the real world, the people living in Norton's summer cottage were a very pleasant doctor, Ralph Drews, and his wife.

In the market, my muse suddenly shat on my head—this happened as it always does, suddenly, with no warning. I was halfway down the middle aisle, looking for hot-dog buns, when I imagined a big prehistoric bird flapping its way toward the meat counter at the back, knocking over cans of pineapple chunks and bottles of tomato sauce. By the time my son Joe and I were in the checkout lane, I was amusing myself with a story about all these people trapped in a super-market surrounded by prehistoric animals. I thought it was wildly funny—what *The Alamo* would have been like if directed by Bert I. Gordon. I wrote half the story that night and the rest the following week.

It got a little long, but Kirby thought it was good and it went into the book. I never liked it that much until the rewrite—I particularly didn't like David Drayton sleeping with Amanda and then never finding out what happened to his wife. That seemed cowardly to me. But in the rewrite, I discovered a rhythm of language that I liked—and keeping that rhythm in mind, I was able to peel the story down to its basics more successfully than with some of my other long stories ("Apt Pupil" in *Different Seasons* is a particularly good example of this disease I have—literary elephantiasis).

The real key to this rhythm lay in the deliberate use of the story's first line, which I simply stole from Douglas Fairbairn's brilliant novel *Shoot*. The line is, for me, the essence of all story, a kind of Zen incantation.

I must tell you that I also liked the metaphor implied in David Drayton's discovery of his own limitations, and I liked the story's cheery cheesiness—you're supposed to see this one in black-and-white, with your arm around your girl's shoulders (or your guy's), and a big speaker stuck in the window. *You* make up the second feature.

"Here There Be Tygers"—My first-grade teacher in Stratford, Connecticut, was Mrs. Van Buren. She was pretty scary. I guess if a tiger had come along and eaten her up, I could have gotten behind that. You know how kids are.

"The Monkey"—I was in New York City on business about four years ago. I was walking back to my hotel after visiting my people at New American Library when I saw a guy selling wind-up monkeys on the street. There was a platoon of them standing on a gray blanket he'd spread on the sidewalk at the corner of Fifth and Forty-fourth, all bending and grinning and clapping their cymbals. They looked really scary to me, and I spent the rest of my walk back to the hotel wondering why. I decided it was because they reminded me of the lady with the shears . . . the one who cuts everyone's thread one day. So keeping that idea in mind, I wrote the story, mostly longhand, in a hotel room.

"Mrs. Todd's Shortcut"—My wife is the real Mrs. Todd; the woman really *is* mad for a shortcut, and much of the one in the story actually exists. She found it, too. And Tabby really *does* seem to be getting younger sometimes, although I hope I am not like Worth Todd. I try not to be.

I like this story a lot; it tickles me. And the old guy's voice is soothing. Every now and then you write something that brings back the old days, when *everything* you wrote seemed fresh and full of invention. "Mrs. Todd" felt that way to me when I was writing it.

One final note on it—three women's magazines turned it down, two because of that line about how a woman will pee down her own leg if she doesn't squat. They apparently felt that either women don't pee or don't want to be reminded of the fact. The third magazine to reject it, *Cosmopolitan*, did so because they felt the main character was too old to interest their target audience.

No comment—except to add that *Redbook* finally took it. God bless 'em.

"The Jaunt"—This was originally for *Omni*, which quite

rightly rejected it because the science is so wonky. It was Ben Bova's idea to have the colonists in the story mining for water, and I have incorporated that in this version.

"The Raft"—I wrote this story in the year 1968 as "The Float." In late 1969 I sold it to *Adam* magazine, which—like most of the girlie magazines—paid not on acceptance but only on publication. The amount promised was two hundred and fifty dollars.

In the spring of 1970, while creeping home in my white Ford station wagon from the University Motor Inn at 12:30 in the morning, I ran over a number of traffic cones which were guarding a crosswalk that had been painted that day. The paint had dried, but no one had bothered to take the cones in when it got dark. One of them bounced up and knocked my muffler loose from the rotted remains of my tailpipe. I was immediately suffused with the sort of towering, righteous rage which only drunk undergraduates can feel. I decided to circle the town of Orono, picking up traffic cones. I would leave them all in front of the police station the next morning, with a note saying that I had saved numerous mufflers and exhaust systems from extinction, and ought to get a medal.

I got about a hundred and fifty before blue lights started to swirl around in the rearview mirror.

I will never forget the Orono cop turning to me after a long, long look into the back of my station wagon and asking: "Son, are those traffic cones yours?"

The cones were confiscated and so was I; that night I was a guest of the town of Orono, that crossword-puzzle favorite. A month or so later, I was brought to trial in Bangor District Court on a charge of petty larceny. I was my own attorney and did indeed have a fool for a client. I was fined two hundred and fifty dollars, which I of course did not have. I was given seven days to come up with it, or do thirty *more* days as a guest of Penobscot County. I probably could have borrowed it from my mother, but the circumstances were not easy to understand (unless you had a skinful of booze, that was).

Although one is now not supposed to *ever* use a *deus ex machina* in his or her fiction because these gods from the machine are not believable, I notice that they arrive all the time in real life. Mine came three days after the judge levied my fine and arrived in the form of a check from *Adam* magazine for two hundred and fifty dollars. It was for my story "The Float." It was like having someone send you a *real* Get Out of Jail Free card. I cashed the check immediately and paid my fine. I determined to go straight and give all traffic cones a wide berth thereafter. Straight I have not exactly gone, but believe me when I tell you I'm quits with the cones.

But here's the thing: *Adam* paid only on *publication*, dammit, and since I got the money, the story must have come out. But no copy was ever sent to me, and I never saw one on the stands, although I checked regularly—I would simply push my way in between the dirty old men checking out such literary pinnacles as *Boobs and Buns* and *Spanking Lesbians* and thumb through every magazine the Knight Publishing Company put out. I never saw that story in any of them.

Somewhere along the way I lost the original manuscript, too. I got to thinking about the story again in 1981, some thirteen years later. I was in Pittsburgh, where the final *Creepshow* editing was going on, and I was bored. So I decided to have a go at re-creating that story, and the result was "The Raft." It is the same as the original in terms of event, but I believe it is far more gruesome in its specifics.

Anyway, if anyone out there *has* ever seen "The Float," or even if someone has a *copy*, could you send me a Xerox copy or something? Even a postcard confirming the fact that I'm not crazy? It would have been in *Adam*, or *Adam Quarterly*, or (most likely) *Adam Bedside Reader* (not much of a name, I know, I know, but in those days I only had two pairs of pants and three pairs of underwear, and beggars can't be choosers, and it was a lot better than *Spanking Lesbians*, let me tell you). I'd just like to make sure it was published someplace other than the Dead Zone.

"Survivor Type"—I got to thinking about cannibalism one day—because that's the sort of thing guys like me sometimes think about—and my muse once more evacuated its magic bowels on my head. I know how gross that sounds, but it's the best metaphor I know, inelegant or not, and believe me when I tell you I'd give that little Fornit Ex-Lax if he wanted it. Anyway, I started to wonder if a person could eat *himself*, and if so, how much he could eat before the inevitable happened. This idea was so utterly and perfectly revolting that I was too overawed with delight to do more than think about it for days—I was reluctant to write it down because I thought I could only fuck it up. Finally, when my wife asked me what I was laughing at one day when we were eating hamburgers on the back deck, I decided I ought to at least take it for a testdrive.

We were living in Bridgton at the time, and I spent an hour or so talking with Ralph Drews, the retired doctor next door. Although he looked doubtful at first (the year before, in pursuit of another story, I had asked him if he thought it was possible for a man to swallow a cat), he finally agreed that a guy could subsist on himself for quite a while—like everything else which is material, he pointed out, the human body is just stored energy. Ah, I asked him, but what about the repeated shock of the amputations? The answer he gave me is, with very few changes, the first paragraph of the story.

I guess Faulkner never would have written anything like this, huh? Oh, well.

"Uncle Otto's Truck"—The truck is real, and so is the house; I made up the story that goes around them one day in my head on a long drive to pass the time. I liked it and so I took a few days to write it down.

"The Reach"—Tabby's youngest brother, Tommy, used to be in the Coast Guard. He was stationed downeast, in the Jonesport-Beals area of the long and knotty Maine coast, where the Guard's main chores are changing the batteries in the big buoys and saving idiot drug smugglers who get lost in the fog or run on the rocks.

There are lots of islands out there, and lots of tightly knit island communities. He told me of a real-life counterpart of Stella Flanders, who lived and died on her island. Was it Pig Island? Cow Island? I can't remember. *Some* animal, anyway.

I could hardly believe it. "She didn't ever *want* to come across to the mainland?" I asked.

"No, she said she didn't want to cross the Reach until she died," Tommy said.

The term Reach was unfamiliar to me, and Tommy explained it. He also told me the lobstermen's joke about how it's a mighty long Reach between Jonesport and London, and

I put it in the story. It was originally published in *Yankee* as "Do the Dead Sing?", a nice enough title, but after some thought I have gone back to the original title here.

Well, that's it. I don't know about you, but every time I come to the end, it's like waking up. It's a little sad to lose the dream, but everything all around—the real stuff—looks damned good, just the same. Thanks for coming along with me; I enjoyed it. I always do. I hope you arrived safe, and that you'll come again—because as that funny butler says in that odd New York club, there are always more tales.

STEPHEN KING
Bangor, Maine

About the Author

Stephen King grew up in Maine and has lived most of his adult life there, both in Bangor and in the Portland area. He and his wife, Tabitha, have three children, Naomi, Joe, and Owen Philip.

He is the author of the best-selling books CARRIE, 'SALEM'S LOT, THE SHINING, NIGHT SHIFT, THE STAND, THE DEAD ZONE, FIRESTARTER, DIFFERENT SEASONS, CHRISTINE, and PET SEMATARY, also published by New American Library.